Praise for
Chapultepec
by Norman Zollinger

▲▲▲▲▲▲▲▲▲▲

"It's great. . . . If you like to learn history painlessly, this is the way to do it. The author really knows the landscape of Mexico. . . ."
—Tony Hillerman, *Entertainment Weekly*

"*Chapultepec* should stand proudly alongside *Exodus, War and Peace, For Whom the Bell Tolls,* and *Dr. Zhivago* as a stirring love story set against the backdrop of a turbulent time in a country's history."
—*The Santa Fe New Mexican*

"History here is as compelling as any I recall in fiction; the characters are in no danger of being forgotten. . . ."
—*San Jose Mercury News*

"An awesome feat. . . . A vivid panorama of the dreams, intrigues, and dangers of the brief, fated empire of Maximilian and Carlota interwoven with the love story of a man and a woman strong enough to survive devastation and build a new world."
—Jeanne Williams, author of *The Unplowed Sky*

"James Michener would probably be proud to have his name on *Chapultepec.* It has the expansive scope of the bloody Mexican Revolution against French arms and Emperor Maximilian the First. It is unsparing in its illuminating detail of deceit, lust for power, and romantic intrigue in the royal court and in the mighty armies it controls."
—Max Evans, author of *Bluefeather Fellini* and *The Rounders*

Forge Books by Norman Zollinger

CHAPULTEPEC

Norman Zollinger

A TOM DOHERTY ASSOCIATES BOOK
NEW YORK

This is a work of fiction. All the characters and events portrayed in this book are fictitious, and any resemblance to real people or events is purely coincidental.

CHAPULTEPEC

Interior illustrations and map by Wendy Zollinger

A Forge Book
Published by Tom Doherty Associates, Inc.
175 Fifth Avenue
New York, NY 10010

Forge® is a registered trademark of Tom Doherty Associates, Inc.

ISBN: 0-812-55541-4
Library of Congress Card Catalog Number: 95-23263

First edition: October 1995
First mass market edition: August 1996

Printed in the United States of America

0 9 8 7 6 5 4 3 2 1

FOR JIM McALLISTER

Who did not run to Samarra

Principal Historical Characters

▲▲▲▲▲

MAXIMILIAN VON HAPSBURG—Archduke of Austria, Emperor Maximilian I of Mexico, 1864–1867

CHARLOTTE VON COBURG—Princess of Belgium, Archduchess of Austria, Empress Carlota of Mexico, 1864–1867

BENITO JUÁREZ—President of the Republic of Mexico, 1859–1872

FRANÇOIS-ACHILLE BAZAINE—Marshal of France, Commander of French forces in Mexico, 1863–1867

LOUIS NAPOLEON BONAPARTE—Napoleon III, Emperor of France

JUAN ALMONTE—Conservative Mexican General, Self-proclaimed President of Mexico, 1862, Regent, 1863

JOSÉ LUIS BLASIO—Private Secretary to Maximilian

DOCTOR BASCH—Czech physician to Maximilian

THOMAS CORWIN—United States Ambassador to Mexico, 1862–1868

IGNACIO COMONFORT—Republican General, President of the Republic of Mexico, 1857

PORFIRIO DÍAZ—Republican General, later President of Mexico

CHARLES DUPIN—French Army Colonel, leader of the *contra-guerrillas*

FELIX ELOIN—Belgian advisor to Maximilian

MARIANO ESCOBEDO—Republican General, Victor of Queretaro

ELIE FOREY—Marshal of France, Commander of French forces in Mexico, 1863–1865

PAOLA VON KOLLONITZ—Lady-in-Waiting to Empress Carlota

MONSIGNOR LABASTIDA—Bishop of Puebla and Tlaxcala, later Archbishop of Mexico

MIGUEL LÓPEZ—Conservative Mexican Colonel

LATRILLE DE LORENCEZ—French commander at the first Battle of Puebla

LEONARDO MÁRQUEZ—Conservative Mexican General, the "Tiger of Tacubaya"

TOMAS MEJÍA—Conservative Mexican General

MIGUEL MIRAMÓN—Conservative Mexican General

ANGELA PERALTA—Mexican opera diva

ANTONIO PÉREZ—the "Plateado," bandit chief

MARIANO SALAS—Conservative Mexican General, Regent, 1863

PIERRE DE SALIGNY—French diplomat

AGNES ZU SALM-SALM—German Princess, thought to be American by birth

FELIX ZU SALM-SALM—German Prince, General in the Imperial Army

ALFRED VAN DER SMISSEN—Belgian aristocrat, Colonel in the Imperial Belgian Brigade

TUDOS—Chef and valet to Maximilian

IGNACIO ZARAGOZA—Republican General, Victor of the first Battle of Puebla

MELANIE ZICHY—Austrian countess, Lady-in-Waiting to Empress Carlota

. . . within the hollow crown
that rounds the mortal temples of a king
keeps death his court . . .
—*RICHARD II*

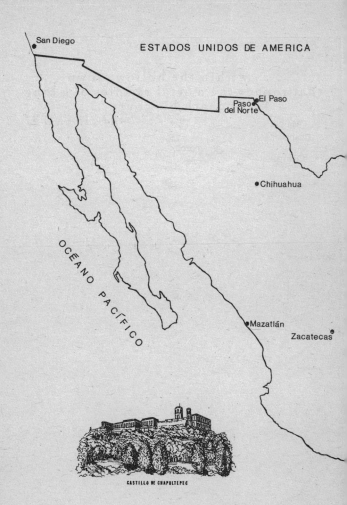

San Diego

ESTADOS UNIDOS DE AMERICA

El Paso

Paso
del Norte

●Chihuahua

OCÉANO PACÍFICO

●Mazatlán

Zacatecas

CASTILLO DE CHAPULTEPEC

PART ONE

THE PEAK

"As if this flesh which walls about our life
Were brass impregnable . . ."

— RICHARD II

1

The colonel awoke to find the girl Sofía pressing a cold, wet rag to his forehead. In the light from the small lamp beside his bed he could read his death in her eyes, and he wanted to tell her it was not true—but there had never been lies between them. Better to say nothing than to tell one now.

There was never, he supposed, a good way for it to end, but it *would* end, tonight, here in this miserable little stone *casa*.

The lamp burned low, the flame feeble, but there was every likelihood it would outlast him.

The stench from the wound in his left lower leg was getting worse, nausea surged over him in waves. Even had he been well and sound he doubted whether he could have kept down a mouthful of the stew Cipi had fixed. The stink of it rivaled the one rising from his shattered leg.

The girl, who had nursed him as the stew simmered, looked into his eyes for a long minute, then returned to the bench at the side of the room. Her birdlike appearance was even more pronounced than usual tonight, but the thing that had happened this morning had robbed her of some of her usual easy grace.

It was too late to worry about what might become of her when he was gone—foolish, too; she had managed very well without him before he came to Mexico with the

Legion. She could do it again. And Cipi would see to her for a while at least.

The pain that wracked him when they dragged him from the farmyard into the *casa* had eased some now, but his memory of the deaths of so many other men with similar wounds told him that was not good news. When the gangrene set in the pain almost always lessened, only to return just before the end.

The downpour which had begun as the pair pulled him from the yard almost twenty hours earlier was beating at the shuttered windows of the *casa*, sounding like an army on the march, and the deep arroyo in the northwest corner of the farm was running full. The bacchanalian roar of the torrent all but muffled the angry pulse drumming in his temple.

The dwarf had come to stand beside his bed.

"Cipi could try to take it off, *mi coronel*," the little man said, pointing to the leg.

"Forget that, Cipi."

"One quick, clean stroke with the *machete*."

"No."

"If Cipi only had a small handful of *los gusanos* . . ."

"I think it's too late for maggots, Cipi," the colonel said.

"*Sí*, perhaps it is too late for everything. How is the pain?"

"Much better now. Almost gone."

The dwarf's ugly face darkened. Cipi knew what that meant too. He patted the old pistol strapped to his waist.

"Then does the colonel wish Cipi to shoot him now?"

"No, Cipi. There is something I must take care of first. Besides, when and if the pain comes again, I shall probably shoot *myself*."

When they first met in that dockside cantina in Veracruz five years ago the colonel, a captain then, would never have believed he and Cipi would last this long together.

"You do not agree with the way I dealt with the general, do you, Cipi?" he asked now.

"*Con respeto, mi coronel*, 'stupid' is the only word to

describe the colonel's decision at the end. But who is Cipi to judge? He does not have the intellectual advantages of his colonel's exalted rank. Of course, the general planned this whole thing well. He is a clever *hombre.*"

Yes, the general had been clever all his life.

Cipi continued. "And he has the luck of a *lunático.*"

That was probably true as well, but more than the luck of a lunatic had brought the general to this wasted little farm. He came here purposefully, intent on execution, and that execution, delayed twenty years, had taken place. All that remained was for the executed man to die.

Cipi's chest heaved. He spread his thick arms in a gesture as close to one of surrender as the colonel had ever seen him make. "Cipi supposes it makes little difference," he said now, "but you *should* try to eat."

"Your food might finish me quicker than a pistol ball, my small *amigo.* I can't eat now. Perhaps later."

"There probably will not *be* a 'later.'" The dwarf was not a sentimentalist. "Cipi went to great trouble to fix this meal. You are not a grateful man, my colonel." He stumped across the room and seated himself on the bench beside the girl.

Sofía kept her black eyes on the colonel's face.

Unless she left soon she would have to watch him die.

But—and this was the case with Cipi, too, for all his show of bitter humor—he knew nothing could persuade her to leave him now. He could not *drive* her away. He had tried to send her away once, tried hard. She had not left him.

He did not deserve such loyalty from her *or* the dwarf—if it *was* loyalty and not just mute, animal acceptance of a warped fate—but he was glad to have it. He could die well enough alone, perhaps should, and make sparing them the sight and sound of his last rattling breath a final gift.

"Sofía . . ." he called.

The girl got to her feet, leaned over and picked up the *rebozo* folded beside her, wrapped it around her shoulders and crossed to him.

"*¿Qué pasa, mi coronel?*" she said. "You are in great pain, no?"

"Not at the moment, *querida*. Would you get me my writing case from the chest, *por favor.*"

She flew to the carved Spanish chest and returned with the case. He took it and looked up at her, searching for the fear that must lurk somewhere there. He did not find it, not in her black agate eyes nor anywhere else on her face. He had seen more expression in the carved features of stone Toltecs in the ruins of Tenochtitlan.

How old was Sofía now? Twenty-one or two? Tonight she looked much older, but with some at least of her fresh youth still furtively apparent, teased into her face by the warm lamplight. How old did *he* look to her? Certainly much older than his thirty-seven years. The lamp could not do for him what it did for her.

What was she thinking? He had seldom known in all their time together. When he had, it occurred only when her temper flared, and that had not happened often. He had not even known what she thought the night he tried to send her away, three years ago.

"You know what will happen tonight, don't you, *querida?*" he said.

"*Sí.*"

"I don't want you grieving for me."

Her eyes narrowed. "When you are dead you will hardly be able to tell Sofía what to do, *mi coronel.*" She reached for him, pulled her hand back before she touched him. "Sofía will content herself with the thought that the *gringa* woman can never have you, either."

Yes, *that* was still there. "There was never much chance of that, Sofía." Was it the truth? Truth or not, he needed to say it. "Leave me for a bit, *por favor*. There is something I must do while I still have strength." He opened the leather writing case. "We will talk again before I sleep."

He felt something tear at his heart as she returned to the bench she shared with Cipi, and then he slipped a sheet of his stationery from the case and shifted himself around until his back was to the lamp. The pain had returned, if only for a while, making every inch he moved a thousand miles of agony. Time for Cipi and his monster pistol? Not quite, but soon. He drew his good knee up to hold the case and looked at the letterhead:

JASON JEREMIAH JAMES
COLONEL, SEVENTH IMPERIAL GUARDS

Under his name he wrote, "Last Will & Testament."

What nonsense. There was little enough for him to leave to anyone: his watch, his saber, the gold penknife he had bought in the Zócalo a year ago, two thousand two hundred forty-odd pesos in the Banco Central in the capital, and this wretched little farm.

The letterhead itself now had become a fraud. He could no longer claim a connection with any army or regiment, and as to his rank of colonel, that was gone as well.

And making a will was a useless exercise.

—for what can we bequeath
Save our deposed bodies to the ground?

He lifted the sheet of stationery to the chimney of the lamp. When it burst into flame the light played over the faces of Sofía and the dwarf. The death watch.

He let the flaming paper flutter to the earthen floor.

The pain began to build in his swollen leg again, and his brain fogged once more. He closed his eyes. The drunken babble from the arroyo grew louder. He would *not* think of death, Cipi, or the girl—and he would not think of the *gringa* woman—as Sofía had called her—either. He had forfeited any right to think of her.

He slept . . .

Then—had he awakened or was it a dream?—the tinny notes of a distant bugle rose above the sounds of the water rushing insanely through the arroyo and of the rain still hammering at the window. For a moment he thought the general had found him again, and there would be no need to ask Cipi to help him leave this life, but there was no mistaking the call he had answered for more than fifteen years in the sands and jungles of two continents and through twenty campaigns in half a dozen wars—the *à l'attaque* of the Foreign Legion.

Coming now it could only be the jangled melody of delirium. No Legion trumpet blew within a thousand leagues. And no one would order him to attack ever again.

When he opened his eyes—and he would open them once more, by God—his two pale, silent companions, the flickering lamp, his mangled leg—everything in the here and now—would be gone beyond recall.

What would take their place? The steamy green tangle of the Niger jungles? . . . the furnace wastes of the desert beyond Sidi-bel-Abbés during the long summer eight years ago when he marched against the Touaregi in one more of those vicious games of hunt and kill, when a third of the regiment—men reduced to drinking their own thin piss— went insane with thirst and no one noticed because they went right on marching? . . . the massed, multi-colored pennants of the doomed charge at Marrakech when everything in Morocco fell on them save the Koutoubya Mosque itself, when bugles had blown retreat across streets awash with blood, and when the muezzin in the minaret called the faithful to their knees in prayer even as the men of the 14th fell back or died?

Or would he see that first mad assault, at Puebla, in *this* chaotic war?

Nothing could ever have brought *that* enemy to its knees. He knew that now. That slick, imperial puppetmaster back in Paris and his fragile, foolishly innocent Austrian marionette—fatally unstrung on the Hill of the Bells in Querétaro by now—had finally known it, too. The mute stone gods of Tenochtitlan surely knew it—as did even that unhinged, relentless general prowling somewhere in the storm.

Would he see the parapets of Chapultepec as he had seen them in his *first* war, long before the Legion claimed him?

Would the parade begin, the long route march of the men he had fought with . . . for . . . and against? Yes, they were coming now: Jean-Claude duBecq, Comonfort, Pierre Boulanger, Miguel López, the magnificent François-Achille Bazaine himself, the bandit *jefe* Antonio Pérez, that consummate ass Marcel Gallimard, and a hundred well-remembered others. Did any of them remember *him?* They gave no sign as they passed in ghostly silence.

For one flashing moment he was sure he saw *her,* but her dear, loved face disappeared in a sudden stab of pain.

He forced his eyes to open, or thought he did.

What he saw was himself, leaning against the rail of the packet steamer *Carcassonne* as it made its sluggish way into the harbor of Veracruz five years ago . . .

2

VERACRUZ, MEXICO—1862

"Mexico!"

Coming from Lieutenant Marcel Gallimard—the St. Cyrian standing next to Captain Jason James on the deck of the *Carcassonne* as it moved into the harbor—it was a throaty prayer.

James could almost see the dreams of glory enveloping the youngster in a cloud as thick and hot as the air they breathed. The boy—fresh out of the academy and with the wax of the Imperial seal on his new commission scarcely set—had dogged James's footsteps every nautical mile of the three-week voyage from Toulon. He had stuck to the Legion captain like a second skin from the first day out, even following him the night James left the officers' evening mess in the captain's quarters during the nightmare storm they weathered a thousand or more nautical miles west of Gibraltar, when dark waves as towering as the Atlas Mountains billowed beyond the prow, and when the rusty old packet pitched and rolled, almost standing on its nose like a performing dog in a circus.

To his credit, the St. Cyrian had delighted in the violence of the wind and water. No surprise. In James's time in desert and jungle wars, the St. Cyrians he fought beside—for all their overweening pursuit of *la gloire et l'honneur*—had never shown the slenderest stripe of cowardice. They may not all have been bright enough to open a tin of bully beef, but to a man St. Cyrians had been brave.

It was a strange sort of attention Lt. Gallimard paid him during the voyage: part puppylike worship once he discovered something about James's combat record in Africa, part the irritating snobbishness he unwittingly revealed in talking about his aristocratic origins in the Loire where his older brother was a count, and even more about his education at the elite French military college. Gallimard, who affected the spiky moustache and goatee of the French emperor, was pleasant enough, but a hopeless bore; his overtures had grown tiresome long before the storm struck, well before the ship touched at the Canaries to pick up the Spanish officers going out to join General Prim.

The Spaniards, doubting partners in this great Mexican adventure of Napoleon III and his Parisian sycophants, seemed to James much more phlegmatic, even cynical, than did the supposedly more sophisticated French on board, about what they would face when they crossed the Atlantic and the Gulf. Few of the Iberians expected they would do any real fighting in Mexico, much less reap glory. They had a nagging national memory. Three centuries earlier their forebears had spilled their blood taming the land toward which the *Carcassonne* now steamed; their New World cousins had milked it of riches ever since. "Why do these damned upstart colonial planters and *vaqueros* need or want us *now?*" a beak-nosed colonel from Estremadura said at the same mess James deserted for the deck in the middle of the storm. "Those bumpkin *hidalgos* and their fucking peasants threw us out forty years ago. Let the French save them." James, leaving the cabin at that moment, had not heard the rest of it. For his part, and for reasons entirely his own, he had less desire to be making this voyage than did the Spaniards.

That night on deck was the only time he saw the *Carcassonne's* most important passenger, Dubois de Saligny, who served with Admiral de Gravière as one of Napoleon III's commissioners to Mexico. He had rushed back to Paris two months ago for meetings on the emperor's latest plans for French intervention in Central America and Mexico, and the *Carcassonne*, slow as she was, turned out to be his quickest way back to Veracruz. His presence on the ship was not exactly a secret, but he kept to himself and out of sight during the entire crossing, dining later than the other officers, with only his two aides in attendance. No one talked about him. James would not have laid eyes on de Saligny at all before they docked if a flash of lightning had not revealed the tall figure of the commissioner touring the slippery deck while the storm raged.

For all the American knew, the reclusive Frenchman held in his slim, manicured hands a good part of the fate of the country toward which they sailed.

Since that one brief glimpse, James had more or less forgotten de Saligny. Gallimard never mentioned him either, not even that night, although James was sure the St. Cyrian knew all about him. Regular French Army officers, even *sous-lieutenants* such as Gallimard, were privy to briefings the Legion seldom got.

James shared a tiny cabin with three other officers and

thanked his stars Gallimard was not one of them. It was as bare and confining as the prison cell in Marseille he rotted in before the Legion rescued him, and he would be glad to end this trip, but he knew how much worse it would be for the enlisted men of the 14th Regiment, coming out from North Africa in two more weeks. When he first shipped out to Morocco with the Legion as a recruit, eleven years ago, he and his new fellow-*bleus* had been stacked in the hold of a leaky four-master as if they had been so much cordwood, with little more than garbage to eat. At least the food aboard the *Carcassonne* had been passable, perhaps because of the presence of the commissioner.

One thing, he remembered the country ahead as a horn-of-plenty where food was concerned.

"Mexico!" Gallimard breathed again. James winced at the boyish exuberance in the voice. "But you have been here before, have you not, *monsieur?*"

The haze that had covered the shore as they slipped into the harbor roads after threading their way through Admiral de Graviere's naval squadron was beginning to lift under the morning sun.

"*Oui,*" James said.

"And that was when, *mon capitaine?*"

He certainly was a formal little priss, nosy, too. "Fifteen years ago."

"*Mon dieu!* You were here with the Americans, then, Capitaine James?" He pronounced it "Capitaine Zhomm," but James had gotten used to that. The Poles and Germans in the rifle company he commanded did even stranger things with his name, and there had been times when he wished he had changed it as had so many other men who joined the Legion.

"Yes, lieutenant." He could feel where the questioning was leading, and he did not much relish it.

"Were you in the army of the great General Winfield Scott?"

Had Scott been so great? It was not an assessment shared

by many of the foot soldiers James had come ashore with back then. Nor was it one James shared himself.

"Yes," he said. "I served under General Scott."

"But, *monsieur le capitaine*, you must have been very young."

"I was seventeen."

"An officer at seventeen? *Sacrebleu!*"

"I wasn't an officer. I was just an ordinary soldier." That would probably drop him a notch in the lieutenant's estimation.

Perhaps—but it would not stop him. "I am almost twenty-one, and I have not yet seen battle," Gallimard said. It was a genuine lament. Then came the question James knew was coming, the one question he feared most of all. "Were you at the siege of Chapultepec?"

Chapultepec.

The name itself brought a shudder.

"*Excusez-moi*, lieutenant. We'll be at dockside in half an hour. I must see to my baggage now."

"I have my man Emile doing that at this very moment, *capitaine*." My man Emile? Maybe it had never dawned on this spoiled youngster that army pay, particularly in the Legion, did not cover servants, or other luxuries. Even a fairly high-ranking officer needed money of his own, or connections to it, to live the life of a gentleman.

James went below deck and secured his portmanteau and his musette bag, wondering if he should strap on his saber before disembarking. It would probably disappoint the eager Gallimard if he did not, and at the moment he felt enough truculence not to, but it would be awkward carrying the weapon rather than wearing it. He hoisted the portmanteau. It weighed a ton. Whether it cost too much or not, he really should consider hiring a servant such as the lieutenant's man Emile. He had employed a surly half-Berber for a while at Sidi-bel-Abbés after his captaincy almost doubled his pay and made him feel rich for a month or two. He had not paid Ali much, but the rogue made up for it by stealing from James and the two lieutenants who shared his quarters. James, a resigned if reluctant realist, had never called the Arab to account.

He sighed, belted the sash that held the scabbard of the saber around his waist, and hauled his belongings to the deck. He could make do very well without a personal servant in Mexico.

Gallimard stood on the bridge, trying now to engage the captain, a taciturn Greek named Bolas, in a conversation the man did not want. The captain was too preoccupied watching the Veracruz pilot they picked up just inside the breakwater guiding the *Carcassonne* toward the long, crowded dock ahead of them.

James placed his gear at the rail near the gangway and slipped behind a lifeboat covered by a salt-encrusted tarpaulin, hoping against hope Gallimard would not see him.

The two hundred yards or so of open water still between the *Carcassonne* and the dock left enough time to look the seaport city over, enough time for all the remembering he *wanted* to do at the moment.

Veracruz had changed little in fifteen years, had only gotten a little bigger and dirtier. The dock itself—where James and his cousin Aaron Sheffield had parted company for the last time—looked much the same, the massive pilings perhaps a slimier, darker shade of brown after all these years, streaked with sickly green sea moss looking like paint laid on with a scraggly brush, and with the water lapping around them the color and consistency of pus. On the quay itself the carts and burros seemed to be the same ones that fifteen years ago greeted Scott's American army and a wide-eyed young rifleman named Jason James, just six weeks away from his father's Kansas farm.

Beyond the waterfront, the stone and mud buildings whose flat roofs stretched away from narrow, cobbled *calles* looked not a great deal different from those of Sidi-bel-Abbés and Oran, and with the huge tent city way out in the open marshland beyond its last muddy alley, and topped by the familiar tri-color flag of France, it could have been either. But the illusion that this might be a desert or coastal town in French Africa was shattered by one glance at the throngs of stevedores and other laborers waiting on the long dock. Save for a detachment of infantry in French Imperial uniforms, fallen out of ranks to smoke in front of a sagging warehouse at the far southern end of the dock, the men he looked at could never be taken for French or Arab. They were Mexican, distinctly and only Mexican, most of them the *mestizos* he had known in '47, but here and there a lone negro or mulatto, *zambos*, he remembered them being called. Some in the crowd had draped *sarapes* in blacks, dull greens and yellows, and a few brighter stripes of the same colors, over their white cotton shirts and trousers, the *obrero* costume that together with the rope-soled sandals made up what was almost a uniform in this country.

And the brown faces had not changed. Almost all of them belonged to men. The few women in sight, withered crones, were vending foods from flatbed carts, or standing in front of smoking braziers, holding out garlands of blackened *chorizos* toward hoped-for buyers. The heady corn odor drifting across the narrowing expanse of oil-slick water on the weak breath of a useless breeze had not changed in that lost decade-and-a-half. It was the ubiquitous smell of this strange land.

The brown faces turned toward the *Carcassonne* showed little interest in the packet or its passengers and nothing in the way of curiosity. They might have been molded from putty.

"Look at them. *Quelles bêtes!* Dumb brutes!" Gallimard suddenly appeared at his elbow again. James felt a bit foolish when he saw the lieutenant was not wearing *his* sword.

"They're human beings, Lieutenant Gallimard!" he snapped, surprised at the sharpness of his voice. Bad tactic. It was not a good idea for a Legionnaire to get on the wrong side of rich, regular army officers, no matter if they were as junior to him as this foppish Frenchman. He had to admit, too, that there was indeed something brutish in the looks of the men and women on the dock. Small wonder, to anyone who knew the sad history of this country. Not that such a history troubled him too much. He was a soldier, a professional; his career would come to a full stop if he ever let the plight of civilians make him forget that.

"But, *monsieur*," Gallimard was saying now, "even if they *are* human beings, how can people who look so stupid and servile possibly stand against a European army? I am assuming, of course, that our enemy in the main consists of this sort of creature."

What lessons the lieutenant had yet to learn! James remembered all too well how goatherds in Algeria and pitifully armed, half-naked black men in the sub-Saharan forests had taken everything a modern army could throw at them, had suffered and survived, and had even beaten that army soundly on more than one occasion.

The fathers and uncles of these dockworkers had fought well enough back in 1847. They might just have won if they had not had too many officers like the one standing next to James. But he had no intention of teaching any lessons about the fighting qualities of indigenous peoples to Gallimard, even if the young man wished him to. The lieutenant in the uniform probably tailored at Soutaine's in Paris would have to learn them for himself. James hoped the boy would not repeat the question.

"Enemy?" he said. "You must bear in mind, lieutenant, that we are not at war with Mexico. We are supposed to be here solely to protect French interests. At the moment we're here with the permission of the Republican government, reluctant as it might be to have us here. If we're lucky we won't fight anyone."

Gallimard's shoulders sagged in apparent disappointment. The sharp look he gave James revealed a certain amount of disdain, too. Clearly he could never regard not seeing combat as "lucky."

The St. Cyrian pulled a square of silk from his tunic and

wiped his forehead. *"Mon dieu!* It is beastly hot and the sun is barely up. Is it always like this, *mon capitaine?"*

"Almost always here on the coast. This is what the Mexicans call *'la tierra caliente.'* The climate at Mexico City, the capital, which is almost two kilometers above sea level, is usually quite pleasant."

The remark about the heat brought to mind some of James's own thoughts on the outward voyage, now reinforced by his view of the sprawling French encampment beyond the town. He had read all the intelligence briefs Legion headquarters in Oran had issued the officers in the regiments shipping out for Mexico, and had wondered at the time why Latrille de Lorencez, the general commanding the French expeditionary force, under whom James had served once in a short, fierce campaign near Colomb Bechar, had insisted on withdrawing forces from as far inland as Orizaba, and holding them here in the swampy country near the coast. The move shrank the French and Spanish perimeter, of course, and made for a better defense, but it exposed the European troops to enemies every bit as deadly as the soldiers of Benito Juárez. The French army, from the last reports, had rotted here for two long months already, could rot here all spring and summer, with no declaration of war in the offing.

In his campaigns in Africa, de Lorencez had revealed himself as a daring, often brilliant tactician, but never a strategist in the grand sense, and too frequently a poor attender to detail. Giving up the inland bastions won here in Mexico last fall without a major fight, even temporarily, might be one such detail. The treaty called the Convention of La Soledad had locked the French here in Veracruz, and if malaria and yellow fever had not attacked French troops yet, they soon could. Dysentery most surely would. The Legion, toughened by long campaigns in hot, disease-ridden lands, might not suffer too much, but regular army units trained in the sanitary, salubrious south of France could wilt in weeks. Surely de Lorencez planned a move to the higher, more temperate interior soon.

Would France bother even to ask the Mexicans to agree to such a move before resorting to hostilities?

With a shiver all along its starboard side the *Carcassonne* bumped against the fenders of the dock, and the boat whistle steamed three enormous blasts into the fetid air in a signal more of relief than of celebration.

Far down the dock the company of infantry struggled into marching order with two trumpeters and a guidon-bearer in the lead. They moved out smartly under the eye of an officer wielding a saber. James's mood brightened when he saw the saber; he would not stand out too much himself now.

"Do you suppose it is a welcoming honor guard for us?" Gallimard whispered, his eyes even wider than they had been.

"Not likely. It is probably for the commissioner."

"*Certainement!* How could I forget."

As the detachment neared the gangplank one of the women vendors rushed up to the column and thrust her wares at a soldier in the last rank of four. The soldier pulled his rifle from his shoulder and without looking at her swung the flat of the stock against her cheek. She crumpled into a heap of rags.

Gallimard laughed. No one else on the dock or at the rail of the *Carcassonne* seemed to notice the incident.

James had no time to concern himself about it, even had he wanted to. The ship's first officer stepped down from the bridge with a megaphone to his mouth and alerted all the officers on deck to go ashore immediately and report to the Customs House. Obviously the commissioner would not disembark until they all cleared out.

The boat whistle blared again, impatient this time— impelling them ashore.

When James stepped from the bottom of the gangplank he felt a tremor under the soles of his boots. Imagination? He could not be sure. After all, this country all too often shrugged and shook as if it were trying to awaken from a nightmare—an attempt that in James's opinion always failed. He had known earthquakes when he landed here with Scott. Real ones, as well as the quakes of battle. A look at Gallimard, right on his heels, of course, told him the lieutenant, at least, felt nothing.

The infantry company formed two lines leading away from the anchored *Carcassonne,* and James, Gallimard, and a broken queue of French and Spanish officers moved between the lines all the way to the steps of a rococo building with a sign reading *"Bureaux de Douane."*

How many times had he reported for duty and assignment like this? It had become old hat. The Spanish officers on board were of a mind that there would be no fighting worth mentioning. Despite his remark to Gallimard, James was not so sure of that. The most sanguine imperialist could have read in the dockside faces that Europeans were not welcome here, even if there was money to be made from these wayfarers from overseas. But—according to the French newspapers he had read aboard the *Carcassonne*— the "people of Mexico" were begging the French emperor to take charge of their affairs. For a year Napoleon III had played coy. Now he was calling for a "new crusade" to establish a Catholic monarchy in the New World, one modeled on the ancient regimes of Mother Europe. *"Republicanism has failed Mexico,"* the press reported him as saying. To make matters worse—or better, depending on one's point of view—a tide of Napoleonic pride had deluged the Chamber of Deputies.

No one, at least no one with a voice strong enough to be heard above the din of hyper-patriotism, had asked precisely who those "people of Mexico" were.

Well, he could not concern himself with that, not the planning of it, at any rate. The fighting that his employers might order him to do—*that* concerned him. And he would do that when ordered. Do it, if not gladly, then with a will. The Legion had treated him with fairness. It had always honored its part of the contract he signed eleven years ago in Marseille—when Legion recruiters saved him from a

Provençal version of the Bastille and quite possibly from the guillotine—and if their honoring of it had sometimes sent him into discomfort and danger, so be it. He would honor his part. It made things simple, manageable—and orderly. If it had not been for the Legion he might still be trudging behind a plow, sweating life out as an ordinary seaman, or worse, fighting against his brothers and cousins in the bloody civil war he had seen coming to the United States even before he left Kansas, the war now ripping his country into two furious, hating halves, the war he had vowed he would never fight in, the war that would have required him to fight Cousin Aaron.

The meeting in the Customs House took less time than he expected. Good thing. The building was an oven, and perhaps the colonel running things wanted to get away from the heat as much as the new arrivals did. James picked up the papers assigning him to a billet in a Veracruz inn called La Posada Rinconada, and an amiable sergeant whose accent tagged him as a native of the Dordogne sketched a map for him to find it. To his mild disgust he discovered Gallimard had drawn La Posada Rinconada for his quarters too.

As quickly as the French colonel had moved things along in the Customs House, James found it was already a few minutes past noon when he stepped back into the hot sun bathing the dock. There had been no breakfast mess aboard the *Carcassonne* this morning and he was ravenous. To his satisfaction Gallimard had become hung up somewhere behind him.

Three shoddy-looking cantinas lined the street facing the dock, but his stomach insisted it was no time to be fussy, and he stepped into the first of them.

A crowd filled the barroom. Most of the drinkers looked like dockworkers, big for Mexicans, hard and tough as leather quirts. Booted feet scraped on the dirt floor. Voices rumbled—a Babel of Spanish and what must be Indian tongues. The air was thick with the blue fumes of *cigarros*, and heavy with the odor of corn, tomatoes, onions, and pork cooking furiously in an alcove away from the bar. One glance told him he was the only non-Mexican there, and he almost did an about-face and left, but as unappetizing as the first smell of the food was, its aroma began to reach right down into his hollow belly. He wedged his way to the bar and ordered a glass of wine to ready himself for whatever assault his eating here in this adobe sewer might make on his sensibilities.

At the sound of his voice, the din faded into silence. He stared straight ahead of him, fully aware that a dozen or more faces had turned toward him as they would in a coffeehouse in the Algiers Casbah. He heard the word "gringo," uttered with venom. The Legion uniform had not fooled them. They knew him for an American. Eyes bored into the back of his head, and he could feel hate in the stares.

"¡Capitán!" A harsh croak came from somewhere behind him.

He looked around, but he could not find or identify the speaker. Nothing greeted him except blank, brown faces.

"¡Capitán!" The same voice, even harsher this time. "Down here, capitán."

He lowered his gaze to see a very small, very ugly man.

The top of an enormous head and even the crown of the straw sombrero the speaker wore hardly reached to James's waist, and under the big hat a bristly black beard flecked with gray failed to hide a lumpy, scored, pitted countenance. Over a naked torso a leather vest only partly covered a chest matted with hair a match for the beard, and from the vest, two simian, heavily muscled bare arms reached down toward truncated legs. A hairy right hand curled around the hilt of a knife which, on the short body, seemed as long as the blade of a Legion saber.

The ugly little creature cleared his throat and spat on the floor, almost hitting James's boots. "You are the Legion *capitán* who came in on the *Carcassonne* this morning, no?"

"Yes," James said.

"The gringo Legionnaire who carries his own *equipaje* like a burro in uniform?" Was there scorn in the man's voice or was it just a congenital rasp?

"I don't think I was the only officer to carry his baggage from the ship."

"Perhaps," the other said, "but the *capitán* was the only one Cipi saw. Permit me to introduce myself, *señor. Me llamo* Cipriano Luis Sebastian Jesus Camargo Méndez y García . . . de Toledo."

"And what does all that mean, *amigo?*" It was all James could do to suppress a laugh.

"Among other things, Cipi is *gachupín.* Unlike these *estúpidos* around us, he was born in Spain. There is not a single drop of *indio* blood in Cipi's veins."

James wondered how this improbable gnome had known to address him mostly in English. "And what may I do for you, *Don* Cipriano?" He could already guess. The little grotesque wanted him to buy a drink.

"You may, gringo—if you have any sense at all—engage me to be your body servant, your *hombre.*"

This time James did not even try to hold back the laughter. "How in *el nombre de Dios* could a midget serve as *hombre* for a full-sized soldier?"

James was unprepared for the way the little man suddenly puffed like an adder. His mouth opened in a snarl. Black eyes sparked. He lifted a clublike right boot, then pounded it down into the packed dirt floor like a pile driver.

"CIPI MÉNDEZ Y GARCÍA IS NOT A *MIDGET!*" The blast shivered glasses on the bar. "A midget is just a Yanqui like you with the *mierda* squeezed out. I am *un enano*—a dwarf—a different and special thing. Men such as I possess black magic, *señor.* Do not forget that—ever!"

The other Mexicans at the bar edged closer, hemming James in. Clearly the dwarf had friends here. This could prove awkward, more than awkward, dangerous. It was still early and most of these hard men were probably only *close* to drunkenness, but near-drunks could turn as vicious here as any he had known on the waterfronts of Glasgow or Genoa. The flare of temper from the dwarf could ignite something deadly in this crowd. The folly of the damned useless saber! He could fall with a dozen knife wounds in him before the blade was halfway out of the scabbard. He could be damned well sure even *French* officers disappeared without a trace on this waterfront from time to time.

Then the dwarf spread his arms. "*¡Basta!*" His voice roared like a cannon. The men moving toward James stopped. The dark, bearded, misshapen face rearranged its corrugations into a saurian smile. "You see, *mi capitán,*" he said. "Cipi told you. He has black powers and second sight. You might need both sometime. Now—lift me up on the bar. I wish to speak with you face-to-face while we discuss the terms of our arrangement."

"Arrangement? I've not agreed to hire you."

"You will, *señor.* Rest assured, you will."

Five minutes later, *el enano* Cipriano Méndez y García, Cipi, entered the service of Jason Jeremiah James. When they ratified their contract with a handshake, James was astonished at the powerful grip of his new employee. Remembering the little man's explosive display of temper, he hoped he had not made a mistake. Servants had been known to kill the men they worked for—out of some black distemper, or for reasons of pure cupidity. Cipi did not look as if thievery or mayhem were entirely unknown to him.

"Now we shall find your *posada,* my captain," the dwarf said, as he hopped from the bar. "*Por favor,* pay for my drinks. Cipi had two. Do not let Esteban here charge you for more than that. I will bring you food from Stebbi's miserable *cocina.*"

What a comic pair they must make, James thought as they trudged along the quay past the Baluarte de Santiago, the small fort Winfield Scott had made his headquarters in '47 until the dampness and a dozen families of indignant snakes drove him and his staff out into the streets of Veracruz.

James took the lead, the ridiculous saber swinging awkwardly at his side as he gulped down the hellishly spiced pork wrapped in a grainy, tough, flat patty of bread that Cipi had handed him when they were in the street. He was glad the men of Compagnie Rouge of the 14th Regiment, and in particular Sergeant Jean-Claude duBecq, were still en route to Mexico and not on hand to see their captain now, stuffing his face like an Arab beggar, juices running down his chin. Behind him the dwarf struggled with the portmanteau. He had lifted it easily enough, but with his hands reaching so close to the ground he could not keep it clear of the cobbled street and had to carry it on his shoulder. James had offered to take it when he saw the effort Cipi was making, but his newly hired *hombre* gave his master a stare that would have melted steel. With the huge bag towering above him and swaying drunkenly with every step the short legs took, he reminded James of a carelessly loaded camel in a Sahara caravan.

At a filthy *calle* leading away from the dockside street Cipi called from behind him. "*Izquierda, mi capitán.* We turn left here."

James consulted the map the sergeant in the Customs House had given him. "That's not the way to the *posada.*" Was the little villain trying to lure him into some back alley to rob and kill him already?

"*Por favor,* do not argue. We must purchase *las cobijas* for you. There is a shop here where they will not cheat us. Not with Cipi Méndez y García watching them."

"*¿Las cobijas? Por qué?*" Some of his Spanish had returned in his talks with his new servant. *Bueno.* "Posada Rinconada does not furnish blankets with their beds?"

"Sometimes. Most often not. If your bed does have blankets you will sleep under them only if you wish company all night. *Los piojos!*"

Lice. The dwarf might yet steal everything he owned, might even use that wicked-looking knife on him as he slept, but for the moment James was grateful to the little knave. He had already had enough experience with lice to last a lifetime.

"The captain will also need *un empalletado*, a straw tick or something like it," Cipi added.

La Posada Rinconada was jammed to the walls with French officers.

Gallimard entered the inn almost on James's heels. James, getting a room key from the owner of the inn in return for the billet voucher, wondered how the Frenchman had gotten to the Rinconada so fast. The stop for mattress and blankets Cipi and he had made must have done it.

There was general laughter as the dwarf staggered through the main entrance hall of the *posada*, carrying portmanteau, musette bag, the now unbuckled saber, as well as the newly purchased bedding—all in one precariously balanced load. Predictably, Gallimard was one of the laughers, the closest to the dwarf—and the loudest.

"What imbecile would employ a little turd like that one?" the Frenchman jeered. Cipi stopped in his tracks. One hand moved to the hilt of the knife, moved back to the load as it shifted and nearly toppled.

James slid around Gallimard with a curt nod and followed Cipi down the hallway toward the room the innkeeper had designated. He guessed Gallimard had not yet linked him with the dwarf.

"Is it permitted for Cipi to take the old *cobijas, mi capitán?*" the little man asked when he finished making up James's bed in a cell-like room. "*Los piojos* never bother Cipi."

"*Sí.* Where will you sleep?"

"Do not worry about me, *mi capitán.* Cipi will find a place." He backed out of the room, his arms loaded with the bedding he had stripped from a wooden cot.

"Cipi will report for duty in the morning," he said. "You will not need him until then."

James laughed when the door closed on the dwarf. An onlooker might be hard put to decide which of the two of them was master and which was *hombre.*

He spent the rest of the afternoon putting his gear in

order and filling out the mile of forms issued to him by the sergeant at the Customs House.

The *posada* served dinner at a pale imitation of a French army mess in a crowded, low-ceilinged room at the back of the inn. James was gratified to discover he had been replaced in the instant pantheon of Lieutenant Marcel Gallimard by a grizzled colonel of Zouaves. The dandified junior officer hung like a trapeze artist on every guttural word the veteran uttered. He did not so much as glance in James's direction.

James recognized most of his fellow diners as having just this morning arrived with him on the *Carcassonne,* but here and there he saw unfamiliar faces. As far as he could tell he was the only Legion officer present, and beyond nods there were no greetings. Starting tomorrow he would have to get to know the men behind the faces he did not recognize. Something told him the new faces had been in Mexico for a while on this campaign, and some of their owners would have answers to the professional questions he wished to ask. Briefings and situation maps would only tell him part of what he wanted; there was no substitute for examining the thoughts and feelings of soldiers who been over the ground already.

From snatches of conversation he learned that although there had been no outbreak of genuine hostilities to this point, Mexican irregulars had made several small attacks on isolated French units. Nothing too bloody. Irritations for the most part. Still, he could feel the tight, under-the-surface tension of men who felt they would soon be going into action, and on a few he could see the look that spoke of recent combat.

After the meal he took a constitutional along the waterfront.

The hubbub of the day had been replaced by the whispers of hot offshore breezes as they moved out to sea, and the noise of the crowd had given way to the pathetic bleats of gulls trying to find an unlikely meal in the oily water. The *Carcassonne*, deserted now, looked to be a ghost ship, a forlorn collection of rusted plates and bolts. There was still some sun on his back, but it was dwindling fast.

The long-before-dawn rising aboard the vessel began to take its toll, and he decided to turn in. There had been no sign of the dwarf. He could not have deserted already, could he? Not likely. Not before his first—and possibly only— payday.

Sleep found the Legionnaire less than a minute after he slid under the blankets bought in the litter-filled shop he and the dwarf had visited, but in less than an hour— he could not be sure with his watch on the chest across the room—a sound at the door jolted him to full wakefulness.

It was a weird, whispering, muffled *swish . . . swish . . . swish.*

His service pistol lay at the bottom of the portmanteau, and he silently cursed the fatigue that had made him too lazy to dig it out and load it before retiring. He eased the saber from its scabbard as quietly as he could, stepped to the door and ripped it open.

Cipi was stretched out on the hall floor just beyond the lintel, his short legs swathed in what appeared to be a brand new *sarape.* The long knife was in one tough, gnarled hand. The other held a whetstone with a deep dish worn into its gray surface. He looked up at James. Was the expression on his gargoyle face grin or grimace? Jesus, he was ugly!

James pointed to the *sarape.* "Why aren't you using the old blankets?"

"Cipi sold them, *señor.*" He patted the *sarape.* "He needed this."

"And you weren't going to tell me . . ."

The dwarf shrugged. James closed the door.

Dinner the night before had merely been a reprieve; he did not escape Gallimard at breakfast. The Frenchman was a different man from the fawning youngster who covered the

Zouave colonel's derriere with kisses last night. His pomaded hair was a wild tangle, and his red-rimmed eyes spoke of a night spent without sleep. One hand dug at an armpit while the other clawed the beard and moustache with manic industry.

"Lice, *monsieur. Mon dieu!* They have taken possession of me. *C'en est de trop!*" His fingernails began another frantic search, of his crotch this time. "It the fault of *mon homme* Emile. My room possessed no bedding of any kind. Emile bought some from that ugly little monster we saw yesterday. He didn't want to sell it at first, but that moron Emile insisted—actually pleaded with him. I believe I shall cane Emile when these creatures leave me." He uttered one more word, the same word he had infused with such breathy fervor at the rail of the *Carcassonne.* This time it carried an absolutely poisonous load of bitterness.

"*Mexico!*"

3

PARIS—APRIL 1862

"Solange!" Sarah Kent Anderson called to the middle-aged Frenchwoman packing the steamer trunk. "I've decided we will take the dark blue velvet after all. It's much too heavy for Veracruz, but if we can go straight on to the capital after we land in Mexico, I'll need it." Her frivolity appalled her. Why was she concerning herself with personal adornment with what lay ahead of her, and with the memory of the tragic recent past still weighing her down?

"*Oui, mademoiselle.*" The maid still had not completely recovered from her first fright at the prospect of leaving Paris. Sarah wanted to tell her to put the two-kilo packet of quinine tablets into the brocade valise, the pills M. Lagarde at the Rue Chapelle apothecary shop delivered this morning, but she knew it might start Solange off on another round of tears. The possibility of malaria could be the last straw for "*pauvre Solange*," as she had begun to call herself this week with the packing under way, lamenting her delicate health with every other breath—even though she had not suffered so much as a runny nose in the five years since the Pelletiers put Sarah in her care.

Solange had swung between giddy anticipation of the trip across the ocean and absolute, quivering terror at what Mexico could hold for them ever since Sarah told her about her brother Samuel's death in Zacatecas and her decision to sail from Calais at the end of April. She had not wanted to tell Solange why they were going, but it was hardly the kind of news one could keep secret, not in a French household knit as closely as that of Auguste and Claudine Pelletier. Besides, Uncle Tobias Kent's letter was still on the escritoire where Sarah dropped it from fingers suddenly turned to ice when it arrived from Boston a month ago. Solange's English was not the best, but it was good enough for her to decipher the heart-breaking message if she read it, something her deep-dyed Gallic curiosity would bring her to sooner or later, if it had not already. The Frenchwoman, whom Sarah knew for a secret, steady, if controlled, tippler, had been at the cognac that she kept in her room even more frequently since Sarah announced the trip.

Perhaps the wisest and kindest decision would be to leave Solange here in Paris; a trustworthy Mexican housekeeper should not be hard to find once Sarah settled in, and it would be difficult for Solange to deal with running a household in a country where she could not speak or understand the language. Sarah herself would have too much to occupy her in becoming a woman of business.

But the thought of leaving this comforting, earnest woman behind in France with the Pelletiers . . . she dismissed it at once. The voyage, without Solange seeing to her needs, and acting as duenna, could turn miserable.

Sarah had always had companions when crossing the Atlantic, and this would be a much longer voyage than the one between Boston and Le Havre. Besides, the one time she mentioned leaving the maid behind, Solange assured her she wanted to go, *insisted* on going, despite her fears of that "*terre sauvage*," as she characterized Mexico. "No black woman can look after you as Solange can, *ma petite*," she said. In thirty-two years of domestic service Solange had never strayed a mile off the narrow path between her village in the Pas-de-Calais and the Pelletier home here in Paris. Where had she gotten the idea that everyone in Mexico was negro?

The Pelletiers, too, had insisted that Solange accompany her when Sarah told them of her decision to sail to Mexico and finally persuaded them it was something she had to do. Monsieur Auguste, of course, had given a little cry of anguished regret, and Tante Claudine had broken into the torrential sobs Sarah knew would come. She almost cried herself, would have, if she had not been drained of tears at the news about Samuel.

The Pelletiers could not have been more of a family to her had they been tied to the Massachusetts Kents and Andersons by blood. She had lived with them every summer for almost nine years, since Monsieur Auguste and his wife had stayed with Sarah and her parents, a time when Pelletier, first secretary of the Academie Francaise, had been a guest lecturer in Bradford Anderson's history department at Harvard. Her summers had turned into a year-round stay the last three years. Even after her father died she had lived a life of satisfying work and play here, studying history at the Sorbonne just as he had, becoming an all-but-legally adopted daughter to the childless Pelletiers.

She had asked Monsieur Auguste only one question about her journey to Mexico. "Do you think it safe for me to go now, with all the trouble building there?"

"*Mais oui*," he had replied. His voice betrayed genuine sorrow at the prospect of her leaving. "While I do not agree with what his Imperial Majesty and the Duc de Morny want France to do in—and to—that unfortunate country, it is certain, *chérie*, that the great strength of our army will keep Mexico safe for Europeans—or Americans. I seriously doubt there will be fighting of any consequence, certainly not a war." He had set his generous, honest mouth in a firm line and added, "However, I do not think I would drink the water if I were you, *ma chère.*" It brought the first smile since the news about Samuel arrived. She knew all about the water in Mexico from her two trips there: her three-month stay eight years ago at the hilltop *hacienda* overlooking the Anderson mine near Zacatecas, when she had spent her fifteenth birthday visiting her brother Samuel; and five years ago, the year before her father followed her mother into the old graveyard in Cambridge where Andersons and Kents had rested since long before the American Revolution. On the second of these month-long visits she met and had two long talks with Benito Juárez, the strange, dark little man who was now president of Mexico, at the time fresh from victory in what his Republican followers called *la Guerra de la Reforma,* a war Samuel—not the pacifist his father Bradford and sister Sarah were—had supported with all the fervor his more distant forebears had shown from Concord Bridge to Yorktown. President Juárez had talked to her as if she were an adult. Women were not often treated that way in Benito Juárez's country—or in Boston or Paris for that matter. Samuel had worshiped the frock-coated little Indian from Oaxaca, had recognized his great worth even before most of Juárez's own countrymen had. Would she see *el presidente* when she arrived in the capital? And would he remember her? She hoped so.

Her first unhappy task when she reached Mexico would be to get Samuel's body disinterred and sent to lie beside their parents in the old cemetery, and arrange for a memorial in Uncle Tobias's First Congregational Church. Uncle Tobias would probably have his assistant pastor conduct the funeral service, saying he could not do it himself since he was related to the deceased. The truth was that the old minister knew he would never be able to officiate without it breaking his heart. He had loved Samuel as he would have loved the son he did not have.

Samuel's body. Funny, she had never felt herself an orphan until she read Uncle Tobias's letter. She had not looked at it since she put it back in its evelope and dropped it on the escritoire, but she remembered almost every brutal word of it.

". . . and Señor Alberto Moreno, Samuel's mine manager, was wounded severely, too. He said in his telegram that Samuel could not have suffered much; it was all over very quickly. The bandits apparently knew exactly when the payroll money would arrive, and they were waiting when Samuel reached his office. Unfortunately, the government of President Juárez, while sympathetic to our great loss, feels there is nothing much that can be done about apprehending these murderers and bringing them to justice. Lawlessness is rampant in Mexico these days.

"My chief regret, my child, is that there is no MAN left in the family to go to Zacatecas State and look after things for you. Harvey Endicott at Peabody, Weston, and McKenzie here in Boston will take care of estate matters in Massachusetts, but he does not seem inclined to leave the city at this time for any consideration. I would go myself, but my age, as well as my duties at the church, preclude that. So many Massachusetts lads like poor Josiah to memorialize these days, with this ghastly war going on. I have, however, written to the American embassy in Mexico City on your behalf, and you should hear from someone there shortly. I have given them your address in Paris. Señor Moreno seems to be a man of utmost probity, and I believe you can rely on him utterly, once he is well again . . ."

"Poor Josiah" was cousin Josiah Anderson from two houses down her street in Cambridge. Sarah and Josiah had been raised together, and he had become nearly as much a brother as Samuel was. He had died at First Manassas. Lord, how she hated war and soldiering! What was going on in her own country now made no more sense than did Samuel's death in Mexico. There were times she was almost glad her father had not lived to see it.

The letter from the embassy, signed by someone named Jarvis Saunders, had indeed come to the Pelletier house in La Rue de Rivoli. It did not tell her any more about Samuel's death than had the sketchy one from Uncle Tobias, but in it Mr. Saunders had promised to arrange her transportation between Veracruz and Mexico City if she decided to come there, and to provide a U.S. Marine officer on duty with the military attache at the embassy to get her through customs and bring her to the capital.

Her countrymen in Mexico were going to a lot of trouble for her. Did every grief-stricken, bereaved young woman receive this kind of treatment? She supposed not. The fact that she was a *rich* young woman probably made the difference.

She did not know yet how rich she was and in her black sorrow did not care. A brief note from the lawyer Endicott arriving in the same post informed her that she was the sole inheritor of the estate of her dead brother, who had never married. The Anderson family trust, which had supported her in comfort ever since her father's death in 1858, still had three years to run before she had to manage all her affairs herself. She only had a hazy notion of what it entailed. During the years since her father died, the law firm of Peabody, Weston, and McKenzie had sent her copies of the financial reports they made to Samuel, her legal guardian, but she had never given them more than a glance. She did not at the moment have the slightest idea where they were; perhaps in her father's old study in the house in Cambridge.

And now she owned a silver mine. As with her brother's money, she did not want it. It was too much like an open grave for Samuel. It would remain just that until she got him back to Boston.

No matter where she came to a stop in Mexico, or for however long, it would not be in Zacatecas. Lovely as the old city was, with its magnificent cathedral crowning a steep hill, it would be for her only another hollow sepulcher echoing with the torments of memory.

"Mademoiselle Sarah, *s'il vous plait.*" Solange had finished with the trunk and was standing by the escritoire. "What shall we do with this? Is it to be saved?" She held the remains of the corsage Henri had brought Sarah to wear to the graduation ball at St. Cyr six weeks ago, when Henri's younger brother Marcel was commissioned in the Imperial Army. It had been pressed in the big French dictionary she kept next to her writing case. Solange had put it there. The maid had never once voiced her opinions about Henri, but Sarah could have been deaf and mostly blind and still have known what they were. Solange's face lit up like a lamp every time the Comte de Bayeux came to call at the Pelletiers.

Monsieur Auguste and Tante Claudine had been as approving of Henri as Solange this past year, since Sarah met him at the Beaux Arts. They invited him to dinner with far more frequency than they asked almost any other friend or acquaintance she had made in all her time in Paris.

She had welcomed Henri's attentions at first, still found them pleasing for the most part, but . . .

There had been times she felt she was only *drifting* toward marriage without knowing in her heart whether or not she wanted it. At twenty-three she *should* want it, should she not? In just a few more years she would stop being a maiden lady and become a spinster, and it was unlikely she would ever find a better prospect than Henri, certainly no man more compatible with her.

Like her, he was a student of history; more than a student, he was working on a mammoth biography of his namesake, Henri Quatre, the "Greengage." Henri was kind, charming, and possessed an unassuming intellect almost on a par with that of Monsieur Auguste, something that placed him very high in the estimation of the man Sarah had come to regard as a second father. Not handsome, but pleasant looking, Henri seemed to dote on her—abandoning his aristocratic reserve whenever they were alone together. She should consider herself a lucky young woman. If she had not quite fallen in love with him, she surely had become infatuated with his background and his family home, an appealing hundred-year-old chateau situated on one of the quiet, slow-moving rivers that fed the Loire. Certainly she would not be the only woman to yearn to be its chatelaine. She had little doubt that someday Henri would ask her to marry him, and almost no doubt at all that when he did, she would say yes. She knew how close he had come to asking her a time or two already. Why did the idea not excite her more? And why had she silently prayed that the proposal would *not* come, either when she told him about Samuel or when she expected it most, when she announced her plans to go to Mexico?

There had been tremors of guilt when she came dangerously close to feeling grateful to Samuel for dying when he did—if he had to die—and sparing her from having to give Henri an answer.

In any event, she would not, apparently, lose him as a suitor because of her forthcoming journey. Henri's brother Marcel, a graduating cadet at St. Cyr, was shipping out to Mexico to join one of the regiments serving under General Latrille de Lorencez, and Henri announced at the graduation ball that as soon as the spring planting was finished at the chateau, he would cross the ocean himself to see them both. This alone made the ball enjoyable—there were far too many uniforms for Sarah's taste and comfort.

She would be ready for the boat train to Calais on Friday. There remained only one last social chore: Charlotte's dinner party tonight.

Charlotte had come to Paris by private car on the train from Trieste, arriving at the Gare St. Lazaire just yesterday.

Apparently Max would not be with her this trip, or at least would not be at the dinner his wife was giving at the nine-room apartment the Belgian court kept in the Faubourg St. Germain.

It would be wonderful beyond belief to see Charlotte again, even if seeing her made her regret her decision to leave Europe now. But seeing her would probably disturb Sarah a little as it always did. How long had they known each other now, six years?

Someone, she could not remember whom, but perhaps it would come to her, had once said, "*With the rich and mighty, always a little patience . . .*" Fortunately, Sarah had never had to exhibit the same patience with Charlotte as the princess's own Belgian coterie did, or, she supposed, nearly as much as the Austrians surrounding Archduke Max had to show.

They had met at the convent school in which the Pelletiers had enrolled Sarah when Monsieur Auguste almost despaired of her ever learning the French of Paris. Drawn together first by a common love of history, Sarah knew the Belgian girl a month before discovering she was royalty. Princess or no, Charlotte had a certain brilliance as a student. She eventually displayed even more brilliance as friend and confidante.

The nuns at St. Catherine's had kept her presence at the French convent school a secret at her royal family's request. Sarah kept the secret, too.

In that summer six years ago the news came from Massachusetts of Sarah's mother's death. Charlotte nursed her through the first and worst of her grief, sitting up with her through an entire week of despairing nights while Sarah sobbed herself to exhaustion, and in the ensuing months the studious dedication, the spirited winsomeness of Charlotte, and always the deep understanding in her black eyes, had almost made Sarah accept her loss. She would be forever in Charlotte's debt for that, no matter what fate brought both of them.

Most of the time she forgot that the dark-haired Belgian

girl was the daughter of a genuine, reigning European monarch. Most of the time, but not all.

Charlotte could turn inward and brooding without warning and seemingly without reason, and when emerging from such states, almost cruelly autocratic. At such times she would allow no one but Sarah near her.

When Charlotte entered one of these dark moods, and during the flare-ups that inevitably followed, when the dancing eyes first turned still as stone and then without warning to hot coals, when she lashed out at anyone at hand for some real or as often as not invented slight—as during the stormy days following her hysterical claim that the teaching sisters at St. Catherine's were stealing from her, and when she insisted the Belgian ambassador call on the mother superior to explain why that kindly old woman was "plotting" against her—she seemed to need Sarah as much as Sarah had needed her.

No sisters, Sarah told herself, could ever have been this close.

Blessedly, Charlotte's consuming fires—whatever their cause—seemed to have ceased when she married Max five years ago, just before she turned nineteen.

This new calmness was hearsay, of course; Sarah and Charlotte had not seen each other since the royal couple honeymooned on Capri and then took up residence in Trieste, where Max commanded the Hapsburg Adriatic fleet. Sarah had only met Max once, in the receiving line at the ball that followed the wedding in Brussels; their brief conversation then had been severely, if warmly, formal—a ritual exchange rather than a talk.

There had been some correspondence from time to time, warm notes and friendly letters, all signed "Charlotte," with no title, and most of them passionate declarations of how wonderful her life was with "my Maxl." Sarah rejoiced for her. Moving in such different worlds she knew she might never see Charlotte again, but it did not matter. There would be a bond between them that nothing could ever break.

The dinner invitation that came a week ago carried a new signature—Carlota—and Sarah was not even sure it was from her school friend at all until she examined the gold embossing at the top of it.

Charlotte always enclosed a list of the guests at any of the more intimate parties she gave, one of her more considerate habits, Sarah thought, and she had done so again this time.

Henri Gallimard, listed as the Comte de Bayeux, was an invitee, of course—Charlotte's Paris circle would have kept her informed of Sarah's involvement with him without a doubt—as was the Duc de Morny, no surprise. The great duke was an intimate of Austrian Emperor Franz Joseph, Max's older brother. Sarah thrilled to find the name of Jenny Lind on the guest list. The "Swedish Nightingale," probably over from her Mayfair home in London for one of her marathon shopping sprees, no longer sang opera, but would doubtless be persuaded to offer an air or two for the guests of the daughter of the King of Belgium. By all reports she had lost none of her lyric splendor.

Also crossing the channel for the dinner was Henry Adams, son of, and private secretary to, the American ambassador to the Court of St. James. Sarah knew Henry, a quiet young man of about her own age who had studied under her father at Harvard and now carried the immense weight of the Adams name on shoulders that did not quite look up to the task. Poor, shy Henry. He always found a seat "below the salt," not so much as if he had been placed there by a hostile hostess, but more as if he had picked it out himself. Sarah liked him.

She noted with relief that no generals or colonels appeared on Charlotte's guest list. Her only quibble about her stays in France had been the never-ending parade of uniforms passing through almost every social and public function in Paris. They always brought uneasiness, perhaps a legacy from Bradford Anderson's deep and devout pacifism—she *was* her father's daughter—and her New England upbringing. Americans in general, and Bostonians in particular, had always harbored a deep distrust of the military, especially the professionals. With the war now splitting North and South, the streets of Cambridge would probably present the same martial appearance as did the boulevards of the French capital. She had better prepare herself for the same thing in Mexico.

And notably missing from the guest list were M. et Mme. Auguste Pelletier.

She wondered about this until she found the name of M. Alphonse de Lamartine halfway down the list.

As alternately insouciant and obtuse as Maximilian von Hapsburg's young Belgian wife could be at times, she would never have the temerity to bring Auguste Pelletier and the celebrated, aging author of *La chute d'un ange* to the same dinner table. Not after the terrible verbal battle the two of them had fought in the past few months, first at the annual meeting of the Academy, then in the opinion columns of the newspapers of Paris, and, in a final, almost fatal bloodletting, right here in the Pelletier home in the Rue de Rivoli, at a *salon* Tante Claudine convened in the forlorn hope she could restore amity between these two old tigers of French culture, who once had fought side by side in the cause of liberalism.

The falling-out concerned, of all things, Mexico, and whether France should intervene in its affairs.

To the surprise of most of Paris and the deep sorrow and then anger of Auguste Pelletier, de Lamartine had praised the imperialist ideas of the Duc de Morny. De Morny had been at the *salon* that awful Sunday, too.

It started only moments after de Lamartine came through the door, and although Sarah wished it could have been otherwise, she had to admit it was Monsieur Auguste who threw down the gauntlet.

"What I cannot understand, 'Phonse, is how in the name of God a man who contested with Louis-Napoleon Bonaparte for the presidency of La Republique, and out of impeccable democratic principles, could become his apologist—almost his *creature.*"

"It is time for France to reclaim the glory it enjoyed under the *first* Emperor Napoleon, *mon ami*. A strong Catholic state in the New World under the sponsorship of France would bring all nations with a Latin heritage to the fore again."

"Bah! You are corrupting the pure Romantic idea you inherited from Rousseau and stand in grave danger of becoming the blind hired pen of the military monsters who have the ear of that pretender. We should leave Mexico to work out its own destiny. Have you no shame, *turncoat?*"

It got worse. In the ensuing exchanges the familiar "'Phonse" and "*mon ami*" deteriorated to "Monsieur Pelletier" and "Monsieur de Lamartine," and finally to plain "*monsieur,*" without a hint of warmth. Sarah watched open-mouthed as her scholarly foster-father and the premier poet-political figure of nineteenth-century France savaged each other like nasty street gamins.

De Morny had smiled an icy smile all through the embarrassing exchanges.

It baffled her that for the rest of the long afternoon Monsieur Auguste went out of his way to be charming and solicitous to the duke, who had never made a secret of sharing de Lamartine's views.

"Unlike Monsieur de Lamartine," Tante Claudine told her by way of explanation when the last of the guests had gone, "Monsieur le Duc has *always* believed in imperialist expansion for France. Auguste sees that as principle, if of a lamentable sort. He feels that Alphonse's apostasy, on the other hand, is nothing short of criminal. It has made him physically ill for months."

When the invitation to the dinner in the Faubourg St. Germain arrived, Sarah's first impulse—despite her compelling desire to see Charlotte—urged her to decline, out of respect for Monsieur Auguste. Tante Claudine persuaded her to go. "It may be the last chance you have to enjoy civilized Parisian society for a long, long time, *chérie.* Auguste will understand."

To be honest, Sarah had hoped Tante Claudine would say something like that. She should tell herself the truth and "shame the devil." She wanted to go for more than just to see Charlotte. Facing the prospect of giving up Paris for the questionable delights of Mexico would have been difficult enough. To give it up without a proper farewell had brought her more than a few moments of despondency since she made up her mind to leave this country. What a distance she had traveled, not only in miles, but in emotional states—which seemed to recognize no boundaries.

Somewhere along the way she had lost a little of the Calvinism planted in her by Bradford and Abigail Anderson, but her love for Paris was still sometimes a guilty thing. Where had the Boston Puritan Sarah Kent Anderson taken the nether fork of the road? The news about Samuel had not quite brought her back to the straight and narrow, but it made her unsure of her footing on the cosmopolitan primrose path her life with the Pelletiers and their cultivated friends had been for her these past few years. Would Mexico wrench her to still another inner journey?

Deep in her misery at her brother's death she spent long hours in her room overlooking La Rue de Rivoli without once ever going to the window.

But would the party tonight be a proper farewell? Well, at least it would not be another political fracas such as Tante Claudine's Sunday afternoon *salon*. Without Monsieur Auguste on hand the gathering would be of one mind about France's course. Oh, Henry Adams would not share the views of the Duc de Morny, but Henry would be circumspect in deference to his father's mission in London. The English did not support Napoleon III in the adventure being talked about with excitement and anticipation in the court's outer circles where Sarah enjoyed a degree of intimacy. The only other soul who might demur was Sarah Kent Anderson herself. Too many generations of good Yankee, antiroyalist Andersons and Kents prevented her from looking with favor on any plan that would add one more country's name to the list of the world's monarchies. And, an only slightly less prompting spur, there was the influence, too, of the democratic thinking of Monsieur Auguste and that of two of her professors at the Sorbonne. But to say that she felt *rabidly* against Napoleon III's Mexican dream? Well . . . no.

She could keep her own counsel tonight without too much compromise. No one at Charlotte's soiree would care about an American woman's opinions, anyway.

No, she would be an American butterfly tonight. She would enjoy Henri's company and, if it came, his good-bye-for-the-time-being kiss, talk about Boston with Henry Adams, gossip like a schoolgirl with Charlotte—or "Carlota" if she were truly serious about the new name—and sate her somewhat unbecoming American appetite on the exquisite food sure to be served at a table such as the archduchess of Austria would set.

And listen to Jenny Lind.

The closest she would come to a political utterance of any kind would be when she asked Charlotte if there was any truth to the rumor rampant in the cafes these days: the certainly idiotic idea that Napoleon III was quietly grooming Max von Hapsburg to be emperor of Mexico. She would not even have thought of asking that—if she had not been practically en route to Mexico herself. In her present frame of mind she did not, deep down, really care what form of government came to Mexico, but the possibility of seeing Charlotte there was strangely comforting, despite her reservations about the Belgian princess.

Carlota? Empress Carlota? It did sound improbable.

"*J'ai fini, mademoiselle,*" Solange called from across the room. "I will not, however, close the trunk until you return tonight and take off the gown you wear to the ball."

"*Merci,* Solange. Which one have you decided to put out for me?"

"The black with the half-train. You are still in mourning, but that is no reason for you to look like a mere *bonne femme.* The black silk makes you look so much more blonde, and it shows just the right amount of bosom. A *poitrine* like yours should be displayed to its full advantage. Solange does not wish them to forget you soon in Paris."

"Solange!" She laughed. "Such a way to talk. *Tu es méchante!* My *poitrine* is not for display, except by accident. And you flatter me. Paris will forget me before they lift the gangplank at Calais."

4
▲▲▲▲▲

A week in the country now and according to Captain Pierre Boulanger, the man riding the black horse next to Jason James, the chance of his seeing action had diminished by the day.

The Chasseurs d'Afrique captain in command of the cavalry unit had not said this in so many words, but he had that frustrated look about him James had seen on other commanders in similar circumstances over the years.

Cipi, on the other hand, *had* predicted action, invoking his black magic and second sight, when James told him he had agreed to ride along as an observer with Captain Boulanger on the mission to Orizaba.

"You will see fighting within two days, *señor capitán.* It will not be a big fight, but it will have importance for you and your army."

James had never expected things to move with any such rapidity, and although it would have been better if he had been riding or marching with his Legion regiment at the head of his own known rifle company, he was moderately satisfied with the turn of events that put him with Captain Boulanger's half-squadron of cavalry. Here on the road from Orizaba returning to Veracruz with a dozen lancers, and as many *sabreurs,* it was back-to-school time, for a class he needed.

The ride out *to* Orizaba yesterday, with Boulanger and his small command detailed to pick up the sick French soldiers left behind in the general January withdrawal to the great encampment at Veracruz, had gone without incident. Boulanger, however, while not visibly nervous since the mission began, had not relaxed for the entire trip, and this morning he had thus far not enlightened James on the cause for his keen attention to the road ahead of them.

With the return trip to Veracruz two hours under way, and after he called a halt so the sick, getting a fearsome jolting in the *carretas* at the rear of the column, could get some relief, Boulanger turned to James. "If the Republicans are going to try to stop us, they will make the attempt in the next half hour," he said, "about when we reach Fortín."

So he did expect action after all. "Where we saw those riders yesterday?" James asked.

"Oui, mon capitaine."

"Why didn't they make their move *then?*"

"The general sent a signal to the Republican authorities in the capital last week that we were going to transport our sick back to Veracruz. The Juarista government protested, claiming any of our soldiers in Orizaba who fought them two months ago are criminals under their January 5 decree, and subject to 'Mexican' law."

"How so?"

"Some of them kept their rifles and sidearms when they went in hospital."

"What about us then? We're armed to the teeth."

"Under the terms of the Convention of La Soledad my command is here quite legally. Or was. Until we loaded up our sick this morning we were just taking a pleasant ride in the country. Benito Juárez is such a stickler for the law he is more of a Frenchman than Napoleon III."

Boulanger, handsome in a lean animal way, with a fierce, full moustache showing the first signs of gray, appeared to be about James's age, and apparently had also come up through the ranks. There had been no way of judging his fighting abilities yet, but the man had certainly shown a good grasp of the situation in Mexico at supper last night. Even on such short acquaintance James mused that de Lorencez and his staff could not have picked a better officer for a mission that gave every promise of becoming a matter of exquisite delicacy.

"Of course they won't attack unless we do something to provoke them," Boulanger continued. "Juárez doesn't want any hostilities at the moment." He shrugged a splendid Gallic shrug. "But now we *have* provoked them and the Republicans *will* try to stop us. I'm counting on it. It would certainly be better for those poor devils in the carts at our rear if they let us pass without protest, but it would be a big disappointment to General de Lorencez, *mon ami.*"

"It's hard for me to believe the general or his advisors would deliberately expose you and your men like this, captain. Yours is not a large force," James countered. What was he saying? Stupid. It was not at *all* hard to believe. James had seen men with less gullibility and more rank than Boulanger's—or his own—used as pawns before. "My apologies."

Boulanger laughed. The Frenchman was quick. He turned in the saddle and looked at the small cavalcade strung out behind them. The road had widened. He shouted an order to the color-sergeant riding a length behind them, and at a sign flashed along the route of march the column split into something resembling a skirmish line. He turned back to James.

"We are almost ready. We cannot fight the Mexicans as we did in January before the Convention. Not that there was a hell of a lot of fighting then. In the treaty we recognized their lamentable cabal as a sovereign government, something we had never done before. Now that we *have* recognized Juárez, de Lorencez must have a reason to declare war, a war the British and the Spanish will tolerate under the rules of international law. And it's not just our weak-kneed allies or their opinions that worry our general. There is always Paris to be considered. We should have pushed on to the capital last winter before half our fighting force came down with fever—and before Ignacio Zaragoza took command at Puebla from that dolt Uraga. Zaragoza knows how to fight and is willing to—*sans doute* eager.

Either way, our great de Lorencez must have his 'legal war.' Perhaps we can provide him with the excuse he needs to declare one."

"But a general in the field can't declare war on his own authority."

"Ordinarily, no, *mon capitaine*. But de Saligny, the commissioner who arrived on the *Carcassonne* with you, carried the authorization for such a declaration straight from the emperor in Paris. You did not know this?"

"No." It was yet another reminder of how much more Imperial confidence was placed in the army than in the Legion. The army was a trusted instrument of policy, sometimes a maker of it; the Legion only a weapon, a cannon someone else would load, aim, and fire. "So, we're to create an incident?"

"Exactement."

So much for delicacy. Boulanger's mission had all the delicacy of a brute machete. "Will the United States hold still for this?"

Again the fine French shrug. "No one knows. The point is moot. Washington is *engagé* at the moment in a desperate unpleasantness of its own. You are an American. You tell *me* if they will, as you put it, 'hold still.'"

James had no idea what might be going on in the minds and hearts of his countrymen these days—did not want one.

He was grateful to Boulanger for the way he shared his views. There seemed little of the elitist about the Chasseur as displayed by so many other French officers when they dealt with Legionnaires.

On the march again the sun was climbing and talk stopped in the mounting heat. Over James's left shoulder the cone top of the volcano El Pico de Orizaba pushed up into a white blanket of cirrostratus. Against its distant, olive-green side, *las buistras*—the turkey buzzards well remembered from his first trek along this road as an infantryman under a forty-five-pound pack back in '47— moved through the oppressive air as tiny, malevolent black specks. It was better to be on the back of a horse, and far better to be an officer, if only a Legion officer, than to be walking this hot *camino* as a foot-soldier private—even on the springy, seventeen-year-old legs that had carried him when he was in Mexico before.

Incident or no incident, this ride so far had been only a processional, but it had not been a happy one for the fevered men lying in the carts bumping along on their wooden wheels at the rear of the column. Boulanger's half squadron had now lost perhaps a hundred meters of altitude since leaving Orizaba and the air was getting close. James felt sleepy. He had nodded in saddles before, on camels as well as horses and mules, and once on an elephant in Tunisia. He closed his eyes for a moment. It felt delicious . . .

"Capitaine Boulanger! Regardez!" It was the voice of the squadron color-sergeant. James's eyes snapped open and went first to the sergeant, then to Boulanger, and then to where the Chasseur captain was staring down the road.

A line of seventy or eighty blue-and-white-clad soldiers stretched across the squadron's line of march, perhaps five hundred yards away. Only two of them were mounted. The rifles of those filling the roadbed from ditch to ditch were all at port arms, but sunlight glinted from seventy or eighty fixed bayonets.

Boulanger's right arm shot into the air, and the horses in the front rank of the squadron reared and stamped as those in the rank behind almost climbed their rumps. The *carretas* way at the rear creaked to a stop.

"Aaaaah . . ." Boulanger's sigh was one of deep satisfaction. *"Enfin.* I hope they will find the courage to engage me." He put his hand to his face and stroked his moustache.

"It shouldn't require all that much in the way of courage on their part, Captain Boulanger," James said. "They outnumber us almost three to one."

"Indeed they do. It was planned that way."

Planned that way? A risky plan in James's estimation. One of the two horsemen in front of the line of foot soldiers blocking the road urged his mount a few tentative paces forward.

"I think he wants to talk, captain," James said.

"We can talk, *mon ami*, but it will change nothing. I will give General de Lorencez his incident *maintenant.*"

"Will you open fire?"

"*Non, non, non, monsieur! Pas de tout.* That would not accomplish my mission. *They* must fire first for a proper 'incident.'"

"With their firepower, a first volley could finish us." James hoped he did not sound too pessimistic.

"Not if we can somehow entice them to open fire at a major fraction of this distance. The Republican Army does not shoot with the skill of Europeans." The horseman facing them moved a little closer. "*Cet espèce de fou* should be carrying a white flag." Boulanger clucked his tongue softly. "All right. He shall have his talk. Would you care to come with me and listen, captain?"

Boulanger and James moved out together, but with the Legionnaire discreetly holding his horse half a length behind that of the Chasseur commander. The Republican officer ahead of them turned to the other mounted man in front of the infantry, beckoned to him, and together they advanced. The four men met midway between the two forces. The rider in the lead—slim, clean shaven, smallish in stature—looked the younger of the two, but clearly was the senior officer. His unfamiliar shoulder insignia made it impossible for James to determine his rank, but that was quickly corrected when he spoke—in Spanish.

"I am *el mayor* Manuel Santander of the Army of the East, *señores*. I must inform you that you are trespassing on sovereign territory of the Republic of Mexico. It is my duty to place you and your command under arrest. I require you to surrender your arms and accompany me and my *soldados* to Ciudad Puebla, *por favor.*"

So he was a major. High rank for one so young. A nervous twitch of his thin lips betrayed that he was not entirely sure of himself. Of course Boulanger had not missed it, and for a second James feared the captain might laugh in the other young officer's face, but the Frenchman revealed an admirable capacity for self-control and kept his own face impassive. Yes, the high command back in Veracruz had chosen well. Still, when Boulanger replied to the Republican major, also in Spanish, he could not keep a caustic tone entirely from his voice. "*That . . .*" he said, "might take a certain amount of doing, *señor mayor.* Please consider *my* suggestion. We can avoid all manner of difficulty if you order your men to step aside and let me and my soldiers proceed freely and unmolested. Surely you can see we are engaged in an errand of mercy. I have sick and injured in those carts back there."

"Impossible, *señor!* Your 'sick and injured' are in actuality criminal prisoners who were under house arrest in the Orizaba hospital. You and your men have now become accessories to escape." The young major was finding steel somewhere in his soul; his boyish voice was firm and unwavering. "I repeat. I am placing you under arrest. Please do not put yourself and the men under you in unnecessary danger. May I respectfully point out that with your few numbers you cannot reasonably expect to offer much resistance." He paused. "I will return now to my troops. You have five minutes to pile your weapons for my men to gather up. *Muchas gracias.*" He saluted Boulanger crisply, made another more perfunctory salute in the general direction of James, wheeled his horse around, dug in his spurs, and cantered back toward the line of infantry. The rider who had come forward with him stared dumbly at Boulanger and James for a moment. Then, as if he were only at that instant discovering he had been left alone, he, too, turned his mount and rode back to join his major.

"What now, captain?" James said.

"We have five minutes, do we not, *mon ami?* I assure you I will be able to use them to better advantage than will the major." He turned his horse back toward his small force.

When he reached it he called to the color-sergeant. "They mean to stop us, Dumont," he said when the sergeant rode up to him. "Move up the three carts our powerful little friends are in. Keep them screened by the horses, though. Lancers in the first rank, saberers in the second. Can you assemble our friends in five minutes?"

"Oui, mon capitaine."

"Très bien. Commencez!"

What were the two references to "friends"? The answer was plain when Dumont and half a dozen of the *sabreurs* dismounted and got busy in the center of the drawn-up *carretas*.

They were assembling a pair of swivel guns, naval two-pounders they looked to be, not much in the way of artillery in any real land engagement, but likely to prove devastating to the obviously unsuspecting major. The parts of the small cannons had been hidden in false bottoms in three of the carts, with pallets and invalid men on top of them. The *sabreurs* had moved the sick men to the side of the road. Small wonder he had not seen the guns.

The guns, of course, explained why the Chasseur captain had been totally unperturbed when James pointed out how badly his squadron was outnumbered.

"I want the lancers to lead us in, with the saberers right behind, Dumont," Boulanger was saying now. "Have the cavalry split at two hundred meters or when the enemy opens fire, whichever comes first. Turn the cannoneers loose even before we sound the charge. But remember, the Republicans *must* fire first! That is an absolute imperative."

Las buistras had flown in closer, were no longer specks. How did those obscene birds *know*? There had been no blood to draw them—yet.

Boulanger had turned to face the Republican infantry again. His keen eyes were fixed on the major, and James knew they would stay there until the Republican gave the inevitable order. James drew his watch from the pocket of his tunic. One more minute. The turkey buzzards were settling into the trees on the left side of the road.

"All right, Sergeant Dumont," Boulanger called out. "Move them forward at a walk. Have your bugler ready. He will sound the charge immediately after I give the order for *us* to fire." He reached down and loosened his saber in the saddle scabbard. James wondered if he should ready his. Could he stop being an observer only when the captain told him to?

Ahead of them the Mexican infantry major was riding back and forth in front of his line of soldiers. When Boulanger's men began to advance he reined in and faced them. He looked back over his shoulder at his own men and apparently gave an order. The rifles with the fixed bayonets came down from blue-and-white shoulders and were leveled against the Chasseurs. The gap between the two forces narrowed. Four hundred meters . . . three. Now James could distinguish individual soldiers in the ranks of the major's command. He tried not to; it served no good purpose to allow yourself to find the enemy was human.

Two hundred fifty meters . . .

The lancers had split down the center and opened a pathway for the swivel guns. They had dropped the steel points of their weapons level with their eyes. On half the lances pennants fluttered. James heard the swordsmen in the second rank pull their sabers free.

His eyes found a young soldier—the boy could not possibly have been sixteen—in the front rank of the Republicans, and he resisted every effort to break them away and look somewhere else. Fifteen years fell away. Would it always be like this for him in Mexico? The boy had not even been old enough to walk when James served here. The youngster was trembling, he sank to one knee, and James knew in an instant that Boulanger's hoped-for shot would come from this frightened lad.

And even as he thought it—it did.

The lone report sent the buzzards in the trees aloft.

"Vive la France!" Boulanger shouted. *"FEU!"*

The heavy thunder of hoofbeats answered the notes of the bugle, all but muffled the sound of the swivel guns and the crashes of rifle fire.

He was in action again. All doubts were gone. But he

veered his horse so he would not ride straight for the kneeling boy. Another man, rifle leveled, loomed in front of him. The saber James could not remember drawing flashed, and he felt the blade slice through flesh, striking bone. Blood spattered his face—and then he was on through the Juárista line with only open road ahead of him.

He reined up and looked behind him to see how the rest of the squadron had fared. One Chasseur, a lancer, lay in the dust where they had breached the enemy line. Scattered around the fallen French cavalryman, a dozen or fifteen men in blue-and-white uniforms lay in the dust of the road. Not one moved. The rest of Major Santander's infantry was streaming off the road, running for the trees, the boy who had kneeled and fired among them. James breathed easier.

One by one the buzzards settled back into the topmost branches. They would have to wait to feast until the dead turned ripe, but they looked as if they had all the patience in the world.

Boulanger rode up beside him.

"My general now has his incident," the Chasseur said. "Someday, I suppose, this minuscule affair will be known as the Battle of Fortín, the opening salvo in the glorious war for the establishment of the Mexican Empire. Perhaps General de Lorencez will make a major out of me for the favor I have done him."

In bivouac that night James gave more thought to the events of the day than he had to most engagements he had seen as a soldier. It troubled him that an unwanted vision had come erupting from the past. The sight of the boy soldier had brought it back. It must not happen again. He could get himself killed if he allowed this sort of thing to distract him . . .

Well, while war was never pleasant he had chosen it as his *métier*, his trade. Nor had he tired of it; he still felt strongly that professional soldiers were needed in this imperfect world, had a useful function—but he had often wondered if the profession of arms, with its all too frequent agonies, was what a *completely* rational man would choose, were he free to make the choice. Had *he* been free when he made his?

Something else: that need of the world for the professional soldier seemed to be growing stronger. Men were learning to kill each other at greater and greater distances, the enemy becoming more and more faceless, its humanness more and more obscured. When, as they inevitably would, men learned how to kill other men they could not even see, an enemy whose presence they divined by some as yet to be invented new *kind* of vision, the process could no longer be entrusted to the hyper-patriot or the blood-crazed amateur. It was one thing to jerk the lanyard of a field gun and blast an enemy you could not see, quite another to club a fellow human being into a bloody pulp.

The professional soldiers he had known—all but one— had known when *not* to kill. Boulanger, for all his practical ruthlessness today, seemed to possess that knowledge, too. He had shown the same reluctance to pursue Major Santander's beaten men James would have shown himself.

Back at the Rinconada a day later he found the "incident" had given de Lorencez and de Saligny all they needed. The seaport had been awash with rumor and speculation when he left for Orizaba, but even before Boulanger's Chasseurs were back in their tents, the commissioner and the general put gossip and guesswork to rest by declaring war on Mexico on behalf of the emperor of the French.

"The general will move on the Republican forts at Puebla within a week, my captain," Cipi offered. "This is his chance to become a great figure in the history of this country. Of course, if he does not *win* . . ." The little man grinned. "And if you ask Cipi, he will *not* win."

"You are predicting his defeat by the use of your so-called black magic powers?"

"*Sí, señor.*"

"Well, if we do lose, you miserable little know-it-all, tell me something. Will I stay alive?"

"*Sí, mi capitán.* Cipi will not let you die for a long time yet. You will be a hero. *Verdad.* Cipi promises."

5

PUEBLA, MEXICO—MAY 5, 1862

Not even a hint of a breeze moved the air, and since the bird chorus died away an hour after dawn, not a sound save the metal-leather-canvas clank and creak of an infantry company on the march disturbed it.

Captain Jason James reined in his horse, raised his right arm, and the men of Compagnie Rouge bunched up behind him. Now silence descended—but the air still throbbed with something. James knew this something, as did every man in the company: the absolute certainty of combat—soon.

This, at last, would be the big attack, not the short, swift engagement of his outing with Pierre Boulanger at Fortín. It was what the French brought him and the battalion across the ocean to do—time for the Legionnaires of Rouge and their captain to earn their pay.

But something was wrong, every bit as wrong as Cipi had said it would be. Alongside James his sergeant, Jean-Claude duBecq, the only other mounted man in his small command, clearly knew it, too. The grizzled noncommissioned officer James had relied on through half a dozen campaigns sniffed the air suspiciously through his enormous Alsatian nose.

James pulled his telescope from his saddlebag and focused on the long, steep hill where the Mexican trenches creased the *maguey*-covered terrain, narrow depressions scarcely visible with the sun now almost overhead. The part of the attack assigned Compagnie Rouge would not be easy; he could not see one place for the company to reach a defilade once they left these rocks. The swordlike leaves of the *maguey* plants could hide a man well enough, but they could not stop a bullet—or a bayonet. Once his men began their advance, there could be no stopping until they reached the breastworks of Guadalupe.

He could see no sign of movement from Guadalupe's high tan wall rising from the top of the hill—not even a banner or a pennant flying from either of the twin towers beyond it.

DuBecq snorted. "It is a little too much like Marrakech to please me, *mon capitaine*," he said. "At least one nervous rifleman in those forward trenches should have fired by now. We are almost within range of them. They either aren't there or they are much more disciplined than the Touaregi."

"I was thinking something of the sort, duBecq." Actually, James had thought specifically of the boy soldier in the road at Fortin. *He*, surely, had been too nervous to hold his fire, probably too nervous to hold his water. "Maybe they're dug in deep, expecting a long barrage from our artillery. I wish I expected one."

"Then what I heard is true? There will be no field guns today, captain?"

"A few, but not as many as I would like. General de Lorencez apparently doesn't think we need them. We only have that Marine Battery and their four rifled 55s and six or seven of the mountain howitzers Lieutenant Bruat's gunners hauled over the pass to Amozoc." He pulled the telescope down and closed it up. Through the heat shimmer rising from the two hilltop forts the glass presented little more than he could see with his unaided eyes—Cerro de Guadalupe straight ahead and Fuerte Loreto angled off behind it—a kilometer northeast of the enemy city. The columns of smoke rising from the forts' morning fires, mere wisps now, quivered like dancers in the souk at Casablanca. "They are there all right, duBecq. I can feel them. *Mais tu as raison*, this General Zaragoza has indeed trained them well. Have you seen the rest of the Fourteenth yet, *mon vieux?*" He kept his eye on the enemy positions.

"They are moving up on our left flank now, *monsieur*. It is a great comfort to Jean-Claude duBecq to have them there."

Even as the sergeant spoke, James could hear the clatter of armed men moving into the nearby rocks. The other company commanders must have seen, as James had, that this was the last broken terrain before they reached the forts themselves, and probably the only spot on the plain affording any protection at all from rifle fire. "Who covers us on the right?"

DuBecq stood in the stirrups. "I cannot see anyone there yet, captain."

"Damn it! The Chasseur cavalry should be in the line by now, and their commander should have sought us out for his instructions."

"*Oui, mon capitaine*. Perhaps the Chasseur commander thinks he can take his Imperial time at a late *petit déjeuner*, ride hard, and catch up with us. Perhaps he doesn't like fighting in the same line as foot soldiers—Legion foot soldiers in particular. The fucking cavalry!"

James smiled. It was as close as duBecq would ever come to criticizing officers. "Just so this tardy captain and his squadron are in place before we push off," he said. "I don't like to move out with our right exposed to Republican cavalry the way it is, and with no hope of a counChasse by our own horse squadrons or even a protecting screen. Without the Chasseurs we'll have less cover than a fig leaf."

And he did not like the idea of moving out at all until he saw some sign of life in the trenches or behind the stone walls ahead of them, either. It gave a rifle company commander much more confidence when he could see his enemies and gauge or guess at their intentions for at least a few seconds before the first volley came. "All we can do for the moment is wait—and hope the general doesn't signal the attack before our cavalry support arrives." Chasseurs? Did he dare hope the squadron—if it did come—would be led by Boulanger? That could be awkward. Boulanger, a skillful soldier and already a veteran in Mexico, might not take kindly to receiving orders from a man he probably assumed had not really fought in this country yet. Fortín did not count. No, it would not be Boulanger. The competent commander James had ridden with three weeks ago would never be late on a day like this.

He turned his attention to the left, to where the other companies of the Fourteenth Regiment hunkered down under the late morning sun. The regimental battle standard hung limp from its staff. God knew he did not want high winds to disturb whatever they threw at the enemy today, but a bright flag, stiff in a good breeze, always did wonders for morale.

If the attack on the *cerro* fort went as planned, his old friends in the other companies, spearheading the attack, would catch it much worse than the Legionnaires of Rouge, unless the Chasseurs did not arrive. It could become a nightmare for the company if no cavalry showed up.

Remembering de Lorencez from Colomb Bechar—and thinking about the order of battle tentatively outlined just after the army moved from Veracruz to Orizaba a week ago, and firmed up just last night—he was fairly sure how the general would make his attack. There were not many tactical choices when going against a walled fort on a hill. Your enemy could see everything you were up to; feints and diversions were virtually worthless. The general would use the guns first, then there would be an all-out frontal infantry advance of at lèast three waves, and not much rest between waves. Cavalry squadrons would guard both of the army's flanks.

He could not carp at the strategy. It was simple, did not depend on critical timing, and had worked marvelously well in the open sand-sea deserts of North Africa, and even against the few genuinely fortified Tunisian towns.

Hell, it had worked well enough here in Mexico under a different general, but with a not much different army—back in '47.

But the lack of field guns . . .

There would not be enough of them by far. And the threat of the cavalry attack from his right. What sort of strength would the enemy horse show when and if they came at him? It most surely would be greater than that of the Chasseurs. The right flank of the Fourteenth—his own Red Company—would be where the first enemy mounted thrust had to come. Without an equal number of French lances to counter them, Mexican riders could roll the right flank up like a bloody carpet.

Few of his fellow Legion officers and few of the supremely confident French regulars of the Tirailleurs and Zouaves had faced the likes of Mexican horse soldiers—no disparagement of the horse- and camel-mounted raiders of Algeria and Morocco—but he remembered too well the superb Tlaxcalan lancers of '47 and '48, who had ridden like the wind against the massive, crushing weight and withering firepower of Winfield Scott's Americans, inflicting casualties all out of proportion to their numbers. At that time Mexico had the finest military riders in the world, and he doubted they had lost their skills. One thing he could count on: the very best of them were not in some unseen staging area behind the stone battlements of Cerro de Guadalupe at this moment, ready to fall on the Fourteenth and the men of Compagnie Rouge. The absolute best—the two thousand cavalrymen the anti-Juarista General Márquez was supposed to be bringing in from the southwest to help reduce Puebla, the army de Lorencez had decided not to wait for—would not appear today. Still, regardless of their quality, if the Republicans turned their cavalry loose before the company reached the shadow of the wall it could be very bad. But not a thing he had not faced before.

At least the day had stayed cool so far, even bracing, despite the powerful, early May sun. The climb through the Cumbres de Acultzingo four days ago had lifted the army to something slightly over two thousand meters above sea level, well above the pestilential *tierra caliente* of the coast. Spirits in Compagnie Rouge had soared; the men talked and joked as they crossed the plain to Amozoc through a countryside green with small farms and lush pasturage, regaling each other with that easy, cynical optimism James always hoped for just before leading them into combat.

Their one brief engagement with the enemy since Orizaba, at the top of the pass, when they stormed the ruined prison that the Mexicans had converted to a makeshift fort to delay any march on Puebla, seemed to have whetted their appetite for more serious action. The Tirailleurs they supported in that small fray lost two men and a score-and-a-half wounded before the Republican garrison abandoned the old jailhouse and fell back on Ciudad Puebla, but not a man in Rouge had suffered so much as a scratch.

There had been an eruption of boisterous heartiness a day later when they approached a village, expecting some enemy resistance, only to find it defended by hundreds of squealing pigs penned up conveniently for the regimental cooks' knives and cleavers. The meal that evening proved easily the best James had known since the officers' mess on the *Carcassonne,* and probably the best the men of the company had eaten in a year.

Memory had dimmed it, but back in Veracruz, before the first move to Orizaba, nearly one man in three in the army had become the victim of *el vómito negro*, the puking sickness that left whole sections of the encampment reeking to the heavens. Even then his company had been lucky. Only Rogusz, the skinny Pole from Lodz, and the albino Austrian Ritter had come down with whatever was eating suppurating holes in French bowels right and left, and the two ailing Legionnaires were already back in ranks. Ritter was new to the Legion, but Rogusz had fought with James five years now. Both were good men, and he was grateful when they returned to duty.

He had been doubly lucky himself. His own belly heaved and bubbled poisonously one night, but Cipi—probably fuming and muttering his all too familiar curses and obscenities right now back at Amozoc where James ordered him to stay with the baggage train—had stoked him with a lumpy concoction of crushed leaves and, James suspected, ground up parts of insects. The remedy stank almost as bad as the Veracruz sea of vomit did. To his amazement and ultimate grudging relief, recovery came soon after his first malodorous belch.

"You need Cipi with you when you attack Puebla, mi capitán. How else is he to keep you among the living?" the dwarf had said yesterday when James told him he must remain at Amozoc.

"I've managed to stay alive without you for thirty-two years, you meddlesome little fart," James replied. "You'll have all you can handle just keeping my gear from being stolen."

He left the little man leaning against the flank of a spavined horse he had purloined somewhere, wiping the blade of his monstrous knife back and forth across his whetstone—beady eyes smoldering.

As James fully expected, neither he nor any of the other company-grade Legion officers had been invited to attend the planning for today's exertions, although their two battalion colonels were. The pair were, of course, St. Cyrians, as were so many of the Legion officer cadre. Thinking of them brought Marcel Gallimard to mind. He had not seen the lieutenant since the move from Veracruz to Orizaba. Maybe Gallimard had been struck by el vómito and had been left behind. James hoped not. He was delighted to be rid of the young fool this past two weeks, but he could not be uncharitable. A man dedicating his life to soldiering, no matter how insufferable he was, should have his chance. He would get his chance at la gloire if he were here today.

The last time James talked with him, Gallimard swelled with pride as he reported he had been posted to the cavalry. Somewhere in Veracruz he had discovered a tailor and now wore a new uniform even gaudier than the Parisian creation of the Atlantic crossing and the first weeks ashore in Mexico, a wild confection of skintight blue riding pants, a scarlet tunic, and a ridiculous white, cockaded shako. He looked like something out of an operetta or from under a Christmas tree.

"Are you going to let the enemy see you in that finery, lieutenant?" James could not resist asking. "It will attract the attention of a lot of snipers."

"Mais oui, mon ami." Gallimard seemed genuinely puzzled at the question. "A St. Cyrian does not hide."

James wasted no breath telling him how little he would relish having such a target anywhere near him on a battlefield.

What a contrast this self-deluding popinjay would make with almost drab-looking Pierre Boulanger. James had found that thoroughgoing professional leaving the meeting at de Lorencez's tent last night and the Chasseur captain obliged him with a *resume* of the general's last orders to his staff. The report his companion of the "incident" at Fortín gave him, however, obscured as much as it revealed.

"De Saligny was there, and so was that *petit chien* Juan Almonte who declared himself president of Mexico last month. Ridiculous! I suppose you could call him regent for the moment. The emperor wants *someone* to be the nominal head of this dismal country until his own choice for the crown gets here."

"The crown? Then it's true? The emperor will try to establish a monarchy in Mexico?"

"Oui, mon capitaine. But not just a monarchy. An empire." The Parisian cocked his head. A saturnine smile broke across his lean features. "Can you imagine this sham of a nation masquerading as an *empire?* Ah well, the history of what happens here in the next few years will someday make a charming revue at *les Folies* in some otherwise dull season."

"But why were de Saligny and the Mexican here? I have heard de Lorencez despises them."

"He does. They had some ideas about how we should proceed against Puebla tomorrow morning. Ideas somewhat at odds with those of our general."

"They aren't military men of any big reputation that I recall."

"No, they are not, but I was impressed with what they had to say. And Almonte did have with him a superannuated little Mexican general whose name I think is Salas. He attacked this city and took it once in what Mexicans call the War of the Reform."

"So?"

"De Saligny, Almonte, and this dear old general are of the strong opinion that we should wait for Márquez and attack Puebla from the south. I am myself persuaded it is the best plan."

"Why?"

"We would not then have to contend with Guadalupe and Loreto."

"Are they so formidable?"

"To hear this *ancien* general tell it, *oui*. Guadalupe was a convent at one time, and still looks like one. But the wall that was once only a giant chastity belt for Mexican nuns serves Zaragoza just as well as the outer shell of a fortress. There is another problem. Look at this, *mon ami*." He pulled a folded map from inside his tunic. "*Regardez*. Guadalupe is girded on three sides by a sort of moat, a ditch perhaps as much as five meters deep. To get up the far side to the foot of the wall, and to surmount the wall itself, will require the use of scaling ladders—and that after crossing a field of fire in front of it. Any units trying to flank the wall on the southern side will come under Loreto's guns. We don't know how many they have, but to blanket this small unprotected area will not require more than half a battery. Guadalupe, too, has artillery we know very little about. One more thing, *mon ami*: I hope you don't consider this ar omen. Whatever guns the Republicans have are old, bought from the British years ago. Some of them are the same cannon Wellington used at Waterloo—and you know full well how that battle turned out for France."

"And if we were to come at Puebla from the south?"

"It would take a little longer than an attack on the forts, but our losses would be smaller. Almonte says we would get help from the populace, who are notorious for their anti-Republican sentiments. I wouldn't count on that myself. But Zaragoza and his General Negrete would have to bring their troops out from behind Guadalupe and Loreto and face us in the city itself."

"Then what is de Lorencez's objection?"

"Mostly he does not wish to use any strategy offered by de Saligny. He feels, *aussi*, that it is beneath the honor and dignity of French arms to fight street-by-street—as we most assuredly would have to do—like the *gendarmes* of Paris or the dockside patrols of Marseille. He salivates for a grand advance—led by the *tricouleur* and the *fleur de lis*. He thinks he can break Zaragoza's back in the two forts. And although he didn't say it, he abhors the idea of sharing the glory with Márquez if and when he gets here. The Mexican probably would arrive in time to help us if we took the slow route through the city. Another case of St. Cyrian ambition and arrogance grafted on the supposed legacy of Bonaparte. *Pour moi-même*, I am always ready to take any help I can get." Boulanger's smile now had become one of amused skepticism. And James had thought *himself* a hard, practical, unsentimental fighting man. He could forget that. Compared to doubting Pierre Boulanger, Jason James of Kansas, was—as the Frenchman would put it—*un naïf*.

"What was the upshot, *monsieur?*"

"Our gallant commander-in-chief's last words before he dismissed us were: '*À demain, messieurs, à Guadalupe!*' He didn't even favor de Saligny, Almonte, or the old general with an apology or a smile. A good part of the disagreement is that our general bears that cordial hatred for de Saligny and the Mexican."

The moat around Guadalupe had caused the late hour of

attack, costing the army the advantage of an early jump-off time, when the sun would be at their backs. The engineers had been sent back to Amozoc yesterday afternoon to find enough wood to build the scaling ladders. The original order of battle, issued by someone who obviously did not know about the ladders, called for the French artillery barrage—such as it would be with only ten or eleven guns in action—to start at nine in the morning, and regimental buglers had blown them all out of their bedrolls at five. No announcement of the new attack time reached the Legion until the two battalions were ready to march, and a monumental chorus of grumbling echoed through the Fourteenth's struck camp when the regiment received orders to stand down until ten o'clock. Two companies were already on the road and had to be recalled, causing six kilometers of marching under full field pack to go to waste.

James, glad he was not the commander of either outfit, looked around at the one he did command.

DuBecq had dispersed it over almost half an acre of the *maguey*, stone, and sand where James halted it. Five or six decks of cards had come out of packs, and smoke from pipes and cigars drifted toward the enemy trenches. Ritter, the eerily pale Austrian who strangely enough never seemed to avoid the sun, squatted in front of a flat-topped boulder, writing something on a scrap of paper. A letter? Probably not. Legionnaires were not given to writing as much as other soldiers. Few of them could write to begin with, and fewer still had anyone to write to. James himself had written home only four times in more than seven years.

"Have one of the men take our mounts to the rear and tether them somehow, Sergeant duBecq. We'll fight on foot with the rest of the company as we always do. *Un moment, mon vieux.* I suppose I ought to keep my Goddamned saber with me."

"If you carry it, *mon capitaine*, the riflemen you are so sure are hiding in those trenches will know you for an officer."

"It's something I'll have to face, duBecq. That's why they pay me a few more *sous* a month than they dole out to you."

To the east of him clouds were building over the top of Pico de Orizaba. Rain had threatened for two weeks now, but had not come—not at Veracruz, Orizaba, nor at Amozoc twenty kilometers behind them, where disgruntled Cipi waited. During the raging of *el vómito* he had watched lightning worry the far side of the distant peaks of the Sierra Madre Oriental every afternoon, hoping with the rest of the army—almost praying along with the most ordinarily blasphemous of them—that the storms they could not see would sweep down into the coastal swamplands—now drying and cracking like mile-wide scabs—drench the filthy latrine Veracruz had become, the *sucio tocador* as Cipi called it, and wash its debilitating waste and detritus out to sea.

"*Mon capitaine,*" duBecq said. "*Enfin.* Something is happening at the fort."

At first glance nothing looked different. He opened his telescope again and trained it on the top of the wall. Not a sign of movement yet. He swung the glass toward the two church towers of the former convent. DuBecq's instincts were as sound as ever. A man poked a green-and-white flag out of the opening of one of the belfries. At that height there must be a hint of a breeze; the banner unfolded into barely discernible ripples.

Then—it was not something heard so much as something felt through the soles of his boots—came a muffled shudder.

Guns! The defenders of Guadalupe were moving their guns.

Sure enough, the black Os of cannon mouths were beginning to appear at the ports halfway up the walls and at the parapets on top.

Then he heard hoofbeats. He turned to the east to see a cloud of dust roiling up in back of the company. The Chasseurs!

A full squadron of cavalry was cantering up on the company's exposed right flank, pennants rippling as the horses ran. He permitted himself a sigh of relief and satisfaction and turned to duBecq.

"Sergeant! Did you test those ladders the quartermasters brought up from Amozoc?"

"*Oui, mon capitaine.* I had Mancuso try them out." Pietro Mancuso was the giant of the company.

"Good. Now perhaps before those guns begin to hammer us we will still have time to greet the commander of these Chasseurs."

Then, as the arriving squadron, still dragging its trail of dust behind it, pulled up even with the company and two or three hundred meters to the right, the horses' heads tossing and a dozen guidons and pennants dancing at the heads of lances, he caught a glimpse of the officer leading it.

The man waved his saber above his head. He sat a fine-looking bay horse as if he had spent a lifetime in the saddle, but James's heart sank into the tops of his boots as he took in the white, cockaded shako gyrating above a splash of blue cavalry breeches and a blood red tunic.

Gallimard!

The youthful ass saw James and urged the bay toward him.

"Well met, Capitaine Zhomm!" Gallimard's smile threatened to devour the ends of the waxed moustache. He brought the saber in front of his face in an elaborate salute. "It is a magnificent day for a trial of arms, is it not, *mon ami!*"

"*Ça va,* Gallimard?"

"*Très bien, monsieur.* And why should it not? This is my first command. The first of many, *j'espère.* My colonel says I am to take my orders from the captain on the Legion's right flank. That is you, is it not?"

"I suppose it is."

"*Alors,* what *are* my orders, sir? When do I and my squadron make our charge?"

"There isn't a damned thing to charge as yet, lieutenant.

Unless you want to charge that wall. I wouldn't advise it. I'm afraid all you can do now is sit tight. Your colonel means for you to protect our right as we advance on foot. That won't even happen until our field guns work the enemy trenches over, and they aren't in place as yet."

"You mean, *monsieur,* that we are merely to walk our horses?"

"To begin with, yes. Keep a sharp eye out for enemy cavalry issuing from behind the fort. Even then you won't be exactly charging. What you will be required to do is hold your troopers in reserve while we overrun those trenches and reach the moat. If my guess is right, we'll see the Mexican horse before that happens. They will try to stop us. When they do, you can have your charge. Hit them on *their* flank. If they don't move on us, you don't move on them. Above all, do not attempt to take your squadron to the trenches. I want you in the open so you can engage any cavalry that comes our way. You understand, do you not, lieutenant? Do *not* ride for the trenches! That is the task of my company, and my company alone."

"*Sacrebleu, capitaine!* Perhaps I should just reconnoiter the side of the fort and seek out targets of opportunity. I did not come to Mexico to hold good French lancers in reserve. I wish to engage the enemy immediately!"

Damn it! All caution with this fool had to be abandoned. "Lieutenant Gallimard, *attendez!* You didn't come to Mexico to lose a squadron and in the process endanger my Legionnaires. Now I suggest you return to your command. I'll signal or send a runner when I want you and your squadron. And for Christ's sake, follow orders and be patient! Just ride even with my company and stay out of trouble until you are really needed."

The young dandy could not have worn a more deflated, crushed look had the scarlet breast been pierced by the saber now hanging at his side. His mouth drooped open. But James knew it was too much to expect the sanguine starch to have deserted Gallimard completely, and he could guess at what was coming next. The lieutenant would not take kindly to this dressing-down in front of duBecq, even though the sergeant had moved a few feet off and discreetly looked away.

Sure enough, the boy's eyes suddenly flashed fire, the moustache quivered like the tines of a tuning fork, and the open mouth curled into rage.

"Patience, *mon capitaine*, is not a martial virtue! Valor demands that—"

Whatever else Gallimard said or intended saying was lost when the ground rolled and bucked under James's feet, and his ears filled with the thunder of cannon. Cerro de Guadalupe had not waited for French guns to open fire. The first heavy salvo from the fort landed between Compagnie Rouge and the main body of the Fourteenth Regiment. A quick reflex look told him no damage had been done.

But the battle for Puebla had been joined. He would have to deal with Lieutenant Marcel Gallimard later.

6

▲▲▲▲▲

"*Mon dieu!*" duBecq shouted into the heavy silence of the fourth lull in the barrage. "How much ammunition do *les cochons* have? They've been at us for more than an hour, *mon capitaine*. And those are not peashooters they are using. I thought all they had was round shot."

James's ears were still ringing half a minute after the last salvo, and duBecq's voice came from a seemingly great distance. His own sounded as faint. "It *is* a little surprising for an impoverished army using secondhand artillery, du-Becq." DuBecq's remark about the Mexican guns was well taken. What artillery the Riffs and Touregi boasted, even at that Marrakech of evil memory, had been diminutive, antique brass stuff that hurled relatively tiny solid balls, stones, and bits of metal scrap, bothersome toys compared with what they faced now. Zaragoza's gunners might be firing antiquated cannon, but they were large-bore pieces, and they were employing them effectively, so effectively there was no doubt in James's mind they had test-fired them days before, zeroing-in on the likely spots where de Lorencez would deploy his troops.

"If I were in command of this army I would attack now, duBecq. We could reach the first trenches before they could depress their guns, and only have rifle fire to face *en route*. But I command only this company. See if you can determine what our losses are, *mon ami*, and if you can hail one of the other companies, find out how things are going with the regiment as a whole—and above all see if there is any chance we'll get our orders for the advance soon. I have no desire to be pounded like this all afternoon."

The sergeant saluted and snaked his way out of the rock defile the two of them had shared since the first missile landed.

Some of the men of the company had hidden themselves in the craters blasted in the plain during the first salvos, believing that since the Mexican guns at the fort probably were not in fixed, hard emplacements the next rounds would not hit in the exact same spots. It did not always work, but it was a damned good rule of thumb.

A pall of powdersmoke was beginning to obscure James's vision of the rest of the Fourteenth. Not only smoke darkened the field; the clouds he had seen building above El Pico were moving westward; in another ten minutes they would cover the sun and shroud everything with an early dusk.

Gallimard had taken his squadron back a couple of hundred meters from their first position, but James could see the lieutenant himself well out in the van of his line of Chasseurs, riding back and forth and waving his saber as if he was daring the enemy gunners to bring their fire to bear on him personally. The damned fool! If the fort had not been concentrating on the main body of the regiment, some devilish cannoneer might just take it on himself to try to land one on him and spray the bay horse, the gaudy uniform, and its posturing wearer over an acre of the hardpan of the plain.

In five minutes duBecq crawled back into the shallow depression.

"It is not good, captain," the sergeant said.

"The company?"

"*We* have taken no hits yet, sir, but Compagnie Bleu and the Greens have already lost more than ten. If the Mexicans change their angle of fire only a few degrees to the left it will be our turn."

"The attack?"

"Delayed. The 55s, however, are in position behind the 2nd Zouaves to the left of the Fourteenth. They will answer the fort in minutes. Unfortunately, Lieutenant Bruat says they have ammunition for only half an hour. The bulk of it is still back at Amozoc. After they fire ten volleys we advance on foot. The Zouaves will march out first, followed by the Fourteenth and then Colonel Hennique and his Marine Light Infantry. We are to begin our advance with the rest of the Fourteenth."

"Where are our ladders now?"

"Two hundred meters in back of us."

"Have them brought up, duBecq."

"It is as good as done, *mon capitaine.*" The sergeant looked at him quizzically. "Is *le premier sergeant* of Compagnie Rouge permitted to give his captain some advice?"

"*Oui, mon ami.*"

"From the regiment's main position I was able to see the wall of the fort better than we can from here. I do not believe our ladders are long enough to scale it to the very top. We will have to break in through one of the gunports halfway up."

"So?"

"I know the captain's habits well. He has always *led* this kind of attack himself. This time I beg him to let someone else try to force entry first. I do not wish to fight the rest of the day without my officer."

"And you have someone in mind to lead the company through the gunport?" He did not really have to ask.

"*Oui, monsieur*. The first sergeant of Compagnie Rouge."

James was every bit as reluctant to fight any battle inside the fort without his sergeant as duBecq was to fight it without his officer. The chances of the first man through the port were not good. "We'll have to see about it when we get there, Jean-Claude. And our enemy will have much to say about whether we come to that point or not." He had not called the sergeant by his first name more than twice in the years they marched and fought together in North Africa, and even now he was not sure how duBecq viewed this sort of slight familiarity. James knew him as a stickler for form with the men of the company, an uncompromising, case-hardened martinet seemingly without human feelings.

"One more thing, duBecq—we will only advance to the closest trench. Drive the enemy out with bayonets, take cover in the trench and regroup. We'll take the others one by—"

The crashes of more cannon fire shattered his thoughts and stopped his words. No matter. DuBecq needed no pictures drawn for him. This time the guns were sounding a different tone, a high, light tenor compared to the heavy bass of the reports from the walls and parapets of Guadalupe; the 55s duBecq had located behind the 2nd Zouaves were beginning the French barrage. Ten volleys the sergeant said.

"Form your skirmish line, Sergeant duBecq. Fix bayonets."

"*Oui, monsieur.*"

"And send me our bugler."

A look at the fort told him the barrage of the 55s and the mountain howitzers was having no discernible effect on the thick wall. As the smoke from the first volleys lifted there were a few inconsequential cavities, nothing more. Six rounds, then seven. Almost time for Compagnie Rouge to move out.

Down the line to the left the standard of the Fourteenth had moved a hundred meters closer to the foot of the hill, but still hung as limply from its staff as it had before. He could not see the 2nd Zouaves beyond the Fourteenth. Wait. The runner sent by Commandant Cousin at ten had relayed *le commandant*'s orders that the Fourteenth would not begin its advance until the Zouaves moved out, so if the Fourteenth's flag had already moved forward it meant *les Zeds must* have left their positions in the first of the *maguey* and begun the attack. He had not heard a bugle, but in the din of the cannonading from both the fort and their own lines that was not too surprising.

Should he take the company forward now? If he had miscalculated about the other commands and Compagnie Rouge went alone, the result could be disaster. The riflemen in the trenches—if his first instincts proved sound—could then concentrate their fire on Rouge. Commandant Cousin, on the other hand, was a hot-tempered, aggressive soldier who would send the Zouaves uphill at a fairly rapid pace. If James did not move when Cousin expected him to move, there would be hell to pay from this senior officer when the battle ended, and a second hell created by Colonel Henri Bonnet, the commander of the Fourteenth.

He saw the bugler a few feet away from him, waiting for his nod. He gave it, and welcomed the call for the general advance.

He pulled his saber free, unbuckled the belt holding the scabbard and dropped it to the sand. If it came to close fighting when they reached the wall or before it, and in the always dangerous climb up the scaling ladders, it would not do to have the damned thing in the way.

"*Et alors, sergeant, allons!*" He pointed the saber toward the wall and took the first step.

White smoke was rising from the first line of trenches. As with the cannonading from the fort, the other companies of the Fourteenth were at the moment bearing the brunt of the fusillade from the enemy infantry. Rouge had led a charmed life so far, but it was only a matter of seconds before the riflemen in the trenches raked the line, moved their fire to the left, and found the company. He could not have the bugler blow the full charge quite yet; the twenty-kilo packs on the backs of the men of Rouge would drag them to the sand well short of their objective if he let them begin running now. This was always the hardest part: holding the company to an orderly walk under the day's first fire.

Gallimard had seen the company move and had urged the Chasseurs forward, too. So far the lieutenant had followed orders. The squadron maintained the same speed as James's men. Would it hold this pace when the company began its charge? Or would the surge of the Legionnaires prove to be too much of a stimulus for the rash young Frenchman?

The fire from the trenches reached the company.

Dust and debris kicked up all around them and in the very center of the advancing skirmish line. On the far left he saw two of his men fall. He could not be sure, but one of them looked like Ritter. One more man, closer to him, pitched forward.

The main slope still lay ahead, but the fusillade from the Mexicans in the trenches now churned its runout into powder. One man on his left opened his walk to a run. Too soon! Would the other men of Rouge break for the trench as well? They should not begin their charge for another hundred meters. Under the howl of the ricochets and the crash of rifle fire he heard the voice of Jean-Claude duBecq.

"*Tenez!* Hold! Stand fast, Rouge! At a walk, *mes enfants.*"

The man stopped in his tracks and for a moment it looked as if he, too, had taken a hit. He began to move forward again, but three more were down.

Something strange. At Fortín, Boulanger, who should know, had said that the Republican fusiliers could not shoot with the skill of Europeans. The fire from the defenders in the trenches should not be this accurate. Not yet.

Then he saw the volleys were not coming from the trenches alone. Powdersmoke rose from the *maguey* just ahead of Compagnie Rouge. The enemy had stationed men behind every third or fourth of the big, spiky plants. The Mexican soldier would fire, then retreat to still another *maguey*, reload, fire again, and finally jump into the trench itself. James realized his company was not advancing against an easily breached thin line; Guadalupe's commander— Negrete? or Zaragoza himself?—had laid down a clever defense in depth, one spread out for nearly a quarter of a kilometer in front of the first of the breastworks. James would be forced to begin the all-out running attack far sooner than he wished—or the company would be picked to pieces in a deadly crossfire. The same thing seemed to be happening to the main body of the Fourteenth, and no doubt to the Zouaves as well. He had to get his men through the *maguey* fast. At least there probably would not be a minefield on the slope. With all those riflemen scattered across the incline in front of the company a minefield would have been as deadly for the Mexicans as for their attackers.

He looked for his bugler and found him off to the right and only ten or fifteen yards behind the van of the company.

"À *l'attaque!*" Could the man hear him? Yes, thank God. He lifted the bugle to his lips.

The notes of the call to battle stirred his blood as it always had, always would. All doubt and misgiving were blown away.

He swept past *maguey* after *maguey*, his eyes searching for hidden snipers, his saber—not such a ridiculous accoutrement now—raised above his head; but on the course he set himself no men were hiding. He stumbled once, sank to his knees, came up fast and continued on.

To the right and left of him the company kept pace. Men were hit, falling or staggering forward.

He had covered fifty or sixty meters before he closed with the first of the enemy, a blue-clad monster of a soldier crouching behind an inadequate clump of ugly vegetation. The man had just fired at a target somewhere to James's right and dropped the butt of his rifle stock to the sand to reload when James's saber flashed across the side of his head. The blade took off the rifleman's ear before it sank deep in his shoulder. James pulled the saber back and buried the point where two white sashes crossed below the big man's heart. The soldier gasped and crumpled.

On the run again, James looked for Gallimard and the Chasseurs. To his horror he saw the squadron had ridden past Compagnie Rouge, had almost reached the trenches and now spread across almost half a mile of front. His lungs were laboring too hard to raise a shout. He muttered a curse under his breath. The Goddamned moron! If the Republican cavalry broke out now, there would be no time for Gallimard to reassemble his riders and contest the slope with them before they took Rouge on the flank. Did the fool not know that charging a trench on horseback was like crawling into the muzzle of a cannon?

He had no time to think about it. His first skirmishers were at the trench while their comrades chased through the *maguey*, bayonetting the few stubborn Republicans who stood their ground. In five seconds more he came to the trench himself.

The long ditch with its twists and turns had filled with smoke from the enemy rifle fire, and coming in quickly on top of the enemy worked well for the Legionnaires; the riflemen in the trench could hardly see to fire at such close targets and had to face steel while looking up at their attackers. Yes, the charge had worked well, but from here the hill slanted sharply upward; the next trench was halfway to the moat. The company would have to jettison their packs before they began the climb.

The bloody work of the company in the trench took less than fifteen minutes, and when the survivors streamed up the slope to the next line of defense, James's Legionnaires brought their own effective fire to bear on the backs of the enemy.

He found duBecq. Somewhere the sergeant had lost his kepi; he looked much older with his gray hair uncovered.

Since the trenches lay open toward the fort, the Legionnaires huddled fully exposed to small arms fire from the parapets. James hoped they were at the extreme limits of the range of the old outdated rifles the Mexicans used. In any event, the company could not linger here. At least he was on his own timetable from here on out.

The guns of the fort were silent now. The commander behind the wall probably would not start them off again until all his forces had secured their positions in the next line of trenches, and perhaps not then. As for the French guns, if duBecq's report on the ammunition shortage was true, he might have heard the last of them today.

Sheet lightning flickered somewhere off to the east, a faint contrast to the repeated flashes of cannon fire from the fort just before the advance began.

DuBecq had found his kepi and once again looked like a Legion sergeant.

"Losses, duBecq?"

"Ten to fifteen who will not fight again today, Captain. Five dead, I think. Hard to tell with some of our dead and wounded out of sight at the far end of this trench."

"We are still a fighting force then?"

"*Absolument, monsieur*. When does the captain wish us to move out again?"

"We'll rest for fifteen minutes. Tell the men to leave their packs. We're facing a nasty climb. Are the ladders with us?"

"Not all. We have lost one of the six they issued us. The bearers of that one took a direct hit from a cannon in the fort."

"See to our wounded, sergeant. Then count off the company in two attack lines." DuBecq had meant it when he suggested *he* be the first through the gunports. James would have to make some small concession to his sergeant's wishes. "You will lead the first and I will follow with the second."

"*Oui, mon capitaine.*"

"When you have formed up the company send a runner to Lieutenant Gallimard of the Chasseurs. Have him report to me immediately." He had not yet looked to see if the St.

Cyrian had stayed alive during the advance. Somehow he knew that the luck most simpletons such as Gallimard seemed to possess would have seen him safely through his initial taste of armed combat. Maybe he had learned something. Probably not.

By the time Gallimard cantered up on the big bay the sky had darkened to lead. More lightning flashed.

"You have orders for my squadron, *monsieur?*" For all the maniacal riding he must have done in the first skirmish, he still looked as if he had just stepped from his tailor's fitting room.

"Only if you'll follow them this time, Gallimard." The young officer looked as blank as a sheet of foolscap. Obviously he thought his comportment during the advance beyond reproach. What the hell did they teach them at sacrosanct St. Cyr? "If you do not follow orders I merely waste my breath. I want you only fighting enemy cavalry, not the foot soldiers in these trenches."

"But I found no cavalry to fight. I felt I must fight someone, *monsieur!*"

"You will find cavalry to ride against soon enough, lieutenant, I assure you. And now, with your squadron scattered over seven leagues of Mexico, you're hardly in a position to contest the field with them. As it is you'll probably be outnumbered."

Something strange flickered behind the moustache. Damned if the young ass did not look pleased at the prospect.

DuBecq appeared at James's shoulder. The company must be ready and waiting for the next stage of the attack. He had to get this business with Gallimard finished quickly. It could not be helped that duBecq would be listening again.

"What losses have you already suffered, Gallimard?"

"I don't know, I—"

"Of *course* you don't know! How could you with the way you've let your command get out of hand? Reassemble your squadron and bring it up behind this trench. And don't damn well move them again until you get the word from me! You will be beyond rifle range just a few feet back of here. We're going to climb the hill to the next trench now, and I don't want enemy cavalry attacking me from the rear. Keep them off our backs. Lead them away. Retreat if you must." He turned to duBecq. "Let's take the company out, sergeant."

In seconds he climbed out of the trench with the second unit. He could only hope for the best now and put Gallimard out of his mind.

The fire from the second Republican line had reached an intensity that made the earlier fusillades from the *maguey* and the first trench pale by comparison. Casualties were bound to soar now. His sergeant loomed ahead of the company's first attack line, moving it along with brisk efficiency. The good sergeant, too, knew that the only way to hold losses down was to reach the trench with all possible speed and begin the grisly hand-to-hand work Legionnaires did better than any soldiers in the world. One thing: the fort's guns would not be brought down on them; the possible target area had shrunk, and the cannoneers behind the wall would fear killing too many of their own.

From this slope to the moat there was no more *maguey* to conceal riflemen, either.

These things, of course, applied only to the one remaining sector through which the company and the Fourteenth would still have to advance. For all he knew, the Zouaves of the Second's center were walking through the hell of both the fort's guns and the firestorm from the riflemen. The far left of the Zouaves—and beyond them Hennique's Marine Light Infantry and the Chasseurs-a-pieds—could also draw the fire of the artillery at Fuerte Loreto, now hidden behind Guadalupe's wall. It sounded as if that could be happening already. Guadalupe's cannon had not smoked since some time before the company reached the trench they had just vacated, but the steady, unmistakable, rolling thunder of big guns echoed from the far left side of Guadalupe—from Loreto.

DuBecq had taken Compagnie Rouge's bugler with him,

and now James heard the notes of the call to charge. The skirmishers ahead of him broke for the trench. A few fell, but not as many as he had feared. DuBecq's timing had been superb. His own second line would have to break into a run in another half a minute.

But before he could give the order a different thunder from that of Loreto reached him. This time it was the genuine article. Drops of rain were spattering the dust of the slope.

"*Attaquez!*"

The second skirmish line leaped forward, straight and unbroken save where the smaller or slower men lagged a pace or two behind.

By the time they reached the trench, duBecq and the first line had almost done their job. It took but a few more minutes to clear the last of the enemy away.

Here in this trench he saw the enemy commander's first small oversight. No one had dug away the back side of the trench as they had with the first. No attackers were meant to get this far. The Legionnaires had a perfect bulwark against small arms fire from the fort. He could take a little more time now, let his men get a real second wind before he ordered them into the steep climb facing them. He could try to determine the positions of the Fourteenth and the Zouaves, and he could wait until Gallimard had done at least a little something about gathering his squadron.

He called duBecq to him.

"We had better pick our gunport objective from down here, sergeant. Once we're in the moat it will be straight above us and perhaps out of sight."

DuBecq pointed to the wall. "I like the look of that galleried one to the right of that row of barred windows, captain. More than one man can get through the opening at once. From here it looks as if it might accommodate as many as four or five entering abreast."

"Good choice. It seems wide enough for both of us to lead."

The sergeant shot him a hard glance, but said nothing.

James turned back to the foot of the slope and found that Gallimard had been able to round up no more than half his squadron. Horses, some riderless, were galloping back and forth behind the Fourteenth and the Zouaves, both clearly visible now that Rouge was two-thirds the way up the slope. The lieutenant himself was slumped in his saddle, his saber sheathed. He must have despaired of finding glory in this battle.

As the rain fell the breeze freshened, whipping the folds from the battle standards of both regiments. The French Army on the attack was an awesome sight. If only there had been enough artillery ammunition for Bruat to hit the old convent once more and give cover to the infantry as they struggled up the last hundred meters between this trench and the foot of the wall. Had that been the case, the Mexicans inside Cerro de Guadalupe would probably have counted the day as lost. But even without the field guns continuing the bombardment, the sight of five or six thousand attackers must be striking terror into the hearts of the defenders. No Mexican troops had faced a modern army since 1848 and very few of the men behind the wall would have had even that intimate experience to fall back on.

"Pick a squad to escort the ladder-bearers, sergeant," James said. "Start them out before I order the rest of the company to leave the trench. When they're halfway to the moat, we'll go. I don't want us up there too early, standing around picking our noses waiting for something to climb on."

"*Oui, monsieur.*"

"Detail a runner to stay close to me so I can send a message back to Lieutenant Gallimard and his Chasseurs." He did not have to spell it out letter by letter for the veteran of Marrakech and Colomb Bechar. If the enemy commander was going to use his cavalry it would be in the next ten minutes, before the first attacking units reached the moat. Whether Zaragoza or Negrete directed the defense from behind the buttressed wall, James admired the tactical restraint the Mexican leader had showed so far. A lesser captain would have sent his lancers out too early. Hitting the advancing infantry as late as possible, when they were engaged in erecting the ladders . . . yes, he saw it now . . . the Republican cavalry could sweep right down the moat itself. James's right flank would be hopelessly exposed, with most of the company's riflemen at the left blocked from firing on the enemy falling on their comrades.

He turned to the runner duBecq had assigned him.

"Get back down the slope fast, corporal! Give the Chasseur commander my respects and tell him to bring his troopers up as close behind us as he can, and ask him to see me when they are in position. *Vite! Allons*, duBecq!"

As Compagnie Rouge poured from the trench the sky broke open.

In the blink of an eye the hill became a filthy, gray sheet of water. The spurts of dust and pulverized rock from the parapet and gunport rifle fire now gave way to splashes, tiny fountains. What would they find when they reached the moat? A rushing stream? Not all bad. It might present more problems for the Mexican cavalry than it would for his Legionnaires.

A horse loomed beside him in the wet darkness. The bay! By God, the Frenchman had certainly moved fast. James could give him full marks for that at least. Gallimard had his saber out again. For a wild moment James thought the St. Cyrian had taken wounds in both his thighs; ghastly red streaks ran down the soaked blue pants and into the tops of his boots. The scarlet dye of the tunic was running madly. The young man would probably want to horsewhip his Veracruz tailor if he got off this slope alive.

Although bedraggled, he still stood out from James's legionnaires in their long, tailcoated blue tunics, making the fine target James forecast back in Veracruz.

Behind Gallimard eight or nine riders had bunched up, all that remained of the forty or so he had led against the first trench. Before James could say a word to him the lieutenant turned his dripping head to the right and stared at something.

The Republican cavalry had now made its first appearance. Fifty to sixty horsemen had rounded the corner of Guadalupe and from the look of things appeared ready to make their first charge on the slope itself rather than entering the moat.

"Engage them, Gallimard!" James shouted, hoping his order could penetrate the noise of both storm and battle. The Frenchman must indeed have heard him for he laid the reins hard across the bay's neck and the big animal turned, rearing as it did.

"À l'attaque, Chasseurs!" Gallimard's voice seemed cut through by the razor-thin edge of hysteria, but it was no cry of fear. He sat the bay as if he were beginning a parade. James could not suppress a welling-up of admiration for him, tinged with immediate sorrow. Only a miracle could prevent Gallimard's cherished military career from coming to a sudden end in the next few minutes.

Then the bay folded under its rider. Blood streamed from under its dead, glassy eye.

Gallimard had rolled clear of the bay's broad back as it fell, but not clear of the mounds of excrement the animal's bowels loosed in its dying spasm.

The last small knot of his Chasseurs unraveled as the few remaining lancers spurred across the slope to meet the enemy.

"Into the moat with my company, lieutenant!" James shouted. He broke for the lip of the wide, deep ditch himself, not even looking to see if Gallimard followed.

The banks of the moat were giving way, crumbling like brown sugar in the downpour, and one step into it was all he could take before his feet shot out from under him, sending him on a swift slide to the very bottom.

As he had expected, the lowest point of the moat already ran like a muddy stream, rising around the legs of the men in the first skirmish line. DuBecq had climbed the far side and now directed the first of the ladder-bearers as they propped the heavy contraptions against the wall. Three of them were already up, leaning against the lower section of the opening the sergeant had selected. They barely reached to the stone ledge beneath the gunport embrasure. There would be hell to play scrambling over the masonry outcropping against any determined soldiers at the guns.

He found Corporal Watkins, the company's reliable Cockney, at his elbow. "Corporal, get your squad at the top of this embankment and cover Sergeant duBecq and me when we mount the ladders. I want a steady fire on that opening until just before we reach it. When we get inside, follow us up."

Farther down the long moat the men of Compagnie Bleu were erecting their ladders, too, but they were far short of the top of the wall, and the gunports at that end were too small for more than one man to enter at a time. The only help for Captain Clermont and the Legionnaires of Blue was for Rouge to make the first sally and draw away defenders. He looked for his last two ladders and found the rushing water had already carried one of them away. The other had skewed against the far bank, both of its bearers down in the muck and water, one of them clearly dead, his companion sitting in the river nursing a bloody shoulder with a face as gray as the torrent now lapping at his waist. They would need that ladder. One end of it had already slipped into the current. None of James's men stood within twenty meters of it. In seconds it would join the other on a trip downstream.

He looked for help, found only Gallimard close enough. "Lieutenant! Give me a hand with that ladder!"

He waded through the stream, almost fell as it slammed against his boots, took hold of one of the ladder legs, and looked for Gallimard, expecting to see him right beside him.

The lieutenant remained on the far side of the water.

"Hurry, man. *Vite!*"

Gallimard stood like a post, the ends of the waxed moustache dripping as if they were water taps. The bill of the cockaded shako spilled a small waterfall down through the pointed beard. He looked paralyzed. Had fear finally reached him?

"*Gallimard!*"

The young officer simply stared at him. Then his mouth opened.

"*Non, monsieur.*"

"WHAT?"

"*Non, monsieur. Je le regrette, mais non.*"

"Why not?"

"I am a St. Cyr officer. A cavalry commander. I do not do the work of common soldiers."

Goddamn it! Fear would have been a damned sight easier to deal with. James reached to his waist, drew his pistol, and leveled it at the Frenchman. "Lieutenant Gallimard, if you don't get over here immediately, I give you my word of honor I'll put a ball right between your eyes. And don't give me any shit about being a cavalry commander. You've let your command slip right through your manicured fingers."

Gallimard crossed the stream, but he did not hurry.

He bent to the ladder, then looked up at James.

"You are humiliating me, *mon capitaine.* I may have to report this to your superior."

"Do what you must, you simple sonofabitch. Now lift this goddamned ladder."

DuBecq and his first unit were almost halfway up to the gunport. When the ladder was against the wall James put his foot on the first rung and looked for the legionnaires who had entered the moat with him. Only two appeared in shape to make the climb. He beckoned to them. Then a dozen or so more appeared through the sheets of rain.

"Come up after us, Gallimard. If you're so damned eager to fight, here's your chance. *Vive la France*, you halfwit!" He meant the "*Vive la France*" as an insult, but the gleam in Gallimard's eye told him it had not been taken as such.

He climbed and did not look back. The body of a Legionnaire, one of duBecq's men, but blessedly not the sergeant himself, hurtled past him from above. It splashed in what now had become a river racing through the moat.

There were other, smaller splashes. The defenders on top were dropping grenades and hand bombs down the face of the wall. It was indeed an ill wind that blew no one good. The fuses of the bombs sputtered out when they hit the water. But it would take the grenadiers on top only one or two more tries before they succeeded in cutting their fuses to a shorter, more effective length.

He looked up and saw no one atop any of the ladders. DuBecq and his men were inside the fort. They might all be dead by now, but they were inside.

A few more rungs put him at a height that gave him a full view of the slope they had charged across. The field was littered with corpses, the two trenches choked with them, the *maguey* looking like floral pieces above the dead. A second wave of Zouaves and what he took to be either the Tirailleurs d'Algerie or the Chasseurs-a-pieds—the infantry arm of the same Chasseurs Gallimard had led so pitifully—were advancing up the hill in the southeast middle distance, taking more fire from Guadalupe, but not, by God, from any of the guns in the gallery above him, thanks to Jean-Claude duBecq.

Directly below and half a kilometer from the moat, the Republican cavalry had finished slaughtering the remnants of Gallimard's squadron, and were now regrouping to make a charge against the near flank of the second wave of Zouaves.

If duBecq was doing good work inside, if James could join his sergeant, and if some of the rest of the Fourteenth—or climbers from the first wave of Zouaves—gained entrance further down the wall, Cerro de Guadalupe would still have to strike its colors before this day was out, the fine Mexican cavalry notwithstanding.

Meantime, the storm rose in fury.

The boots of duBecq and his climbers had coated the rungs of the other ladders with greasy mud, and one of the men on the next one to James lost his footing, falling and taking a comrade with him.

James was at the top. He had to lay his saber on the stone

ledge and haul himself up and over it. He tripped over a body and staggered against the still hot barrel of one of the two cannons just inside the opening. It seared his arm through the sleeve of his tunic.

There were at least five hand-to-hand fights going on across the stone vault inside the fort. Smoke had rolled to the farthest corners, but he made out duBecq in furious combat with two Republican soldiers, gunners probably. One of them wielded a club while the other tried to swing a long artillery tamping rod at the Legionnaire sergeant. Poor devils. They would be no match for duBecq and his bayonet. Even as he thought it, the Alsatian dispatched them with two swift thrusts.

He had to think fast now, find the door or gate that led to the rest of the fortress, and plan the company's next move before infantry poured in to seal this dangerous wound to their defenses.

Out of the corner of his eye he saw Gallimard clamber over the edge. If he could make himself heard, it might give the Frenchman useful work to do and keep him out of the way.

"Spike the cannons, Gallimard!"

A blank look greeted him, then, "What with, *mon capitaine?*"

"Find something, you stupid bastard. Use your cock if nothing else!"

Then he saw the expression on Gallimard's face change. He smiled. Incredible! Even after James's treatment of him today, he still overflowed with hero worship.

In something under five minutes the company had killed or wounded every enemy soldier James could see. All resistance crumbled. Bodies sprawled across the stone floor, some French, some Mexican, but at least three squads of the men of Compagnie Rouge were still in fighting order. The assault had succeeded beyond James's wildest dreams.

Now to find the route into the heart of Cerro de Guadalupe.

The comparative silence in the gunport gallery allowed

James to hear something from outside the fort that turned his blood to water.

He could not believe his ears, did not want to, fought against belief.

No, no, no! Not now. We are about to win!

But what he heard could not be mistaken. A French bugle. Blowing the general withdrawal.

Latrille de Lorencez, the gallant author of the victory of Colomb Bechar and a dozen other French triumphs, had decided that he had lost the Battle of Puebla de los Angeles.

He was calling his army home.

Jason James of La Legion Etrangere wondered how history would speak of the fifth of May, 1862 A.D.

The rain outside the gunport cascaded down even heavier than before.

It would be a long, wet march back to Amozoc.

7

▲▲▲▲▲

"Sarah, *ma chère.*" Charlotte von Coburg beamed. "It has been *years!* Let us promise each other we will never be separated this long again."

"I feel the same way, Charlotte . . . or should I call you 'Your Royal Highness' now?"

"Nonsense! We shall always be Charlotte and Sarah to each other."

Sarah Anderson felt even more affection for the woman smiling at her now than she had at any mere memory of her in the five years they had been apart. "But you are an archduchess of Austria now. And soon, from what I hear in the salons of Paris"—did she dare broach the subject of the rumors—"to perhaps become an empress."

"It is a little premature, but yes, it is true." Charlotte waved to someone across the huge, crowded sitting room of the Faubourg St. Germain apartment. "I am excited far beyond words. Maxl has already talked with His Imperial Majesty, *chérie.*"

Charlotte's taking Sarah into her confidence so quickly, during the first private moment the two of them had together, right after dinner and just before Jenny Lind was due to sing, made her feel as warm as in their days together at St. Catherine's.

"It *will* be Mexico then, Charlotte?"

"*Oui.* There is much to be settled, of course, but it is almost a *fait accompli.* Maxl *will* be crowned Emperor of Mexico. Papa is now in London, in close negotiations with the queen. It is important we have the support of England as well as France."

Sarah had not forgotten that King Leopold of Belgium was a Coburg uncle of Queen Victoria, but when Charlotte mentioned her father it always came as a slight shock, causing her to consider her strange, sometimes dreamlike life in Paris, making her wonder how a Bostonian commoner had drifted into the lofty circles of European royalty the way she had. Every third person in this glittering gathering tonight possessed a title of some sort.

Henri Gallimard—appearing the "Comte de Bayeux" more than ever—had engaged himself deep in conversation with the Duc de Morny. Henri looked elegant in his evening suit, his manner with the powerful nobleman easy, intimate.

They would be separated for a long time when she boarded the steamer at Calais on Friday. She would miss him.

From the way Henri and de Morny glanced at Charlotte, it seemed the sort of things the probable future empress was telling Sarah were the subject of *their* talk, too. The dinner party had buzzed with speculation about what the dreams of Napoleon III meant for the archduke of Austria and his wife. Max, of course, was still at Miramar, the Adriatic seaside castle Sarah had yet to visit.

"Can you bear to leave Miramar, Charlotte? Can Max?"

"I will be the happiest princess in Christendom when we are at last on the high seas and bound for what is Max's best chance to fulfill his destiny. Miramar, as much as he loves it, has not been altogether good for him. His great talents go to waste there. He should lead a nation, not dabble in botany and poetry, or live in the shadow of his brother."

"What do you know about Mexico?"

"I remember all the things you told me when we were at St. Catherine's, of course, and I have read everything in the Imperial Library in Vienna. Friends at the Sorbonne have been helping me as well. I have begun learning Spanish. Mexico is by all accounts a marvelous Catholic country with good people and great riches. It only needs the strong, capable, kind hands of Max to guide it. We have had so much help from so many people we cannot fail."

"Have you talked with any Mexicans, Charlotte?"

"Oui. Of course! Senor Gutiérrez, whom you may know, has been of great assistance in that regard."

Sarah knew Gutiérrez de Estrada all right, or more precisely, knew of him, through Monsieur Auguste. The Mexican had at one time been foreign minister of his country, serving under that old scoundrel Santa Anna. Gutiérrez had made millions from his hennequen plantations in the Yucatan, and had lived in Rome for a number of years, ingratiating himself with the Vatican circles closest to His Holiness. He spent his days advancing the causes of the Mexican church and his conservative friends and relatives back in Mexico City, and plumping hard for a monarch for his country to anyone who would listen to him.

Auguste Pelletier thought little of Gutiérrez. "He is an ineffectual dilettante in international politics," the professor had told her once, "a rich expatriate who has been away from Mexico so long he knows less of his native land than I do, and certainly less of the Mexico of the common man than you learned in your visits there, Sarah."

Perhaps Gutiérrez was not quite as ineffectual as Auguste

Pelletier, for all his perceptiveness, judged him. His tireless campaigning for a crowned leader for Mexico seemed about to succeed.

But there was no point in perhaps spoiling the evening for Charlotte in even the tiniest way by mentioning Monsieur Auguste's damning assessment of her informant. Or by revealing what had just now crossed her mind: a talk with Gutiérrez de Estrada hardly constituted a dialogue with *Mexicans*.

Sarah had never seen her friend so radiant, or so full of purpose. It had not come about overnight. Even the most vital woman did not blossom like this as a result of some sudden whim.

"When will you and Max go to Mexico, Charlotte? Soon?"

"Oh, it will take a while. Our good friend at the Tuileries, Emperor Napoleon, must make certain guaranties. And there is the full permission of Max's brother in Vienna to be secured, too. Both should come as a matter of course, but you know how Franz Joseph and Napoleon III can be at times."

She did not. It almost made her laugh that Charlotte would assume she had the same familiarity with the French and Austrian Emperors that a genuine member of a kindred royal house enjoyed. Friends of Sarah's father, the fierce old faculty members at Harvard College, whose true religion was republicanism—and probably Uncle Tobias Kent as well—would sniff their suspicion of Sarah Kent Anderson if they could be here listening now. An Anderson of Cambridge consorting with the kind of people her forebears threw out of the colony in 1776!

"Did you know that I leave for Mexico myself in three days time, Charlotte?"

"*Oui*. I heard. Henri Gallimard told me. Marvelous! Perhaps you will be in our capital when Maxl and I arrive. If that is the case you must come to call. We must see a lot of each other."

Sarah nodded. Then the utter absurdity of her place in

this society shocked her like an icy bath. Come to call? She could just hear herself. *Just dropped over to borrow a cup of sugar, Char. Are Max and you doing anything next Saturday night?*

She almost sighed aloud. "I'll look forward to seeing you in Mexico. *Bonne chance,* Your Highness." Charlotte did not even seem to notice that Sarah had slipped back into the formal mode of addressing her.

Henri and de Morny had finished their talk and were coming toward them.

"Mademoiselle." The duke made a little bow to Sarah, another subtly different one to Charlotte. "Your Highness. *Votre présence nous honoré.* May I have a word in private?" He didn't *slip* into the formal mode. He never left it, although by virtue of his rank he certainly had a greater right to call the princess by her given name than anyone in this drawing room. There was, as a matter of fact, infinitely more intimacy in his "Your Highness" than in any "Charlotte" Sarah had ever uttered.

When Charlotte and the duke moved off together, Sarah turned her full attention to Henri. This might be awkward. He looked as if his world were coming to an end. He had been like this since he called for her tonight to bring her here.

Henri took her hand. "This is the next to last time we shall see each other, *ma chère.*"

"We shall have a long time together on the boat train when you take me to Calais, Henri. And I will see you when you come to Mexico next summer."

"It will seem ages, Sarah. *Quel dommage!*" he said.

Not for the first time she realized what a startling resemblance Henri, Comte de Bayeux, bore to Maximilian von Hapsburg. He was of a height with Max; his prematurely thinning hair glinted with the same golden color as did that of Charlotte's absent husband—looking as if it had been combed in place by the same hairdresser—and with the same luxuriant beard, side whiskers, and moustache framing his soft, kind face. He carried himself in Max's shy stoop, too, becoming, as did the archduke she remembered from the wedding and reception, suddenly erect when addressed—as if he had just remembered who and what he was.

Again there came the apprehension, almost fright, that when Henri returned her to the Pelletier home on the Rue de Rivoli tonight he would ask *the* question.

What on earth was wrong with her? She had never, until her thoughts about almost *everything* darkened after Samuel died, had one uneasy moment with this gentle man. The commonality of their interests, his look and manner, the great warm feeling of being truly cared for whenever they went to dinner or the theater, the envy she saw in the eyes of every woman who saw her on his arm—as here tonight at Charlotte's dinner party—should have conspired to bring her paroxysms of desire, and if not that, at least throbs of loving comfort. And she did love him, did she not?

Enough. There was still this one last Parisian evening to enjoy. She would have all the time she needed to sort things out on the Atlantic crossing that would begin this weekend.

The great diva was huddling with her accompanist, and Henry Adams, looking bemused, was signaling for Sarah and Henri to sit beside him during the performance. Decent Henry Adams, the sort of man she had known well as she grew up in Cambridge, could bring her out of these clouds of perplexity with good talk of home and London after the recital. But it would mean a temporary abandonment of Henri Gallimard. She smiled at Adams, but not in invitation or acceptance. Tonight was Henri's night with her, his alone.

De Morny and Charlotte had apparently finished their private word and the duke was now in earnest discourse with a sallow little man Sarah did not know.

Henri apparently noticed the direction of her gaze. "The man with Monsieur le Duc is Monsieur Jecker, the Swiss banker who has just become a citizen of France," he said. "I have heard that he is deeply involved in the finances of Mexico."

She was already acquainted with the name. M. Auguste became incensed whenever he heard it. "These *mauvais* freebooters, these clever conspirators in this Mexican adventure of the Emperor, bring me to the point of nausea, *ma fille*," he had said. "The plans they have for that poor land are couched in talk so noble, so lofty—and so completely false. Catholic monarchy, bah! In the end it comes down to money, as it always does. The affairs of this Monsieur Jecker are an excellent case in point. He has floated enormous bonds to put Benito Juárez in France's debt. Now there is a whisper that the Duc de Morny has received a gift of some thirty percent of Jecker's Mexican loan paper in return for his support for a war of intervention to squeeze the money from the Republican government. France will soon become a country without a soul if we embark on this wicked course. And now that President Juárez has quite properly declared a moratorium on repayment of foreign debt in order to put his impoverished nation back on its financial feet, we also run the risk of becoming a country without a *sou*. It will serve us right."

Jenny Lind was, as expected, marvelous, but by the time Henri left her at the house on the Rue de Rivoli she found herself strangely ready to leave Paris . . .

On the voyage across the stormy Atlantic, with Solange seasick a good many days, and with their caretaker-recipient roles consequently reversed for most of the crossing, there had been more gossip about Jecker, de Morny, the two Hapsburgs and their fortunes, and France's part in their futures, and of course even more wild surmises about the war that had been declared after the "incident at Fortín" last month. There had been, too, a welling-up of patriotic fervor at the prospect of the impending first great battle of the war—Puebla de los Angeles. The martial pride of the French voyagers on board was not confined solely to those wholeheartedly behind Napoleon III's grand design. Even the few doubters of the Emperor's policies and politics eagerly looked forward to celebrating what would surely be yet another triumph for the "finest army in the world." The talk made her shudder.

The *Strasbourg*'s captain had learned of the imminence of the French attack on Puebla from signals flown from the bridge of a homeward-bound packet they passed somewhere off the coast of Cuba. He had fired a victory salute with the *Strasbourg*'s signal gun. The date had been May fifth, the hour close to the very one when—unknown to the captain or his passengers—General Latrille de Lorencez was pulling his badly mauled troops away from the shell-pocked walls of Cerro de Guadalupe and out from under the furious guns of its companion stronghold, Fuerte Loreto.

When the *Strasbourg* docked in Veracruz and its passengers learned of Puebla's stunning rebuff of French arms, even as they stepped from the gangplank, that depressing port became in an instant a doubly depressing place for the new arrivals. It had been a well of gloom for the French garrison for days, apparently.

Even Matthew O'Leary, the U.S. Marine lieutenant from the Mexico City embassy who was to serve as Sarah's and Solange's escort to the capital, seemed nonplussed by the defeat when they met him at the Customs House. It was as if Americans rather than the French had suffered the setback. He probably felt a professional kinship with the smart Zouaves and Chasseurs d'Afrique of the Imperial French Army he could not possibly feel for the ragtag peasant- and worker-soldiers of Ignacio Zaragoza.

"It was a disaster," he said. "I've heard some crazy estimates of French losses. Up to a thousand, according to a Zouave major I met in a *cantina* yesterday while I was waiting for your ship. It isn't quite that bad, but the figure *is* something over five hundred—almost all killed, not merely wounded. The Mexicans lost only half as many. The French attacked with amazing courage, but there's no hiding the fact they blundered badly. Rumors are flying thick and fast that General de Lorencez's days as commander-in-chief are numbered, that the Frogs will have a new general on the scene within a month."

"Will they even stay in Mexico after such a defeat, lieutenant?"

"Oh, I think so, ma'am. They're a proud bunch. But now they know beating Juárez for that Austrian what's-his-name won't be the cakewalk they thought it would. My Zouave friend says he's heard they're going to up their forces here to something over thirty thousand men. They intend to bring in a lot more artillery, something they were sadly lacking at Puebla. An army like that will get them to Mexico City without too much trouble, but I'm not sure about the north. One thing surprised the French right after Puebla."

"What was that?"

"Because they're so much against the Church, Europeans have always looked on the Juaristas as a lot of heathens, but they sure acted like good Christian souls after they'd won the battle."

"How so?"

"They sent all their French prisoners to Orizaba where de Lorencez had regrouped, and without even asking for an exchange. The ones who were wounded too badly to make the trip will be coming out of captivity, too, soon as they're fit again. I understand the Little Indian himself, Juárez, gave the order."

She wondered if one of the dead or wounded could be Henri's younger brother, but in the bustle of getting ready for the next stage of their journey, she had not investigated. From what O'Leary said, if Marcel had fought at Puebla and lived through it, he would be at Orizaba when they got there with their Marine lieutenant escort. If something terrible *had* happened to young Gallimard in the fighting, she did not want the news to add to the fears of *"pauvre Solange,"* who had met Marcel when she and Sarah journeyed to St. Cyr for the graduation ball.

The one night and the following morning they spent in Veracruz had already provoked pure horror in Solange, and had been no picnic for Sarah. But even had the port been a seaside resort of ease and luxury she would have disliked it. That utter revulsion about war and soldiers inherited from her father came to the fore again. Except for the natives and the commercial travelers who had arrived with her on the *Strasbourg*, every man she saw wore a uniform. She stiffened at the sight of every one of them. And not just her father's ideas haunted her, either. She supposed her *total* New England upbringing made her wary of soldiers. Yes, she would always be a thoroughgoing Yankee if she lived abroad for the rest of her days, at the very least uneasy around military men.

O'Leary found them a *posada* in the dock area, but too far from the waterfront to expect an ocean breeze, and installed them in its last free room, a cramped, windowless cell no bigger than her dressing closet at the Pelletiers', populated by enough crawling and flying insects to keep Solange up and on guard the entire night. French soldiers and business travelers from the steamer filled the small inn and its walls rocked with carousing until almost dawn, the sounds of breaking glass, curses, and furniture being badly mangled making the tiny room vibrate. Sarah slept little more than did Solange. The bath the innkeeper, who looked a cutpurse, offered them next morning was rejected out of hand when Sarah learned they would have to walk to an unwalled pumphouse in a palmetto grove a hundred yards behind the establishment. They went together to the other outbuilding, a foul-smelling wooden affair that looked like an upright coffin, one of them standing guard while the other used the facilities, each in record time.

Matt O'Leary joined them for breakfast. Good thing, too. What passed for a dining room at the *posada* was a murky, smoke-filled barroom, jammed with men—some at the bar, a few seated—who quite obviously had not used the pumphouse-bath, either. Sarah never could have persuaded Solange under threat of death to enter any such place without some strong, friendly male presence. As it was the Frenchwoman scarcely ate a bite.

Snatches of conversation gleaned from the three other tables, and O'Leary's footnotes to them, filled Sarah in on just how bad things were here in Veracruz.

First, there was something called *el vómito negro*, which Matt explained was the local jargon for yellow fever. He said the death toll from the ailment had in all likelihood been as high as the men around them claimed. If so, Sarah decided, the Battle of Puebla had been the second engagement the mighty French Army had lost since disembarking on these shores, and the smaller one as far as casualties were concerned. Only the wounds gouged in French pride made Puebla the more significant.

"There's been a lot of other sickness here in Veracruz, too. Food has been scarce until this spring, and what there was of it didn't exactly suit French stomachs," O'Leary said. Solange sniffed as if to say she could well understand that.

Veracruz had become for the French expeditionary force as wicked and dangerous a port as Marseille or Genoa had ever been. No one strolled the waterfront alone after dark. Men of all ranks had been found with their throats cut or were reported missing and presumed dead. Seven bodies had washed up on the curved southern shore of the city. The missing had not deserted. "There's no place here in *la tierra caliente* where it's safe for a European to hide," the Marine said. "Like Veracruz itself, the whole state is a hotbed of Republicanism."

After breakfast and a pitiful attempt on the part of Solange to organize a *toilette* for the two of them, Matt O'Leary had a sullen porter haul their luggage to the railway station in a mule-drawn *carreta*. They followed in a buggy Matt hired.

Away from the dock area the streets were empty except for a few mangy dogs and a lone beggar who looked to be suffering from leprosy.

Sarah reflected that Charlotte, empress though she might be by then, would have to make her entrance into her realm along this same sordid route. It would be a far cry from Brussels, Paris, Vienna, and Miramar.

Once at the railway station Solange brightened when she discovered the locomotive and the two coaches were of French manufacture, brand new, the locomotive glistening in black enamel and gold paint, and their carriage fitted out superbly. A sign in gilt letters on the coach's side read *"Ferrovia Occidental—Veracruz-Méjico."*

"It only runs twice a week," O'Leary said as they boarded. "We were lucky the *Strasbourg* docked when it did so we could catch it."

The train got under way in good order. There was no schedule, Matt told them, so it was hard to tell if it was actually pulling out on time. They had the entire second coach to themselves.

Hot and steamy as the air inside the carriage was, Solange began to relax as the train made its way across the marshlands west of Veracruz. Their seats were vis-a-vis, and she leaned forward and patted O'Leary on the knee with her gloved hand. "It is almost as nice as the boat train from Paris to Calais," she said. *"Merci, monsieur* Matt. Perhaps Mexico will be better than I expected. This is the only way for a civilized person to travel."

Strangely, Matt looked uncomfortable at the remark and the friendly touch.

The low, soggy *ciénagas* of the coastal plain gave way to a scrub rain forest bright with red and yellow flowers, and groves of banana and mango trees. In about an hour out from Veracruz they pulled into a small village of attractive white-washed buildings and the train squealed to a stop. A sign on a beautifully stuccoed wall as white as the buildings proclaimed the place to be Pueblo Soledad.

"This is where the French and the Juaristas signed the agreement that let de Lorencez's army out of that sinkhole last fall," O'Leary said. "The village women here will stock us for lunch and supper quite reasonably, Miss Anderson. I suggest we buy everything they offer us. It's a long trip before the next real town, Córdoba."

Two pretty girls about eight and ten years old were already proceeding down the aisle toward them, carrying huge baskets of fresh fruits, bread loaves, sausages, and flasks of wine wrapped in straw.

When the two girls reached them, they curtsied and

pushed the baskets toward Solange, evidently deciding that as the oldest member of the party she would have the say—and probably the money.

"*Charmantes,*" Solange muttered.

O'Leary took charge of the purchasing and bought the two baskets and all their contents to the shy but wide smiles of the youngsters. The girls raced back up the aisle, their red skirts swinging, and barely made it off the train before it was under way again.

In only three or four kilometers Sarah discovered the reason for Matt's discomfiture at Solange's earlier thanks.

The train screeched to a stop in the middle of the jungle and loosed three piercing blasts from its whistle.

"I'm sorry, folks," Matt O'Leary stared out the window as if he were afraid of meeting the eyes of his two companions. "This is it—end of the line. It's as far as the French have managed to lay track in the last year."

The soaring spirits of half an hour earlier fluttered and fell to ground.

It took three more days to reach Orizaba, mostly in stiff, lumbering coaches with no springs, brutal affairs pulled by four to eight mules over roads which seemed to Sarah little more than dried up, rocky river beds. Nights found them in farm homes in rooms as tiny as their confining box back in Veracruz and as smelly, and once, to Solange's complete and speechless embarrassment, all three of them had to share sleeping quarters, with Matt bedding down on a straw pallet on the mud floor. He insisted at first on staying outside, but their host, a genial little highway robber who was charging them a small fortune for the cramped quarters he provided, told the marine—in Spanish that Sarah was beginning to understand again—that the tangled, green forest outside his door teemed with poisonous snakes. She would not hear of Matt stepping a centimeter beyond the sill until daylight broke again.

They did get one bath, at a watering trough shielded from prying eyes by *sarapes* hung on lines stretched between small trees, where they were waited on by an elderly woman Sarah decided was Indian or *mestizo*, the hardworking, prototypical Mexican such as those she had seen working for Samuel in Zacatecas. Solange and the old woman were friends before the Frenchwoman toweled herself off, even though they could not make conversation.

But Solange did not quite forgive O'Leary for the indignities he had inflicted on her until they reached Orizaba and he took her to Mass in the multidomed cathedral of San Miguel.

Orizaba was a paradise compared to Veracruz and the decaying villages near the coast. Sarah was only slightly disappointed when Matt decided they could not continue on immediately.

"I'm sorry, Miss Anderson," O'Leary said. "I know how anxious you are to get to the capital, but the ambassador would see me tossed out of the Marine Corps if I tried to take you one more step until the roads are safe. After the French took that whipping at Puebla and pulled back to Orizaba here last week the whole countryside has swarmed with Republican troops—or bandits. Actually, we couldn't even get back to Veracruz."

"I understand," Sarah said. "It's just that Solange and I have been traveling so long. But I can see the danger. We heard that fighting on the mountain two nights ago."

"That was sure an incredible little action, ma'am. After his victory at Puebla, Zaragoza sent about a thousand troops up that big hill north of here they call the Cerro del Borrego to cannonade the town. Some captain from the Foreign Legion's Fourteenth led a company up the mountain in the dark of night, just reconnoitering. He stumbled on the Mexicans by sheer chance. He had no idea of how strong they were, and apparently they didn't know how few Legionnaires *he* had. He drove them out of their positions before they could even set their guns, inflicting hellish casualties on the Mexicans. Only lost one man himself. Rumor has it he is an American, and had already been some kind of hero in the attack on Guadalupe at Puebla and in fighting a rear-guard action during the retreat to Orizaba—

the sort of utterly fearless, ruthless officer generals dream about."

"An American? With the Legion? A *mercenary* in other words." She made the word mercenary sound like an obscenity.

"Yes, ma'am. He's a mercenary, all right. I suppose there's worse things in this world."

"But an American? Selling himself to French imperialists? I can think of *nothing* worse. Why isn't this money-grubbing hero north of the border, fighting in his *own* country's war, whichever way his allegiance lies?"

The sudden, stricken look on the Marine's smooth young face told her it was a matter of some distress to this pleasant officer to be posted to Mexico City instead of battling for the Union. Of course, she was making an assumption that his loyalties were with the North. Union partisan or Confederate, it was heart-rending to be an American these days, wherever choice or blind fortune placed one, doubly heart-rending for anyone who despised war and soldiers as much as she did.

"Well, I suppose Solange and I will just have to be patient, wait until you tell us it's safe to proceed, Matt." At his urging back in Veracruz the Marine had very quickly become Matt to both her and Solange, but he had never bowed to her insistence that he call her Sarah. "Miss Anderson" and "ma'am" made her feel so *old*. O'Leary probably was her age, give or take a year, but he seemed at times an adolescent, boyish and innocent.

"Please don't worry about us, Matt. We'll be all right. Solange can do with the break in our travels." Sarah, with her previous experience of Mexico, was at least modestly prepared for the strange sights, sounds, and smells of this still largely unknown country, but the Frenchwoman, born into and reared in the ordered rural life of the Pas de Calais and eased into middle age in the civilized home of Auguste and Claudine Pelletier, had nothing in her European background to ready her for a primitive country made even more savage by the war now raging. Orizaba had confounded Solange a bit. She had flatly refused to believe that Veracruz was not typical of what they would have to live with on these shores. She was a deceptively courageous woman, though, and until the gunfire from the mountain here in Orizaba, she had become somewhat mollified. She saw Orizaba, compared with Veracruz and the arduous journey inland, as a haven of peace and comfort, even when the "alarums and excursions" of war rolled down the canyons from the mountaintop two nights before. Not that Solange, for all that she was enamored of uniforms and tales of soldiering, had not come close to hysteria when the noise of bombs and rifle fire echoed through their windows at the *posada*.

"We will be killed, *ma chère!*" she had shrieked. "Or much, much worse—raped!" Sarah suspected that some of the courage Solange found after this outcry came from the occasional cognac she sipped, supposedly in secret.

The duenna found solace in the cathedral. O'Leary, also a Catholic, took her there to Mass again the day after the nighttime fighting. "I will admit," she said when they returned, "this *sale* country at least seems religious, even if the church the lieutenant found for us looks nothing at all like Notre Dame and has no seats for the worshippers."

Sarah did not have the heart to tell her how Benito Juárez and a good many of his fellow Republicans had tried, with their Constitution of 1859, to set the unshod feet of Mexico's *mestizo* masses on a secular path. The new laws forbade Holy Mother Church to own property, a matter Sarah heard about when crossing the Atlantic. With this news she learned the name of the savagely anti-Republican cleric her more liberal-leaning French traveling companions worried about, Archbishop Labastida, who sounded as if he were as dedicated an enemy of the French as he was of Señor Juárez.

She hardly thought it right or wise to ask good Catholic Matt about the Archbishop. But it made her think of Charlotte at her last *soirée* in Paris.

The Belgian princess, now an archduchess of Austria,

was every bit as staunch a communicant as Solange, and certainly a more militant one. She had been at her devout Roman best at the dinner in the Faubourg St. Germain, and at her most aristocratic.

Staying in Orizaba a little longer than planned meant she might be able to get in touch with Henri's brother.

"I have a French friend serving with General de Lorencez's forces here in Mexico. A Lieutenant Marcel Gallimard. He's with the Chasseurs d'Afrique. Could you find him, Matt?"

"I'd be glad to, Miss Anderson."

It made Sarah a bit angry when Henri's younger brother sent a note instead of presenting himself in person. The note invited her to dinner at his officers' mess in the dining rooms of El Reposo, the largest *fonda* in Orizaba, with no mention of how she was to get herself to the hotel. She was tempted to ignore it. She had met Marcel exactly twice, and on both occasions he had struck those lurking Boston sensibilities as a fop, a startling contrast to his older brother. She could do very nicely without seeing him, and without being thrown in with any large gathering of uniformed men.

But a sudden guilty memory of her last moments with Henri and how she had temporized about his proposal of marriage—which came more or less as expected during dinner in Calais the night she boarded the *Strasbourg*—made her send an answering yes by the corporal messenger who brought Marcel's invitation.

She explained her uneasiness about getting across Orizaba alone to Matt O'Leary and he promised to escort her to El Reposo and return to take Solange to dinner somewhere.

She had Solange lay out the midnight-blue velvet gown she had not really intended wearing until she reached the capital.

O'Leary saw her inside the oversized foyer of El Reposo. He wore a wistful look as he gazed around him. There were men in uniform everywhere. She could guess he would like nothing more than to see what a French officers' mess was like. She wished Matt could take her place.

The *fonda* was surprisingly impressive, not quite the equal of a Paris or London hotel, of course, but stately, and by any standards Mexican or European, tasteful. From the foyer she could see through to a tile-floored patio behind a huge brick arch closed off with filigreed wrought iron. A fountain played in the middle of the patio, and fronds of greenery drooped from a wooden lattice-work covering. The baroque masonry of the side walls seemed exotic to eyes more accustomed to the understated red brick and fitted stone-work of Mayfair or the Champs Elysées, at a glance more Italianate, but with a difference even from that flamboyant style. A pair of bright red, white, green, and yellow macaws perched on one of the verdant garlands. Charlotte Coburg-von Hapsburg would enjoy this vista—Max, too. It called to mind a courtyard garden in one of the photographs Charlotte had sent her once of Castello di Miramare, the fairytale Miramar.

She recognized the Zouave uniform on most of the men milling around in the foyer, but there were several others unknown to her. She wished Marcel had asked her to dinner in some slightly less martial atmosphere, but perhaps none existed in the armed camp Orizaba had become.

Matt stepped to the desk in the foyer to inquire about Gallimard. The inquiry was unnecessary. The Chasseur was descending a curving staircase into the foyer.

"Mademoiselle Sarah!"

The military finery was the same, but this was in no way the Marcel Gallimard of the Loire, St. Cyr, or Paris. The Napoleon III moustache and goatee were as immaculately waxed and trimmed as she remembered them from France, but they did not stab the air with the same jauntiness as when she had first met him with Henri, a week before he graduated. Something had happened to him. She knew in an instant what it was. An old friend of her father, a gentle soul who was studying at Harvard Divinity after half a life in the business world, had fought in the war against Mexico in 1848. He had once said within her hearing, "I hated every minute of my military service, but I will admit that I felt better about myself that I faced enemy fire without showing the white feather too prominently. War does make a man feel like a man. Pity we've never discovered another, better, more Christian rite of passage."

Yes, Marcel Gallimard, former Parisian dandy and youthful boulevardier, was now a veteran.

O'Leary joined them, Sarah made hurried introductions, and the Marine asked Gallimard when he should return for Sarah.

"That won't be necessary, Lieutenant," Marcel said. "I shall bring the *mademoiselle* back to her *posada* myself." A haughty tone made it an outright dismissal. He had not even asked the Marine to join them. Veteran or not, some things about him had not changed. Marcel had divined, with that sixth sense Sarah had seen too often in the society which produced him, that Matt had even less blue blood coursing through his veins than she had.

The officers' mess at El Reposo was a far cry from the dismal dining room at the *posada* in Veracruz, and even farther from the farm kitchens which had provided their catch-as-catch-can meals on the way to Orizaba. Like the foyer, the dining room teemed with men in uniform and her uneasiness returned. As Marcel led her through it she discovered she was the only woman in the place.

Smaller rooms branched off from the main *salle à manger*, and she breathed more easily as they turned into one of them, where a headwaiter, a French enlisted soldier, gave a middling imitation of a Parisian *maître d'*hotel as he seated them. One other table in the small room, set for two, stood empty.

She would have to admit, when Solange asked later, that the meal was wonderful. The French army had somehow managed to ferry the culinary arts of France across the ocean. A baked Mexican fish the waiter claimed was a sea bass, every bit as good as one from the Mediterranean, was teamed with a bottle of Pouilly Fuisse that had withstood its Atlantic and Caribbean travels well. Despite her slight pique with Henri's younger brother and the disgusting noises of martial camaraderie from the main dining room, she began to enjoy herself. Marcel bubbled with talk. He recounted the battle for Puebla in more detail than Sarah wanted, of course, but like women all through history she had a sixth sense about how much his first taste of armed conflict meant to the St. Cyrian, and she feigned an interest.

As they ate dessert, a delicious *poire Helene*, two officers, with perhaps a few more years showing in their weathered faces than her companion, entered the private room, and the *maitre d'hotel* showed them to the empty table. One of them, who looked every bit as Gallic as Marcel, but with a much harder countenance, wore a Chasseurs uniform much like Gallimard's, but without the high, platform epaulettes and gold-cord tassels the young lieutenant affected. The other officer was dressed in the even simpler navy blue and white of the Foreign Legion.

Trying desperately to hang on Marcel's words, distasteful words like enfilade, defilade, barrage, and howitzer, she had not paid any particular attention to the second man as the pair entered the small room, and with his back to her now she could not see his face.

As the two new arrivals stepped to the other table to take their seats, Henri dropped his fork into his plate and exploded, "*Formidable!* It is my *bon ami* from Puebla." He stood up and called, "*Capitaine Zhomm!*"

The officer with his back to her stiffened perceptibly. He turned to them, and it took no second sight for Sarah to decide that the turn was made with reluctance.

If the Chasseur officer's face had struck her as hard, the Legionnaire's was flint.

He was taller than either Marcel or the man standing beside him, with dark hair touched with gray—although he certainly had yet to pass his mid-thirties. Handsome? Well, at the very least women who did not share her prejudices would think so. Unlike Marcel or the other Chasseur, no beard or moustache adorned his faintly lined, deeply tanned face.

"Lieutenant Gallimard," the Legionnaire said. *"Comment ça va?"* The French lift at the end of the question, the nasalization of the *"comment,"* were both flawless, and yet she knew in an instant that French was not his native tongue.

"Très bien, capitaine," Marcel said, and then, in English, "What brings you to El Reposo, Captain Zhomm?"

"A small, *private* dinner for Captain . . ." he turned to the other officer. "Forgive me, *mon ami* . . . Major Boulanger. To celebrate the promotion he received today." The stress on *private* told Sarah unmistakably that this captain had every intention of keeping his small dinner just that way. He had little use for Henri's brother, that was clear. The officer named Boulanger looked quietly amused. Zhomm or Jomm, or whatever his name was, had not yet looked at her.

"Permit me to introduce my dear friend Mademoiselle Sarah Anderson, *mon capitaine,"* Marcel said. "She arrived just this week from France. She is the excellent *amie* of my older brother. Mademoiselle Anderson . . . Captain Zhomm!" The words were ordinary enough, but the tone Marcel used with the tall Legionnaire's name spoke of absolute adulation.

The Legion captain turned to Sarah. *"Enchanté de faire votre connaissance, Mademoiselle. J'espère—"* He stopped. "Forgive me. Your name just registered with me. You speak English, do you not?" Behind the almost adamantine brightness of his eyes she detected an ineffable sadness. "Lieutenant Gallimard has trouble with my name. It's James, miss, Jason James."

She knew this man.

Of *course* there could be other Americans serving in Mexico with de Lorencez, but she knew this one. This was the mercenary Matt had painted as a hero with his few gleaming brush strokes, the "*. . . utterly fearless, ruthless officer generals dream about.*"

"What, may I ask, Captain James, is an American soldier doing here in Mexico, fighting France's dubious battle? Why aren't you in Mr. Lincoln's or Mr. Davis's army?"

He stared at her a full second before responding, without a trace of anger or exasperation.

"And may *I* ask with the utmost respect, Miss Anderson, what business it is of yours?"

"*Touché*, Captain James." Her voice seemed shrill, not the voice of Sarah Kent Anderson, Boston maiden lady. Something had torn loose inside her. "I withdraw the question. It indeed is *none* of my business . . ."

8

▲▲▲▲▲

The morning after the troubling dinner, Matt O'Leary surprised Sarah by telling her to be ready to move on by noon.

"Not that I don't want to get to the capital," she said, "but why the sudden rush?"

"I'll explain tonight, when we reach our first stop, ma'am."

It troubled her that for the first time since he met them at the Customs House in Veracruz, Matt had armed himself with a monstrous pistol.

Solange protested at the burst of work required to get all their things packed and into the coach O'Leary had at the front door of the *posada* at eleven-thirty, protested again when Matt told her that no, he could not promise they would reach a church for the pair of them to attend for at least two days. Under other circumstances Sarah would have smiled. Solange had not been this ardent a churchgoer back in Paris; she must have decided she needed more divine protection in the wilds of Mexico than she did in France—or perhaps she just liked the special attention she got from the Marine when they went to Mass together. At any rate, she clearly hated to leave Orizaba.

Sarah had her own reluctance to leave Orizaba and she might just as well admit it—if only to her mirror.

She felt ashamed of her small scene with the Legion captain James, the more so since, aside from his one gentlemanly admonition that she mind her own business, his manner had been courteous, almost courtly—not at all in keeping with what she would have expected from a mercenary soldier.

Marcel Gallimard had witnessed the scene. Her only hope was that he was too obtuse to recognize just how gauche she had been with her challenge to Captain James. The other onlooker, the Chasseur captain—Boulanger if she had çaught his name right—could not have failed to register what a shrew she made of herself with her petty attack on the American. From the Frenchman's sardonic look he must have thought her a schoolgirl consumed by pique and completely out of her element.

As for Jason James, she could unburden herself of any feelings of guilt at what she *felt*, if not at the things she said. He certainly was not her type. He would be as easy to forget as she now assured herself he was easy to dislike. But—she *would* like to have stayed just long enough to make something approaching an apology, and as the coach rolled past El Reposo on its way to the road to the capital, the feeling haunted her that she was leaving something unfinished—unexplored—in this handsome town.

"How did the road to Mexico City get to be safe so quickly, Matt?"

"Sorry I had to rush you, but I discovered this morning that Zaragoza has pulled most of his cavalry and all of his infantry a little to the north of the main roads west, and completely unblocked our way. It may not stay like this past tomorrow daybreak, though." He pulled a map from inside his tunic, unfolded it, and placed it in her lap. "We've got about thirty kilometers to put behind us before dark, Miss Anderson. We'll be met here tonight," he pointed to a spot on the map and she read the name Acultzingo, "at the foot of the *cumbres*, by the people who will take us as far as the Valley of Mexico. Once we reach the valley you'll be as safe as if you were in God's pocket."

"Couldn't we have set off just as well tomorrow morning?"

"I have my reasons, ma'am. We have a sort of timetable."

"Lieutenant!" she said, her tone nearly as sharp as it had been with the other American at the dinner last night. "Why do I get the feeling there is something you're not telling me?"

"Please, ma'am . . ." His eyes pleaded with her. "Trust me. I've made some arrangements I might not ordinarily make, except that I want you and Miss Solange out of Orizaba before another round of fighting starts. If Zaragoza and Negrete attack, we might never get through at all. And as I told you, the road back to Veracruz is even more dangerous than the one to Mexico City. We go now or maybe never."

Solange gave a small, strangled cry. *"Mon dieu!"*

Sarah would have pressed for more from Matt, but they were driving past a row of shops and in the doorway of one stood two men. The tall one with his back to her wore a Legion uniform something like the one that had brought her so much distress at El Reposo. The other, clearly the Legionnaire's companion, was an outlandish little creature wearing a broad, straw sombrero. A dwarf, the most spectacularly ugly dwarf she had ever seen, and she had seen a number of them in Paris over the years. She wanted to turn and look straight down the *avenida*, but the little man had caught her stare, and she feared a sudden aversion of her eyes might be taken as fright or contempt. The dwarf grinned. His hand moved to his sombrero and swept it from his head. He bowed. With his torso so much longer than his stumpy legs, the bow brought his head perilously close to the ground. When he straightened up again and clapped the big hat back on his outsized head she found a suggestive leer had replaced the grin, and her cheeks burned.

He raised his right hand toward the carriage and made a gesture with the middle finger such as she had seen only once before in her life, the night after the opera when Henri had taken her to Les Halles for the traditional after the theater onion soup. One of the produce vendors had offered a finger to her in the same disgusting, frightening manner, and Henri had hurried her away from the man's booth, found a *gendarme*, and sent him back to deal with the offending tradesman.

Now she hoped Matt had not noticed. He might just want to play the gallant as Henri had, and they could not take the time. Not with thirty kilometers to cover before darkness fell.

She held the dwarf's gaze and tried to smile an indifference she was far from feeling.

Then the man who faced the dwarf, obviously alerted by the gesture and the look on his gnomish companion's face, turned.

It was the American from El Reposo, Jason James.

It would not be as easy to forget him now, but it had become even more imperative that she do so.

It did not matter that his look at her was one of embarrassment, or that the look he turned next on the dwarf was one of fury.

They reached the coaching stop at the foot of the Cumbres de Acultzingo just as the sun slipped over the rim of the huge high mesa that cradled Puebla de los Angeles.

Matt settled them in their room, another of the confining boxes she had come to expect, where they freshened themselves before the promised supper, and when they returned to the front of the inn they found Matt in conversation with the ostler.

"You have had trouble with *bandidos* the past few days, *amigo?*" the Marine asked.

"No, señor." The man laughed. "Not with *el jefe* Antonio Pérez and his *plateados* operating on this stretch of road. He is the great hurricane that blows small winds like *bandidos* all to hell. They would not dare rob a traveler while Tonito is in the neighborhood. He would look on it as if they were stealing from *him.* He would not like that. *Es un hombre muy violento!"*

When Matt translated, Solange gasped. How many more dislocations of her sense of security could the poor woman take?

Sarah got Matt to one side. "Who is this Pérez? And what exactly are *plateados?"*

"Well . . . Pérez is a big shot bandit of a sort himself. He often has as many as a couple of hundred men riding with him, hard cases I will admit. The name *plateado* comes from the fact that for years he's been waylaying the silver trains that come down to Veracruz from Zacatecas and San Luis Potosí."

"And he's operating in this area right now?"

"Yes, ma'am."

"Matt! I thought we left Orizaba today because the roads were safe."

"I can understand your concern, Miss Anderson. Please. I beg of you. Trust me a little longer."

They sat down to supper. The *mestizo* girl who served them appeared every bit as uneasy as did poor Solange. The girl glanced nervously at the door with every trip she made to the rough plank table.

They had almost finished when a drumming noise filled the room. Horses—it seemed like an entire cavalry troop from the sounds that rattled the walls of the inn—were charging into the courtyard. The girl stepped to the one tiny window.

"¡Los plateados!" she cried. *"¡El Jefe Tonito está aqui!"*

In a moment the inn door flew open, framing a large man dressed in black, with silver mountings adorning his costume. He wore a mammoth sombrero as black as his clothes, and a beard and moustache even blacker. A pistol bigger than the one Matt carried was jammed into a wide, black belt. His eyes swept the room. He carried a leather quirt as thick as his hairy wrist, and now he pointed it at the Marine.

"Lugarteniente O'Leary!" If he had drawn and fired the huge pistol it could not have shocked Sarah one bit more than did the cannon boom of his voice. *"¡Como está, amigo?"*

He looked at Sarah and Solange for a fraction of a second before Matt could answer.

"¡Hola, Señor Perez!" There was no fear in Matt's voice. Perhaps she could relax.

"Are these the *señoras* I am to escort to the capital?" He waved the quirt in Sarah's and Solange's general direction, but he did not look directly at them.

"Sí, jefe."

"You know I like to ride only at night, *amigo.* In this case I will make an exception, but I still don't like being *en el camino* in the middle of the day. Have them ready to go at dawn." He turned and looked at the girl who had served their meal. "Luz, I have twenty-two starving *hombres* in the courtyard. Feed them. Feed them well, not with the *mierda* you gave us last time." And to the ostler. "See to my men's horses, José."

It struck Sarah that the demands would put a terrible burden on the tiny coaching stop, but neither the man nor the girl displayed so much as a touch of dismay. They were both grinning—broadly. She looked from them to the bandit chief Perez just in time to see him step back through the door and pull it closed with a powerful yank, shivering the jambs. She could surmise this forbidding man did nothing gently.

"Il est très formidable, n'est-ce pas?" Solange whispered. My God! Sarah would have thought the Frenchwoman beside herself with terror at such a moment, but instead Solange seemed smitten.

Sarah turned to Matt O'Leary. "Am I not due an explanation, Lieutenant?"

"Not much to explain, Miss Anderson. I was scared that if I told you about Tonito back in Orizaba you wouldn't have come."

"You're very likely right!"

"And if you hadn't come then, there's no telling when we could have started for the capital."

There was a stiffer tone to his voice then he had ever used with her before. The Marine was taking charge.

"Just how did you arrange this, Matt?"

"Pérez has an informant in Orizaba. Forgive me now. I must have a word with *el jefe.*" He left the table and went to the door, turned back. "I believe you and Miss Solange had better retire for the night. When Tonito said 'dawn,' he meant it."

The climb from Acultzingo up through the Cumbres was spine-jarring and at times frightening, especially when the coach leaned sickeningly out over deep, apparently bottomless gorges filled with morning fog.

The French Army under de Lorencez had come this way but a few weeks ago, on its passage to defeat at Puebla and again on the humiliating way back down, and the record of both trips appeared on either side of the tortuous route. Perez's horsemen led them up through rocks and scrub littered with broken cannon, their barrels ripped from the carriages; discarded knapsacks; carts with one or more of the wheels missing; carcasses of horses and mules in various states of decomposition, half-devoured by predators and scavengers and now glistening black with flies and crawling insects; parts of uniforms.

She caught sight of a Legion *kepi* such as the mercenary captain had worn yesterday on the street in Orizaba. Jason James . . .

The bandit chieftain Pérez had provided Matt O'Leary with a horse and the Marine changed his place in the procession from time to time, sometimes riding with the *plateado* leader, but more often dropping back beside the coach.

She had to admit she was pleased with this living embodiment of the Marine Corps motto.

They came up out of the last section of the Cumbres at noon, and when they stopped for lunch in a field dotted with giant daisies—very much like the black-eyed Susans of New England—it almost seemed as if the air was filled with the heady fumes of some mountain wine. Sarah opened the hamper packed for them by the girl Luz back at the coach stop and asked the Marine if he wanted to invite Pérez to eat with them.

"Kind of you, Miss Anderson, but I don't think so. Tonito doesn't care much for foreigners. French, Austrian, or American, we're all basically one to him."

Actually, when she discovered how skimpy the fare inside the basket was, she was happy he answered as he had.

"He seems accommodating enough to *you*, Matt."

The Marine shrugged. "The embassy has done him some favors in return for what you might call intelligence reports. Even with its troubles in the United States, Washington is vitally concerned with what happens here. He's a robber and a ruthless brute, but he's also a staunch Republican. Our nation likes that. He still doesn't like *us*, but he's a practical gent as well. And surprisingly enough, he's close to Benito Juarez."

Pérez was eating with his men, those he had not posted ahead of and behind the cavalcade on its line of march. Even at a hundred or more meters away he was a brooding, immediate presence. He seldom so much as glanced at them. The men of his command, if you could call this aggregate band a command, were an unsavory looking lot, each of them bristling with assorted weapons: pistols, rifles, knives, or *machetes*; sometimes all four. Ruffians, marauders. How could a leader and statesman such as President Juarez permit this *jefe de bandidos* to come close to him?

Her two previous visits to Zacatecas went for naught. She was still a great distance from understanding Mexico.

Why did Charlotte and her Maxl want to become the

crowned heads of such a bloody, nightmarish, fragmented country?

An hour after the restful but abbreviated meal they passed Puebla on the south at a distance of two miles or more. With its cathedral spires it did not strike her as a warlike place. To the north and east of the city itself she could just make out the twin forts Marcel had described to her irritation at the dinner two nights ago. The larger one with the two church-like towers must be the Cerro de Guadalupe where young Gallimard and Jason James had fought.

She busied herself by making a thorough study of the map Matt had given her as they left the *posada* in Orizaba.

Southwest of a large village west of Puebla, a place the map identified as Cholula, if she were reading it correctly, the coach stopped.

Matt had been riding alongside and he now rose in the stirrups and stared down the road to the west. Sarah poked her head through the window and looked, too.

A group of armed riders had moved into the road ahead of them, men in blue uniforms, carrying lances.

"Republicans," O'Leary said. His hand went to the pistol on his hip, but he made no effort to pull it from its holster.

Solange had snugged her head next to Sarah's and now she emitted her usual gasp. "We'll be killed yet, I know we will." She crossed herself. "We should have gone into that *ville* with the cathedral so Solange could pray."

Pérez rode out ahead of his men and conferred with the officer who seemed in charge of the cavalry unit. There were handshakes and salutes and backslapping and in minutes the half-squadron or whatever it was moved off the road and the officer waved them on. He saluted the coach and its occupants as it rolled on past him. She was going to have to make it up to Matt somehow for doubting him.

That night they slept in the coach, piled with robes Matt pulled from the boot. Or rather she and Solange did. The Marine, from the look of him next morning, did not sleep at all. He must have guarded them through the entire night.

At breakfast O'Leary smiled over a cup of weak coffee the driver brewed at a tiny fire and said, "We've put any real danger behind us now. From here to the capital it will still be tedious and boring, but it will be safe."

Perhaps Matt had traveled this road too many times; it did not bore Sarah.

Lovely—if a touch melancholy—vistas opened to the far horizons on either hand. In the distance straight ahead of them, what she guessed must be the great volcanoes which hung over the capital pierced clouds which had surrendered their early morning gold to a rich, hammered silver.

Maybe Max and Charlotte were right after all to want this jewel of a land as the gleaming ornament for their wished-for and now apparently attainable crown.

Mexico might very well be the most beautiful country she had ever seen.

Even the ragged, desperate men making up their escort had taken on a different, more appealing aspect. Suddenly they looked almost noble in their rustic simplicity—and above all else, free.

9

▲▲▲▲▲

JALAPA, MEXICO—NOVEMBER 1862

"It is hard to believe six months have gone by since we limped back to Orizaba from Puebla, *mon ami*," Pierre Boulanger said as he and Jason James shared a bottle of Mexican wine in the crowded cantina in Jalapa, northwest of Veracruz. "A wasted half year. *Merde!* Well, perhaps things will improve now that Forey and Bazaine have replaced our unfortunate de Lorencez." He held his glass to the light. "This red piss is disgusting. I should only imbibe in the Zouave mess where they have *French* wine. Swill like this, or *ennui*, will kill me far sooner than will Juárez's army." He sipped his wine and shuddered. "Jalapa has even less to offer than Veracruz, never mind Orizaba."

"This northern route *is*, however," James said, "the road to the capital we took in '47, Pierre. It would have been much more difficult to go straight west from Orizaba, with Puebla always threatening us on the flank."

"*Mais oui*, Jason. I will not quarrel with General Bazaine's strategy. With Douay coming from Orizaba and up through the Cumbres again, we will have Puebla in a nutcracker, even if it *is* a tough nut to crack. If Forey and Bazaine will let us fight."

James had grown close to Boulanger in these six months, closer than he had become with any shipmate or fellow-soldier in the years since Kansas. Perhaps as close as he had been to anyone he had ever known except his cousin, Aaron Sheffield, who had fought here in Mexico with him in '48 and was now fighting again somewhere north of the border in that other, much larger, more deadly war. Perhaps Aaron was dead now. Letters from James's mother had placed him at Bull Run and Antietam. Aaron—at age nineteen and a West Point cadet—had been the scholar who started James in the classics he had gone on reading at sea and in North Africa. Even though he and Aaron had suffered that terrible falling out, if Aaron *had* died, James could take some comfort that *he* hadn't killed him. If they ever met again, Aaron would have to do what killing would be done. While James had killed countless men for the Legion, he never could have pulled the trigger with Aaron in his sights—no matter who the commander or what the cause. Aaron, ever the soldier, would not have hesitated to kill James if his orders required it. He would not have hesitated to kill James at Chapultepec or on the dock at Veracruz in '47 before they parted, if things had been just a little different.

Boulanger poured another glass of the Monterrey red,

shuddered, tossed it off with a grimace, and refilled his glass. "I have been drinking far too much. *Mon foie* complains. I need work," he said. "But things do seem to be happening at last. We have now landed another fifteen thousand troops at Veracruz. They will march to Orizaba as soon as the Egyptian regiments on the troopships following them disembark next week. It will bring us to something over thirty thousand men, and with enough new artillery to defeat even Márquez and his marvelous cavalry."

"Tell me about Forey and Bazaine, Pierre."

"Forey. Major General Elie Forey. Frankly, I think him as incompetent as Latrille de Lorencez. But he will probably be commander-in-chief at least until the Austrian and his Belgian wife arrive, and I don't think Maximilian will be inclined to tamper with Emperor Napoleon's appointments for a long, long time. Without us his crown would only be a *papier-maché chapeau*. Forey will be here primarily for the politics of this ridiculous adventure. The real military strategy to deal with Juárez will be left to the First Division's François-Achille Bazaine, another major general and a *premiere classe* fighter. Let us pray that Forey seeks his counsel. I doubt he will. They do not get along too well. Forey is openly jealous of Bazaine's reputation. The latter would not prove as rash as our departed de Lorencez, but he wouldn't let things drag out all fall and winter, either. Do you know anything about him, Jason?"

"A little. I know he went to the Crimea for France, and he fought in Spain and North Africa, but before my time. I really remember him only as a colonial administrator in North Africa."

"Oui. What I like about him—" Boulanger stopped, looked around at the other tables filled with French officers in the smoky cantina, then went on, lowering his voice. "—is that he is an up-from-the-ranks commander, not another fucking overdressed, parade ground St. Cyrian. However, that is not a sentiment I necessarily wish to share with the toy soldiers at these tables. *Vous comprenez, n'est*

ce pas?'' He raised his glass. "Let's drink to him, *mon ami.* I think he will give us professionals useful work to do." He took another drink. "There is some interesting gossip about Bazaine, not that I think it would diminish his effectiveness. When he served in Spain he married the daughter of some Spanish grandee. She remains in Paris. It is said she does not pine for him. Her bed, the wags of Paris say, is not empty when the general is off somewhere with the army. An actor from the *Theatre Francaise* occupies his half. No one, they say, has ever told the general. Knowing his temper, I would not wish to be the one who eventually tells him. Even Forey, his nominal commander, does not dare."

In the six months since the retreat from Puebla, Compagnie Rouge—where new arrivals from North Africa had replaced the twenty-two casualties of the Puebla disaster— had recovered fairly well from its beating beneath the parapets of Guadalupe and on the way back through Amazoc and Acultzingo to Orizaba. Now, after the uneventful move to Jalapa, James had busied himself with the routine of reshaping his small command.

Under blazing summer skies the relentless duBecq drilled and double-drilled the men of the company, newcomers and veterans alike, marching them across rocky fields and along burning roads until almost every one of them dropped or wanted to. James looked his company over with a hard eye every day and accompanied duBecq on both the regular and surprise inspections of the company's makeshift barracks, a stable a few miles out on the road down toward Fortín where he had first seen combat with Boulanger on this second trip to Mexico.

The Fourteenth had done no fighting since James led Compagnie Rouge up the steep sides of Cerro del Borrego that first week back in Orizaba, surprising Negrete's sleeping Republican battalion in the dead of night, a marvelous piece of blind luck, he told Pierre.

"Luck?" Boulanger said. "Your modesty is *très convenable, monsieur,* but a good captain *makes* his luck. If he cannot, he should take advantage of it when it comes his way. Take the credit, *mon ami*, and the promotion that should come with it."

"Promotion?" James laughed. "Non-French Legion officers almost never become majors."

"Ordinarily that is true. But this is Mexico, not North Africa. Someone will take note of what you did."

"Too much time has gone by. It's ancient history now."

"We shall see."

Boulanger, at least, his complaints of inactivity notwithstanding, had taken Chasseur squadrons into engagements twice in just the past month. They were small operations to be sure, neither of them even as big as the affair at Fortín that won him his majority—but genuine combat nonetheless. The gods of war smiled on the cavalry even while they blandly ignored the infantry. Juarista cavalry squadrons had nibbled at the French perimeters at Orizaba, and now here at Jalapa, three and sometimes four times a week since another daring young Republican general, Porfirio Díaz, had harried the retreating Zouaves and Tirailleurs across the *maguey* plains east of Amozoc and down through the passes all the way to Ciudad Mendoza. The Chasseurs d'Afrique were learning the hard way about the excellence of the Mexican cavalry.

Even Marcel Gallimard had seen fighting.

He was seconded to Pierre Boulanger shortly after Puebla. Their association began in Orizaba on a sour note and had not improved here in Jalapa. Apparently the St. Cyrian botched assignments from Boulanger as badly as he had at Puebla, and the tough Parisian did not possess a forgiving nature about faulty soldiering. He snorted contempt for Gallimard every time his name came up in conversation, or when he and James chanced on him in the Jalapa cantina, or anywhere else they found him—as often as not in another new and more glittering uniform.

"That pitiful creature represents every one of the few things I despise about my country," Boulanger said. "St. Cyr—money he never earned—the whole aristocrat business—his clownish, clothes-horse silliness—and the fact that as an officer he will some day lead good men to unnecessary death. And on top of it all, there is something else very special and personal about him I dislike intensely."

"What's that?"

"Do you remember the night we celebrated my promotion, *mon ami?* Do you remember the woman he was with?"

All too well. There was a strange uneasiness now that Boulanger had brought her up.

"Yes."

"I do not, of course, know exactly what he has to do with her, but it offended me to see them together. You told me you were a sailor before you joined the Legion. Was not the *liaison* we witnessed at El Reposo that night somewhat like taking a boy from the tiller of a dinghy and putting him at the wheel of a racing yacht? She is altogether too formidable a woman for a *jeunet* like Gallimard. Do you not agree, my friend?"

"I didn't really speculate about it." That was only partly true. When the Anderson woman threw down the gauntlet about his profession, Gallimard did fade from James's awareness as if he were not there at all.

But good friend or not, James did not want Pierre inquiring into his memories of Sarah Anderson too closely. The worldly Parisian was entirely too perceptive. James, of course, remembered the woman from more than just the dinner. If anything, the sight of her the following day had been even more distressing.

' Would you consider her too formidable for *you,* Pierre?"

Boulanger laughed heartily enough to turn heads at nearby tables. "*Sacrebleu! Pas de tout.* No woman is too formidable for me, *mon ami.* But I was thinking of *you.* I saw the sparks fly between the two of you. Under the right circumstances such sparks could ignite something *très interessant.* It could produce great heat, and I do not mean the kind that burns down houses."

"I don't have the time. Besides, a woman like her would have no interest in a man like me. You heard her."

"Don't have time? Nonsense! Ah, but I forget you are not a Frenchman, *monsieur*. As for what interest she might have in you, do not be so modest about that, either."

All through this Boulanger had worn a look of peculiarly Gallic glee.

"It is unlikely that she and I will meet again."

Boulanger just looked wise.

The Chasseur had touched an already unquiet nerve. James, too, had wondered about Gallimard's connection with the Anderson woman. The few more bits of conversation with the pair of them after the edgy moment brought on by her first remarks had elicited nothing of consequence. He let Boulanger pose the polite, socially acceptable questions, but gleaned little from the replies of the St. Cyrian and the American woman except that she was en route to Mexico City and then, for some reason she did not offer, north to Zacatecas.

By the time he reached his quarters that night he had persuaded himself that he would forget Sarah Anderson in short order, but when he saw her on the *avenida* the following afternoon he knew how wrong he could be.

And then that little monster Cipi pulled that ugly, despicable, unforgivable indecency. James came close to flogging him, and now wondered why he had not. He did give him a dressing down much worse than he had ever given any soldier he commanded.

At the beginning Cipi fumed with outrage at the blistering James gave him. To listen to his rationale one would have thought James himself at fault.

"Men need to act that way with *las mujeres, mi capitán*. It has always been that way, and it always will be. She did not mind it as much as the captain thinks. Part of her probably liked it. The captain must know the part Cipi means."

James had never considered himself particularly fastidious where thoughts about women were concerned, but Cipi's remarks made the original offense mild by comparison and he threatened to fire him on the spot.

At that Cipi looked genuinely contrite. *"Por favor, mi capitán!* Do not dismiss Cipi. You would be making a big mistake. Cipi will work for nothing for a month. Besides, Cipi's finger was not meant for the American gringa, but for the older one riding with her."

"That makes no difference. Miss Anderson saw you do it."

In any event, James relented. He did put the dwarf on probation.

Cipi's show of humility over the next week would have been comic if the Legionnaire had been able to forget quickly the wounded look on the face of Sarah Anderson as the coach rolled away that day. The memory of it did fade at last.

What he could not forget was Boulanger's characterization of her as *formidable.* As Pierre himself would have said, *c'etait le mot juste.*

Yes, formidable was the precise word, not that she had appeared unwomanly, or that there had been, despite the brief flurry of combativeness at El Reposo, the least thing unappealing about her. By any standard, the blonde woman was uncommonly attractive, even beautiful, with a slim but stunningly female body and blue eyes of amazing voltage. They had snapped hot sparks when she accosted him.

The memory of her scent had lingered all the way back to his room that night. James did not consider himself an authority on colognes, nor did he consider himself an authority on *anything* concerning women. Those he had known best were of an entirely different sort; in North Africa, Arab women were little more than slaves, and some of them were slaves in fact in spite of France's efforts to stamp the practice out.

His own more intimate experiences with women had taught him little. A few had satisfied appetite, but there had been no other involvement—and no desire or need for it.

Sarah Anderson differed from any and all of them; this he knew in the few minutes of their encounter at El Reposo. Her speech hinted at an Eastern seaboard rearing; the few words in French she addressed to Boulanger and Gallimard were gems of fluency, if a bit stiff and formal and smacking of the schoolroom and the *salon*. Nothing had told him what she might be doing in southern Mexico, traveling a country ravaged by war over a highroad infested by cutthroats.

James did not know what Cipi thought, but that the dwarf would sooner or later voice an opinion he had no doubt. Whatever success he had in withholding his thoughts from Pierre, he failed with Méndez y García. He had unwittingly revealed that interest in Sarah Anderson to Cipi when he chastised him for his lewdness even before the coach was out of sight.

As humbled by James's flaying of him as he might have been at first, Cipi rebounded to his best, or worst, irreverent self by week's end.

"Cipi has made inquiries on behalf of his captain," he told James, "about the woman we saw in the *avenida* a week ago."

"Why would you do such a thing, you nosy little meddler? She . . . was . . . *is* . . . none of your concern. Have you learned nothing? Besides, I am not particularly interested."

"*¿No, señor?*" he asked with a sly look. "*Perdon*, but Cipi certainly thought otherwise. Do you not wish to hear what I have discovered?"

"No."

"I think you should hear it anyway. Cipi has been useful to you already, *señor*, and you have but scratched the surface of his talents. Did I not predict the downfall of your General Lorencez at Puebla? And did I not promise I would keep you alive through the battle? Cipi can make more predictions, but at the moment he does not wish to."

"Good!"

"All he wishes to do now is pass along what he has learned."

"Must you?"

"*Sí.*"

"And where did you uncover this vital information?"

That did it. There would be no stopping the little brute now.

"From that *estúpido* Emile, the *hombre* of Lugarteniente Piojo."

Since that second morning in Veracruz in April, Cipi had never—despite half-hearted rebukes from James reminding him that Gallimard was, after all, an officer—referred to the young lieutenant by any other name than "Lieutenant Louse," or more simply, "*the* louse." How had he learned of the connection of Sarah Anderson to Marcel Gallimard? Best not to ask another question. Bad enough that he would have to suffer what Cipi was already primed to say. A smug, arch look lit the bearded face.

"The *señorita* comes from somewhere in Los Estados Unidos called Boston, but she lives and studies in Paris. She has no interest of any kind in El Piojo, but *el lugarteniente*'s brother, a French nobleman of some kind, wishes to marry her. Emile thinks he will. They are both *ricos*. She has inherited silver mines at Zacatecas from a dead brother. Also, back in France the *señorita* was a familiar of the woman who would be Empress of Mexico."

He had not wanted Cipi's revelations, but now he was ruefully glad he had them.

He could at last banish any lingering curiosity about her. What possible common ground could a sketchily self-educated, rough soldier of misfortune, without a *sou* or a *centavo* to his name, occupy with a rich young woman who was all but betrothed to a member of the nobility, and who was an intimate of an archduchess of Austria to boot?

As for Cipi, never had James encountered a man of such exquisite confidence, or such boundless ego—not even in Pierre Boulanger, who seemed singularly free of self-doubt of any shade. Vexed as the Legionnaire often became with Cipriano (and that exhausting string of other names) Méndez y García, he would be the first to admit Cipi was a man of amazing parts, parts that added up to more than his ugliness and truncated body.

To James's utter astonishment, despite Cipi's lack of

those physical attributes which ordinarily would signal attraction to women, the dwarf apparently lived an erotic life of some magnitude. On more than one occasion since the army settled into its enervating stay in Jalapa, James found him in cantinas in the company of sensuous women, all of them big for Mexican women, voluptuous. From the way these ample *señoritas* fawned on Cipi, climbed into what passed for a lap, and encircled him with their fleshy brown arms, there was little doubt in James's mind that these were not innocent, playful affairs, but forecasts and echoes of couplings of a more torrid sort. He tried not to imagine what such seismic grapplings might be like, could not help himself, and shook with laughter.

Pierre remarked on Cipi's amorous adventuring. "*Vraiment, mon ami,* that man of yours is a Casanova of accomplishment. Does it not trouble you that you, my friend, live like a monk, while that deformed little *avorton* samples the world's true joys to the full? Perhaps you may someday rectify your dismal celibacy with someone like that woman we saw with Gallimard—"

James cut him short with a growl, getting in return an irritating, knowing smile from the Chasseur.

Cipi went his merry way with women. Then one day, a month or more ago, James chanced on something that told him Méndez y García lived yet another life.

James returned from a hot, fatiguing day of drilling with duBecq and the company to find the dwarf lying in the shade of a mimosa tree at the stables. The omnipresent wicked knife and the whetstone were on the ground beside him. He was reading. The book in his hand was a thick, leatherbound volume he snapped shut as James approached.

"I need clean shirts, you lazy little turd," James said. "Do a wash, or have one of your overblown women do one for you. I am dining with Major Boulanger tonight and I do not wish to look and smell like a mendicant."

Cipi shrugged, got to his feet, and moved toward James's quarters, taking the knife and the whetstone with him, but leaving the book behind. When the dwarf disappeared inside the stable, James picked it up. He opened it and leafed to the title page.

"*Traite des passions de l'âme*," he read, "*par René Descartes.*"

The thought of Cipriano Méndez y García as a Cartesian scholar brought a smile. Miracles, as James's mother had been fond of saying, will never cease. He wondered if Cipi had not left the book behind intentionally, knowing he would examine it.

He had heard the dwarf speak French, of course, with an execrable accent, but now it dawned on him that, as with the little man's Spanish and English, it had been French of a fairly elevated rhetorical style, if with a vocabulary pretty much limited to the uses of the workaday world. Certainly he had no idea of how much Cipi understood of Descartes's weighty thought, but surprises at his servant's hands had come with frequency since Veracruz and Orizaba.

He did not mention his find to Cipi, but he did discover him at his Descartes on two other occasions, and the dwarf fell strangely silent for hours after his reading.

There had been with Cipi, too, a contretemps James at the time judged minor, but which apparently meant a great deal to the other man.

On the long retreat from Puebla, when Díaz and his squadrons had harassed the column, James kept him well away from any of the hot action. Cipi seethed as he had when James ordered him to stay at Amozoc before the assault on Guadalupe.

"You do not know, my captain, what a superb fighting man Cipi is. He could be *muy soldado*, given the opportunity."

"Forget that. Just do what I hired you to do, *pequeño*, or I'll give you a *bastinado* you won't soon forget. You're not big enough to be a soldier!"

"Cipi's size in no way limits his ability to fight and kill."

"Look after my comfort and my kit and be content."

As far as James was concerned the subject was closed.

Then he made a discovery that drove the notion of the

cloistered Cartesian philosophy student and the pint-sized, industrious womanizer, too, right out of mind.

He found still another Cipriano Méndez y García.

On a sultry night in late August James made a tour of Jalapa's cantinas, again in the company of Pierre Boulanger. The Frenchman made no secret of the fact that he was on the prowl for something other than wine.

"My beard is growing like wheat in Provence, Jason. Boulanger must have a woman, *maintenant*. Are you so inclined, *mon ami?*"

Boulanger had ragged him a number of times in the past after he had turned down similar invitations, with the Frenchman almost always making some oblique reference to Sarah Anderson and some imagined claim she had on James. He could not turn his friend down forever.

"All right," he said. "I'll go with you, Pierre—but we'll have to wait and see about any women."

They started at the cantinas nearest to their quarters, drinking places of a marginally higher class than those back in Veracruz and frequented by French officers, but the few women they found who appealed to Pierre—prostitutes for the most part, but with a couple of seemingly willing and perhaps talented amateurs already known to the Chasseur—were paired for the evening. It must have been the height of the growing season for Tirailleur and Zouave beards.

"*Alors,*" Boulanger said after his hopes were dashed in the first three cantinas they visited. "It is lucky that I am a realist. We must lower our sights. Let us attack targets in what I believe Mexicans call the *barrio*. One gets less particular by the minute."

In the seamier section of Jalapa they found a bar called *Sombras de las Flores*. Shadows of the Flowers? A romantic, even poetic name for what James was sure would turn out to be just another grimy, *sarape*-draped cesspool—albeit a lively one. Noise from within fairly shook the walls of the place.

"This bistro looks promising," Pierre said.

They had to push their way in through a log jam of voluble Mexicans and a scattering of French soldiers from the lower ranks.

The small mob looked as if it were made up more of spectators than drinkers. Something out of the ordinary seemed to be going on near the bar itself. Sure enough, after Pierre and James wedged their way closer, James saw, but only by peering through a cloud of smoke past men and women jostling each other, that a section of the dirt floor had been cleared to make a small arena. James's first thought was that he and Boulanger had stumbled on a cockfight. With two huge men in front of him blocking his line of sight he could not be sure, but yes, several of those crowding nearest him had banknotes folded between their fingers in the manner of gamblers everywhere. There were shouts, catcalls and curses rising on all sides of the make-shift arena.

It was a fight, all right, but not between birds.

Pierre, who had a clearer view of the bar and the area in front of it than James, was the first to see it.

"*Mon dieu!*" he shouted in James's ear, barely making himself heard above the din. "*Ces hommes-la* are using the biggest knives I have ever seen in a fight!"

"Perhaps we should leave," James yelled back. "Pretty damned silly to get ourselves caught in the middle of someone else's squabble. Let's go!"

"*Non, non, non, monsieur!* We must stay. What is going on here is a matter of some importance to *you* at least."

James edged around the larger of the men in front of him and the move gave him a good look at one end of the bar.

A young woman cowered against it, a slim, dark creature not truly a woman, but a girl, a birdlike girl—beautiful, James decided in a flash, were she cleaned up and dressed in anything but the rags she wore.

Another half step gave him a clear view of the open space.

Two men faced each other. One was a six-foot giant with shoulders as broad and bulky as those of a fighting Miura bull; James would have thought him a *carretero*, but he did not wear the high boots of a muleteer. His right hand clutched a monstrous knife which he jabbed in the air toward the other man—an ungainly, bearded imp not four feet tall.

Cipi!

The dwarf was naked to the waist. His greasy leather vest was wrapped tightly around his left hand and wrist. The right brandished the knife James had seen him honing almost every day for five months now.

The combatants were six or eight feet apart, but now they moved toward each other, the giant on the balls of his sandaled feet, moving lightly for so big a man, the dwarf dancing from side to side as they closed.

"I think, Jason," Boulanger croaked, "that the first order of your day tomorrow will be a search for a new body servant!"

The Frenchman had it right. Little Cipi could in no conceivable way prevail against the brute he faced. The girl cried out; it was easy to determine the cause of this struggle.

James stepped forward, felt Boulanger's arm slam across his chest.

"*Non, non!*" the Frenchman screamed. "Not unless you wish to join *votre petit nain* in death."

He was right; and in any event it was too late to stay this execution.

The big man lunged, his knife reflecting light from somewhere behind the bar, causing James to blink.

When he opened his eyes again he saw that Cipi had flopped on his hairy back, shoved his feet between two tree-trunk legs, scooted forward on his rump, and was drawing his blade across the backs of the big man's legs almost as casually as he wiped it over the whetstone. Good Lord! He was severing his opponent's hamstrings, the knife slicing through heavy cotton trousers, muscle, and sinew as if they were all made of butter.

The giant found nothing but air with *his* knife. His thick legs buckled. He toppled, his weapon falling free, blood spurting from the slits in his *pantalones*. He sagged to the floor, covering Cipi, flattening him.

The dwarf struggled from under the weight of the enormous body and in a second he was on top of his fallen enemy with the knife at his throat.

James leaped forward.

"No, Cipi, no!" He reached the pair on the dirt floor. "Don't—for God's sake! They'll hang you, *estúpido!*"

The little man looked up at James and grinned.

"*¿Como esta, mi capitán? Qué relaje.* Relax, *por favor.* Cipi does not mean to kill him. But this *sucio marron* badly needs a shave if he is to appeal to the *señoritas* he craves so much." He looked down at his erstwhile foe. "You would like that, would you not, Fermin?"

They sat at a table in the corner of the barroom, Méndez y García, James and Boulanger. The girl still hovered at the bar, silent, and to all appearances unmoved by what had happened.

The *cantina* owner and two old men had dragged the bleeding man named Fermin to a room in back of the bar. The crowd now moved to tables or to the bar itself. One of the old men reappeared with a bucket of water he sloshed across the pool of congealing blood.

When the owner returned, he announced from his post behind the bar that Fermin would be all right, but ". . . it will be some time before he walks."

"Cipi—" James said. "What started this?" He nodded toward the girl. "Her?" The girl returned his look with a brooding gaze of her own.

"In a way, my captain. Fermin wanted her. Cipi did not blame him, but Cipi was making her a business proposition at the time. He could not allow Fermin to interfere."

"Women will someday be the death of you, you stupid little bastard." He could guess at the nature of the business proposition. "Don't you have enough women as it is?"

The dwarf's eyes widened. "Cipi did not want her for

himself, *señor!* Sofía is not a *puta*. And anyway, she is far too *flaca* for Cipi's taste. He does not care for the skinny ones. Cipi wanted her for you."

"What?"

"When we move into the *casa* you will rent in the capital next year, we will need someone besides Cipi to look after you, a woman to clean and wash, and cook our meals. Cipi is strictly your body servant. He has done enough of the work of women since we met."

James's mouth fell open. "I can't afford more help, you simpleton. My pay is hardly enough to keep *you* working for me. And what *casa* in the capital?"

"Ah, *sí*. That is right. Cipi forgets he has not yet made his prediction of the *casa grande* on the Paseo." He shrugged. "As for the *dinero*—you will have money to burn."

"Another prediction?"

"*Sí.*"

"And just where will all this money come from?"

"By this time next week the captain will be a major. And by the time we reach Mexico City he will be a colonel."

James laughed. "And before that happens elephants will fly. You'd better tell the girl to seek employment somewhere else."

The dwarf smiled. "If you do not become a major by exactly one week from today, Cipi *will* send Sofía away." He sighed. "But then you would lose the chance to have her share your bed. Cipi thinks she will be *muy mujer* when we fatten her up a little—and you instruct her in what pleases you."

"No! We have no need of her."

Pierre Boulanger clapped his hand over his mouth to no avail: laughter burst out in a cascade.

"God damn it, Pierre!" James exploded. "I have absolutely no intention of—"

"*Attends, mon ami.* Are all Americans such dreary, joyless Puritans? As with the sage advice I gave you to take the credit for Cerro del Borrego and to look for the promotion which I am sure this clever little *monstre* is absolutely right about, you should accept the good things that come your way. The *jeune fille* looks delicious. If you are discreet, as any Frenchman would be, this *liaison* will in no way interfere with the quest you will make for the attention of Mademoiselle Anderson." He laughed. "You see, *Major* James—Boulanger, *aussi*, can make predictions."

10

▲▲▲▲▲

The army was getting ready to march again.

James felt his life swing back into balance, but precarious balance—the needle on the scale still quivered, but he had kept his equanimity all through the long months of inactivity that chafed Boulanger, and with the prospect of action looming, and with his mind now focusing on the rumored new offensive, he itched for marching orders.

Then, a week to the day after the savage night in the cantina, a message arrived summoning him to First Division headquarters in Jalapa and informing him that he and Compagnie Rouge had been detailed to an unspecified "special mission" to be carried out at an "as yet undetermined date." The message bore the signature of the division's commanding general, François-Achille Bazaine, all very formal. And slightly odd. Legion officers, except for St. Cyrians, generally got their orders from their superiors as almost casual asides, as when Colonel Bonnet told him he was assigned to Mexico while they were both at the same barber shop back at Sidi-bel-Abbes.

At Bazaine's headquarters an even odder surprise awaited him.

"*Monsieur le General Bazaine* wishes to see you personally, Captain," a smiling corporal-clerk said when he reported.

Alarm that the second-ranking general of the French Army in Mexico wanted his presence was offset by the deferential, almost obsequious manner in which the corporal steered him to a bench to wait. The big room was filled with other officers, mostly of higher rank, and James prepared himself to cool his heels for God knew how long before the general worked his way down to him. He reached for a Parisian newspaper lying on a table next to the bench.

At that moment Bazaine himself burst from an inner office, crossed the room to where James sat, strode through a crowd of officers suddenly at a rigid attention, and pushed out a meaty hand. James sprang to his feet.

"*Comment ça va*, Captain James?" It was not quite the "Zhomm" of Marcel Gallimard, but close enough. Holding James's hand in a strong but easy grip the general turned to the clerk. "Cognac and two glasses, Lemonde." Back to James, "Let us retire to my office, captain. I wish to hear directly from the hero of Guadalupe and Cerro del Borrego." With his hand fast in the general's the Legionnaire could not salute, and he was not able to get out the *"Très bien, monsieur le general"* which common courtesy called for. He was too much taken aback that this great general, so recently arrived in Mexico, knew about his two actions of nearly seven long months ago.

With a dozen pairs of Chasseur and Zouave eyes on him he followed the general through a buzz of speculative talk cloudy with mild outrage and obvious envy and into the inner office, almost reeling at the thought of what had just occurred. High-ranking commanders such as Bazaine simply never came to lowly captains, not even were they blueblood graduates of St. Cyr instead of Legionnaires.

Bazaine's desk, save for an ornamental dagger crusted with gems and laid aslant a stack of papers aligned to perfection with its beveled mahogany edge, was gleamingly clean. Behind it the far wall was covered by a phalanx of flags and regimental standards, one the tricolor, the others a

draped history of France's wars and military adventures of
the past thirty or forty years, with streamers carrying the
names of regiments and battles familiar to any old soldier
and to some, like James, not so old: Balaclava in the
Crimea, Italy, Spain's Saragosso, Damascus, North Africa.
Grime coated a few, turning the once gaudy reds the color
of dried blood, and *genuine* scabbed blood stiffened a
particularly tattered one, that of his own Fourteenth, but
from some battle before his time. Cannon fire had pierced
two others, leaving holes with burnt, blackened edges—
debauched eyes staring at James as if he were an interloper.

"*Asseyez-vous, mon capitaine,*" Bazaine said.

James forced himself into a carved Spanish chair. It was
the first time he had ever taken a seat in the presence of a
general officer, anywhere. He could not sit with any degree
of comfort. Crouching in the rocks at Guadalupe with
duBecq, awaiting the first Mexican barrage from those
forbidding walls, had been easier.

Corporal Lemonde entered with a crystal decanter and
two glasses.

"*Merci,* Lemonde," Bazaine said.

James had seen the general once before. It had been only
a momentary look from an "eyes right" five years earlier,
when the Fourteenth had passed in review in Casablanca,
and his memory of the moment had dimmed. At the time
Bazaine, immersed in his duties as a colonial administrator,
had not involved himself in Legion affairs that concerned
James, except in the remotest way. Now, as Lemonde
poured and left the office, James studied the general as
closely as he dared.

Amazing. Pierre Boulanger might look like this some
day. The general's body, thicker than Pierre's, verged on
portliness, but with no hint of softness. Years of good living
in the realms of the rich and influential had not diminished
its strength and power.

Bazaine's dark brown hair, cropped closer than the
current fashion among senior French officers, and his trim,

rounded beard, were beginning to gray. The face, for all its slight fleshiness, looked as wolfish in its own way as did Boulanger's, and betrayed the same sensuality. Piercing jet black eyes under heavy lids fixed on James. Two strong hands, looking as if they could still wield a saber or run a lance through an enemy breastplate, rested on the desktop.

After Lemonde closed the door behind him, the general pushed one of the glasses toward the Legionnaire's side of the desk and lifted his own.

"À votre santé, capitaine. I do not ordinarily take strong spirits this early in the day, but this is a special occasion." He did not sniff the cognac, or savor its amber clarity; he tossed it off in one swift, efficient swallow.

"À la vôtre, mon general," James said. A special occasion? He took a careful sip of the fine brandy—a Napoleon without a doubt—the bouquet drifting up from the globe glass heady and seductive. He had only tasted a cognac such as this once before, when he and his fellow Legion officers had celebrated his captaincy in Sidi-bel-Abbés. The bottle they consumed that night devoured a whole week's pay, he remembered.

Bazaine reached forward and stabbed the stack of papers with a forefinger as stiff as a bayonet. "I have been reading your dossier, Captain James." He picked up the bejeweled dagger and began playing a light drum tattoo with its point on the topmost document. "You have done great credit to yourself here in Mexico. And to . . . France."

France. There was something almost worshipful about the way Bazaine uttered the word. In that instant James knew he had just discovered the most salient single thing about the character of François-Achille Bazaine. He must never forget it.

The dagger still tapped the papers. "Now, Captain James, I wish you to tell me—with no false modesty—of your two splendid achievements in this campaign, particularly of your assault on the fortress of Cerro de Guadalupe in the Battle of Puebla. Spare me no detail."

As James talked he had the sure feeling that the man across the desk was reliving some feat of arms from his own past. He now might do the bulk of his fighting from behind desks or from horseback on a hill a discreet distance from the immediate perils of shot and shell, but he was at heart still a combat warrior.

From time to time Bazaine would hold up one of his huge hands, stopping James's narrative to ask a question. His interest, as judged by his intense, unwavering gaze, did not flag at any point, but it seemed to heighten as James described the events surrounding the hellish climb to Cerro de Guadalupe's battlements and the forced entry into the fort itself. James wondered if Bazaine had assaulted a fortified position such as Guadalupe at some time in his career. Of course he had: Sebastopol.

Bearing in mind the general's admonition to "spare me no detail," James made the report as meticulous and painstaking as he could. The only thing he omitted was the name Marcel Gallimard. It would serve no point to tell this general—up-from-the-ranks or not—of the derelictions of any St. Cyrian.

Toward the end Bazaine's hooded eyes closed as if in sleep, but James knew sleep and this general were virtual strangers.

Done, the Legionnaire leaned back in his chair, immediately pulled himself upright again, and took another small, cautious sip of the cognac. He dared not relax.

"Tell me something, Captain James," Bazaine asked. "Had you been General de Lorencez on the fifth of May, would you have called for a withdrawal from Guadalupe and Loreto when he did?"

Risk rode on *any* answer, but this was not a man to countenance a lie.

"No, sir, I would not. But I and my company were already inside the fort. I didn't have the view of the entire battle General de Lorencez had. Perhaps the general did not know the Legion had breached the walls. He possibly had other and larger concerns. Puebla was a huge, complex battle-field."

"That is very generous of you, *monsieur*. But the fact remains. You would not have had your buglers sound the retreat, *n'est-ce pas?* Be utterly candid, *si'l vous plait.*"

"No, *mon general.* I would not have."

"Do you think the day could ultimately have been won for France?"

Again an almost undetected but religious breath of fervor invested the word "France."

"Yes, sir."

Bazaine smiled. He pulled the dagger from the papers and laid it down in front of him. *"Zut alors.* Your dossier says you fought here in Mexico with Scott and the Americans. General Scott's campaign was far more successful than ours has been thus far. From your recollections of that war, do you have advice for your general in waging *his?"*

"No, sir. When I served with General Scott I was just an ordinary soldier. I gave no thought to the strategy of that conflict, and even if I had, generals are not in the habit of confiding in men—boys, really—such as I was then."

The general's hearty laugh eased him. *"Touché, capitaine.* In the main that is a sound observation. I must differ with you on one small point, however. In my view there is no such thing as an *ordinary* soldier. I have marched many a brutal kilometer under a twenty-kilo pack. Did you know that?"

"Yes, general. It is common knowledge in the army."

"Good. Now let us return to the Battle for Puebla and to the officers and men who fought it. This paragon sergeant of yours *par exemple*—his name again?"

"DuBecq, sir."

"Would he make a good officer?"

Jean-Claude would forgive him for what he had to say. He might even thank him. "No, sir. As with many men in the ranks, duBecq distrusts officers and could not function as one. He truly believes wars are won by sergeants."

The laugh this time was even heartier than before. "I agree with him. You and I exist only to put sergeants in the right place at the right time." He picked up the dagger and tapped the papers again. "I see in your file that your term of enlistment with the Legion ends on the first of April."

James had forgotten the date.

"Will you re-enlist, captain?"

He had not thought about it; actually, there was not much to think about.

"Yes, general."

"Why?"

"I am a soldier, a professional. The Legion has been good to me."

"You realize, do you not, that you have already risen as high as you will ever rise in France's service? Few foreigners become officers in the Legion, fewer still reach the rank of captain. Thinking about this, will you still enlist again?"

"Yes, sir."

So much for Cipi's prediction and Boulanger's confident expectations. This interview must be coming to a close.

"I have orders for you, Captain James, but not specific ones—and none dealing with matters that are imminent. The message that brought you here was sent merely so I could get a look at you. As you must have sensed, the First Division will be moving against the enemy soon. Our first task will of course be a return to Puebla. That is why I wished to be sure you intended to re-enlist. I need officers like you when we avenge last May's defeat at the hands of General Zaragoza."

Yes, any new commander would feel it necessary to stitch up the gaping wound Puebla had ripped in the French Army's pride. "As far as you are concerned," Bazaine continued, "I do have something in mind for you and your company, but I am not ready to tell you of it yet. I do wish to see you here two weeks from today."

"I understand, general. Am I dismissed now, sir?" James prepared to rise.

Bazaine raised a big hand.

"*Mais non, monsieur.* There is one more thing to be taken care of before we part." Bazaine reached forward, slipped one sheet of paper from the bottom of the pile, turned it around, and placed it on the desk in front of James.

The Legionnaire leaned forward.

His promotion to the rank of major!

"Felicitations, *Major* James!" Bazaine said, thrusting out his hand. "France places her trust in you. Now—you would please me if you stopped being so ridiculously abstemious and took a genuine, soldier-sized drink of my excellent cognac."

When he reached his quarters in a stable virtually indistinguishable from the smelly one on the road to Fortín down in Orizaba, he found Cipi crosslegged on his bed with his spare tunic draped across his lap. The dwarf was sewing bits of gold braid and red-white-and-blue ribbon to the shoulder boards. He grinned at James like a triumphant Beelzebub.

"If you take off that tunic Cipi will sew the insignia of your new rank on it as well." Would he gloat? Would James now have to begin believing in his claimed "powers"?

"How much do I owe you?" he asked, reaching into his pocket.

"Seventy-five centavos."

"For these miserable rags and tags?"

"Twenty-five for the braid and ribbon and fifty for the *cerveza* with which I will drink your health and celebrate your promotion."

"You have a big heart, *Don* Cipriano—and an even bigger thirst. For fifty centavos I should become healthy enough to live forever."

"Certainly. Does the *major* think I would drink that much *cerveza* just to please myself?"

James felt good. He placed a peso note on his bedside table near the dwarf's elbow. "Keep the change, you mendacious little runt." Cipi *was* gloating, but it warmed him. He stripped off his tunic and dropped it on the bed. "I want you to take a note to Major Boulanger when you finish your needlework."

"It is already done, *mi mayor.* He congratulates you. You will be his guest at the Chasseur mess tonight. I will need to press a tunic and *pantalones* for you and black your best boots."

"I am to dine with him? What will Major Boulanger order for us to eat?"

"How should I know? I am not a *sortilego.* I do not tell fortunes."

"You certainly try to. It baffles me that you can foretell the fate of an entire French army, but you don't know if I'm to get a souffle tonight or not. Do I have clean linen?"

"No, but do not worry. Shirts and things will arrive momentarily."

"Arrive? Did you send them out? Your extravagance will ruin me. Are you taking *la mordida* from whomever you have doing my laundry, too?"

The injured innocence that suffused the imp's swarthy face was a work of art. "Is that what *el mayor* thinks of Cipi? That he would squeeze *dinero* from another member of the major's household? Never!"

"Another member of my *household?* What are you talking about? *You* are my household, you *solamente.*"

"That was true this morning, *señor.* But an hour ago, about the time the major received his promotion, the girl Sofía entered his employ."

"What?" Why did he not feel more anger, or at the very least irritation? "You hired her without my permission? You have overstepped yourself."

The little man shrugged, his ugly countenance now composed into smugness. "The major would have come to this decision himself. With his new rank he has a position to maintain. Besides, although Cipi has many talents, cooking is not one of them. Sofía will more than earn her pay in what the major saves by not eating out so much."

Cipi had a point. On the march to Puebla and since James found himself driven more and more frequently into the costly French Army messes and the *posadas* of Orizaba and now Jalapa.

He thought it over. "We'll try the girl then—but I warn you. Make her no promises!"

"I knew someone high on the ladder of command would sooner or later pay attention to you," Boulanger said at dinner, "but Bazaine himself? *Sacrebleu!*"

"What do you suppose this 'special mission' might be?"

"I do not, of course, know, Jason, but from your account of the meeting I have an idea: perhaps the keen interest the general expressed in your tactics at Cerro de Guadalupe might be a clue. He may look upon you as an expert in attacking forts. It is certain that our first objective will be Puebla, but I had assumed that he would not repeat de Lorencez's mistake and attack from the north. You may be asked to repeat your heroics at Guadalupe. I will be disappointed if either Forey or our worthy Bazaine succumbs to pride as did de Lorencez."

"Bazaine struck me as a more pragmatic soldier, Pierre. Well, perhaps I'll know in two weeks time."

He told Boulanger then of the general's question about Jean-Claude. "I confess he worried me for a moment when he talked of my first sergeant becoming an officer. Not that I wouldn't be happy for duBecq, but it would not be Compagnie Rouge without my stubborn old Alsatian."

"Ah, that perhaps is another clue, Jason. Perhaps Bazaine has something in mind for you that does not involve your company. He might have been thinking of duBecq as your replacement. It's in character from what I know of the general. *C-est un mystère, n'est-ce pas?*"

The thought of anything being a mystery to the probing, skeptical Chasseur was an odd one.

It had been a wonderful dinner, with only two minor rubs. When James and Boulanger sat down their mess boy informed them that their meal and a bottle of champagne were already paid for. "Compliments of Lieutenant Gallimard, *messieurs.*"

Across the room Marcel stood by his table, smiling and saluting. He picked up a glass of wine, lifted it in James's direction, and then drained it off. For a second the Legionnaire's heart sank. Would the young ass try to join them? The last time Gallimard had inflicted himself on them at dinner the result was a minor catastrophe. But before he sat down again the St. Cyrian, wearing tonight yet another bizarre uniform probably of his own design, flicked his eyes toward Boulanger, and winced.

"No," Boulanger said as if he had read James's mind. "*Le fou* won't bother you while I am with you. Lieutenant Gallimard and I had more angry words just this past week. I admit most of them were mine. He has had a painful time at my hands, and I make no apology. He is easily the most inept officer I have ever encountered."

James should have felt relief, but did not; the memory of Gallimard's unwanted intrusion half a year ago with his American woman companion came flooding back.

The second rough rub came when he tried to change the subject by telling Boulanger about his defeat at Cipi's hands in the afternoon over the hiring of the girl Sofía. The moment the words left his mouth he regretted it; the Chasseur seized on it like a ravenous wolf.

"*Magnifique!* Have you given thought to my suggestion after that *très interessant* piece of theater that night in the cantina? Do not, I beg you, dismiss it out of hand. A soldier needs this kind of *divertissement*. This *gamine* Sofía looks as if she could provide more important nourishment than food." The look on Pierre's saturnine face, casual as an onlooker might have thought it, was nonetheless a leer.

Something blazed in James. "Why the hell don't you try for her yourself?"

"Ah, but I have, *monsieur*." The Chasseur's mouth widened to a smile. "*La jeune fille* would have none of me. She apparently will not take a Frenchman to her bed."

"That must have hurt."

"*Pour un moment*. There are, fortunately, others who are not so discriminating."

As he descended the steep, cobbled, crooked street leading down to his quarters, James considered himself fortunate that the Parisian had made no mention of Sarah Anderson.

11

▲▲▲▲▲

He became uncomfortably aware of Sofía's presence in the stable the next few days, but—probably without any intention on her part—the girl made his gradual acceptance of her fairly easy. A week passed before he realized that, except for her one terrified cry in the cantina when Cipi seemed to be in mortal danger, he had not heard her voice. The only sound she made as she went about her duties—making up his narrow bed, cooking meals he was delighted to discover were simple but satisfying marvels, or hanging out the wash—was the whispering rustle of her loose white cotton dress, belted at the waist with a twisted green and blue silk scarf. Even her bare feet, as she made her swift passages through his living area, did not make the soft thuds he might have expected to hear. They did not seem to touch the packed earth floors. It reinforced his first impression of her. She *was* birdlike. Her half-glimpsed, silent movements were the dark, easy glides of a swallow.

He had not really seen those immense eyes since Cipi hired her; she never looked at him. If she did, he failed to detect it.

When asked if Sofía did indeed talk, Cipi observed, "It is not to be encouraged, señor. Like all women she will some day talk us to death if we allow it."

"Only if she can wedge a word into your magpie chatter," James said.

For his part, he never made a request of her for a particular chore nor did he give her a single order. He left that to Cipi. He saw her only when she worked; when she was not working he never saw her at all. Of course it was none of his business what she did with her free time. Still, he wondered about it.

"Where does Sofía sleep?" he asked the dwarf one morning.

"In one of the *caballo* stalls, at the far end of the stable."

"You haven't provided her with a bed?"

"She will put down fresh straw every Monday, *señor*. Cipi insists. We cannot have her bringing *los piojos* into the major's living quarters. And what would she need a bed for, anyway?" His thick lips curled into a Rabelaisian leer. "Aaah . . . *sí*. Stupid of me. There *are* things she could use a bed for—although I have found straw often does just as well." James stared balefully at the dwarf. "All right, all right! Do not fall victim to distemper over such a small thing. Cipi will see to a bed for Sofía *pronto*. Of course I will need more money . . ."

James's first clots of anger dissolved into curiosity when he speculated on the girl bedding down in a filthy horse stall. With the grease and smoke from her kitchen fire and the accumulated detritus of her sleeping place, how did she manage to appear so immaculately clean every time he saw her? Her white dress—and she seemed to own no other garment—stayed unsullied.

That question was eventually answered, too, but not by consulting Cipi.

The answer, when it came, raised more, and more vexing, questions.

He returned to the stable late one night, after still another dinner with Boulanger. They had dined with a captain newly arrived from France, a likable, knowledgeable cannoneer schooled in the grand tradition of French Army artillerists, a man who took great pride in the new breech-loading, rifled 55s he had brought with him on the rusty old *Carcassonne* of James's own voyage to Mexico. James and the Chasseur were both fascinated by the captain's mastery of his profession.

It promised at the outset to be a long evening, and James skipped the customary post-prandial cognac and drank beer instead. But the length of their session with the captain brought a lot of beer, and by the time the evening ended and James walked home, his bladder was swollen.

A full moon had bloomed above the stone houses that lined the Calle del Flor, and to the west the usually dark head of El Pico de Orizaba, seldom seen in Jalapa's perpetual, late winter, daytime haze, was a mammoth, looming *massif* of gleaming silver, the clouds around the peak itself bright ingots prized from it and held aloft by the hand of some ghostly sculptor. Brilliant moonlight turned the dull cobbles of the narrow, twisting street to a scattering of burnished coins.

When he reached the stable his need to relieve himself led him around the corner toward the outhouse.

On the clothesline where he saw his own linen hanging just that morning, a single article of clothing caught the moonlight, reflecting it as a splash of pristine white.

It was Sofía's cotton dress. It came to him that she must wash it every night, and it answered the question about her.

She stood next to it, staring at him.

The loose dress she had worn night and day since he had known her had hidden a body of classic elegance. The light of the moon drenched the nakedness of it now in liquid mercury, making it appear frozen in time and place. His breath caught and stopped. Hers seemed to move easily enough; the only motion the exquisite form showed was the light, even rise and fall of her chest, where the nipples had stiffened in the chill night air. Other than that there was not a tremor. The gleam of one tantalizing curve melded into the sheen of the next and his eyes followed them all, came to rest at last on the dark delta in the shadows of her flat belly.

Then his eyes lifted and found hers.

If the sight of her luminescent body had stopped his breath, that of her eyes now stopped his heart.

Two wide lakes of pure white with coal black centers, they were leveled on him, the gaze unwavering, holding no embarrassment, no shame, and above all, no fear. Nor was there in it even the faintest hint of deliberate exhibition. She seemed to invite *his* look as passively and unconsciously as might the distant mountains or the moon.

How long did they stand facing each other? It seemed like hours—and it seemed, too, as if no time passed at all. Did she really see him as he did her, was she assessing *him?*

At last she moved, turned and walked slowly toward the far end of the stable. Just as she reached the horse stalls and disappeared, a cloud crossed the moon, and it disappeared as well.

He felt as if a gift had been torn from his grasp.

She served his breakfast in the morning as if the silent meeting the night before had never happened. She did not look at him the rest of that day nor through all the next, nor did she utter a word. Not to him at least; if she spoke with Cipi it was out of his hearing. Nothing had changed.

He could put that midnight, blinding sight of her out of his mind. He had work to do. Bazaine would ask for him again in another week and he wanted the company razor sharp for whatever the general had in mind.

He went determinedly about his business in the next few days, driving the veterans of the company as well as the new men—part of the huge contingents of reinforcements arriving from Veracruz—through killing drills, with an unrelenting vigor that made even tough duBecq blink and shake his head. In the past such frenetic attention to soldiering would have emptied his mind, but he found that the moonlit vision of Sofía had somehow burned itself into the back of his brain, and into every nerve and muscle of his body, too.

If he faced things squarely and honestly, he wanted her.

It wasn't a question of need. He had never needed a woman, had never thought of women as something to be needed. Wanting one was something else.

Of course he had wanted women—and taken them—in the years since Kansas. There had been any number of them in the seamy Atlantic and Mediterranean seaports where the half dozen ships he sailed on anchored, fewer perhaps in the souks of French North African cities. None had ever *mattered*. If he could not now remember one single name or recall a single face, it was just as certain none of them remembered his.

This girl Sofía would in the long run be no different. For all the quicksilver purity he had glimpsed that night, it was likely not the purity of virginity or inexperience.

In Kansas, when he first began studying with Cousin Aaron he had been too young to even think about these things. Aaron, for his part, never spoke of girls or women in their early years together.

There had been no girl in his life as he grew up back home. None walked the roads and paths between the vast Sheffield farm and the smaller place Jason's father worked, and those in Jason's one-room school were either years older than he was or far too young to be considered girlfriends, much less sweethearts. He blushed now at his own innocence and ignorance back then. He had not even had the wit to connect those first troubling stirrings of his body with members of the other sex except in a vague and utterly baffling way.

When it came to women and Aaron Sheffield, things were more complex.

In the James and Sheffield families a well-worn story related that Cousin Aaron had once had a girl whom he met at a dance in his last term at West Point, and to whom he wrote fifteen- and twenty-page letters once a week for a year. The girl had, it seemed, said no when Aaron asked her to marry him, but it all happened when Jason was only twelve and he had quickly forgotten the matter.

He first became aware of his cousin's feelings about women when Aaron insisted he memorize Keats's poem "La Belle Dame sans Merci."

Jason had thrilled to the eerie beauty of the verses, had conjured up visions of himself as the knight-at-arms, but the poet's strange, dark meaning eluded him.

In his first recitation of the poem for Aaron he raced through nine stanzas of it without an error. He slipped at the beginning of the tenth, the one which had troubled him most. He took a breath and began again.

> "I saw pale Kings, and Princes, too,
>   Pale warriors, death pale were they all;
> They cried, 'La belle dame sans merci
>   Thee hath in thrall!' "

He stopped.

"What does 'in thrall' mean, Cousin Aaron?"

Aaron Sheffield turned and gazed through the kitchen window and out across the table-flat, winterbound Kansas wheatfields stretching eastward to a dull infinity. When he turned back to Jason his handsome face had clouded to match the dead gray January sky, but the eyes flared with dark fire.

"You won't fully understand for a long time, Jason, but for your eventual good I shall try to explain. 'La belle dame' is *all* women. They enslave men, put them 'in thrall,' strangle them in the coils of their own abiding evil!"

This explanation puzzled young Jason James. Aaron could not *mean* that. He seemed the very soul of chivalry where women were concerned, gracious and charming, in Jason's view the perfect "knight-at-arms," a figure straight out of Camelot itself. This notion was reinforced when Aaron, the summer after he graduated from West Point, received his first assignment, to the U.S. Army fort at nearby Leavenworth.

Jason's parents permitted him to attend the rare formal dances when Aaron came home on leave, and he sat against the ballroom wall with the few other farm and town boys his own age—when they were not loitering outside behind the parked buggies and carriages sharing a forbidden pipeful of tobacco. He watched the girls and women shamelessly, and he watched Aaron, who in his dress uniform and with his demeanor seemed indeed a knight.

If Aaron hated and distrusted women so much, how could he touch them, kiss their fluttering hands, and take them into his arms as he did for the waltzes he managed with courtly grace. Was Aaron not stepping right into those "coils" he had spoken of with such black intensity?

In truth, Jason had earlier doubts. In the days following his cousin's sinister warning, Jason studied with a sharp eye his hard-working, uncomplaining mother, his sister Elizabeth Mary, and the pastor's unselfish wife Mrs. Temple, his teacher at Sunday School, with a sharper eye. If any of them were *"la belle dame sans merci,"* he failed to detect it. Try as he might he could not see any trace of the "abiding evil." And if any of them cast coils about Jason James, they were coils of love and caring.

Early on in his time at sea, and despite Aaron's too-well-remembered warning, James determined to take women as he found them. It was not the fault of those he found that none were the likes of Addie Sheffield James, her daughter Elizabeth Mary, or Mrs. Tyler Temple.

Well, one perhaps . . . now.

The American woman was probably back in Boston, or in France, or if she were still in Mexico, probably somewhere in the north. Six, almost seven, months had slipped by since his two fleeting collisions with her. She would not have spent a solitary minute thinking about him. Besides—remembering Cipi's gossip—she already belonged to Marcel Gallimard's brother. Even if she did not, she could never tolerate involvement of the smallest kind with a rough-edged mercenary soldier.

Still, he had spent no few moments conjuring up the sight of her compelling face and clear blue eyes, even more of them in recalling the way those eyes had flashed with

challenge in their few—and in the main uncomfortable—
words together.

The only sane thing for him to do was to erase the
memories of both Sarah Anderson and Sofía from his
thoughts. With the war against Benito Juárez and his
republican government about to begin again, that should
not prove too difficult to do for a bought-and-paid-for
"knight-at-arms."

He did not, however, have to erase them himself.
General François-Achille Bazaine did it for him in their
second meeting.

On the top of the general's mahogany desk James's dossier
and the ornamental dagger had been replaced by a yel-
lowed, tattered map. Dark stains, much like the dried blood
on the Fourteenth's colors there against the wall blotched
its surface in several places.

"Sit down if you please, major," the general said after
nodding a return to the Legionnaire's salute. Bazaine began
drumming the thick fingers of his right hand on the faded
map. "I have your mission for you, Major James—if you will
agree to undertake it."

"I will accept any mission the general assigns to me."

Bazaine shook his head. "Don't be so hasty, James. Hear
me out. The first stage of this mission cannot be considered
usual for a fighting soldier. Some French officers, particularly my fastidious St. Cyrians, might even think it inconsistent with their personal codes of honor." He paused, as if to
let the last sink in. "But let me begin at the beginning. You
must have divined that with the additional troops which
have arrived here in Jalapa, and with the new cannon and
artillerymen who disembarked this past month at Veracruz,
the First Division is almost ready to begin hostilities again."

"Oui, mon general."

"Our first objective will be Puebla. You have guessed that,
too, of course."

"Yes, sir."

"It is a pity that the general who defeated us last May,

Ignacio Zaragoza, will not be facing us at Puebla this time. His untimely death cheats the French Army of some of its planned revenge. General Zaragoza was too young to die of such a pedestrian disease as typhoid fever, but in a way he was fortunate. The last battle of his life was a resounding victory. There is, I believe, a special heaven for great captains." He closed his eyes for a moment. Was he thinking of himself as well? "Now—" he said as he opened them, "let us get down to cases. I may want you to take a fort for me, Major James."

Guadalupe again? So much for Boulanger's hopes that Forey and Bazaine would not repeat the grand folly of Latrille de Lorencez.

Bazaine was proceeding. "You will have three additional companies of the Legion placed under your command, something commensurate with your new rank in any event, and as many of the new field pieces as you think you might require. But first, you will have to scout the objective thoroughly. The reconnaissance may take weeks."

Bazaine's caution seemed odd. And how could he possibly think an action such as this could be inconsistent with any soldier's "personal code of honor"? He took the plunge.

"Begging the general's pardon, I feel I already have all the knowledge of the fort I need for an assault."

"*Oui.* I forget. You have been there before."

"When will I attack it, general?"

"Not for many months yet, major."

"But—again begging the general's pardon, I thought the new offensive was imminent."

Bazaine laughed. "I should beg *your* pardon, Major James. I said I would begin at the beginning, and I did—but then I jumped leagues ahead of myself. The offensive will begin within a week. If you accept this mission, you will not be part of it. You will be operating nowhere near Puebla."

"But Guadalupe—"

"Your objective will not be Guadalupe." Bazaine stood. "Come to this side of my desk and look at this map with me."

James rose and moved around the desk. He leaned across the map. It was not a map in the ordinary sense, but rather a detailed drawing of an enormous set of stone fortifications. His eyes moved to the legend at the lower right hand corner.

PLAN DE LA FORTALEZA DEL CASTILLO DE CHAPULTEPEC
1846

Chapultepec!

"As I indicated," Bazaine was saying, "we will not reach the gates of this fortress for some months, but I wish preparations for its investment and eventual reduction to begin now. As much as I would wish to have an officer such as you with me when we take Puebla—from the south this time—I am willing to forgo that luxury to insure our complete success when the two divisions of the army reach the capital."

He heard every word, and his mind registered the meaning of each of them clearly enough, but some part of him was no longer in the same room.

"We have no way of knowing," Bazaine continued, "just how much of a defense of his capital President Juárez intends to make, or even if he will defend Chapultepec at all, but if he does I want the castle taken." His big hand doubled into a fist that pounded on the map and shook the heavy desk. "Wars are not won or lost by besieging castles any more. We are not medieval knights. In some ways wars are not even won or lost in the field. Triumphs and defeats are confined more to the hearts of men. This immense heap of rock, impressive as it looks, is now only a symbol. But it is a symbol France must have if the Emperor's great plan for Mexico is to be realized. And it must be taken in as close to an intact state as possible. Chapultepec will be the residence and seat of government of Archduke Maximilian when he comes to Mexico.

"What I would like you to do, Major James—and this is why I asked you to take a moment to consider—is to go to Mexico City now. This sadly out-of-date map is typical of all our intelligence about this country and our enemy. I want you to scout Chapultepec, devise a plan for taking it with as little damage to it as possible, and then lead the assault on it when the main force reaches the capital. Of course you would have to go there now as a civilian. I will not try to euphemize. *You would be a spy.* If you have the same sense of honor the St. Cyrians have, you may have no wish to serve your general and your flag this way. I cannot, of course, send a French officer, even were I to find one with your qualifications. As an American, you would have certain advantages, but make no mistake—discovery will mean an ignominious death. If that prospect is too repugnant to you I will understand."

Bazaine was offering him a choice that in truth was no choice at all.

His eyes explored the map. Yes, he knew every inch of that southern wall. It had been awaiting him for a long, long time. Its stones were patient, but not silent. They never had been as mute as the graves around them.

"When do I leave for the capital, *mon general?*"

12

▲▲▲▲▲

He sat in the yard and watched the sun go down over El Pico de Orizaba, stayed there until the great volcano swallowed the last sliver of orange in the western sky.

Cipi came to stand beside him. "The major has lost all appetite?"

James waved the dwarf away.

The sunlight had fled the high plains stretching between Jalapa and Puebla, and the last glimmer had probably left Guadalupe, too, but hundreds of kilometers to the west it would still be touching the parapets and battlements of Chapultepec itself, turning the walls a mordant red.

"*. . . this heap of rocks . . . is now only a symbol . . .*"

A column of Tirailleurs-in-training, beaten and bedraggled, trudged past the mud wall that separated the stable from the road. In the gloaming, the pack-laden men, rifles skewed in a dozen different directions, looked as if they had just come from actually engaging the enemy rather than merely from some harmless exercise in a friendly field. Their officer waved to James. He made no reply.

"*. . . we are not medieval knights . . .*"

Darkness fell suddenly, seemed to crash noiselessly, but with troubling echoes.

"*. . . triumphs and defeats are confined more to the hearts of men . . .*"

He went inside. Cipi was sitting at a table in the alcove kitchen. The girl Sofía was serving. She had set a place for James, but he *had* lost all appetite. She did not look at him, just moved toward the door as swiftly as she always did. Well, he had gotten used to that. Cipi ignored him, too. That he was *not* used to.

In his room he tried to read the Montaigne he had bought on that brief shore leave in the Azores. No use. The words blurred. He shut down his oil lamp and undressed.

Chapultepec!

He tried to sleep, gave it up. He lit the lamp again for another try at his book. Twice Cipi came to his door and looked in. If he had not known him better James would have thought him worried. The faint twist of mockery that normally played across the familiar ugly countenance seemed to have gone into hiding. The third time he appeared in the doorway James barked savagely at him. "Close my door! And don't even make a sound until reveille if you place any value on your position here." He turned off the lamp again. He had to get some sleep. Tomorrow would be a difficult day. He had not yet told the dwarf of the trip to the capital they would begin tomorrow night. Cipi could be ready at a word, but James would have to find civilian clothes, return to headquarters for the false passport and the money Bazaine had ordered for him, say good-bye to Jean-Claude, find good horses for the journey, pack, and leave.

Sofía would stay behind. By the time they returned—if they did—she probably would have found service with some other officer or in one of the Zouave or Chasseur messes. Perhaps Boulanger would employ her, but he would not speak with Pierre about it—the shrewd Parisian would be too full of questions about his new assignment. Bazaine had not sworn him to secrecy, but James knew without being told that the general wanted silence from him. It would not be hard to keep the seal on his lips. Silence right now was his only ally. Silence . . . and sleep—if he could find it.

He did at last. It was not a dreamless sleep. Bodies hurtled from high, gray crenellations. Rockets flared and round shot blasted craters within craters inside of still other craters. Cannon fire beat a heavy counterpoint to the mingled screams of men and horses, and fragments of every war he had ever known fell around him in a rain of fire. The smell of burning flesh was an invidious, debilitating gas that reached every fiber of him . . .

He awoke, every nerve tingling and alert.

Someone was in his room.

At some other easier time he would have done an unthinking, reflex half roll off his bed as he reached for his pistol. This time he lay and waited. He could hear, or possibly just feel, someone's or something's breath.

He could not move. His instincts and his strength had not failed him; his will had. If there were a knife poised above him now, so be it. Chapultepec would cease to matter. He sat upright, turned and put a match to his lamp.

Sofía stood at the side of his bed.

"Cipi said Sofía should come to you, *mi mayor.*"

He raised his hand to protest, held it there as if he were taking an oath.

The rays from the lamp had turned her naked body to gold this time, but some of the silver of the moonlight still lingered.

"Cipi sent me, *señor,*" she said now. "He said you needed me."

Looking at her in the lamplight he had no doubt

whatsoever that she could satisfy any *want*, and he did want her. What living, breathing man would not? But was wanting her enough?

"And you, Sofía . . ." he said. "Do you *know* what I need? You said Cipi sent you. Did you want to come?"

"*Sí, señor.* Or I would not be here."

He lay awake for an hour after she left. It took a long time for the memory of her to fade. If she had not yet learned of the extent and depth of his need, perhaps *he* had. And he knew where it all began.

> O what can ail thee Knight-at-Arms.
> Alone and palely loitering?
> The sedge has withered from the Lake
> And no birds sing.

PART TWO

▲▲▲▲▲▲▲▲▲▲

THE VALLEY

"For we must do what force will have us do . . ."

— RICHARD II

13

▲▲▲▲▲

MEXICO CITY—FEBRUARY 22, 1863

What happened to Sarah Anderson on this rare bright February morning caused her to reassess everything else that had happened to her since her arrival at Veracruz last May.

The gloomy months following the equinox, while not exactly the "winter of our discontent," had nonetheless been a season of genuine frustration. Oh, there had been compensations. Without them she might very well have abandoned her entire Mexican adventure and returned to Paris by way of Boston as soon as she could book passage. That, of course, was what she intended doing in any event, once she successfully concluded her family business in Zacatecas.

But while nothing had gone encouragingly right, nothing went disastrously wrong, and more and more heartening signs surfaced every day of the change in attitude of *"pauvre Solange"* toward their temporary home. The Frenchwoman, to Sarah's amused amazement, had begun by midsummer to cast on the capital of Mexico and its surrounding countryside the same approving, cheerful glances she had once reserved only for Paris and the Pas de Calais. Matt O'Leary could—had the modest young Marine been so inclined—take most of the credit for Solange's metamorphosis. The way he danced attendance on the maid, who was old enough to be his mother, and who in fact acted like one when she was with him, worked a quiet wonder.

Sarah herself saw little of Matt in her rented apartment at La Fonda Mirador, but from their first week there he called for Solange every Sunday at the Mirador in sober civilian clothes, to take her to early Mass while Sarah attended the Protestant "go-to-meetin'" services of the chaplain at the embassy.

At first Sarah wondered about his solicitous attention to Solange, but once, when they were all three having dinner, the Marine fished out pictures of his family in some strange place in Ohio named Chillicothe. His mother bore a striking resemblance to the Frenchwoman. Even Solange herself commented on it. "And you could be *mon fils*, Matthew."

By summer's end the odd pair must have knelt in every cathedral and most of the mid-sized *iglesias* in the entire city and its environs, two devout and dedicated theological tourists. Nor did they confine their worship to only those churches offering regular services; Solange was enraptured by the vine-covered, ancient semi-ruins at Tlatelolco, Acolmán, and Xochimilco, which Matt characterized as the "fortress monasteries."

"They remind me of the old temples in Provence, *chérie*, when we went to the Midi three years ago with Monsieur Auguste and Madame Claudine," Solange said, blithely ignoring—or more likely simply ignorant of—the fact that the Roman stones of the south of France were vestiges of a paganism her staunch Catholic beliefs would reject out of hand.

At Matt's suggestion she made a crude rubbing of the worn sandstone date-plaque at Acolmán and hung it reverently next to the crucifix she had brought from Paris. Matt, counter to what Sarah might have expected, was as excited about such small treasures of discovery as was Solange. This revelation went some distance toward erasing Sarah's niggling, Boston-bred perception of Matt O'Leary as just another military man—a slightly more palatable professional soldier than that Legion Captain Jason James.

Solange's ecclesiastical peregrinations with Matt prepared the older woman for the arduous trip north to Zacatecas, a journey as physically grueling as the one from Veracruz to the capital, if not quite as dangerous. The week-long stay at Samuel's mine, La Mina de la Sierra Verde, and at the once lovingly remembered *hacienda* where he had lived, sapped Sarah emotionally, particularly after the rigors of the exhausting pilgrimage north.

Despite the efforts of Señor Alberto Moreno, Samuel's manager, to make her time there easy and pleasant, she felt drained and beaten the entire week.

When the mine manager opened the office door for her and followed her in, her mind and body went numb. This was where Samuel had died. She knew how right she had been back in Paris: no matter how long her affairs kept her in Mexico, no matter the ecstasies of Solange at the sight of Zacatecas's lovely old baroque cathedral, she could not live anywhere near this place, not even at the *hacienda* on the heights of La Bufa, a place she had loved on her earlier visits here. After her despairing look at the mine office she decided against looking into Samuel's bedroom.

Moreno was a sad-eyed, dapper little man—"sweet" in Sarah's mental description. He revealed himself as a competent, hardworking mining engineer, a perfectionist of sorts whose records of the mine operation and the books he kept on the *hacienda* household accounts were impeccable and up to the minute. Examining them—and feeling herself almost an intruder with Moreno looking over her shoulder—she did not have to be an accomplished businesswoman to see that Samuel Anderson's company had faltered since his death. The payroll robbery at the time of his murder had only been the beginning of a downward turn in its fortunes. A string of minor disasters had plagued the operation: the downpours of an unusually severe rainy season had flooded three of the mine's four main shafts; an epidemic of measles had swept out of nearby El Bordo and decimated Moreno's work force; and an explosion in the mine's tipple had stopped work for three weeks earlier in the year. None of it, of course, was the fault of earnest Alberto Moreno, although he seemed willing, even eager, to take the blame. Revenues from shipments had fallen to where the poor man had to make a valiant struggle merely to meet the payroll of a radically diminished work gang out of an even more diminished bank account. For a year he had only drawn half the salary due him under the terms of his contract with Sarah's brother. There were, though, she discovered to her relief, enough funds in Samuel's personal account in the Banco Central for her to rectify Moreno's sacrifice immediately, over the manager's sincere objections.

"But, *señorita*," he said, when she held a cheque out to him. "I can wait until the company is once more showing a profit. *De Veras*. I have some small savings of my own to live on."

"Unthinkable, Señor Moreno," she told him. "As the old saying goes, 'a workman is worthy of his hire.' Of all people you should know this is exactly what Señor Anderson would have wanted me to do. Now, what will be required to get us on our feet again? New equipment? An effort to recruit new miners by offering higher wages?"

"Those things would be of great help, *señorita*, but we have one problem I fear you cannot do anything about."

"And that is . . . ?"

"*Los bandidos*. We cannot even get the silver we have been able to extract to our agents on the coast. Three of our pack trains have been attacked in just the past six months. I have miners who should be digging ore serving as armed guards even here in the compound." He looked apologetic, as if to assume yet more guilt that such precautions had not been put in effect in time to thwart the attack that took Samuel's life.

Something went off inside her head. "*Los Plateados*, Señor Moreno?"

The somber little mine manager smiled. "Antonio Pérez? *Pero no, señorita!* Tonito is guilty of many outrages, but none against Señor Anderson. He would never take a gram of Sierra Verde silver. He and your brother were great *amigos.*"

"My brother and a bandit . . . friends?"

Some sharpness in her voice, no doubt, brought a blush and then a troubled frown to Moreno's face. "I think it was politics, *señorita.* Señor Anderson and Tonito were both dedicated supporters of Presidente Juárez."

Proper Bostonian Samuel Kent Anderson . . . Benito Juárez, the intense little Indian politician . . . and the probably bloody-handed *plateado* Pérez?

If Max von Hapsburg did not yet know of the transforming power of Mexico, he had better learn.

Going through Samuel's desk in his study at the *hacienda* she made other discoveries, principally in some personal letters Señor Moreno and Arturo, Samuel's aged *mayordomo,* had not forwarded nor opened.

It was typical of self-effacing Samuel that he had never in all his letters to Sarah—nor to Uncle Tobias Kent— mentioned the orphanage in Mexico City he was helping, with money, time, and personal effort. The oldest letters from Sor Francisca, the Mother Superior who was the home's administrator, were effusive in their thanks, but the ones since his death lamented the fact that they had not heard from him in so long. There was no criticism at the way his contributions had dried up, but there were hints of desperation. Apparently the bells heralding the victory at Puebla in May, joyous as they were, had also rung out small, sad echoes from the good sister's convent walls. The great battle had created more orphans or half-orphans clamoring for her order's help—and by extension, Samuel's. One last letter, of condolence, was addressed to La Familia Anderson.

Sarah had not yet stuffed the letters back in the correspondence box before she knew how this discovery would alter her plans for the future. She could not return to

France or Boston until the mine was running well again. Samuel's body would have to make the trip home alone; there were things she had to do in Mexico City. She and Solange would have to find more permanent quarters than the apartment in the Mirador.

Back in the capital a letter from Henri Gallimard awaited her.

He would not be coming to Mexico for a while, he wrote. The defeat of de Lorencez at Puebla and the resulting turmoil had made the roads between the coast and the Valley hazardous for any traveler these days and particularly unsafe for those carrying French passports. The horror stories current in Mexico City about the fate of wayfarers of any nationality had reached as far as the Loire.

The letter was phrased with Henri's usual delicacy and taste, but a strong current of passion and love pulsed through it. Paris and the life she might someday lead with Henri seemed so far away. It troubled her that since Orizaba she had actually thought of Jason James—however inconsequentially—more often than she thought of Henri.

The capital puzzled her. Even with the tremendous victory in May, things were clearly unsettled, awry, in Benito Juárez's Republican government, and indeed on any stratum of society in the city. Although she sent notes to the Palace on three different occasions she still had not seen the president. Perhaps he did not remember her, but that seemed unlikely; talks with Alberto Moreno before she left Zacatecas revealed that Samuel's support of the Juárez regime was not an arm's-length affair. Her brother apparently had been deeply involved on Juárez's behalf, had contributed money to the Reforma and to the president's last run for office. He had even campaigned for Juárez personally in several towns in Zacatecas State, his status as a foreigner apparently forgotten or forgiven by the voters he addressed.

She knew her own position on Mexican politics to be anomalous.

Deep inside her—prompted to her views by her upbringing, and by the continuance of her political education at the hands of liberal Auguste Pelletier—she had whole-hearted sympathy for the Republicans. As a realist, though, she wondered if ordinary Mexicans might not fare as well, even better, if and when Charlotte and Max ruled here. Perhaps it would be better if Benito Juárez gave up his struggle. England and France had monarchs, and both were free, decent nations. She knew that what she had seen at Veracruz and Orizaba of the gargantuan French military buildup promised to bring defeat and misery for the Juar-istas, and untold suffering for the *obreros* and *campesinos* who had elected them.

Matt told her it looked as if the army Forey and Bazaine were putting together would be moving on Puebla again soon. "The French won't repeat the mistakes of last May," he said. "They've brought a hell of a lot of new artillery in from France, and maybe as many as twenty-five thousand additional troops, with possibly more to come. If the Republicans don't hold them at Puebla, the capital itself will come under siege—provided, of course, that the Indian wants to make a stand here. I personally think he would be foolish if he tried. There are two armies of conservative Mexicans hanging over Toluca just to the west of us. If the French break through on the east he'd be in a vise."

With the trip north to Zacatecas and in immersing herself in the business affairs of the mine even after returning to the city, she had not as yet found her way into the social life of the capital. O'Leary arranged an invitation to an embassy dinner and she jumped at the chance to thank Ambassador Corwin and his deputy Jarvis Saunders—the man who had written her when she was still in Paris—for the way they had looked after her, and particularly for assigning the young Marine lieutenant to her and Solange. In Paris she had thought she was getting this seemingly special treat-ment only because she was wealthy. From the ambassador and his deputy she discovered that poor dead Samuel had been held in very high esteem at the embassy. "He was the kind of American I delight to see abroad. He gave his country a good name everywhere he went," Saunders told her at the dinner.

A good part of the American colony of Mexico City attended the affair. It proved much more difficult to fix her countrymen and women in the scheme of things here in Mexico than it would have been had she met them in the United States or even back in Paris. President Lincoln, of course, had made no secret of the fact that Washington was firmly on the side of Benito Juárez and democracy, indeed would have taken an even firmer, possibly more forceful, anti-French position were its own desperate war north of the border not going so badly at the moment; and as far as she could tell, that was the fixed attitude among the Americans living and working here.

It did seem to her, though, that with a few exceptions, Jarvis Saunders and Matt O'Leary among them—and to her not very great surprise the ambassador Thomas Corwin himself—their devotion to the cause of republicanism was in inverse proportion to the length of time they had been stationed in Mexico. She became more and more sure, as the evening wore on, that many of them looked forward to the day Max and Charlotte would land at Veracruz. None of the high-born Mexicans present actually vouchsafed such sentiments in as many words, of course; revealing their strong desires for a crowned head for their country might be risky with Juárez still occupying the Palacio and Republican troops walking every *calle* and *avenida*.

The Americans she spoke with at the dinner felt no such constraints. At home they were probably thoroughgoing egalitarians; here, the aristocratic life they brushed against, and in some cases lived themselves, had transformed them into something else. One reason, she supposed, was that it was only the members of Mexican *criollo* high society—the rich and the Catholic churchmen—who felt enough confidence in themselves to mix with foreigners to any great extent. A scattering of the members of both groups broke bread with the Americans and their other foreign guests that night. She did not meet a single representative or adherent of the government of Benito Juárez—and of course *el presidente* himself was absent.

She wondered if the same seduction had worked on her in her years in Paris, the democratic leanings of M. Auguste and Tante Claudine notwithstanding. Certainly a small part of her at least longed for the grace and charm which would attend a European-style court such as the one the Archduke and his young wife would fashion in this ancient capital when and if they got here.

True, Max's ascension to a throne was by no means a foregone conclusion. The French would have to secure a solid military base at least here in central Mexico before that could happen, and the announced demands of the archduke—the support of England and Spain as well as guarantees from Napoleon III, backed by a request of the Mexican people that he become their monarch—would have to be met. And now she learned that England and Spain were pulling out of Mexico. France's two, and from the outset lukewarm, allies had not entered the conflict on the side of the Tricolor, and apparently Whitehall and Madrid had no intention of doing so at this late stage. Strangely, she did not hear this at the embassy dinner or in any of her talks with Matt. It baffled her that here in the capital the people most involved knew less than she did. A long letter from Auguste Pelletier brought her up to date on the view from the Quai D'Orsay and Miramar. M. Auguste wrote:

I have no doubt that Archduke Maximilian will succumb to the entreaties being made to him by that inveterate Mexican meddler Gutiérrez de Estrada who has beaten a triangular path from Rome to Paris to Miramar. Señor Gutiérrez, with the blessing of the Holy Father, has already hoodwinked His Imperial Majesty into lending France's power to this misadventure, and as for the Archduke, wishful thinking will suffice for the rest. Emperor Napoleon is pretending that the studied silence of London and Madrid constitutes agreement with France's aims, and he refuses to recognize that England and Spain are acting honorably, something not necessarily endemic to the conduct of great nations. Of course, France has enough armed strength all by itself to take care of the military part of this farce—the defeat at Puebla must be looked upon as only a temporary derailment of the Imperial locomotive—and any counterfeit "plebiscite" the French Army and the reactionary elements of the Mexican aristocracy ultimately concoct will, I fear, be given full credence by the Austrian and Princess Charlotte. They are dreamers. Max von Hapsburg is at heart a decent man, but he is much given to self-delusion. Mark my words. If the army succeeds in what they now are calling the "stabilization of Mexico," the Catholic monarchy our watered-down Napoleon lusts for will become an edifice in Mexico's capital within a year. That it will be a house of cards goes beyond saying.

He added Tante Claudine's love to the message and passed along the news that they had seen quite a bit of the Comte de Bayeux in the house on the Rue de Rivoli.

Then a note from the Palace arrived at the house on Avenida Moctezuma Sarah rented shortly after the return from Zacatecas, telling her that President Juárez would not only see her, but looked forward to their meeting. She was to present herself to General Ignacio Comonfort, the Minister of War, who would usher her into the president's office.

She found General Comonfort, in spite of his martial demeanor, to be a genuine charmer. He seemed reluctant to pass Sarah along to his superior, not because he did not want her seeing Juárez, but obviously from the delight he took in her company himself. His attention was flattering, but she could not wait to see the grave man who had impressed her at Samuel's dinner table.

Benito Juárez had changed little since she had seen him years ago in Zacatecas. She had been hardly more than a child then, but he had seemed to her then and now to be one of those rare creatures who are born middle-aged and never grew a day older or younger. If memory served, the brooding, stocky Indian in the undertaker-black frock coat and the starched white shirt must be fifty-six or fifty-seven years old, but he looked no more than a dark, flinty forty, in spite of the few streaks of iron gray in the otherwise raven-hued, severely combed hair. The eyes were the same riveting ones she remembered, too. He stood to shake hands with her, but he did not smile. He had not smiled much at Zacatecas, either. There seemed nothing truly cold about his soundless greeting, though. From their previous brief talks she knew him for a kind man, one of genuine if never blanketing warmth, but there was no escaping the fact that the President of the Republic of Mexico was a man completely devoid of humor. He was rock-like, never yielding; still, it was hard to believe this quiet man was capable of waging a war on two fronts against a determined enemy. Nor were his enemies all outside the city. His own capital was shot through with conspirators who lived for the day he lost his power. But, she felt, alone and without friend or supporter, this man from the green mountain wilds of Oaxaca would never completely lose his power. It was not something chance had bestowed on him or lent him.

"I learned of your brother's death with great sorrow, Señorita Anderson," Juárez said from behind a massive desk that almost hid him. "He was a good friend to my country and my people. I regret that his murderers have never been brought to justice. There was little my government could do at the time. Perhaps less now."

It was a terrible, utterly honest admission.

"I have just returned from Zacatecas, Señor Presidente," Sarah said. "I know you have many more things with which you must concern yourself, but I wondered if you are aware of the depredations against persons and property still occurring in that state. They did not stop with my brother's death."

"Sí, señorita. It is perceptive of you to understand that los bandidos operating between here and the coast and in the northern states are not very high on the list of my government's priorities these days. Until we repel the foreign invader I fear their atrocities will continue. The armies of the Republic have little time for police work with what faces us in these critical moments." As he spoke, nothing in his face moved except the full, beet-dark lips. "Tell me, is it true that you were escorted to our capital by el plateado Antonio Pérez?"

"Yes." Interesting that the little head of state, with all he had to juggle in that solid, square head these days, would know and remember that. "I do not know," he continued, "how you contacted Tonito, but it might be wise to get in touch with him again. He had mucho respeto y affeción for your brother. Perhaps he would be willing to afford some minimal protection for the Sierra Verde pack trains. Nothing goes on in the silver country without his knowledge."

She had thought about this while still in Zacatecas, when Alberto Moreno mentioned Pérez. Perhaps Matt could reach the bandit again. Comforting to know that the man across the desk was giving the notion some sort of approval.

She did not have time to pursue the idea with him before he spoke again.

"You are, I am told, newly arrived from France. Is that not so?"

"Actually, I landed at Veracruz nine months ago, Señor Presidente."

"That is not precisely a lifetime." A touch of humor at last. "Have you had regular correspondence with anyone in Paris?"

"Yes, sir." She went on to tell him of Auguste Pelletier and her connection with the former secretary of the French Academy, of his letters with their guesses and predictions— and of his views.

"Your friend, then, does not approve of the policies of his Emperor and the so called Second Empire?"

"He does not. He thinks France would be better served if it allowed Mexico to seek its own destiny without European intervention. Monsieur Pelletier is a great admirer of yours, and of President Lincoln."

"Your friend and I are alike in that last, *señorita*. It is sad for Mexico that your countrymen are at war with one another. If that were not so, I do not believe the United States would tolerate for an instant French troops defiling our soil. But tell me, do *you* feel as your friend in Paris does?"

She was not accustomed to men in high places asking her opinion, had forgotten how earnestly Juárez had listened to her half-formed notions on fairly weighty matters at Samuel's when she visited Zacatecas six years ago. Some inner storm signal told her she had to be honest with Benito Juárez.

"I am an American, Señor Juárez, and I am dedicated to democracy, in my own country and everywhere. I would be overjoyed to see it survive and prosper in Mexico. But I must confess I also feel there would be many advantages for a— forgive me—somewhat technologically backward state such as Mexico seems to be to have a sponsor with the art and science, and economic strength of France. A partnership with Paris would do much to bring this country into the last third of the century as a full-fledged modern nation. My own United States, as you know, was nurtured to something approaching nationhood by Great Britain for one hundred fifty years before our Revolution."

"And those advantages would outweigh the blessings of universal freedom and equality?" The black eyes bored into her.

What sort of poppycock had she just delivered to this dedicated patriot? "Well . . . *that* I am not so sure of. Forgive me, sir. I had no right to pontificate the way I just did. I am as much an outsider here as any Frenchman."

"*No, no, no, señorita.* Do not apologize for speaking your

mind. The full and free exchange of ideas is one of the things I want most for Mexico. But you are quite right in one respect. It must come principally from *Mexicans*. It cannot ever come while my people are under the muzzles of Imperial guns. You spoke of a 'partnership'. *Sí*, such an eventuality would fail to tempt only a fool, but a true partnership cannot be forged by conquest."

She left the palace in a slightly shaken state. If she had learned anything about Benito Juárez she had not known before it was how absolutely uncompromising the little Indian would be in dealing with his enemy. If there were a dozen more like him in Mexico, France and Charlotte's "Maxl" could not, in the long run, hope to prevail. But there were not a dozen. France would triumph, and the Oaxaca *indio* would fade into faint, dusty legend.

All she could do now was look after her own affairs, and stay out of trouble until the mine, and then the orphanage, were in good shape again.

Juárez's remark that his beleaguered troops did not "have time for police work" took on a new and disturbing meaning as the pale winter days lengthened into early spring.

By day, with the never-failing sun brightening the Valley of Mexico and bathing it in gold, the capital could almost have been any other busy city in late nineteenth-century Christendom. Two hundred thousand and more souls thronged the broad *avenidas* every day on their way to and from their labors, most on foot, but with score upon score on horseback or in the driver's seats of carriages or mule-drawn *carretas*. Shops and cantinas engaged in a lively, noisy commerce. If there were too many soldiers carrying rifles with fixed bayonets through the side *calles* of the central city, lounging in the parks, or drinking far too much *pulque* at crowded tables on the Paseo terraces, it could not be a great deal different in Washington, D.C., today. But in Washington would the populace have betrayed such an almost willful ignorance of the dangers facing it? No one seemed to notice the legless beggars, many of them former soldiers mangled in the Cinco de Mayo at Puebla, who sprawled against the walls of the churriguresque buildings fronting on the main streets and boulevards and on the dished stone steps of the cathedral, holding out tin cups. The newspapers hawked at kiosks and open stands carried little news of the war and even less of politics.

Moving from the Mirador to the house on quiet, leafy Avenida Moctezuma had allowed Sarah and Solange to escape from some of the seamier, more depressing sights and sounds of the city, but leaving the teeming downtown section for the supposed peace of this residential neighborhood presented another problem.

Although birdsong and sparkling sunlight blessed every morning and most afternoons, and although their new neighbors were comfortable and comforting, the two became semi-prisoners once darkness fell. Unless O'Leary or someone else from the embassy escorted them, they dared not stir from the house at night, keeping every door doublebolted and every window latched. Avenida Moctezuma, as did most thoroughfares away from the comparative security of the brighter lights and the evening crowds, became a tunnel of petty terrors—and some not so petty—after sunset.

Robberies and holdups were epidemic across the entire city; not infrequently accompanied by a brand of violence she struggled with determination not to think of as typically and peculiarly Mexican. There were cutpurses and footpads to a horrid sufficiency in Boston and Paris, God knew.

In one incident reported to them by the Marine lieutenant, a gang of young toughs accosted a German couple from the Bavarian delegation as they were returning from a musical evening at their embassy, robbed them of everything they wore or carried, and stripped them down to the skin in the process. They drove off in the couple's buggy, firing pistols wildly into the night air. The German and his wife suffered the humiliation of having to knock naked and

shivering at a dozen silent doors before anyone answered
their pleas for help. At that the Bavarians had been lucky;
thieves killed three people in such attacks during the week
between Christmas and the New Year. In January bandits
raided a coaching stop at the capital's eastern edge, took
five travelers hostage, held them overnight by burying them
up to their necks in the sand of the courtyard while they
caroused in the cantina attached to the small inn until
dawn broke over Popocatepetl. Packed tightly to the point
where they could scarcely breathe, two of them died.
Stabbings and beatings, one of the latter here on Avenida
Moctezuma in February's first, forlorn week, occurred frequently. No one talked about these horrors. They would
never have been mentioned to her at all if it were not for
Matt.

She heard regularly from Señor Moreno in Zacatecas. He
sent two copies of every letter, by separate post; bandits
respected the Republic's mail service no more than they did
the rights of travelers or silver trains. The manager was
modest in his requests for financial assistance, again almost
apologetic that he had to trouble her at all. By mid-
February the reports of ore tonnage extracted showed that
the operation of the mine at least was beginning to improve.
Matt promised to see what he could do about getting word
to Antonio Pérez. She felt no compromising of her principles in considering enlisting the aid of a common criminal—well, perhaps an uncommon one. If she had qualms,
they disappeared after her first of several visits to the
orphanage of San Sebastian.

At her first tour of the home with Sor Francisca, together
with the wrinkled nun's laments about of the plight of the
orphanage and its charges, something else disappeared as
well: the last vestiges of any Boston Puritan prejudices about
the Holy Roman Church. She had already abandoned most
of those prejudices during her years with devout Catholics
Claudine and Auguste Pelletier and during her short, happy
sojourn at St. Catherine's in Paris, when Charlotte and she
were students there.

She missed Paris, she sometimes longed for Boston, but all in all she could count herself uneasily content.

On the morning of February 22 she scheduled a shopping trip to the Mercado Merced to look for a lighter evening wrap than the one she had brought from Paris, something she could wear to the embassy tonight for the celebration of the birthday of George Washington, which Matt said was the biggest event of the American legation's late winter season.

"Everyone of any consequence from back home will put in an appearance," the Marine said enthusiastically. "Most of the foreign bigwigs will be there, too, as well as the more important Mexes. Juárez will have people there, which doesn't often happen. Might make for an interesting evening since I hear Archbishop Labastida is coming. The conservatives must feel pretty confident about things if he's going to hobnob with the American unbelievers *and* the Republicans, Miss Anderson."

On the way to the market she directed the driver to take her by the Banco Central so she could retrieve her pearls from her safe deposit box.

They pulled in behind a fiacre parked at the bank's front door, and as she alighted she cast an eye at the vehicle's driver and single passenger.

The first thing that struck her about the occupant of the rear seat of the horse-drawn cab was the incongruity of seeing someone in the white peasant costume of all working class women in Mexico—except the widows—sitting in a fairly resplendent carriage as though she had every right to be there. The second and more powerful impact was that the girl in the carriage was one of the most beautiful young women she had ever seen. She held herself as proudly as an Aztec princess. Dark hair streamed down her back in cascades. Her face was as set as stone, but there was about it a secret shimmer that took Sarah's breath.

Then Sarah's eye drifted to the fiacre's driver. Even seen from the back the little man with his short legs draped across the dashboard was as ugly under his straw sombrero as the girl was beautiful. He was scraping a wickedly enormous knife back and forth across a whetstone. Her mind raced back to Orizaba.

It could not be! There must be dozens of dwarfs in Mexico who were indistinguishable from each other . . .

She turned toward the front door of the bank. Framed in its fancifully carved jambs and lintels, a tall man in a dove gray frock coat, and carrying a matching, broad brimmed felt hat in a powerful right hand, stared at her.

There was no mistaking *this* man.

Jason James.

14

▲▲▲▲▲

"I am sorry, ma'am—or miss—but you must be mistaking me for someone else," Jason James said.

He heard the alarm in his voice, hoped she had not. Her greeting had stopped him in his tracks, and his hat, halfway to his head, almost dropped from his hand. "My name is indeed James," he said, "but I do not hold the military rank of captain." Not that she would believe him, but he had to go through the motions, otherwise his mission for Bazaine might end at this moment. If she, her Marine friend, or anyone else of consequence were to learn of a serving Foreign Legion officer wandering around the capital, the news could streak through Mexico City like a prairie fire—right into the corridors of the Federal Palace and across the desk of Benito Juárez.

"Please," Sarah Anderson said at last, "do me the ordinary courtesy of not prevaricating, Captain James. I am not a child, and I am *not* making a mistake. You are the same Legion officer Marcel Gallimard introduced me to in Orizaba!" Her voice throbbed with barely controlled anger.

He could not blame her; the style of his lie was as insulting as the substance.

Behind her he saw Cipi had become alerted to the meeting—as had Sofía. The dwarf grinned impishly; the girl's face betrayed nothing, but her eyes bored into the American woman's back. Sofía had no more than a few words of English, but James knew she had caught the gist of the exchange.

It was not the first time he had felt misgivings that he had allowed Cipi to talk him into bringing Sofía along—something he had to admit he had not at the time struggled against too industriously—but the feeling now was sharper.

His only remote chance of repairing the damage caused by this unexpected meeting was to tell Sarah Anderson the truth, or at least as much of it as he could tell without putting his neck in a noose and his mission on the block.

"You are quite right, Miss Anderson. We have met before, and yes, I was a Legion captain then. You are not compelled to do so, but I would appreciate it if you could forget that."

She frowned, perplexity written in her face. Cipi's grin from his seat in the carriage grew wider. Sofía turned her gaze straight up the *avenida*, a deliberate show of indifference.

"Am I to take it, then, Captain—*Mister* James if you prefer—that you are no longer connected with the Legion?"

He had to say something to stop more questions.

"I wonder if you would have dinner with me tonight, Miss Anderson. We could discuss things more comfortably that way than standing here in a public street."

He could see the proposal surprised her.

"That's a very unexpected invitation, Mr. James. Under the circumstances I'm not entirely sure it's a welcome one." Then, as if she had been tapped on the shoulder, she turned her head toward the fiacre. To his amazement, when she turned back to him there was a hint of a smile on her face. "I have what I think is a better idea. There is an affair at the American embassy tonight, *our* embassy if you still think of yourself as American, Mr. James. Perhaps you already know about it, since all of our countrymen here in the capital have been invited. I would be pleased to have you escort me."

His mouth must have opened like a cave. Her faint smile widened. He recovered quickly. This gave him more than he dared hope for, a chance to stay close to her at least long enough to determine whether or not she would give him away to Republican authorities, either by design or accident. It was a tiny, momentary, but very real victory.

"I would be delighted, Miss Anderson."

"Good. Oh—one thing. It will be full dress, I'm afraid. Does that present a problem?"

"None at all."

She looked him up and down. "*Civilian* full dress, Mr. James?"

"Of course." He nearly laughed.

She reached into a huge, tooled leather bag and brought out a small case.

"My card, sir. Please call for me at eight o'clock. Dinner is at nine. You may wish to hire a larger carriage. There will be two others in our party."

From inside the open door of the bank Sarah watched the dwarf whip up the horses drawing the fiacre. James and the Mexican girl talked as the vehicle pulled away, or rather James talked and the girl listened, her face turned full on his.

There was no doubt in Sarah's mind that even if the girl did not, the dwarf understood what had just taken place. When she turned to look at the pair in the fiacre, the bold, knowing smile on the little man's bearded face and the flicks of his shrewd eyes from Sarah to Jason James and back shouted complete understanding of every word.

Had she done a wise thing in inviting James to the embassy affair tonight?

Matt would be accompanying them, and now she had decided Solange would be going, too. They would want to know about Jason James. She had enough curiosity about him herself, no doubt of that, and she would speculate enough between now and tonight to produce even more—and probably shape the questions about what he was doing in the capital and why he was in civilian clothes to try to satisfy it. He had certainly avoided answering when she asked him if he was still connected with the Legion.

But curiosity alone did not account for the way in which she had blurted out the invitation.

She certainly had not *meant* to ask him. At first, still in the grip of anger, she had merely wanted to turn his offer of dinner down with a minimum of courtesy and be done with him; make him pay a little something for his half-truths or whatever they were. When she looked away from him and toward the carriage, she found the Mexican girl examining her with a frankness she had never before seen on the part of native women, who usually averted their eyes when dealing with Europeans. Something in the look spun her back to James, and the words came tumbling out.

As the team sped the fiacre down the avenida from the bank under Cipi's furious whip, the dwarf yelled back over his shoulder.

"Do you suppose the *gringa señorita* will put you at risk, *mi mayor?*"

"No more than you will, calling me 'major' at the top of your lungs on a public thoroughfare. Mind your tongue!"

"*¡Sí!* Cipi is sorry, Señor James. *De veras!*"

"Get us back to our *posada, pronto.*"

He had not told Cipi the details of the mission Bazaine had given him, but he would not wager that the dwarf had not figured them out for himself, either by those uncanny divinations that even Pierre Boulanger had begun to believe in, or by the nonmystical application of what James had long before now recognized as a truly shrewd mind. All he had told Cipi in Jalapa was that they were going to the capital to do some scouting for the general. The dwarf had winked at him and nodded sagely.

In the wake of his discovery by Sarah Anderson, he did not consider leaving the capital, although Bazaine would understand if he abandoned his mission now. The general might insist on it if he knew.

Cipi had beaten the horses without mercy ever since they left the bank, but now he reined them in front of a shop whose gold-lettered sign read, "Tienda de Vestidos."

"We must procure your dinner clothes immediately, señor," the dwarf said, "if el sastre is to have time to make alterations before tonight. Do not rent—buy. It is after all, the money of General Bazaine, and you will need a full dress suit anyway when we are living permanently here in the capital."

"You still have that dream, Cipi?"

"It is not a dream, señor. It will come to pass."

They entered the tailor shop and, with Cipi running things as usual, a tiny, timid proprietor brought out three different tailcoats for James to try before the dwarf was satisfied.

"Your figure was made for evening clothes, señor," Cipi said. Without even so much as looking to James for approval he began to haggle with the tailor. "And, of course," he finally said to the little shopkeeper, who was desperately outmatched in the face of Cipi's bargaining skills, "all alterations will be gratis, no? And I feel it would be only fair if you furnished a walking stick for mi caballero, también!"

It turned out the tailoring would take an hour, and James decided to drive himself and Sofía back to the posada while Cipi waited for the finished garments.

The dwarf seemed a bit reluctant to let him go. "I do not think it a good idea to tell Sofía what you have in mind for the gringa woman, señor."

"I have nothing in mind for Señorita Anderson!"

"¡Sí! Of course. But Cipi wouldn't tell Sofía that, either. There are strict limits to what women will believe when another woman makes an entrance."

"There are also," James snapped furiously, "strict limits to the kind of impudence I will take from you!"

Back in the carriage he took the reins and started up the avenida. He did not look at the girl, but he remained conscious of her every meter of the journey back to their quarters.

At the *posada* the hypocrisy of their housing arrangements embarrassed him as much as it had every day of the three since their arrival in the capital. When they took the rooms, his fronting on the *avenida*, theirs well at the back, Cipi told him the girl and he would always enter the building from the rear. "We can be casual in the provinces, *señor*, but not here in the capital."

He drove the fiacre into the alley behind the inn. Sofía alighted first.

She looked up at him. "I will do a wash, *señor*. You will need fresh linen for tonight. When Cipi brings your new evening clothes I will press them, too."

He searched her face.

"Gracias, Sofía," he said.

"De nada, señor."

"After you are finished I will not need you until tomorrow morning."

"Bueno, señor."

Señor, señor! That was one of the myriad things they had yet to discuss: what she should call him. So far she had used the same *senor* or *mi mayor* when they were alone as when Cipi or any other listener was present. Once, though—it was at the coaching stop at Atlixco southwest of Cholula, where they spent the second night out from Jalapa and when she had slept next to him—he thought he heard her mutter "Jason" just before returning to her own bed.

In a way, her mode of addressing him was somehow typical of everything in their brief relationship.

Sarah Anderson dressed with as much nervous fuss as she had for her first dance at Miss Pettibone's School when she was sixteen.

It would be the dark blue velvet, the pearl necklace, and Aunt Louisa's zircon dinner ring. Solange once said the blue-white stone made her eyes an even deeper blue when she raised her hand to her face.

The knottiest problem was her hair. She piled it up, pinned it, tore the fastenings loose, and let it down a dozen times. There was now a downside to her having made a friend and equal instead of a servant out of Solange; the change in their relationship had robbed her of the French-woman's ministrations as a hairdresser. Solange, at Sarah's insistence, now had herself to get ready whenever they went out together.

Even when living in the Rue de Rivoli with Tante Claudine Pelletier, who, while not a slave to it, was a typically French devotee of fashion, she had not taken such pains with her appearance.

She gave up on the hairdo for the moment and turned her attention to Aunt Louisa's ring. Louisa Kent had been a tiny woman, with wispy frail hands; the dinner ring was a snug fit, almost too tight, even when she soaped her knuckle and forced the ring past it.

She should have been a great deal more vexed with the Legionnaire James this morning at the bank than when she fenced with him in the Chasseur mess back in Orizaba. He had lied to her today, a bald-faced, *clumsy* lie.

In Orizaba he had turned her unwarranted attack on him aside with grace and dignity—and left her fuming. She had acted toward him then like a shameless virago. What had he thought her then . . . some Lady Macbeth or Lucrezia Borgia in her midnight-blue velvet gown?

Oh my God! She had worn the velvet to the Chasseur officers mess that night!

"Solange!" she called, her voice teetering on the edge of panic. There was no answer. Solange must still be in the kitchen, soaking herself in the same wooden tub the new girl Rosa had filled, perhaps even having a nip from her cache of cognac.

She would just have to decide by herself for once. The lavender organdy? Yes. The pearls went well with it, too, as did the zircon.

She had to laugh. For a moment there, a grown woman who was running a silver mine, who had traveled half the width of Mexico in the company of bandits, and who could—if she was not giving herself too much undue credit—engage the interest of the president of a sovereign nation and a landed noble of the Loire, had become girlishly unhinged at the prospect of showing a man the same gown.

Jason James . . . that sudden look of vulnerability which she had seen on his face even as he tried to lie to her.

He *was* attractive. Her father and her uncles would have called a him a "fine figure of a man." The touch of early gray at his temples, the straight nose set so well in the tanned features, the clear eyes, also gray, she thought. He wore his fine, herringbone-tweed frock coat with casual ease, even in these probably awkward circumstances.

Something else bothered her, and she should face *it*, too. Her more tolerant view of him had not been shaped by *his* looks alone this morning, but by those of someone else as well.

When she turned and looked at the ravishing young woman seated in the carriage she found her looking back with that utterly candid, fearless gaze, one of challenge.

It was half past six. She had come no closer to solving the problem of her hair than when she began; she would have to ask Solange's help, no matter how busy she was with her own *toilette*.

At Sarah's second call for her—this one less distraught, but still breathing urgency—Solange entered the room wrapped only in a towel. Yes, things had changed between the two of them. In all their time together with the Pelletiers, Solange had never appeared before her in such a state of *deshabille*.

"My hair, Solange!" She followed her panicked cry with the eternal lament of women everywhere: "I can't do a thing with it."

It took Solange fifteen minutes to put her hair in order

with familiar, skilled, still loving hands, including the inevitable retouching needed after Sarah pulled the organdy gown over her head and smoothed it into place.

"*Vous etes très jolie ce soir, chérie—magnifique!*" Solange said. "Monsieur and Madame Pelletier would be proud of you. I hope this American is worth the way you have dressed yourself."

"I have not dressed for *him*, Solange!"

"Of course not, *ma chère*. This elegance then is only for the benefit of the absent Monsieur le Comte de Bayeux, *n'est-ce pas?*"

15

▲▲▲▲▲

His arrival at the house on Avenida Moctezuma proved just a bit unsettling when a Mexican girl ushered him into the parlor and he found Sarah Anderson in the company of two other people. The same two had shared the wagon with her that day in Orizaba. He breathed more easily when neither of them seemed to recognize him.

Sarah Anderson introduced him—blessedly as "Mister James" rather than "Captain"—to the Marine lieutenant Matthew O'Leary, who seemed all soldier but pleasant enough, and whose steady, wide, blue eyes held a great deal of unmistakable curiosity.

"You're new in the capital, Mr. James?" O'Leary asked.

"Yes, Lieutenant. I arrived here just three days ago." He would have to be very careful with any more questions, and to that end he had prepared a story that would vaguely confirm his having *once* served in the Legion should Sarah Anderson bring up their meeting in Orizaba.

He also became the object of searching looks and a wary smile from the older woman. Mademoiselle Tournier—Solange, if he'd heard correctly—seemed more friend than servant. He would not have judged her to be the latter at all except for the way she fussed over her "Mademoiselle Anderson," picking a loose thread from the American woman's lavender gown as they both donned evening wraps in the foyer for the ride to the embassy.

"Have you just come from the States, then, Mr. James?" O'Leary asked.

"No, Lieutenant. I haven't been home in some years."

The Marine shook his head disappointedly. "I was hoping for some firsthand news about *our* war."

James doubted if O'Leary would make an issue out of his not being back home, wearing the blue or gray; the embassy man was probably slightly embarrassed, perhaps even heartsick, that he was not fighting somewhere north of the Rio Grande himself.

"What are you doing in Mexico, and in particular here in the capital?" O'Leary asked now.

James readied his story, but help came unexpectedly, and from an unlikely quarter.

"Mister James is in the capital to do his banking," Sarah Anderson said. Her eyes seemed to sparkle with humor. "But it is now well past eight, gentlemen. We had better get started for the embassy."

At the street he and O'Leary helped the two women into the big carriage Cipi had rented. The dwarf shot the Marine a glance, cast another even briefer one in the direction of Sarah Anderson, then focused far more intense attention on Mlle. Tournier. With some horror James recalled that back in Orizaba Cipi claimed he thrust out his obscene finger solely for the Frenchwoman's benefit. He took a tight grip on his cane.

Once they were all settled the dwarf snaked a long black whip out over the backs of the two horses and the carriage fairly leaped down the *avenida*.

It was a rattling, creaky, ancient vehicle and there was little in the way of conversation as Cipi drove them through streets arched over with black branches.

"Are you armed, Lieutenant O'Leary?" James asked.

The Marine grinned and held up his right hand. A set of brass knuckles encased his fingers. "I've found these are often more useful than a pistol in close quarters, Mr. James. They don't misfire—and I can't shoot myself in the foot with them." Nothing in the statement smacked of boastfulness; it displayed the high confidence James remembered well as the universal attitude of young American soldiers of virtually every rank.

At the wrought-iron gates of the embassy compound a Marine private saluted O'Leary and waved them on through to the stone steps of the building where another private helped the two women from the carriage and directed Cipi to take the vehicle to a park at the rear.

A liveried footman announced the four, and James saw heads turn at the stentorian "Mr. Jason James!" No one he could see showed any such curiosity at the footman's "Miss Sarah Anderson," or even at "Mademoiselle Solange Tournier," although several welcoming smiles were directed at the two women. Apparently Sarah and her companion were already fairly well known in this small, tight society.

Once past the reception room Solange and O'Leary disappeared in the crowd.

Small as it might be for embassy parties, it was far and away the largest gathering of his countrymen he had been a part of since he left the redolent crush of the Seaman's Hiring Hall in Newark more than a dozen years ago to ship out on that filthy Portuguese ketch.

It occurred to him that Sarah Anderson, if she did not betray him—something she at least had not done with O'Leary—was the finest camouflage he could have worn this evening, cloaking him even against the ambassador himself when she introduced him.

"May I present Mister Jason James, Mister Ambassador? Mister James is a friend of an old friend from France."

She certainly seemed to James to have solid *bona fides* with U.S. Ambassador Thomas Corwin. He sounded the soul of sincerity as he said, "Any friend of Miss Anderson's is a friend of mine, Mr. James. If I or my staff can be of help during your stay in the capital, please let me know." James had known of this distinguished looking man for a long time, and it was not just that Corwin had been a Governor of Ohio nor a respected, hardworking Senator from that state, and later Secretary of the U.S. Treasury, that stuck in the Legionnaire's mind. Corwin was one of the very few Americans of any stature who had unequivocally opposed the Mexican War of 1846–48. His opposition had ended his career in public life until Abraham Lincoln revived it. "Have you heard from your friends at Miramar, Sarah?" Corwin asked.

"Not a word directly, Mr. Ambassador. I have had no letter from Princess Charlotte. I expect she and Max fully intend to come here, though. The view in Paris is that they're only waiting for some signal from the people of Mexico."

Miramar? A possibly *expected* letter? Max?

Cipi's gossip, garnered from Marcel Gallimard's manservant Emile, was fact. This American woman knew Maximilian and Charlotte von Hapsburg. Sarah Anderson, of "a place in Los Estados Unidos called Boston," in all probability the fiancée of a French nobleman from the Loire, *knew* them! Corwin was listening to her out of more than mere courtesy; clearly he placed some value on her ideas.

"The Austrian and his wife are two very naive young people," the ambassador said. "I hope they don't come to grief here. Mexico, in my experience, is seldom what it seems. Now, could you please excuse me, Sarah? I see Archbishop Labastida has arrived. Making him feel welcome will not be the easiest of my diplomatic chores this evening. I have mixed feelings about the archbishop. He is a hard, obtuse, uncompromising man. Thoroughly opposed to the United States. But he does have one saving grace in my opinion. Labastida is easily the best friend the Indians of Mexico have had since Bartolomé de Las Casas, three centuries ago." He turned to James. "I hope we meet again, sir."

James watched Corwin walk toward a tall, rake-thin man

in the cassock of a senior churchman. This was the forbidding priest spoken of with such awe by the Spanish officers on the voyage from Toulon in the *Carcassone*. He scarcely had time to register the silent, hawklike presence of the Catholic prelate before Sarah tugged at his sleeve. He turned and followed her as she moved across the embassy's ballroom floor, nodding to an occasional man or woman, stopping finally in front of a bulky, bespectacled man whose wispy hair made a delicate white circlet on his bald head. From the red, white, and blue sash girding his tailcoat he appeared to be another member of the embassy delegation.

"This gentleman is the deputy ambassador," she said. "He is—"

The older man put his hand out and spoke before she could finish. "Jarvis Saunders, Mister . . . ?"

"James, Jason James."

"Mr. Saunders arranged to have Lieutenant O'Leary meet Solange and me in Veracruz, Mr. James," Sarah said. "Without his help I doubt if we ever would have reached the capital."

Saunders was looking over his shoulder to where his superior still engaged Labastida in conversation. Sarah's eyes followed his.

"The ambassador is doubtless getting an earful of what a boon Archduke Maximilian will be to Mexico," she said.

"Don't be too sure of that, Miss Anderson," Saunders replied. "I don't believe Labastida is exactly in the Hapsburg-Bonaparte camp."

"But isn't it the intention of the emperor to establish a new Catholic monarchy in Mexico?"

"Yes," Saunders said.

"Well, Max von Hapsburg is as devout as any prince in Europe. Hasn't the Roman Catholic hierarchy always felt more comfortable in a monarchy? It's fared a great deal better in the France of the Second Empire, for instance, than it did under the Republic. Archbishop Labastida should be pleased at the prospect."

Saunders chuckled. "Oh, I daresay His Excellency would

prefer such an eventuality to President Juárez's Republicans with their anti-clerical views. But his and Emperor Napoleon's ideas on what constitutes a *true* Catholic state differ in some important respects, particularly where Mexico is concerned."

"How so, Mr. Saunders?" She glanced briefly at James, who was riveted by the conversation.

"The emperor and the Austrian apparently are willing to let some of the reforms of the Juarist Constitution of 1859 stand, Miss Anderson. They don't seem to favor returning the properties the Mexican Republic forced the Church to sell. Archbishop Labastida has never wavered in his threat that *no* government will enjoy the support of the Church until that happens."

"Does that make a lot of difference?"

"Yes, indeed. The archbishop commands no troops, but he commands generals who do—that unholy terror Leonardo Márquez for one. A number of other conservative commanders are under his control as well, some harboring strong anti-French sentiments which could be turned against any government the archduke forms here."

"That wouldn't be entirely bad news for President Juárez, would it?"

"No. A three-way struggle would give him breathing space. It's not apt to happen, though. My guess is that the Archbishop and the French will resolve their differences."

James watched Sarah's face all through the deputy ambassador's recitation. She listened every bit as well as she talked. Saunders's eyebrows had shot up at her incisive questions. Men like Jarvis Saunders, decent as he appeared to be, all too often rejected the opinions of women on such matters.

Out of the corner of his eye he saw the ambassador and the churchman had parted company for the moment. The American diplomat's place was immediately taken by, of all people, the two others who had shared James's carriage, Solange Tournier and the Marine O'Leary. The Frenchwoman curtsied and Labastida held his ring out for her to kiss.

"Solange must be in seventh heaven," Sarah whispered. "The people I lived with in Paris and who were her original employers, were good but not fanatic Catholics. This is probably the first archbishop she's ever gotten close to. Matt's a devoted churchgoer, too."

Jarvis Saunders excused himself and hurried off to circulate among the others present.

"I expect Mr. Corwin has invited the Archbishop here tonight for reasons which have little to do with what he called his 'diplomatic chores,'" Sarah Anderson said.

James was alone with her. It had been a long time coming and now he could not be sure whether he welcomed this turn of events or dreaded it.

"Let us find somewhere comfortable to sit, Mr. James," she said, "and then perhaps you could bring us some punch."

He steered her to the side of the huge room, found an unoccupied settee, and headed for the far wall and the table with the punch bowl.

He could smell the punch even before he reached it. He guessed it to be a Fishhouse or one of the other wickedly powerful concoctions from the hard-drinking revolutionary era of the man whose birthday they were celebrating.

He purposely passed close to where Solange and the young Marine were still deep in conversation with the Archbishop.

"We have heard nothing to that effect here at the embassy, Your Excellency," he heard O'Leary say. "Our communications have not been good, what with the condition of the roads between here and Veracruz."

"I assure you my information is reliable, Lieutenant." The prelate's voice was deep and held strange echoes. James wished he could pause by the small group and hear more, but he got his two cups of punch and returned to Sarah.

"All right, *Mister* James," she said when he sat down beside her, "I suppose I can't expect to get the whole truth from you, but will you kindly go part of the distance toward enlightening me about what you are doing here in the capital?"

Something—not the drink, though—had brought a high flush of color to her face. Things had proceeded with great rapidity this evening when he called at Avenida Moctezuma. With no real opportunity to study her then, or afterward during the ride through the dark city streets, he had gotten no chance to reflect on what a beautiful woman she was.

When she lifted her cup to her lips again a blue-white ring flashed pale fire and lit those startling blue eyes, and over the strong aroma of the punch he thought he detected a faint whiff of the same perfume which had followed him home from that first meeting with her at Orizaba. The scent, something like orange blossoms in the south of France, but whatever it was, suited her well: fresh and forthright but not overpowering, and not at all cloying. The hand with the ring was well-formed, graceful but by no means delicate. He took in the slight curve of her forehead and . . .

"I am waiting, sir," she said now. "Have you anything to tell me?" With this her bosom lifted and fell. His breath caught.

"Would you prefer lies to nothing at all, Miss Anderson?"

"Of course not!"

"Then I'm afraid it must be nothing."

"You are here on behalf of the Legion, aren't you?"

"I do have *personal* business in Mexico, I assure you, Miss Anderson."

"Do the Republican authorities know of you?"

"I think not."

Had all his chances of carrying out Bazaine's mission gone glimmering? One word from Sarah Anderson in the wrong ears and he was as good as dead.

No matter how he might try to put it from his mind, even here in the United States embassy he was in the midst of enemies. Despite the fact that the American legation wined and dined a sworn enemy of Juárez tonight in the person of Archbishop Labastida, he could not forget that the *official* feeling here backed the Oaxacan and his government.

And Jason James was pledged as a soldier of France to bring that government down.

"We are getting nowhere, Mr. James," she said.

"Must we get *somewhere*, Miss Anderson?" For the first time in his life—or at least since he watched Cousin Aaron at those half-forgotten dances back in Kansas—he wished he had an easy way with women. "I am not free to tell you the things you wish to know. I have made promises I must keep. I'm sure you've done the same."

Suddenly she laughed—a cascading laugh that warmed him and at the same time braced him as a splash of cold water might. Her face had softened, and the eyes veiled with doubt now twinkled with something approaching friendliness and with a touch of that same humor he thought he had glimpsed before.

"Why did you ask me to dinner this morning?" she said.

"Why did *you* ask me here?"

"This is childish, Mister James."

"Yes, it is, Miss Anderson."

"Well," she said, "let's *be* children tonight, Mister James. As a matter of fact let's start by dispensing with this Miss Anderson, Mister James nonsense. My name, as I hope you remember, is Sarah, and yours is Jason, isn't it?"

He was about to answer when she pulled her eyes away from his. He turned and found Solange Tournier hurrying across the room to join them, her eyes bright, rapturous even at a distance.

"Did you see, *ma chère*, did you *see?*" The Frenchwoman's excitement defied containment. "An archbishop. *Sacrebleu!*"

"Yes, I saw, Solange. Where is Matt?"

"He stopped to talk with some Mexican general he knew."

"Ah, yes. I see him now. That's General Comonfort." She turned back to James. "I met the general when I called on President Juárez. Perhaps you would like to meet him, too," she paused, then smiled, "—Jason."

The quizzical look of Solange Tournier at the "Jason" did not escape him.

The danger had not passed. Sarah knew Comonfort— and *Juárez!* That she was totally imperialist in her sympathies suddenly seemed unlikely, despite her likely tie to the Austrian couple.

Beyond the immediate peril, the feeling that he was out of his depth with this remarkably connected, intelligent woman was suddenly overpowering.

"Yes," he said. "I would like very much to meet the general—Sarah."

She turned and led the way across the floor to where Matt O'Leary was engaged in conversation with a handsome, older man in the blue uniform of the Republic of Mexico.

"General Comonfort," she said when the Mexican officer faced them, "this is my American friend Jason James and my companion, Mademoiselle Tournier."

The general gave James a curt nod, bowed to Solange, then turned his full attention on Sarah.

"El Presidente sends his felicitations, Señorita Anderson. He predicted I would see you here tonight. He hopes you will call at the Palace again soon."

"I shall, General. Give him my very best regards, *por favor.* Will I see you there again, too?"

"I regret you will not, *señorita.* I was just telling Lieutenant O'Leary here that my duty assignment changed only yesterday and that I am no longer at the Palace with the president. I now command at Chapultepec."

The name thundered in James's head.

He heard the general's next words well enough, but they seemed to be coming from somewhere else. "Why do you not come to the castle," Comonfort said, "and visit me there, Señorita Anderson. Bring your friends. We can have a *partida de campo*—what I believe they call in England and the United States a picnic." His arms opened wide, as if he might gather James, Sarah, Solange, and Matt O'Leary into them. "But you must come very soon, of course," the Republican general said next. "I have no way of telling how long my soldiers and I will be in the Castle. Presidente Juárez received a signal this afternoon from General Ortega at Puebla. Three days ago the French commander-in-chief, General Forey, marched his army to the gates of Gonzalez Ortega's city. Yesterday the invaders began a bombardment much more destructive than the one General de Lorencez brought to bear against Puebla's garrison on the fifth of May.

"The war is beginning again in earnest. Puebla *must* hold. I may have to march my command to the support of our brave *compadres* there at any moment."

Jason James did not remember much of the rest of the evening at the embassy. His mind was far too occupied with other things.

16

▲▲▲▲▲

"*Vraiment*, Monsieur James is an attractive man, *ma chère*—but what about Monsieur Le Comte?"

Sarah looked up from her writing table. "There is no reason to link them, Solange. Mr. James does interest me, but it is not a romantic interest. I'll thank you not to mention him again."

It had been Solange's first reference to the Legionnaire since the party, but three times within twelve hours now she had spoken of Henri by name—or, more pointedly, by his title. She was meddling, but perhaps it would not hurt to have *someone* keep Sarah Anderson on the sensible path toward marriage. She had certainly wavered in her determination to keep the Legionnaire at arm's length last night.

She had issued her invitation in front of the Banco Central as a challenge, and had first viewed the evening as a contest. It remained that from the time he called for the three of them until something she said at the party brought the look of a man listening to far-off voices. He finally made a reply of sorts.

"I have made promises I must keep."

As little as she still knew about him, she decided one thing in that second: this indeed was a man who kept promises.

In their talk with General Comonfort another puzzling thing happened. Something the general said—perhaps the news that the conflict was raging again at Puebla—seemed to strike the American so forcibly he almost reeled. He recovered quickly, his face a mask, unreadable.

At any rate, it did not spoil the rest of the evening.

"Solange," she said now, "did you hire that old *jardinero* Pedro?"

"Oui, chérie. He started on the garden this morning."

"Could you send him in to my study, please? I have written to General Comonfort asking if Tuesday is all right for his picnic. And there's a note for Matt. Pedro can't be too busy in the garden yet. If he could deliver them . . ." She paused. "There's another for Mister James." There was an arch look from the Frenchwoman, but nothing more, thank heavens.

"Ignacio Comonfort was there in all his military splendor, was he not, *mi mayor?"* Cipi said as Sofía served James's breakfast in the parlor room of the hotel apartment. "And so was Labastida, *no?* My major was treading a very high and risky wire to enjoy the company of Señorita Anderson."

Sofía refilled his coffee cup and left the room without a word or a look at James.

The dwarf seemed especially pleased with himself this morning. "While Cipi took Comonfort's driver's pesos in a game of monte," he said, "he also discovered that the general, who is not the worst of Benito Juárez's commanders, has been reassigned. He now commands at Chapultepec."

Comonfort's proposed picnic—if it came about—had not exactly delivered the commandant of Chapultepec into James's hands, but it could prove valuable. The general, in his transparent attempts to impress Sarah Anderson, had been talkative enough, perhaps would be talkative at a picnic to the point of indiscretion.

James had forced himself to appear calm at the embassy, but his perceptive companion must have noticed his reaction when Comonfort said "Chapultepec." He was fast wearying of the lie he was living with her.

"Your army will win at Puebla this time, *mi mayor,*" Cipi said now. "It will take a long time, but the big guns, the new generals, and the reinforcements which have arrived from France and Africa will make the difference."

"Will I live through this battle, too?"

"Of course, *señor. Pero*—the major will stay alive principally because he will not be as prominent in this one as in the Cinco de Mayo last year."

"I will not fight?"

"Not at Puebla itself."

He felt a little as if something or someone had cheated him. If what Cipi said proved true, who would take Compagnie Rouge into battle?

It was time to get back to being a soldier again—or, more distastefully, a spy.

He had not received so much as a solitary signal from Bazaine. The general had told him he would be in touch by means of coded messages delivered to his hotel through the ordinary Mexican mails. To this moment nothing had arrived. It seemed strange in light of the news of the new battle for Puebla passed along by Comonfort last night. Forey's army had now been at the city's breastworks for half a week. Surely Bazaine wanted him to hurry, assess the possible future target with all due speed, and then return to prepare for the assault on Chapultepec.

Perhaps he should not wait for the picnic; strike out on his own, get the espionage over with, and rejoin Compagnie Rouge with all possible speed. But . . .

The obvious advantages of having the Republican commander as a host, and possibly touring the castle and its
approaches in a way he could never hope to on his own,
made him reject the idea.

Despite a stern effort to keep his mind solely on his duty,
it ran back over the rest of the evening following Sarah
Anderson's talk with Comonfort, when the long hours
shrank to minutes. A string quartet played Viennese waltzes
and at her teasing insistence over his stammering disclaimer
of any ability on a dance floor, he actually took her in his
arms and somehow moved her around the ballroom without
too many embarrassing missteps, wishing all the while he
had a tenth of the art of Cousin Aaron. She seemed
weightless, and yet when he took her hand, and when his
arm circled her waist, he felt an almost electric charge of
energy.

The Marine Lieutenant O'Leary, who was quartered
somewhere on the embassy grounds, did not return with
them to the house on Avenida Moctezuma. The temperature had dropped and Cipi dug lap robes from the boot of
the old carriage. James wrapped them around the shoulders
of the two women, and when his hand touched Sarah's it
was an even more electrifying moment then when they
danced.

When they passed the rare lighted corner or stretch of
roadway, he found her eyes turned full on him. He fought
away all curiosity about what she might be thinking.

Now he finished breakfast and looked for more coffee. Sofía
appeared in the arched opening leading from the parlor
to the bedrooms. She stepped to the table and refilled his
cup.

"The *gringa señorita* Anderson is beautiful, *señor may-
or*," she said. Without looking at him she retraced her steps
to the arch. Once there she stopped and turned to face him.
Their eyes met, and there was something fierce but not
necessarily accusing or forbidding in hers.

"Will the major want Sofía to come to him tonight?"

It was the first time she had *asked*.

17

▲▲▲▲

General Ignacio Comonfort's picnic at Chapultepec produced two uninvited guests before the day was out, one Jason James expected, one he did not.

Neither, however, waited with the general when he met James's carriage—with Cipi at the reins—at the iron gate opening on the long drive leading to the castle. But one arrived very shortly after Comonfort, on horseback, led Sarah Anderson and her friends directly west of the citadel to a table set in a clearing in a forest of young *ahuehuete* trees, saying, "We will tour the castle after we dine, *amigos*."

That, James knew, was when he would see the uninvited guest he *expected*, the one who had waited for him in the shadow of the south wall for fifteen years.

The surprise guest, on the other hand, came upon Comonfort and his party just as they settled in to what by Republican standards promised to be a Lucullan banquet. The corporal and his private soldier assistant detailed to serve the noonday meal of roast pig both fidgeted nervously when an unescorted, unpretentious closed carriage rattled up to the picnic table.

"*El Presidente . . .*" the corporal breathed in an ecstasy of adoration. Old soldier Comonfort looked a little ruffled as the tiny, one-horse coach creaked to a stop. He snapped to attention as did his two soldier-caterers.

Benito Juárez stepped down unassisted from the running board. The driver settled his whip handle into the socket beside his high perch and smiled broadly at the two enlisted men.

Under the brilliant noon sun the carriage was as black as its passenger's costume, and in the shade cast by the nearest trees James got no clear look at Benito Juárez until he moved away from it—darkness emerging from darkness.

James saw instantly that the stocky, black-clad Indian in the stove pipe hat did not subscribe to such frivolity as his general's *partido de campo*. He pointed his brass-knobbed walking stick toward the table with its gleaming cloth, mountains of food, and rich appointments.

"Do not let my arrival put a halt to your *fiesta*, Ignacio," Juárez said, acknowledging Sarah's and Solange's curtseys by lifting his hat a scant inch above his black hair and making small separate bows to the two women. He did not so much as look at James or Matt O'Leary, obviously did not see the Marine's smart salute; he just turned and began walking away from the group, speaking softly to Comonfort over his shoulder as he did. "May I have a word with you, general? It will not take long."

The commandant hurried after him, caught him at perhaps twenty paces distance. When they huddled together the tall general bent toward the shorter man and all James could make out was the low, muddied rumble of voices.

The conversation presented a strange tableau. Comonfort was doing most of the talking, but impressive as the general was, he seemed to be bending into an attitude of supplication. Juárez, for his part, became rooted in the soil of the clearing while he listened, as if he were one of the rocks that dotted the glades and openings of the park-like forest.

"He is a magnetic little man, isn't he?" Sarah whispered in James's ear. "The general must be trying to explain just who we are and what we're doing here."

"He knows who *you* are, Sarah, doesn't he?"

"We've met three times. And he probably knows more about Matt than Matt does himself. I suspect it's you he wants to know about."

James turned his eyes from Juárez and Comonfort and looked her full in the face. "What can General Comonfort tell him?"

Her eyes flashed. "What you really mean is what have *I* told General Comonfort."

"With respect, yes."

"Nothing. But then I didn't have anything to tell, did I?"

He glanced at Comonfort and his uninvited guest again just in time to see Juárez fix his eyes hard on *him*.

Even from about twenty meters he could feel the intensity of the gaze. Magnetic little man, had Sarah said? There was more than magnetism to Benito Juárez. No commander in James's memory had carried with him a field of force to equal that of this somber, solid man—not even François-Achille Bazaine.

Comonfort and the president had apparently finished with each other and now approached the table.

"It is Señor James, is it not?" Juárez said. "General Comonfort says that, as is the case with Lieutenant O'Leary and *Señorita* Anderson, you are a *norteamericano.*"

"Yes, *Señor Presidente.*"

"And you are an *hombre de negocios,* a man of business, *no?*" James hoped that did not call for an answer. Juárez continued. "Ignacio also tells me you have recently arrived in our capital from the coast. Did you come by way of Jalapa or Orizaba?"

"I stopped in both those cities, sir." Risky—but less risky than outright lies that could trap him even more easily. This man would be as difficult to lie to as Bazaine.

"I realize, Señor James, that as an *hombre de negocios* you perhaps cannot answer my next question, but—were you able to observe the strength and disposition of the French forces assembled in either city?"

"To some extent, Señor Juárez."

"Did you—again only as a businessman, of course—form any opinion as to how our armies might fare against them?"

"I am not privy to the French order of battle, sir."

"Order of battle, *señor?* Such an esoteric phrase. My generals, including Ignacio here, use expressions like that all the time. Are *you* by chance a military man as well as—"

"Señor Juárez!" It was Sarah Anderson. "Mister James is in the capital looking for investments. I am going to try to interest him in shares of the Sierra Verde."

Juárez flicked his sharp black eyes to Sarah, then back to James. Even if the Indian let the "order of battle" slip pass without further remark, and even if he believed Sarah's vouching for him, he did not trust the American. "Will you, like so many foreigners, only invest in Mexico if France is victorious here, Señor James?"

"Mexico and its people will prosper no matter who governs them, Señor Juárez. Investors will swarm to its shores."

The agate eyes bored deep into James's. Juárez seemed at the point of saying something more, but he shrugged instead and turned to Sarah again.

"I would like very much to spend the afternoon with you and your friends, Señorita Anderson, but duties in my office call me. *Por favor,* enjoy your stay at Chapultepec."

Comonfort, who had followed Juárez to the coach and stood braced to attention as the stocky man climbed in, motioned the corporal and his soldier helper to begin serving the rest of the luncheon.

James could not relax; there were far too many things to consider in the wake of Juárez's departure. He was fully aware of how close the stroke of the sword had come before Sarah blocked it. The reference to "Sierra Verde" puzzled him, but it must have had meaning for the President of Mexico; it was the one thing that stopped the probing.

The general and Sarah had taken seats at the far end of the table and she was now saying something to him, earnest words if he could judge from her look, but words he could not hear above the animated conversation between Solange and O'Leary, and the clatter of dishes and silverware. Suddenly Comonfort brightened at something Sarah said and James heard his response clearly enough.

"Ah, but *señorita,* they will never get this far. General Ortega will see to it that Puebla does not fall. I will never have to fight them here at Chapultepec."

O'Leary must have picked up on this last. "That's good to hear, General Comonfort. The new French siege guns would play hell with those old walls of yours," he said.

"You are certainly correct about that, Lieutenant. The castle, for all that it looks impregnable, is not an easily defensible redoubt. You *norteamericanos* proved that in 1847."

"I don't know much about that engagement, sir." The Marine laughed. "I was only six years old at the time, barely old enough to *play* at war."

"Some who *should* have been only playing fought here—and died." Did the others at the table catch the bitterness in the general's voice? "Perhaps . . . ," Comonfort went on, "Señor James remembers . . . ?"

It was as if someone had triggered a land mine in James's head. "I—I have read about it, *señor general.*" He prayed his stammer had gone unnoticed. "It must have been a tragic day for Mexico." He *had* read about it, but the accounts of what had happened here had not begun to tell the story as it had been lived that day.

"Gentlemen!" Sarah said. "Would it be too much to ask to let the past sleep on a lovely afternoon like this?"

It was another rescue, if only for the moment.

Why, Sarah wondered, had she rallied to his side the way she had?

She owed him nothing. He remained a soldier of the most contemptible kind, a hired sword; that he was a fellow American could not change that.

But at Comonfort's remarks about the castle and the terrible battle fought here fifteen years ago, she had seen much the same look cloud his face that darkened it at the embassy affair. It touched something deep inside her.

Blessedly, the mood at the table turned lighter in the wake of her admonition to the three men to forget the past. Comonfort's officers' mess, or whatever the provenance for the meal, had outdone itself. The roast was splendid, the side dishes and condiments superb, as was the wine whose label read "Romanée Conti." She had last tasted this great French red at Charlotte's in the Faubourg St. Germain.

The general smiled when she complimented him on his choice.

"I should not take too much credit, *señorita.* It came as a gift to me from General Porfirio Díaz. One of his cavalry patrols surprised a French provision pack train near Orizaba and the wine was a pleasant dividend. I confess I am glad *El Presidente* did not see it. Even though I know he has a great love for champagne, Benito Juárez is in most ways what I believe you Americans call a Puritan. I love and respect my president, but it is often hard to labor under his somewhat disapproving eye."

Jason's dwarf coachman-servant, still seated in the carriage in the shade of the *ahuehuete* trees, was now feasting from a plate the corporal had taken him. He had kept his distance since their arrival in the clearing, but he had also fixed his glittering eye on Solange the entire time, save for when Benito Juárez had drawn everyone's attention. Solange had not returned his gaze.

Jason James might possess much the same roving, assessing eye his servant did, even if it had not yet been turned on Sarah Anderson in any uncomfortable way.

For one thing, it could well be that he was already deeply involved with the Mexican girl she had seen in the carriage at the bank, something one could expect from a soldier, from everything she had heard. There had been tiny signs that Matt was up to the same sort of thing on the nights he did not wait on Solange and her. She knew very little of the ways of men in this regard, certainly could not trust the meager knowledge gleaned from the risque burlesques witnessed at the Folies, nor from reading *des romans,* the French novels she had told M. Auguste she perused only to improve her skill with the sophisticated French of Paris. Reticent Henri Gallimard, who had bestowed on her exactly three chaste kisses in all their time together, had not been much help, either.

Something about the self-possessed look of the girl in front of the bank spoke of intimate, personal knowledge of all these things.

Sarah Anderson—sitting with friends who valued her and a high-ranking, cosmopolitan Mexican officer, festively wined and dined in this pleasant, softly shaded grove, rich, well-dressed, bejewelled and parasoled, young and healthy, traveled as much as any Bostonian of her acquaintance, and from comments heard all her life attractive, perhaps even beautiful, certainly intelligent—knew a paralyzing moment of blinding, jade-colored jealousy . . . of a mere girl in a cotton peasant dress!

"*¡Ahora, mis amigos!*" Comonfort exclaimed. "It is time to show you all the castle. Señor James, if you could have your driver follow me, we will enter through the western sallyport. After a look at the old residential apartments on the second floor we can mount to the roof for a tour of the high battlements. I have prepared some entertainment."

James beckoned Cipi to bring the carriage around. Clouds were beginning to roll in above the western reaches of the forest and a thin mist was snaking into the clearing.

Do not storm now, he pleaded silently. He had steeled himself as well as he ever could for the things he would see and remember in the next hour.

Let's get this over with, Cousin Aaron. We've both waited long enough.

18
▲▲▲▲

The last hollow roar of Comonfort's rooftop "entertainment," his seven gun salute for a mortified Sarah Anderson, died away. James watched with momentary amusement as she pulled her slim white hands from her ears.

The Mexican general had made a big mistake if he thought he could impress this woman with such a feeble if noisy display of firepower. All the artillery of the entire

French Army crashing at once probably could not have brought a greater look of discomfort and disapproval from her. She had recoiled at each of the seven reports as if she had taken a direct hit herself. Comonfort, monitoring the performance of his gunnery team, had not seen her reaction, and likely thought her overjoyed by the salute he had arranged *"solamente* for you, *señorita."*

The eighteen gunners swabbed out the barrels of the six old artillery pieces, formed in two ranks at the sharp order of a Republican captain who looked even younger than Matt O'Leary, and left the roof at a silent command from the captain's saber.

"If they can do a gun drill as smartly with someone shooting at them," Matt said as the last of the team disappeared, "they will give the Frenchies all they can handle, general."

"I assure you they are more than *tropas de procesión*—parade soldiers—lieutenant." Perhaps, James thought. There seemed more hope than assurance in the general's voice.

"I must say, though, sir," Matt added, "that they look a little young for combat troops in the kind of war facing the Republic. The French Army under General Forey consists almost entirely of veterans, particularly the Zouaves, the Chasseurs, and the Legion."

"Younger soldiers than these have fought with *mucho valor* for Mexico before—and from this very spot. My Chapultepec garrison has the tradition of *los niños heroes* behind it."

James had by this time girded himself well against what was to come.

The trip through the apartments downstairs revealed to his professional eye a series of possible small, closet battlegrounds to be fought for at bayonet point one by one when and if Bazaine gave the order. For his companions the tour was every bit the pleasant stroll Comonfort intended it to be. In the old living quarters and the more public chambers of the castle were heavy, carved Spanish furniture, floor-to-ceiling tapestries flecked with gold thread, dusty statues, and in the grand ballroom with its gleaming parquet floor the full length portrait, not of a Mexican or a Spaniard, but of the great Colombian, Simon Bolívar. The Liberator seemed to be smiling a faintly cynical smile down on Comonfort and his little band of sightseers.

"The castle is like something out of a storybook, general," Sarah said as she gazed up at the painting.

"Not always a noble story, señorita, nor a comforting one for my poor country," Comonfort said. "Look at the portraits on the far wall, por favor. The one just to the right of San Sebastian is that comic old fraud Agustin de Iturbide. This was to be his throne room when he declared himself emperor forty years ago, conveniently forgetting that the people of Mexico, having just shaken off one monarch, would not take kindly to bowing their heads to still another. It cost many lives to get him there, but in the end he went ignobly to the wall. The Austrian Archduke the French intend to install on a similar false throne here in Chapultepec should keep that usurper's fate in mind."

James thought he saw Sarah shudder at this last.

If she had, she recovered quickly. "I forget, even with all the daily reminders in the capital, just how old Mexico is. Where I come from we flatter ourselves that we are the cradle of liberty in the Americas."

"Ah, but you are, señorita. We were a little slower here in Mexico, even if my country was something resembling a nation much, much longer than the United States. Cortés and Mendoza and the gachupines and criollos who followed them through the corridors of power were not what any astute observer would call los demócratas. Some were Republicans, sí, but hardly democrats. Not like El Presidente."

James would have listened willingly to more of this, particularly to anything Sarah said in reply, but he had a job to do, one he should begin now, before the last guest arrived.

With the last echo of Comonfort's salute gone from the rooftop, he looked around him. He was a soldier, not a tourist. He had to assess these defenses now—if his memories permitted him to do it.

This had not been a roof over living quarters in 1847, but an open courtyard with four stories of gun galleries along the southern side and with stairs and ladders connecting them. Here Lance Corporal Jason James and Company C of the Fourth Kansas Rifles, Captain Aaron Sheffield commanding, fought their way to the top and wedged the Siege of Chapultepec into the history books.

The half dozen pieces of antique artillery used for Comonfort's salute to Sarah, round-shot muzzle loaders that belonged more in a war museum than in defense of a vital strong point, poked their mute black barrels through the crenellations on the south wall. If forged metal could look tired, these ugly old weapons appeared to have collapsed into fatigue long before today's ceremonial salvos. That had not always been the case. They were probably some of the same guns that poured fire down on the Fourth Kansas in '47. They had not stopped Winfield Scott's army then; they would not even *slow* Bazaine's if it came this way.

Unless he uncovered some new plan of defense, Chapultepec in 1863 would present even less of a problem than Cerro de Guadalupe at Puebla last year, and certainly less of a problem than it posed in '47. A true fortress then, it was now more palace than redoubt, "storybook" as Sarah called it. To be sure, James had discovered that Mexican military engineers had replaced the flimsy postern gates of fifteen years ago with new ironclad timber ones, stout enough at a glance, but which would yield in seconds to modern sappers. There were a score of other ways into this warren of weathered stone for determined attackers, too.

It was a matter of exquisite irony that if he ultimately had to take this castle for Bazaine, the French general would want him to do it without turning it into a ruin, in order that French goldsmiths, masons, cabinetmakers, and other artisans could prepare it for the new Emperor and his Belgian wife. From what James had just seen on the lower floors, the Mexican governments of the last fifteen years have already done a large part of the remodeling Bazaine might be considering.

He detached himself from Comonfort, Sarah, and the other two and began walking toward the edge of the roof. He knew what he would look down on when he reached it, and who would look down with him. He knew, too, how differently they would respond to what they saw.

Unlike the slopes fronting Cerro de Guadalupe last year, the approaches to Chapultepec back in '47 held no clumps of barbarous *maguey* to hide snipers, no trenches to impede the skirmish lines, and no sluiceway moat where men might drown. The field leading to the castle's high southern wall when the Fourth Kansas Rifle Regiment under Colonel Selman Hawkins reached it was a grassy slope, hardly more difficult to ascend than crossing some parade grounds. It *was* a parade ground in '47; this southeastern section of the castle housed the military college then, the "Mex West Point" according to Sergeant Danno Sullivan, the tough old regular from Topeka who had saved James's life at Cerro Gordo. "Don't reckon many of the class of '48 will live to graduate," the sergeant said that day.

At the parapet James felt the last guest come to stand beside him. He did not turn to look; he knew exactly who had come. This phantom has waited for him at this same high parapet for more than a decade and a half.

"Let us talk a bit about that day in 1847, Jason."

It was the same strong, clear voice that uttered commands as easily in battle as it did in barracks, and James feared that if he turned he might actually *see* Aaron Sheffield, wearing that same look of threat and retribution he wore in the twilight of that day in '47 when the killing ended and the echo of the last shot died on the toxic wind.

"You failed me that day, Jason. You failed yourself."

James placed his two hands firmly on the battlements, leaned far forward, and looked down.

The mist that had begun to seep into the picnic clearing as they left it had reached the slope at the foot of the wall. It was thicker now, and it might have been the lingering white pall of powder smoke of fifteen years ago.

"Yes, Jason, that's where we broke out and finished the attack, down there under those three trees opposite the postern gate. Things look different from up here than they did then, but as your new masters would say, 'plus ca change, plus c'est la meme chose.' Do you remember that day?"

The three trees were much bigger now, and all leafed out again. They were black skeletons when the smoke cleared in '47, their branches stripped clean of greenery by the cannon and rifle fire.

"In spite of your failure it was a splendid day, Jason. Pity all of them up here on the parapet had to die. They could not match our fighting qualities, of course, but in the way they died they were as fine as any soldiers I have known—oh, so fine! Remember?"

James pushed himself back from the parapet, but his eyes stayed fixed on the three cypresses spiraling up out of the earth.

It is suddenly September 12, 1847.

He is crouched down there a quarter of a mile short of the three trees, getting ready to mount the slope leading to this wall. As a lance corporal in Company C of the Fourth Kansas Rifles of Shield's Brigade, Captain Aaron Sheffield commanding, he is to start his climb to the castle heights exactly half a minute after the New York Volunteers' field guns stop pounding the Mexican position.

If Cousin Aaron is right—and he nearly always is—this could be the last combat I will see in Mexico.

I fix my bayonet. I am ready. Today is my eighteenth birthday, and it will be wonderful to celebrate it with the last victory of the war.

Cousin Aaron, saber drawn, will lead the company from well out in front as he has done in every engagement since we left the frigate Raritan in Veracruz.

"The Mexicans would be insane to continue this war once the castle falls," Aaron said yesterday. "And it will fall." He was in high spirits then. But my cousin and captain does not share my eagerness this morning. Last night he begged, pleaded, with Colonel Hawkins to let Company C lead the main attack, but at our cold mess this morning he told us Hawkins gave us only this far southern wall. "It is a sop, a sideshow compared to the main thrust to the west." Aaron sounded as bitter then as I had ever heard him. "I wanted to go in against their best. I wanted the main flag tower. I have earned it. It is an outrage!"

But that was this morning. Now Cousin Aaron is frozen calm, and I know somehow I should fear this even more. Since Veracruz something dark has grown in my cousin when he does not get a chance for some greater glory, something dark that I cannot understand.

Off to the west, and around the corner from the flag tower, the Voltigeurs' howitzer battery of Lieutenant Reno has wheeled into place, and from the sudden thunder of the guns I know they have already brought the west wall under fire. The dragoons of Clarke's Brigade must now be in the saddle, lances lowered toward the sallyport, ready to charge on through it once the field pieces blow off its wooden doors. The New England Ninth will stream in on the heels of the dragoons. It will not last long after that, Aaron says.

As lance corporal, I am to move out with the regimental colors, only a pace behind my captain.

He gives us our last instructions. "When we reach those three trees, take cover. Dig in deep. The riflemen on the wall will try to keep us pinned. In the long run they will fail. Once we are in position, the guns will move up close behind us and begin a second barrage. Our first task is to keep the sharpshooters from getting at our gunners. When the artillery has finished its work on the postern gate, we shall make the final attack, such as it will be."

Then he says something else. "Once inside . . . I want no prisoners!"

No prisoners? The words are a bludgeon, and the men of

the company stir uneasily. This is something new, even for the dark side of the Cousin Aaron which has come out in our time in Mexico.

The New York guns have stopped. I count the thirty seconds to moveout time.

"Forward the Fourth!" Aaron shouts. His voice rings above the din of the rifle and cannon fire from the gunports.

I stride out, my eye on my captain's beckoning sword.

The regimental drummers somewhere behind the company begin their tattoo as the captain, the colors, and the first skirmish line move through the woods, stepping over exposed root systems as high as Kansas fences. Field gun and small arms reports muffle the drumbeats to something I feel more than hear. Heavy fire comes from the wall and from time to time, when the smoke drifts away, and before new smoke rolls in again, the wall itself becomes a sheet of flame. From the shrieks and curses around me I know some men of the company have already fallen, good friends, probably; but I cannot turn to see who or how many have been hit. My captain has trained me too well for that.

The Mexicans on the wall mean to make a fight of it, even if the men behind the guns up there are not those "best" Aaron hoped to face. I have not seen a single enemy soldier yet. The smoke hides even the infantry protecting the men working the heavy guns. A dark head shows now and then, only to disappear after a flash of fire. But a slight wind is stirring, and sooner or later the gunners on the wall and the riflemen defending them will be exposed.

Miraculously, no one in the color guard next to me has been hit, and in less than a minute I reach the three trees. The men of the first skirmish line surge around me; I drop to my knees behind a monstrous root, lay my rifle down, and begin digging with the short-handled shovel from my pack. Even before I finish, the repositioned guns at the rear of the Fourth Kansas begin throwing round shot at the parapets. At the top of the wall, huge blocks of masonry break loose and fall away, partly uncovering the guns and the Mexicans who tend them.

"Fire at will when you are under cover, Company C!"

Captain Sheffield calls. He towers over us, his saber sheathed for the moment, his telescope trained on the wall. He will dig no hole himself. He never hides.

Three minutes of hard shoveling produces a small revetment just deep enough to hide me. I have been too busy to see if any more of my comrades have died or taken wounds. Now and then a ricochet screams off a nearby rock or a ball thuds into a cypress trunk. Fire from the top of the wall is tearing through the trees. Fountains of dirt spout from the ground around me. I am down on my belly in my shallow trench, my rifle stock at my shoulder, the barrel laid across the root.

My captain's voice soars above the noise again. "Fire! Drive them from the guns. Kill them!"

Heavy fire breaks across the last line of woods on either side. The poor devils atop and behind that wall have never faced an onslaught like this before.

Volley after volley rips through the men on the wall, but the company and I are firing blind and there is no way to tell what effect our fire has.

"Cease fire!"

Now I hear the caissons of the New York guns rumbling up close behind the company. One of them almost rolls right over me; its iron-rimmed left wheel breaks down the side of my revetment.

When it comes to a stop the crew leaps to feed the gun, falls away as the match is set. The blast almost pitches me from my trench, smoke pours from the cannon's muzzle, and in half a second the postern gate at the base of the wall is ripped to shreds. The New York men are good. Two more thundering reports follow, and now I can see far into a courtyard behind the wall.

"Through the gate, Company C. Follow on!"

I am on my feet and running for the opening before the bugle sounds, but even so my captain is out ahead of me.

Half the company regroups with the captain and me inside the tunnel leading to the courtyard from the postern gate, and now I hear the noise of the even larger battle at the west end of the fortress. Something new and different must be happening *there; mixed with the sound of gunfire I hear men shouting. Americans.*

"Clarke and the New Englanders must have forced their way in, too," Cousin Aaron says. "The castle will fall in minutes." There is no joy in his voice, only the bitterness again. His eyes are wilder than I have ever seen them.

Across the courtyard from the tunnel a covered walkway faces the wall above us. Without a word this time my captain races for it, I and the company on his heels. I throw myself behind a gun carriage, turn and see the inner side of the whole south wall, the connected gun decks, the rifle ports, and, at the very top, the platform of the long gallery we kept under fire until our guns opened the postern gate.

And for the first time today I actually see the enemy.

Lined up as if in an honors formation on the long deck just below the top of the wall, standing against what still remains of the crenellations, or huddled in the gaps blasted in the battlements, are thirty or forty uniformed figures I take at first to be toy soldiers, honest-to-God, actual TOYS.

But then I see that the tiny men in the crisp white trousers and bright blue tunics, and wearing chin-strapped, hard black shakos, are not men at all but boys, little more than children— the cadets of Chapultepec! As I watch, one of them pulls a flag from the stonework.

Some are still busy at the guns, trying desperately to answer those of the New Yorkers still battering the wall from the other side. The rest carry rifles half again as long as they are tall.

They are totally exposed, and apparently as yet unaware that Company C has broken through the gate.

"Bring them under fire!" Aaron says.

Good Lord. Does not he see what I see?

My reflexes make me aim. The cadet who fills my sights cannot be twelve years old. The others look as young.

For the first and only time since Cousin Aaron swore me in as a recruit back in Kansas, I ask myself questions.

Can I squeeze the trigger on a child? Can I follow my captain's orders and take no prisoners? Are these questions a soldier under oath has any right to ask?

Then the boy in my sights crumples to his knees. Some other man in the company has found the same target and asked no questions.

Three more of the little soldiers on the wall are hit; two sag into the arms of comrades, the third staggers as if drunk, then pitches sideways and off the edge, toppling crazily toward the bottom of the wall. I feel myself sicken as the small body thuds on the courtyard's fieldstone floor.

I shift my rifle a few inches to the left, look for and find another target, another doll-like soldier.

I cannot squeeze the trigger.

"Corporal James!" Captain Sheffield looms above me, a blue ghost in the smoke. "Fire, soldier! That is the enemy up there." The captain bangs the flat of his saber on my rifle barrel, and somehow I find the strength to pull the trigger, but my eyes close even before the report, and when they open again the cadet is still in my sights, still standing. I have not missed a target this easy since my first day on the firing range at Leavenworth.

I lower my rifle and look up at my captain.

"If you do not employ your weapon to better effect, Corporal James," he says, "I will have you shot, or what should be worse for a man of honor, drummed out of my command as soon as this is over—kin or not!"

It is the blackest reproach I remember hearing from the man who has taught me just about everything I know.

There is no time to think about it now.

"Captain! Look!" It is the big voice of Sergeant Danno Sullivan. He is pointing at the tower at the center of the castle, well to the left of the courtyard. "They've struck their colors, Captain! We can break off our action now, can't we, sir?"

Sure enough, the Mexican flag is dropping. The halyards whip and clang against the metal flagstaff.

"I do not see that, Sergeant." Cousin Aaron's whisper is savage. "Nor do you. Tell your men to continue firing!"

Rifles bark all across the company front. Mine is not one of them. The cadets on the gun deck high above the company try to return the fire, but are cut down one by one. After half a dozen deliberate, but almost leisurely volleys, only seven or eight still stand. Only the one with the flag still holds a weapon.

"Are they surrendering, Captain Sheffield?" Sergeant Sullivan asks.

"I will take no surrender, sergeant. Fire!"

The September heat has become unbearable.

But what happens next chills me to the bone.

The Mexican cadet with the red-green-and-white flag drops his rifle and gathers the banner's folds around him. The boy lifts his head, cries "¡Viva Mexico!" and steps out into the air as if marching to an unheard drum.

His companions hesitate for only a fraction of a second before following him, echoing his cry of "¡Viva Mexico!", then dropping from the gun deck like birds shot down in flight.

The bodies of the children lie helter-skelter on the flat stones of the courtyard. Only one moves. He pulls his slim, broken body half upright, and blood gushes torrents from his mouth.

"Corporal James," Captain Aaron Sheffield says. "You now have a chance to redeem yourself. Finish that man with your bayonet."

I cannot move. I am down on my knees, vomiting until there is nothing left to vomit. Somehow I bring myself to speak from a throat burned raw with bile.

"No, sir."

Cousin Aaron's look of contempt for me is an even stronger acid than that which still scalds my throat.

He walks toward the fallen boy with his saber.

True to his word, Cousin Aaron takes no prisoners.

I feel a hand on my shoulder and look up at Danno Sullivan.

"He's crazy, you know," the old sergeant says. "Our captain is an absolute raving looney."

I am leaving Mexico. My war is over, and perhaps it will be my last. Aaron finds me on the dock at Veracruz where I have been talking with Danno Sullivan and another man from the company. My cousin will go home on another ship, the one for *officers. He motions me to him and I step away from the other two.*

"I have a few things to say to you before we part, Jason," Cousin Aaron says. *It is the first time he has spoken to me since Chapultepec. "If you have ever entertained the idea of becoming a soldier, forget about it. You do not have the talent for it, and from what transpired at Chapultepec, certainly no calling. You must know the only reason I did not have you court martialed after your insubordination there is because of the personal shame it would have brought to me. But do not think you can escape the judgment I have made forever. I would kill you this very instant for what you have done to me, for the way you have jeopardized my career, but I cannot risk further damage to it now."*

"What have I done, Cousin Aaron?"

"You know."

"But I don't . . ."

"Do not add lying to your other failings, Jason. Just remember this. Someday . . . when all my wars are over, and my career is not at stake . . . I will find you. And on that day we will fight each other."

"I could never fight you, Cousin Aaron."

"Yes, you could, Jason. And you will. One of us will die that day. It is carved in stone."

He turns away before I can say another word and walks toward his vessel's gangplank.

In minutes the transport he has boarded leaves the dock. He stands at the rail and stares down at me. His gaze is more deadly than any enemy fire I have faced. Why does he hate me so? What does he think I have done to him? Perhaps I failed him as he says, but surely not so badly as to bring on this.

I want to shout my questions out to him, but now the ship has moved too far off for him to hear me.

Danno Sullivan is at my side again.

"I'm sorry," the sergeant says. "He's a great soldier, and I know he's your cousin, but like I said, he sure is crazy." He falls silent for a moment, then goes on. "I'm a little ashamed of myself, Jason. I wrote a letter to General Scott about what

happened at Chapultepec—but I didn't have the guts to sign my name.''

My heart empties when I realize I can never tell Cousin Aaron that—and put the man who saved my life at risk.

"Jason . . . Jason!" The woman's voice comes to him softly, but with deep insistence. "Are you all right, Jason?"

The gentle question pulls him back from the parapet and out of the depths of 1847.

It is the third time in their brief acquaintance Sarah Anderson has provided rescue of a sort for Jason James.

19

▲▲▲▲

"Antonio Pérez in my back garden at nine in the morning, Matt? Why didn't he come to the front door? He'll terrify poor old Pedro. He'll collapse right into his rose bushes."

"Tonito doesn't want to embarrass you with your neighbors, Miss Anderson."

"How could he embarrass me? My neighbors couldn't possibly know who or what he is."

Matt grinned. "Wait until you see him. *El Jefe* isn't ordinarily this considerate of people's feelings, but you made a mighty big impression on him during our trip here from Orizaba last year. Tonito's a very independent cuss. He despises the city, and would probably have turned down anyone else's request to come here." A look of apology and sympathy erased the grin. "I wouldn't get my hopes too high, Miss Anderson; he expressed reluctance when I told him roughly what you wanted. It was all I could do just to get him to listen to you. I hate to say I told you so, but I never thought trying to enlist Pérez was a good idea."

"I know, but he just *has* to help us! Go on back through the kitchen, please, and bring Mister Pérez in." She turned to the maid who had just shown the marine into the parlor. "Rosa, could you make coffee, *por favor?*"

Matt frowned. "I think things would go better if you offered him something a little stronger."

"Well . . . we have the wine General Comonfort gave me and a bottle or two of *cerveza*. No spirits, though. Which shall I have Rosa put out."

"I *hope* beer or wine will do the trick, but I wouldn't bet much on it."

"Wait. Solange might just have a bit of cognac."

"Can you persuade the old girl to part with it?"

Matt disappeared through the hallway leading to the back of the house.

Liquor or no, how was she going to deal with Pérez if they got down to cases and she somehow managed to maneuver him somewhere near agreement? An offer of money was probably in order, but some sixth sense whispered it would be politic to make sure he looked on it as *pay*, and not as bribery or some disguised gratuity.

She hurried to Solange's room, where the duenna sat by an open window mending the shoulder strap on a chemise.

"We have company, Solange."

"Quelle personne, ma chère?"

"Do you remember *le brigand* Señor Perez who escorted us here to the capital last year?"

"Mais oui! Est-ce qu'il est ici, maintenant?"

"Yes. He came with Matt."

The Frenchwoman's eyes widened; she was clearly excited, and perhaps even a touch frightened, but she looked pleased, too. She had been taken by the bandit at her first sight of him. Sarah took the plunge.

"Forgive me, Solange, but do you by any remote chance have any cognac or other spirits we could offer him?"

The chemise slipped from Solange's lap. She reddened and sputtered. *"M-mademoiselle!* Why . . . why would you think . . . ?" Then she pressed her mouth into a firm, thin line of defiance. "But, of course, *chérie.*"

"Merci."

She returned to the parlor to find Matt and Pérez already there, and saw immediately why the lieutenant made his sly remark "wait until you see him."

The *plateado* seemed even bigger and more brutish than she remembered him. He was dressed in the same black *charro* outfit he had worn every day on the journey to Mexico City; it was even more grease-stained than on the long ride, and now grimy with trail dust. The heavy beard, touched with gray, bristled. Two enormous bandoliers, with cartridges looking as if they might be the teeth of some voracious antediluvian creature, made a threatening X on his barrel chest, and a gunbelt sagged from the weight of an enormous pistol. He had not removed his sombrero.

Matt was right. Her neighbors would have taken him for exactly the fearsome thug he was had he knocked at her front door in the full light of the morning sun. And they would indeed have *heard* him knock. A discreet, light tap would be impossible for this intensely physical man whose every breath and movement hinted at unbridled power. She heard a tiny, throaty gasp from Solange, now at her elbow. Sarah could understand it; Pérez looked even more dangerous in this bright parlor with its civilized atmosphere and appointments than he had when he burst into that dark, smoky coach stop that night on the road from Orizaba.

The last place Antonio Pérez belonged was in a room festooned with lace and filled with china, porcelain, and doilies.

"*Buenos dias*, Señor Pérez," Sarah said.

"*¿Como esta, señorita? Perdon—señoritas.*"

"Sit down, please, sir."

The bandit looked around the room, and Sarah wondered if it was because he wanted to choose a seat where his clothing would not be as apt to leave a stain. He picked the davenport whose cushions were covered by a dark *sarape*, and lowered his giant body into it.

Solange almost leaped to him with her half bottle, showing more courage and elan than Sarah might have expected. The Frenchwoman had taken only one cut-glass goblet from the sideboard; obviously she was not going to offer any of her precious nectar to Matt or Sarah. She had, judging by her suddenly nearly bold comportment, fortified *herself* with a hasty swallow on the way to the parlor.

"Lieutenant O'Leary says he's already told you what my problem is, Señor Pérez," Sarah said.

"*Sí, señorita.*" He drained off the small draught Solange poured him, squinted first at the empty crystal glass with something like contempt or at the very least disappointment, fastened his black eyes on Sarah as Solange refilled it—to the rim this time, bless her—and went on. "In my business we are not in the habit of stopping fellow *plateados* from making a living. I am a strong man, and a feared leader, but if it looked as if I was trying to take all the Zacatecas silver for myself, the other *jefes* might band together against me. I do not think I can be of help, *señorita.*"

It sounded final, but she could not give up this easily.

"My manager at the Sierra Verde, Señor Alberto Moreno, tells me you were a friend of my brother Samuel. Is that so, Señor Pérez?"

Pérez said nothing, but his eyes bored into her, and his huge hand reached up to stroke his beard. "Now I make the association, *señorita.* Your resemblance to your *hermano* Don Samuel is very strong. *Sí, el patrón* of the Sierra Verde was an *amigo.*" He fell silent and Sarah held her breath. Twice she started to speak, but kept in mind something she had learned about this country in her nine months here: a prototypical Mexican male such as Pérez could never be pushed or made to appear too readily persuaded by a *woman*, particularly not with another man looking on.

Matt coughed into the silence, and it was like a gun shot. The bandit chieftain's glass was empty again and Solange took notice of the signal, crossed to Pérez as she might have approached the effigy of a saint in one of the churches she and Matt frequented, and poured him another drink. It was the last one in the bottle.

"Did the lieutenant also tell you, Señor Pérez, that President Juárez himself suggested I seek your help?"

The big man grunted. He put his glass down on the small table at the side of the davenport.

"*Señorita,*" Pérez said, "what need have you for so much silver? Are you not rich enough?"

"I know of no reason you should believe me when I say that I don't want any such treasure for myself, but I beg you to. I live on my own money, not on the earnings of the Sierra Verde. My brother's mine employs something like one hundred fifty people who wouldn't otherwise have jobs, and whatever profit the mine makes goes to the unfortunate here in the capital and to the poor in Zacatecas. There can be, of course, *no* profits if bandits continue to prey on the silver trains."

"*Bandidos* must eat, *también, señorita.* How can I be sure that if the French *puercos* succeed in their war against my country those same profits will not go to feed *them?*"

"Because you have my word on it, *señor.*"

The giant on the davenport stirred, pushed his great head toward her, and the salt-and-pepper beard and mustache took on an even more bristling look. Her heart fell; he was going to turn her down.

Pérez cleared his throat. "You must write a letter for me to take to Alberto Moreno at the Sierra Verde, *señorita.* My men are highly skilled at getting information, but Don Alberto is an *hombre muy dedicado,* and very brave. Even if we beat him half to death, without your permission he would never tell me the things I need to know—the exact days and hours he will make shipments of ore, and their precise routes—if I and my *compañeros* are to protect your silver trains from *pícaros* like us."

Another surprise awaited her—or rather two.

First, and possibly the more astonishing of the two was the first smile to light the face of Antonio Pérez.

The second came at the end of his next spate of words. "We must now discuss the matter of *compensación,*

Señorita Anderson. I would be the object of much unpleasant laughter if *la fraternidad de los plateados* ever thought I worked for nothing. I would be obliged to deal harshly with those of my *amigos* who dared to laugh. *Con qué*, the payment—since the *señorita* assures him she desires no *dinero* for herself—will be one fifth the value in *pesos* of every shipment I see safely to its destination—"

She opened her mouth to protest, but only managed one sharp "*Señor*—" that died as his heavy voice continued to roll over her.

"—to be paid directly to Sor Francisca Angélica Olivares, the Mother Superior of the orphanage at San Sebastian . . ."

She floated on a cloud of euphoria and self-satisfaction the rest of that day, feeling that for the first time since she had arrived in Mexico she had actually accomplished something.

But throughout the evening the visit to Chapultepec began to nag at her with even more persistence. Something deeply troubling had happened in the aftermath of General Comonfort's ridiculous cannonade.

Jason James at the parapet kept emerging in her inner vision.

After the general's tour of the castle Jason suddenly, and with an abruptness which a few days earlier she would have put down to a disregard of common courtesy, left Comonfort, Matt, Solange, and her to stride to the low, crenellated wall, standing then between two of the cannons as if at attention—as if reporting for duty to some ghostly commander. She in turn had moved to his side in curiosity about what he might be looking at, but drawn, too, by something much more compelling.

The biting odor of powder smoke still poisoned the air, and with his erect bearing he looked for a second the quintessential military man surveying with cruel satisfaction a devastation he himself had ordered.

Then he leaned forward, placed his hands on the top of

the parapet, and bowed his head, but not in an attitude of prayer; it was more as if he awaited the blade of the guillotine.

He twisted his head as if he were listening to something, and the slight movement turned his face toward her.

He looked ravaged, his eyes two deep wells of pain. He made no sound.

Jason James was a man in desperate need of comfort. He was also, she knew in a sorrowing flash of insight, a man who did not know—much less admit to—any such thing, and one who would have to be almost beaten into accepting it.

Only the rashest of women would have the temerity to speak to him now and to venture into the dark recesses of such suffering.

She called his name.

In the middle of a night when sleep eluded her until the small hours, and when the crackle of the cicadas outside her window sounded like the burning leaves of a New England autumn bonfire or like the cocking of a thousand pistols, Sarah Kent Anderson reached a decision.

Perhaps the success of the meeting with Antonio Pérez had something to do with it. There was no doubt the discovery that the bandit wanted to help Sor Francisca and her abandoned children had shown her the narrowness of at least some of her views of men in general, and of those she had met here in Mexico in particular.

It was high time to come to terms with the feelings she was beginning to have about Jason.

"I think I shall serve him that roast kid our Mexican friends call *cabrito*, Solange. Pedro can dig the pit to cook it in at the back of the garden. You liked the kid when we had dinner at the Montenegros, as I recall."

"It is all the same to me, *mademoiselle*," Solange sniffed.

The Frenchwoman had been stiff-necked ever since Sarah told her that she wanted to give Mr. James an "intimate" dinner. It was impossible to tell whether her attitude was due to her loyalty to Henri Gallimard or to the fact that *she* was being excluded. Either way, there had not been a single *ma chère* or *chérie* since Sarah asked her if she could join Matt at one of the evening services they frequently attended.

"Rosa can do the serving, Solange," she said.

"Oui, but Rosa is a disaster in the kitchen with anything other than those satanic swills Mexicans call food, *mademoiselle!"*

"Don't worry. Except for the *cabrito,* which Pedro will look after, I'll do the cooking myself."

Solange snorted. "If a woman wishes to catch a man with her *cuisine,* she had better make certain it is *nonpareil!"*

"Good grief, you old busybody! I'm not trying to catch a man."

"Non? Then Solange is not French!"

"You could make a *soupe a l'oignon* or a *potage bonne femme* before you and Matt leave for church Friday night, but only if you really want to."

"We'll see."

She went to her desk, penned and sealed the note to Jason inviting him to dinner, found Pedro weeding the kitchen garden at the sunny edge of the back patio, and asked him to take it to the *posada* where Jason lived before Rosa fixed lunch. That done, she went back to the desk and began a list of things for Solange to pick up at the market.

That would not do. She would have Pedro hitch the buggy for her and she would drive to the *mercado* and do the marketing herself. Aside from sparing Solange any more irritation, it seemed somehow fitting that *she* do almost everything connected with the dinner. And going to the market alone would give her a chance to look for a decent cognac for Solange to replace the bottle Pérez finished yesterday. She had already chosen the wine to accompany the *cabrito.* It pleased her even more now than it had at the time that General Comonfort had not listened to her protests, and had pressed on her three bottles of the wonderful Romanée Conti they drank at the picnic in Chapultepec's woodland park.

There could be no thoughts about the man who would sit across the candlelit table from her, no deep reflection on what the two of them might talk about. There could be no planning for anything other than the thoroughly innocuous, possibly mundane, conversation of two grown people who simply wanted to know each other a little better.

It would have to be as if they were meeting for the first time. In plain fact they should, of course, step swiftly along a pathway to a serious consideration of each other.

Pedro stood in front of her, his battered straw sombrero clutched across his waist.

The old gardener, always shy to the point of agony, turned the big hat in his two brown, wrinkled hands.

"I am very sorry, Doña Sarah. The Norteamericano *Señor* James left La Posada Mirador this morning." He fished in a pocket of his mudstained white shirt. "I brought back *una marca* from Señor James which *el proprietario* said he would have delivered himself tonight if I had not come along."

She tore the letter open.

Dear Miss Anderson—

First, let me explain the manner of the greeting of this note. I feel I have forfeited the right to use your first name, as you so graciously insisted.

By the time you read this, I shall be gone from Mexico City, perhaps for good. I could not leave without making a clean breast of things.

As I am sure you suspected all along, I have been far from candid and truthful with you.

I will not hide behind the fact that I told you no actual lies; withholding the *complete* truth with someone I hold in such esteem is every bit the falsehood a lie would be—it is dissembling at the very least.

It *is* true—as I told you that morning at the bank—

that I am no longer a captain in the Legion, but only because I hold the rank of major now.

But this admission is trivial beside my real disservice to the truth—and to you.

I have been here in the capital on an errand for my army that cannot be characterized as other than espionage. Please believe that I had no wish to use you as it may seem to you I did in the furtherance of my mission.

It is doubtful that you and I will meet again in any real sense of the word.

I will, however, possibly be coming to the city again at some point in the future.

I will certainly try to avoid embarrassing you, but should we, by pure chance, be put in each other's company, and should you, as would be proper and by me expected, choose not to recognize me, I will understand, indeed approve, not that you would need any such approval.

I have but one more thing to say, but say it I must, since this letter purports to be about truth.

It is admittedly presumptuous of me, but I must tell you that, for reasons of my own best left unsaid, I am grateful to you; you have affected me more profoundly than has any man or woman I have known.

With this note I am in no way asking for forgiveness; I expect and deserve none.

> Your obedient servant—
> J. J. James

20

"I have not had an enjoyable time while you were gone, *mon ami*," Pierre Boulanger said. "I've been sitting on my ass in front of this tent ever since we came here. The inactivity will kill me yet. But, look!" He pointed toward Puebla's southern walls. "It begins again . . . without you and me."

James gazed at the walls from the makeshift canteen in the tent city south of Puebla and the incredible warren of trenches General Forey's engineers had dug in the last month. A vast network of tunnels and ditches snugged against Puebla's shell-pocked southern walls—such sections of wall still standing after the opening artillery barrages— conduits now of ammunition and supplies for the attacking troops already wreaking havoc within those walls. Forey might not, as Boulanger had said once, be a first-class strategist, but in this battle at least he was being thorough—and professionally ruthless. Smoke rose from a score of places in the nearest *calles* and *avenidas*. The defenders of Puebla were catching it again. So were the attackers.

Boulanger raised a glass to his lips, while keeping a tight hold on the neck of a bottle of cheap cognac.

He had been a steady drinker when James first met him, but had confined himself to wine, not spirits, then. In the days since James's return to the army, his friend had turned to cognac—and when he could not get it, the native poison, tequila—and had done little *but* drink, managing to keep himself reasonably sober by sheer will.

Now he apparently caught James's look at the glass and bottle. "*Oui, mon ami.* I *am* drinking too much. I probably will go right on until they make some use of me."

"I understand," James said. "I suppose, like me, you have never been this close to action without being part of it."

The Frenchman made no reply, but a look of utter disgust soured his lean face. He raised the glass to his mouth again, and James looked away and began monitoring what could be seen of the battle.

This was not the failed, all-out, lightning attack of a year ago, but the unrelenting grind of street-by-street and house-by-house struggles where men died in clouds of dust and cascading rubble. Not one battle raged, but fifty or a hundred at any given moment. The Zouaves and the Tirailleurs were busy in the maze of stone nearest them. Angry bursts of small arms noise reached James and his companion. Few wounded were coming out from behind the walls; most of those hit were dying on the spot. James knew from sad experience how ghastly it must be for the musketeers and grenadiers contesting every bloody inch with an enemy who knew the ground so much better. For the foot soldier this was the worst kind of war. From what he had seen and heard since his return from the capital it was highly likely the spring and a good deal of the summer could pass before French arms prevailed over this stubborn city—an outcome as yet far from certain. With the Chasseurs unemployed and unlikely to find employment in this kind of fight, it could also be that long before Pierre entered the conflict again, unless James made the decision Bazaine asked him make at their last meeting.

The massed field pieces used to such devastating effect while James was comfortably spying for Bazaine, were silent now, and the task of taking Puebla had passed from the hands that jerked the firing lanyards of the howitzers to those carrying rifles with fixed bayonets.

Boulanger waited while another racketing of fire died away before speaking. "I have been so idle I am getting fat. The attack this time has little use for cavalry. Of the Chasseurs only *les pieds* have gone into battle. Since the first days, even the artillerymen are sulking beside their guns. Forey has deployed every Tirailleur, Zouave, and all the engineering troops, of course, but the horse Chasseurs haven't seen combat since this siege began almost two months ago."

"They haven't put Compagnie Rouge into the line, either," James said. "DuBecq tells me my men are getting rusty."

"I thought you had three companies now."

"In a manner of speaking I do, but I am not to take them

into combat yet, just hold them ready for Bazaine's orders, which apparently do not include this engagement."

"I am surprised. Legionnaires would be superb at this kind of work. What did Bazaine say? Is the attack on Chapultepec still a probability?"

"The general has not told me otherwise. Of course it will likely have to wait until we are done here."

"Bah! It should wait forever. The castle is the same useless objective now as it was for your Winfield Scott in 1847. It is of no military value. When we take Puebla and enter the Valley we should strike straight for the heart of the capital itself. I thought Bazaine of all people would understand that." He took another drink.

"Chapultepec has a *symbolic* value."

Indeed it did, and not just for the First Division of François-Achille Bazaine or for Napoleon III's intervention in Mexico. It had now become a double symbol for Major Jason James: Bazaine's objectives aside, it had also become an indelible cipher for 1847—it would be forever that; he had laid no ghosts to rest on that haunted rooftop—and the time he had spent at the parapets with Sarah Anderson had become a cachet for what life might possibly have held for him had he lived it differently.

Beyond inquiring quite decently, and for him innocently, whether Jason had seen the American woman while in the capital, Boulanger had not pressed him about her since James's return. The Frenchman had good instincts.

Cipi, too, seemed to have divined that his master had placed her off limits as a subject of conversation, but while not privy to its contents, he had seen James's deep despair as he wrote the letter to her. The dwarf shook his head in something approaching sadness—almost as if he had read the letter himself—when James sealed it and gave it to him to pass along to the owner of their *posada*.

Marcel Gallimard, still smarting under the command of the contemptuous Boulanger, had also learned that James had spent time in the capital, and had persisted in trying to discover the whereabouts and present circumstances of his brother's lady—fiancée, friend, or whatever in fact she was to the nobleman. James fought a running battle with himself for a week before he broke down and gave Gallimard the address of Sarah's house on Avenida Moctezuma. After all, he had no right to withhold such information; the insufferable young dandy—who might soon be her brother-in-law—at least had legitimate claims on her.

He knew *he* had no business keeping her in his mind—or his heart. He had meant every syllable of his farewell letter, and meant with even more fervor what he had written between the lines. The place to which he had forced her in the recesses of memory was now forbidden ground to him.

It was better this way.

Although Sofía had never mentioned Sarah since that one time at breakfast, she had not come to his bed, either, in all their time in Mexico City. Perhaps it meant nothing. Neither she nor Cipi could be here in the Legion's tent city, where James was billeted with the company. DuBecq assigned a Legionnaire—so silent he might have been mute for all James knew—to look after the wants of his major, simple and few enough in the rough camp.

But he missed the odd pair that formed his household. As for Sofía, he had foregone her easily enough during the stay in the capital. His sworn divestiture of Sarah had opened a door to the Mexican girl again he had at the very least partly closed while in Mexico City, probably out of some murky, mistaken fidelity to a passing dream. Perhaps he should close the door again, and this time latch it.

But Sofía, putting the best possible construction on it, was a camp follower. She had initiated this business, had never by word or look demanded more from him than had camp followers since long before the time of Caesar.

He still knew almost nothing about her or her antecedents; his few queries about where in Mexico she came from and what her life had been like—made on the trip to the capital and the one back to the nameless village where he dropped her and Cipi—met with vague and cloudy responses.

If Pierre Boulanger, with admirable circumspection even when in his cups, avoided any references to Sarah Anderson, he was far less fastidious about Sofía. To the Chasseur a woman was another item of an officer's equipment, as vital as a saber, a canteen, or a telescope, if requiring much less care and maintenance. While James was gone Pierre had taken a mistress of his own, a fleshy, blowsy creature from Jalisco misnamed Paloma—there was nothing dove-like about her. James only saw her once, in the same village where he deposited Cipi and Sofía, before he moved up to join Pierre.

"Your new lady friend," James said, "is a woman of considerable substance. I would have thought her more to my man Cipi's tastes than yours."

Boulanger turned lusterless eyes on him. "*Vraiment.* Paloma is not of course the same lissome nymph your Sofía is, *mon ami,*" he said, "but she will serve the purpose until we reach the capital. When this beastly, stubborn town is at last a heap of smoking gravel flying the *tricouleur,* Boulanger will doubtless find opportunities to sample women of a more elevated sort. Making love with Paloma is like riding a barge on the Seine. As is the case with such vessels, she is not too maneuverable, but if she answers the helm somewhat tardily, she has an amazing capacity to transport *les matériels.* In comparison with my *boule de suif,* your Sofía is a swift, graceful corvette. And I do not even have my dove's minimal comforts at the moment. This," he said, holding his glass toward James, "is virtually all I have. But enough of my complaints. You have not yet told me in detail about your report to Bazaine and what he said when you submitted it."

"Not sure I can. Some of it at least was confidential." He made the statement with misgiving, but he could not tell his friend quite yet how the name of Major Pierre Boulanger had figured in the meeting with the general.

"Forget I asked, *si'l vous plait.*"

When James arrived at the First Division encampment a week ago duBecq had handed him a summons from the general, and he hurried to the huge tent which served as headquarters and nerve center for Bazaine's division. The tent was large enough to hold a circus ring, pieced together with gaudy, red-white-and-blue canvas panels that made it look like a pavilion at a fourteenth-century tilting ground. The flags James had seen at Jalapa were stacked just inside the main flap, where a carpet which looked to be a genuine Oriental covered the dirt floor. Bazaine, plain, pragmatic soldier most of the time, was also a grand devotee of style. Sitting behind his field desk he appeared even fitter and younger than the Legionnaire remembered him from Jalapa. The action here at Puebla, demanding enough for his First Division, must have been a tonic for him.

The general looked up from the written report James had sent ahead.

"Major James! *Bien entendu!* I have just finished reading your excellent *précis* of your sojourn in the capital. May your old commander ask how you managed to get so close to General Comonfort?"

"By purest chance, *mon general,* not by any brilliance on my part."

"What is your assessment of that enemy officer, major?"

"He is by reputation and probably in fact a soldier of uncommon valor, general, much the same as General Ortega who commands against us here at Puebla. Word in the capital has it, however, that he would never defend a fixed position with the tenacity Ortega shows. He prefers the set-piece battle of movement in open country, and as a matter of fact is impatient for just such a fight."

Bazaine tapped James's report with his forefinger. "But he stays behind the thick walls you describe at Chapultepec."

"Yes, sir, but only because President Juárez has ordered him to do so. The president has, however, given him some latitude to respond to any perceived threat to Mexico City."

"You think then, *mon ami,* that he could be *lured* out by the prospect of a more classic engagement of charges and countercharges than by some dirty grueling business such as we are engaged in here?"

"Yes, sir."

"How?"

"If General Forey feels he can spare some major part of the First Division for an initial advance on the capital, say one that penetrates some leagues beyond Cholula, both General Comonfort and President Juárez might feel obliged to come out and meet the challenge. I don't think either of them want a fight in the city itself."

Bazaine laced his fingers together. "And when you say a major part of my division, you mean a force that would include your three companies of Legion infantry, *n'est-ce pas*? Go on, Major, and be quite specific."

"Yes, General. If I do not presume too much, that is exactly what I mean, except that I feel such a force would have more credibility as a lure to those of General Comonfort's scouts who operate between here and the Valley of Mexico if a few squadrons of Chasseurs and perhaps a battery or two of field guns could be detailed to it as well. This force must appear large enough to be a genuine threat, not merely a probe for gathering intelligence, but not so large that Comonfort and Juárez decide to hang back and choke the passes between here and the capital. If they do that we could be held up perhaps for months. Comonfort's army, even augmented by the reserves the Republicans have at Tlaxcala, must be drawn down from the mountains, met in the high plains beyond Cholula, and annihilated there."

"But the force you describe cannot possibly hope to accomplish any such annihilation."

"No, sir. But it could hold our enemy long enough for the rest of the First Division to join the action."

"*Zut alors, mon ami!* You wish to participate in the grand strategy of this war?"

"I do not think this suggestion qualifies as grand strategy, sir."

"You have selected a commander for this force, as well, major?"

"No, sir. My thinking has not gone that far."

"But if I were to agree to create such a command, would you then have at least a suggestion?"

"With the general's permission, I would rather not." ·

"Suppose I will *not* agree to your plan until I hear your recommendation for its commander? Come, come, major! Do not be coy." The tone was insistent.

"There *is* an officer I think would be ideal, general."

"And he is . . . ?"

"Major Pierre Boulanger of the Chasseurs d'Afrique."

"Un de vos amis, non?"

"Yes, sir. But I don't mention him solely out of friendship. I fought with Major Boulanger here at Puebla last year and know him for a brave and intelligent soldier. He also is the officer General de Lorencez trusted with the mission to Orizaba that prompted hostilities in this war."

"Ah, *oui*. The 'incident' at Fortín. I have been told of that. The good major is an excellent choice. But is it modesty that prevents you from making an even better one? Yourself, *par exemple?"*

Bazaine proceeded. "I see it is modesty, major, and I admire that. *Maintenant*, do not for one small moment consider it a disparagement of your abilities if I agree that you are *not* my man. I have something quite different in mind for you, something far more commensurate with your talents. Did you not tell me that your period of enlistment with the Legion is up very shortly?"

"Yes, sir."

If the general's eyes pinioned him before, James was now as fixed as a butterfly to a collector's board.

"It would please me," Bazaine said then, "if you did not re-enlist."

Until this moment the meeting had gone as well as any he had ever had with a superior officer; better in fact. Leave the Legion?

"With all due respect, *mon general*, it is my unshakable intention to re-enlist. As I believe I told the general once before, the Legion is my home. I know no other."

"Ah, *monsieur!* The strong tone of your voice tells me

you think yourself *persona non grata* with your general. Such is far from the case. Let me explain my wish to have you leave the Legion: as you doubtless know, his Imperial Majesty plans to establish a Catholic monarchy on these shores, and to that end has secured the agreement of Archduke Maximilian von Hapsburg of Austria to ascend a French-guaranteed throne together with his wife, Princess Charlotte of Belgium . . ."

"I have heard this, sir . . . yes."

"Your loyalty to the Legion—and France—is commendable, major, but hear me out, *si'l vous plaît*. This is what I have in mind for you, Major James. I will not press you for a decision at this moment, but I would like an answer soon. We French do not mean to stay in this country indefinitely. When Max von Hapsburg becomes Emperor of Mexico he will need an army of his own. Although General Forey is nominally our commander-in-chief now, Emperor Napoleon has asked *me* to form the cadre of the Emperor's forces. Unfortunately, the most capable officers of any significant rank and experience he could hope to get from among his subjects are the very ones facing us at this moment, and it is doubtful in the extreme they would abandon their commitments to President Juárez for any consideration. At the start, Emperor Maximilian will have to rely on French officers seconded to him, myself among them. We can—with sufficient help from Paris—forge a splendid army for him. There is one rub, though. Not all of our natural allies here are as fond of Frenchmen as I would like, nor do they care much for the Belgians and Austrians who will arrive with the archduke. That bloodthirsty monster General Márquez, for instance, the one Mexicans call the Leopard, hates us quite cordially, as I am sure does Archbishop Labastida, the cleric which you said in your report you met at the American embassy. Do you see where all this leads in regard to you, major?"

"I think I'm *beginning* to see, general."

"*Très bien!* As an American, but not as a Legionnaire, you would have great value to me—and to France." Bazaine fixed his huge, brooding eyes on James. "I want you with me in the Emperor's army as my liaison officer. You would become a colonel within a year, something I assure you can *never* happen if you remain in the Legion." He held his hand up, meaty palm toward his listener. "I can see in your face that you want to turn me down, but I beg you to consider my offer for a week before you tell me of your decision. In the meantime—and please keep this to yourself—I will form the expeditionary force you have suggested. That is all for now, major."

James stood, saluted, and turned to leave. When he pushed aside the flap of the tent Bazaine's voice reached him again. "One more thing. I am not a man who sulks when he doesn't get his way. If you decide not to accept this appointment, it will in no way militate against your career in the Legion. As a matter of fact, you *will* then be the new force's commanding officer. Should you decide the way I hope you will, your friend Major Boulanger will have that honor."

Now, with the week Bazaine gave him to come to a decision at an end tomorrow morning, he watched Pierre toss the empty cognac bottle into the desert scrub growing at the edge of the tent and then finish off the last drop in the glass. The reason the general could so confidently characterize himself as "not a man who sulks when he doesn't get his way" was clear—that eventuality had never come to pass.

Boulanger kept his eyes on where the cognac bottle had come to rest. A scorpion crawled across the label. "I must find another bottle, quickly, *mon ami*," he said. "Even if it has to be one of the several varieties of *urine* the Mexicans drink." James had heard many things in his friend's voice, but what he had just heard came close to desperation.

And hearing it, Jason James made the decision.

"Pierre," he said, "at the risk of appearing immodest, and unlikely as it may strike you, I might by late tomorrow morning be in a position to offer you a combat command, one of more significance than any you have ever had."

21

Bazaine gave Boulanger his friend James as his second-in-command of what he dubbed Force Soixante-Trois, together with James's three Legion companies of infantry, four squadrons of Chasseurs d'Afrique with—a minor but genuine irritation—Marcel Gallimard commanding one of them. Two batteries of mountain guns, brand new breechloaders not two weeks off the transports docked at Veracruz, two companies of Tirailleurs, one of Chasseurs-a-pied, and a baggage train—with many more wagons and caissons than the command actually required for supply, to make it look more imposing and add credibility in the eyes of spies—rounded out the force. Almost every man who marched west with Boulanger and James—Gallimard, too—had been in action in Mexico at some time in the last year, but as was the case with the Legionnaires, none had seen combat in a month or more.

As the column cleared Cholula on the second day out from the encampment on the southern side of Puebla, James could feel the eyes of Republican scouts on his back; Boulanger and the other officers and men felt them as well. He confided to Pierre it would probably take no more than a day before Comonfort knew of their movements.

"You've made this trip recently," Boulanger said. "What is your guess, *mon ami*, as to how long it will take our enemy to respond once he knows about our little excursion, and in what strength do you think he will come at us?"

"If he takes the bait, he will bring every man he has. We'll see his outriders in three days time, skirmishers in four."

"You should be commanding this venture," the Frenchman sighed.

"Nonsense, Pierre. I have never taken anything bigger than a company into action. You were conducting sizable operations on your own here in Mexico while I was still patroling the desert in North Africa with no more than a half dozen men."

"But I do have you to thank for my good fortune, *n'est-ce pas?*"

James admitted that yes, he had suggested Pierre to Bazaine, but "the general investigated you pretty thoroughly, my friend. You won this command on merit, I assure you. And you obviously passed the test of your face-to-face meeting with him."

"*Merci,* my friend. Three days then until we meet Comonfort?"

"I think so."

"And he will fight?"

"You can count on it, *mon ami.*"

Pierre clucked in appreciative wonder when the sun rose behind them three mornings later and four blue-uniformed lancers appeared on a distant rise, with the great, cloud-draped volcanic peaks that brooded over the Valley of Mexico in the distance.

"*Tu a raison,* Jason. Incredible! Exactly three days," he said. "Did General Comonfort take you into his confidence completely when you dined with him at Chapultepec? Or do you have second sight as does that dwarf of yours?"

"It was a lucky guess, Pierre."

"Your modesty is sometimes *de trop, mon ami.*"

Boulanger dispatched a dozen Chasseurs at a gallop to check out the enemy lancers, perhaps catch and take them prisoner, a hope James knew to be forlorn. Good as they were, Chasseurs could not *begin* to ride with Mexican *hacendados, peones,* or professionals such as Oaxacan cavalrymen or *charros* born and raised as centaurs.

"And now—" Boulanger went on as they waited, "Can you tell me if we will do battle in the morning?"

"*Je pense que oui.* Yes. Those lancers were not scouts. Armed as they were, I think they are part of the vanguard of Comonfort's army."

The Chasseurs returned by nine o'clock, empty-handed as expected and exhausted from their hot ride, but with the sergeant leading the detachment confirming James's speculation. He reported a *"grande armée,* encamped less than half a kilometer beyond the rise, an army consisting mainly of cavalry, Major Boulanger, with what appears to be full artillery and many more infantrymen than we have, sir—at the very least twice as many. It is a new camp. They haven't even pitched tents, and supply wagons are stretched into lines a mile to the west of it."

"Merci, sergeant," Boulanger said. He turned a delighted eye on James. "Your plan has worked, *mon ami."*

Comonfort had risen to the lure with amazing speed. To come east in such strength meant he was sure he faced a massive French threat to the capital. It was the outcome James and Bazaine had hoped for. Boulanger would give battle, retreat if he had to, but hang on until General Bazaine swung in from the northeast with the rest of the First Division.

Comonfort, somewhere across the rise, must have licked his chops when his cavalry detail rode back into his camp and reported the apparent strength of his enemy. His first reaction to the news must have been suspicion, but he would also probably decide he had more than enough time to crush the French units facing him before a trap could close its jaws. He could well be right. Pierre had only one choice to make that would give Force 63 any chance at all.

Pierre stared intently at the distant rise. "Were you seen by the enemy camp, sergeant?" he asked the sweat-drenched Chasseur.

"Almost certainly, *monsieur.* They broke out most of a squadron to give chase for a while, and despite our lead nearly caught us. These peasants ride like the wind."

Boulanger turned to James again. "In that case, *J'atta-querais,"* he said. "But you are at last wrong about something, *mon ami.* We shall not fight tomorrow. I will not *wait* for morning. Since our friend Comonfort now knows how small a force we are, we cannot give him a moment to consider how he might plan his attack on *us*. We shall engage him before the sun is in our faces, and, if we are lucky, before he really settles in."

The decision to go on the offensive without delay was the one James had hoped for.

Pierre deployed his infantry companies, and half an hour later ordered them on a brisk march straight for the low ridge, with instructions to stop just before they reached the crest. He called up his batteries of field guns, sent them bumping along behind the skirmish lines of riflemen, and split the Chasseur cavalry into two main wings with a squadron in reserve under the command of the glum Marcel Gallimard to escort them as they moved into position. These things done he sent a courier racing back to Bazaine to tell him of the Chasseur sergeant's discovery.

"All we can do now, *mon ami*," Pierre said, "is come to grips with the enemy, and hope our general thinks enough of us to rescue us before we all perish. When I said I would attack, that was not quite true. My attack *pour le moment* will be mainly a *defensive* move." He sniffed the morning air. "What is the name of that village down there behind the rise?"

Somewhere south of where the four enemy cavalrymen had disappeared the two blunted towers of a mission church nosed above the ridge. James checked his map. "San Lorenzo." It was the small village where he left Cipi and Sofía, and where ample Paloma waited for Pierre. "With your permission, Major Boulanger, I will move up now and join the infantry."

"*Non, non, monsieur!*" Pierre drew a deep breath. "There is something General Bazaine told me in our meeting he did not tell you. It is of course one of the reasons you are not commanding Force Soixante-Trois. The general knows that left to your own devices you would expose yourself to enemy fire too closely and readily. He said his plans for you demand that I keep you alive. I am quite frankly amazed he did not hold you out of this action altogether. *Excusez-moi* now. I must signal the cannoneers to bring the enemy under fire. Since Comonfort is still engaged making camp, they will be able to loft several salvos right into his lap with impunity so long as our infantry can keep the enemy off the ridge." He dug his spurs into his horse, moved a few feet toward the guns, turned back and said, "You may follow me, *mon ami*, but please, only to the foot of the rise. Stay behind the guns when I ride to the top to assess the effect of our first barrage. I would not like to face Monsieur le General Bazaine if you are killed or even wounded, and I must now regretfully *order* you to stay out of the line of fire. *Si'l vous plait*, do not think unkindly of me."

James had noticed how Pierre distanced himself from Marcel Gallimard ever since this march began. The St. Cyrian almost cried when Boulanger told him he and his squadron were to stand by the guns while the rest of the cavalry probed the enemy lines from the flanks.

The guns were already in action by the time James joined Boulanger, Gallimard, and the officer in charge of the two batteries, another St. Cyrian named Chouinard, a captain he knew by reputation as a fine artilleryman, and who seemed from his sour looks at Marcel to take no more pleasure from the young lieutenant's presence than did Boulanger or James.

Between rounds Gallimard eased his horse over to James. *"Et alors, ça va bien*, Major James . . . ?" It was a more subdued greeting than any in the past.

"Oui, pas mal. And you, Gallimard?"

"You have great influence with Major Boulanger, *n'est-ce pas?"*

"We are friends, but he is also my commanding officer." He could guess what was coming.

Behind Gallimard, Pierre edged his horse close to the two of them, just in time for the Parisian to catch the lieutenant's next words.

"I beg you, *monsieur*, please persuade Major Boulanger to give me a more honorable duty than merely guarding these guns."

"Guarding the guns is vital to our mission, you idiot!" Boulanger roared. "Much depends on it. You may have more to handle here than you could ask for when the enemy comes across that ridge."

Gallimard, looking whipped and disconsolate, drifted off toward the farther of the two batteries, but well away from Chouinard.

The gun batteries loosed their third volley now. It passed above and shivered the slope where the French infantry, duBecq and Compagnie Rouge among them, crouched in readiness. As yet no enemy soldiers had appeared atop the rise.

DuBecq was facing back down the incline. The trustworthy old sergeant stood to attention and saluted James.

Salvo number four shook the earth and echoed from the ridge.

Boulanger urged his horse up the slope toward his most forward and exposed troops, preparing, James figured, to order them even closer to the top to seek whatever slight advantage a few more feet of height would give them when Comonfort's men began to move.

Then the scream of enemy shells overhead almost ruptured his eardrums. Craters opened on each side of him and a shower of dirt and debris erupted from them. A French field piece took a direct hit and a wheel from its carriage rolled in circles around its mangled crew.

How long would Comonfort content himself with a duel of guns? In 1847, Santa Anna's commanders had shown little patience in similar engagements. The essential character of Mexican generals could not have changed much in seventeen years. Any second would likely bring the first sight of that superb Mexican cavalry.

Everything depended on Comonfort's nerve and on how well the French had fooled him into thinking Force 63 was all he would have to face. If he did believe that, and if his initial losses were not severe, he would send his infantry out quickly, supported by most if not all of the cavalry squadrons he held in reserve. When that happened, it was imperative that Boulanger's riflemen shoot fast and well, play havoc with the enemy's front line, and buy the time needed for Bazaine and the Division to march from the east and north and join the action.

The Legion, duBecq and Compagnie Rouge in the van, had now reached the top of the rise, with the Tirailleurs and the Chasseurs-a-pied on either side of them.

Men in the front rank knelt, rifle-stocks at their shoulders, the gun barrels of those in the second rank aimed above their heads or in some cases even resting on their shoulders. A Chasseurs-a-pied officer standing between his own company's position and the Legion held his saber aloft. Men rigid and motionless from this distance must now feel their spines vibrating like the tines of tuning forks. Boulanger, with his avowal that he would be on the defensive even though initially advancing, would have to show the patience James did not expect from Comonfort. It would not be easy for Pierre to restrain troops eager for combat after months of inactivity.

When his eyes found the figure of duBecq moving with ease and confidence behind the ranks of Compagnie Rouge he knew the men he had trained and with whom he had fought would not break.

Then the heads of enemy horsemen began to bob below the line of the ridge, now shimmering in the late morning sun.

The next hour or so could decide the soundness of the grand plan he and Bazaine had worked out. It all seemed so simple back in the general's gaudy tent with its multicolored record of French Army triumphs. The cavalry ascending the other side of the rise could upset that simple plan in the blink of an eye.

Blue-clad torsos with crossed white straps now came into view under the bobbing Mexican caps, but only in two or three places did a horse rear its head above the rim of the rise. The riders out in front were holding their advance to little more than a walk. None of the mounted men had as yet lowered his lance. The Mexican tacticians might not be as impatient as James remembered them; their cavalry's discipline right now seemed exemplary.

Boulanger had taken a station a mere fifty meters directly behind the Legion and could have been an equestrian statue in the Bois de Boulogne, his saber held against the sky.

DuBecq and the rest of the riflemen in the nearest skirmish line should begin to fire any moment.

The oncoming cavalry were in full view now. A trumpet call seeped through the din; the Mexican squadrons broke into a chaotic, full blown charge, and the entire scene exploded into fury.

Smoke boiled up above the heads of the French holding the ridge line, and the rolling rattle of musketry filled the air, all but smothering the sound of the few enemy shellbursts still echoing around him. Chouinard's two batteries threw volley after volley over the heads of their forward line, but the enemy guns beyond the rise stopped now. Disdaining the effect of Boulanger's forward marksmen on his attacking cavalry, the unseen enemy commander must have been certain it could ride unchecked into the cannonaded area where the French gunners still worked their weapons.

The fusillade from the Legion and the Tirailleurs had a deadly effect; horseman after horseman tumbled from his mount, pitched over its head, or slipped limply to one side or the other. Several, their feet caught fast in stirrups, were dragged along the ground to where French bayonets finished them.

Another call from the trumpet rose unsteadily above the noise of battle. Most of the enemy still in the saddle reined up, wheeled around, and headed back in fair order to where they began their advance, the two wings of Chasseurs on their heels. Boulanger would not let his precious cavalry follow the enemy too far down the other side of the rise. Their real work would not begin until the second Mexican charge.

One Mexican rider, his lance parallel with the ground in classic threat, had made it through the lines of infantry, and now pounded down the slope straight for James. This soldier had no intention of heeding the bugle calling him home. The Legionnaire drew his saber, a futile weapon against the lance.

When the horse and rider were within thirty yards of him he saw that the tunic of the man's uniform was no longer the bright Republican blue with the white straps. Blood spewed from an ugly canyon in the center of his chest. His eyes were wide open, dead as stones, his face not now the deep *mestizo* bronze it might have been moments earlier, but a drained, pale, sepia mask. Some last, fantastic, iron determination, forged probably only one gasp before Legion or Tirailleur bullets stopped breath and heart, had shored up his charge through the French ranks and held him as erect as if he were on parade. His horse carried him past the Legionnaire and out of sight.

When James turned his eyes to the rim again, he found that for all the heat and thunder of the Mexican attack, things had gone surprisingly well with the infantry. Men were down, but "supportable losses," some closeted general might call the casualties. He held his breath until his eyes fell on duBecq, tending a wounded Legionnaire whose face James could not see. The veteran sergeant himself appeared untouched.

The great crashing noises of the battle fell away, but the humming silence promised no real quiet.

Boulanger rode back down the slope and reined in beside him, eyes gleaming. "So far, so good, eh, *mon ami?*" He had situated himself so close behind his infantry that powdersmoke had blackened his wolf's face. *"Quelle heure est il?"*

James pulled his watch from his waistcoat pocket. "One fifteen."

"Quel dommage! I had hoped that *notre ami* Comonfort would use up much more time, be more persistent. Appar-

ently he is not that stupid. Breaking off his first attack as quickly as he did leaves him the rest of the afternoon to come at us again at his leisure. His second cavalry charge will be followed by an advance of infantry across the entire line. It is *exactement* what I would do were I in his place."

"Could you see the enemy's main camp from where you were on the heights?"

"*Oui.*"

"And . . . ?"

"My Chasseur sergeant was right. It is a large force indeed. They occupy every inch of land from just over the rise on south to the village. I suspect Comonfort has been joined by La Garza from Ocatlan, and we can be pretty sure the Oaxacans are with him, too. With the addition of La Garza's army and the others, it gives him perhaps as many as eight thousand men."

"And we have what, Pierre? We began with seven hundred seventy-five. We must now be down to something less than seven hundred."

"*Oui.* But this is what we wanted, is it not? Even if the Division doesn't get here soon enough to save our *culs,* they will still be able to demolish the only sizeable force between us and the capital. I'm going to shift our whole defensive front half a kilometer to the south. Comonfort will have to attack obliquely. It will give Bazaine a better angle when he brings the full division in."

If General Bazaine had entertained any doubts at all about his selection of Boulanger to lead Force 63, they would remove themselves in a hurry when he arrived and found Comonfort's entire left flank opened to him by the Parisian's tactics.

"If we can hold them one more time," Boulanger said, "they will probably break off hostilities for the night, and with any luck at all, early morning at the latest will see the entire First Division take the field."

He rode off to gather his company commanders, take their loss reports, and issue orders for the new troop dispositions. Litter bearers carried the dead and wounded to the rear. James looked in vain for the dead enemy horseman who had ridden as if he were still alive. Perhaps the man was riding yet, perhaps forever . . . in a sense he would—for Jason James at least.

As the right wing Tirailleurs, the Chasseurs-a-pied and the three Legion companies took up their new positions further south on the ridge and the field guns lumbered in behind them, James located duBecq in the drifting smoke. Surely Pierre would not object to his riding to the top of the rise to speak with his longtime sergeant now that no firing was going on.

He had been wrong about duBecq coming through the first action entirely unscathed; the sergeant's right sleeve clung in bloody tatters to a lacerated upper arm bound in a makeshift dressing.

"How badly are you hurt, duBecq?"

"It is but a scratch, *monsieur,* a deep one, but a scratch."

"Do you wish someone to replace you?"

"Mais, non, non, non, monsieur! This battle must still be fought."

"You said this battle must still be 'fought,' sergeant. You did not say it must still be 'won.'"

"Oui, Major James. I am a realist. I saw the enemy camp quite clearly from Compagnie Rouge's position."

"Yes, we face a formidable task, duBecq. Do you have regrets?"

"Only one, sir—that the major is not commanding and fighting with the company."

He had not told duBecq that he was under orders not to expose himself directly to enemy fire, probably did not have to tell him; they never had made excuses to each other. "Carry on, duBecq. Perhaps we can talk again when the company's work is done." He did not tell duBecq, either, of the expected or at least hoped-for arrival of the division. He and Boulanger, on the odd chance that some of the Mexican wagoneers were spies, had kept that information to themselves. They had not even told trusted officers such as Chouinard and they certainly had not told Gallimard.

Now came the time soldiers dread above all others: the long, enervating wait for combat.

He steered his horse behind the now-silent guns, dismounted, hitched the animal to what was left of the carriage of the gun knocked out of commission by the enemy shelling, and looked for some smooth place in the rocks to stretch.

Damn it! There could be no rest: Gallimard, as long-faced and woebegone as before, rode up to him.

"*Sacrebleu, monsieur!* Their cavalry did not even get as far as the guns Major Boulanger ordered me to guard."

"Be of good cheer, Gallimard. They will next time."

"You think there will *be* a next time, Major James? You do not think they have had enough?"

"No, I don't." The St. Cyrian had not as yet ridden to the ridge, had no idea what Force 63 still faced. Whether he liked the man or not, James would have to credit his eagerness for combat to an otherwise overdrawn account. "They will not only come again, their next charge will make the first one look like child's play."

Gallimard's face lit like the Champs Elysees during an imperial *fête*, his Napoleon III goatee wagging like the tail of a delirious puppy. Then he turned somber again. "But I suppose Boulanger will still find a way to keep me out of action."

"Whatever the major plans for you, I expect you will see enough combat in another hour or so to last you a lifetime, lieutenant."

James decided he should have a word with Pierre about the St. Cyrian; the treatment Gallimard had received the last nine months at Boulanger's rough hands and even rougher tongue would not in the long run do *him* any good, either. Personal connections counted for a lot in the French Army, and this was no ordinary, lowly lieutenant of Chasseurs. Who knew what influence Gallimard's older brother had with general officers such as Forey and Bazaine and the pearl-hard layers of rank between those two and Pierre Boulanger?

Ridiculous as Marcel Gallimard might appear, the differences between him and Boulanger were more of a degree than of a kind. At bottom, both were caught up in the idea of *la gloire*. It troubled him some. He had once seen an insane lust for personal glory turn a man into something sinister.

He was blown out of these ruminations by a shell landing only twenty yards to his left and another falling between him and the ridge. The Mexicans were beginning the softening-up for their second attack.

"Get back to your command, Gallimard!" he shouted against the roar of incoming artillery. The St. Cyrian became as erect in his saddle as a lightning rod, dug in his spurs and cantered around the rear of the two batteries of mountain guns.

The French infantry ahead of James re-formed into new skirmish lines facing more to the right than they had during the earlier conflict, spreading an umbrella of rifles and bayonets back down the slope between the enemy and the guns. When the Republican cavalry broke across the top of the rise, they would find nothing facing them, at first. The right wing Chasseurs d'Afrique, three hundred yards to the north, were motionless but clearly ready. Pierre's gun captain, Chouinard, had reset his breechloaders so they could blanket the ridge north of the Legion and the Tirailleurs, and was waiting for the second appearance of Comonfort's blue-uniformed lancers before he gave the command to fire.

And then, rising like the surf at Oran, they were there. Two hundred riders, three? This significantly larger force might be checked, but there was no chance of stopping it this time. The phalanx moved across the top of the rise like a blue tidal wave. Shellbursts from Chouinard's guns blossomed in their center, giant red orchids, and men and horses flew skyward or fell to the ground, but the wave rolled on down the slope. James could almost feel the surprise of the officer leading the charge as he discovered how Boulanger had shifted his defenses. The entire line of enemy horsemen wheeled to the right and now closed on the infantry, behind whose ranks Pierre sat his horse, saber drawn again, directing the rifle fire of the Legionnaires and the Tirailleurs. The enemy riders had almost reached the front rank when the right wing Chasseurs came on. The Parisian's tactics would not perhaps turn things much in his favor in the long run, but they were for the moment marvelously effective. Any sense of two distinct, opposing forces vanished when the French cavalry rode into the blue curl of the Mexican wave. The battle suddenly became a melee. A hundred small, bloody fights—between two men, four, six, often as many twenty—raged at once. French riflemen and lancers were bringing down many of the mounted enemy, but not nearly enough. If Comonfort sent his infantry up from beyond the rise now, this struggle would end in half an hour despite the fact that Boulanger was wisely holding his left cavalry wing out of the fight to deal with Mexican foot soldiers when they arrived.

A small group of enemy cavalrymen, ten or a dozen, somehow broke loose from the swirling, grappling knots—by turns hidden and revealed in the smoke and flashes erupting on the ridgetop—and galloped obliquely down the slope, not at the guns, but straight at Jason James.

He raised his saber. His sense of futility left him. It would be his last fight, but for a few more seconds he would be a soldier. Bazaine could not keep him out of this one, nor could Pierre protect him.

Then, rising thinly above the blare of battle, a shout, a shriek really, reached his ears from close on his left.

"Have no fear, Major Zhomm. Gallimard is with you!"

Why in the name of God had the idiot left his post? He would merely die with James; the two of them would be no match for the determined horsemen bearing down on them.

The fact that the fast approaching riders wielded sabers and not lances would only delay what would turn out to be a summary execution. There were eight of them now. French rifles had emptied three saddles, but the remaining cavalrymen were now out of range of the Legion and Tirailleur fusiliers. They would get no more help. James braced himself. The eight men would not reach them all at once. Perhaps he and the foolhardy Chasseur could take a pair or more with them.

The first enemy horseman was almost on him when the man's chest exploded. In the deafening noise James had not heard a shot. There was no time to turn and see who had fired it. The nearest of Chouinard's gunners had no rifles or sidearms—and would not have had time to come to their aid in any event.

The second rider fell from his saddle, his body hurtling against the forelegs of James's horse. The third made directly for Gallimard and the faint, tinny sounds of saber striking saber reached James's ears through the din just as the fourth rider slumped across the neck of his animal, another victim of that unknown and unseen gunner. The last four attackers were riding abreast, and James spurred his horse toward a narrow gap between the third and fourth, slashing on both sides of him as his mount responded, feeling the resistance of muscle and bone on his left, but nothing but air on the right. If he could force these riders to turn about to get at him, perhaps they would separate a little and give Marcel and him a fraction of a chance.

When he wheeled his own horse around he found that another of the enemy had fallen, not the one his saber had struck, but the other.

And he saw what had happened and the miracle worker who had made it happen.

Fifteen feet away, not atop an army mount, but on what appeared to be an enormous draft horse on its last aged legs, holding a smoking pistol that loomed as large as any of Chouinard's mountain howitzers, sat Cipriano Méndez y Garciá.

No time to wonder. Gallimard was doing fine with his adversary, and the victim of James's saber rode slumped in the saddle, carried from the scene by an obviously unguided animal. The remaining two, to James's surprise, veered away and now bounded past him and on up the slope, just as Marcel swung his blade into his man's neck, bringing him out of the saddle in a torrent of blood.

Now a new sound reached his ears.

Guns. And not the cannons of Chouinard or those of Comonfort beyond the ridge. These reports came from half a kilometer to the north. The commandant of Chapultepec would not have moved *his* batteries that far from the immediate action.

Bazaine and the First Division had joined the battle.

Yes, squadron upon squadron of Chasseurs were riding down the ridge from the north. A regiment of Zouaves were in a hard double time close behind them.

Bazaine had arrived at precisely the proper time, when Comonfort's field guns were turned in the wrong direction and the rest of his army, particularly his infantry, had probably strung themselves out and opened an unprotected flank nearly a kilometer in length.

James urged his horse down to an idiotically smiling Gallimard, brought his saber to the brim of his *kepi* in salute, and pushed on toward Cipi, whose ancient nag, unflustered by the mounting crescendo as the Division moved to the attack, was calmly nibbling at a bunch of grass.

"Cipi! How on earth did you . . . ?"

The dwarf pushed his sombrero from his head to his back and grinned. "The Major did not think for one second that Cipi would allow him to make a liar of me by getting himself killed before he became a colonel, did he? Even had I permitted it, *nuestra amiga* Sofía would not have countenanced it for half that long."

"But—"

"I heard the sound of the guns this morning. I would have been here earlier, but it took time to steal this sorry Rosinante." He patted the big horse's neck. "What does my major think of my qualities as a fighting *hombre* now?"

James drew a breath. He did not know how he could keep the promise he was about to make, but he *would* keep it. "I'll never ride into battle again without you by my side, *amigo.*"

The Battle of San Lorenzo ended at sunset.

Bazaine had brought tremendous firepower with him, virtually all the guns silent since the early days of the Second Battle of Puebla, when Forey's army began the first of its assaults inside the city.

After dispatching elements of the Chasseurs d'Afrique to cut off any retreat Comonfort might think of making toward the Valley of Mexico, and then deploying raiding parties to harry the remnants of his army as the Mexicans made what escape they could to the north and west, General Bazaine rode into Boulanger's command post. He wore a slouch hat, a nondescript tan vest, and a pair of baggy trousers that made him look more an African explorer than the commanding general of a modern army. Riding with him were thirty-five or forty other officers, his entire general staff, it seemed.

"Your forces are relieved of all duty for a week, major. Well done," he said, and to James, "I am glad to see you looking well and fit, *monsieur.*" He cast a quizzical eye past the Legionnaire to where Cipi still sat his monstrous warhorse. He shook his head, but said nothing about the dwarf. Without a doubt, whatever informants he had in the lower echelons had told him all about Méndez y Garciá, too. His eye fell to the scabbard of James's saber with the blood on it now dried to scabs.

A team of engineers had the general's resplendent tent pitched in minutes. "We will have a meeting in my quarters at ten tomorrow morning, *messieurs,*" Bazaine said before he disappeared behind the main flap.

Boulanger must have read James's mind or sensed his disappointment. "Do not belabor yourself, *mon ami.* Our general is very pleased. From what I learned about him at

Puebla, he is usually even more critical after victory than defeat. He always thinks there have been mistakes his lieutenants can learn from."

"What now?"

"After I have visited the wounded, I for one am heading for the village. I suggest you come along. Bazaine will not be calling you tonight."

Méndez y Garciá grunted in assent. "Cipi, too, thinks that an excellent idea, *mi mayor*. Besides, I promised Sofía I would bring you back."

James spent a long time at supper with Cipi and Pierre in a farmhouse on the edge of San Lorenzo, and an even longer time in a small, grubby cantina where Paloma draped herself across the Chasseur. It was as if he were deliberately postponing seeing Sofía although Cipi reminded him through the evening she awaited them.

By midnight Boulanger and Paloma had left, and soon afterward Cipi, too, announced he was leaving.

"*Por favor, mi mayor,* do not expect me to wait on you again until daybreak. It is time for you to go, *también*. The major does remember my directions to the inn, does he not?"

He rose to leave directly after Cipi disappeared through the cantina's doorway in the company of two of the bulging beauties he had flirted with for the better part of the last hour. James was paying for his last drink when Marcel Gallimard stepped inside the door.

In light of the St. Cyrian's rallying to his side in the nearly fatal afternoon, he could not very well dismiss him out of hand as he had on almost every other occasion since the early days in Veracruz. Perhaps they should make a new beginning.

"*Salut,* Marcel," he said as Gallimard reached his table. "*Assieds-toi.* I would like to buy you a drink."

The young French officer's face came alight as it might have had James just awarded him a medal.

Actually, and to his surprise, James felt a glow of bonhomie toward the Frenchman.

He had been in no great hurry to get to her, but when he saw her standing by the rumpled bed in the small room he wondered why.

Moonlight streamed through the one window and he saw her as he had that night in Jalapa. If anything, the sight was even more overpowering now.

"Jason . . ." she breathed. It was the first time she had addressed him by his name except in sleep.

Afterward, as he lay beside her, he knew he had not yet unraveled the essential mystery of her—perhaps never would.

A great battle, largely of his planning, had been fought and won, his future in his profession held promise he had never even hoped for, and above all, he had faced his personal demons on the rooftop at Chapultepec, and if he had not vanquished them he had at least survived. His soul had been battered, but it was still intact. This girl was enough for any man's desires. She was possible; the other was clearly not.

He should not ask for more.

Three days after the rout of Ignacio Comonfort at the Battle of San Lorenzo, Puebla fell.

Pierre had not stopped drinking entirely, but his death grip on the cognac bottle relaxed, and his daily intake of alcohol diminished to pre-Puebla levels.

Bazaine had been ecstatic the day after the battle. "The road to the capital now lies open before us!" he said. "France is in your debt, Major James. You have demonstrated brilliant military thinking."

Boulanger and forty other officers of the division heard the general's words.

Yet James felt almost nothing, no sense of accomplishment, no pride and joy.

22

▲▲▲▲▲

"Wake up, *mademoiselle!*" Solange whispered.

Sarah had been sure the duenna had put behind her the nightmares that came so regularly before they reached Mexico City a year ago, but something had frightened her badly tonight.

"A bad dream, Solange?"

"It is not a dream, *mademoiselle.*"

"*Que'est-ce que c'est?*"

"*Je ne sais pas!* Listen!" Solange crossed herself.

Sarah sat up. She heard nothing. "*Ce n'est rien, ma chère.*"

"Come to the front room windows and see, *mademoiselle,* I beg you. Something strange and terrible is going on in the street."

"But what?"

"I do not know. I have not dared look. I could hear it from *ma chambre.*"

Sarah struggled into her peignoir, pulled on her slippers, and let the Frenchwoman push her down the hall to the parlor. She started at the tremor in Solange's hand in the small of her back as the older woman pressed her forward and jumped a little when the hall clock struck two as they passed it.

When they reached the front sitting room she kneeled on the couch and looked out through the large window behind it toward Avenida Moctezuma.

The moon had gone behind clouds, and pitch darkness hid the shrubbery outside the window and completely blotted out the street itself.

She heard—or perhaps only felt at first—what had terrified Solange—a nearly undetectable rumble of dull, soft thuds as faint as distant rolling thunder, as if hundreds, perhaps thousands, of shuffling feet were walking across her lawn.

"You hear, *mon ange?*" Solange breathed. "Ghosts! There must be a horde of them."

Then the night clouds split and full silver moonlight spilled over a scene that caught her breath and held it as if in a vise.

What met her eyes was not Solange's spectral "horde." She saw hundreds of people, a broad, flood-tide river of humanity that choked the street from side to side and from left to right as far as she could see, a sluggish river of shuffling figures that lapped up on the lawn and except for the muted drumming of those relentless feet made no sound at all.

No one in that human river turned or looked aside; every one of them stared dumbly straight ahead as they moved.

Solange leaned against Sarah as if the contact might give her strength and courage. "What does it mean, *ma chère?*" The Frenchwoman crossed herself with trembling fingers that clutched a rosary.

Sarah dreaded the effect of her answer. "I can't be sure, Solange, but I think President Juárez has decided not to defend the capital. The last of the Republican Army is leaving us!"

"*Mon dieu!*" Solange crossed herself again. Her rosary caught on something and broke. Beads scattered across the couch, spilled from the cushions, and bounced across the tiled floor of the parlor. In the silence, eerily disturbed by the muffled sounds from the street, the tiny, tinkling noise they made seemed that of hail on a window pane.

In Avenida Moctezuma's shadows, men in the blue uniform of Juárez's Republican Army, but with a great many in the flowing *calzoneras* of Mexican irregulars, their feet bare or in *huaraches,* padded northward, a tide of white- and blue-clad lemmings. Leather cartridge cases drooped from sagging shoulders. The ragged column trudged at a pace that could go on forever, a shapeless mob, no ranks, no files, no leaders—and seemingly no purpose.

Now and again women, balancing sagging bundles on their heads or carrying them slung across eloquently bent backs, walked in silence alongside the men, and every so often children, half-naked boys and girls from three to twelve years old, shuffled along in the same disconsolate fashion as their elders. Nondescript dogs by the dozen walked in and with the crowd. As if the hush were contagious even for animals, not one barked.

The procession up the moonlit *avenida* went on unabated all night long.

Sarah and Solange did not leave their post at the window until the river dwindled to a trickle and dawn blazed its way into the now mostly empty street, and until it seemed as if all of Mexico had drifted by.

Matt O'Leary arrived in an embassy carriage at ten minutes before eight o'clock, and made his way through the few stragglers still crossing the front edge of Sarah's lawn.

Solange flew to him and embraced him. When the Marine freed himself from her grasp he looked at Sarah.

"Would you like breakfast, Matt?"

He shook his head. "Get enough things together to last the two of you at least a week, Miss Anderson. You won't need food. Ambassador Corwin has already sent just about all the staff out for provisions. He's asking all the Americans in the capital to come in to the embassy until the French arrive. There's bound to be a crowd, so we ought to get moving *pronto* if you're going to have a choice of quarters. Besides, you could be in grave danger now from here on out."

"Matt! I'm not leaving my home. If Antonio Pérez comes into the capital to report to me I've got to be here. He'd never come to the embassy."

"He can find *me*."

"No. Thank you, Matt, but that just wouldn't work. I must see him myself. I haven't heard from Señor Moreno at the mining company, but I'm sure I owe Señor Pérez more money than I've sent to the orphanage so far. Someone else—might want to get in touch with me, too." She drew her breath in sharply.

Even if Jason James arrived with the French, assuming he was still alive, it was doubtful in the extreme that he would venture anywhere near Avenida Moctezuma. His letter to her when he left the city had been painfully final.

"I can't talk you into leaving here?" Matt said now.

"No." But the pageant she had witnessed during the long night was not a reassuring memory, and she had no right to think only of herself. "You can take Solange with you if she wishes to go."

Solange heard this exchange. *"Non, non, non, ma chère! I will not leave you. C'est fou, certainement,* insanity beyond belief, but if *you* stay here, I stay, too. Besides, my Emperor's men are coming."

"All right," Matt said, "I'll try to get myself freed from duty so I can bunk in here and look after you, but the ambassador will probably turn me down. He'll remind me that it would be easier if you did the sensible thing and came in under the embassy's wing with the other Americans."

"Thank you, Matt. We *are* grateful, and we're sorry to cause you so much concern. I know we can't dismiss *all* thought of danger out of hand, but our—at least *my*—decision is firm. Should Solange change her mind, I'll send her along to the embassy with Pedro. Now, tell us what exactly has happened to cause the Republicans to desert the city?"

"Ignacio Comonfort foolishly took every man garrisoned at Chapultepec to a place sixty or seventy miles east of here called San Lorenzo, leaving the capital guarded only by the second line troops you saw last night. Last week the First Division under General Bazaine absolutely crushed Comonfort and General La Garza who had come down from Tlaxcala, and cut off any possible withdrawal back to Mexico City. I think Comonfort is finished."

"It must be a bitter pill for that proud man, Matt," Sarah said.

"He wasn't the only Republican commander who had to

swallow one. Ortega folded *his* tent at Puebla and surrendered the city three days later and General Forey took a raft of Mexican generals prisoner, including maybe the best of them, Porfirio Díaz. It means there is no longer any force that can rightly call itself an army between the French and the capital, just scattered units with nobody to rally around. President Juárez has moved his government—if he can truly be said to still have one—north to San Luis Potosí. As much as Washington likes Juárez, I don't think it likely they'll send an envoy there. I expect we'll see the tricolor flying over the National Palace here within a fortnight . . ."

Solange sighed with unmistakable pleasure. O'Leary smiled wanly at her and continued.

"Realistically, Ambassador Corwin will have the French and their conservative friends to deal with until a new government is formed. Before long it will be the government of the Austrian archduke. I think this war is over. Until the first units of the French Army get here and take charge there won't be any civil authority to speak of, certainly no military one . . ." His voice trailed then into silence. The Marine lieutenant did not seem a particularly happy man.

"Fix Matt something to eat, Solange, *s'il vous plait*," Sarah said, "no matter how he protests. He's earned it by merely coming here. Besides, he'll be less gloomy with something in his stomach."

When O'Leary had eaten Sarah saw him to the front door. The empty *avenida* signaled that the procession of the night and early morning was over.

Another visitor arrived at noon.

This time Antonio Pérez entered through the front door. Two of his *plateados* looked after the bandit's horse while their own mounts nibbled at the grass in the front yard.

"The French have put me out of work *por de pronto*, Doña Sarah. Their patrols will shortly start to ride every trail through the silver country, and Señor Moreno and your people at Zacatecas will have little to fear. I do not think this will hold forever, of course, and I will keep an eye on things. *Ahora*, I can earn some of my pay guarding your house until the French come in to police this stinking grid of sewers."

For a moment Sarah thought he perhaps had received a message from Matt O'Leary, but there had been no time for that. The bandit had come on his own. It made his offer of help just that much more touching—and valuable.

"Once I feel you are safe," Pérez went on, "I will take *mis hombres* and ride north to San Luis Potosí. I have no wish to become a common soldier, but El Presidente will soon need every man he can find if he is to carry on the struggle against the oppressor. *Pobre Mexico*. It will be a while before I can ply my trade again."

"But if you stay here to look after Solange and me, are you not afraid you will be caught by the French, either here or on that ride north, Señor Pérez?"

"No, *Doña*. The French look only for big armies to fight. They will not trouble themselves with small bands like mine. There is no glory in shooting thieves. My only regret is that after I join Don Benito's forces I will not, as I said before, be able to look after your silver trains. Fortunately, for a time they should not require my protection."

"How much do I owe you now, Señor Pérez?"

"*Nada, Doña*. That last *dinero* you sent to Sor Francisca puts me in *your* debt."

It did not take long after the bandit said "*adios*" for her to be doubly grateful to him.

The two men Pérez brought with him stayed on to guard the front of the house, and old Pedro came on a limping run from his potting shed an hour later to tell her that there were three strangers camped out in the back garden. She quickly established that they were *plateados*, too. All five were as rough and unsavory looking as Antonio, if not quite as imposing, even though they bristled with weapons as did their chief. It irritated her some to begin with that they lounged, smoked, and drank in full view of the neighbors and any passersby, and she almost stepped outside and sent them packing.

But the news that ran through the city by the following morning put an entirely different face on things, and she decided in a hurry that she could not afford to be fastidious. Her neighbors should not complain, either. Pérez's men had made a haven of tranquillity and security out of Avenida Moctezuma. Not one frightening incident occurred.

There seemed no such other haven in the capital. No one seemed to know how many people footpads and thugs killed that first lawless night, or how many dwellings and businesses fell victim to single marauders and roving bands. Heavily armed riders shot up and robbed Sarah's bank, killing the bank manager who tried to stop them and terrorizing the staff and patrons.

Mexico City had been restive and far from free of crime when she and Solange first settled into the house on Moctezuma a year ago. Now the mayhem and pillage reported around the city in the week following the departure of the Republican military forces and their volunteer allies brought a sense of vulnerability of a much greater magnitude. No one made even a modest attempt to halt the depredations. The foreign community tried to organize a civil defense-cum-police force, but only the U.S. Embassy had any appreciable number of trained men such as Matt O'Leary in residence, and Matt and his fellow Marines had their hands full looking after the Americans who availed themselves of the sanctuary offered by Ambassador Corwin.

O'Leary reported that several foreign embassies had issued an appeal to General Forey to send his soldiers in as fast as possible to take over the administration of the capital. The most harrowing fear was an unspoken one: that General Leonardo Márquez, the ruthless conservative commander known as the Leopard, might storm in with his cavalry and commit even worse atrocities against the Liberal professionals and working people who remained behind when their erstwhile protectors left. The French, with their own agenda, at least were not seeking vengeance for the years of the Reforma.

By the third day of the violence erupting in every district of the city, Sarah had not only become accustomed to the presence of Antonio Pérez's ruffians, but was happy to have them. She regretted the need for them, regretted even more the reason the need had arisen—the abandonment of Mexico City by Juárez and his government. She doubted she would ever see the President again unless the French or their conservative allies brought him back to the capital some fine day in shackles. And even then she probably would not see him before they executed him.

Beyond an idle conversation or two with Matt, she had not talked politics at all since Jason left the city.

Solange seldom voiced her opinions, but when she did she revealed it was all very simple for her. While she more or less followed the political line of her long-time employers the Pelletiers in most things, she had no objection to Louis-Napoleon's grandiose imperial design for Mexico. Her emperor *was* French. He favored the cause of Max and Charlotte. That was good enough for her. "Let them come," she said once. "They will be good for this country. I would like French soldiers patrolling the streets when I go to Mass with Matt."

Matt, although he had evinced mild sadness when Juárez's forces fled the capital, seemed not to have terribly strong feelings of his own. He showed a good deal of admiration for the French Army and its leaders. "As a professional military man," he said, "I must say they have conducted a brilliant campaign since the first disaster at Puebla. Forey and Bazaine have done a great job so far."

"But as an American whose government backs President Juárez aren't you uncomfortable with their success?" she asked.

"A little. Far as I'm concerned it's six of one and seven of the other. Juárez *does* get the seven."

It vexed her a bit that the two people closest to her gave such little thought to the great events going on in Mexico, that both formed outlooks on affairs of such importance almost casually. There might have been an excuse for Solange; she, after all, had little formal education and could not even qualify as a member of the *petite bourgeosie* back home in France. Her simplistic remarks were understandable. O'Leary, on the other hand, surely as steeped in the pure waters of republicanism as she was, had graduated from the Naval Academy, where he must have studied under that splendid old liberal professor of government, Abner Long McCann, a longtime friend of Sarah's father.

As for Sarah herself, there came a slight tearing of her emotional fabric which threatened to become a wide rip if Juárez failed.

Her heart had ached for him and the people of Mexico the night she and Solange monitored the sad exodus of the Republican Army and the women and children who trudged beside it as it proceeded toward some *oubliette* of history.

At first, as the legatee of the pure democratic ideas and ideals of Bradford Anderson and those of Auguste Pelletier, she had desperately hoped for some rekindling of the flames of fortune for Juárez and his followers. She knew—particularly after Matt's glum remarks on the government's military predicament—that it was probably a hope without the slenderest chance of realization. Perhaps, cruel as it might seem, it was just as well. Her horror of war, and fear of more killing, a fully admitted desire for her personal safety and that of Solange and all their friends and acquaintances, brought her close to praying that Benito Juárez would bow to what seemed inevitable and give up the struggle. As she had mused once before, the French would not prove to be monsters as governors of this country. Nor would Maximilian von Hapsburg and his wife.

She awaited the arrival of the French resignedly to begin with; her resignation turned to expectancy as the day of that arrival neared.

But she faced one thing squarely at least. Jason James played no part in her expectancy. He was a closed chapter in her life. He had made it easier by writing *finis* to everything himself in that heart-scalding letter.

It was not the only troubling letter pigeon-holed in the Spanish writing desk in the unadorned room that served her as an office.

One had arrived from Henri Gallimard a week before the Liberals left the city.

Ma chère Sarah—

My plans are about made for my trip to Mexico to see you and *mon frère* Marcel. I intend to sail at about the same time as the Archduke and Archduchess so I can be a witness to their historic coronation. Oh, I know there has as yet been no official invitation from the Mexican people, nor has Prince Max avowed that he will accept such an offer when and if it arrives, but the talk in Paris and indeed in all of France has it that it is only a question of time before both things occur.

I am not one of those Frenchmen who opposes our Emperor in this matter. A Catholic throne in a New World country would have a stabilizing effect on great affairs around the globe.

Now—I must confess a certain amount of deviousness on my part in planning my journey to coincide with that of Archduke Maximilian. It has to do with another invitation and acceptance. You gave me no answer to my proposal of marriage the night I put you on the *Strasbourg* in Calais Harbor, but the fact that you did not simply decline it out-of-hand gave me soaring hopes.

I will not implore you to say yes in writing. I live for the day when I hear that word from your lips.

I leave you with but one more thought. Would it not be a thing of wonder and beauty to be married in that marvelous city where you are now living at about the same time Holy Church of Mexico sanctifies the coronation of Emperor Maximilian and Her Imperial Majesty Empress Carlota? Since you are an intimate of the Archduchess, I am sure it would be entirely possible she could persuade her Emperor husband to give the bride away. I am not a military man, but as Le Comte de Bayeux it would be a simple matter for me to secure a brevet commission in the Chasseurs d'Afrique. Marcel tells me he and his brother officers would be overjoyed to serve as our male attendants. I am sure the by then Empress would furnish those on the distaff side from what will surely and quickly become a brilliant court, one to rival any holding sway in decadent Old Europe.

I will say no more on the subject until we are together once again.

Avec tout mon coeur,
—Henri

When she first read the letter she almost laughed at this sweet, earnest man's sudden turn to some kind of hearts-and-flowers romance.

Henri, bless him, would apply no heavy direct pressure for marriage. Perhaps he would not have to.

Would she even be considering Henri's latest proposal as a remote possibility if Jason James had not written *his* letter?

Five mornings after the visit from Antonio Pérez, Sarah awoke to find his men gone.

At ten the bells of what seemed to be every church and cathedral in the capital began a low persistent carillon that by noon had risen to such an insane clamor she feared the bells would fly wild from the steeples.

The French had arrived.

Reliable, predictable Matt O'Leary showed up on her doorstep at three in the afternoon. An embassy carriage stood at the side of Avenida Moctezuma.

"Forey will parade his troops up the Calle de San Francisco just before five o'clock, Miss Anderson. Word has it they're going to put on quite a show. I thought you two might like to take a peek. I've reserved a place for you both on the embassy's portico."

She turned to Solange and found the Frenchwoman quivering with ecstasy, looking for all the world as if her Emperor himself was riding in on a charger to rescue her in person. "Can we dress quickly enough, Solange?"

"Mais oui, chérie! Absolument!"

While the Marine strolled in the garden and chatted with Pedro, the two woman made their *toilettes* and dressed.

Before she joined Matt—and a Solange who had accoutred herself in her most precious brocade gown in a small miracle of speed—Sarah spent a last moment in front of her dressing room mirror, putting the final touches to her hair.

She was not entirely sure she recognized the young woman who stared back at her. The face was subtly different from any she remembered, wearing an expression half of sadness and wholly of excitement.

Solange, her eyes signaling undisguised high pleasure looked out of place in the strange, quiet crowd gathered on the steps of the embassy. Sarah saw that the women under the bright parasols supposed to guard them from a punishing sun, but unneeded here under the overhang of the portico, were turned out in dresses fancier by far than any she had seen at the embassy's evening parties. The soldiery who would appear any second now were, after all, *Frenchmen* who had seen no women other than Indians and *mestizos* in more than a year, or any dresses more fashionable than the shapeless white shifts peasant women wore.

Certainly no one here under the portico would shout or cheer or flirt when the French regiments came in sight; outwardly at least, each and every one would abide by the dictates of their masters in Washington and hold themselves aloof from the conquerors. After all, the French marching into the capital today were tramping over the sacred platform of U.S. foreign policy: the Monroe Doctrine. Certainly Ambassador Corwin knew tiny pangs of humiliation today, and certainly Matt and his fellows in the Marine guard felt the same frustration all good soldiers feel when they are withheld from a righteous battle. Crisp and firm as they looked in their uniforms, they must inwardly be as limp as the Stars and Stripes hanging from its angled staff at the peak of the embassy roof, where no wind blew.

Solange had moved down the steps and almost into the broad boulevard itself, leaving Sarah alone with Matt.

"We'd never stand for this in a million years if we weren't fighting for our lives north of the border," the Marine lieutenant said. "This is the day of the French. We'll just have to grin and bear it."

Then, from far down Calle de San Francisco, from beyond the jutting masonry fronts of the shops and offices where the wide street angled off to the southeast, a bugle sounded, followed by the shrill insistency of fifes, and a steady roll of snare drums.

A larger drum beat a counterpoint to the hammering of hundreds of booted feet striking the sunbaked cobbles somewhere beyond the bend of the *calle*, echoing from its stone and brick facades.

No real crowd clogged the sidewalks as she had expected. Most of the people welcoming the French must have gone to the Zócalo and its great plaza or to the steps of the cathedral.

Down the *calle* toward the bend wide-eyed little girls in white guarded by nuns held bunches of bright gold *flamenquillas* in tiny hands, and behind them a pair of silent *padres* in plain black mitres cast glances to where the conquerors would make their first appearance. No *obreros* or working women made up any part of the scattered knots of people along the route of march.

"It's not what you could call a rousing welcome, is it?" O'Leary whispered. "I don't think my fellow Catholics here in the capital will show the eagerness today the French expect."

"Why not?" Sarah asked.

"According to Ambassador Corwin, General Forey sent

word to Archbishop Labastida yesterday that the French have no intention of backing his demand for the return of the property Juárez's Liberals forced the Church to sell."

"How do *you* feel about that?"

"It's high time Mexico took a step out of the Middle Ages."

"You surprise me a little." She had thought Matt bright from the beginning, but certainly not reflective. Only a few days ago she lamented the fact that he seemed to have an almost old prejudice of hers against all soldiers and the dark gods they served, she supposed. "You're a good Catholic. I would have thought you agreed with the archbishop."

Matt grinned. "I wouldn't want my confessor or Miss Solange there to hear me say it, but I'm a damned sight more *American* than Catholic." The grin disappeared. "I've got some pretty strong feelings about what's happening here today. My heart's always been with the President and his Liberals, and I hoped the French would leave Mexico after First Puebla, but with Juárez suddenly and perhaps finally eclipsed, I do find myself hoping something good for this country and its people can come of this—" He broke off and gazed down the *calle* and Sarah turned her eyes to follow his.

A color guard of Zouaves in dark blue tunics and flaring, blood-red pantaloons had rounded the bend.

Heat waves throbbed up from the cobbles and turned the tricolor and the other flags and pennants into a shimmering dance of light and color.

Behind the Zouaves—in perfectly aligned ranks and in files so straight that each of the lead marchers, seen head-on and at a two hundred yard distance as Sarah saw them now, completely hid the one in the rank behind him—came three companies of smartly uniformed Tirailleurs, bayonets gleaming in the sun. The companies were separated by their officers, all on horseback, all with sabers drawn.

"Vive la France!"

Sarah blushed when she realized the shout came from Solange. Matt O'Leary groaned. "That's not guaranteed to win her many friends in this crowd, Miss Anderson. Can't say that I blame her, though. They do look fine, don't they?"

Despite the heat, she felt chilled.

Matt stirred beside her. "Here comes the victor of Puebla, General Forey. That's Juan Almonte on his left and Dubois de Saligny on his right. If I were Emperor Napoleon I'd get de Saligny out of here before he wrecks everything for the French. I wonder where Bazaine is?"

She only saw the supreme French general, Forey, dimly as he rode past the Americans under the portico without a turn of his head; her eyes were too busy searching for someone else.

A squadron of Chasseurs d'Afrique followed on the heels of Forey's horse.

Behind the squadron and its dancing, pennant-headed lances rode two officers she recognized. Marcel Gallimard, fitted out in a uniform that put the sun to shame, was the only one in the column who deigned to look at the Americans gathered on the steps of the embassy. On the horse alongside Marcel's, looking as if the company of Henri's young brother had given him dyspepsia, the Chasseur major she had met with Jason in Orizaba stared sourly up the *calle*.

A battery of field guns followed the Chasseurs. Through the thin soles of her pumps she could feel the tremors caused by their grinding passage.

"I'm glad now that President Juárez decided to leave, Matt. Those poor devils the other night could never fight this army."

Before she could wave to Marcel the Chasseurs and the artillery had moved on past the embassy.

There was no point in looking for *him* yet. He would ride with his Legionnaires.

No more soldiers marched in the wake of the guns. The Americans on steps began to move toward the giant doors.

She felt emptied. "Is it over, Matt?"

"I don't think so. We've only seen a fraction of them.

And we haven't seen Bazaine. Of course, some units, the Chasseurs-a-pied and the Foreign Legion in particular, might be taking another route through town. They can't all bivouac near the Zócalo. Bazaine may be deploying forces *around* the city, too. Maybe we had better go. The ambassador wants to give us supper."

"Wait just a moment." She held her breath.

There were more faint sounds of marchers coming from beyond the bend. These echoed from the old stones of the buildings lining the Calle de San Francisco with an eerie resemblance to the noises Solange had awakened her to the night of the Republican exodus.

Then she saw them: the wounded.

The French had not meant them to be seen. Broken men, seemingly never-ending lines of them, men in the same uniforms of the vanguard troops: Zouaves swinging awkwardly on crutches; Tirailleurs swathed in bandages or with arms in slings and sometimes with a limb missing hobbled along beside them or huddled together on mule-drawn *carretas;* Chasseurs d'Afrique looking lost without their mounts; Chasseurs-a-pied, one leading another man whose eyes were covered by a bloody dressing—and Legion-naires.

Her heart froze. For the first time she made the connection between his profession and the dangers he must have faced since he left the capital. Even when Matt or *La Prenza* reported the heavy fighting leading to this day of French triumph, she only once considered the possibility of anything happening to him . . .

"I don't feel too well, Matt," she murmured. "Do you suppose you could find me a place to sit inside?"

"Certainly, Miss Anderson."

She turned and started up the steps, only to be halted by O'Leary's suddenly excited voice. "It's Bazaine!" She had no genuine wish to see another general, but Matt's next words forced her to turn back toward the *calle.* "And would you look at who's riding on his right! It's an old acquaint-ance of ours."

A tall major with black hair grayed a little at the temples rode beside the only officer who could possibly be Bazaine. The major looked unmarked by battle. If a heart can truly sing, hers did now.

"I'll be damned!" Matt said. "I think our companion and fellow tourist at Chapultepec was playing games with us that day, Miss Anderson. He's no more plain *Mister* James than I am."

23

Even before the grand French entrance into the capital Cipi nosed into the city and found quarters for the three of them in a rundown but spacious old house near the Plaza Mayor, a stone's throw from the Zócalo and the Palacio Nacional where Bazaine and General Forey made their headquarters. The general insisted that James live no more than five minutes away.

The dwarf made a mild apology that it was not the apartment on the Paseo he still predicted they would occupy before the year ended.

"We will get there, *mi mayor!*"

"There is nothing wrong with this place. Besides, I will be leaving for the north soon with my new regiment."

"*Pero,* you will *not* go north, *señor.* General Bazaine will, of course, but you will stay behind."

"Why would I stay behind when there's a major action?"

"Cipi does not know *everything.* As to our quarters, you are right. These *will* do for the moment. But you are still only a major, *señor.*"

"Let's get back to that business about me staying behind."

"You doubt Cipi?"

"I most certainly do. But supposing for a second you are right, when do you see all this taking place?"

"The promotion? Soon, very soon. *La Casa* on the Paseo? Not until autumn, when the general returns from his victory at San Luis Potosí."

"You think we shall defeat the Republicans by then?"

"No. President Juárez will simply move his government somewhere farther north."

"And General Bazaine will fight at San Luis Potosí without me?"

"*Sí.* Your general will once again have special, and more important, tasks for you. Your fighting will come later. The French high command will want to get as much of Mexico in their hands as they can before the Austrian arrives. *También,* that high command will be much different from the one we know now."

"How so?"

"General Forey's days here are numbered, *señor.*"

"Nonsense. He's just taken an important city, maybe a whole country, for his emperor."

"Be that as it may, do not doubt Cipi, *por favor.* Wait and see."

"Well, let's suppose it were true. Is someone else coming out from France to take General Forey's place?"

"No. The principal players in this comedy, save for the Austrian and his wife, are all on stage and in their places. General Bazaine will rule Mexico. Your *carreta* is now drawn by a very bright star, *verdad.*"

"Don't be ridiculous. General Forey is firmly in command. There has been no word that the Emperor contemplates any changes until the archduke takes over."

Cipi shrugged. "We shall see."

It gratified James—at first—that there was also room in Casa Mimosa, as the ramshackle dwelling was called, for Pierre and Paloma and he asked the absurdly mismatched couple to move in with him.

He found that Boulanger had no opinion on Cipi's forecast of the departure of General Forey, and the Chasseur looked perplexed when James had the little man repeat it, but he fell solidly in line with the dwarf's prediction about

James's new position with Bazaine and about the general's place in Mexico. "He will run this country whether Forey leaves or not, *mon ami.*"

James had some restive moments thinking about Cipi's conviction that his master would not see combat soon. That simply could not be. His only genuine value to Bazaine was as a fighting man. But he finally faced the fact that since his enlistment ran out two days after San Lorenzo, he was no longer a Legion officer.

Bazaine had no sooner settled into his office in the Palacio Nacional than he posted James to the command of an Imperial Guards regiment forming soon, but at the moment he was actually a man without official military standing, although still in his old uniform. He felt rootless.

One thing made life a little easier. With the back pay accumulated while he sat in the tent city south of Puebla and during the Battle of San Lorenzo, he now possessed more small wealth than at any time in his life. He raised Cipi's and Sofía's wages. The dwarf took it as his simple due, but the girl actually deserved it more. She had her hands full running Casa Mimosa since Paloma turned out to be a lazy slut. Sofía pressed uniforms and ironed shirts for Boulanger right along with the ones she did for James. The situation enraged Méndez y García. "I do not know why Major Boulanger keeps that sow. She makes love no better than she cooks or cleans." James wondered how the *brujo pequeño* knew that.

Although Sofía never breathed a word of displeasure at the extra work, James made a mild complaint to the Chasseur.

"*Tu a raison.* I will look for another servant, Jason. My dove will leave us soon, anyway," Pierre said. "And not merely because of her slothful housekeeping. With a new order shaping in Mexico, Boulanger will soon enter circles barred to him in Paris. Paloma would be an embarrassment. A man needs a woman of standing." It occurred to James that the Frenchman may have been hinting that James, too, should look to insuring his social position by ridding himself of Sofía. Pierre went on. "Which reminds me, the woman you and I met at Orizaba and whom you told me you met again during your time here for Bazaine—did you see her when we marched in?"

James *had* seen her—but only for a heartbeat. She and the Marine who accompanied them to the Washington's Birthday gala and later Chapultepec had stared at him from the steps of the American embassy on Calle de San Francisco, but he had not returned their look beyond a flick of his eyes so rapid neither of them could have detected it.

Thank God he had soldiering to do—even if it was soldiering from behind a desk for the moment.

As Cipi pointed out, it would only be a matter of weeks before Bazaine ordered the First Division north to San Luis Potosí in pursuit of Juárez's government and what army remained to the Indian president. The little rogue's predictions notwithstanding, James would be on the move with it. It would be too much to bear were he locked in Mexico City, so near and yet so far from her. It was not likely he would see her before the army went on the offensive once more.

Near the end of the third week of July, Bazaine surprised James by asking him to report for a meeting at seven on a Sunday evening. He could not remember the general working on a Sabbath. Something out of the ordinary must have happened.

There were two other generals and perhaps a dozen colonels and majors in the anteroom of Bazaine's office in the National Palace and James prepared to wait, but as had been the case at Jalapa, Bazaine appeared in the doorway and called him in by himself before he had a chance to sort out any of the others.

"I am going to astonish those officers out there, Major," Bazaine said as James closed the massive carved door behind him. "Perhaps you, too." Always energetic and forceful, he seemed extraordinarily so tonight. "The *junta* which . . .

General . . . Forey appointed has finally named the regents who will govern until the archduke gets here."

Odd, the way the usually precise, articulate Frenchman stumbled as he uttered the words "General . . . Forey." He continued. "We can deal easily enough with that compliant pretender Juan Almonte, and that old *champignon* General Salas will follow Almonte's lead on almost any matter, but I fear the third, Archbishop Labastida, will present problems. His Catholicism, unlike the reasonable religion we know in France, would return Mexico to the time of Torquemada. I wish the *junta* would have included a trustworthy Frenchman in its triumvirate of puppets—even de Saligny—but I suppose it matters little to General Forey. He is too busy playing *grandpère* to the children in the Zócalo!"

James had heard about Forey's attempts to woo the citizenry. Bazaine—if Cipi was right in his prophecy that the general would soon be the genuine ruler of Mexico—would be different. He would only pay court to his Emperor and to France.

Bazaine was trying to disguise his feelings at the moment, but James knew he still smarted from the snub Forey had given him by not allowing him to be in the van of the triumphal march up Calle de San Francisco. Feeling himself to be the real architect of the victory at Puebla that opened the portals of the capital to France and the conservatives, he must have lusted to take the cheers at the Zócalo, too. Instead, the Legion and the wounded, Bazaine and James with them, were shunted off the *calle* to a bivouac on the Alameda.

But if what Pierre reported to James represented the actual tenor of the greetings from the small conservative crowds that turned out to welcome the army, they had not missed much. There had been nothing like the roars that erupted two days later when Leonardo Márquez and his cavalry swept into town from the wreckage of Puebla and hammered their way, pelted with flowers, up the same cobbled streets where Forey, with Juan Almonte and de Saligny on either side of him, made their more stately progress. Even with the French presence to hold the Leopard and his horsemen in check, fearful Liberals of every stripe kept themselves indoors and out of any possible harm's way when Márquez and his fierce soldiers rode in, but it did not diminish the size of the crowds. Without a pro-Juárez Mexican anywhere in sight, masses of people who backed the church and the Conservatives lined the streets and jammed the plazas, shouting variants of "¡Viva Mexico! Death to Juárez!" as the surprisingly tiny Márquez and his horde cantered to the Zocalo.

It should have told Forey something, but apparently it had not.

Bazaine heeded the warning, though. "We are not nearly so popular here, even with the Conservatives, as General Forey thinks."

It had been a hectic month.

Bazaine—as if he took no umbrage whatsoever in the role of civil administrator Forey had assigned him—set to work like a whirlwind. He concerned himself with the smallest detail of the French governance of the city, even down to rewriting traffic regulations for the public carriages on the Paseo and its tributary calles, and issuing orders banning games of chance, which he maintained kept the populace from their work. He had the more unwelcome changes underwritten by the junta.

Boulanger roared with laughter when James told him of the general's activities. "Scratch a Frenchman of even the loftiest rank or station and you will find a bureaucrat."

James wondered how Salas, Labastida, and Almonte occupied their time. With Bazaine such a dervish, there surely was not much left for them to do except sign off on the general's decisions. No word came from their conference rooms in the National Palace, a floor above Bazaine's office. They might as well have conducted their affairs—were there any to be conducted—on another planet. The silence would not hold, he was sure of that. He remembered the steely archbishop from the party at the embassy; the intense clergyman would not remain a figurehead for long.

This Sunday night meeting, though, must be confined to military matters; James had seen no civilians in the anteroom. Bazaine confirmed it now.

"Bring the rest of my staff in for our little meeting, *s'il vous plait*, major. This, of course, will not be an administrative conference. It is time to plan for the next stage of the stabilization and pacification of Mexico."

Without Forey?—James wondered.

"We have received orders from General Forey, sir?"

"We shall not bother ourselves about the *general* or any orders he might give, major."

James's jaw dropped.

Bazaine smiled.—"Bring in my officers, major."

My officers? One of the generals and two of the colonels James had seen in the anteroom were on *Forey's* staff, not Bazaine's.

James went to the door, nodded to the group in the anteroom, and a superbly confident lot of French officers, with Mexican general Leonardo Márquez in their midst, trooped into Bazaine's office. The appearance of Márquez came as a surprise. He had not been in the anteroom with the others when James arrived.

If the Leopard looked tiny on horseback, he was minuscule in this roomful of tall, privileged, well-fed, and so recently conquering French officers, even in his braid-festooned uniform. It was almost impossible to reconcile Márquez's almost childlike appearance with his reputation, but in modern warfare a commander's size was not nearly as important as his reach and grasp. James glimpsed in the Leopard's countenance something so frighteningly messianic it brought a slight shudder. It was more than a guess, of course; stories about Márquez's ruthlessness had abounded since James came down the gangplank at Veracruz.

Bazaine stood to address the gathering.

"*Bien entendu, messieurs* and *bienvenida*, General Márquez. You must all realize that we have much military work to do here in Mexico before we rest. But before we get to that, there is a dispatch from Paris I must share with you. I have the honor of informing you, gentlemen, that his Imperial Majesty Louis-Napoleon has named our General Elie Forey a Marshal of France."

In the silence that followed, and through the first mutters of high pleasure from Forey's own three staff officers present, James smiled to himself. *So much for your black powers this time, Cipi. Forey's days cannot be "numbered" after this promotion.* The inner smile faded when Bazaine went on.

"*Aussi*, the new marshal has been recalled to France in the same directive." There was nothing turned inward about Bazaine's smile. "The emperor has expressed his trust in me by giving me command of all French troops in Mexico." He turned to Márquez again. "In his message, General Márquez, the emperor expressed the wish that you will continue to serve our common cause as faithfully and valiantly as you have. Together we can prepare this land for the new sovereign of Mexico."

The Mexican said nothing. Bazaine turned now to the rest of the group. "One other thing before we begin: most of you are acquainted with the officer on my left, my aide, Major Jason James, formerly of the Legion Etrangère. Major James, although he began life as a citizen of *Les Etats Unis*, is the first French officer appointed to serve in the Imperial Army of Mexico—where he will hold the rank of colonel and command a regiment of Guards. I am taking the First Division to San Luis Potosí, but Colonel James will stay here in Mexico City, *pour le moment*. Those of you not marching with me must keep something in mind. Colonel James will be a great deal more than my aide while I am in the north. He will be my deputy, with full powers of command. Not even the new marshal can countermand his orders. Now—let's get to work! We still have an enemy to defeat."

James could not have been more deafened had a battery of Chaumont 75s gone off in the crowded room. Every eye now rested full on him. Not all seemed friendly.

All right, Cipi, I can hear you . . .

The thought never reached completion. Leonardo Márquez was fixing General Bazaine with a penetrating look. It was not the sort of look James would have expected from an ally.

Bazaine had not been gone to the northern front a week before James had his first meeting with the erstwhile commander-in-chief of all of Napoleon III's forces in Mexico, the newly named Marshal of France, Elie Forey. He came to the office in the palace, and Bazaine's Corporal Lemonde showed him in to where James stood at attention behind the mammoth desk he occupied in the general's absence.

Marshal Forey had aged since James's previous glimpses of him. He looked more stooped, grayer, his sharp old nose a blue latticework of bright veins—but James still did not dare count too heavily on Bazaine's admonition, *"Not even the new marshal can countermand his orders."*

"Asseyez-vous, Colonel James," the marshal said. "No need to stand on ceremony with an old discard such as Elie Forey." They sat, with James feeling a jump of uneasiness, occupying his general's chair in front of more rank than any he had ever faced. But the marshal was speaking again. "You then, *monsieur,* are François-Achille's young paragon." He searched James's face with a pair of rheumy eyes. "I fear I have an awkward chore for you."

"Yes, *mon maréchal?"*

"My personal dispatch pouch from Paris contained disturbing, tragic, news from Paris concerning your commanding officer. General Bazaine may wish to return to France forthwith." If his news was so disturbing and tragic, why was this toothless old tiger smiling? Forey went on. "It seems that Madame Bazaine has died." He reached inside his tunic and brought out an envelope. "My *aide-de-camp* has written down the details of the unfortunate lady's last hours. Can you send a signal to General Bazaine at his First Division headquarters?"

"Yes, sir."

"Merci beaucoup, Colonel James." He laid the envelope

on Bazaine's desk. James watched the tired eyes stray to the array of battle flags. "This is a splendid office," the marshal said now. "A *bureau* fit for a Marshal of France—*propre*."

James decided that in spite of the delay it would bring, it would be prudent to send the bad news north by courier in a padlocked pouch rather than by telegraph. Bazaine's wire codes were known to too many members of his staff. Remembering the gossip about Madame Bazaine which Pierre Boulanger had passed along when the general first came to Mexico, a sixth sense told James the general might not be happy to have any mention of his wife, even that she had died, made in public before he heard it himself. Fortunately, as far as James knew, Forey had not bruited it about the capital, not yet, at least. James could guess a possible reason for his silence. There was no love lost between Napoleon III's two senior commanders here, and perhaps the marshal feared a welling-up of sympathy for Bazaine. Forey was already speaking to everyone in the Palacio who would listen about his reluctance to return to France and probable retirement.

James would not learn of Bazaine's reaction to the death of his Spanish wife for months.

As for Colonel Jason James, *his* loss had already taken place—in truth, he had lost something he never had possessed.

24

▲▲▲▲

After a brief rainy spell in June and early July, the weather in the capital turned clear and hot. The succession of bright, fair days, pleasant enough when they began, soon assumed for Sarah a deadly monotony, the blue of the sky piercing and very nearly cruel. There were times when she longed for the low, soft, gray-and-pastel canopies of spring-time Paris and even the pewter, late fall overcast of Cambridge.

The house on Avenida Moctezuma which had begun to seem like home was fast becoming a cushioned prison.

She caught glimpses of Jason James—once outside the Hotel Mirador where Matt took her and Solange to dinner, and again with General Bazaine in a carriage on the Calle de San Francisco, but on neither occasion did he seem to see her. Both occasions occurred before the first of August, and with no more signs of him in September and October, she became persuaded he had left the city and was with the army again, campaigning in the north.

Unlike her, Solange was perfectly happy now that her compatriots were completely in charge of the capital. "It will never be Paris, of course, *ma chère*, but this city is beginning to look and feel a little more French."

Indeed. Wives of ranking French officers arrived in the capital on an almost daily basis, and the *avenidas* and *calles* thronged with French engineers, architects, and construction crews making changes that promised to be more than the mere cosmetic ones such as the louvered shutters appearing everywhere on buildings in the more fashionable and better traveled boulevards. Freight wagons clogged the streets, delivering goods from Europe, including plumbing fixtures hitherto seldom seen in Mexico, and new shops sprang up on the Paseo and the sidestreets around the Zócalo. Solange pushed her nose into every one of them almost before they opened their doors for business, and spent a small fortune on perfumes and other toiletries they had not seen since she and Sarah boarded the *Strasbourg* at Calais.

While the capital became more French by the day, there were still constant reminders of the real identity of the country.

Under the aegis of Archbishop Labastida and Juan Almonte, the Conservative newspaper *El Cronista de México*, which Juárez's government had suppressed, began publishing again even as the mournful footfalls of the departing Republican troops and their women, children, and dogs seemingly still echoed. Another journal, *La Sociedad*, even more firmly in the archbishop's camp, sprang up overnight. While nominally backing the designs of Napoleon III, neither paper left it in doubt that the genuine ruler of the country should be Holy Church. The explosive matter of returning the properties Juárez had forced the Church to sell was the linchpin of Labastida's plan. Conservatives, who for whatever reason—power, pelf, or pure idealism—might otherwise have backed Maximilian as emperor, were splitting their support between the French and the brooding archbishop, pending the outcome.

The Liberal newspaper *El Siglo XIX* had ceased publication when Juárez and the Republicans fled, but a new journal, *La Independencia Mexicana*, soon circulated from San Luis Potosí. Bazaine and the Regents banned it from Mexico City. The American embassy, however, subscribed to it, and Matt O'Leary delivered it to Avenida Moctezuma semi-secretly. Its dimly printed editorial columns seemed pathetic flags for the cause of La Reforma, declaring that the Republican government would never surrender. In spite of the weekly brave scribbles of the Liberal writers, Sarah remained convinced that it was probably only a question of time before Juárez's hopes collapsed. Matt's prediction that the United States would not accredit an envoy to San Luis Potosí proved accurate. No representatives of the other powers, large or small, were sent north, either.

To make the outlook even gloomier came the news of Ignacio Comonfort's death in an ambush north of Guanajuato. Bad as she felt about it, Sarah's chief reaction was to wonder if the news had reached—and had any effect on—Jason James.

The prospect of complete Republican defeat failed to sadden her in any *new* way. It fitted too well with her listlessness.

Some strange, small things happened.

Until general, now marshal, Forey named the thirty-five

member *junta* to reign until the Mexican people chose the form of the new government they wanted, the capital's civil affairs had been run by antiquated General Salas, now a member of the Board of Regents with the archbishop and Juan Almonte. One of the old general's first pronouncements had made it mandatory for men in the streets to doff their hats whenever the Host was carried by in religious processions of any size, and for women of every station to cover their heads and kneel on the cobblestones.

General Bazaine countermanded the edict, provoking a heated editorial in *La Sociedad,* which painted the French Army authorities as godless. Sarah had already made up her mind that *she* would not kneel.

Another religious contretemps—again centering on the unresolved issue of the former church holdings and again reported by O'Leary—occurred in October and threatened for a few teetering days to bring a far more serious confrontation.

Bazaine, in the company of Zouave guards, virtually forced his way into a meeting of the regents and ordered them to validate the transfer by sale of the properties at issue. Juan Almonte agreed immediately and General Salas, too, not surprisingly, fell in line with the French demand, which Bazaine told them had the full backing of Napoleon III.

In cold fury Archbishop Labastida refused to comply. Bazaine, by Matt's account, smiled and informed the cleric that he was now dismissed from the Regency. "'Excused' is the way the general put it," Matt said. "But the archbishop was sacked all the same." Two days later Labastida excommunicated all the men who had taken office under the Regency. That, Matt said, would probably not have bothered Bazaine in the slightest, since only two of them were French, but the determined prelate then heated things up by closing the cathedral on Sunday during the hours the French Army had set aside for its soldiers to go to Mass.

Bazaine rode to the cathedral with a battery of artillery, had his gunners train their weapons on the great doors from point-blank range, and vowed that if the *padres* did not open them in five short minutes, French cannons would.

The doors swung open only seconds before time ran out, and Labastida, apparently fearing arrest, went into hiding for the next several weeks. Not one word about this contest of wills appeared in either *La Sociedad* or *El Cronista*.

What did appear was the result of the plebiscite on the form a new government for Mexico should take. It spoke overwhelmingly, according to the newspapers and the pro-French elements, for empire, and ordered the Regents to extend an invitation to Archduke Maximilian von Hapsburg to ascend the throne. For all the splash made about it, the news failed to impress O'Leary. "I won't say it's an out-and-out fraud, but the vote was only counted in areas like Puebla, Querétaro, and Cuernavaca, where the Imperialists were pretty sure of the sentiment. I suppose it will look like a mandate to the Austrian, though, and certainly will to Paris."

No titanic battles were being fought anywhere in the country, but a score of villages had already fallen to the French. "There hasn't been a lot of resistance by the Republicans," the Marine said. "It's a walk in the sun for the Frogs. They're conquering this country more with their feet than with bayonets or field guns. At the moment it's not what I'd call a real war. Bazaine isn't even meeting much opposition at San Luis Potosí."

But there was enough real *killing*, seemingly on every highroad and byroad from Oaxaca to Veracruz and to the north and west.

Two names kept emerging in that respect: one, that of General Leonardo Márquez, variously the "Leopard" and the "Tiger of Tacubaya"—in reference to his carnival of death in that city in 1859 when he was serving under General Miguel Miramon—was familiar; the other belonged to a newcomer to the carnage, Colonel Charles Dupin, leader of the French *contra-guerrillas*, a handpicked force whose unsavory reputation had grown with each passing month.

The Leopard's huge cavalry forces were advancing north-by-northwest toward Zacetecas in an attempt to outflank Juárez if the President decided San Luis Potosí was untenable and moved his government again. Not many details of the diminutive Márquez's battles reached the capital, but that they were bloody, merciless affairs seemed certain. Dupin, on the other hand, was ranging far to the east, back toward Veracruz and then to the north of the port city, firming up the French hold on the hinterland they had ostensibly brought under control after Second Puebla.

These were small actions, but every bit as murderous as those of Márquez.

Dupin's conduct in the small towns and villages he and his raiders swept through disturbed Matt O'Leary deeply. The flamboyant colonel was hanging and shooting scores of the Liberal officials and civilians left in the wake of the Republican's withdrawal—in some few appalling cases women. "Atrocities," Matt said. "There's no other word for it. France's military leaders have always been big on waging 'civilized' war. When Bazaine took over from Forey I thought he would put a stop to this sort of thing."

Sarah tried to distance herself from the worst of the news by taking an even keener and more intimate interest in Sor Francisca and the orphanage. Every Monday, Wednesday, and Friday she had Pedro drive her to the mission and its crumbling old buildings on the road to Cuernavaca, where she helped mend and alter donated clothing the sisters had solicited from all over the city, read to youngsters with sad, hollow faces—surprising the Mother Superior and the other nuns at her newfound command of Spanish—and presided at different tables each week for the big noonday meal. She performed these self-imposed duties faithfully, but with less and less enthusiasm as fall limped into winter.

Invitations to the embassy still arrived at the house on Avenida Moctezuma with regularity, but as the months crept by she found herself accepting fewer and fewer of them.

When she learned of the Tiger of Tacubaya's advance on

Zacatecas she sent an urgent message to Alberto Moreno at Mina La Sierra Verde, fearful that the earnest little manager, who had made no secret of his Republican sympathies, might find himself and his crew in danger. She cautioned him not to do anything rash or foolish out of loyalty to her dead brother's principles, but his return letter begged her not to worry about things at the mine nor at the *hacienda*. His reply eased her mind, but only to a degree.

> . . . and I foresee no trouble here, Doña Sarah. No Republican troops are stationed in the city now, and I fully expect General Márquez and his army to pass us by and concentrate on Durango. I will, however, heed your kind advice. We at La Sierra are too much in the debt of La Familia Anderson—*hermano y hermana*—to invite trouble for the enterprise that means so much to *los pobres* here—*and* in the capital. With Tonito Pérez no longer escorting our silver trains, there is nothing to call particular attention to us. More to the point, I have found that Conservatives such as General Márquez always assume that owners and managers of mines and *estancias* are of their own class and in total political agreement with them. I suspect the same is true of the French. Besides, *their* agents are now collecting the extraction taxes which formerly went to the government of Don Benito. I made no argument about this as I was sure you would agree, since refusal to pay might bring down the wrath of the new authorities, but if I have not acted in accordance with your wishes, let me know and I will refuse payment on the very next collection date . . .

She hastened to send him word that he had done exactly right; if he turned away the Conservative-French tax collectors he might find himself against an adobe wall.

Mine revenues, Señor Moreno informed her in the same letter, were on the upswing, and that brought her some satisfaction; it enabled her to tell Sor Francisca to begin construction on a new classroom wing for the mission school.

And if her outlook on life in Mexico stayed uniformly dismal through the summer, fall, and now early winter, it became mired in a bog of gloom at Christmas.

Wistful memories—of a Boston frosted in white, of sleigh rides and skating parties, carolers, and pine branches shimmering in the light of candles, of the gathered Kent and Anderson families holding pleasantly wicked eggnogs in loving hands, of mistletoe and merriment—did nothing to raise her spirits. In fact they made her feel achingly alone, as when her father died—even more alone than when Samuel died.

She had not heard from Henri. Not a word arrived about his projected trip to Mexico.

She wondered why this did not disturb her more.

Her dull mood worsened when the news reached the city of Bazaine's victory at Guadalajara and when General Tomas Mejía—the tough little full-blooded Indian who, surprisingly, considering his up-from-poverty history, had fought as a Conservative all through the War of the Reform—captured Guanajuato without his troops firing a shot.

For his part, Matt O'Leary turned gloomy and silent at the report that Bazaine and the French had joined forces with Mejía and succeeded in dislodging Juárez from San Luis Potosí, causing the president to moved his government even farther north to Saltillo. Republican resistance was crumbling everywhere. It was exactly as she had expected. She hated the prospect of Juárez's complete defeat, but she *would* welcome an end to the killing.

The third week in February, on an impulse, she hired a carriage and had the driver take her down to Chapultepec. Solange wanted to make the short trip with her, but Sarah insisted on going alone.

Her driver balked when she directed him to take her to the sallyport where she had entered the castle with Comonfort, Solange, Matt O'Leary—and Jason James. "*Pero no, señora . . . los Franceses!* Too many Frenchmen. They are working on the castle to get it ready for the new tenants. I do not wish to go anywhere near them." Obviously the man had Republican sympathies. It was getting easier and easier to forget there *were* such feelings in the capital any more.

She had him take the road that led through the deformed ancient cypresses under the north wall, where she had watched the Legionnaire's tortured face, and where her last nagging discomfort in his company finally turned to something else.

The ride back to Avenida Moctezuma seemed dreary.

On the first of March she made her decision.

"We shall break up housekeeping here," she told Solange, "and begin our return trip to France the first week in May, or as soon as I can book passage from Veracruz. If I can arrange it we'll stop in Boston before going on to Paris."

She knew how loath Solange would be to leave the Marine she had begun to refer to as her son—*mon fils*—but she could not allow it to dissuade her.

Her news devastated Matt. "It isn't that I blame you, Miss Anderson. I'd like to get out of this country myself before it becomes another European power, but every request for transfer I've made has been turned down flat. I'll sure miss you and Mademoiselle Solange."

The Marine did not mention his real reason for asking for a transfer. He had never said much about it, but she knew he desperately wanted to get back to the United States before the terrible war between the states reached a conclusion. In July of last year, while everyone at the embassy celebrated the great Union victory at that little town in Pennsylvania called Gettysburg, Matt fell victim to mild despair. "I think it's the beginning of the end for the Confederacy," he had said then. "I don't suppose I'll see action before it's over."

She would miss the young man, too. He had become almost family now, hers as well as that of Solange. She was beginning to understand his sorrow that he probably would never take part in the fighting still going on north of the border. She now had too *much* of an understanding of the feelings of men who had dedicated themselves to the frightening profession of arms, but she rejoiced in the thought that as long as Matt served in his present post he was far more likely to stay alive. She could only wish for the safety of another soldier.

Then she caught sight of that soldier again.

Alberto Moreno had come down to Mexico City from Zacatecas in mid-April to confer with her for the last time about the affairs of Mina La Sierra Verde. Pedro drove the two of them to the Banco Central to arrange for what constituted a power-of-attorney in Mexico, and to see to it that all of the mining company's funds were available to Moreno to keep a steady stream of money flowing toward Sor Francesca and the orphanage.

As they pulled to a stop across the street from the bank, Jason James emerged, just as he had that day more than a year ago. He was in uniform, not that of the Legion, but one that had begun to appear with increasing frequency in the city streets in recent weeks, the uniform worn by officers of the new Mexican Imperial Army.

He stepped to a carriage driven by his man Cipi, and before she could call to him, the dwarf whipped up his pair of horses and the carriage rattled down the cobbles of the *calle*.

She trusted Alberto Moreno so completely she allowed him to take charge of all the negotiations with the youthful bank manager who had taken the place of the one bandits killed during that week of anarchy in May. Papers the young banker pushed toward her across his desk received her signature without a thought and with no more than a cursory glance.

Back at the house on Avenida Moctezuma she hurled herself into a frenzy of packing.

She and the sorrowing but silent Solange were ready to travel within a week.

The confirmation from the Franco-Transatlantique Shipping Company in Veracruz confirming the reservation of their stateroom arrived on May fifth, in the same post as another letter, one in a rich vellum envelope bearing the great seal of the House of Hapsburg, the return address Castello de Miramare, Trieste.

Miramar
April 11, 1864
Ma Chère Sarah—

At long last the people of Mexico have spoken and asked Maxl and me to become their Emperor and Empress.

Paris and Vienna are all aflutter about the great adventure upon which we are ready to embark. The same is true in Brussels, where dear Papa declared that April 10, yesterday, the day Maxl signed the agreement delivered to Miramar by Señor Gutiérrez, will now be a Belgian national holiday.

We leave Miramar for Rome and the blessings of the Holy Father in another week, and then on to Mexico!

Emperor Franz Joseph has graciously offered the use of the Austrian frigate *Novara* to transport us to our new realm. Maxl and I feel this to be a good omen. The *Novara* was his flagship when he commanded the Adriatic Fleet.

We should reach Veracruz very near the end of May.

Of course I hope to see you immediately upon our arrival, but beyond that there is a very great favor I wish to ask.

I would be pleased and grateful if you would agree to become a member of our court.

Beyond the affection in which I have held you since our school days together at St. Catherine's, there is my esteem for you due to your intelligence and charm. While the latter—with your so well-remembered beauty—would serve to make you an ornament among my ladies-in-waiting, it is the former characteristic that recommends you to me most strongly.

You have lived in Mexico for two years since we saw each other last at my *petite soirée* in the Faubourg St. Germain, and your knowledge of the country over which Maxl will reign with wisdom and abiding gentleness would prove invaluable to us and, it scarcely needs saying, to our new subjects.

I have gathered a truly brilliant group, many of whom are already friends or acquaintances of yours, to serve me and present Mexico with a court worthy of it. None of the women in my personal entourage, however, is intimate with the country or its manners, and most of them, regrettably, do not at this juncture have more than a smattering of the language.

You would be first among equals.

I am sorry that this letter will arrive too late for you to give me your answer by return post.

If you agree to serve me, you can say yes by meeting the *Novara* at Veracruz and then accompanying Maxl and me when we make our imperial progress to the interior and our capital.

J'espère you *will* agree.

> *Je t'embrasse très fort*
> Carlota
> Empress of Mexico

The offer tempted her, as her old love for Charlotte welled up.

But her life in Mexico was over. Even if it had not been, there was no way she could ally herself with the imperialist designs of Napoléon III, not and keep faith with the lifetime dedication to democratic ideas and ideals fostered first by her father and strengthened by her association with wise and tolerant M. Auguste.

But—in the millionth of a second between asking herself

if she could say yes, and answering that she could not, a peculiar notion coursed through her. As a member of Charlotte's inner circle she might find herself in a position to be the voice of decent, humble Mexicans such as Alberto Moreno, Sor Francesca, her gardener old Pedro, and the coachman who had driven her to Chapultepec on that solitary pilgrimage.

But how, she wondered, could commoner Sarah Kent Anderson—not even French, Austrian, or Belgian— influence someone as headstrong as Charlotte von Coburg, or direct any small part of the thinking of someone as distant from Sarah Anderson in person, power, and tradition as Emperor Maximilian I of Mexico? No matter how much value Charlotte placed on her intelligence and "knowledge of the country," or how invaluable that knowledge would be to the royal couple's "new subjects," one word in the letter weighed more heavily than all the others—"ornament."

In no way could she ever resign herself to being a mere ornament to even the most brilliant gathering.

She put the letter in her desk with her Sierra Verde papers and the letter from Jason James, and opened the one from Franco-Transatlantique.

The steamer line had booked Solange and her to voyage out on the *Strasbourg*, the very vessel which had brought them to Mexico. The packet would sail from Veracruz on the fourteenth of May—comfortably in advance of Charlotte and Max's arrival at the Gulf Coast seaport—and drop them at Havana where they would board the New England Lines' S.S. *Paul Revere* for Boston.

Her future was set, perhaps not in stone, but in somewhere far from the Mexico that had brought her such mixed joy and pain.

Ordinarily, and this had been true her entire life, even her strongest dreams faded before she had been awake an hour.

But not this last one.

Three days after she first tried to shake it away it remained etched at the backs of her retinas the way lightning hangs in a dark sky long after it strikes the earth.

She was at Chapultepec again, but this time not gazing up at its parapets as she had from her hired carriage, but behind them on the roof, as she had been that first time.

And almost as exactly as the first time, Jason James was there, with but one difference in his appearance. He wore the uniform of the Imperial Guard he had worn at the Banco Central last month.

The look on his face would have cracked a stouter heart than hers.

In the dream he turned from the guns and took her in his arms.

In the morning of the tenth of May she retrieved Charlotte's letter and reread it. Half an hour later she called Solange into her study.

"Start putting things back together in our house, Solange. I have to see our landlord and renew our lease."

The Frenchwoman's face reflected a mixture of ecstasy and perplexity. "We are not leaving for Veracruz tomorrow?"

"Oh, we're going to the coast, but we shall return to the capital by the end of May."

The happiness on the duenna's features gave way to suspicion. "Am I permitted to ask *why* this change of plans, *ma chère?*"

"No, you're not."

It was not that she felt any reluctance to tell the Frenchwoman.

She had no answer for her.

PART THREE

▲▲▲▲▲▲▲▲▲▲

THE PLAIN

"Allowing him a breath, a little scene,
To monarchize . . ."

— RICHARD II

25

▲▲▲▲▲

VERACRUZ, MAY 1864

While still displaying the squalor and misery Sarah remembered from when she and Solange landed here more than two years ago, the Gulf port had changed considerably.

The French had constructed new docks and piers to accommodate the military buildup for their forces of the interior and to speed the flow of the increased commerce between here and the capital. To the casual eye the port seemed cleaner and more orderly, but a closer look revealed that *las buistras* still hovered over garbage-strewn back streets and alleys. The coachman who drove them in on the last stretch of road from La Soledad—the train they rode two years ago was now reserved for the transport of the royal party—informed them that the feared *vómito negro* endured in the coastal lowlands. "It is harder on the French," he said. "They are not used to it as we Mexicanos are."

Despite the brave gaiety of the banners and other signs of welcome along the waterfront, Veracruz at least in its barrios remained the pest hole which greeted Sarah and the terrified Solange back when they first stepped ashore.

They found accommodations now in an inn with a good view of the harbor, a new building fitted out to a much closer approximation of comfort than the *posada* with the airless room they occupied in '62 after disembarking from the *Strasbourg*; the money pouring in to the gulf port because of the still-growing French presence had somewhat improved the lot of travelers. Even Solange seemed marginally content, fatiguing as the trip had been.

Their innkeeper reported that the Austrian frigate *Novara*, not expected for another week, already lay at anchor in the harbor, but that the Imperial party would not disembark until the next day. Apparently the entire city had been taken by surprise. She left Solange at their *posada* to supervise a maid doing their laundry and set out on foot to see if she could divine what was apt to happen.

Inquiries made of a haughty colonel at French headquarters in the Baluerte on the waterfront were met first with stony silence and then only a few grudging words. The colonel put no stock in Sarah's claim that the new empress expected her, and she could not bring herself to tell him that she would actually be a member of the court. He probably would not have believed her anyway. He flatly refused her request to send a note out to the *Novara* on one of the launches she could see running from shore to ship every fifteen or twenty minutes. Leaving Charlotte's letter in the desk in her study back in the capital could bring about a minor disaster of missed connections in the ceremonial pandemonium planned for the royal couple's arrival tomorrow.

She and Solange would have to rise at an ungodly early hour, get their baggage carted to the Customs House at the docks, and wait there until she determined where and when to attempt the meeting with the friend she was finally beginning to think of as the "Empress." Matt might have thought of a better plan, but he was in the capital. He had wanted to make the trip with them, planned to, but at the last second Ambassador Corwin, fearful of sending misleading signals to a watching world, decided no one from the embassy should be at the landing, particularly since President Lincoln had at the moment no intention of recognizing the Austrian's Mexican government. The United States Consul at Veracruz, as a matter of fact—as if his Washington superiors were putting an exclamation point to turning a cold shoulder to the new regime in Mexico—had been ordered back to his own country, had already shipped out on an American warship, and had probably passed the inbound *Novara* on the high seas.

Sarah returned to the inn frustrated and out of sorts.

By nightfall dreary Veracruz became a place of luminous magic.

The ingenious Bengal lights Sarah had first seen in *fêtes* in Paris hung from every lamp post, and workmen had erected bamboo and silk arches on all the street corners near the waterfront to welcome the Austrian couple now taking their last dinner aboard the *Novara*, five hundred yards offshore in the oil-slick water which darkness turned to gleaming onyx. The small city itself gleamed in the soft gaslight which spread an amber glow over the principal *calles* and *avenidas*.

Out in the harbor roads the *Novara* sparkled lamplight from stem to stern, and reflections of the lanterns suspended from the frigate's rigging danced in the barely rippling water as if they were a second, low lying band of stars. Now and again the faint sound of string music floated over the harbor.

After a pair of steaming sitzbaths to soak away the aches and pains of the four-day trip from the capital—in the same sort of lumbering, stiffly sprung coaches of that first journey inland—a fine meal, by Veracruz standards, left them ready for bed.

Sleep eluded Sarah, but she was kept awake not only by the prospect of tomorrow's celebration of welcome.

On the last stage of the journey here, somewhere between Cordoba and La Soledad, a regiment of lancers had passed their sluggish coach at a furious gallop, intent, she realized now, on getting to Veracruz before their new monarch did. The officers leading it wore the same new Imperial Guards uniform she had seen on Jason James when she nearly met him again at the Banco Central. She searched for his face to no avail.

The incident made her wonder if Maximilian would pack his court at Chapultepec with uniformed men. The French soldiery certainly intended making more than a mere appearance there. According to Matt, François-Achille Bazaine fully expected to station himself at the emperor's side practically night and day once the new monarch was crowned in the Cathedral. Surely the Emperor would want his own ranking officers in attendance, too.

Well, Jason James, until recently a mere Foreign Legion captain, probably did not possess sufficient rank or stature to be posted to a palace garrison, and perhaps, given the nature of the court Max and Charlotte would create, he lacked, in sophisticated Viennese eyes at least, the polish such a posting would require. Still, anything could happen in Mexico. For instance, who would have thought that plain Yankee Congregationalist Sarah Anderson would perhaps be trading intimacies with Her Imperial Catholic Highness Charlotte von Coburg, her ultra-noble Hapsburg husband, and the lords and ladies of what she just knew would be a glittering court?

In the afternoon the arrogant colonel had revealed that the early arrival of the *Novara* had caught the French Army completely unawares.

Bazaine, campaigning with his army in the north, and after his triumph at San Luis Potosí seeking battle with President Juárez's Republicans at Saltillo, would not apparently be able to make an appearance here in Veracruz, and only a tiny fraction of the Council of Notables, whom rumor back in the capital said would be falling all over each other to greet Max and Charlotte, had as yet arrived. None of the Regents were on hand, not even Generals Almonte or Salas. Almonte, probably as much in the dark about the early arrival of the *Novara* as were the French, was expected to ride in from Orizaba sometime today according to the French colonel. With no one coming ashore from the Austrian frigate before seven in the morning, those supporters of the crown who did not make it in to the city tonight or by shortly after dawn tomorrow would never be able to tell their grandchildren of seeing Maximilian I place his imperial foot on the earth of his realm for the first time.

Other rumors in Mexico City reported that Archbishop Labastida, while allowing a formal welcome by the Bishop of Puebla, had subtly discouraged too big a Mexican fuss over the Austrian *entrada*. The prelate had no intention of being on hand himself; an article in *El Cronista* quoted the churchman as regretting he would be unable to undertake the journey to the coast because he was completely occupied preparing for the coronation in the cathedral. The author of the piece, however, let slip that Labastida was running those same preparations from his summer residence in Manzanillo on the far Pacific coast.

Which all reminded Sarah she had not heard a church bell since she and Solange arrived. Perhaps they would ring tomorrow.

Restless and wide-eyed, she went to the window and gazed out over the water toward the *Novara*.

A wind had risen, had already extinguished two of every three of the Bengal lights adorning the quay, and was stripping the bright silk from the triumphal arches directly in front of the inn, revealing their essential flimsiness. The streets were empty. For the sake of her old friend Charlotte she hoped they would fill by the time she and Max left their ship.

As she watched, the wind picked up, and by eleven became a full scale, roaring *norte*, which fortunately died away by two o'clock.

At last she found sleep, or rather sleep found her, but not before the outriders of doubt about her decision to stay in Mexico made a determined run at her.

During the last hours of the night the *Novara* had moved to dockside. The flare of the trumpets died in the still air on the waterfront as Maximilian von Hapsburg waved to the crowd from a break in the frigate's rail.

"He looks *merveilleux, n'est-ce pas?*" As far as Solange was concerned, she was looking at a viceregal surrogate for her *own* monarch, Napoleon III.

"*Oui,* Solange. *Et elle, merveilleuse, aussi.*" Once again Sarah—watching from the steps of the Customs House as the archduke descended the gangplank of the *Novara* with Charlotte on his arm—was struck by the strong resemblance between Max and Henri Gallimard, Comte de Bayeux. Yes, they could have been twins, or at the very least, brothers. The tall figure elegantly dressed in the same uniform worn by the Imperial Guards—its tunic front splashed with decorations—and bent into the slightest of stoops; the thin, fair hair and wispy beard; and, more than any other feature, the soft, sad eyes: all might have been Henri's, too.

In Max's shadow Charlotte gleamed like a dark jewel, the radiance Sarah had noted at the party in the Faubourg St. Germain heightened and magnified. The same colonel who had said Sarah could not approach the couple during the actual landing was now striding up and down in front of the Customs House with three armed soldiers. They had already stopped a portly middle-aged man in his attempt to find a place on the dock near the foot of the gangplank, three or four hundred yards away from where Sarah and Solange had taken up their positions.

Now the gun salute boomed across the water from the island fort of San Juan de Ulua, drawing an answering cannonade from the French frigate *Themis,* which had escorted the *Novara* across the Atlantic and through the Caribbean. Sarah's mind raced back to the last time she had heard this kind of martial thunder—on the roof of Chapultepec.

Max and Charlotte stopped on the quay. Half a dozen civilians, four men and two women, came down the gangplank behind them. The women, one a spectacular reddish blonde, were no doubt part of that "brilliant group" of Charlotte's in which Sarah was supposed to be an "ornament."

The emperor-to-be and his dark-haired consort seemed absorbed in the sights and sounds greeting them, but there was also about them a strange hint of detachment, of otherworldliness perhaps.

What was probably part of the same regiment of the Imperial Guard that had raced past their coach on the road between Cordoba and Veracruz, on foot now, was drawn up in impeccable lines on the dock where the Austrian couple alighted. Again—probably because of those fleeting thoughts about Chapultepec, rather than with any real expectation—she looked at the faces of the officers for Jason James.

Two companies of Zouaves, certainly not an imposing force, were lined up behind the Guards. It *would* be wise of the French not to make too overwhelming a presence today; it was, after all, *Maximilian* making his entrance to Mexico, not Emperor Napoleon, no matter how much Solange or her countrymen might have wished otherwise. But there should have been more welcomers—military *and* civilian—and there should have been a military band in evidence.

A small gathering of well-dressed people stood on the dock itself, but there were not half a dozen around Sarah and Solange on the steps of the Customs House. Most of them, from what conversation Sarah had heard as they waited for Max and Charlotte, were French. The Mexicans of Veracruz, *criollos* and *mestizos* alike, seemed to have stayed at home or at their work today. Matt had told her how strongly the citizens of this town supported the forces of Benito Juárez during the War of Reform. Apparently that sentiment had not changed or weakened since the French landed here almost three years ago.

And why were the church bells still silent? Orders from Labastida? The few times she had seen royalty on public display in Europe bells and chimes had played a counterpoint to every step they took.

At the end of the pier a flower-bedecked open carriage waited with several mounted officers who had just moved into place. Hard to tell from here, but they looked to be wearing the same uniform as the soldiers of the Guards nearer her. Stately, indeed leisurely, as was the pace of Max and Charlotte as they reviewed the troops, they would reach the conveyance in little more than a minute.

How could she position herself where Charlotte could see her? The Imperial Guard, and Max's and Charlotte's French Army host-guarantors as well, would probably not let anyone not actually a member of the imperial party anywhere near the couple, and probably intended whisking the pair straight to the railroad station at the central plaza to board the train. There would be far too much danger from the *vómito* to risk exposing the new royal arrivals to its ravages one second longer than absolutely necessary, and there was always the possibility, however remote, that they could find themselves in other, more immediate kinds of physical danger in this basically unfriendly city. There could be an Antonio Pérez or someone else as dangerous and threatening lurking behind every corner.

With no transport available to her and Solange, she could not arrive at the station in time to find out what Charlotte planned for her. A check with the officials in the Customs House had turned up no message from the frigate. It had not worried her too much at the time, but it began to now.

With the gap between the Customs House and the royal entourage widening, she could not just grab Solange's hand and run to greet her old school friend. Such a display, particularly since they would have to push their way through all those uniforms, would look ridiculous.

Then her feeling of helplessness disappeared in a momentary vexation with Charlotte.

Princess, archduchess, empress, whatever, no matter how preoccupied, she had no right to treat a friend so cavalierly. She had asked Sarah to meet her here in Veracruz. With all the resources of two great empires behind her, Charlotte could have arranged to get word ashore from the *Novara* last night, or this morning at the latest.

Max and Charlotte stepped up to the running board of the carriage, and the cavalry officers detailed to escort it saluted. The vehicle pulled away, made a sharp U turn, and began to roll back toward the Customs House in front of the troops the pair had just reviewed. The ranks of uniformed men looked seamless. The civilians down on the dock had surged forward, but the colonel and his three soldiers—their bayonets fixed—moved in front of them and barred their way. Even if she threw dignity to the wind and tried to push her way past the colonel and through the Guard's close order ranks, she could never reach the roadway before the carriage and its mounted escort passed. It would do no good to call out, either, The soldiers between Sarah and the vehicle had grounded their rifles, raised their caps, and were filling the air with *"Vivas!"* loud enough to blanket all other sound, even though in some strange way they seemed more sighs than shouts.

She heard her own despairing sigh. It could be she would be back in Mexico City before she and Charlotte met. Hemmed in by their military guard as the French obviously intended the couple to be on every foot of the journey to the capital, it was unlikely in the extreme she could get to them before then.

Damn! If she had not renewed the lease on the Avenida Moctezuma house, the temptation she felt now to wait here in Veracruz for the next vessel setting sail for Havana might prove irresistible.

"Señorita Anderson, *por favor!*"

The voice from behind her was as much the growl of an animal as any human utterance.

Sarah turned to find Jason James's servant Cipi grinning at her.

An altogether different little man from the carriage driver of the trips to the embassy and Chapultepec, he was dressed in the full regalia of the Imperial Guard lined up on the waterfront. His crooked grin, though, was the same marvel of impudence she remembered. He removed his military cap and made a sweeping bow that brought the top of his big head perilously close to the step he stood on. "*¿Como esta, señorita?* Colonel James sent Cipi to take you and the other lady—" he nodded toward Solange. *Good Lord! Was he winking, too?* "—to *la ferrovia.* He said to tell you the empress will receive you in the imperial private car once the train leaves the station."

"But, *señor,* how did—"

"*Perdon, señorita.* We do not have time for the lengthy conversation Cipi would like. He has already secured your *equipaje* from the idiots who work inside this building and has placed it in the buggy he has waiting in the *calle* at the back. The *muchacho* who is supposed to guard it looks only marginally reliable, so Cipi suggests we hurry."

With that he spun around on black boots polished to a mirror finish and swaggered toward the front door of the Customs House. The knife she saw the night of the Washington's Birthday celebration at the embassy was belted swordlike to his side.

It did not even occur to her to question his right to take charge of their luggage the way he had; the words "Colonel James sent Cipi . . ." still echoed. Jason must be here in Veracruz. And *Colonel* James? She burned with curiosity.

She nodded to the open-mouthed Solange and started after Cipi, taking one quick second to cast a glance behind her to the pier, where the royal carriage and its escort had now reached a point even with them.

One officer of the Guard, his saber slanted across his right shoulder and ablaze with reflected sunlight, led the way for the entourage.

Jason . . .

Before she even realized she had moved, she found herself at the bottom of the stairs, going toward him. That colonel and his men be damned! From the lower vantage point she could see nothing of the carriage or its escort.

"Señorita Anderson!" Cipi's voice was harsh, commanding. "*Adelante, señorita!* There is no time to waste."

At the top of the steps again she looked for Jason. He was gone, as was the carriage and the other officers of the escort.

She turned and followed Cipi and Solange through the doors of the Customs House.

26

▲▲▲▲▲

"The emperor and the empress have gone to the cathedral to attend Mass," Cipi said as he helped Sarah and Solange into the buggy at the rear of the Customs House. "It will be their first in Mexico."

"Can *we* go, *ma chère?*" Solange pleaded. "The cathedral here is the one with the famous 'cross with the hands' Matt told me about. To attend Mass there and take communion with Emperor Maximilian would be something to—"

Sarah was grateful when the dwarf intervened. "*No se puede, señorita.* You would not be allowed in the cathedral while their majesties are at worship, and they will have an escort to get them quickly from their devotions to the station. The army won't hold the train once they are in their private car. If Cipi does not take you and Señorita Anderson straight there now, he might not be able to get you on board before they pull out. *Vamanos.*"

The little man rushed them through the back alleys of Veracruz to the railway station with the same lightning whip hand he had used on the night trip to the embassy. The streets were empty.

The train was much longer than the one they had taken with Matt. A baggage car had been added, as well as several for animals and freight. Cipi showed them into the very coach they had ridden in before, now the third behind the locomotive. He handled their heavy bags as if they were feather light, garnering a look of admiration from Solange.

The car had nearly filled by the time Cipi left it and the crowd of trackside crowd workers swallowed him.

Solange gazed after the dwarf until he disappeared. "Where do you suppose he got that uniform, *ma chère?*"

Sarah had a question of her own. How had Cipi, or more to the point, Jason, known of their whereabouts, or even that they had *come* to Veracruz?

Civilians jammed the car looking for seats, but none among them seemed to be any of those who came ashore with Max and Charlotte. None, that is, until the strawberry blonde from the gangplank, older than Sarah, but still not past her early thirties, with a very American duster draped across her arm, came to their seat and perched casually on the arm of the one opposite her and Solange. Not beautiful, but boldly handsome, the woman wore a stunning gown of silver lamé and several strands of pearls. The red-gold hair, rounded into a chignon at the back, was topped by a small black felt hat with a rolled brim; the very style of hat Napoleon III's Empress Eugenie had worn to the races at Beauchamps in Paris the last time Sarah saw her.

The woman surveyed Sarah through narrowed eyes with a hint of green or hazel, eyes with a spirited twinkle.

"*Wie geht es ihnen?*" She curved full lips into a winning smile. "I am Paola Kollonitz, lady-in-waiting and wardrobe mistress to her majesty. I *think* perhaps we met at Charlotte's dinner in the Faubourg St. Germain two years ago. I had a lot of champagne that night, but I know I *saw* you there. Even if my memory fails me, *fräulein*, you are easily the most beautiful young woman in this car, so you just *have* to be the empress's Sarah Anderson. She has instructed me to bring you to her once she is settled in the private car, the one ahead of this one." Her greeting in German and the slight accent tinting the rest of her words spoke of Austrian, probably Viennese, origins.

"I remember you well, countess." Actually, she had only a faint recollection of seeing this woman at Charlotte's soiree. The countess was a marvelously attractive creature she *should* have remembered better, a woman of a fine full figure and from these first hints an open, breezy manner. It was a stroke of luck that Sarah did recall hearing her name, and particularly her title, somewhere; there must have been some mention of her by M. Auguste or Tante Claudine. Flattering that the Kollonitz woman would remember seeing *her*. The countess barely glanced at Solange.

Sarah placed her hand on Solange's. Things would be different for the Frenchwoman now that her friend and once-again mistress was entering Charlotte's inner circle. There had been a steady escalation of the duenna's position with Sarah over the past two years, but with the strict adherence to protocol she presumed Charlotte would expect, Solange would have to withdraw to the same well-kept place she had occupied in Paris. It could hurt.

"Call me Paola, *bitte*," the countess said now. "And with your permission you will be Sarah to me. In serving Charlotte . . . the empress . . . we shall become like sisters, *nein?*" She seemed sincerely warm—but it did not bring about a complete resolution of Sarah's doubts. Great care had to be taken with anyone she met from here on out.

"How is . . . Her Imperial Majesty?"

"Splendid. Exhausted, of course. It was a difficult crossing. The *Novara* is not precisely a passenger vessel, and we had severe storms in the Atlantic. The empress occupied herself mostly in study for her new tasks here in Mexico and in helping the emperor compile his book on the protocol and etiquette for the court. I, on the other hand, not so industrious as the empress, learned about nautical life from a most engaging young first officer. I should not be surprised to find that—" Paola Kollonitz broke off and stared out the window. "But I see Their Majesties have arrived."

Sure enough—although Sarah caught no sight of Max or Charlotte—horsemen of the Imperial Guard were passing by the window. Sarah looked for Jason again, but did not find him.

She would in very short order face one of the two or three

most defining moments of her life, and she could not keep her mind on it. Jason had to be out there somewhere. Sending Cipi to her could only have been done with Charlotte's, and perhaps Max's, knowledge and approval. How had he come by either? For that matter, how could Charlotte or Max even *know* about Jason James?

Paola Kollonitz stood up.

"General Almonte and a group of the emperor's new Mexican subjects are with Their Majesties at the moment. I am not sure how well they will be received after this dismal welcome. In any event, they should not be much longer. I shall come back here for you, Sarah, when the time comes for your audience. *Wiedersehen.*"

As the countess made her way down the length of the car, Sarah marveled again at the stylish, silver dress. After two years in Mexico, her own wardrobe was probably hopelessly out of fashion. A few French couturiers had already opened ateliers in Mexico City and Solange had pestered her for months to go in for fittings. She would now.

The Guards Paola had seen through the window were gone, and the train left the station in minutes, but it was the better part of another hour before the countess returned for her.

When Sarah entered the Imperial car in the perfumed wake of Paola—who then stepped gracefully to one side—Charlotte rushed from a chair at the far end and wrapped her slim arms around her. She kissed Sarah on the cheek and leaned back to look at her.

"Sarah! *Ma chère!*" Charlotte's voice had lost the musical ripple of schooldays, or even of the Faubourg St. Germain. Now it carried a new air of wary maturity, something evident in her jet black eyes, too, although a hint of the banked, moody fire of the headstrong Charlotte of St. Catherine's still glowed in them. "Yours may be the first friendly face Max and I have seen in Mexico. You have met Paola?"

"Yes, Charl . . . Your Majesty."

The emperor was gazing through a window facing the station side of the tracks. A milky white hand rested on the gilt scrollwork of an upholstered upright *chaise* the Imperial car's outfitters must have thought a reasonable approximation of a throne. He did not look at Sarah.

She had expected the car to be filled with people, but save for a liveried servant bearing a silver tray with empty glasses who ducked into what appeared to be a pantry of some kind, no one else was in sight. A solo audience? Gratifying, after the strong feelings of neglect that had dogged her through the morning.

"So . . ." Charlotte said, "that handsome Guards colonel found you. I am so pleased. I was worried about you." She turned then to the emperor. "Maxl. It is our Sarah. Sarah Anderson. My good friend from Boston. You remember her from Brussels and our wedding, *n'est-ce pas?*"

When Maximilian took his eyes from the window and faced her, it was instantly clear to Sarah that this man in the medal-spangled uniform coat did *not* remember her, but his perplexed look disappeared rapidly. Apparently her name and the fact that she was American had brought some kind of faint remembrance or at least the show of it. He nodded and smiled. The smile seemed warm enough, but . . .

Freed from Charlotte's embrace she curtsied.

Charlotte spoke again over her shoulder. "Sarah has agreed to join Paola and Countess Zichy as one of my ladies, Maxl."

"Ah, yes." Max von Hapsburg sent a pale smile in Sarah's general direction. "We are delighted. It is not only the desire of Empress Carlota, but *our* sincere wish as well, Mademoiselle . . . Anderson, that you join our court. Empress Carlota has told us of your time together at St. Catherine's. You were a good friend to her then when she needed one; she may need a friend such as you even more in the days ahead." Well, he had remembered *something* about her. "Yes, we will need every friend we can find."

The graceful little speech sounded a trifle pathetic, but perhaps that was uncharitable.

"Empress *Carlota*" brought the question of exactly what she should call Charlotte now. No problems would arise in public, where it would be easy to stay with "Your Imperial Majesty" or some such stiff locution, the same as she would with the emperor himself, but even secluded, private discourse such as this one would demand something other than "Charlotte." "Carlota" perhaps? The answer might be found in that book of court etiquette in progress Paola Kollonitz had spoken of, if and when she got a look at it.

"This colonel of Guards—his name is James, *n'est-ce pas?*—" Charlotte said now, "seems to know you, *chérie*. Understandable, since you are both Americans here in Mexico."

"We have met, Your Majesty."

"He is a strange, quiet man, but so attractive. Like other Americans, he is very outspoken when he does speak, extremely capable, too, from what General Bazaine said in the letter the colonel brought to Maxl as his credentials. He acted *un peu* embarrassed when we asked him to look for you. Reluctant, too, although he apparently is too much of a dutiful soldier to say so. Have you two quarreled over something?"

"No, no, Your Majesty!" One could scarcely call either her first edgy meeting with Jason at dinner in Orizaba—or the momentary set-to outside the bank when she met him the second time—a quarrel. "We hardly know each other well enough to quarrel."

"We are pleased, *chérie*. Both you and Colonel James will be important to us, and the two of you will doubtless be thrown together frequently in the days and years ahead."

Sarah wondered what her face had betrayed at that last.

The emperor had regarded her with a bemused countenance all the way through this last exchange. Now he turned to look through the window again.

The train had left the sand dunes and *cienagas* of the

coastal lowlands, now rolled through the denser sections of the rain forest. The celebrated "botanist" of Miramar was becoming captivated by the trackside foliage and blossoms: mangoes, banana trees, a wild variety of orchids, bombax, peeping colorines—pinks, yellows, flaming reds, phantas-magoric blooms almost incandescent in the darkness where the trees arched together to form a sweeping canopy of deep blue-green—all against a luxuriant background of towering coconut palms. As she watched the emperor, Sarah felt a sudden glow of proprietary pride in the chromatic glories of Mexico. Nature was putting on a far more dazzling show for the new monarch than the French, for all their sense of style, had been able to mount this morning on the waterfront.

"*Wunderbar . . . magnifique . . .*" he said. "Splendid beyond description." The words were barely breathed, uttered for his own ears alone, but Sarah heard the rapture in them.

For a moment she could almost share his joy. This luxuriously appointed car was a magnificent theater-box from which to survey the beauty of the countryside, but she wondered then if anyone had bothered to tell their majesties that the track would still run out where it had two years earlier, a few miles beyond the village of La Soledad. For all their diligence in trying to reshape this country, particularly the capital, in their own national image, the French had yet to add so much as a paltry kilometer to the railroad line.

Countess Kollonitz had by this time discreetly absented herself from the imperial carriage as had the servant, and Sarah was alone with the two sovereigns. With what was facing them, and with the short journey aboard the train, this was probably all the time she would get with them before they transferred to the brutal coaches and had to face the rigors of the three hundred miles still ahead of them. At every city, village, and hamlet on this journey there would be crowds, deputations, Te Deums sung in the cathedrals, long queues of petitioners to receive, meetings, dinners, private chats with sycophants and political figures, and never-ending speeches and proclamations to be made. It could take weeks to reach the capital.

"Maxl!" the empress called.

"Yes, my dear?" He turned to her as if awakening from a dream he had no wish to leave.

"We wanted to talk with Sarah."

"We did?" His look was vague, distant, as if he were listening to secret voices. "*Mais oui.* We remember."

"Of course we do, Maxl. Sarah is the American who has lived in our capital these past two years."

"Ah, yes."

"She could become our most valuable and trusted guide to Mexico."

Now his look did focus on Sarah, and she knew he was really and truly seeing her for the first time, the earlier sweet greeting notwithstanding. It came as a shock that her truest perception of *him* was being formed in this instant, too; when she entered the car with Paola Kollonitz there had been too many impressions to register and catalogue at once.

Looking at Maximilian von Hapsburg now, she realized she had been wrong this morning and those other times when she likened him to Henri Gallimard.

Outwardly, they might appear as brothers to a casual, first-time observer, but there was one very real and frightening difference between the Comte de Bayeux and Maximilian von Hapsburg.

Quiet and serene, Henri throbbed with life compared to Max. For all that the emperor of Mexico's court physicians would doubtless assure him he was entering the prime of life glowing with the pink of perfect health—he seemed a dying man.

He was thirty-two years old. If he had been sickly as a child or youth, the gossip mills of aristocratic and bourgeois Europe would have ground the news out *en fine* from Dublin to the Danube. He had never, so far as Sarah could remember hearing, surrendered to the excesses that not too infrequently undermined the health and vigor of royal personages in the courts of the old continent, particularly the men. To her almost certain recollection, he had not lived only the sheltered, sequestered life of Schonbrunn. He had been a sailor on active duty in the Adriatic even before he commanded the Austrian fleet, was an accomplished horseman by all reports, and even in what could easily have been a soft life at Miramar had eschewed ease and repose, to the point of actually performing heavy manual labor with the stone masons who restored the old castle near Trieste. His love for botany, which had shone forth a few moments ago as he gazed at the tropical forest outside the car window, had emerged first on a trip to South America in his young manhood, when he had explored the back country of the Amazon jungles with his hosts. He certainly should be sound enough, and in what his doctors would surely call "robust health."

Still, Sarah could not shed the feeling that she was observing a man already in decline, a decline that could steepen precipitously at any moment.

"When Sarah and I studied together at St. Catherine's," Charlotte said now, "she told me much about this country, Maxl. Her brother owns silver mines in Zacatecas, and she made visits to his chateau, or *hacienda* as it is called here. I believe she once dined with Señor Benito Juárez. That is so, *n'est-ce pas*, Sarah?"

Sarah nodded, but kept her eyes on the emperor. She had only the vaguest memory of telling Charlotte about meeting the little Indian. Had she also told her of her deep admiration of him? Charlotte must have remembered Sarah's tenuous link with Juárez long before she wrote her letter asking Sarah to join her at the court.

"Tell us, *si'l vous plait*, Mademoiselle Anderson," the emperor said. "Have you seen President Juárez since you have been in Mexico *this* time?" Strange that he would use the term "President." Her understanding was that France, having abrogated the Convention of La Soledad, was now withdrawing its recognition of Juárez's government. For the

French, and surely for Maximilian, too, there could be no *President* of Mexico.

"Yes, Your Imperial Majesty," she said. "I have seen . . . the president . . . on two different occasions since I took up residence in the capital, once quite by accident, but . . . I must confess that *I* initiated the other meeting."

"And what are your feelings about Señor Juárez? Please be utterly candid, *mademoiselle*."

Now she would just have to send the whole truth out naked and unguarded and see what response it provoked. Only the truth would do.

But before she could launch whatever that truth was, someone else entered the private car. The emperor turned from her to look at the new arrival.

"Felix! *Quel plaisir, mon cher ami*."

The newcomer was dressed in a sober suit of black wool, far too heavy a garment for the hot, humid Veracruz they had left behind, one which would probably prove every bit as uncomfortable until they reached the relative highlands of Cordoba. Even so, she knew at once that its wearer would not suffer in it. A slim man, something about him made him seem as cold as ice, a man who would not allow himself to perspire even in the midday Mexican sun. His clean-shaven face was bland under an abundance of dark hair, but with a faint sheen—an altogether unremarkable countenance if it were not for eyes which glittered and snapped under startling, ebony brows as if fires raged behind them. His head, facing the emperor and empress, was tipped forward, his chin almost on his chest, his back bent slightly in an obvious show of subordination, perhaps too obvious a show.

"Mademoiselle Anderson," Max von Hapsburg said, "may we present our advisor, Monsieur Felix Eloin? Felix is a Belgian, a countryman of the empress. Mademoiselle Anderson, Felix, is a long time, dear friend of the empress, and an authority on our realm. You must get to know her. She has lived in Mexico for the past two years."

Felix Eloin stepped, glided really, to where she sat.

She raised her hand to him. Eloin bent over, took it in his, and kissed it. Yes, his lips *were* frigid. Her hand went cold.

"*Enchanté, mademoiselle,*" he said as he straightened up.

He had not straightened up entirely, holding his upper body in a half bow, the identical attitude he had just displayed toward the imperial couple. Something told her it was a much-practiced thing. Felix Eloin probably bowed to everyone he met, pauper or potentate. His face was wreathed in a smile she could only characterize as unctuous.

She murmured an acknowledgment of his "*enchanté, mademoiselle*" and turned back toward the emperor and Charlotte. They had both fixed Eloin with a gaze of expectation and she felt drawn to turn and look at the Belgian again herself. His face was hidden from the couple, and he was still looking at *her,* but the ingratiating smile was gone, replaced by an intense regard that smacked of distrust, or at least suspicion.

"You have the reports on Chapultepec for us, Felix, do you not?" the emperor said now.

Eloin gave Max his full attention. "*Oui,* Your Imperial Majesty. The last of the rebuilding work at the castle will be completed in time for—"

"Maxl . . ." Charlotte broke in. "May we not give Sarah our permission to withdraw?"

"What, my dear? Oh. *Oui, oui,* of course."

He did not look at her as she curtsied and backed toward the vestibule. Charlotte followed her and kissed her on the cheek when they reached the end of the car.

"Maxl has perhaps too much to occupy him these days, *ma chère,*" Charlotte said.

She stepped out onto the platform between the two cars and found Paola Kollonitz leaning over the railing into the breeze. A few strands of the reddish hair had escaped the imprisonment of the chignon and were streaming out from under the Empress Eugenie hat. If anything, it made her even more appealing. The lively eyes were taking in the passing scene Maximilian had surveyed, but with what appeared to be only mild interest, not the revealing passion of the emperor. At the sight of Sarah the countess left the railing.

"Ach, wie gehts, Sarah liebchen? How did it go in there? Are Their Majesties in a slightly better mood?"

"It would seem so . . . Paola." An almost audible release of the tension she had not realized she was under accompanied the sound of the door of the imperial car closing behind her.

"You met Felix Eloin, did you not? I saw him enter the car."

"Yes, I did." Did her tone reveal that Eloin was the cause of her uneasiness and tension? It was the Belgian who had soured the audience which had begun so well. Actually, things might have turned awkward enough without him. His appearance, after all, had stopped Max's questioning of her in regard to Benito Juárez.

"Be very careful with Felix, Sarah."

Sarah searched the Austrian woman's features. "Tell me about Monsieur Eloin, Paola—please."

"He is a Belgian who seems to have gained the imperial ear to the detriment of my old friend from Vienna, Sebastian Schertzenlechner, the emperor's private secretary. It makes this Belgian a very powerful man. I understand he was a mining engineer in Australia and Fiji and his work impressed the empress's father. Gossip has it that his main duties in Mexico will be to watch for investment opportunities for King Leopold."

Investment opportunities? What was it Monsieur Auguste said before Sarah left Paris? "Catholic monarchy, bah! In the end it comes down to money, as it always does."

"Felix is a clever, sophisticated schemer," Paola continued. "I think he had more than an advisor's role in the emperor's repudiating the Family Pact he agreed to at Miramar, in which our Max renounced his rights of succession to the Austrian-Hungarian throne if he accepted the one in Mexico. At any rate, Felix and poor Sebastian—

who must have quaked in his boots at the time—were witnesses to the document of repudiation the emperor signed during the crossing on the *Novara*. When the news of *that* reaches Schonbrunn it could have disastrous consequences. I can't prove this, but I think Felix wrote it. Also King Leopold's idea, I suspect." The countess laughed. "In spite of all that, I must admit there are times when I find Felix devilishly attractive. If you knew me as well as you will, I am sure you would say, 'You say that about every man you meet, Paola.' There would be some truth in that."

A faint alarm sounded. Did Paola Kollonitz have the right to pass along the private, compromising, and perhaps dangerous information which she had told Sarah so breezily? And how could *she*, a brand new acquaintance, have inspired the kind of confidence Paola Kollonitz had just reposed in her on such short acquaintance? Perhaps Charlotte had told Paola that Sarah Kent Anderson of Boston and La Rue Rivoli could be trusted. But trusted with Charlotte's *secrets*, among which the Belgian influence of Felix Eloin might very well be one?

"Your maid or companion or whatever Mademoiselle Tournier is," Paola said now, "told me you are well acquainted with the Guards colonel who came out to the *Novara* last night."

"Solange told you? When?"

"I sat with her while you had your audience with Max and Charlotte. She is a very interesting woman. Very humorous. Very, very French."

Perhaps Sarah would have to revise her assessment of this Viennese woman as some terminally rigid aristocrat. Another thing: the countess let the names "Charlotte" and "Max" bubble from her lips quite blithely, her eyes even livelier if anything. It sounded as if they would always be Charlotte and Max in Paola's lexicon, and in whatever company.

Again it was too early in their acquaintance to make some hasty judgment, but it was not going to surprise Sarah too terribly if she and Countess Kollonitz did become friends, perhaps even the "sisters" Paola an hour-and-a-half ago forecast they would become.

A throaty laugh from Paola rose above the clatter of the wheels. "How did you ever find this American colonel, *liebchen?* When I met him last night on the *Novara* I was immediately struck by some deliciously naughty thoughts. At the empress's mention of your name, however, his look was such I knew I had to abandon them. Paola Kollonitz does not engage in competitions she has no chance of winning. But if there are any *more* like this Jason James in Mexico bring them to court."

"Surely . . . *you* don't need any help in finding admirers, Paola."

"Nein, nein—but a woman can scarcely have too *many.* But why am I telling *you?* Charlotte says that Henri, the Comte de Bayeux, is a serious suitor of yours . . . and now you have this marvelously attractive Guardsman to fill your life here in Mexico until Henri gets here. A splendid way to have your *kuchen* and eat it, too." The arch look on Paola's face left no doubt what she meant by "fill your life." Sarah felt a blush begin as Paola's earthy laugh came again. "Henri Gallimard, the *kuchen* in question—or in this case the *gateau*—is coming to Mexico, *nein?"*

"I haven't heard from him recently, but I think he plans to get here some time this summer."

"I don't know Henri well, but I do know men, I assure you. He is a shy, quiet man, but he *is* a Frenchman. Now that I have seen you, I *know* he will come to Mexico. Believe me. But I must confess I cannot understand what is keeping him."

Sarah wondered if she should be disturbed that Paola and Charlotte had talked so much about her.

"Do you know exactly what my duties will be?"

"We will both get instructions from Melanie—Countess Zichy—whom you have yet to meet, when we reach . . . what is the name of the place? Orizaba . . . *ja."* As she spoke the undercarriage of the train began the low squeals signaling an approaching stop—and the end of the line. "But I see we will have to save much of what we want to say to each other until later in the journey. I hope our accommodations will be within walking distance of each other."

Sarah curtsied to the countess, and hurried back to the seat where she had left Solange.

When the train stopped a swarm of railroad workers entered the coach to carry out the hand baggage which had not been loaded in the cars behind them, and in moments the passengers were trackside. There half a dozen wagons like the one she and Solange had taken to Veracruz from Cordoba yesterday were drawn up waiting for them.

Back down the line a crew of men had attached a ramp to one of the freight cars and were unloading quite a different sort of coach, easing it down to the crude stone platform that held the rain forest at bay.

Gold filigree gleamed from the carriage's black enamel sides, and through spotless huge windows with silver damask curtains plush red upholstery was visible. The lovely contraption, with graceful leaf springs under the body, could have been crafted by a watchmaker in Bienne.

She had last seen such a conveyance as Henry Adams's guest on the balcony at the United States Embassy four years ago, when they watched the Queen's Birthday parade in London, as the Coldstreamers and the rest of the Household Guard escorted Victoria through Grosvenor Square.

But she feared whoever had planned their Imperial Majesties' processional to the first extended stop in Orizaba had never made the trip himself. Unless the French Army's corps of engineers had performed some miracle of road rebuilding since she and Solange passed this way only yesterday, this delicate, proud marvel of a coach could not possibly hold up as far as Orizaba. The rock-strewn roadways lying in wait ahead of them would shake it into kindling and send its passengers into shock before the sun set tonight.

From near the animal cars farther back down the tracks a

groom in a uniform as resplendent as that of the Guards at the station in Veracruz led four jet black horses with gold plumes at their foreheads up the platform toward the imperial carriage.

Once there, the groom backed the team into the traces under the eye of a shako-capped coachman brandishing a long whip.

Another carriage leaped to mind: the squat, drab, funereal black cask-on-wheels in which Benito Juárez rolled into General Ignacio Comonfort's picnic in the park at Chapultepec. The president's little one-horse coach—for all that it appeared as unprepossessing in the shaded grove of *ahuehuete* trees as a sentry box in some frontier outpost—was sprung like a field artillery caisson and looked capable of rolling forever over the fiery cobbles of Hell itself.

But she did not want to remember that day at Chapultepec—not now.

Paola had come to stand beside her and Solange.

"The real adventure begins now, *nein?*"

27

When Jason James saw Cipi put Sarah Anderson and her companion aboard the imperial train he made a retreat, turning his horse and riding swiftly to the far end of the line of coaches and cars. He stayed there until the train left the station.

He would have gone to her and made an utter fool of himself if it were not for what he had learned aboard the *Novara* last night. He should be grateful to the troubling and seemingly faintly troubled woman he had learned it from—the empress.

Meeting and talking with imperial royalty would have been an uncomfortable experience for a man who still knew himself as an unremarkable, workaday soldier, despite the successes of the last year which had left Pierre Boulanger shaking his head. Under the circumstances he felt he had handled himself well with the emperor and his wife.

To be sure he had some understandable trepidation as the launch carried him over the oily waters of Veracruz harbor to the frigate. Bazaine had prepared him thoroughly for this particular mission, rehearsing him carefully in the manner of address acceptable to the new sovereigns and what topics of conversation were safe.

Maximilian himself seemed to want to put him at his ease when they met moments after he was piped aboard the *Novara*.

The emperor alone received him in the salon of the vessel. The small oak-paneled room, lighted by a single oil lamp set in gimbals hanging over a mahogany table limned Maximilian in its weak gleams. He returned James's salute with an almost imperceptible nod, motioned him to a ship's chair, took one himself well away from the table with its flickering lamp, and opened and read the sealed letter from Bazaine which James had carried with him from the capital, tipping it toward the lamp, then holding it close to his eyes—very close. James wondered if this was due to the poor illumination or if the emperor disdained spectacles out of vanity.

It looked to be a lengthy document, and James studied the emperor closely. The chance might never come again.

Either Max von Hapsburg merely scanned the long letter or he was a lightning reader. In seconds he lifted his eyes and smiled when he saw those of James on him. "General Bazaine expresses great confidence in you, colonel. He also informs me you are an American. Is that so?"

"Yes, Your Majesty."

"Yours is a great country, and will become greater if it survives its present troubles. But President Lincoln and his government do not look with favor on what we are beginning here in Mexico. Since you are in the uniform of our Imperial Guard, may we take it you do not share their views? Do you perhaps wish the Confederacy to triumph in your country's struggle? You must know that we do, although this feeling is not a strong one. Slavery is an abomination under heaven, and it revolts us, but *our* cause has met with far more understanding and support in Richmond than it has in Washington. We truly bear neither side ill will."

"My only oath is to La Legion Etrangère, Your Majesty."

The emperor leaned back in his chair, placed his fingertips together and gazed upward toward the ceiling of the salon. "We suppose we will then have to be content with your answer for the moment." He leveled his gaze on James again. "But you are no longer a Legion officer, colonel?"

"No, Your Majesty,"

"Then you are free to take an oath to us."

"I suppose I am, sir."

"Would you object to that"

"No, sir."

"Would you take such an oath now?"

"Right here and now, Your Majesty?"

"Yes."

He had expected this to happen sooner or later. Bazaine had mentioned it once, saying that it could wait until the new monarch arrived in his capital. He would have liked to give the matter more thought, but . . .

"Will you not want witnesses, Your Majesty?"

"We require none, Colonel James, nor do we need a Bible. Your word alone is good enough for us."

"In that case, Your Majesty, I will gladly take an oath to you—and your realm."

In fifteen more seconds Jason Jeremiah James became a sworn servant of Maximilian I, Emperor of Mexico. For all that he pledged his fealty without "any inner reservations," his heart thudded strangely when he raised his right hand and said, "I swear . . ."

James's eyes had now adjusted completely to the light.

What little of it reached the emperor's features revealed a coolly passive face above a full beard. He looked exactly like the man in the daguerreotypes and newspaper sketches James had studied in Bazaine's office in the palace. The face was as pale as the one in the pictures, too. His first instinct, when meeting someone new, had always been to assess them by what their eyes revealed, but that was no easy task in this dimly lit room. He had the impression those of the man in the shadows were dark blue—and dead.

Then the emperor lowered those eyes to James again and they suddenly sparked with life.

"Tell me, colonel, do you command the Imperial Guard regiment which we have been told will escort us to the capital?"

"No, Your Majesty, not officially."

"But General Bazaine asks in his letter that we place our person completely in your hands for the next stage of our long journey. We thought surely he would send the Guards' commanding officer to meet with us."

"Colonel Miguel López commands the Guards regiment which has come to Veracruz, but during the trip to Mexico City he will report to me. I am the liaison officer between Your Majesty's military forces and General Bazaine. At the moment my sole duty is to get Your Majesties safely to the capital."

"There is danger?" There was no fear in the voice.

"There is always *some* danger, Your Majesty. Although the French Army has been successful this past year, this is a huge country. Complete pacification will take a long while. There is no enemy *army* to be concerned with in southern Mexico now—with the exception of that of General Porfirio Díaz in Oaxaca who is in no position to go on the offensive—but there are guerrillas and bandits in the countryside, and an undetermined number of dissidents still to be reckoned with."

"Dissidents? It was our understanding that the welcome extended our reign was universal and heartfelt. We were told that the people of Mexico want us to be their emperor, that they beseech us." Again there was no sound of fear, but something else came through this time: pain.

The emperor's last remark was too delicate a matter for a practical soldier; things such as this were best left to someone like François-Achille Bazaine.

Before the emperor could utter another word the door to the salon opened and two women stepped inside. James rose.

Only one of the newcomers could he classify simply as a woman: a handsome bright-eyed female with a shock of red-blonde hair who favored him with an engaging smile. The word "woman" was inadequate for the other, Charlotte von Coburg, Archduchess of Austria, Princess Royal of Belgium, and as soon as the gold circlet settled on her head, Empress of Mexico.

It was as if the lamp in the gimbals had suddenly grown brighter, but perhaps it was only the contrasting darkness of the empress herself—dark hair, eyes whose irises were as black as the shadows in the farthest corners of the tiny room, the severe midnight-hued long dress on the slim, perfectly erect body, and the onyx or obsidian of her necklace. Only her face was alight, a pale, proud beacon in the lamplight.

"This officer is General Bazaine's Colonel James, my dear," the emperor said. "He and a regiment of the Imperial Guards have come to Veracruz to escort us to the capital."

"Ah, bon! Vous etes bien venu, ce soir, monsieur."

It was a strange thin voice, with a pulsing counterpoint. The picture which hung alongside her husband's in Bazaine's office failed to do her justice; she was a placid, chiaroscuro cloud, but one he guessed had the power to release a stab of lightning.

"C'est un honneur, Votre Majesté."

She motioned him back into his chair with a delicate china-like hand. "Permit us to introduce our second lady, colonel. This is Countess Paola Kollonitz."

James inclined his head first to the empress and then to

her companion, whose smile had turned broader and whose eyes now widened in curiosity.

The empress continued. "Perhaps you are the one we should talk to about our friend Sarah Anderson, *monsieur.*"

The name shook James inwardly.

"Mademoiselle Anderson is to meet us here in Veracruz, colonel," the empress said. "Unfortunately, I do not know how to get in touch with her, or even if she has arrived. Since we are going ashore and then on to the train so early tomorrow morning, we are afraid we might not make contact with her. She will join our court as one of our ladies along with Countess Zichy and Paola here, and we wish her to travel with us to the capital, but she, of course, does not know that yet. Could you possibly . . . ?"

"I . . ." Did she, or the emperor, notice his consternation? The countess apparently did; she seemed to be struggling to suppress laughter. "I shall be happy to oblige, Your Majesty."

"It is imperative that you find Mademoiselle Anderson, colonel." Each of her words rang with the sound of struck metal, a far more imperious tone than he had heard from the emperor.

"Certainly, Your Majesty. I will find Sarah . . . Mademoiselle Anderson . . . for you."

"You sound as if you know her, colonel."

"Slightly, Your Majesty."

"Then you will be glad to see her, *n'est-ce pas?*"

"Yes, Your Majesty."

"And she will be glad to see you?"

"That I do not know, Your Majesty. Mademoiselle Anderson and I have not been in touch with each other for some time."

There was a soft, deep chuckle from Countess Kollonitz.

On the deck of the *Novara* a strong wind had come from the north and by the time he boarded the launch to go ashore oily waves were breaking over the bow and gunwales, buffeting the small craft.

One thing he had decided: he was not going to search for Sarah himself. Cipi could attend to that, even if he pulled a face at being excluded from the reception on the docks tomorrow. The dwarf had been in high good humor ever since James had gotten him somewhat tenuously enlisted into the Guard back in the capital, where he put most of a month's pay into new uniforms. He had bubbled continuously since they began this trip, leaving a resigned Sofía to look after the house.

Cipi would probably rant and rave, but he would find Sarah, give her the empress's message, and somehow get her aboard that train tomorrow.

If he had thought her the occupant of a different world from his in their three meetings, the news he had gotten from Empress Carlota last night placed her in a different *universe*.

28

▲▲▲▲▲

Bazaine returned from the north to ride alongside Maximilian and Carlota when they entered the capital.

The capture of San Luis Potosí now an accomplished fact, his First Division was moving on Saltillo in tandem with the army of Tomas Mejía. Bazaine demonstrated his high confidence in the Mexican general by leaving Mejía in sole command of the main thrust against Juárez, with full authority over the proud Frenchmen and other Europeans of the First Division, regulars and Legionnaires alike. "I could never have placed such trust in Márquez, but that is strictly between you and me, colonel," he told James.

James was glad to have the general back in his office at the National Palace to shepherd him through the intricate maze of court procedure and administrative detail already miring him. Since he rode with López and his Guards regiment, escorting the new monarch from Cordoba to Puebla and from Puebla to the capital, he had found himself carrying a leather document case far more frequently than a weapon. His new duties kept him away from his own Guards regiment for all but ceremonial occasions and the endless Saturday morning inspections. It would embarrass him to face Jean-Claude duBecq now. The good Alsatian sergeant and Compagnie Rouge were nearing the gates of Saltillo, and even were the city to fall soon, they would be in the north for a long time. Boulanger, Gallimard and the Chasseurs were in the line there, too, but due to return to the capital for the coronation.

Bazaine must have guessed at how his being held away from combat duty chafed him. "Do not let it corrode your spirit, *mon ami*. I am a fighting soldier in the same predicament myself, and—as I am sure you see—on a much grander scale!"

But the general, with undisguised zest, occupied himself almost entirely with social matters during the establishment of the imperial court and the grand affair soon to take place in the cathedral. Balls and receptions were taking place under Bazaine's aegis as regularly as the sun set.

James begged to be excused from as many of the social events as he dared, *all* of those where the court was most in evidence, and consequently his and Sarah Anderson's paths had not crossed since the return from Veracruz. It would only be a question of time before they did. He could not tell Bazaine "no" forever on the parties and galas the general sponsored.

The general, on the afternoon before one of the balls which James did agree to attend with him, finally mentioned the matter of his wife's death in Paris.

"I have never told you, Colonel, how much I appreciated the intelligence and tact you showed in sending me the news of Madame Bazaine. *Merci* a thousandfold."

Perhaps the general only brought the subject up because of what he knew James would learn that night.

Bazaine danced every dance with the same young woman,

an absolutely stunning creature no older than Sofía, considerably less than half the age of the general. Obtuse as James considered himself in assessing things of the heart, had he been blind he would have seen that the general was deeply, desperately in love. Bazaine introduced the young woman to him when he found himself alongside the pair at the punch bowl.

"*Ma chère*," Bazaine said to the girl. "Permit me to present my most valued officer, Colonel Jason James. This lady, colonel, is Señorita Josefa de la Pena. Two days ago she honored me by agreeing to become my wife. We will announce this happy *accord* before the last dance this evening."

Their two rapturous faces caused James to wish, for a split second, that Sarah had been in attendance at the affair.

He had not caught sight of her once during the trip from the coast to the capital.

Escorting the emperor and empress had gone smoothly, although once, in a cloud-choked side canyon of the Cumbres de Acultzingo, on the slow climb to the great mesa that cradled Puebla, the Guards had a brush with guerrillas. No one in the Imperial party was even aware of the short, fierce fight that took place a mile ahead of the cavalcade and almost a thousand feet above it. Miguel López, the Guards commander, an aristocratic, handsome Conservative colonel who had come out of nowhere to a position of relative importance in the new Imperial army Bazaine was forging for Maximilian, impressed James with the way he handled the dangerous small action.

The lackluster, well nigh insulting reception given the Imperial couple at Veracruz had been more or less forgotten—by their escorts, at least, if not by the monarchs themselves—by the time the caravan reached Córdoba in the middle of a rainy season downpour, late on the second night inland from the coast.

The exhausted emperor and empress seemed touched by

the throng that had waited for them for uncounted hours in the city's dark, muddy streets, lighting and patiently relighting drenched pine-knot torches between cloudbursts. The couple stayed out on the balcony of the big stone house vacated for them by Córdoba's Conservative *alcalde* and waved to the soaked crowd until it seemed they could no longer lift their arms or keep their eyes open.

James, bivouacking with López and the Guards in a grove of dripping trees on the outskirts of Córdoba, received a note from someone in the imperial party named Felix Eloin, commanding his presence in the gatehouse of the Spanish colonial home the emperor and empress were occupying. As he rode to the residence he girded himself against the possibility of an encounter with Sarah Anderson, only to discover he had concerned himself without cause. According to the servant who admitted him there were a limited number of rooms available in Córdoba. Half the civilians accompanying the court to Mexico City had been shunted off to lodging places in Orizaba and were not expected to be in the procession again until they all reached Puebla. Sarah, it turned out, was one of them. He breathed relief, but a little disappointment burned in him that he would not at least get a look at her from some safe distance.

Eloin, a highly citified Belgian with a supercilious manner that set James's teeth on edge, demanded assurances from him that a great crowd of the emperor's subjects would gather for the grand entrance into Puebla. Surely the little functionary he assumed was some sort of high level majordomo realized James was in no position to give such assurances.

"By and large, Monsieur Eloin," he said, "the citizens of Puebla support the Crown wholeheartedly, but there is no telling in what numbers they might turn out to greet Their Majesties."

"But, colonel, you could send word ahead regarding the emperor's expectations, could you not?"

"I wouldn't have the faintest notion of who to send it to.

Civil administration has not yet been fully restored to Puebla and the French Army commander there certainly won't feel he has the authority to *order* a reception, or the ability to gather a crowd, for that matter."

"Is this the sort of cooperation His Imperial Majesty can expect from a highly placed officer of his Guard?"

James made no answer, but suspected he might hear a lot more from Felix Eloin in the future and little of it to his liking. In a petulant silence Eloin showed him out of the hallway.

When the morning broke bright and clear, promising fair weather for the next stage of the journey, the emperor and empress were ready to travel again, remarkably revived. They looked only a trifle disconcerted to find that the fine English carriage which brought them from the railhead to this mountain town had broken a spring in a pothole as it was being brought around from the stable. It could not roll another league. Without complaint Their Majesties switched to one of the huge, spine-jarring, mule-drawn coaches furnished the rest of the entourage for the rocky trip up through the Cumbres to Puebla.

At Puebla, Maximilian and Carlota at last reached the Mexico which Bazaine—who had exchanged perhaps a dozen letters with the emperor while he was still at Miramar—said was the land of their dreams. "They are romantic young people, *mon ami*," he told James just before he left for the north to join the First Division. "When they are at last in the country I fear I will have to teach them that this adventure is no dream."

The general, of course, had not been there to begin their education, and James certainly could not appoint himself Bazaine's surrogate for the task. Even had he wanted to acquaint the monarchs with the realities of their realm, he never found himself alone with them again as he had on the *Novara* that night in Veracruz harbor. The weasel-like little Felix Eloin in Córdoba stood between all comers and his imperial master and mistress at every point on the trip to Puebla—night and day.

After Puebla, *nothing* could have persuaded the couple they were not beginning a reign over an earthly paradise.

The assurances Eloin sought from James were unnecessary. If Archbishop Labastida had tried to restrain the churchmen of the city in their welcome, they certainly paid him no heed, nor did the populace.

The cavalcade, with James and Miguel López out in front of the Guards, had just passed Amozoc where James had ordered Cipi to stay before the battle at Guadalupe—the little man, jubilant, was riding a mere two lengths behind him now—when the sound of Puebla's bells reached them. Their route to the northeastern gate would take them right under the walls where Compagnie Rouge had bled so profusely two years ago.

When they neared to about six kilometers, still far short of the slope on which he and the company had struggled that day, a low, wide, boiling cloud of dust seemed to be moving down on them.

When the cloud came close enough for his eyes to break it into its elements, he saw it was made up of horsemen, wagons and carriages, all manner of conveyances filled with waving, cheering people. The gentry of Puebla, at least, were riding out to greet their emperor and empress.

Eloin should be pleased.

In the center of the onrushing vehicles, men, women, children, and animals that bore down on James, López, and the column of Guards, six of the whitest horses he had ever seen, caparisoned in purple silks with gold tassels bouncing in the sun, pulled a flower-bedecked carriage, empty save for the driver. The lovely conveyance made straight for the ugly, cumbersome coach flying the personal banner of Maximilian with its ancient Hapsburg device. Six horsemen, multicolored streamers trailing from raised lances, accompanied the Puebla carriage. Their long, graceful weapons notwithstanding, none of these riders wore a uniform: all had decked themselves in the silver-studded, jet black *charro* costume of so many of the men of south-central Mexico.

The transfer of the imperial couple to the carriage completed, the procession got underway again. The sound of the bells rose in a deafening crescendo.

James had López order the Guards to a canter. As splendidly affectionate as the reception for the emperor and his empress promised to be, he could take no chances with this entrance.

"Send your men right on through the gate, colonel," he told López. "Once they are in Puebla itself, have them fan out into every side *avenida* and *calle* between the city walls and the cathedral. Make as clean a sweep as if you were on a battlefield. I expect no trouble, but if it should appear, deal with it with sabers and lances. I want the sound of no gunfire reaching the ears of their Majesties."

When James and the first of the Guards reached the Cathedral de Santo Domingo, still vibrating with the sound of the bells, the crowd already gathered there astonished him, not only by its size, but by its makeup.

He had not seen this many human beings congregated in one place since the end of the grand review when he entered the capital with the First Division. And he had never seen this many Indians before—ever. Not one man or women in ten who stood there as if rooted to the stones seemed *mestizo* or *criollo*.

They made up a human, frozen, sun-washed sea which much earlier must have heaved and billowed from every alley opening on the Cathedral Plaza and lapped almost onto the steps of the great church itself. They looked as if they had been waiting here for days. Hundreds of children brown as chestnuts carried bouquets and garlands almost painful to the eye in their chromatic brightness. No one in the immense gathering moved, save for those making a way for his horse as he guided it across the plaza. None spoke. If the bells were to stop their clamor he thought the ensuing silence might be that most ominous silence of all: the muteness of the dead.

He could see the Imperial couple behind him, coming into the enormous cobbled square, could feel every head in the multitude turn, and he knew what every one of them saw.

Quetzalcoatl!

They were looking at the pale, promised, blue-eyed god from beyond the sunrise, as their ancestors had looked at him three hundred and fifty years before, when Hernan Cortes came ashore in Mexico and burned his ships on the beach behind him. He wondered if Maximilian had closed off any exit for himself that way.

James also knew that no matter how high the fortunes of Maximilian von Hapsburg and his Belgian wife soared in this "empire" that had come their way largely by default, they would never again know a moment quite like this one.

The fanfares, fireworks displays, and floral tributes of Mexico City, while spectacular—and gratifying to Bazaine at least, who since his return from the front at San Luis Potosí had orchestrated all the festivities in the capital except the coronation itself—were the expected things. But clearly, from Maximilian's frequent mentions of Puebla after he reached the capital, none of them ranked in his well of emotions with the sight of that worshipful, silent array of simple people.

It was one thing to be a sovereign—quite another to be a god.

And it was no great surprise to James that Bazaine groused at Maximilian's repeated references to the entry into Puebla.

"I am pleased, of course, that things went well, but His Majesty may need reminders that it was France that placed him on the throne, not God, and certainly not any horde of illiterate peasant savages."

Since the emperor settled into the drafty upper floors of the palace, Bazaine had insisted that James accompany him upstairs for almost every appointment he had with the monarch. He only rarely excluded him from the imperial presence for private sessions, and it pleased James that Eloin, influential as he seemed in everything else, had no power to bar the general. The Belgian acknowledged the

French general's importance readily enough—with a mildly disgusting unctuousness—but he made no attempt to hide his resentment of the American.

None of James's visits to the palace with his commanding officer produced a glimpse of Sarah, and of course he did not ask for her. As it turned out, he did not have to. Eloin—who shadowed him like a hawk in a silent hunting stoop if Bazaine closeted himself with the emperor on one of their trips and James was left alone in one of the public chambers—let slip her whereabouts. "Countesses Zichy and Kollonitz, and your compatriot, Mademoiselle Anderson, have already installed themselves at Chapultepec, and are overseeing the preparations of the new apartments for Their Majesties." The Belgian then remarked with undisguised glee that "since you will be working in the general's office at the palace, we will probably not see as much of you when the imperial household moves from the palace to the castle, colonel . . ." He always made a *point* of not remembering James's name.

It required no gift of prophecy to know that in spite of Eloin's smug prediction, James would indeed see her when the emperor and empress made the move to the great castle just four miles beyond the western edge of the capital.

A subtle change in his position was taking place, paralleling the not so subtle one occurring between Bazaine and Maximilian.

Until the *entrada*, as the Mexicans closest to the court called the couple's arrival, James had been the highest ranking officer in the new army of Imperial Mexico, with the exception of Leonardo Márquez and Tomas Mejía, both still campaigning in the north. He fully recognized this could not last. In early August the emperor, with Bazaine's approval, announced the appointment of General Miguel Miramón to the post of commander-in-chief of all of the Imperial Army of Mexico. Nominally, this put James under Miramón's command.

Miramón, of some vague French origin, had fought

valiantly against Juárez in the War of the Reform. Darkly handsome and young—he was a year younger than James— he was a man of keen intelligence and charm, dedicated to the church, a fact which had probably recommended him to Maximilian more than any other single thing—and possessed of an ego to match Bazaine's. He had been Márquez's superior officer at the time of the massacre of Tacubaya in 1859. The Tiger in that bloody affair executed every officer and a host of the common soldiers taken prisoner after the town's surrender, extending his orgy of killing to medical students caring for wounded Liberals. James had heard rumors that Márquez had gone about his business not only with Miramón's knowledge and blessing, but by his specific order. The British had taken Miramón prisoner at Veracruz in the earliest days of the intervention, charging him with absconding with money they had advanced him to pay his army. Released to Spanish authorities in Cuba when Queen Victoria's government washed its hands of Mexico, he had returned to the capital after the army of Benito Juárez left it.

"I don't quite trust the man," Bazaine grumbled. "He strikes me as entirely too self-serving, but I suppose I can't disregard every single one of the new monarch's wishes. Things will be slightly different for you now, *mon ami*, as an officer of the Imperial and not the French Army. However, do not concern yourself. I still command *all* French and Conservative forces for the emperor. *Monsieur le beau general* Miramón will give you one order, and one order only. At the emperor's request he will relieve you of what few garrison duties you presently have as a colonel of the Guards, assigning you as the emperor's personal *liaison* officer to me. Things between you and me will not change."

Here was a strange arrangement. Exactly whom was he working for? His new oath no longer bound him to France, but to Maximilian.

In the days immediately following this meeting Bazaine began showing James the dispatches that arrived from Napoleon III. The general did not make the American privy to his replies to Paris, but the changing tenor of each successive missive from Napoleon—delivered to Bazaine's office once or twice every week—made it clear that the French emperor was disturbed over certain aspects of the Mexican situation. A number of the exchanges had to do with the fact that Marshal Forey, recalled to France months ago, had not yet left for Europe. Reading between the lines of Napoleon's comments and directives, and making guesses at what Bazaine fired back in return, James realized his general would never feel entirely comfortable until Forey left the country. But it seemed that neither the French emperor nor his principal commander in the New World could summon the will to give the old marshal his marching orders. As a soldier, this indecisive attitude toward an officer who was being at least mildly insubordinate puzzled James. He had never before found Bazaine less than firm and confident. Perhaps the germs of Napoleon III's *own* indecision had been ferried across the Atlantic in the padlocked despatch case.

James knew that Benito Juárez, besieged in his northern stronghold, would never waver on any such matter.

Then Bazaine confounded him by assigning him a task of much greater delicacy than his espionage mission to Chapultepec before San Lorenzo.

"Archbishop Labastida has not forgiven the emperor or the French for refusing to return the church properties," he told James. "He has not, of course, declared himself opposed to Maximilian's ascension to the throne of Mexico, but he has apparently decided to show his displeasure by not officiating at the coronation. The bishop of Querétaro is to perform that function. We must change Labastida's mind. Louis-Napoleon will stand for no one but the primate placing the crown on the head of the new monarch. I would come to grips with him myself, but after the affair at the cathedral and my dismissal of him from the Council of Regents he has turned aside every attempt I have made to meet with him. Miramón fears him, and the emperor, for reason surely obvious to you, Colonel, cannot be perceived for a moment as *begging* his indulgence. Consequently it would be folly to send Felix Eloin."

James listened attentively, but wondered what all this had to do with him. The answer came immediately.

"I would like *you*," Bazaine said, "to change the thinking of this obstinate prelate."

James, dumbfounded, swallowed his first impulse to protest. "I will do anything the general wishes, but . . ."

"No 'buts,' colonel. I can guess what you are thinking. Your stubborn modesty cannot come between any reluctance you might have and France's needs. You are now an Imperial Army officer. That will have to serve as your credentials."

"Is it permitted to remind the general I am not a Catholic."

"That can work to our advantage. This cold, lofty priest surely will understand you have no theological prejudices in this matter. Get his agreement for me within two days." Bazaine smiled. "Bring to bear the same powers of persuasion you used on *me* before San Lorenzo."

James refrained from pointing out how much this differed from planning for a battle.

The archbishop received him in an shadowy office which seemed in its severity as empty as James's mind in his uncertain state. The cleric wore the simple gray cassock of a village *padre*, and the face above the stiff white collar appeared in the dim light to match the garment's somber hue. He sat absolutely motionless, without a flicker in his black eyes, betraying not a sign of emotion. His two bloodless, fragile hands lay folded on the desktop, one of them bearing the huge ruby ring—which Solange Tournier had kissed at the Washington's Birthday celebration at the United States Embassy—the only dot of color in the room.

"The church cannot alter its position, colonel," he said when James told him the reason for the visit. The archbishop's voice rose barely above a whisper and in its dryness contained more rustle than resonance.

The talk did not go well.

James put forward all the arguments Bazaine had rehearsed him in: the possibility of France taking its case to the Holy See; the political desirability of supporting the crown fully against the Republicans in the north; the fact that since the properties were now in private hands they produced tax revenues the new government sorely needed; the compelling wisdom of a show of solidarity against any and all enemies of the realm and its church.

The response was the same to all of them: nothing, not a tremor.

James dreaded taking the report of his failure back to the palace and the general, but even as he fell into the clutches of something like despair and prepared to ask permission to withdraw, he suddenly remembered again his first full evening with Sarah Anderson at the embassy.

". . . *Labastida is easily the best friend the Indians of Mexico have had since Bartolomé de Las Casas, three centuries ago . . . ,*" Ambassador Corwin had said that night.

"Your Grace did not come to Puebla de Los Angeles for the emperor's entry there, I believe," James said.

"No."

"Surely Your Grace has received reports about His Imperial Majesty's welcome in that city."

There was no answer. James tried not to hurry as he continued.

"It may have been the largest gathering of *indios* your country has seen since Aztec times. I have never seen an outpouring of affection for a public personage to match it, Your Grace. Not even among the fanatic Mohammedans of North Africa."

Bazaine quivered with jubilation.

"I have no idea how you managed it, James. Fine soldier that you are, I think your diplomatic talents far outweigh your military ones. I am not sure who should be complimented more, you for your superb performance as an envoy, or your general for his uncommon genius in selecting you for the job."

Boulanger returned from the north when Mejía pulled the Parisian's regiment out of the new Saltillo line for rest and refitting. He breezed into James's office in the palace late on a Friday afternoon, lean, fit-looking, bronzed to a russet glow from long days in the sun with his Chasseurs, warm in his congratulations about his friend's promotion to colonel, and with no laments that his own colonelcy had not as yet come through. He refused an offered drink.

"Do not despair, *mon ami*," he said in response to James's mild complaint about being kept away from the action. "Remember when you gave somewhat the same advice to me? Bazaine will not waste your fighting skills in administration and petty diplomacy forever."

"How are things in the north?"

"Quiet. My regiment won't need me for at least a month. But it looks good for our army and that of our Mexican allies at the moment." There was a faint but unmistakable sneer underscoring the word "allies." "But we would be rash to underestimate the Republicans. As you know from your years facing the faithful in the desert, there is always something to fear from fighters who think they have a holy cause. Now, tell me the situation here in the capital. Has the reign of Maximilian *le Bon* begun with the brilliance Paris expected?"

"It is certainly a brilliant beginning insofar as appearances go, Some things are troubling General Bazaine, though, and although he doesn't speak of them, I have an inkling of what they are."

"So?"

"The Emperor has already made many friends, including some among the more liberal elements of the city who, while not active supporters of Juárez, have until now leaned in the president's direction. Perhaps he has made *too* many friends of that persuasion. Some of them are people who bought the property stripped from the church by the

Republicans' constitution in '57. He has not backed away from his *pronunciamiento* that those holdings will not be returned. Labastida, I fear, will continue to fight him tooth and nail on this. On the other hand, he has come out in favor of a number of very conservative initiatives the *French* dislike. There are times when, actively or by simply ignoring what Bazaine tells him, he seems almost deliberately intent on alienating the two factions he must bind closest to him if his empire is to become a reality—the Catholic conserva-tives and his Napoleonic sponsors."

"*Est il fou?!* From what I saw in the north, there is no way he can control this country *without* us. You say you have met him. How does he strike you as a man?"

"I can't answer that completely. He is a very complex human being, warm and human for such an aristocrat, but sometimes with a sharp, sarcastic tongue. And just when I think I can make a good guess as to how he will react to people or events, he does or says something unpredictable. He professes a love for the common people of Mexico I believe to be truly sincere, and yet . . . well, for example, this appointment of Miramón as commander-in-chief in the face of General Bazaine's doubts about the man. I just don't know."

"Do you *like* him?"

He had not thought about this before.

"Yes."

"Unreservedly, *mon ami?*"

"Yes."

"And the empress?"

"I've seen her only once. Bazaine, for his part, seems to think that her capabilities, in the more practical matters of governing a country, at least, are, if anything, greater than the emperor's. I found her a strange woman, but that is only on the shaky basis of my one audience with her."

"Was Boulanger right when he predicted—along with your *homme* Cipi—that the real ruler of Mexico will be Bazaine?"

James gave that some thought before answering. "All in

all, yes. There is a secret stubborn strength in these two people, though, that amazes me when I consider the sheltered life they've led."

"They will need all the strength they can muster, and of the not so secret kind, *mon ami.*"

"I suspect you're right again. Now—let me ask if Bazaine will see us. He'll want to hear how things are going in the north."

"I can't add much to the official reports he must have already received from General Mejía."

"It would be perhaps better if you *subtracted* from them. Mejía sends no *bad* news, and there must be some of that. If we can see Bazaine now, be candid. He doesn't believe in killing the messenger. Besides, you are French. That makes all the difference."

"You could be French, *aussi,* my friend, with your pragmatic outlook. By the way, is there truth in the gossip that came north? Is our *grand general* actually affianced to some seventeen-year-old Mexican beauty?"

"Yes."

"He likes them somewhat younger than I do. It seems a reprise of the unfortunate amorous alliance he made in Spain. I sincerely hope *this* one does not fit our good general with another set of horns."

"From the little I've seen of the lady, it doesn't seem likely. I'm not a reliable judge in these things, but she seems to worship him."

"Bon!"

They walked the twenty feet to the general's office, and Corporal Lemonde in the anteroom had scarcely gone to Bazaine's door to announce them when Bazaine burst through it.

"Major Boulanger! *Bienvenu, mon ami. Tout va bien?"*

"Mais oui, mon general."

"Come inside. Come, come! And you as well, colonel."

They were seated, with Boulanger's eyes straying to the battle flags—new to him, James realized—when Lemonde came through the door with the inevitable decanter of cognac and three glasses. Boulanger did not demur when Bazaine poured and pushed a generous glass of the liquor toward him, but neither did he lift it to his lips.

"A toast, major," Bazaine said, lifting his. "And there is but one toast for French officers serving in Mexico. *Vive l'Empereur!*"

"*Mais lequel, mon general?*" Pierre responded. "*Which* emperor, sir?"

Bazaine looked slightly surprised. "Of *France*, of course. There is no other emperor."

"Ah, *oui. Vive l'Empereur.*" Boulanger did take a careful sip now. James, a trifle taken aback at Bazaine's last remark, brought *his* glass to his mouth, and followed suit with a more subdued "*Vive l'Empereur*" of his own. A glance at Pierre told him it had been a revealing moment for the Chasseur.

No other emperor? Then who and what exactly *was* the man Bazaine had pressed him to serve when he left the Legion?

He had to force his attention back to the conversation beginning now between Bazaine and Boulanger. They had launched themselves swiftly into a technical discussion of the siege of Saltillo, something which ordinarily would have absorbed him, but somehow he could not fasten his mind to it.

"And General Mejía?" Bazaine asked the Chasseur.

"Sound, *mon general,* perhaps even gifted when a battle situation allows him to use his cavalry. It is excellent, of course, as is all Mexican cavalry. I fear I cannot say the same for his infantry. And the Mexicans do not understand artillery or its employment at all. The only losses of any consequence we sustained in the last several weeks came about when General Mejía's guns fired on our own troops by accident."

"Your assessment of the enemy?"

"Hard to judge, sir. Juárez's general at Saltillo, Manuel Doblado, is as headstrong as his dead predecessor, General

Comonfort, whom you defeated at San Lorenzo. Since they are on the defensive at the moment he is prevented from taking any kind of initiative, and his soldiers perhaps *seem* to perform better than they in fact do."

"*Oui.* All other things being equal, defenders do indeed have the better of it in fixed position combat. Recommendations, major?"

"May I speak freely, *mon general?*"

"Do. *J'insiste.*"

"While I realize we have an entire country to pacify, I think we dissipate our power by going off in too many directions at once. I do not think we take full advantage of our victories of the past year when General Mejía has us dig in and merely outwait the enemy as we seem to be doing at Saltillo. If I may be so bold as to make a suggestion . . . ?"

"By all means."

Pierre hesitated the merest fraction of a second. "General Márquez should be pulled out of the west and sent north to join General Mejía and the First Division. I believe the Republicans will soon give up Saltillo and attempt to move deeper into the northern states. That will look like a retreat and as if we are winning, but it lengthens our supply lines dangerously. We should not just drive Juárez to the north, we should crush him before his next move, perhaps by tempting Doblado into the open in some fashion as we did Comonfort. That done we should direct our attention to Porfirio Díaz in Oaxaca. We will have to bring our full strength against Díaz if we do that, so it is imperative we finish the business in the north as soon as possible. I fought Díaz sporadically around Orizaba two years ago and I respect his abilities enormously."

"*Merci beaucoup,* Major," Bazaine said. His voice indicated he had taken no umbrage at Pierre's advice.

More followed, but not until the two Frenchmen finished did James realize he had paid close attention to only about half of it. Bazaine had one final question for Boulanger.

"You are not a St. Cyrian, are you, major?"

"Non, mon general"

"Nor am I. That is a cross we both bear. I hope I bear mine with the same insouciant fortitude you bear yours."

One solid satisfaction had come from this meeting. If he had developed any insights at all about Bazaine, Pierre's promotion to the rank of colonel was now almost a certainty.

The Chasseur took James to dinner in a dimly lit cantina in a side *calle* leading away from the Zócalo.

"The American lady we met at Orizaba, Jason," Boulanger said when they were taking coffee. "Is she still in Mexico?"

"Yes."

"Have you seen her?"

"I had a glimpse of her at Veracruz."

"Will you see her again?"

"I have no plans to do so."

Pierre's sardonic face suddenly seemed that of a conspirator. "Look, *mon ami,*" he said. "I have no wish to insinuate myself into your personal affairs, but unless I am mistaken, we have become good friends in the past two years, and now I feel I *must* intrude." Boulanger sighed. "I have some idea of how taken you are with Mademoiselle Anderson. Although you possess an admirable *sangfroid* when facing an armed enemy, you do not have, in regard to members of the other sex, what I have heard Americans call—for what arcane reason *je ne sais pas*—the 'poker face.' You have the look of a lonely man. Do you not think it is time for you to press forward with the lady seriously? Do not simply dismiss what I am saying out of hand. I know that you felt great irritation in the past when I taunted you about her, but this is not my intent *maintenant. Il faut me croire,* I speak from the heart. It is a short life. Do not discard what could be the better part of it."

If he had not known it before, he knew now that Pierre Boulanger was the best friend he had ever had.

He surrendered.

For the first time since those adolescent days as Aaron Sheffield's worshipful student he felt the need to talk with someone about his deepest feelings, and he finally knew, too, how badly Aaron had damaged him—had wounded him in a way far worse than the horror he inflicted on him at Chapultepec. It could happen again if he let the Chasseur get to close to him.

But he would have to take the chance.

"I'm sorry, Pierre. I should thank you, and I do, but I am afraid there's nothing to be done. I know it sounds cowardly—if these things are ever a matter of courage—but Sarah Anderson is now far beyond me, not that she was *ever* truly within my reach. Simply put, I am not good enough for her."

He told Boulanger then of the farewell letter he had written Sarah, of her new position with the court, of his behavior in virtually hiding from her on the railroad platform at Veracruz, and of his trepidation at the inevitable meeting. "It is quite easy to avoid her here in the capital. But when their Majesties take up residence at Chapultepec we will undoubtedly be thrown together frequently. You would not believe how many balls and *fetes* we have had here at the palace and at almost every wealthy home on the Calle de San Francisco. On some occasion I may be required to meet with her. I can only hope it doesn't cause her too much embarrassment or discomfort."

"*Sacrebleu!* Why should you *embarrass* her?"

"I lied to her, Pierre. I used her good offices for furthering my mission without informing her."

This said, he felt suddenly and strangely better, as if some tight constriction in his chest had been dissolved.

"Ah, *mon cher ami . . .*" Boulanger looked genuinely sad. "You have such a totally unwarranted low opinion of yourself. I will say no more on the subject now, but I reserve the right to enter the lists on behalf of *l'amour* again."

As good as his word, Pierre made no more mention of Sarah the rest of the evening.

Over a cognac he seemed to relish far more than the

drink he had only toyed with in Bazaine's office—"That was an aberration; I no longer drink before sundown except for reasons of politics, such as was our *tête-à-tête* with the general this afternoon"—he became again the delightful, deliciously cynical Boulanger of memory.

Paloma, he told James, had gone. "*Oui,* my dove has flown. She gave *me* a lesson in humility. I did not get around to discarding her; she divested herself of *me.* She is now out of Boulanger's dovecote and on the wing—if I may attribute to her an ability at odds with her configuration—with a burly sergeant of Tirailleurs, dedicating herself to *liberté, egalité,* and her own version of *fraternité.* Fortunately, her flight clears the way for Boulanger to begin his own soaring hunt for a woman of position."

He inquired about Cipi, roaring with laughter as James described the dwarf's strutting around the Zócalo during the evening promenade hour in his Imperial Guards uniform, but—perhaps due to the talk about Sarah—he pointedly did *not* ask after Sofía.

Nor did he need to. A nagging voice inside James kept whispering her name all through the balance of the evening and well after he and the Chasseur parted, echoing in his head with every step he took through the dark, silent streets of the capital on his way back to the house.

The light from her candle showed under the bottom of her bedroom door.

He went to bed without calling her.

In August and September things happened that had nothing to do with Jason James on the surface, but which promised changes for him eventually.

Marshal Forey finally returned to France and obscurity.

Maximilian I, Emperor of Mexico, gave the bride away when General François-Achille Bazaine and Josefa de la Pena took their matrimonial vows in the biggest wedding the cathedral had seen in twenty years.

Maximilian made a gift of the rambling Castle of San Cosmé to the newlyweds, Emperor Napoleon III conferred the rank of Marshal of France on the bridegroom, and Marshal François-Achille Bazaine announced plans for "*le plus grande fête* this country has ever seen."

In the north, Saltillo surrendered to General Tomas Mejía, and Benito Juárez, President of a Republic of Mexico that surely could not stay afloat much longer, sought another new anchorage for his listing ship-of-state.

29
▲▲▲▲▲

"Marshal Bazaine has made a *wunderbar* tribute to his young bride with this grand affair, Sarah," Paola Kollonitz said. "As old as he is, he is still a true Frenchman—a great player in the game of Love."

"It surely *is* grand," Sarah said. "There must be a thousand people here."

Indeed, the ball at San Cosmé was a wondrous thing, and the old castle glowed in incandescent splendor. Sarah could not remember a social function of such brilliance, even in Paris.

Imposing in the harsh and all too often betraying Mexican sun, the castle with its lofty spires had become a place of baroque magic by night. Its rooms and halls were not nearly large enough to host a gathering of this magnitude, but Bazaine had brought in an army of workmen to erect a roof of lattices, propped up by gaily painted timbers threaded with greenery, over its immense patio, which before tonight had been a walled courtyard open to the sky. Over the years since some transplanted Spanish grandee first laid it out, the patio's two or three acre expanse of cobblestones had felt the tread of far more horses' hooves than the feet of men in evening boots and women in delicate dancing pumps.

A polished hardwood dance floor, hammered together

this week by fifty or more *mestizo* carpenters, covered a full third of the cobbles between the ironwork gate in the high wall and the front of the castle. Under the portico that opened from the castle's three-story stone facade a dais had been set with two thrones for the royal couple. Torches blazed from sconces in the patio walls and flames leaped from a candelabra hung from the temporary roof.

"There is little doubt," Paola said, "that this party is being given by a Marshal of France—the Hero of Sebastopol. San Cosmé is stupendous, but there is still an air about it of a beautifully decorated barracks. I certainly do not object to that. As with any barracks it is filled with young men in uniform."

Sarah saw what she meant. Behind the thrones, what looked to be the massed battle flags of the French Army caught the light in their silken folds. At intervals throughout that part of the patio not covered by the dance floor, French soldiers had piled up perfect pyramids of cannonballs like the ones she had seen on the high battlements of Chapultepec, and then wheeled artillery field pieces into all the corners, their black muzzles trained for some unfathomable reason on the dais and its twin thrones.

The orchestra was half hidden on the roof of the portico, the musicians' heads silhouetted against the light streaming through the tall, arched casement windows behind them. The music drifted down on the dancers—there were at least three score pairs on the floor at any given moment—as if from the dark heavens themselves.

The thrones had not as yet seen service. The Imperial couple would of course be the last of the guests to arrive.

Paola sighed. "I doubt if the men who might be drawn to me here in Mexico will ever have the means to declare their love in such a fashion as this. Not that I am in any hurry to marry, you understand."

There were certainly enough single men in attendance to satisfy even what Sarah had come to learn was Paola's enormous appetite for masculine attention.

A dazzling assortment of uniforms greeted Sarah's gaze

everywhere she turned: Zouaves, Chasseurs d'Afrique, Tlaxcalan Hussars who had fought the French before changing sides after Comonfort's defeat at San Lorenzo, Imperial Guards—her breath caught every time her glance fell on one of *them*—Austrian Lancers, Legionnaires—another little catch—and any number of others she failed to recognize. The civilians all wore full evening dress: the men with explosions of decorations on their chests, something that had not been true at many of the affairs at the American embassy in her early days in the capital; the women in dresses with the unmistakable stamp of Paris and Vienna on them.

"Should we not find somewhere to sit?" she said.

"Nein, nein, liebchen. I am not—what is your ridiculous English expression?—a flower of the wall. Let us seek the table with the punch bowl. That is where we shall find the men. When they are not in barracks they drink. Besides, I would like a drink myself."

With Sarah in her wake, Paola sailed across the cobbles as smoothly as a racing schooner cutting through gentle swells off Nantucket, some unerring inner compass leading her directly to a long mahogany table hemmed in by sturdy young men in fitted tunics. "The Belgians are here in force at last, I see," she whispered when they reached it. "We might have expected that. King Leopold is a very fond papa. He will surround our empress with as many of her countrymen and women as he can persuade to leave Brussels for Mexico. I am not all that terribly taken with Belgians, you understand, but I do have a high regard for Alfred there." She nodded in the direction of a tall, exceedingly handsome man in one of the uniforms Sarah had not identified, chatting with two other officers.

"Who is he?"

"Alfred van der Smissen. A dashing and very courageous officer. I know him only slightly from visits he made to Schonbrunn when all this imperial splendor was just a dream of Max's and Emperor Napoleon's, but that can be rectified tonight. He is a colonel in one of the Belgian regiments. Pity he is busy at the moment. I must introduce you if the opportunity arises, although that constitutes something of a risk, the way you look. That gown is ravishing."

Immodest, perhaps, but Sarah agreed with Paola. She did look good tonight. She had put herself together for the ball without the help Solange had provided for years; with little help at all in fact. With most of the ladies of the court invited to San Cosme there had hardly been enough Mexican maids to go around.

Paola turned from the table with two crystal cups of punch, and almost spilled the one she held out to Sarah; her swift eyes had not stopped their perusal of the Belgian officer.

"Do I detect a very special kind of interest in Colonel van der Smissen, Paola?"

"Certainly. But I have that special kind of interest in almost every man I know—and a great many I do not." Her laugh throbbed above the sound of the orchestra. "Do not worry, *liebchen*. Your Jason James is not one of them."

"He is not *my* Jason James."

"*Nein?* Somehow then I received the wrong impression. I wonder why." The laugh came again, this time with an even deeper throb. "And I wonder where he is. As a colonel of the Guard he must have been invited. Besides, I have heard he is extraordinarily close to the marshal. I would not have expected such rapid advancement for an ex-Legionnaire. He is doubtless a man of parts. Delicious parts."

Sarah hoped her blush had gone undetected in the torch and candle light. There had been a great deal of this sort of mild teasing from Paola ever since they moved down to Chapultepec with Countess Zichy. On a trip to the rooftop to take the *tierra templada* early evening air, after a particularly busy day supervising the work of the drapers in the imperial living quarters, she told Paola of her visit there as a guest of General Comonfort. Paola looked at her with something like suspicion for a moment, and Sarah realized it was because she had said she was acquainted with the late Republican general. She hurried to tell the Austrian woman that Jason had been there that day, too—and the reason for his presence. She had not meant to talk too specifically about him, or *his* part of that experience, but obviously— from Paola's remarks in the days that followed, and the one a moment ago—she had told her far more about the American than she intended, if not in actual words.

"We must arrange to have your Colonel James invited to Chapultepec for one of Charlotte's *thés dansants*," Paola remarked a few days after the unwitting revelations Sarah had made on the rooftop. While wondering how a Sunday afternoon tea dance might appeal to a veteran of so many bloody campaigns, the countess casually tossed a lighted bomb. "Have you slept with him yet?"

After the adventures and misadventures of the past two years Sarah thought herself proof against almost any shock.

"For Lord's sake, no! Whatever would give you the idea that—"

"*Ach, liebchen,* but I *always* have that idea. In some ways—and at least with some men, it is all that matters. If you have not slept with him, it will only be a question of time. And why not? What is there to fear? You are not some simple village girl. There are ways to guard against—"

"Something like that would never occur to me."

"But Sarah, it may be a long time before you are married, and you are already a grown woman. At any rate, if you do marry, I doubt it will be to a professional soldier. You have Henri Gallimard for marriage, do you not? In the meantime . . ." Her eyes widened and so did her ready smile. "*Gott im Himmel!* Can it be you are a virgin?"

Sarah went numb. She certainly would not dignify the question with an answer, and as for whether she had slept with Jason, she had never even considered such a possibility. For that matter, had *he*? Nothing in his behavior had ever smacked of his desire for what was, according to Paola, "the one thing every man wants, more often than not to the exclusion of all else, no matter what fine things they say to hide it from us."

Sarah made every effort to remain scandalized . . . or at least appear so. It did nothing to stop Paola's smiles and sallies, which alternated between even more teasing and a sympathy Sarah did not want, or feel she needed.

She *had* wondered about Jason's possible presence at San Cosme tonight, but there had been no sight of him.

"The marshal and his lady are coming out now," Paola said. "I should think Max and Charlotte will not be far behind."

On the dais the thrones bracketed Bazaine, wedging his way between them with his new wife on his arm. Sarah stared at them in fascination as they came into full view. It was the first time she had seen the former Señorita Josefa de la Pena, now the second lady of the land. She had heard of the new Madame Bazaine's extreme youth, but it had not prepared her for the sight of the seventeen-year-old bride and her Marshal-of-France husband together. His cropped, grizzled hair contrasted dramatically with her glossy black tresses, and his weathered face seen against her totally unblemished, creamy skin, made the gap in their ages seem even greater.

The marshal paused beside the slightly larger of the two thrones, the one clearly intended for the emperor. He gazed for an instant at its gilt, carved frame and red plush upholstery, and then placed his big hand on the top of the gleaming scrollwork back. He patted it as one might pat the head of a child, then he pulled his hand away to face the thundering ovation breaking from the crowd on the dance floor, a resounding storm of applause mixed with shouts of "*Vive le Marechal . . . vive Madame Bazaine,*" and swelling above everything else, "*Vive la France!*"

Sarah searched the faces of the uniformed men and fashionably gowned women seeking punch at the table. Had none of them seen Bazaine's patronizing hand? Did no one but Sarah Anderson hear the marshal's secret voice? He *had* spoken, without uttering a word, whether or not *anyone* in this insouciant crowd heard him.

"*Do not delude yourselves*, mes amis," he had said. "*France and I decide who sits here . . . and for how long . . .*"

Bazaine led his wife well to the side of the dais, but without seeming to abandon his place in the center of the crowd's attention.

The music stopped, and pair by pair the dancing couples left the floor.

Then the emperor and the empress appeared at the back of the portico.

The ovation which had greeted the Marshal and Doña Josefa had been one of triumph; this new one for Max and Charlotte was something else, not necessarily lesser, but different—a deep, warm, rolling sigh of affection that flowed to the farthest reaches of the patio and spread then through what seemed to be every group, large or small. Sarah waited for the first shouted "*Vive l'Empereur*" or its equivalent in any of the other languages spoken in this latter day Babel. None came.

The Imperial couple took their seats on the thrones as the orchestra began the first strains of the anthem Sarah thought she recognized as the ancient "Hymn of the House of Hapsburg."

When the last notes died away Bazaine stepped to the thrones, saluted His Imperial Majesty, and bowed to Empress Carlota. She rose, and the marshal led her to the edge of the dais, hopped to the hardwood dance floor with surprising lightness for such a thickset man, turned, took her hand, and, it seemed, lifted her down beside him. At the opening measure of the waltz they moved together across the floor.

"Now Max will have to waltz with the child bride," Paola said. "He hates this sort of thing. As a matter of fact he usually has retired by this time. It might have been different if Madame Bazaine were some unmarried *señorita*. Max, as you perhaps already know, is not perhaps as faithful to our Charlotte as he should be, but then, can you blame him when so many young women throw themselves at him."

Sarah felt a tremor of mild shock. Paola continued. "Do not bother to finish that punch, *liebchen*. When His Majesty begins to dance it will be champagne for the rest of this affair. *Ja*, he is taking Madame Bazaine to the floor now. He looks so *Austrian*. Ruler of Mexico? He will always be a Hapsburg to those of us who are Viennese."

The tall Belgian colonel, van der Smissen, moved in front of Paola when, true to the countess's prediction, the first champagne cork popped.

"Countess Kollonitz," he said. "We are acquainted from a visit to Schönbrunn a few years ago, *n'est-ce pas?* May I have the honor . . . ?"

"The honor is mine, colonel."

Then they were gone—without the promised introduction, but with a wink from Paola unhidden from her partner.

Sarah felt pathetically abandoned. Not so alone, however, that she was ready to welcome the approach of the preening young officer now bearing down on her at a gallop, with a "may I have this dance" gleam in his eyes.

"Mademoiselle Anderson . . . Sarah, if I may . . ." Marcel Gallimard loomed above her, a grinning peacock. "Since Henri is not with us tonight, I feel it my duty to represent *la famille Gallimard*. Shall we waltz in the new Madame Bazaine's honor?"

At least, as she discovered when they were on the floor, Henri's foolish younger brother—decked out in an absolute caricature of a Chasseur uniform, all iridescent scarlets and yellows, and deep, jolting blues—*could* dance. They drilled them well in the social arts at St. Cyr.

He was indeed a good dancer, but perhaps too rash, his steps too bold. He insisted on talking, too, causing other dancers to turn their heads in their direction, bringing the kind of attention that made Sarah uncomfortable. "You have heard from Henri? He is coming to Mexico next month, you know. He says he has written you. No? My letter came, of course, on the military packet, so it is no surprise it arrived before yours," Marcel said as they twirled and glided toward the center of the floor, perilously close to where the emperor and Madame Bazaine were taking their first tentative turns, almost colliding with them. Max looked startled, his easy dignity deserting him for a moment.

"Marcel!" Sarah whispered in fright. "Move us away from here . . . *now!*"

He did—right into the path of the marshal and the empress, knocking them aside as if they were wooden pins on some village bowling green. Sarah's stomach knotted. Everyone on the floor was staring at them.

Marcel released her and began what under other circumstances would have been an utterly comic series of bows and scrapes in the direction of the marshal and his imperial partner. The titters, and in a few cases the full-blown guffaws of the waltzers nearest them rose above the music, a rippling counterpoint of ridicule. Sarah could have died on the spot.

"Stop that grotesque business, Gallimard! It does not become a Chasseur officer," Bazaine barked. "Resume your dance—but far away from Her Majesty and me." He nodded toward Sarah. "Mademoiselle . . ." he said with a tight small smile.

Charlotte, meantime, while not actually laughing, seemed more amused than angered by the incident. "We can forgive them, can we not, Monsieur le Marechal?"

Back in Gallimard's now much less confident embrace, and blessedly at the edge of the floor, well away from the other couples, she felt sharp pangs of disappointment. She had looked forward to Marshal Bazaine's ball with eagerness, catching fire from Paola's enthusiasm, dressing herself tonight in a frenzy of happiness and expectation in the new violet satin gown with the discreet bustle and, for her, fairly abandoned decolletage. She admitted freely to herself that her high excitement was due in no small part to the likely chance that she would see Jason.

And now it seemed as if she might be stuck with the ridiculous Marcel for the entire evening. She could not even hope to look to Paola for rescue. The Austrian woman and her Belgian colonel had disappeared.

"Capitaine Gallimard!"

At the sound of the voice behind her the St. Cyrian stiffened. She barely had time to register that Marcel must have been promoted before he whirled her around quickly, turning his back on the speaker.

"Capitaine . . ."

Over Gallimard's epaulettes she looked into the lean face of Jason's dinner companion at Orizaba, Pierre Boulanger. There was no mistaking the sympathy in the smile he gave her.

"If the lady does not object, Captain," he said to Marcel while not taking his eyes from hers, "I am—how do you say it in America, *mademoiselle?*—'cutting in.' It seems I must do this before you mount another attack on the emperor or the marshal of France and their ladies."

Marcel said nothing, but his eyes went wild.

"Shall we leave the decision to Mademoiselle Anderson, Gallimard?" Boulanger said.

Without a word Marcel bowed to her, spun on his boots, and stamped off, sparks of fine fury arcing up from every step he took.

"Your young *ami* does not care much for me, Mademoiselle Anderson," Boulanger said as his right arm encircled her waist. "I cannot for the life of me imagine what prompts such strong feeling." The wicked look in his eyes betrayed that he imagined it very well.

But the last person in the world she wanted to discuss at the moment was Marcel Gallimard.

She did not have to. Boulanger must have read her mind.

"If you were wondering, Mademoiselle Anderson, *oui*, he *is* here tonight. I left him but a moment ago." The

Chasseur's face did not wear the ironic mask she remembered from Orizaba.

"In fact, I *was* wondering, Major Boulanger, but I assure you it was merely idle curiosity. Colonel James and I have not spoken for more than a year."

The smile that broke under Boulanger's elegant mustache was far too knowing for comfort. "I would wager *he* did not talk much at that time. Jason is not a great talker to begin with, and he has a difficult time letting others know what is in his heart on anything. *S'il vous plaît, mademoiselle,* forgive a perhaps too blunt soldier for speaking of intimate matters that are your and Jason's affair alone, but what do I have to do to bring you two together? *Mon ami* Jason thinks himself unworthy of you. Ah, *bien.* Your face tells me you find that as preposterous as I do."

The Chasseur's tone was one of unmistakable affection. He fell silent for a bit, then began again. "Is it possible, *mademoiselle,* that you share the strong feelings he is having such difficulty admitting to?"

She almost fell away from him. "Major Boulanger, I . . ." she began. "Would you find somewhere for us to sit? I would appreciate it if you could also get me a glass of champagne."

"Certainement, mademoiselle."

He led her to a wooden settee in a remote corner of the patio, bowed when she was seated, turned, and began elbowing his way through the crowd in the direction of the table where she and Paola had parted company in what seemed hours ago.

The settee nestled in the shadow of one of the fearsome artillery pieces. Boulanger, demonstrating a sensitivity she would never have suspected he possessed, must have chosen it to afford her as much privacy as it would be possible to get at the ball. He must have seen how his remarks had shaken her.

The field gun was parked between her and the nearest wall torch, and it was a bit darker in this small alcove than almost anywhere in the enormous patio, particularly out on the brilliantly lighted floor still a kaleidoscope of waltzing couples.

She caught a glimpse of Paola whirling around the floor with her Belgian colonel.

Then her champagne arrived.

But not in the hands of Pierre Boulanger.

Jason James stood before her.

"M-miss Anderson," he stammered, "forgive me. I had no intention of accosting you. Pierre said Madame Bazaine . . ." She had never expected to see this stern soldier so completely shaken. "He tricked me. But I should have guessed . . . there is no acceptable excuse for this intrusion."

"Do not apologize, Jason. I am very glad to see you. I had given up hope we would meet again, even casually, after your letter . . ."

"I meant every word of it . . ."

"I know you did. And thank you for your discretion, although I never felt it necessary." She reached up toward the glass of champagne he seemed to have forgotten. "Please . . . I am dying of thirst. It was very warm dancing with Major Boulanger."

He surrendered the glass. "I had better leave you now, Miss Anderson."

"No, no! Stay. And will you *please* stop that 'Miss Anderson' nonsense? I realize we never got a chance to come close, but when we talked last there wasn't such a wide chasm between us that we had to hurl our last names across it. Sit down . . . Jason."

He sat, stiffly, using only a scant few inches at the front of the settee. The wooden bench was barely wide enough for two, and her hip and thigh were snug against his. It was the first time they had been this close since that awkward, hesitant dance at the American embassy during the Washington's Birthday celebration. They both stared straight ahead.

She turned toward him slightly and took an inventory of everything about him.

From the tips of his polished boots with their high, shield-like fronts to the broad shoulders encased in the midnight blue tunic of the Guards, he was still every inch the soldier she remembered from Orizaba, the rooftop, and the great parade up Calle de San Francisco. That no longer distressed her as it once had.

Solange had once called him "attractive." The adjective was of more use in some less intimate assessment. Compelling—that fit. A few more strands of gray had appeared at his temples since they met last, a year ago, but at this moment, perched on the settee, all hard, masculine angles and strength, he looked handsomer than ever. She looked straight ahead again.

Now the warmth from his body seeped through the layers of his uniform and through her ball gown.

"Have you slept with him yet?"

Would she ever get close to him again without hearing Paola's question?

The only way she could stop it now was with questions of her own. They would not be, as Boulanger had phrased it, rhetorical. She did not want to let the evening run out in social inanities. She sipped her champagne.

"How is Cipi?" she asked. Safe enough, and since their meeting on the coast, when the dwarf put her and Solange aboard the imperial train with such care and diligence, she genuinely wanted to know.

"He is fine . . ."

Would he say more without prompting? Was he really smiling? The answer to both was "yes." "Cipi fancies himself a great soldier now," he said.

She chanced a small laugh. "Yes. I saw him in his new uniform at Veracruz. Which reminds me, I have yet to express my gratitude that you sent him to look after Solange and me. Without him we would have missed the train and been put to all sorts of bother."

"No thanks are necessary. To be perfectly honest, I was under orders from the empress. And Cipi enjoyed taking care of you."

"Even so, I am grateful."

"Her Majesty told me in Veracruz that you and she are friends."

"Yes, we are. I was in school in Paris with her for a while."

"And you are now a member of the court at . . . Chapultepec."

He had said the castle's name as if he always had to force himself to say it. Memories of the darker moments of that day on the rooftop came streaming back. Something told her that to ask about it might be like taking a nettle in her hand and trying to make a fist.

"And you," she said, "are now an aide and confidant of Marshal Bazaine. Do you like your work?"

"Well . . . it is not precisely what my training and experience fit me for, but . . . yes, I like it. Actually, it surprises me that I do."

"You are at the center of things, Jason. Will the war in the north end soon?"

He looked around, as if to see who might be listening. "I don't think so. But most of the military men here, and practically all of the European civilians, expect a quick, easy victory."

"The French *are* a confident lot."

"No more so, unfortunately, than the Conservatives and the emperor's other allies. And not without some reason, of course. The marshal's army, and those of Generals Miramón, Márquez, and Mejía have a great superiority in numbers and materiel over the forces of President Juárez, particularly since our country's own war north of the border prevents him from getting any foreign help . . ." He stopped, looking a trifle discomfited. "But if my memory of some of your views serves me, you must have no wish to discuss distasteful military matters."

"Quite to the contrary, Jason. That might have been true

once." By and large it was *still* true, but there was no way she was going to show anything but utter fascination with *anything* he said tonight. She wanted to keep him talking. Not only for her sake—for his, too. Boulanger, with his comment that Jason should "unburden himself more," had thrown down a gauntlet for her. Something strange had happened to the daughter of that uncompromising pacifist Bradford Anderson. She was taking the counsel of a soldier about the emotional well-being of another soldier.

"And *your* work at the castle," he said. "Are you enjoying it?"

"Some of it . . . most, I should say. The day you and I were there with General Comonfort, I was so dazzled by Chapultepec's rich history and the general's carefully engineered tour of the public rooms I failed to see what miserable condition the rest of the old place was in. We found the living quarters a shambles. It has been an Augean agony getting them fit for the emperor and empress, even though our Indian servants did all of the worst drudgery. Paola and Melanie—that's Countess Kollonitz and Countess Zichy—and I . . ." This would not do. She was talking too much. The idea was to let *him* talk. "I am *deeply* interested in your views of the political and military situation in Mexico, Jason. I find myself terribly confused by what is happening to Mexico."

Paola danced into Sarah's line of sight. Another officer had taken the place of Colonel van der Smissen, a thin, bald Zouave with a black, waxed mustache extending far to the sides of his narrow face. The ball was going very well for Paola, and she looked it.

"If the French Army stays in this country long enough there is probably no way the Republican government can survive," he said. "Once hostilities end, the emperor will be able to institute his reforms—if he's patient. The trouble is he is trying to establish an enlightened rule while the fighting still rages. No one doubts his sincerity, but he will, I fear, always meet with a certain amount of distrust among his Conservative allies. They can't understand why a supposedly devout Catholic prince won't give the Mexican church everything it asks for. I sometimes think they would accept his thwarting them with a good deal less fuss and perhaps even with resignation if he *weren't* a Catholic, or at least if he wasn't as religious as he claims and appears to be."

"You are talking about the properties the church used to own?"

"Among other things."

"How would you advise His Majesty, Jason?"

He paused, looked at Sarah intently. "I would never presume to advise him, Sarah, even if asked. I am just a soldier. I hope I will soon be relieved of my duties here and sent north. I am half afraid my Guards regiment will be ordered into battle without me. How would *you* advise His Majesty?"

"Like you, *I* would never presume to give His Majesty advice, and he certainly would never ask it of me. Oddly enough, even though I live at the castle now, I am less well positioned in that regard than you are. We seldom actually *see* the emperor at Chapultepec. He rises even before most of the household servants do, rides with his equerry or walks in one of the terrace gardens until breakfast, then busies himself with affairs of state almost until the dinner hour, if he is not at the National Palace with Marshal Bazaine. Only the empress and Monsieur Eloin are permitted to disturb him when he is working in his office."

"Felix Eloin?"

"Yes."

"I suppose it's not my place to say so, but I think *he* is responsible for most of the irritation between Marshal Bazaine's people and those around the emperor. Does *Her* Majesty accept Eloin's advice?"

"I don't really know, but I fear so."

"Will she listen to anyone else?"

"I keep hoping." Uncanny that he should ask her about something which had brought the only genuine rub she had felt since the move to Chapultepec. She had almost abandoned that foolish hope that she could make a difference, a pathetic, idealistic dream kept fluttering by that first conversation with the Imperial couple aboard the train to La Soledad.

It pleased her that she and Jason seemed to be of a mind about Felix Eloin.

"The emperor and empress are so *innocent!*" he blurted out now.

"I hadn't thought of them that way," she said. "But, yes, I suppose they *are* innocent. Is that so bad?"

"They are dealing with experienced schemers, people with quite a different agenda from theirs."

"And you feel they should listen only to Marshal Bazaine?"

"I think it would not be their worst course. If they want to secure the empire, the war against the Republicans must be won. Only the marshal can give them such a victory."

"Would it be so terrible for this country if President Juárez were to triumph?" She wondered how much she was giving away of her still nagging doubts about where justice might be found in all this chaos.

"Probably not, but only if he could triumph completely. Defeating the French-Conservative alliance would only be the beginning of his struggle. With the exception of the United States and possibly Great Britain, every major country in the world will be arrayed against him, not in a military way, but in the secret ways nations conduct their affairs." He stopped, stirred uneasily, and she felt his body move against hers. "Please, Sarah, forgive these dreary pontifications."

"They don't sound like pontifications to me."

She meant it. The man reluctantly revealing these perceptions was "just a soldier"? Pierre Boulanger's awed description of him as a quiet man whose modesty discounted his own intelligence and integrity seemed more apt than ever.

All of the things he said fascinated her, but when she thought about where they were tonight, and how long it had been since she had attended a party such as this, she wished silently that he would ask her to dance.

Failing that, she certainly wanted something from him other than politics, and she knew what it was. She wanted to hear about Jason James the *man*.

"Tell me, Jason," she said. "Did you always want to be a soldier?"

"Well . . . no. I . . ." He hesitated, then went on. "Strange to think about it in these surroundings, but there was a time when I wanted nothing more than to be a farmer. I still like growing things. I had a garden at my last post in Africa, but there's been no time for that sort of thing since I came to Mexico."

"Why *didn't* you become a farmer?"

"It's a long story, a boring one I fear. After the war here in '47 I went to sea, fully planning to go back to Kansas where I was born. Something happened and I joined the Legion. I have not regretted it, but sometimes . . ."

He broke off and glanced toward the dance floor. A couple was leaving it and coming toward them. Pierre Boulanger, with Paola on his arm; the countess had changed partners again, and from her look it was a change that pleased her. For his part, the Frenchman seemed a different creature altogether from the wolfish officer of Orizaba or Sarah's dancing partner of just a few minutes ago. He could not take his eyes from Paola's face.

"*Liebchen!*" the countess cried when she and Boulanger were still fifteen feet away from where Sarah and Jason sat. "Look what I have found, or rather what found me. Is he *nicht schön?*"

Jason rose as Paola and Pierre stopped in front of them.

"Colonel James!" Paola said. "I hope you remember me. We met aboard the *Novara.*" When Jason bowed she winked at Sarah over his head. "Fräulein Anderson, let us send these handsome officers for more champagne."

When the two men moved off, she turned to Sarah again. "You did not tell me that your Jason had such an attractive friend. Pierre is the complete Parisian. He can make a woman forget the differences in their stations. Mexico has turned immeasurably brighter for Paola tonight. And you—what did you and your Guardsman find to talk about?"

"Politics."

"Politics? How incredibly dull. It appears I must take a hand in your education, *liebchen*. There are so many things they do not teach one at the Sorbonne. Some things are best learned in the drawing room—and the boudoir."

"You astound me, Paola." She was not nearly as shocked as she made herself sound. The sudden light-heartedness she felt persuaded her it was *her* turn to tease. "I would not expect to hear such scandalous talk from a woman Melanie told me is a Canoness of the Order of Savoy. Isn't that a religious title, you wicked thing?"

"What? Oh, *ja*, that. I suppose it began as a religious honor. It has little meaning for me. It is just something I inherited. I do not have the same outlook as my sister Savoyards. It is not much different from my hunting lodge in the Tirol—which I also owned the day I was born, and which I have never paid much attention to, either. But here come our *caballeros*, as our Mexican friends call them. Let us both make the most of the next few minutes."

The Chasseur and Jason had made a quick trip to fetch the wine. "They are preparing the buffet tables," Boulanger said. "I expect the emperor will leave us soon after we dine. His Majesty looked bored the last time I saw him. I feel a little sorry for the empress. She appeared as if she wished she could mingle with the rest of us."

"Indeed," Paola said. "Charlotte loves a good party, and this *is* a good one." She gave Boulanger a broad smile. "Now."

And at that moment it became a good party for Sarah Anderson, as well.

As much as she wanted to spend more time alone with Jason, there was something satisfying having Paola and Pierre for company.

She had a sudden notion.

"Jason," she said. "Is Cipi here tonight?"

"Yes. He is with the carriage."

"Could you possibly send him to Avenida Moctezuma with a message for Solange? Countess Kollonitz and I can furnish transportation for the four of us later. I realize it's an odd time to bring this up, when we are about to eat, but I have an idea the marshal's ball will last till dawn. When it is over I should like all three of you to be my guests at breakfast."

She held her breath until the answers came—quick nods from Paola and the Chasseur, a bit more hesitation on the part of Jason. Tardy as it was in arrival, his acceptance seemed wholehearted. "I will be glad to come."

"Wunderbar!" Paola exclaimed. She looked at Jason, then back again at Sarah. "You are an excellent student, *liebchen.* And now, let us finish this champagne—we will require more, of course—and we will also dance the night away!"

"I fear we shall have to delay our dancing for a bit," Boulanger said. "The Marshal is going to light the Mexican night with a display of fireworks such as this country has never seen."

Fireworks indeed, Sarah thought. She might just have set a match to a few herself. . . .

30

▲▲▲▲▲

In the spring of 1865 two things happened north of the Rio Grande that affected millions of Mexicans and even more millions of the countrymen of Jason James and Sarah Anderson.

A fanatic Confederate loyalist named John Wilkes Booth assassinated President Abraham Lincoln, and General Robert E. Lee surrendered his sword and his army to General Ulysses S. Grant at Appomattox Courthouse in Virginia.

The war was over.

Sarah reduced it to understandable human terms when she told Solange, "It will upset Matt terribly, but thank God our good friend will stay alive."

Jason James greeted the news of the end of his country's bloodiest war with a passionate sigh of relief. Now he would never have to fight his Cousin Aaron. *"Carved in stone"* had lost its meaning.

Over the course of the six weeks after the ball at San Cosmé James and Boulanger saw Paola and Sarah every third or fourth evening or with even more frequency, something made easier when James invited Boulanger to bunk with him again until orders sent him north.

James made no attempt to seek Sarah's company on his own, as Boulanger did with the Austrian countess, and Sarah did not suggest any private meetings, either.

An inner voice cautioned him not to push too hard, too soon. For one thing, he would have to come to a decision about Sofía, a decision he was loath to make, but one that *had* to be made. For the moment he could only try to be content.

If James was content, Boulanger seemed in the grip of ecstasy.

The Parisian's pursuit of Paola—if it could properly be characterized as *his* pursuit of *her*—was close, sure, and seemingly successful, accomplished at the speed of light. Since the night of the ball at San Cosmé there had been no more prowling of the cantinas for female "targets of opportunity."

James smiled at the only threat to Pierre's soaring *joie de vivre*. Clearly the countess was also taken with Pierre, but she was an inveterate flirt, driving the Chasseur mad with comments about—and bold, inviting glances toward—almost all the other men the four met in their travels about the city. The theaters, restaurants, and other gathering places of the capital thronged with men, most of them single, and most in the uniforms she admired with unabashed enthusiasm.

"This city," Paola said once, bringing a painful flush of agony to Pierre's face, "is a horn of romantic plenty for a single woman."

Sarah, out of Boulanger's hearing, but not out of James's, took the carefree countess to task for her behavior and remarks. "Aren't you running a risk that you might lose him, Paola?"

"Not at all. It keeps a man on the *qui vive* if he sees other men interested in his woman. I could not abide a man who quailed in the face of a little competition."

More and more often Paola took a room by herself at the Mirador rather than stay with Sarah and Solange, if Sarah returned to Avenida Moctezuma, and on one of these occasions James knew almost to the exact hour when Pierre first took the Austrian woman to bed.

Not that Boulanger had reverted to his old, open, "kiss-and-tell" habits, as was the case with the now long gone and unlamented "barge on the Seine," Paloma. But the Chasseur's almost catatonic look of reverie one morning when he and Jason met for breakfast, coupled with the fact that he was still wearing the uniform he had worn the night before when he set out to see Paola, spoke all too eloquently of what must have happened.

Rather than showing the eagerness to get into the northern action which James expected, Boulanger actually expressed regret that the day would soon arrive when he had to return to his regiment. Before Paola, he had already begun to chafe at the easy, uneventful life of the capital, complaining in the same bitter way he had before the second battle of Puebla. Now he grew more and more wistful, and at times abruptly resentful, at the prospect of leaving the city. He was no longer altogether the skeptical, cavalier Pierre Boulanger of Fortín, Puebla, or San Lorenzo. The Pierre Boulanger of those (certainly for him) bracing conflicts had not completely disappeared, but had been submerged. Jason, after the advent of Paola Kollonitz, wondered if the old Boulanger would ever break the surface again.

He also wondered if *he* was the Jason James of those days and places.

At the ball he told Sarah he found his work with Marshal Bazaine at the palace enjoyable. He had already discovered in himself a talent for administrative work, and—since the meeting with the archbishop—negotiation. He was surprised to find that his effort had not gone unnoticed. He received a note from the empress thanking him, and Sarah mentioned it with admiration, too.

In some ways his new job was far more demanding than soldiering in the field, but the regular and task-filled hours, the pleasure of watching over a project other than one of destruction from inception to fruition, and the engaging young Mexican officers of the Guard who reported to him— in particular gifted Miguel López, the colonel who had commanded the emperor's escort from Veracruz to Puebla and the capital under Jason's supervision—kept his interest from flagging.

Even before reconnecting with Sarah at San Cosmé, life had turned moderately pleasant for him. He did not delude himself. There had been, as well as his enjoyment of the work itself, the steady growth of some secret inner satisfaction at finding himself in a position of power and authority. It worried him a little. He had always been content to be a subordinate, a soldier.

Each succeeding dinner with Sarah, the Frenchman, and the breezy, fun-loving countess served to intensify a sense of well-being he had seldom felt before. The other couple became a catalyst in a strange, satisfying chemistry.

The chemistry had been neutralized for a few minutes the night the four of them attended the opera at the old Teatro Nacional—renamed El Gran Teatro Imperial since the emperor's coronation—and heard the Mexican diva Ángela Peralta sing Halevy's "La Juive."

The great soprano, an astonishingly beautiful, black-haired creature with flaming, passionate eyes, shocked the *criollo* and French audience into dumbfounded silence when she stepped in front of the curtain even before the overture, nodded to the conductor, and launched herself into a full-throated rendition of the Republican anthem "La Libertad." As she sang she waved a tiny flag with the colors of the Republic of Mexico, and turned a hostile, defiant eye on the Imperial box and its shaken occupants. Finished—she shouted the old *grito*, "¡Viva Mexico!"

The royal couple departed forthwith, as did all the other occupants of the loges, and half the audience on the orchestra level.

Paola expressed her outrage at the top of her lungs, screaming "Shame! Shame!" at the stage—to the applause of those few around them who had remained in their seats after the singer disappeared behind the curtain and the orchestra began the overture. The evening, James was sure, would turn out to be a disaster, but when Boulanger suggested they leave, the countess protested, "No, no! I came to see and hear an opera—and I will!"

At the late supper afterward the Chasseur proposed an excursion for the four of them the following Sunday to see the bullfights.

Boulanger, it turned out, had learned a bit about bullfighting while with the army in Spain, but James had seen his first *corrida de toros* only a month before with Cipi, who turned out—no surprise—to be a highly knowledgeable, critically demanding *aficionado*.

The dwarf had sneered at all but one of the fights James and he saw. "Pitiful *faenas*, pure butchery, *mi coronel*. This is not bullfighting in the classic style of Sevilla, it is assassination. Only the *rejoneador*, the *torero* on horseback we saw first, was any good."

The horsemanship of the *rejoneador* also impressed James, but he was fascinated more by the matadors who faced the horns on foot. The fights had indeed been bloody, and even to James's uninitiated eye, artless, but he found himself strangely drawn to what he had seen, and he had plied Cipi with questions about the *corrida*.

As part of Cipi's course of instruction, and to gales of Sofía's laughter—the first James had ever heard from her— he and the dwarf played "*toro y torero*" out on the patio, with Cipi as matador, of course, and James charging him with a footstool held to his forehead, its curved legs serving as horns. In these sessions James became familiar with the language of the spectacle, and at least could now identify a few of the intricate passes with the cape Cipi called *suertes*.

At the end of one of these charades, with James on his knees on the tiles as the defeated bull awaiting the last thrust, and Cipi holding the cane he had extorted from the tailor, the dwarf's face turned as dark as dried blood.

"*¿Que pasa, Cipi?*" James said.

"This is ridiculous, *señor*," the dwarf said. He began to stamp his way back into the house. Sofía looked as puzzled as James felt.

"Get back here, you little piece of *mierda*," James called.

The dwarf stopped. He did not turn as he spoke. "Cipi has no time for this childishness. He has work to do."

"None that I know of. What's gotten into you?"

"Cipi would rather not say."

"But I want to hear it. Damn it, look at me!" Cipi turned back, but still avoided James's eyes. James had seen the dwarf this brazenly defiant before, but never quite so evasive.

"Out with it, Cipi!"

There was a long, deadly silence.

"No, *mi coronel*." His look said there would be no surrender. He turned on his heels and stalked into the house on his short legs without another word.

Paola greeted Boulanger's idea about the bullfights with a cry of utterly abandoned pleasure and quick acceptance. James, after a glance at Sarah, and remembering the torrents of blood at the fights he had seen with Cipi, decided it was not the best idea the Parisian had ever had, but he withheld his objections. He was confident that Sarah, with her abhorrence of violence, would demur, but she confounded him by welcoming the idea and agreeing to it almost as speedily as Paola had.

On the following Sunday James had Cipi buy tickets and hire a carriage for the outing. As the dwarf drove the two couples to the Plaza de Toros he echoed James's doubts at the supper. "Cipi does not think this is a good idea, *mi coronel. Norteamericana* and European women are not very stoic at the sight of blood."

Paola hooted in derision. Sarah said nothing.

"What can we expect today, Cipi?" James asked.

"There will be six bulls killed, the first by a *rejoneador*. There is no need for the *señores y señoritas* to rush to their seats for that one."

"A *rejoneador?*" Sarah asked.

"The mounted *torero, señorita*. They are most often amateurs, highborn *caballeros* who think this sort of nonsense makes them more appealing to *las mujeres*."

"I saw one such fight with Cipi a month or two ago, Sarah," James said. "Unbelievable horsemanship."

"The work of this mounted clown today," Cipi interrupted, "will not be worth watching. There is little *emoción* in such a fight—and no sense of the tragedy a great fight should have. The *rejoneador* is of such little consequence he most often performs when the seats are only half full and usually even before the president arrives."

"President?" Sarah asked. Was she thinking of the man who had met them at Chapultepec?

"The dignitary who runs the *corrida*." Cipi looked at James, shook his head skeptically, then brightened as he turned back to Sarah. "Ah . . . but the killing of the second bull, *mi doña*, right after the *paseo*, the parade of *toreros*, could be of genuine beauty and importance. El Viti, who will take this one, is *primera clase*. He is not one of these slovenly Mexican matadors. He learned his trade in España—Sevilla. Whenever El Viti can, he takes *el toro* in the manner we call *recibiendo*, where he does not truly kill it, but draws it to him with the *muleta*, the smaller red cape he uses only at the end. If the bull is brave and follows well—and this one today should be brave; he is, after all, a son of the great seed bull Negro Grande—he will kill *himself* with his final charge. Such a triumph does not come twice a season, you understand. If it happens this way, and Cipi predicts it will, do not bother to stay for the other fights. Even if they are moderately good they will be of little interest after a *recibiendo*." He turned to James. "Cipi will meet you back where he drops you off, colonel."

James pressed the dwarf to sit with them. "You can explain the *corrida* to us."

Cipi shook his head. "I have *amigos* I must meet. You will not need me, anyway, *señor*. I have taught you well." He stopped the carriage at the entrance of the Plaza de Toros.

James, helping Sarah alight from the carriage, had seen her turn a shade paler at Cipi's description of his hoped for outcome, and again felt misgivings.

At his first fight he and Cipi had been high up in full sunlight, but their seats this time were in the *sombra* side of the ring in the midst of a number of upperclass Mexicans, three of whom Jason knew slightly from one of the intimate small dinners Bazaine had given France's more reliable Conservative allies in the first weeks of the French occupation. These *aficionados*, and their immediate neighbors, were a noisy lot, their behavior quite at odds with their sober comportment at the marshal's parties; they cheered, jeered, and howled at the bullring servants who raked the sand of the arena, and welcomed the arrival of the *presidente* with boisterous applause when he took his place in his box above the highest row of seats behind them. Their applause drowned out the few catcalls that came across the ring from the cheaper seats in the sun on the opposite side of the ampitheatre.

The Mexicans around them gulped down enormous amounts of food of ghastly redolence, drank wine that from its harsh, raw, sour smell was not really old enough for consumption, and in general acted much as his own Kansas neighbors had at the Fourth of July celebrations of his boyhood. Some of the Mexican men and even a few of the women smoked the ugly, twisted *cigarros* Cipi sometimes indulged in. Sarah looked askance for a moment, then erupted in laughter when Paola begged one from the man next to her and disappeared in a blue cloud when he held a match to it.

Sarah refused James's offer of refreshment. "I don't think I could possibly eat," she said. "I am not made of the stern stuff Paola is."

The *rejoneador* was an amateur, sure enough. James recognized him as his associate at Guards headquarters, Colonel Miguel López. Just two mornings ago he had appointed López to the command of the Imperial Guards stationed at Chapultepec.

He need not have worried about López's performance disturbing Sarah. It was mild and inoffensive enough for all but the ultra-squeamish. The bull was small, with an unimpressive set of young horns. The picadors were almost casual as they used their lances to weaken the unfortunate animal for the last part of the *faena*. López—in a short black jacket spangled with silver and wearing pants so tight the muscles of his legs pressing against the horse's flanks rippled as visibly as if he wore nothing at all—awaited his turn. Blood did not stream down the bull's flanks as it had on nearly every animal when James watched with Cipi. López fought the bull with a long, slender lance, and most of his work took place at the far opposite side of the ring. The young colonel was a gifted rider, and his horse uncannily adept, with incredible reflexes, jerking its hindquarters under it and away from the bull's horns whenever he charged.

After a dozen such charges, and with his mount and his

body concealing the lance and its target from Jason and Sarah, López moved in for the kill quickly and cleanly; only a small amount of blood stained the yellow sand when, after the last lance thrust from López, one of the bull ring servants stepped in and gave the animal—already down on his knees—the final *coup de grace* with a short, thick-bladed dagger plunged into the spinal column.

When the triumphant López spurred his horse to a canter and made a circuit of the ring to the *olés* of the crowd—even while a team of mules was still dragging the carcass of the bull away—he saw James, reined in his horse, swept his sombrero from his head, and bowed across the horn of his saddle. Straightening up again, he favored each of the women with a separate smile.

Paola Kollonitz heaved a vast sigh from within her wreath of *cigarro* smoke. "He is quite something, Sarah, *nein?*" Her stage whisper reached for several seats around them. Heads turned and smiles appeared. "With a body like that I can think of things he should be able to do at least as well as he kills dumb brutes."

Pierre snorted. "He is not a real bullfighter, Paola! He has no reason to parade himself with such disgusting pomp and pride. His victim was little more than a calf!"

Paola smiled—and waved her *cigarro* in the direction of Colonel López. Boulanger's words were poor disguises for his jealousy, and the coquettish Austrian woman apparently had no intention of putting that jealousy to rest until she had wrung every personal dividend from it she could.

Except for Pierre's discomfort, the afternoon seemed to be going well so far, better than James had expected.

At the sound of trumpets, a gate across the expanse of freshly raked sand opened and three men on foot, brilliant, sparkling parade capes folded over their left arms, began the *paseo,* a stately march across the sand toward them, sunlight dancing over the gold and silver braid and sequins of each of what Cipi had called the *traja de luces,* the "suit of lights." They were followed by more men on foot and even more on horseback, the riders carrying lances much heavier than the one López had used. They stopped directly below Paola, Sarah, Pierre, and Jason. The three men in the front rank looked up to the president in his box and saluted.

"They are asking his permission to begin," Boulanger informed the women. "They will ask it again when it is time to make the kill."

Two of the *toreros* moved off to the sides of the ring. The third—slender, solemn, with the prominent beaked nose of so many Spaniards—took up a position in front of one of the barriers which formed passageways between the sand and the first row of *barrera* seats. James had seen more than one man dive behind these shields to escape the bull in the earlier *corrida*.

Paola leaned across Sarah. "Is the man in front the one they call the *matador,* Jason?"

"Yes." He smiled. The countess really should stop torturing poor Pierre and ask *him*. James might have said it aloud—if Sarah had not been next to him. "That is El Viti, whom my man Cipi spoke of."

"Is he the one who will kill the bull?"

"If he is brave, skillful enough—and lucky."

"I wasn't really sure *who* killed the first one."

"Nor was I, to tell the truth. I believe the credit goes to Colonel López."

"Will this next *matador* ride a horse."

"No."

"Pity. I like men on horseback. I have another question. If they want the bull dead so badly, why don't they just shoot it instead of going to all this bother—colorful as it is?"

"*Oui!*" Boulanger's voice was an explosive rasp. "Shoot the damned thing. And then we can all go home."

James told them then what Cipi had said about what they would see—that the lone man on foot facing the bull only with a scarlet rag and about a meter of steel was the truest test of *torero* courage.

"This next fight will present such a test?" Sarah asked.

"Presumably. One can't always be sure, according to Cipi."

"The *matador* is not alone now—although I will admit he *looks* alone."

"He will be alone at the end. His two helpers, the other men with the capes—who are also the matadors who will fight the rest of the afternoon's bulls—will help him learn about his enemy—how he charges and employs his horns—before the beginning of the *faena,* the last stage of the fight. He will have other helpers: the same two matadors acting as *banderilleros* and those men on the padded horses, the *picadores.* But when he reaches what Mexicans and Spaniards call 'the moment of truth' he will be totally alone."

"It is strange to hear truth and death linked that way."

"Every sport has its own arcane language."

"This seems more ritual than sport."

"It may be just that. Cipi calls it art. I do know that here and in Spain there is an almost religious worship of bullfights—and the men who take part in them."

Now the *matador* El Viti and the two other *toreros* stepped to the wooden barriers and spread the capes they carried in the parade across the tops, shook out the rose-and-yellow fighting capes their servants handed them, and walked to what must be strategic points of the arena, with El Viti in the center, directly below James and Sarah.

None of the three men casting black dagger shadows on the sand moved, until El Viti crossed himself.

Across the ring servants swung open a solid, wide door with the word TORIL painted on it, revealing the mouth of a cavernous, black tunnel. A hush cloaked the arena. He felt Sarah stir beside him. She leaned against him, and for a moment he forgot everything happening in the ring and fought off an almost overwhelming urge to put his arm around her.

The second bull burst out of the blackness.

Compared to the first small animal this was a monster

straight from a nightmare: mammoth, black as primordial sin.

James heard the quick intake of Sarah's breath.

The bull's first blind charge took him a third of the way into the ring. He stopped there, his hooves rooted to the sand. Then, his eyes apparently now fully adjusted to the sunlight, he caught sight of the man straight across the arena from him.

El Viti lifted his cape.

The bull began to move; a measured, almost mincing walk at first, accelerating next to an oddly delicate trot, and then to an all out, hammering run. The ring did not actually shake, but it seemed to.

Sarah lifted her gloved hand and placed it on Jason's upper arm. Unconscious and surely unintended as it was, it was a far more intimate touch than her hand on his shoulder in any of the waltzes at San Cosmé.

El Viti met the bull's first charge with a swirl of the cape—a poetic move Cipi had called a Veronica—taking the rushing dark mass of the animal under the folds as if he was gathering him to the silk *faja* sash around his waist, bringing him out then with a straight right arm, turning slowly and letting the cape trail down the entire length of the bull's back as he charged on past him toward the nearest barrier right below them. He faced the huge brute then, and with the cape flowering, drew him back again. He led the bull past him this way four more times, finishing the fifth pass of the series with a much tighter curl of the cape that turned the bull in half his length and brought him shuddering to a stop.

The passes were not so much continuous motions as single, separate, frozen images, with the great cape welding man and animal together as one in isolated works of sculpture.

A throaty, almost ghostly "¡Olé!" from the crowd met each of these passes.

This first act did not last nearly long enough for Jason

James; when it ended, Sarah pulled her hand back into her lap.

More intent on her, he was fully conscious of very little in the second part, although he watched every pass, looking for the things Cipi pointed out when they were here before and in their mock fights on the patio: the swift, sure, sometimes dainty placements of the *banderillas*, and the serious, deep thrusts of the pics in the bull's hump as the picadors stood in their stirrups and leaned their bodies into the terrible work of their weapons as they broke down the great head-tossing muscle to prepare the bull for the sword.

Unfortunately, there were also the gushing, probably fatal wounds the horns made in the belly of the second picador's horse. This would doubtlessly be the worst of it for Sarah.

But the placing of the bright, beribboned barbed sticks by the other matadors now working as *banderilleros* was carried out with satisfying style, and he knew El Viti's *suertes* with the cape were good, perhaps brilliant, possibly even touched with genius; he would have to ask Cipi later about just how good they were.

But he did not marvel at any of it as he felt he should; today only Sarah and her reactions could claim his full attention. He barely heard the cries of the people closest to him. Except hers. He heard every faint gasp, every breath she took, felt every tremor from the body still pressed against his.

A trumpet blared.

El Viti, alone when his helpers left the ring for the barriers, looked up toward the *presidencia* and received his signal to proceed. He stepped to the wall of the ring below them, removed his hat, the boat-shaped, black *montera*, and sailed it toward the first row of shaded seats, where it fell into the lap of a stunning young creole woman in a white *mantilla*.

"El Viti is dedicating the bull to her," James whispered to Sarah.

El Viti moved to the barrier and laid the rose-and-yellow cape across its top. When he turned to face the bull again he held the red *muleta* in his left hand and the naked sword in his right.

"Is it time now for what Cipi called the *faena?*" Sarah asked.

"Yes. The last act. And the most dangerous." He kept his voice as soft as possible. She had borne up so well so far it would have been unforgivable to frighten her now, but he had to prepare her for the distinct possibility of something going wrong.

"Most dangerous? But why? The bull is tired, badly wounded, and he's lost a lot of blood. He doesn't move with the frightening speed he did at first. He must be weakened terribly. And he doesn't look as if he knows what is happening to him."

"He is weaker, Sarah, but not *truly* weak. And he has begun to understand something about the man he faces. He charges more slowly, true, but that means he may ignore the *muleta.*"

"And if he does ignore it?"

"He will try to get the matador. You see how much lower the bull holds his head than when he first came into the ring? He can lift those horns in less time than it takes to blink. He is only slower when he runs; his reflexes are still lightning fast."

The bull had fixed himself foursquare, six or seven meters to the right of El Viti's barrier. His shoulders and flanks now streamed with blood from the wounds the *picadores* had inflicted, the red running through the short, black hairs and creating a new color as dark as death itself. The great beast stood motionless. Had he found his *querencia*, the secret place in the ring where Cipi said he felt most secure and where he was most dangerous?

El Viti, half turned toward the animal, held the *muleta* low and the narrow sword pointed straight down at the sand, its slightly curved tip almost touching the white silk stocking above his black sandal. The bull turned his big head slowly from side to side, as if assessing some walled space invisible to humans.

El Viti stepped toward him. When he reached him his left hand and the *muleta* dropped even lower. With his wrist stiff he placed the red cloth under the animal's muzzle and with slow moves of his forearm began to bring him out— step by step.

Once away from the side of the ring, but still straight beneath James and Sarah, El Viti seemed to pull the bull to him as if on cords. He led the animal past him, sent him on his way. The bull turned back on him and El Viti faced him with his back arched in arrogance.

Now one pass led directly and smoothly into another, and in the final one, the matador wound the huge animal around his waist as if he were a monstrous belt. Silence had blanketed the arena so completely James could hear each deathly scrape of the monster's hooves. El Viti stepped clear and turned his back on his adversary, now stock still again and bolted to the sand. The matador's chest was smeared with the creature's blood.

The "moment of truth" came suddenly.

The matador turned, took two steps back to the bull, draped the *muleta* under his nose, brought his head even further down, sighted the length of his sword between the horns, and placed the point on the ridge of the bent neck. He drew the red cloth down to his knees and the bull made his last, slow, surging charge.

The sword was buried to the hilt.

Recibiendo! Exactly as Cipi had predicted.

The ring shook. Tidal waves of "¡Olé! . . . ¡Olé! . . . ¡Olé! . . ." flooded it.

She still had not spoken when they met Cipi waiting with the carriage outside the bull ring. Paola and Pierre had stopped to visit with a well-dressed Mexican couple who seemed to know the countess and were still fifty paces behind them as James helped Sarah into the vehicle. Cipi turned in his driver's seat when she was settled in the cushions.

"¡Como estas, señorita?" He fixed Sarah with an eye as sharp, glittering, and penetrating as El Viti's sword. "And how did you like the fight El Viti made?"

Her gaze at the dwarf was, if anything, even stronger and steadier than his. "It was ghastly . . . hideous . . . terrifying . . . and *absolutely beautiful*. You were right, Cipi. After watching El Viti's artistry, there was little point in staying." She turned to James. "I can't begin to thank *you* enough, Jason."

At the Mirador a dismal disappointment awaited James.

He had planned supper down the Paseo at El Gavilan for the four of them, and he and Pierre had taken Sarah and Paola back to the hotel to freshen up, but as they entered the lobby a cadet messenger from Chapultepec approached them with a summons from Countess Zichy commanding Sarah's immediate return to the castle.

"Nothing important, Jason," Sarah said. "But as a soldier you certainly understand an order is an order."

To Boulanger's immense satisfaction, Paola's presence apparently was not called for. The Chasseur asked James to dine with him and the countess, but it was clear there was little heart in the invitation and he declined with thanks.

James walked Sarah to the court carriage which Melanie Zichy had sent to pick her up and which now stood next to his own rented one, where Cipi was nodding in sleep in the driver's seat.

When James took her elbow and helped her up to the runningboard she paused and turned to him.

"Did I measure up, Jason?"

The question set him back on his heels. "Good Lord, Sarah! It wasn't a test."

"Not of *your* devising, surely—but of my own."

"Then you alone know if you passed it."

She smiled. "At the risk of seeming immodest . . . I

believe I did pass, the most difficult part of the test, at any
rate—and the part I wanted to pass above all the others."

She bent over and kissed him on the cheek.

He had never struggled harder than at this moment, as he
fought the urge to take her in his arms and return her kiss—
but not on the cheek.

Before he could do any such thing there was something
else he must do first.

He watched the carriage until it rolled out of sight down
what now had become with her departure the early evening
gloom of the Paseo.

A snorting cough roused him from his musings.

"*Señorita Anderson* is a remarkable *mujer, mi coronel.*
Beautiful, too."

James climbed into the carriage. "Take me home, Cipi,
por favor."

"*Bueno, señor.* Sofía will be glad to see you back so early
in the evening. I have no doubt she will welcome you with
special ardor tonight."

The meddling little rascal had almost spoken the names
of the two women in the same breath. And every suggestive
implication was clear. It was not a slip. Cipi never slipped.
It was best to ignore it, turn any talk—if there had to be
talk at all—to something else.

"Cipi . . ." James said. "That day on the patio . . .
when I started to play the part of the *rejoneador.* You
suddenly lost interest in the game . . . no, it was much
more than a loss of interest . . . you looked very . . .
disturbed." He could not accuse the dwarf of fear. "Why?"

Cipi stiffened, then raised his whip and cracked it over
the horses' backs, causing the carriage to leap forward and
throwing James hard against the back of his seat.

Cipi glanced back at him. "In Spain the advice they give
young *hombres* is: 'take a woman to the bullfight and then to
bed.' In the colonel's case it will be a different woman, but
it does not matter. For all their surface differences, one
woman is much like another."

* * *

He did not wait for Sofía to come to him that night. He called her to his study, not his bedroom—even before he could frame what he would have to tell her.

"¡Sí, mi coronel?" It was some small comfort she had only once called him "Jason" in waking moments; it was no comfort at all that she had never looked lovelier—or more vulnerable.

"We must talk, Sofía. It is a talk long overdue." He paused, nervously. This would not prove easy. "You have meant a lot to me, still do—always will. But . . ."

Except for whatever dissonant echoes might come, the worst of it was over just that quickly. Her face told him she already knew the essence of everything he intended saying. Still, it had to actually be said. He could leave no open ends, no possibility of doubt or misunderstanding. He knew she would say nothing.

"I think you will want to leave my service when I finish what I have to say, Sofía. Things cannot go on as they have. I have taken terrible advantage of you, and it must stop. The fault is not yours. Cipi will see to it that you are provided for until you find another position. With your skills, and with whatever references you need from me, that should not take long."

Her eyes had not left his—had not wavered.

"It is the gringa, is it not, mi coronel?"

He could not lie to her.

"Sí, Sofía." It was the second "moment of truth" of the day, and by far the more deadly one.

She nodded.

To this point she had remained standing just inside his study door. Now she took a seat in the upholstered chair opposite him. Her black eyes held his again.

He went on—lamely, he knew; disgusted with himself. "Please try not to hate me, Sofía. Although I could never reproach you if you did." He cringed at the words and the sound of his voice; he was no different from all the other cruel, unfeeling men she must have known before Jalapa.

"I will never hate you, my colonel." She paused. "And—unless you *order* me to go, I will never leave you."

"But—"

She raised her hand, palm toward him, as one would hush a child. "One day you will need me. Not for the things we have done, but for something even more important. Until that time I will be your servant—and your servant only. The things we did together in the night were wonderful, *mi coronel,* but I will make do without them. They are *nada* to what you will need me for if what Cipi . . ."

She stopped, stood up, and turned to leave.

"What were you about to say, Sofía?"

She turned back.

"I think perhaps Cipi will beat me if I tell."

"Tell what?"

She stood as stock still as El Viti had when he turned his back on the bull seconds before he killed it.

"He will not beat you, Sofía, I assure you."

"Do you remember the day on the patio when the colonel and Cipi played at bullfighting, *señor?*"

"*Sí.*"

"Cipi told me what he saw in his mind's eye as he looked at you that day."

"And?"

"He saw the colonel in a place far away from here. A storm was coming. He saw the colonel facing death at the hands of a man the colonel has known for many years. He saw the colonel dying. He saw me caring for you and trying to save your life . . ."

The smile he gave her belied the cold chill below his breastbone. "And you believe all of this will actually come to pass?"

"Cipi has the gift."

She became suddenly the wild bird in flight again, disappearing into the hallway blackness as if she were flying into the vault of night.

No, she was not leaving.

And he knew he could never send her away.

There would be nothing intimate between them from here on out, forever. That denial, he regretted, would make her no less a threat to the promise now entering his life— but he could not, would not, send her away.

31

▲▲▲▲▲

"Most of the Mex conservatives who come to the embassy on business," Matt O'Leary said, "seem to think Bazaine is every bit as bad for their country as Juárez. What does your . . . friend . . . Colonel James, have to say about him, Miss Anderson?"

Sarah reddened at the Marine's probably entirely innocent use of "friend." Matt sent a smile in Solange's direction and tried to hide it by lifting his breakfast coffee to his lips.

"Jason doesn't say much about his work. I'm sure he admires the marshal greatly, for the most part, but now and again I think he has some tiny doubts. Marshal Bazaine is a puzzling man. The way he has so far opposed the archbishop in nearly everything doesn't exactly fit with the impressions I've gotten over the years about good Catholics. And his professed Christian outlook certainly doesn't square with the absolute ruthlessness he appears to allow his commanders like Márquez and Dupin. Of course, public figures have displayed this sort of hypocritical behavior before. Being good Catholics didn't keep any number of Europe's tyrants from orgies of killing down through the centuries. I'm not offending you, am I?"

"Not at all," O'Leary said over his coffee cup. "You know I'm no fanatic, Miss Anderson. Catholics come in all shapes, sizes, and flavors. Labastida, for instance, is a throwback, in my opinion. This business of allowing his priests to bar Frenchwomen from the Mass unless they dress like Mexican women is right out of the Dark Ages. I guess I'm firmly on Bazaine's side where the archbishop is concerned. Incidentally, Leonardo Márquez serves at the emperor's pleasure, not Bazaine's, although the Frenchman does have the say over his military actions."

It was good to have this week off from her duties at Chapultepec and to spend it with Solange in the relaxed atmosphere of the house on Avenida Moctezuma, doubly good to have the Marine come to call as he had today, ostensibly to tell her and Solange of his promotion to captain. But he had brushed their congratulations aside nervously. He clearly had something else on his mind from the way he fidgeted on the divan from the time he sat down.

The week would turn even better if she could see Jason. Since the bullfight her hopes for them had soared, even though they had not as yet seen each other alone for more than a dozen minutes. There had been brief *tête-à-têtes*, yes, but none of the *truly* private moments she longed for. He had come to the castle twice, once bearing messages from the marshal to the emperor, and once to one of Charlotte's *thés dansants*, and there had been more evenings at the theater and dinners with Paola and Pierre.

But Jason's manner with her did seem marginally easier if not intimate, almost as if he had reached a decision about the two of them.

Paola, typically, had scoffed at any such forbearance. "You've got to bring things to a head with him, *liebchen*. Life is all too short as it is. Do not make such a face. I am not talking about your climbing into bed with him. You have made your feelings plain about that. And in your case I wouldn't call it prudery. But I can guess the depth of your feeling. You must make him aware of it."

That frightening outer limit of intimacy Paola hinted at still remained out of the question, and she was glad Paola finally realized it, but the thought of it no longer sent her into the embarrassed, unraveling panic of her responses to the earlier teasing. For the first time in a life that, until Mexico at least, had been as sheltered as if she were in God's pocket, she knew she was no longer the schoolgirl-student of Boston and Paris. She had become a woman. Scary, but with stirrings of some newfound, satisfying sense of strength.

But would that pulse of strength be sufficient to see her through an adventure she was still unsure she could handle?

"How is the campaign in the north going, Matt?" she asked. "Does Juárez have any chance at all?" The second question was one she would never dream of asking at Chapultepec. No one in the grim old fortress Max and Charlotte had transformed into a Miramar-like fairyland would dare ask it.

"Good question, Miss Anderson. Ambassador Corwin turns almost despondent every time Colonel McClellan, our military attache, goes over the situation map with him. I can understand it. The Frogs have sure gobbled up a lot of territory in the central and northern states, and the way their engineers are extending the rail lines, it would appear they are well on their way to the complete pacification and control of Mexico for the emperor. Mind you, though, I only said it would *appear* so. I have a few ideas of my own—they're not worth much, I expect—about how deceiving those appearances could be. I'm no military genius, and I'm sure not a political one."

"What *are* your ideas? I do want to hear them. You've never been too far off the mark."

"Well, it all turns back on the man we were talking about a moment ago—Bazaine. Or rather on the marshal and Napoleon III."

"How so?"

"Bazaine still seems rigorous enough in his prosecution of the war—with only one lapse in his attention—but news from our embassy in Paris indicates that Napoleon himself might be losing interest. He's under heavy pressure from his subjects to pull out of Mexico. Should that happen, the prospects of the Republicans would improve enormously. Of

course, that would probably mean even more bloodshed."
He paused and took a last sip of coffee, staring then into the
cup as if he were seeking answers to some as yet unasked
question.

Suddenly she realized that whatever was on his mind he
would not bring it up with Solange in the room.

"Could you have Rosa fix more coffee, Solange?"

The Frenchwoman had made a wry face at Matt's
remarks about the report from Paris. She was still firmly
wedded to the idea that whatever Emperor Napoleon had
set his heart on must be the best thing for the country she
had come to love almost as dearly as she loved her sacred
France. It must be wounding her that her monarch might be
losing heart for his ambitious adventure here.

"The coffee . . . ?" Sarah said.

"Certainement, ma chère."

When Solange left the parlor Sarah fixed her attention
on Matt again. "Can't Maximilian's own army continue
without the French?"

"Oh, sure. They can and will. But both the French and
their Conservative allies, Márquez, Mejía, and now Miramón, lost their best chance when they let Juárez's army
under General Doblado move north from Saltillo without
drawing it into a battle where they might have crushed it
completely. That's the lapse I just spoke of. The Republicans' latest retreat looked like a tremendous victory for
Emperor Max's government forces, but it allowed the Indian
to withdraw and consolidate. He's jammed up against the
border with the United States, true, but it gives him better
access to American arms and supplies, and focuses all his
efforts in one direction only. He'll be in a better position to
squelch Republican infighting, too, without having to deal
with petty satraps running their own shows up and down
the country. Only Díaz in Oaxaca would not be under his
direct control then, and there seems to be no question of *his*
loyalty. As for Juárez's enemy in Mexico, something unexpected seems to have happened. At the embassy we hear
that the emperor is considering negotiating, since he thinks

he would be doing so from a position of strength. I think he's reading Juárez all wrong. If his past performance is any indication, the president will never quit in this struggle—and he most assuredly won't compromise. Any thoughts, Miss Anderson?"

"Well, I *have* heard mutterings around the castle that Max and Charlotte might indeed look for some kind of accommodation with President Juárez, but so far it's only speculation. *You* ought to be on the imperial staff."

The captain chuckled. "If I were, and despite the 'mutterings' you've heard, I'd still tell the emperor to pack it in and go back to Miramar."

"Not much chance of that. He and the empress are very happy in Mexico. And, as you say, they are fully confident they're winning everywhere. Whether or not they're right about that, they feel quite sincerely that the people of Mexico *want* them, and that they have a divine mission to rule this country just as the Hapsburgs have ruled Austria and Hungary."

"Well, I have grave doubts about the Mexican people wanting them—even some of the conservatives they count on—and as for that 'divine mission' stuff, I guess I'm too much of an American to do anything but gag at that. But so far as their military situation is concerned, I have to admit that for the moment at least, they have the upper hand. I suppose that happy state of affairs will last as long as Bazaine and the French stay." He paused again. It was an even longer pause this time. "I don't mean to pry, and I certainly would never compromise your position at the court, but I've wondered about something for some time now." He looked embarrassed. Clearly, whatever he was going to say was the bigger part of why he had come here at this early hour.

"Go on, please."

"From the first time we met, way back in Veracruz, I thought I had your feelings about a lot of things pretty well pegged. We've become good friends, I trust, but I'm still not sure I have a right to ask certain questions."

Matt had never struck her as an overly forward young

man, certainly not a pushy one, but he appeared at the moment even more unsure of himself than usual.

"You may ask me anything you like. I do reserve the right not to answer."

"You spoke once," Matt said, "of your admiration for Benito Juárez. You said you met him on two or three occasions. I was with you on one of them, of course. He seemed to have great respect for you."

"I don't know why he would."

"You're too modest, Miss Anderson."

"Matt . . . whatever it is you're leading up to, for Pete's sake get to it!"

"I suppose I'd better." He paused. "In the time we've known each other, I've gotten the impression that deep in your heart you would like to see the little Indian's dream for Mexico become a reality."

"True enough, but with my position at court I wouldn't want to be quoted to that effect. I'm sure you understand."

"I certainly do," he continued. "And I would never take anything you say away from this house to where it could possibly put that position at risk. But please tell me something. Do you really think the imperial government could come to some kind of . . . accommodation, I believe you called it . . . with the Republicans?"

"I have no idea. But to stop all the killing going on, it sounds like something that somebody should try."

The Marine placed his empty cup on the table in front of the divan. "Would *you* try?"

Her mind stopped working.

"What did you say?"

"Would you talk to the empress? Or better still the emperor himself? About offering terms to Juárez? Could you possibly find out if the rumors that Maximilian would consider some mutually agreeable arrangement have any basis in fact? And, if so, could you persuade him to get negotiations under way?"

She caught only half of it.

He could not possibly be serious!

"Why have you come to *me*—of all people—with such a request?"

"Ambassador Corwin asked me to. I guess you could say he's asking you to do this for your country."

That put the seal on it. Time to be realistic. The extent of her involvement in political matters at the castle had been the mere voicing of a few purely personal opinions to Paola, who seldom looked as if she heard, and she had not volunteered any of those in any chat with the empress. Interceding for the ambassador with Charlotte, and possibly with the emperor himself, would be different in kind, not merely in degree.

"I can't for the life of me understand why the ambassador would think *me* capable of accomplishing anything of this sort. It pains me no end to say it, but women aren't often listened to by powerful people very frequently about such matters, if ever."

"The ambassador thinks that in this particular matter they *will* listen to you. You are the only American citizen in Mexico who has even a small part of their attention these days. The ambassador himself is very uncomfortable with the emperor's court. He's too much the common man to hobnob easily with royalty."

What had Charlotte told her husband on the train from Veracruz? That Sarah *could become our most valuable and trusted guide to Mexico.* Well, it had not happened yet. Since that one short conversation in the imperial private car she had never spoken of politics to either of the imperial couple. The biggest task Charlotte or Melanie Zichy had entrusted to her at Chapultepec so far was serving as hostess for a tea dance neither the empress nor the older of the two Austrian countesses could attend. That she had never been even so much as consulted about Mexico or Mexicans had been a disappointment, but with Jason on her mind she had not troubled herself too much about it.

Was this at last the kind of thing she had dreamed of so wistfully? It would go a long way toward erasing the anomaly of her position at court. Even moving closer to Jason had done little to make her feel good about what had in essence put her in the service of two opposing urges: her own wishes for Republicanism to triumph, and her genuine regard for the fortunes of her good friend Charlotte.

At first hearing it seemed outlandish to think anything could possibly come as a result of Matt's overture. Still, the idea held enormous appeal for her. Something occurred to her.

"I'm a little puzzled about something, Matt. I have always been firmly convinced of the distaste in the United States for the idea of a monarchy in Mexico. Why is our country suddenly willing to give some credence to the emperor's government and lend it even minimal legitimacy? I had the opinion the United States would back President Juárez unreservedly to the end—to the *bitter* end, if it came to that."

"That's still so. Or it might have been if Lincoln were still alive. I guess with what's happened in our country the past few years President Johnson is sick to death of war, in the States or anywhere. And I think our country is just plain tired out. Perhaps our new president feels that Maximilian, working *with* Juárez instead of against him, might come close to giving Mexico something like a democratic society, even if it remains a monarchy in form. The United States could live with that for a while at least."

"Precisely what do you—and the ambassador—propose I tell the emperor and empress?" Actually the beginnings of an approach were already beginning to prod her.

Matt answered quickly. "If you could persuade them to pick an envoy to go to the north, and give him at least a little power to negotiate, the ambassador thinks he can talk President Juárez into receiving him. Mr. Corwin stands in pretty good with Juárez. The man the emperor picks should probably not be a Frenchman, though. Not the marshal, it goes without saying, and not even any of the old Frog crowd that failed at Puebla two years ago. The most important thing of all, though, is that Maximilian has to feel *he* has picked him—whoever he might turn out to be."

"Did you just say Ambassador Corwin doesn't want Marshal Bazaine as a negotiator?"

"Yes. I mean *no*, he doesn't want him."

"Why not?"

"As a marshal of France, Bazaine would never be open to the kind of delicate compromise this situation might call for. In order to maintain his credibility with Paris and in the armies he commands, he has to be seen as going all out for total military victory. It would be better, too, if the envoy didn't hold such high rank as his. The man selected should be a soldier, a colonel maybe. He would have to explain the military realities to the president. And if he's a soldier, it would make it easier for Maximilian to disavow the poor devil if things turned awkward."

This was too good to be true. Matt was underscoring the very thought that had already begun racing through her mind. Could he be thinking *exactly* what she was thinking? That Jason James was the envoy the ambassador was seeking?

Her decision and the words to seal it came without another moment's hesitation. "I'll try, Matt."

"You sure don't fool around, Miss Anderson. The ambassador will be pleased to no end."

"Before we go further on this. Would a colonel of the Imperial Guard, an American, be acceptable?"

O'Leary grinned. "I was hoping you'd say something like that, Miss Anderson. Ambassador Corwin was mightily impressed with what he heard about . . . this colonel . . . and his handling of Labastida."

"Don't think for a moment that my suggestion means I speak for Colonel James. Even if *he* agreed, I am sure he would have to get the approval of Marshal Bazaine, to say nothing of the emperor's."

"I know that. So does the ambassador, but he wants to make a start." He stood. "I have a position paper he wrote yesterday, as well as some other notes I think you'll want to read before you return to Chapultepec. They're in my carriage. Excuse me for a moment. I'll bring them right in."

While Matt went to the carriage Sarah tried to settle herself into a calmer state.

But this was no time to dream or drift. She had allowed herself to be carried along in a torrent of excitement from the moment of Matt's first approach, and small wonder, but there were some practical things to be considered. To whom should she speak first, Jason or the imperial couple?

She could in no way offer Jason to Maximilian without getting his permission, and then have him turn the emperor's offer down and leave her stranded; it would hardly be better to enlist Jason first and have Max veto the idea and in doing so embarrass or compromise Jason. There were a number of hurdles to be cleared.

Then, some of Matt's words came back as delayed but persistent, nagging echoes: that choosing an envoy of lower rank than Marshal Bazaine's, a colonel perhaps, *"would make it easier for Maximilian to disavow the poor devil if things turned awkward."*

Decent and humane as he appeared, if Max was cast in *anything* like the same mold which had formed most other monarchs in history, it would more likely be cynical abandonment than disavowal, no matter how deep were the Hapsburg wells of decency. To what sort or degree of personal danger would she be exposing Jason?

She would have to ask *him* first.

Matt, a sheaf of papers under his arm, let himself back in through the front door.

"I want some help on this," she said. "I want you to come to dinner with me—and Colonel James. I'll get in touch with him and let you know just when. I would like Ambassador Corwin to be there as well. Can you arrange that?"

The Marine's broad smile answered her question.

For her dinner she found a small, secluded inn on the edge of the Ciudadela section of the city seldom frequented by Europeans. She knew the ambassador would not want this preliminary meeting noised about.

Her note, sent around to Jason at his house on the Paseo, had nothing in it concerning the purpose of the gathering, merely that she wanted to see him on "a matter of some importance to both of us."

She arrived at Posada de las Golondrinas before the others and sent Pedro and the carriage back to Avenida Moctezuma, feeling herself more of a conspirator than at any time she could remember. She told the old gardener he need not return for her.

O'Leary and Ambassador Corwin joined her within a minute after her arrival, and Jason came into the candlelit dining room hard on their heels.

He wore a questioning look when he saw the two American men seated with her. He had an awkward grip on an exquisite bouquet of roses, and he blushed a little when she took them from him and had the waiter find a vase and place them on the table.

If Jason was disappointed, she certainly more than shared the feeling. The inn was tiny, intimate, and delightful, the kind of place Paola might have picked for a romantic dinner, and it seemed a shame to waste the moment by talking politics, even politics of such tremendous portent.

It took no time at all for Corwin to get to the heart of things when they finished their meal. At their first meeting two years earlier she had figured the Ohioan for a man who wasted no time, but it did surprise her at how he must have anticipated her agreeing to the appeal he had sent through Matt, and how much groundwork he had already done. It surprised her even more that without any probing he accepted Jason as a possible emissary in what would most certainly turn out to be a mission of the utmost delicacy.

Oddly, it did not occur to her to wonder whether or not *Jason* would fall in with the ambassador's plan. He had been silent throughout the meal, but she sensed his keen interest in what the American minister had to say. Somehow, his attentive silence seemed to constitute approval.

"I've been in touch with President Juárez, colonel,"

Corwin said. "He has given tentative approval to what my government has in mind. This will not be easy for him. Certain arrangements must be made before he will meet with anyone. Of course you see the need for extreme secrecy."

"Yes, sir."

"If the President agrees to your going north, it will not be all the way to Chihuahua, where he is now. There would be a lot of suspicion on the part of his Republican supporters if he received you there. He didn't come right out and say so, and he didn't put it in writing, but he probably has a meeting somewhere in the mid-northern states in mind. He seems willing to leave the exact location up to us, which is more evidence of his courage."

"Do you have a place in mind, Ambassador Corwin?" James said.

"I confess I do not. I would like to leave that up to you. You no doubt have full knowledge—or can get it—of where all the French and Conservative troops are deployed, and I'm not asking you to reveal that information, but there must be an island of security for you and him somewhere in Mexico that is reachable for both of you."

"No such place occurs to me immediately, sir. Not all risk to the president's person could be eliminated, of course, whatever the chosen site, but I suppose he knows that."

"If the approval of the emperor is forthcoming, colonel, will you undertake this?

James took his time in answering. He looked gravely at Sarah and then turned back to the ambassador. "Yes," he said at last. "But only if my superiors allow me to—and only if a safe place for the meeting can be found."

His concern about some possible risk for Juárez touched her; had he none for the risk this journey north might pose for *him*? Again the thought of what she might be getting him into assailed her. There had to be *some* secure haven in the deserts and mountains to the north for Juárez and this man she had begun to love more with each passing moment.

Then it struck her. She knew such a place.

"Perhaps I can help with this," she said. All eyes turned on her. "The meeting could take place at my *hacienda* at La Mina de la Sierra in Zacatecas. Señor Juárez knows it well. He was a guest there on a number of occasions when my brother Samuel was alive. My manager, Señor Alberto Moreno, says that Imperial and French troops have all moved well away from his city. I believe Zacatecas is situated so that the president could make his way there through the mountains to the north and west undetected for most of his journey and in comparative safety."

There came a boyish, happy chortle from Matt O'Leary, and Ambassador Corwin nodded his head. Jason smiled.

"I would like one thing understood before we go any further, gentlemen, even before I talk with the empress—and, I hope, the emperor himself. I will only make the *hacienda* available for this meeting if I am permitted to accompany Colonel James."

She could not have brought more silence to the table had she struck a gong. The three men's faces were pale ovals in the candlelight. Jason seemed the first to recover, but it was Corwin who spoke.

"I couldn't sanction a woman putting herself in such danger, Miss Anderson! No, I could not allow it."

"It's not a matter of *allowing* it, Ambassador Corwin. The decision is mine alone."

Matt stirred uneasily. "There's . . . something else, Miss Anderson," he stammered. "There's the matter of . . . impropriety."

She felt the first simmer of a fine fury.

"Nonsense, Matt! I am a grown American woman. Matters of propriety or some imagined lack of it should be left to me. What we are planning here is a chance to stop a war, not begin an assignation. It would be a far greater impropriety to let that chance slip away. I don't by any means wish to portray myself as indispensable to this venture, but I have known President Juárez longer than anyone at this table. I genuinely feel I could be of use to

Colonel James when and if he meets with him. As far as any danger is concerned, there would probably be less of it with a woman in his party. Republicans, even Republican bandits, do not ordinarily attack women. And even if they did, are men still so stupid they think women unable to face danger for something they believe in?"

O'Leary and the ambassador seemed stunned. She could not read Jason's look.

She turned to Matt and continued. "If the emperor agrees to use the good offices of Colonel James, I would like you to get word to Antonio Pérez before the two of us leave for Zacatecas. Perhaps he and his men could even provide an escort for us when we leave the area where the French Army holds sway. I think that would be somewhere just west of Querétaro.

"I return to my duties at Chapultepec tomorrow, and I'll speak with the empress before the weekend." She had better not leave the chance for at least one moment alone with Jason to pure luck. "Now . . . if Colonel James could drive me back to Avenida Moctezuma, I'll say good night."

She had expected to find Cipi in the driver's seat of a carriage like the one they had taken to the bullfights, but a groom brought a small, trim buggy around to the front of the inn, and after helping her into the cushioned seat, Jason took the reins himself. Once they left the lights of Posada de las Golondrinas his face became invisible. He had not uttered a word since they entered the buggy. It seemed odd that he would not discuss the important and perhaps dangerous things they had committed to. She might have disturbed him with her assertiveness at dinner. It had disturbed the Marine and the ambassador, for a moment, anyway.

His quizzical look as she spoke her piece to Matt and the ambassador—with a determination which surprised *her*— had not seemed one of criticism. Wonder, yes, but not criticism—nor disapproval.

The alternating light and dark of their passage through

the shaded streets on the next part of the way back to Avenida Moctezuma put her in mind of their first carriage ride together, to the Washington's Birthday ball at the U.S. embassy. She was a much different woman now; she wondered if he were the same sort of man.

All too quickly he turned the buggy into Avenida Moctezuma. The short ride was not going to grant her anything like the "moment alone" she sought.

At her door she raised the heavy brass ring in the mouth of the lion's head knocker to summon Solange rather than dig in her bag for the key, but before she could let it fall she felt his hand grip hers and the ring, too.

"No . . . please, Sarah. Not quite yet."

His hand moved from hers, and she lowered the knocker ring as gently as she could.

Then she felt *both* his hands on her shoulders, felt him turn her, knew that no matter that he had used no more strength than he would need to wipe away a tear, she could no more have struggled against it than she could have flown across the night sky.

They kissed.

It was a long kiss.

She did not knock for Solange.

In the parlor she hurried to the big front window to watch him drive away down Avenida Moctezuma, but there had been no need to hurry. The buggy was stock still, and although she could not see his face in the darkness and at this distance, she knew he was looking at her door, perhaps even at her window.

She moved to the table at the end of the divan, struck a light, touched it to the wick of the glass-shaded lamp she had bought just last week, and stood in the luminous orange cloud that filled the parlor.

There . . . he could see her now.

With the lamp reflected in the window, she could not see *him*, but her inner eye still held the image of his face when the long kiss ended. Her body still felt the pressure of his and the tender iron circle of his arms. There was nothing in the least bit passive about the man who had turned her into his embrace with such sureness; nothing timid or uncertain about the kiss he gave her.

She moved to the lamp again and turned the wick down until the room was plunged in darkness.

Out on Avenida Moctezuma the buggy moved away.

A light came from the hall behind her, and with it Solange's excited voice.

"*Ma chère!* I thought you would never return. I have watched for you for two long hours."

The intrusion into perhaps the deepest feelings she had ever known brought an unaccustomed irritation. "What are you doing up this late, Solange?"

"A court courier brought a letter which came to the castle for you, *chérie.*" Solange held out an envelope in a hand that shook noticeably. "It is from Monsieur le Comte!"

What on earth was the woman babbling about?

"For heaven's sake, exactly which 'Monsieur le Comte,' Solange? We must have a dozen French and Belgian counts in Mexico, to say nothing of the Austrians."

"Le Comte de Bayeux. Monsieur Gallimard."

She took the letter and tore it open.

Sarah, *ma chère*—

Please forgive the brevity of this missive, but I will soon be able to place the contents of my heart at your feet in person and at any length you will permit. By the time you receive this, it will be only a matter of a day or two before we are at long last together again.

I shall arrive at the domicile of my brother Marcel in Mexico City on 15 Aug.

Avec tout mon coeur,
Henri

As the letter slipped from her fingers Sarah Kent Anderson uttered a word in French she had never so much as breathed in English, even when alone . . . had never heard from the lips of any woman in her family, and probably never would.

"*Merde!*"

32

▲▲▲▲▲

When the time neared for Jason and Sarah Anderson to leave for Zacatecas, she found to her dismay she would be taking far more encumbrances than she would have liked—emotional baggage, mostly.

The embrace and kiss at her door on Avenida Moctezuma was not repeated—getting ready for the journey had denied her and Jason any time to be alone—but the memory of his lips on hers lingered.

She wanted to keep her mind and heart clear for Jason's meeting with Juárez. If she were to be of any help to him on this mission she could not get snarled in her own personal feelings, particularly those that revolved around him. But adding to the uncertainties which bubbled up about where their relationship would lead them next was the prospect of Henri Gallimard's arrival.

Her talk with Charlotte promised a good beginning.

The empress clapped her hands together in unfeigned happiness and exclaimed, "But of course, *chérie!* Maxl has been waiting for *someone* to come forward with just such a proposal. We supposed it was *de trop* to expect any similar suggestion from the marshal. Am I being immodest when I tell you that this was my idea to begin with? It took some persuasion to get Maxl to agree with me over Felix Eloin's doubts. I sometimes think you are the truest friend I have." She clasped Sarah to her.

* * *

The conference with Maximilian himself took place with so little fuss and with such brevity it was almost an afterthought to the one with Charlotte. That was to be expected. What was not expected was something she had more or less forgotten—the reminder of where Jason took his orders from now that he was no longer a Legionnaire.

"We shall talk with your colonel as soon as we inform Marshal Bazaine how we might employ him in this matter, Mademoiselle Anderson. Colonel James now serves the Mexican Crown instead of France, but courtesy requires we inform his former commander. We recall meeting the colonel aboard the *Novara*, and of course we have caught glimpses of him here at our castle from time to time. A most impressive soldier. He could almost be an Austrian."

Two days passed before she heard more, but Felix Eloin finally summoned Jason to the presence of the emperor for an audience at a private tea. It pleased her that she was to be included. The still somewhat sinister Eloin would sit in on the session in the Imperial office, too.

One important figure would be notably absent: Marshal Bazaine. It would not be the first time the emperor undertook something without seeking the marshal's counsel, but it was far and away the most important. She wondered if Jason had talked to his erstwhile—and possibly still—commanding officer about the mission.

But it was at that meeting with the emperor and Eloin that she had another tiny, troubling misgiving about the venture. Before it was over, the whole "*Affaire de la Paix et de la Reconciliation,*" as Charlotte had dubbed the proposed conference in Zacatecas, had taken on a highly personal cast.

After Charlotte's ecstatic endorsement of the overtures made by Ambassador Corwin through Sarah, it was a letdown to find that the emperor, by comparison, seemed almost lackadaisical. He bestowed on Jason almost *carte blanche* for any dealings with Juárez, true, but he did it with a disappointing, casual wave of his pale hand that depressed her.

Eloin began the talk. "You may tell Señor Juárez, Colonel James, that to show the Crown's good faith, His Imperial Majesty has relieved General Márquez of his command in the north and sent him to Europe on a special diplomatic mission. His Majesty will also prevail on Marshal Bazaine to curtail the activities of Colonel Dupin."

The emperor did not appear to have heard a word Eloin said. He gazed through the window and sipped his tea as if it were the most important thing on his mind.

When Eloin stopped there was a long silence until the Belgian whispered to the emperor.

"What . . . ? Oh, *oui*, Felix." He turned to Jason. "Ah, Colonel James . . ."

"The mission, Your Majesty," Eloin prompted.

"Yes . . . the mission, colonel. Tell the Indian whatever you think will satisfy him. The details can be attended to at our leisure. We have no doubt he is a man of a high order of intelligence; he must see that halting this war is even more in his interest than it is in ours, no matter what sacrifices of petty principles must be made."

Jason leaned forward. "May I offer President Juárez a substantial share of power in governing Mexico, Your Majesty?"

Maximilian turned toward Eloin, who shrugged as if it were a matter of complete indifference to him, and when the emperor returned his gaze to a waiting Jason, the pink-and-white imperial face showed the beginnings of a smile, and something else. Sarah fought down the feeling that the fine beard and moustache covered a face that could harbor deceit. Even anti-royalist Monsieur Auguste Pelletier had always maintained that Max von Hapsburg was a man of unyielding honor, singularly free of duplicity of any kind. She wanted to believe it.

"The answer to your question, Colonel James," the emperor said, "is that President Juárez can become our first minister. You may tell him that."

"I do not believe he will be satisfied with a sinecure, sir.

As first minister will he be granted a genuine share of authority?"

"We shall endeavor to make the president's position in our government a useful one. See Felix here before you leave. He will give you all the credentials to negotiate you feel you need. It should not require much in the way of guarantees for this noble savage."

A glance at Jason told Sarah it was no more the unequivocal "yes" about Juárez's possible future position he sought than it had been for her.

But if Jason felt the shallow stabs of doubt she did, his strong face did not show it. The long years of discipline were standing him in good stead.

Felix Eloin, she shivered to discover, was looking at her intently.

"Have either of you," he said, "decided on just where this meeting will take place? El Paso del Norte?"

"Yes we have," Sarah said. "We can send word to the president that we can use my *hacienda* at Zacatecas. He knows it well."

"And when, exactly, will you try to meet with this troublesome little man?"

She looked at Jason. He had not liked the "troublesome little man" a bit.

"I think we can make our travel arrangements and get word to Señor Juárez in a day or two," Jason said. "If we can offer him ironclad assurances of his personal safety, then we can be ready for him in about two weeks' time. We *can* offer him a safe conduct, can we not?"

The emperor reached for some papers on his desk and riffled through them in a bald pretense of reading which Sarah knew signified dismissal.

"Godspeed, Colonel," he said, without favoring either Jason or her with another glance. "Bring me Señor Juárez's promise of cooperation." Then he looked up, and his smile almost made everything all right again. "*Au revoir . . . and à bientôt*, Mademoiselle Anderson. *Merci beaucoup.*

With subjects such as the two of you, we cannot fail in Mexico."

The lift of her spirits brought on by his winning smile and the soft-spoken *adieus* failed to last.

With the emperor's "thank you" dying away, Felix Eloin, who had remained silent throughout the meeting, rose, and with fluttering gestures actually shooed Jason and Sarah from the office.

From start to finish the conversation had not consumed five minutes.

It hardly seemed enough time for the serious consideration of such an important initiative. Maximilian's comportment during the meeting had not seemed serious enough by half, either; she had heard him discuss the menu for a state dinner with a greater display of interest and urgency.

As she and Jason stood alone in the anteroom, looking for all the world, she feared, to be two tradesmen asked to use the rear entrance, she was mortified that she had been the instrument of any embarrassment or disappointment for her tall, silent companion.

He was gazing at the full length portrait of the emperor on the far wall. Clearly, from the calm appraisal he seemed to be making of the painting, he felt none of the resentment burning her, or had hidden it with more success than she could. She readied herself to apologize to him, but he spoke before she could open her mouth. His voice was pitched so low she had to strain to hear it.

"Well, sir, it wasn't what I wanted or expected, but it can't be helped. It *is* your show. For me, *Il faut d'abord durer.*" Mumbled as they were, she knew the words were not meant for her. He turned and faced her then. "Can you be ready to leave for the north in two days' time?"

Today was the twelfth of August. Henri would be in the capital in only three more days. She had planned to use those three days preparing herself to tell him about Jason, and to telling Jason about Henri, a thing she dreaded.

An invitation to a dinner welcoming his brother had

come to the castle from Marcel yesterday and she had already replied, accepting.

Jason waited for her answer.

"Two days?" she said. "Why not three, or better yet, four?" Yes, she had to be at that dinner of Marcel's, find time alone with Henri, and unburden herself. Little as she wished to go to Marcel's, she wished less to put off this painful task.

"I'm afraid it *must* be two days, Sarah," Jason said. "Your Captain O'Leary called on me this morning to tell me the *guerrilla* leader you asked him to contact is willing to meet us just northwest of Querétaro next Sunday afternoon. He says this man Pérez will not wait for more than the rest of that one day. I can understand that. He and his men could not possibly linger for any protracted period so close to a strong government position."

"I'll be ready," she said. She would send her regrets to Marcel the moment they left here.

"Of course," Jason said, "if you should decide not to go, the escort he has agreed to provide for us will not be quite so necessary. I must confess that my mind would be easier if you stayed here in the capital." He looked down at her from what suddenly seemed to her a dizzying height and never in her life had she felt so tiny. The feeling was only momentary.

"Stay here?" No matter how much she loved him she would have difficulty capping the fountain of irritation rising in her. They had better come to an understanding without another moment's delay. "Oh, I'm going, Jason. Set your mind at rest about that. As I said, I'll be ready. Count on it."

He smiled. "That doesn't surprise me a bit."

Only the fact that Felix Eloin had come from the emperor's office into the anteroom and was fixing them with a sharp, possibly suspicious eye kept her from seeking his embrace.

That—and telling Jason about Henri—would have to be

left for the trip to Zacatecas. With packing to do there would be no time until they were on the road.

"I feel terrible about not seeing Henri before I leave," she told Paola that night.

"He'll be here when you return."

"I know. But I wanted to tell him about Jason the very moment he arrived."

Paola recoiled with a look of disbelief and even of something close to outrage.

"Are you utterly mad, *liebchen?* If you tell him, you will be burning a bridge you may someday wish to cross. I swear you ridiculous Americans are beyond all understanding. You, Sarah, are so . . . *bourgeois!*" She covered her mouth with her hand for a moment. "I am sorry. I should not have said that. You are too dear to me to have to suffer such an insult at my hands."

In the Austrian woman's lexicon the word *was* an insult.

"Don't apologize, Paola . . . I truly am *bourgeois* and there's no point in denying it. Don't you see I *have* to tell Henri the truth? It's bad enough he has gone to all the trouble and expense of coming to Mexico. It would be unconscionable of me to let him go on thinking—"

"Nothing we do or say to men—or don't do or say—" Paola broke in, "can be called unconscionable. The rogues do much worse to us with every breath they take. In my opinion you owe Henri Gallimard no explanation whatsoever. What he doesn't know can't hurt *you.*"

That, Sarah thought, was a matter of opinion.

33

▲▲▲▲▲

"I am Pérez," the giant astride the splendid black horse said. "I am pleased to meet you, colonel." Antonio Pérez did not *look* pleased, he was scowling, his face as dark as the black flanks of the distant sierras, but there was no hesitation as he pushed his big hand out. "We will get along *muy bien*," he said, as if he had read James's mind. "Señorita Anderson has vouched for you, and if that is good enough for my president, it is good enough for Pérez for the moment."

As they talked, Cipi began to draw the carriage up to where James and Pérez sat their horses in the middle of a dozen or more clumps of *maguey* whose spikes reached higher than their boot tops. Sarah rode alongside the vehicle, and Solange Tournier's head was sticking out of the window. Despite her strongly voiced misgivings about this trip, due to the news of Henri's imminent arrival, the Frenchwoman had not missed a single thing at any stage of the journey.

Sarah reined in the horse Cipi had saddled for her back in Querétaro when she insisted on riding "at least," she told Jason, "until we make contact with Señor Pérez. I'll ride in the carriage when it cools off a bit." When she first saw Pérez a moment ago, from a distance, she had not been sure of his identity, seeing him in the uniform of the Republic for the first time. She waved to him with her riding crop, and Pérez gave her an unexpectedly smart salute. The way he had tipped his hat forward until its rolled military brim almost covered them, his eyes were hard to see. She wondered what Jason made of him.

For his part, James had already decided he would have to stop thinking of Antonio Pérez as a bandit. He was one, of course, or had been. His reputation as a *plateado* in the days before the French secured the eastern half of the silver country was the biggest—and to the French and the Conservatives the most contemptible—of any freelance marauder in central Mexico, and after the nasty beating he and his irregulars had given a unit of Dupin's *contra-guerrilla* command six months ago, he had become much more than a bandit, even in their eyes. He now wore the uniform of the Republican Army, and James guessed the three pips on his shoulder said he held the rank of major. Of course, guerrilla leaders often awarded themselves high rank. James had heard of ex-highwaymen, originally lone wolf bandits such Pérez had been, who made themselves full generals once they turned soldier and gathered a dozen armed, uniformed men around them. But such grandiose self-promotion hardly seemed likely in Pérez's case. From the respectful attitude shown their *jefe* by the three riders with him—also in Juarista uniforms—it was clear he commanded by force of character, not by means of some trumped up military title. He had not appended any rank to his name when he introduced himself to James, either.

Sarah had eased her horse alongside them. "*¿Como estas, Don Antonio?*" she said. Her use of the familiar *estas* meant she had more than a passing acquaintance with this forbidding former bandit. Riding sidesaddle, her long skirt falling straight from her hips to somewhere below the stirrup, she made a strange picture, but more appealing than he would have ever thought a woman could be in a khaki riding habit, perspiration streaks running down her back and from under her arms, with her fair skin burned a little blotchy, and with the wisps of spun gold hair under her broad-brimmed hat coated with high desert dust.

There had only been chaste good night kisses since they left the capital. With the sharp-eyed, distinctly unfriendly and watchful duenna Solange so much in evidence, he had not expected more. He wanted more every time he looked at her or thought about her, but it was just as well that Solange had come along, even if she had been markedly cool in her few dealings with him since the trip began.

Pérez now boomed a reply to Sarah's greeting that blasted James out of his thoughts.

"*Muy bien, Señorita Anderson, y usted?*" The swarthy, bearded face broke into the broadest of smiles. It was hard for James to find the scowling brute of a moment earlier. "Is it possible for you to tell me the state of things with Sor Francisca?"

"I am happy to report she is in excellent health . . . and in high spirits, too."

"Then all must be well with *los niños, qué no?*"

"Yes, indeed. The new wing on the orphanage is at last completed, and three very capable nursing sisters, young, strong ones, have joined her staff."

"The money supply is good then, no? I regret I have not helped much since the French put me out of business. Soldiering does not pay as well as robbing silver trains—or guarding them."

"No need to express regrets, Don Antonio. Sor Francisca's treasury is in excellent shape at the moment."

"I suspect she has you to thank for that, Doña Sarah."

"Por favor, jefe. Do not give me too much credit. The empress has helped enormously, as have several other ladies of her court. The French Army has contributed to the orphanage as well."

Pérez growled. "As much as I wish to see the home and convent prosper, I am not sure I want any help from that quarter, Doña Sarah."

"Forgive me for intruding, Señor Pérez," James said. "I don't think we need rush, but we're only a league out of Querétaro, and dangerously in the open. I would not care to have one of General Márquez's Tlaxcalan cavalry patrols stumble upon us. Tell me, are these three *soldados* our entire escort?"

"Pero no, colonel. The main body of my *tropa,* another twenty mounted *guerreros,* will parallel our line of march, out of sight in those low *lomas* to the north, but ready to ride instantly to our aid should we encounter trouble. They will not come out of the hills and ride with us until we enter Zacatecas State. However, you are quite right. We should move out *pronto.* We will be in the saddle until dark."

He wheeled his horse around and set it on the road that pointed north and west through the *maguey* like a Chasseur's lance. James signaled Cipi to get the carriage under way.

The dwarf had pranced and preened for the benefit of Solange ever since the trip began. It might even have had some effect; the Frenchwoman had shown herself to be a good deal happier with Cipi's company than she had with James's.

All in all it was an odd band of travelers that made its way across the wide, sere, tilted plain that led to Zacatecas.

The meeting with Pérez had almost made Sarah Anderson forget her misery. She had been entirely too stubborn about riding this unforgiving horse under the blazing sun all day long, with her back aching and stiff as a board, and with sweat streaming down into her eyes.

She supposed she was still trying to prove something after Ambassador Corwin's remark about some presumed "place" for women, and it would have been an agony of strained silence riding in the carriage with Solange. The Frenchwoman, thinking about Henri, no doubt, had been in a high dudgeon ever since they left the capital.

At any rate, it was a grueling afternoon and evening until they stopped for the night at a nameless crossroads somewhere west of French-garrisoned San Luis Potosí. She felt what she soon found to be an entirely unjustified sense of euphoria that the day's ride had ended.

Pérez led them from the road into a farmyard, where poorly constructed pens teemed with gaunt pigs emitting plaintive squeals, a manure-covered yard alive with squawking, molting, sickly poultry. The farmer, his mute wife, and a stairstep brood of half-naked children vacated their dwelling to move out into the fields.

Their shelter for the night could hardly be called a house. It consisted of little more than several semi-connected *jacales*, mere huts thatched over with the broad leaves of the ubiquitous *maguey*.

Solange whimpered at the prospect of the night they faced. "I would sell my soul for a chance to bathe, *chérie*." At least the "*chérie*" had returned to her vocabulary.

Even after a liberal dousing with toilet water, the embrace Sarah hungered for from Jason might not be a good idea. She knew she was being too fastidiously sensitive, but she wondered how soldiers in the field could stand each other. After a single day she was finding it hard to stand herself. But she wanted his arms around her, wanted him to crush her to him as he had done so thoroughly if fleetingly that night outside her door.

They did talk. Mostly about the forthcoming meeting. She prayed for another kind of talk. He had been almost maddeningly circumspect from the outset of the trip and she knew why. Solange. More than once in the three days out from Mexico City Sarah had regretted bringing her along. They had shared rooms in the close confines of the two tiny inns they stayed in the first two nights. There was virtually no chance to be alone with Jason and when they did manage to sequester themselves for a few moments, she— and probably Jason as well—was all too conscious that the Frenchwoman might pop right out of the woodwork if they went to each other's arms.

But there was not even any woodwork in *this* warren of hovels, and if Solange did not appear like a genie when Sarah and Jason watched the sun set after the meal, all sorts of other humming and buzzing creatures promised to be maddeningly effective chaperones.

The way Solange had behaved toward Jason at every stop for food, water, or rest, and again when they were all together at day's end, vexed Sarah, but there was little she felt she could say.

In their early days together in Paris, Solange, probably feeling it a duty imposed by the Pelletiers, had often been harsh about some real or imagined breach of etiquette on the part of her young American charge, but had never teetered so close to the precipice of rage as she did when Sarah announced her plans. "But Monsieur Le Comte is arriving!" she had screamed five days ago as she reluctantly began packing. "Monsieur Auguste and Madame Claudine would be disgusted if they were to discover you were going off on some *folie de coeur* with this . . . this mercenary . . . I cannot bring myself to say what he is . . . when a French nobleman has come across the ocean to pay you court. *Ma fois,* you do not deserve him. It is shameful!"

"Don't you dare speak to me like that! Our trip north is not a *folie de coeur*, it is a serious venture of real importance to this poor country."

"*Oui*! And Solange is the empress of France!"

Even without her long-time companion reminding her, Sarah had felt guilt about Henri since his letter arrived, more of it during the journey, but had persuaded herself that it could not be helped. Henri should have given her more in the way of notice. It did little to free her conscience; she knew the truth of the matter all too well.

Assignation? *Folie de coeur*? Remembering the blistering fury of Solange's tirade about her seeming disregard for Henri's feelings, and suddenly, almost uncontrollably rebelling against it, she almost wished this trip *were* one or the other—or both.

34

▲▲▲▲

"I remember you quite well, Colonel James," Benito Juárez said. "We met the day you were the guest of Ignacio Comonfort at Chapultepec. No one told me you were a soldier at that time, but something told me you had some connection with the military. You say you serve in something called the Imperial Guard. The uniform you must wear now when you are not being a diplomat had not, I believe, even been created at that time. There was no so-called Empire then, and consequently no Imperial Guard."

James need not have wondered if Juárez would remember him; this man forgot nothing. He felt a faint tremor of worry when the hard black Indian eyes flicked to Sarah at the words "no one told me you were a soldier at that time." The president looked back at him and went on, "The mere fact that you *are* a soldier makes you quite a different sort of *norteamericano* from Señorita Anderson here. If I remember correctly, she is not enamored of soldiers and soldiering, but perhaps you and she have come to some meeting of the minds on that." It was James's turn to glance at Sarah.

Juárez sat in a high-backed rattan chair whose seat was so high off the tiled floor of the *portal* of the *residencia* the square toes of his black boots barely touched it. Some short men would have felt uneasy about that, unsure of themselves and at a distinct disadvantage, particularly when they faced a man so much taller. Tiny Alberto Moreno, sitting next to Sarah, and whose short legs rested on the tiles no more firmly than did the president's, probably knew the feeling well. James would wager his last peso that any misgivings the president had about his own lack of height would not give him pause for half a breath; he would not measure size by physical dimensions—his own or others'.

Juárez accepted Sarah's offer of wine and then he surprised James—and probably Sarah, too, although she did not show it—by inquiring in almost the same breath, "Could we possibly have champagne, señorita?" It was doubly surprising when James recalled the Puritanical blanket he seemed to cast over the picnic lunch Comonfort served in the forest of Chapultepec.

"*Sí, Señor Presidente,*" Sarah said. "I would prefer champagne myself. Arturo, *por favor.*" The old *mayordomo* nodded and padded off.

It surprised James that the cellar of the *hacienda* could yield a bottle of champagne so readily. While not as large and sumptuous as so many great houses in Mexico, the home building of Sarah's Mina de la Sierra Verde was tastefully luxurious beyond his experience, and he felt another of those pangs of inadequacy which had plagued him for a year. Sarah Anderson was a wealthy woman.

He was bracing himself to ask the president when they might begin to talk about the things which had brought them here, when Juárez addressed himself to that very subject.

"I do not wish to consider the details of what the Austrian offers Mexico this evening, Colonel James," he said. "For the rest of this day I want rest, a chance to enjoy Señorita Anderson's hospitality, and that of Señor Moreno." The mine manager sat up as if something had prodded him. Clearly he thought his presence had been forgotten. The president favored Moreno with a look that, while not precisely accompanied by a smile, came close to revealing one. About as close, James speculated, as Juárez would ever come to smiling.

The president continued, "As you may or may not know, colonel, I was a guest here many times when Señor Samuel Anderson was alive. I regard this *hacienda con mucha affeción*. The *señorita* was a charming and considerate hostess, even at . . . how old were you when we first met, *señorita?*"

"I was sixteen, *Señor Presidente.*"

"Ah, *sí.* Sixteen. A very mature, intelligent sixteen. I wonder if I was *ever* sixteen." He seemed to drift off for a moment, returned his gaze at last to James. "You did not know the *señorita's hermano?*"

"No, sir." As a soldier, Jason wanted to advance straight to the heart of the matter which had brought him north, but he recognized that the man swallowed by the huge chair was not a military objective. Not now at least.

"He was a truly remarkable man, colonel," Juárez went on, "a friend I am proud to say, an early supporter of mine, and a genuine lover of freedom, as so many of your countrymen are. But with a difference. Unlike some shaped by life in that wonderland north of the *rio,* he believed that liberty is not a special right or property peculiarly limited to *norteamericanos* and only to some of *them.* It is a blessing that is not—or should I say should not be—rationed. If I sound critical of some of your countrymen, *lo siento,* colonel. All too many of my people err in their thinking in just that manner. And of course I am afraid that for all that he seems a genuinely compassionate, and sometimes a paradoxically democratic man in many respects, the Austrian, unfortunately, even with the noblest of intentions, feels that way, too. Am I wrong in assuming that he believes the

Trinity is his electorate and the heavenly host his only true constituency?"

James said nothing; the question had not seemed to call for an answer. Alberto Moreno was nodding fiercely. The earnest little manager was another Republican patriot like Antonio Pérez, now bivouacked with his troops out near the corrals and tackrooms of the *hacienda* and apparently determined to stay there, in spite of a valiant effort on Sarah's part to have him join them all at dinner. Juárez had expressed regret at that. He must put great store in Pérez. "Antonio fights much better than he socializes," he said as the erstwhile road agent rode off to join his men.

While the president had not touched on anything of any substance, he had brought Maximilian himself into the conversation a dozen times in this first half hour, but he had yet to refer to him as anything but "the Austrian." Juárez was making no attempt to disguise the way he was laying the groundwork for the discussions yet to come by subtly denying Max von Hapsburg any real official standing in the governance of Mexico. He was also letting James know, and without any subtlety, that the negotiations tomorrow would proceed from the solid terrain of his own unshakable convictions.

Considering the long struggle this man had made against enormous odds, nothing about Benito Juárez smacked of the messianic; there was not even a hint in his manner of the semi-religious fervor James had seen in the tribal leaders he fought as a Legion *bleu* in the sand seas of North Africa. The swarthy face—only passive in the way an outcropping of granite in a canyon wall can be considered passive— seemed free of all emotion, with a look shaped and hardened by pure thought alone.

James had dealt with any number of highly intelligent men before, men with quick, incisive minds capable of slicing through the thickest curtain of obfuscation with a single stroke—Bazaine, for instance—but he knew he was now in the presence of a truly formidable intellect, the magnitude and strength of which he could not recall facing since the long, deeply troubling talks with Aaron Sheffield, when James was far too young to cope with such a force.

Juárez had come up the winding road from Zacatecas to the hilltop *hacienda* in a small, black, cube-shaped, one-horse carriage identical to the one in which he had made his entrance to Chapultepec Park that day. James had seen no armed guard, no escort of any kind, although there must have been one on the long trip down from the north. James was struck by the outlandish notion that Benito Juárez did not actually travel as mortals do, that he simply *appeared* by magic wherever he had to be. His quicksilver peregrinations of the last two years, moving his government one step ahead of the guillotine blade of the French Army in a succession of last-second, vaporous disappearances, did seem to be a kind of sorcery.

"I think Arturo is calling us, gentlemen," Sarah said. "Let us just forget everything while we dine. There will be time enough in the morning for politics. May I take your arm as we go in to dinner, *Señor Presidente?*"

Her voice brought James back to reality. He could keep quiet, surely, but she must know that with every bite he took and with every sip of wine, his mind would race through twenty-odd possible approaches to the serious talk tomorrow. His one unsettling thought remained: were they plodding along some false, dangerously mined road with no real hope of it leading anywhere?

Sarah was grateful that Solange—consummate actress that she could be when it suited her—maintained a level of fairly persuasive affability as they ate and talked afterward. Her performance made it hard to remember her absolutely foul mood of earlier in the day, when, to Sarah's astonishment, she also suddenly revealed a prejudice Sarah had not known she harbored. Solange expressed in bitter tones that it was beastly of the *mademoiselle* to ask her to accept the man in question as a social equal. "After all, he is *un homme de couleur*," she said.

A man of *color?* Sarah could not quite believe her ears.

She had found the French people of every class and division, at least Parisians, a good deal less conscious of color than Bostonians had been, for all her townsfolk's public stance on abolition, and she would have sworn Solange, as a good servant in Maison Pelletier, where negro Tunisian and Algerian students of Monsieur Auguste frequently came to dine, would be *singularly* free of bigotry.

"You shock me, Solange."

"Ordinarily it would not bother me, *mademoiselle*, but *à ce moment* . . ."

"But *à ce moment* what?" Solange's continued use of *mademoiselle* clearly indicated her pique.

"We should be back in the capital where we belong, entertaining Monsieur Le Comte. I have been uncomfortable about this since we left Avenida Moctezuma."

It was not, after all, the little "man of color" who vexed her.

Sarah had not seen Solange since that conversation, which had taken place when they arrived at the *hacienda* and before President Juárez's somber little black carriage rolled up the hill. Although invited, the duenna had not joined the gathering on the *portal*. She was spending her free time with Cipi at the bunker-like stone building where he was living, somewhere near Perez and his riders. Solange had not had much chance to talk with the dwarf on the road, even though on one short early morning stretch, she had ridden beside him on the driver's seat of the carriage.

Sarah had no idea what they found to talk about, or what else they did, and she was not about to ask. Disturbed as she might have been about Solange's conduct, she still had to grant her control of her personal life. After all, it was something she fiercely coveted for herself.

She slept in Samuel's old bedroom, something she had not done on her tour of the *hacienda* with old Arturo at her elbow almost two years ago when the wound of her brother's death was still raw and bleeding. On that visit she had only peeked mournfully into the dusty room from the door and then had Arturo close and lock it. On this trip, with

Solange, Jason, the president, and herself to house, she was forced to press Samuel's room into service. It was situated at the end of the hall running from the balcony above the foyer, far from the other sleeping rooms, up its own half flight of stairs, affording her something of the solitude she feared she might need before this sojourn ended. She knew she would need the great, high bed with the thick down-comforter tonight. Last night at that pitiful farm had been an agony of wakefulness.

When Arturo carried her and Solange's bags upstairs this morning she had been too preoccupied and too rushed to take a real look at the room beyond noticing that the old *mayordomo* and the Indian maid Isabel had apparently followed orders about cleaning it. It looked spotless. This afternoon, when she went upstairs again to dress for the arrival of the president, she took a much better look around.

Even if the wound caused by Samuel's death had now more or less begun to stitch itself together, it pulled and hurt when she opened a magnificent mahogany armoire to put her clothes away and discovered *his* still hanging there, faintly redolent of moth crystals and tobacco. She stroked the friendly, rough sleeve of a Harris tweed jacket Samuel had apparently kept from his school days, then drew her hand away, deciding to leave everything as it was and find some other place for the things she had brought with her from the capital.

Her slight melancholy gave way to quite another feeling when just before she closed the armoire's graceful double doors she found a silver lamé evening gown and a sheer, lacy peignoir draped next to Samuel's full dress suit.

She smiled.

There had never been the slightest hint in letters home that her bachelor brother was involved with someone in a way which would have raised eyebrows in the staid New England that had shaped him. At the parties and dinners she remembered here in the *hacienda* there had never been a woman among the guests she could link with her brother.

The woman who wore this gown might have been at one of those small affairs without Sarah seeing her. After all, her sixteen- or seventeen-year-old pre-Paris eyes were fixed on people like Benito Juárez or some other exotic male friend of Samuel's.

Why should she be surprised at the prospect of a woman in Samuel's life? When he was still living at home there had been girls aplenty, and she had fond recollections of him dressing for balls and cotillions. Beyond some idle girlish speculation and inner giggling, prompted no doubt by Bradford Anderson's gentle teasing of his son about the possibility of a purloined goodnight kiss or two on some spring evening when Samuel left the Cambridge house with a spray of tea roses clutched in his white-gloved hands, she had never thought . . .

She combed the bedroom, looking for more signs—and found them. In an alcove that must have been used as a dressing room, she found a three-way mirror a man would not be likely to need, and on a kidney-shaped table with a floral print skirt a hairbrush with a mother-of-pearl back nestled behind a porcelain wash basin and water pitcher. A few long, glossy black hairs were tangled in the bristles. Samuel had been blond. Near the brush a gay little enamelware pot held rouge that had probably once been a bright incarnadine paste, now dried to a dull red cake.

Across the room another alcove beckoned, and she moved to it for a closer look. This one was exclusively a man's terrain; a pair of Mexican riding boots leaned against the heavy, carved leg of a much sturdier table than the one she had just turned from, and on its top she spied the teakwood rack with its seven straight razors—one for each day of the week—which her father had given Samuel when he moved across Cambridge to the apartment just off Harvard Yard . . . thirteen, no, fourteen years ago! A black leather strap with a solid ivory grip at the end—did men call such a thing a "strop"?—hung from a brass hook clamped to the table's edge, right under a small square mirror in a filigreed pewter frame.

She lingered a moment longer. Then, out of some sudden, inspired curiosity, she pulled open the drawer in the table.

A pewter picture frame that matched the mirror held a sepia daguerreotype of a woman. There was a message and a signature written across the bottom: *"para Samuel, con amor, amor, y mas amor—Ángela."*

With something suddenly ringing in her ears, Sarah realized she *knew* this woman. She had never seen her here at the *hacienda*, but she knew her, or at least knew about her.

The raven hair, the dark, piercing eyes, the cool brow, the slender throat and unbelievably sensuous mouth belonged to the Ángela Peralta whom she had heard at El Teatro Imperial with Jason, Paola, and Pierre, when the passionate Mexican diva drove Max and Charlotte from the theater with her anthem to her country.

But the Ángela Peralta of the daguerreotype in the drawer was something other than the one of the opera.

She was leaning back against a marble table in a room of shadows, her back arched like a dancer's, and with one brilliant shaft of light turning her upper body to sepia flame.

And she was nude.

Unlike the few other daguerreotypes of nudes Sarah had seen in Paris—she remembered no fuss about such "undraped" pictures, even at the Pelletiers—nothing seemed somber or "arty" about this picture. A look of expectant eagerness played across the woman's face, something almost lustful. This was not the sorrowing Rachel of "La Juive," nor the militant beauty who had sung "La Libertad."

Dark brown nipples jutted from aerolas which spread halo-like over perfect breasts. Her legs, slightly parted, one foot in front of the other, were in shadow, as was the dark delta where they came together. The shaft of light had been directed upward and away from it—in a failed attempt at decorum—by whoever stood behind the camera. The effort had been solely that of the photographer; this woman would hide nothing.

She closed the drawer.

Samuel, her very own dignified brother—and La Peralta, the great soprano who had offered Maximilian and Charlotte that gratuitous insult at the opera?

She left the alcove, telling herself it was time to get her mind back on the delicate undertaking which had brought her and Jason here. Tomorrow, if she could find time either before or after their talk with President Juárez, she and Isabel could clear things from the two dressing tables and pack them away.

The picture would stay where Samuel kept it.

It was time to dress; the president could arrive any moment.

When she shook out the gown she would wear to dinner and laid it on the bed, she found Isabel had already bunched the bulky down comforter against the footboard and turned back the coverlet.

As tired as she expected to be by nightfall, she wondered how well she would sleep in Samuel's and Ángela Peralta's bed . . .

Through dinner she watched Jason every bit as much as she did Juárez, more perhaps, keeping her eyes covertly on him even when the president was talking. She only turned her attention on the Republican leader when he directed one of his few remarks to her. But she missed nothing.

At table, Solange, stuffing her pique about Henri under some Gallic blanket of resignation, talked more than any of them, easy to do in the case of Alberto Moreno, who, out of awe for the company he was keeping, Sarah supposed, did not utter a word during the entire meal. The president and Jason were hardly more talkative.

She knew Jason was eager to start on the business that had brought them north, but he was holding himself in check remarkably well. He seemed to have taken her urgent wordless message about patience just before they came to the table from the *portal* very much to heart.

"Doña Sarah," Alberto Moreno said when Isabel brought

coffee and while Arturo opened another bottle of wine, "there is something I must ask, *por favor.*"

"*Sí, señor?*"

"One of my best miners took a bride this afternoon. These young people beg to pay their respects. They feel God has smiled on them by bringing El Presidente and the gracious Doña Sarah to Zacatecas on their wedding day. *Por favor,* may they present themselves?"

"*Magnifique!*" Solange cried. "You must say *oui, chérie!* Weddings *sont le bonne chance,* the very best of luck."

Sarah would have agreed to Moreno's request with or without Solange's outburst, but it was nice to find her companion pleased at the prospect after their mild but irritating estrangement of the last few days.

"*Sí, Señor Moreno.* Have them come in."

"*Lo siento,* Doña Sarah, but they will not come inside *su casa,*" Moreno said. "They are waiting in the garden under the *portal.* I believe they and their families have arranged some entertainment for La Doña and her guests."

"Then by all means, let us step out to the *portal* and welcome them."

This time she offered her arm to Jason.

Children in the considerable group around and behind the bridal couple held torches against the dark gray night and as he looked at Sarah's face, bathed in the torchlight, James thought no woman could ever have been lovelier. Down below them, the young couple, in bright white wedding clothes, their necks circled by flowers that glowed incandescent in the torchlight, held hands, their upturned faces suffused with happiness.

The gathering around them seemed a mix of the few field hands Moreno kept at the *hacienda* itself, their wives and children, and the subtly tougher looking men who worked the mine.

Sarah had Arturo take champagne down from the *portal* to the newlyweds, smiled as they shyly raised their glasses to her, and said, "Pity there is not enough for everyone out there." She turned to Juárez. "*Por favor, Señor Presidente.* Could you make a toast to the bride and groom? They will treasure the memory all their lives."

Across the valley a full moon was just nosing above the brow of the brooding, steep hill James had heard her call "La Bufa" when they rode in through the small city this morning. In seconds it cleared the hill's topmost ridge, its scarred surface as yellow as a pale, veiled *calabaza*. It would turn platinum before it climbed another hundred meters. The valley was filling with light that would in moments wash over everything and make the torches unnecessary.

Juárez raised his glass. "*Salud y pesetas para siempre, niños . . . y viva la libertad.*" The first part of the toast was sincere enough, but the second sounded like a prayer. A heartfelt sigh rose from the gravel drive and the gray-green, grassy slope stretching down and away from the *portal.* It seemed to grow louder as it echoed from the stone facade of the *hacienda* and met another wind of sighs rolling upward from the drive. "*Viva la libertad . . . Viva El Presidente . . . Viva Mexico!*"

Three old men in identical woven straw sombreros stepped out of the small crowd's loose ranks. Two carried violins, old, crudely homemade, but bright and warm in the flickering orange light from the nearby, softly exploding brands; the other held a dented but lovingly polished trumpet across his chest as a soldier might hold his rifle at port arms. The young couple, knowing perhaps that for a moment anyway not everyone would be looking at them while the musicians tuned their ancient instruments to a counterfeit of pitch, released their handhold and gazed at each other. The boy's arm had found its way around the girl's slender waist, and now he kissed her—twice. The first was as shy as the dart-and-retreat approach of a humming-bird to an unfamiliar flower, but the second . . .

James's arm moved around Sarah's waist in an involuntary motion he never could have stopped. She turned her face toward him and he knew she, too, had seen those torchlit kisses.

They could not kiss. Not now. Not with the president, the mine manager, the ever watchful, suspicious, and very likely inimical Solange, and this curious *campesino* and *minero* crowd looking on.

The music began.

The first two pieces were simple *canciones* James vaguely recalled hearing somewhere, but to neither of which he could put a name. A few voices out there, mostly women's, enlivened the second one, a song of *amor* and roses and moonlight, and all the expected if seldom realized emotions such music was written to evoke, but realized perhaps for a few moments here tonight, if only by the newlyweds. Both pieces were done with something approaching artistry coming from the mouth of the old trumpeter and the bows in the hands of his two equally old companions.

For the third song, a slim boy, no more than eleven or twelve, stepped out from the throng as the instrumentalists had. He nodded to the three old men, bowed deeply to Juárez, and began to sing. The three oldsters followed him—with far more vigor than they had shown in the two earlier songs—into the anthem of the Republic, "La Libertad."

As his clear soprano floated up to the *portal* James felt Sarah's shoulders stiffen under his arm. She turned her head first toward the president, and then her face up toward James again. There was some kind of question in it. Was he missing something here?

"This song, Jason," she whispered. "You have heard it before?"

"A few times, yes."

"But one time in particular. We heard it together on that occasion."

Then it came to him. The opera. La Peralta. He saw the great singer now with full recall, heard her ringing challenge with these same notes and words, saw the emperor and empress leave the imperial box in full retreat, saw the chagrin and outrage in nine faces out of ten in the boxes of the horseshoe and in the loges, heard the screaming diatribe of Paola Kollonitz.

"Yes, I remember."

She was pleased when, shortly after the wedding party and their fading torches disappeared from the lawn, the president announced he would retire, and almost at once Moreno asked her permission to withdraw. Solange left, too, looking back over her shoulder with a withering glance at Jason. The dinner truce had ended.

They were alone now.

Jason sat in the big chair the president had occupied before they all went in to dinner. She perched herself on a cushion-covered wicker hassock just a few feet away from him.

She had almost gone to him, but knew that would not do. She regretted it, but she knew she had to hold her ground. If he could not wrestle into submission whatever frenzied inner demons still beset him—the same furies which plagued him on the rooftop at Chapultepec perhaps, or the imps of self-doubt whose barbs he must have felt intermittently ever since, as he had in that one brief, ecstatic moment at her door on Avenida Moctezuma— there was no hope for them.

The night came alive with sounds that had been muffled by the gathering of the wedding party, the music, and the gentle crackle and snapping of the torches. The hum of insects filled the air.

Now the only thing she heard above the sound of the cicadas was the rustling of his clothing as he left the chair.

He took her hands in his and pulled her to her feet. She folded herself into his arms when his hands left hers and sought the small of her back. Their mouths met, as did their bodies, and she could feel the marvelous heat of his through clothes that seemed to slough away.

How many kisses now? She could not count. Did not want to. She pressed against him with strength she had never known before. All the hesitation of the past had fled. From both of them.

It was minutes before she could take a breath and speak.

"The answer is yes, Jason."

"Are you sure, Sarah?"

He waited then, his face in the moonlight filled with hope and desire, but with patience, too.

"Oh, yes. More sure than of anything in my entire life."

35

▲▲▲▲▲

When James met Sarah for breakfast in the dining room and discovered no one there, he tried to make the kiss he gave her something separate and different from the ones of the all too short, sweet night. What had happened in the half darkness of her room had changed his world, and so the hurried kiss this morning was no casual brush of his lips on hers. None he would ever give her would be.

If he feared her response would reveal second thoughts, it did not. Her body returned the pressure of his with every bit of the fervor of the night's embraces.

"I love you, Sarah," he said. If she had been lovely in the torchlight last night, and later in the moonlight streaming through her window, she had become, if anything, even more so in the full light of day. He could look at her forever.

But he somehow had to keep her out of mind when he met with Juárez. He would find dealing with the president demanding enough were the skills he had honed in his work for Bazaine since coming to the capital at their sharpest. His bargaining position was not a strong one; he had brought north with him a pathetically slim portfolio of offers. But a beginning must be made. He would have to tell the president of the emperor's disappointingly vague proposals and then sit back and listen. If Juárez rejected Maximilian's offers out of hand they might be through with each other before the sun was very high over La Bufa.

His plan for this morning's meeting was simple. He had discarded every one of the elaborate scenarios which ran through his mind on the journey from the capital, a process made more difficult then by all those tormented moments when his mind and emotions were tangled with thoughts of Sarah.

After the first full warmth of his kiss subsided a little and they sat down to breakfast, Sarah looked at Jason across the old Spanish table. She supposed convention demanded that she should feel some guilt about what had happened between the two of them, but she did not. This was far more than something physical. She had loved Jason before this morning, but now it seemed as if their hearts and nerves drew life from the same deep well.

What a distance they had traveled from Orizaba.

Here in Zacatecas they were two different people from the embattled pair in the officer's mess with Marcel and Pierre back then, she waspishly combative, he guarded, parrying but never thrusting as she had, bless him, both of them walled away from each other for almost two long, empty years by their separate histories. Well, no more walls would rise.

What the two men would discuss this morning held so much heavy portent for Mexico—and for her and Jason, too—that it seemed almost shameful to let her private, intimate concerns get in the way. She had to pay attention. And she had to play her part.

"How much do you know about President Juárez, Jason?" she asked.

"I've known *of* him for years, of course." It would be hard to keep his mind on this. "And Eloin sent a *précis* about him to my office before we left."

"The usual polemic, I suppose?"

"Yes, for the most part. His birth in Oaxaca, his Zapotec Indian roots, how he studied for the law and became a judge, the high points of his political career. He's fifty-eight now. He doesn't look it."

"No, he doesn't. What else?"

"A capsule history of his political career, a somewhat slanted one, I fear. Eloin does not like him, but I expected that."

"Does it mention the two years he spent in New Orleans when Santa Anna exiled him?"

"Yes. And thank you for reminding me of that. I had better watch myself. He probably knows how Americans think much better than I know how Mexicans do."

She smiled. "New Orleans. I've often wondered what they thought of him there. I think that's where he got his taste for champagne. Someone in our country must have been courting him even then; from things my brother told me he could never have afforded to buy fine French wines himself during what amounted to an exile. He's been poor most of his life. His long fight for the people of Mexico is . . . well, there aren't really words for it."

"He might have fought *me* once, in '47, somewhere on the road from Veracruz to the capital, although Eloin makes no mention of what he did back then, and I don't recollect any talk about him when I came here with General Scott."

"Then there's not a lot of new information to prepare you for this morning?"

"No. Most of Eloin's *précis* was pretty much what I expected, but one thing it said about the president did make a very deep impression on me."

"Oh?"

"After he returned from New Orleans he served as minister of justice under our host at Chapultepec, Ignacio Comonfort, when *he* was president. It speaks volumes about Juárez's capacity for leadership that a proud soldier like Comonfort could show such willingness to take second place to a former subordinate. He was clearly in awe of the president that day at lunch."

She would not have to worry about Jason this morning. He had read everything between the lines Eloin had written. She had been right at San Cosmé. He was much more than a soldier.

"Anything else?"

"Not really. Eloin's account pretty much ends there. He and the emperor probably assume I'm knowledgeable enough about what has happened to Juárez since the French got here."

"Jason."

"Yes?"

"You want this accord very badly, don't you?"

"Yes. Since I came to Mexico I've begun to learn how ineffective war is as an instrument of policy."

Some men who acquire power use it as a hammer; some bring their listeners close to them, elevate them above of and beyond themselves, and often make them more than they really are. Jason James had already decided which one of these Benito Juárez would prove to be.

They met on the *portal* at ten.

Sarah had insisted it was too fine a day to stay indoors and Juárez was quick to agree. In his eagerness to get on with things, it was all one to James; he would have met with the Republican president in a canyon or a cowshed.

"By all means let us go outside," he said. "Since we will be discussing the future of Mexico, I suppose it is fitting that we actually look at some of it as we talk."

Once on the great stone porch of the *hacienda* Juárez pointed to a *campesino* crew marching out to the *hacienda*'s nearest fields carrying shovels, hoes, and mattocks, their cotton clad bodies shimmering white in the haze rising from the crushed stone drive sweeping down below the *portal*. The last wisps of the haze would soon be burned away as the sun climbed above the spires and roofs of Zacatecas and the tops of the near and distant hills.

"Yes, let us look at Madre Mexico, colonel," Juárez said. "We should also keep in mind those *pobrecitos* during our discussions. If I were half the democrat some of my countrymen have been generous enough to claim I am, I would call those good people up here to listen to us, and if I had enough courage, allow *them* to determine what fate should bring them. They are not stupid, nor incapable of deciding for themselves, but it has been so many centuries since anyone has so much as permitted them the smallest say in their own affairs, that I fear they would not know how to respond. I *can* pray their day will come—and I can work for that day, *por de veras.*''

James girded himself for the task at hand. Inferior in rank as he was to the man facing him, he could thank God he had the vocabulary for this morning's exercise, and knew a little something of the labyrinthine geography of talks such as this one might turn out to be. Bazaine's confidence in him had helped buoy his own, but really, if he now had any talent at all for this sort of thing its development had begun long before he became a soldier. He had Aaron Sheffield to thank for the marathon sessions in that Kansas kitchen where Aaron rehearsed him for debates and elocution contests, drilling him as his Legion sergeants in his days as a *bleu* in Sidi-bel-Abbés and the desert never had, scalding him with abuse and scorn when he faltered in his logic or forgot a line.

This would be a stern test, but no sterner than those devised by Aaron.

Juárez turned his gaze back from the *campesinos* to James and Sarah. "We do not need to fence with each other this morning, do we Colonel James?" he said. "I was aware of your impatience last night, and I apologize for my seeming indifference."

"No apology is needed, sir."

"Let us go straight to the heart of the matter then." Juárez's gravity was contagious. ''*Por favor*, give me one single reason why this talk should take place at all."

"Because your forces are bleeding to death, Señor President, and there seems no prospect the hemorrhage will stop. I betray no state or military secrets when I tell you that the French under Marshal Bazaine, together with the emperor's own army, will shortly mount an offensive which will make the earlier ones mere skirmishes by comparison. Your own intelligence should have told you that by now. Scouts must already have reported the massive French buildup in Chihuahua State. Perhaps you even saw some of those preparations yourself on your way south to Zacatecas. The opening salvos of the new push may have sounded by the time you return to the north, and the loss of life among your soldiery could be devastating. Your people's blood could very well run out before the next few battles end."

Juárez had nodded as James spoke, almost in emphasis of every word. "Sí, colonel. Honesty—together with my own practical military sense, such as it is—compels me to admit that what you say is true. But in this country new blood has a way of pooling up where and when our enemies least expect it. If our reservoir is somewhat drained after so many years of war, we can always wait for it to fill again. We have great patience. Do our enemies have such patience?"

"Enough for their purposes, I think. But can we not, sir, for the moment, and for the sake of this discussion, dispense with talk of enemies?"

"Sí. But only for the moment. Words are de importancia, but one cannot dispense with real enemies by playing semantic games. Now, tell me what the Austrian is prepared to offer Mexico."

"The emperor . . ." That would not do, but neither could he bring himself to say "the Austrian" as Juárez had. "The head of the Mexican government now installed in the capital and at Chapultepec . . ." There was no discernible change on the dark face of his granitic listener. ". . . wishes you to join that government, Señor Juárez."

Did this enigmatic Zapotec never show surprise?

"In precisely what capacity?" Juárez might have been asking James the time of day.

"As His Imperial Majesty's first minister, sir."

"And for this exalted post the lawfully elected government of Mexico is expected to cede exactly what?" The president had trumped his ace with the use of the word "exalted," but it was too early to throw in even the worst of hands. "Proceed with the Austrian's proposal, colonel. We can consider any possible benefits after that."

"Yes, sir. Your Republican government would either have to disband its army, Mister President, or have all its units come in and serve under the Imperial flag."

"We would have to disarm completely then?"

"Yes."

"Muchas gracias, Colonel. You have indeed presented the worst of the offer. Is there any 'best'?"

"In return for swearing fealty to the crown, all surrendering officers and their men would receive the benefits of a general amnesty, together with no loss of rank or privilege. Many, but of course not all, of the civilians serving under you would find rewarding situations, too. The government pledges its word on that."

The dark, square face did not betray a tremor when Juárez spoke again. "And you are asking me to take the Austrian's word on that, Colonel?"

"Yes, sir."

"His word is his bond?"

"I have not known of it being otherwise, sir."

"This part of the offer is designed, of course, to tempt me, colonel. But I and my followers will only be tempted by substance. Let me ask you something. If I agree, there would of course be a duly constituted, democratically chosen legislature safe from any so-called *imperial* sanctions and prejudices as well, would there not? Something on the order of the Congress of your United States, the English Parliament, or France's Chamber of Deputies? Would this be the shape of this new *junta?"*

"I am not authorized to guarantee that, *señor.* The emperor feels that any new lawmaking body should probably act for the most part only in an advisory role—for a while at least. However, he fully expects that in only a few years Mexico will have a constitutional monarchy resembling in most respects that of Great Britain."

"Genuine parliaments are more than mere advisors to the executive, colonel, as I am sure you, as an North American, will agree, and constitutional monarchies, however benign, are still monarchies. And a few *years?* How many? Why not now, with no wait at all?"

"Once you are first minister, sir, I feel sure that you and the . . . present head of state . . . can agree on limits to the wait. May I respectfully remind the president that he said he and his people have great patience."

"That patience is not inexhaustible, Colonel." Juárez continued. "*Sí.* My people do have an enormous fund of patience. It is perhaps their most abundant resource, together with the bottomless capacity they have shown for accepting hardship without audible complaint down through the centuries."

"The complaint was audible enough during the War of Independence sixty-some years ago, *Señor Presidente.*"

"That was not a complaint from the people, Colonel. The part of our society that waged that war was that same part that supports the Austrian and his French mercenaries in this bloody conflict today. When the Spanish were driven from Mexico, the people merely found themselves bending their backs under the lashes of a different set of masters, despots such as Iturbide and Antonio de Santa Anna."

"I stand corrected, *Señor Presidente.*"

"Yes, we are patient. *Pero* . . . although I have just included myself in the general fund of this patience, I might not have been speaking the entire truth. I am not at all sure their president has as much patience as do his people. Sometimes it makes me wonder if I am fit to serve as their leader."

Arturo walked onto the *portal* with coffee, and Juárez fell silent as the *mayordomo* bent his old back to pour. The black eyes took in every move the servant made. It gave James the chance to look at Sarah. Beside the need to see her just for the sight of her alone, he wanted some reassurance that he was handling matters well.

She smiled, nodded almost imperceptibly. Then, with a quick shift of those blue eyes forced his attention back to the president.

"We must come immediately to grips, Colonel," Juárez said now, "about the proposed size, strength, and political power of the . . . ministry . . . the Austrian says he is ready to entrust me with. Exactly how much authority would I have as first minister? Would I control the military? No, I can see by your face I would not. The money then? The last say on taxes and other levies? You do not know, do you, Colonel James?"

James had to ignore that, or avoid it as the matador would the bull. "There would be a whole range of civil matters about which the emperor would seek your counsel, sir. You may rely on it in fact."

"Counsel? A true first minister does more than counsel." The black eyes bored deep into James's now. "Come, come, colonel. Please be as forthright with me as I know you *meant* to be when we sat down together. Are you prepared to call what the Austrian proposes a genuine offer to share power with him?"

There was only one tack to take now. It called for brutal candor.

"No, *Señor Presidente.* But I think that with the military situation as it is, the emperor is being extremely generous in offering you *any* share of power." Dangerous as what he would say next might sound, he had to say it. "May I, with all respect, remind the president that nothing *compels* His Imperial Majesty to give you anything. I am, of course, only a messenger, but my candid, personal opinion, which you just asked for, sir, is that you and all of Mexico would be best served by coming to some accommodation with the emperor and his government. If this war continues it will bring disaster to the people of Mexico, no matter which way things go, and at the present they most assuredly are not going *your* way at all. The Mexico of the president's dreams and hopes will die."

"Forgive me if I disagree with your last remark, colonel.

Mexico—and my dreams and hopes—will never die. I assure you *that* is a given. *Esta es la tierra de la vida, de veras.* And even if some as yet by-no-means-certain military reverses happen, and should the Mexico we are engaged in creating, despite my perhaps too sanguine prediction, die— like the phoenix it will rise again."

"But wouldn't it be better, sir, if, *un*like the phoenix, it did *not* have to die and burn as a prelude to its rising? There is always the likelihood that if Márquez and Mejía and the French under Marshal Bazaine kill the bird they will also scatter its ashes to the four winds with no chance for those ashes to be reunited."

The coppery Indian visage could have been solid rock, the line between his compressed lips so thin a razor might have cut it there. The rock James looked at could be cradling the same pressure and heat a volcano does in the moment before it erupts. The American knew he could provoke the eruption with his very next words, but again, some unpalatable things had to be said.

"You and your army cannot win, Señor Juárez."

In the silence that followed he heard the quick intake of Sarah's breath. Had he gone too far?

"That is possibly true," Juárez said. "It is possibly every bit as true, however, that we cannot *lose*, doubtful as our chances of a triumph of arms appears at the moment. Not all the battles in this struggle will be fought with weapons. You strike me as a man who might be able to deal with paradox, colonel. Are you such a man?"

"Possibly, sir. I am willing to be tested."

"Then attend me for moment. This is the paradox: it is not only possible, but probable, that we shall lose and win at the same time in this struggle. Another paradox: there is no way the Austrian can win, *even if he does*. I fear you have not been persuasive enough thus far, Colonel James."

There had been to this low point no outright rejection of Maximilian's offer, but the last surely meant it was imminent.

But even with failure looming as an immediate certainty,

James felt no sense of loss or disappointment. There was, instead, quite another feeling. Something had descended into the bright morning air of the *portal*, the same invisible cloud which had hovered around him before and during the journey north and which he could neither run nor hide from any longer—his oath to Maximilian. He was the envoy and sworn creature of the emperor, and it was time now to face and fight against something trying to emerge from deep in some cellar of his soul.

Benito Juárez and his unyielding, stone-faced adherence to the intellectual—and surely moral—high ground, together with his undoubted courage, was almost seducing him. In another time and place . . .

The most exacting test of his principles was beginning now. He had to pass it or make a lie of more than half his life. The thought brought a shiver he hoped went undetected.

Sarah Anderson could not even guess what caused the shadow of a shudder that passed through Jason at the president's last words, but something very strange and powerful had happened to him.

"There is still something else to be considered, President Juárez," Jason said now. His tone had changed. Where before he had been firm if respectful, his voice had been that of the petitioner. She heard a new ring of steel in it now. "You have made your wishes known in unmistakable terms, sir, but I must ask you one more question, even if I am hardly in a position to ask it. This is not the emperor's question; it is *mine.*"

"Ask," Juárez said.

"With the terrible fate you could bring down on your people, *do you have the RIGHT to refuse the emperor's offer and allow this war to continue?*"

Juárez did not move, nor did his expression change, but in the deathly quiet that spread across the *portal* she could feel the working of his mind, a distant, imagined, ghostly rumble.

At last he spoke.

"*Por favor*, Colonel James, would you tell me why I might *not* have that right?"

Jason, erect in his chair through the entire talk, seemed suddenly evenmore so.

"Yes, sir. I will gladly tell you. Please do not think me presumptuous, but . . . we have talked largely of abstractions this morning, things such as democracy, constitutionally elected governments, ministerial powers, freedom, and equality. The sort of thing that fills the speeches of leaders who all too often do not remember the plain, practical wishes of the people. I have no quarrel with such ideas in principle." He pointed to the nearest *hacienda* field. The *campesinos* visible a few moments ago had shrunk to the size of ants with the distance and moved out of sight over a rise as they worked their way to the ends of the rows they were tilling. "Those workers we saw earlier may not see it quite that way. Without denigrating them one iota—and I never would, since *I* once worked the land and loved it just as they seem to do—is it not possible that after so many years of struggle, poverty, and suffering, they might welcome the chance to eat their fill for once and to stay alive?" He paused. "They are indeed, your 'people.' Please, Mr. President, I beg you, for their sake, walk a few feet in their shoes. I know you remember what it was like. Then a march few more in whatever hall of power the emperor marks out for you. There are always exits if the hall leads nowhere."

Juárez left his chair abruptly and strode then to the edge of the tiles of the *portal,* and fixed his eyes on the same field Jason had pointed to. Other workers, women this time, were coming back over the top of the rise, their backs bent, huge sacks dragging on the earth beside them.

The president's short body was as rigid as any of the carved wooden posts supporting the *portal,* and he remained that way for long seconds in which it seemed to Sarah Anderson that she did not draw a single breath.

"The land . . ." Juárez breathed. He still looked out over the nearest field. "*You* worked the land, Colonel James? I would have thought you were *born* to the life you lead now. Where *was* this land you worked?"

"In my home state of Kansas, sir."

"Why did you leave there, colonel?"

"I did not want to see that land soaked with blood. Nor do I want more blood spilled on the soil of Mexico. There is a better way."

At last Juárez turned and looked at Jason.

He was smiling, the first smile since his arrival, the first smile from him Sarah had ever seen.

"You have won me, Colonel James. You may return to the capital and tell the . . . head of your government . . . that Benito Juárez will serve as his first minister."

Far down the crushed stone drive a pillar of white dust was rising above a single horseman. The rider was flailing both flanks of his mount with an enormous quirt and the sun reflecting from the cartridge belts crossed over his chest flashed pale, winking, warning fire in the late morning sun.

Antonio Pérez.

Horse and rider thundered to a stop at the edge of the *portal*.

"*Señor Presidente!*" the huge ex-bandit shouted. "*¡Lo han traicionado, jefe!* You have been betrayed!"

"How, Tonito? Explain, *por favor*."

Pérez looked at Jason with eyes full of hate. "Perhaps it would be better if this *coronel puerco* in the pay of the usurper explained." The black eyes of Juárez followed those of his guerrilla chief. "The scouts I posted at Guadalupe just rode in with the report that five, maybe six squadrons of Imperial *caballería* are entering the gorge, headed for Zacatecas and riding hard. There are no troops in the city for them to attack except mine. They cannot have seen them yet. *Sin duda* they are coming here to take you prisoner or kill you, *jefe*."

The president's eyes were leveled on Jason now. "*Can* you explain, Colonel James?" he said, his voice remarkably calm.

Jason had turned chalk white, but Sarah in her newfound knowledge of him knew he was consumed by rage.

"I am as much in the dark about this as you are, sir."

Antonio Pérez exploded. "He lies!" His meaty hand went to the pistol at his belt. "¡Madre de Dios! I will kill him now." The gun was out and in Jason's face. He made no move to avoid the weapon.

"No, Tonito," Juárez said, the level Indian voice as soft as before. "Colonel James, do I have your word of honor that you did not know of this?"

"Absolutely, sir."

Now Jason reached up and with a firm hand pushed the barrel of the gun to one side. "How long before they arrive, Señor Pérez?"

The pistol was back in the belt, but even with the danger gone for the moment, Sarah began to tremble.

"Two hours, perhaps much less," Pérez said. He turned then to Juárez. "When they reach the plaza I will try to stop them, but I cannot hold them for more than another hour, Señor Presidente. We must get you on the road north at once."

"That won't do," Jason said. "With five or six squadrons they could find a mouse on the road." He turned to Sarah. "Is there somewhere in the hacienda or on your land where we could hide the president, Sarah?"

"We cannot hide him!" Pérez roared. "The only chance El Presidente has is if he starts out now, with Pérez and his men to escort him. Leaving this trap and riding fast is the only way."

Jason shook his head. "If this cavalry is from the regiment garrisoned at San Luis Potosí it is the First Tlaxcalans. You know how good they are, Señor Pérez. There is no way you could outrun them, and certainly not with the president's coach."

"El Presidente will have to use my horse, cabrón!"

"Tonito . . ." Juárez said. "You know I have never ridden anything except a burro, and that when I was just a niño.

Caballos are not for me." He turned to Jason again. "Colonel, you sounded just now as if you had a plan."

"A crude one, sir. It may not work."

"Tell me of it."

"If Señorita Anderson can find a safe temporary haven for you, we can perhaps lure the Imperial squadrons out onto the Camino del Norte with your coach. With luck they will not overtake it until nightfall. Once they take the bait the president can strike out on another route, one well to the west and to the *sierras*."

Juárez nodded. "But how can we make sure they *take* the bait?"

"Someone can pose as the president. When the coach rolls through Zacatecas to reach the Camino del Norte, a score or more of the villagers will see him, or think they see him. Señor Pérez and his men will lend credibility when they ride beside the coach. He will have to go shorthanded, of course. The real president will need an escort, however small. We will have to hide them, too, until the Tlaxcalans leave the city in pursuit of the impostor."

"*¡Idiota!*" Pérez snorted. "Who would be fool enough to impersonate *El Presidente?*"

"Find my man Cipi. Have him shave his beard off. Tie him down if you must. *Señor Presidente*, may we have your coat, shirt and cravat? And your hat. I am sure Miss Anderson can find a conveyance and a driver for you when you leave tonight. You should not have to ride a burro."

Juárez nodded, and understanding and grudging agreement began to dawn on Pérez's big, brute face.

"I suppose it is as good a plan as any. But hear me, gringo. If for *any* reason *mi presidente* does not reach his destination safely, I will find and kill you if it takes a lifetime."

"I know you will. Now, let's find Cipi! We cannot waste another second."

In an hour Jason returned to the house.

"Where have you put him, Sarah?" he asked.

"Arturo hid him behind a wall of racks in the wine

cellar—with the champagne." She chuckled. "Forgive me. I know how serious this is. I'm afraid I'm a bit hysterical. Have Antonio and Cipi started out?"

"Yes."

"The Tlaxcalans?"

"They reached the plaza half an hour ago and have begun to question people. Their commander will not be a stupid man. Even if they do set out in pursuit as we hope, he will send a detachment up here to make sure the president is really gone. But that will cost him time, and Pérez and Cipi already have an hour's start. They can maybe get well beyond Fresnillo before they're caught. While Pérez and his men make their fight, Cipi can perhaps strike out for Sombrerete, reach it with luck, abandon the coach, and become a harmless dwarf again."

"It just might work then?"

"I pray so."

"Poor Cipi."

"Do not worry about him yet, Sarah. After the shock and humiliation of losing his beard faded a little, he began immediately to look upon it as a lark. He's resourceful—and still mendacious, too. Once he was in the coach—looking very presidential I must say—he asked for a rise in salary."

When they said good-bye to Juárez and the four men Pérez had assigned him, James silently cursed the full moon he had marveled at, reveled in, the night before.

"It goes without saying," the president said when he shook James's hand and accepted Sarah's full embrace. "that I will not come to the capital to see the Austrian. Not without an army."

"I know, sir."

"When I come there with my army I shall have to fight you, shall I not?

"Yes, sir."

"There is a way we can avoid that, Colonel. Have you considered it?"

"Briefly, sir."

"And . . ."

"I believe you know, *Señor Presidente,* why considering it is all it can come to."

With a grave nod Juárez entered the *hacienda*'s old carriage and waved as it moved off through gaps in the *maguey* that made a forest of silver spikes in the moonlit dry flats behind the *hacienda.*

When it was lost to sight, Sarah turned to James.

"How did the Tlaxcalans know where to come, Jason?"

"Felix Eloin knew."

"Oh, my God, yes! And I was the one who told him."

"Do not blame yourself for a second. It was every bit as much my fault. Someone else knew, too."

"Yes, but surely you don't suspect for one moment . . ."

"I guess I can't allow myself to. But perhaps I relied too heavily on the word of a man I did not really know. There are questions I must ask when we return to the capital. As a civilian advisor, Felix Eloin has no authority to order an Imperial Army cavalry action of this magnitude on his own."

"Jason! You can't possibly think . . ."

"I'm afraid I do."

His voice was hollow.

36
▲▲▲▲▲

Every meter of the long road back to the capital seemed to stretch out to a dreary kilometer.

That they had so quickly won everything they came to Zacatecas for, and then so quickly lost it, made the journey even more tedious.

Once they left the *hacienda* Jason never spoke again about a part the emperor might or might not have played in the attempt on Benito Juárez, but his mood, already dark when they set out, worsened with every kilometer. Sarah grew progressively more somber and withdrawn herself, but she lifted herself out of depression with brief flashes of righteous anger about the unfairness of it all.

There had come, for that one brief, giddy moment, a rising sun of hope for both of them—and for Mexico—which Antonio Pérez's warning had eclipsed as quickly as it appeared. She tried to persuade herself that even without the threat of the Tlaxcalans something else would have torn the prize from Jason's grasp, and that in any event the raiders' arrival was coincidence, a stroke of unhappy luck. She failed. Someone had deliberately and effectively wrecked the delicate accord he had engineered. The worst of it: there would never be another chance.

Yes—it was a dismal trip back down to Mexico City, and a frustrating one for another, entirely personal, reason.

To the moment of Antonio Pérez's appearance at the *portal* with the horrifying news about the Tlaxcalans she had been in ecstasy over the discoveries they had made of each other, or rather that *she* had made. Now such explorations would have to wait.

There would not be many opportunities when she was back with Charlotte, Paola, and the court at Chapultepec, either.

She ached to have his arms around her longer than in the few stolen moments of the return home. She wanted his embrace to linger, to last, wanted to hear his voice again exactly as it had sounded that night when they gazed at the moon afterward, before he left her room for his. He had assured her, if not in so many words, that he could and would be patient. She needed no such assurance. She trusted him. How could she not, with the memory of his gentleness fresh and new each morning since it happened?

As their small caravan turned into Avenida Moctezuma to deliver Solange home before going on to Chapultepec, she finally decided that all the questions to which she did not yet have answers were part of a mystery deliberately posed by love itself.

The answers would come. Love, she suspected now, had its own irresistible, glacial logic, one that could grind to powdery terminal moraine everything that blocked its way.

She said good-bye to Jason near dark at the great entrance to Chapultepec. With uniformed guards and servants looking on, no chance came for that longed-for embrace; he was hurrying to the emperor's office suite to report on the meeting at Zacatecas.

The loving smile breaking through his grave and troubled face when they said good-bye would have to suffice her until they met again.

A note from Charlotte telling her of Henri Gallimard's arrival at Chapultepec and commanding her presence at a dinner honoring him in the empress's private dining room that very night waited on the foyer table in her chambers.

Impossible that she could so quickly have forgotten Henri, but she had.

It was going to be a long, trying dinner before they were alone and she could tell him about Jason James.

Paola, already in a dinner gown, burst into the sitting room just as she finished reading Charlotte's note.

"Welcome home, *liebchen.*"

"Paola!" She handed the note to the countess. "Have you seen Henri?"

"*Ja.*"

"Was he angry at not finding me?"

"Disappointed—and absolutely crushed when you did not appear at his brother's *soiree* for him."

"I feel terrible about that, Paola."

"You should—but only until you make it right with him. He thought perhaps you had forgotten him. I told him that was not a possibility. I was right, *nein?*"

"Certainly. I just couldn't be here." What else could she say?

"You know my feelings about Henri, Sarah. You cannot

afford to let him get away. Get that look off your face, *liebchen*. I've told you before, you can have them both if you are clever."

"How *is* Henri?"

"Very handsome, as always." Something did not ring true. Paola turned away. "I must confess he did not seem to me to be the same *bon vivant* I remember from Paris and Vienna, but perhaps it was the long journey. I understand he suffered through the same bad storms as we did on our crossing a year ago." She turned back, and now her face had regained its customary radiance. "*Ja, ja*, he is fine. You will see for yourself tonight. Now—tell how your trip with your dashing Guardsman went."

"Not much to tell." Nothing much she *could* tell, at any rate. She could say nothing, of course, about the meeting with Benito Juárez until after Jason reported to the emperor, and as for the other, well . . .

Paola had gone to the door. "So good to have you back, *liebchen*, but you do not have much time to dress. I will send Florita to help you. Wear the velvet."

"This will not be a ball, Paola, just a small dinner, according to Charlotte's note."

Paola sighed. "No matter. Wear what you like, of course, but the sight of you in that deep blue is a tonic for a man. Hurry now, *liebchen*. *Wiedersehen!*"

Despite Paola's insistent but too rushed assurances a moment ago, things might not be well with him, but it would be useless to pursue the matter with the countess. When she said "you will see for yourself" the message had really been "you will *have* to see for yourself."

Henri's letters of the last three years had never once hinted that there was anything amiss with his health, but then he would have suffered the most debilitating, agonizing disease in utter silence rather than burden anyone close to him. What would she find in him at dinner tonight? Probably just the malaise of a grueling voyage as Paola conjectured.

She had just now girded herself to tell Henri about

Jason—*tonight*—but what had happened to her sincere intention of telling Jason about Henri when they left for Zacatecas? Had she really just forgotten Henri on the trip north and during the stay at the *hacienda*? Had she deliberately *avoided* any thought of him? Either way, her memory was showing alarming signs of becoming an instrument of personal convenience.

No matter what had happened in Zacatecas, she had to think about Henri now. She owed him that much, maybe more.

When the girl Florita arrived to help her dress she decided she would wear the velvet after all.

"Comment ça va, ma chère?" Henri said as he released her from a wordless, breathless embrace greeted with warm sighs by almost everyone in Charlotte's sparkling little dining room.

"Bien, Henri, et toi?" she said. His face, even suffused as it was now with the joy of seeing her, revealed unmistakably that something was wrong. It was pink enough, but it looked to be the chalky, roseate flush of fever she had seen once or twice in victims of consumption. In the past she had harbored the wild notion that the principal difference between Henri Gallimard and Max von Hapsburg had been Max's faint look of decay and imminent death, something that in his case had nothing to do with anything as temporal as his physical condition. Now Henri wore that same clouded look.

She wished Maximilian were at hand at the moment to compare with Henri, but the chair at the head of the table obviously meant for the emperor was empty. Perhaps he was still in conference with Jason. The place set for him surprised her a little. She had not really expected him; he seldom attended Charlotte's more intimate dinners. What made this occasion different?

Charlotte motioned them to their seats. "The emperor has sent word that we are not to wait for him. An affair of state," she said.

As much as her mind seethed with thoughts of Henri and Jason, old habit made her take stock of who the diners were at Charlotte's table: Melanie Zichy of course; the elegant Belgian Colonel Alfred Van der Smissen whom Paola had pursued so shamelessly at San Cosmé before she discovered Pierre Boulanger; another Imperial Army colonel, an Austrian named Brunner and his wealthy Italian wife; Princess Agnes Salm-Salm, the exotic beauty who had made a splash at court in recent months that rivaled the glitter of Paola Kollonitz; a newly arrived Belgian couple she did not yet know except by sight. Most held glasses of champagne. None were seated yet. She heard the insistent, grating voice of the guest of honor's brother, Marcel Gallimard.

As they dined, Henri maintained a smiling silence. Charlotte held the floor alone for the most part, discoursing strenuously on her—and Max's, she was at some pains to add—latest plan for schools for the Indian children of the realm.

From time to time through the meal, Henri's hand strayed to Sarah's. She detected a tremor in it. Once he turned from the table to cough into his napkin until his face seemed drained, but after a moment's alarm she decided it was not consumption. If he suffered from anything that serious he never would have attempted the trip across the Atlantic. She could hope it was something trivial and temporary.

Perhaps the ways in which the Henri now at Chapultepec differed from the Henri of the Loire, Paris, and Le Havre three years ago were only visible to her. She saw no questioning or pitying glances directed at him from the others at the table. No other eye but hers apparently caught sight of the forbidding pill he washed down with a careful sip of Charlotte's Le Chambertin. On the other hand, Paola Kollonitz missed nothing.

While they waited for dessert Henri did manage a word or two—about Marcel. He seemed particularly proud of his brother, a pride clearly traceable to what the ingenuous young fool must have told him of a few real, and many more imagined exploits while serving the flag of France and the cause of Emperor Max. Pierre Boulanger would surely prick the balloon of the junior Gallimard's ego regardless of who might be listening. Thank heavens Jason's Chasseur friend would never find himself invited to this sort of dinner.

Even with her concern with Henri, her mild irritation with Marcel—who had chattered like a lunatic macaw even as Charlotte spoke, prompting an ill-tempered glance or two from the empress—and her longing for Jason, she found she was enjoying herself immensely. Truth to tell, she would miss at least some of this lofty fuss were she to abandon her place at court.

Henri nodded toward the empty chair. "What is keeping our Max?" he whispered. *Our Max?* Yes, this was indeed an exclusive circle, the empire *en famille*. Sarah was one of only two or three of those present who did not call the Emperor of Mexico by his first name to his face.

And, yes, where *was* he? How had Jason's meeting with him gone? She would not rest easy until she heard. While nowhere near as outspoken as Pierre, Jason would not hold his tongue today. He would be circumspect, of course, but what she now knew of him told her he would insist on knowing who had ordered the Tlaxcalan raid. If it had come about by the way Jason suspected, the matter presented a nasty problem. How did one tell one's commander-in-chief he has committed a breach of honor?

As much as the prospect of such a confrontation frightened her, she would not want Jason to avoid it, would never ask him to. His courage and resolve when facing up to unpleasant tasks defined him as a man as much as any other single thing about him. These were soldierly attributes she would never want him to lose.

"Maxl! At last, *ma chère!*" Charlotte cried.

As everyone at the table rose, the emperor made his way to the head of the table, nodding to each of the guests in turn. He seemed every bit as amiable toward Sarah when he passed her as he had been with the others, but it did not escape her that his pale eyes lingered rather longer on her than they had on anyone else at the table.

"Sit down, everyone, *bitte, bitte!*" he said when he reached his chair. "Please accept my apologies for my inexcusable tardiness." Once seated himself, he put both hands out to clasp Henri's. "It has been far too long, *mon ami*. You bring us news of our beloved Paris, *n'est-ce pas?*"

"Actually, I have not seen much of Paris these last two years, Max. When I have not been attending to the business of the chateau I have spent a good deal of time in Switzerland."

"Ah, *La Suisse!* Such a lovely land. My forebears should never have let it get away from Austria. Did you climb, paint, what?"

"I was mostly confined to Zurich. You see, I—" He stopped and cast a hurried glance at Sarah before continuing. "But that does not matter. What matters is that I am at last in Mexico with Sarah . . . and with Your Imperial Majesties as well."

Sarah had never seen the emperor quite this carefree and talkative. Of course she had never seen him with an old *friend* before. She looked in vain for a sign that his meeting with Jason had upset him.

Then, after another smiling glance at *her* he beckoned a servant to him and in a moment everyone's glass brimmed with champagne.

The emperor rose, glass in hand, and tapped a spoon against a crystal goblet.

"*Attention, s'ils vous plait, mes amis!*" He looked down at Henri, looked out over the table again. "As you all know, we are gathered tonight to honor our esteemed and valued friend, Henri, Le Comte de Bayeux and Chevalier de La Legion D'honneur de la France." He held his glass out toward Henri. "*Bienvenue a Mexico, notre cher cousin!* It is proper that we honor you. You do *us* honor by visiting our realm."

Cries of welcome echoed the length of the table and

several voices shouted "*Vive, Henri,*" but it all stopped when the emperor called for silence with another tap on the goblet. "What only one or two of you know, however, is that we have another reason for celebrating here tonight, and someone else to honor. Her Imperial Majesty has informed us that *le bon* Henri has come to Mexico not only to visit. There is a far more significant reason for his long journey to our capital . . ." He paused, for dramatic effect—and it *was* effective; no one at the table seemed to breathe. "Monsieur Le Comte has come to our shores to claim a bride . . ." Now the glass was extended in the direction of Sarah. ". . . the beautiful and *très charmante* Mademoiselle Sarah Anderson, our dearly beloved, surrogate daughter and devoted, faithful servant!"

A dozen glasses were thrust toward her, and a Babel of voices wished her well. Then she felt Henri's arm circle her waist. At the foot of the table Charlotte looked as ecstatic as if all the warm racket echoing from the walls of the dining room was for her.

"*Attention, mesdames et messieurs!*" It was the emperor again. "There is but one more thing. We shall not press the lady Sarah to set a date, but if she and the Comte de Bayeux are man and wife by first October, we shall—as a token of our esteem and love—make them a wedding gift of the beautiful *hacienda* of La Mesa Encantada which adjoins ours at La Borda Quintas at Cuernavaca."

Sarah gasped. Paola had once told her that La Borda Quintas was Max's favorite of all the Imperial estates. "So much so in fact that he has had the Imperial Exchequer purchase every one of the nearby *haciendas* to insure his privacy. Mind you, I said *his* privacy. Charlotte almost never goes down to La Borda."

She wanted to flee, run blindly from this suddenly confining room.

She could not move.

Down the table Paola Kollonitz was smiling like an imp of Satan.

37

"You have made your report to the Austrian, James?"
Bazaine looked as much amused as curious. Odd that he
would refer to the emperor in the exact words Juárez used,
and with the same icy tone he had heard from the
diminutive president.

"Yes, sir. Last night."

"Your audience went well, despite the failure of your
mission?"

"I have little idea how it went, sir. His Imperial Majesty
gave me only a moment. He was hurrying off to a dinner in
honor of a visiting French nobleman, the older brother of
one of your Chasseur officers, a Captain Marcel Gallimard."

"This nobleman must be of some importance, to put a
dinner for him ahead of the business you had with the
crown. What is this visitor's title?"

"Le Comte de Bayeux, I believe." He *knew* who Marcel's
older brother was, and knew all too well the French count's
possible claim on Sarah.

"Les Bayeuxs de Normandie? A great old name in La
Belle France. Do *I* know this Captain Gallimard, James?"

"There is no particular reason you should, sir." Actually
there was. James had learned long before now how the
marshal's political instincts worked. That one of his officers,
no matter how junior, had a nobleman for a brother—a
French nobleman at that—would be a compelling reason
for Bazaine to know him. The marshal confirmed this
unspoken observation with his next words.

"Perhaps you and I should cultivate this Captain Gallimard, James. Are you by any chance acquainted with him?"
Unapologetic interest and excitement lifted his voice.

"Yes, sir. Quite well."

"Bon! Tell me, if you can, how long he has been a captain."

"I do not know exactly, but not really long enough for promotion if that is what the marshal is thinking. Promoting him ahead of some of the more experienced officers in his Chasseur regiment could provoke morale problems." That assessment with its careful hint of advice would probably disappoint Bazaine. James found he did not give a damn. He was in a well nigh rebellious mood this morning after the brief, fruitless session with the emperor last night. He had stopped his report to the monarch just short of being actually rude. He certainly had been critical, and His Imperial Majesty must have felt it. If the emperor had *not* noticed, Felix Eloin certainly would sooner or later have pointed it out to him.

His foul mood had also to do with not seeing Sarah before he returned to the Paseo—that and the appearance in the capital of the Frenchman Cipi had told him of more than two years ago, a man who might still be a rival.

"Pity." Bazaine sighed. "It would please the brother, and probably the emperor, too, were we to advance the young man's military career post haste, but of course you are right, colonel. Now . . . would you care to reprise your report to the emperor for your old commander?"

He told Bazaine then of the two near misses at Zacatecas: first, how close he had come to securing Juárez's agreement to the Imperial offer, and then how much closer the attempt had come to kill or capture the Republican president.

Bazaine's bushy eyebrows seemed to stand to attention. "The attack was not just a fortuitous accident?"

"No, sir. Not in my opinion. It had all the earmarks of something planned."

"Planned? By whom?"

"That I do not know, sir."

"But you have suspicions?"

"I am not entitled to have suspicions, sir."

"No. Not in the hearing of anyone at Chapultepec, I suppose. But here . . ." He paused. His amusement became even more pronounced. "How did you deal with this in your report to His Imperial Majesty?"

"I made him acquainted with the facts as I know them, sir."

"And without holding any of those facts back, am I right?"

"No, sir."

"Was Eloin present this time, too?"

"Yes."

"Perhaps that obsequious Belgian jackal engineered this idiocy."

"I considered that a possibility, but now I think not. It may have begun with him, of course, but he cannot order a military operation like the one at Zacatecas without the full approval of someone of higher rank."

"*Tu as raison.* And although he is a civilian, there is no one of higher rank in the Imperial government than Monsieur Eloin, except . . ."

Even safe from eavesdroppers here in Bazaine's banner-bedecked office it would be wisest not to respond to this.

"What was the emperor's reaction when you told him what happened at the *hacienda?*" Bazaine asked.

"He dismissed the entire incident with a wave of his hand."

"Was the wave a dismissal of the try for Benito Juárez—or for the failure of your mission?"

"Both, sir. It seemed that neither were of consequence to His Majesty."

"And you were furious, no? Be candid with me, James. You and I have never kept things from each other."

"I wasn't happy, *monsieur.*"

"And you said so?"

"I am afraid I did."

The marshal leaned back in his chair, put his fingertips together, and gazed up at the ceiling. The earlier look of tolerant good humor had vanished. "This, unfortunately, is the way the Austrian conducts his business. He is not a stupid man, and he certainly means well, but in his casual manner of coming to decisions, he trivializes even the most portentous matters. He has instituted government by whim, reserving his serious efforts for things such as that laughable thousand-page book of etiquette and protocol he has written for that assemblage of perfumed *mollassons* he calls a court. He pulls Márquez, his most effective general, out of the war, makes this overture to the Indian, throws it all away with this ridiculous attack—and then merely waves his hand. In the long run this cavalier attitude will cost him dearly. I might not always be here to save him from the consequences of such folly. And France might not be here. Emperor Napoleon does not intend us to maintain a presence indefinitely, in any event."

James would be here. His oath would keep him in Maximilian's service, and even if by some unthinkable concatenation of events or forces he released himself from his oath—and an apostasy such as that *was* unthinkable, was it not?—he would stay just as long as Sarah stayed.

Lord, how he missed her.

They had been together—or tantalizingly close to each other—for ten straight days and nights, and this first day of total separation hurt as much as would pulling a dressing from a wound that was not quite healed. He knew now he would never again breathe freely or happily in air she did not share. He had tried to see her after making his report.

When the emperor had left the office with a pleasant but brisk farewell and Eloin ushered him out, he had found the new Imperial secretary José Luis Blasio and asked if he could see her, only to be told that she had gone to the same dinner as had His Imperial Majesty. He had returned to the house on the Paseo in disappointment.

He hoped now that Bazaine would have some errand for him at the castle, something that had to be done this very morning. If not, he would simply have to dream up an excuse to go there on his own.

"Quite frankly, James," Bazaine said, "I never expected even as much as you got from the Indian. I was fully persuaded from the start that your mission would be an exercise in futility, but for a different reason. I thought the little Titan would reject the emperor's offers out of hand because of those Republican principles he espouses. He and his army must be in an even weaker position than I thought."

"With all respect, sir, I do not think the president came so quickly to agreement out of weakness. His military position is weak, of course, but I think he ultimately made the decision he did because he realized for the first time that he could do more for this country working with the Imperial government than against it."

"Well, in any event the die is cast. After what happened he will never change his mind, will he?"

"No, sir."

"It is now a duel to the death then. I look forward to it. We should strike hard without further delay. The United States, now that its own civil war is over, might feel free to indulge its quixotic idealism on an international scale again—increase its support for the Republicans, perhaps even enter the conflict on the Indian's behalf. Tell me something. You are still an American when all is said and done; that could happen, could it not?"

"Yes, sir." Not for the first time James considered the possibility that he might be asked to fight against his own countrymen. He had considered that back in Kansas. Aaron. How binding would his oath be if the United States did march on the empire? Thank God the possibility was remote.

Bazaine continued. "We must not waste another minute in this war." He left his desk, went to the window, placed his hands on the sill and looked out over the Zócalo. "And France will have to do it for that imbecile down at Chapultepec." James had never expected to hear anything like this, even from the outspoken marshal. There was more of it. "My emperor is getting sick of the way this one spends money on balls, dinners, and pomp. He must have given his favorites at least five costly *estancias* or whatever they are called this past year alone. He is draining his treasury as if it were a bathtub he could fill at will. Mark my words, James, one of these days he won't have the wherewithal to pay you—or *any* of his soldiers." He returned to his desk and sat down. He tilted his head toward the ceiling. "Please forget that, but let me know if it happens."

"Yes, sir."

"Enough of this. I am a little out of sorts today. Now to something much more important. Prepare yourself for travel, colonel. I want you to go to the northern front with me. Tomorrow." Bazaine had pulled his gaze from the ceiling, and had fixed his eyes on James again.

Never before had he felt reluctance about getting close to action or going into it. Now he could understand Boulanger's attitude in those first days after his discovery of Paola Kollonitz.

Bazaine went on. "My generals in the field there—especially those who are nominally under the command of the emperor—do not possess the Western world's finest military minds. We shall offer them the opportunity to make use of my intelligence and fighting skills . . . and yours."

The fact that Bazaine was thinking of returning him to combat, or at least to some proximity to it, and perhaps with a larger command position than he had ever held before as a likelihood, did have something to recommend it. There would be a chance at the one promotion he had never even dreamed about, never truly wanted until now. He had no doubt Bazaine's recommendation would ultimately wind up on the desk of Maximilian, and would probably outweigh any disadvantage brought about by his critical report last night—the emperor had shown himself a magnanimous ruler from the very start, when he must have been heartsick at the disappointing welcome accorded him and Empress Carlota.

James's ecstasy over what had happened between him and Sarah at Zacatecas had been tempered by a hard, honest, searching look at the respective places they occupied in the rigid Imperial society. She belonged there, he did not. Not only her wealth put her there; far more, it was her background, her place with the empress and her court, and

the genuine, soul-deep aristocracy she herself possessed, a
nobility infinitely more permanent than any brought about
by the bluest tint of blood.

Becoming a general officer of the Imperial Army would
not close the gap between them, but it would narrow it. For
one thing, crass at it seemed, money mattered. He had
done moderately well financially these past two years, but
there would be an enormous increase in his salary should
this once impossibly distant promotion come about. The
social advantages that would accrue could not be taken
lightly, either.

"When we go north together, sir, will I have a field
command?"

"I should not be too surprised, *mon fils*, if you had an
army of your very own." Jason James felt more confidence,
joy, and hope in that moment than he had ever known.
François-Achille Bazaine, Marshal of France, ratified it.

"You are a far cry, James," he said, "from the courageous
but relatively unsophisticated Legion captain I first met at
Jalapa. I look forward to having such a distinguished
Imperial officer serving with me as we bring this war to a
glorious conclusion."

38

▲▲▲▲▲

When they left Charlotte's dining salon Henri turned
strangely quiet.

She dreaded shattering that calm, but telling him of the
monumental change in her life and affections could wait no
longer. Her first wrenching inclination to postpone inflicting pain would not in the long run lessen it.

He walked her to her living quarters in what seemed a
cloud of silence, and at her door she turned to invite him in
to her sitting room.

"We must talk, Henri."

"I know, I know, *mon amour* . . ." he said. "Of course we must talk. And at great length. We have much to discuss, about our past, and of course about our future. But—*pardonne-moi, ma chère*, I am too tired to embark upon a protracted talk tonight. *Oui, je suis très fatigué.*" He did look tired, worn almost to exhaustion. The dinner must have taken a toll on him, too, if in a different way. He smiled a wan smile. "I promise we *will* talk, and soon."

As much as she wanted to put a difficult moment behind her, she could not hold him here to the point of possible collapse. "All right, Henri. What I have to say can wait until morning . . . I suppose."

"*Merci, ma chère.* You are the most understanding *fiancée* any man could ask for. *Bonne nuit.*"

She offered her cheek as she had so many times in Paris, expecting the same soft, affectionate brush of his lips that ended an afternoon of touring a new exhibit at the Louvre, an evening at a *fête*, or one spent at dinner with the Pelletiers or at the opera. Now, to her mild surprise, he took her chin in his hand and turned her face toward his firmly. His free arm slid around her waist. For gentle Henri it seemed extraordinarily bold behavior.

Her thoughts flicked suddenly to Jason as their lips met, but she decided just as suddenly that there could be no harm in this old and familiar farewell-for-the-moment, and she returned the kiss.

Was there on his part a touch of desperation in his kiss? It would not make telling him of her love for Jason any easier, and it heightened the embarrassed confusion in which she had left Charlotte, Max, and the others, all of them still buzzing from Max's expansive pronouncements.

She was still dizzied by them herself, and still embarrassed, first by her own necessary silence about everything Max said, and her persistent self-accusation about the hypocrisy of the situation forced on her.

As if all that were not embarrassing enough, she had next squirmed through an endless round of best wishes from the women. Worst of all, she was finally and absolutely shocked to the core at Max's offer of La Mesa Encantada as a wedding gift. What sort of ingrate would she appear if she turned it down? Not if—*when*.

"Good night, my love," Henri said.

She stayed in her doorway for a moment, and as she watched him walk down the lamplit corridor, her regret that she had not insisted on the talk that *had* to come was washed away by a wave of gratitude that—other than the embrace and kiss—he had made no move to press any advantage he might have thought the evening had given him.

Before he reached the end of the hall leading to the wing holding the suite of rooms prepared for him he suddenly staggered, put his arm against the wall to steady himself, and leaned there for a long moment. She almost ran to him, but before she could move he righted himself and moved on out of sight.

Henri did not appear at breakfast nor at any time during the long morning.

As she might have expected, Paola had the answer when they met before lunch. "The emperor abducted your sweet cavalier at dawn, *liebchen*. They have gone down to Cuernavaca to inspect your wedding gift, the *hacienda* near La Borda Quintas." The countess's smile was a deliberately teasing one.

"He didn't tell me."

"He probably did not learn of the trip himself until the emperor sent for him. You know Henri. He would never awaken you that early."

"But he could have left a note." She very nearly blurted out her irritation to Paola, but, after all, Henri had not left her in the lurch for a frivolous day of wagering on the races at Beauchamps; it was a trip with the Emperor of Mexico, a command performance. "When will Max and Henri return?"

"Not for a week or more, I should imagine."

"Why so long? A day down and a day back should do it."

"I think perhaps the emperor has interests in Cuernavaca besides your wedding gift."

Unless Sarah saw Jason, a week loomed before she could have the talk with him *or* Henri.

"I'm in trouble, Paola."

Paola eyed her shrewdly, then her full mouth popped open. "*Gott im Himmel!* You're in *trouble*? Don't tell me you've gotten yourself pregnant on the first try! Why did you not listen to Paola?" Her eyes widened. "It's Jason, isn't it? *Ja!* You two must have been up to something long before you left last week."

"No, I'm not pregnant! It certainly isn't *that*, Paola. It's just that I must tell Henri about Jason. If I wait much longer, it will be even worse for him."

Paola's face clouded. "You have no need to tell him, *liebchen.*"

"Yes, I do. He is entitled to—"

"Patience. I'm not giving you unwanted advice again. I did not say you *shouldn't* tell him, even though that still *is* my thought. I merely said you *needn't*. The truth is that Henri already knows about Jason. At least he knows you two have been frequent and, for all he knows, intimate companions these last few months."

"But how . . . ?"

"*Mein Gott!* You are such an incredible *naïf*. If some compulsive, troublemaking busybody here at the castle—and they hide in every closet and lurk behind every last bush in the gardens—did not make *sure* he knew, his brother Marcel would have felt it his duty to tell him."

"None of this alters the fact that I should have written Henri about Jason long ago. I should never have left it to the last minute as I did, but I wanted to tell him face to face."

"Do not be so hard on yourself. Henri's finding out in that way also was quite unnecessary. Sooner or later he would have guessed—without *anyone* actually telling him. As innocent as you say your *liaison* with Jason has been,

Henri Gallimard is no fool, nor is he totally unworldly. As a Frenchman, he certainly must realize a desirable young woman could not be left alone with her own quite natural urges for this length of time without getting involved in some way with *someone*. If I know French noblemen—and I do, in every way it is possible for a woman to know them— he has surely had involvements of his own this last three years that he expects *you* to wink at, some that would make someone like you blush. But do not let any of this worry you. His look last night told our small world he still has every intention of taking you to the altar, even if you and Jason *have* become lovers."

Sarah felt slightly sick to her stomach. She would never think as Paola thought, and if she had not known it before, she knew she would never want to.

But . . .

Paola's news about Henri already knowing cropped one horn of her dilemma, if not as neatly and cleanly as she had wanted. With Henri gone to Cuernavaca for a week or more, she now had plenty of time to saw off the other horn by telling *Jason*.

The opportunity did not come.

There was a brief note from him the morning following the dinner, informing her that until some things about the Zacatecas trip were sorted out he would be on call for Marshal Bazaine and staying in one of the rooms for transient officers at the Marshal's headquarters in the Imperial Palace. She waited all afternoon of the day after Charlotte's dinner, and all through the following day and night without another word from him. She grew impatient, and ached with longing. She wrote to him, sending her letter to the palace by Imperial courier. She begged to see him, here at Chapultepec, at Avenida Moctezuma, at the Mirador or anywhere he chose—and at anytime.

After another three hand-wringing days of waiting, no answer from Jason had as yet arrived at Chapultepec.

An exquisite irony marked the simultaneous absences of

both Henri Gallimard and Jason James. At the door to Charlotte's gem of a *salle-à-manger* Paola had assured her that she looked *wunderbar* in her dark blue velvet gown. At the end of the affair she had been inundated by the envy growing in at least some of the women there after Max's generous remarks and even more generous offer of the Cuernavaca *hacienda*. She had left the dinner with two handsome men in tow, one of them at hand and obviously doting on her, and the other—from what Paola had just said—no secret to anyone in the gathering, and no secret, it seemed, to Henri, either.

Yes, she had two men then. Now, if only for the moment, she had none.

She was finally able to rid herself of a major fraction of her impatience with some unexpected help from an unlikely quarter, that of the Empress of Mexico.

In the days since the dinner Charlotte had begun to pay more attention to her than at any time since she came to the castle. The empress insisted she join her at breakfast the second morning after the dinner, and today had sent word through Paola that she was to accompany her in her ritual late twilight stroll through Chapultepec's gardens, an honor formerly reserved for Melanie Zichy and in recent days the new arrival at court, Princess Agnes Salm-Salm, to whom Paola seemed to have taken an instant dislike and with whom Sarah had not as yet exchanged a dozen words. Charlotte never had taken more than one of her favorites with her at such times, and even Paola—to that ordinarily insouciant lady's chagrin—had not yet received an invitation to these quiet promenades at vespers.

"I will admit I am jealous of the Salm-Salm woman," Paola said after she relayed Charlotte's request. "She is an upstart, and is now intruding more and more on Melanie's and my running of the household. She fastens herself to Max like a leech every chance she gets. I have no wish to start gossip, but there are times she acts as if she wants to take *Charlotte's* place."

"But Agnes has never had so much as one audience with Max."

"*I* have seen to that. I put a bug in Melanie's ear and she has managed to keep the Salm-Salm from bothering the emperor, but the trollop is using all her false charm on Blasio and everyone else close to him."

There was no doubt that Princess Salm-Salm was every bit as confident and flamboyant as Paola at her best—or worst. Actually, Sarah herself had seen little of Agnes since her arrival at the castle. She had moved in during Sarah's trip to Zacatecas and had quickly gathered about her a coterie of new, admiring friends, some of them, unfortunately, former intimates of Paola's.

"Why do you refer to her as an upstart?" Sarah asked.

"She is common, *liebchen!* An impostor. Not really one of *us.*"

"For heaven's sake, Paola, neither am I."

"You case is quite different. You do not pretend. No one knows much about her. She lets people think she is an American, but the way she speaks French and German gives her away. She rode her way into the court on her husband's back, just as she rode trick horses in the circuses of Europe. She puts him through his paces when he is here at the castle, and he can't shake the bit from his teeth. He is a gelding! I think that is why he keeps a room in the Imperial Palace. Agnes Salm-Salm is a social climber of the most despicable sort. A horseback rider, bah!"

Sarah did know the stories which had run through the castle about the graceful Agnes having been a circus rider at one time, but her understanding was that it was as an amateur, something not too much at odds with the eccentric behavior of other aristocrats in this day and age. Colonel Miguel López, for instance, was a gentleman bullfighter, and he was by all appearances no Mexican commoner. It was unlike usually tolerant Paola to even bring this up.

Although Paola disparaged Agnes's husband along with

the princess, there seemed to be no doubt about the social standing of Prince Felix Zu Salm-Salm, at least in the view of the other residents. Sarah had seen him only once since the couple arrived in the capital as latecomers to the court at Chapultepec. Prince Salm-Salm had busied himself on maneuvers with a regiment in the army of General Miramón.

The prince, youngest son of an old family in southern Germany, had come into Austria to escape an avalanche of debt. He had then served in the army of Franz Joseph as a cavalry officer until detouring through the United States to fight as a Union general until that war ended. No one at Chapultepec asked why a *Union* officer would choose to come to Mexico to wield his sword in the service of Maximilian rather than Juárez. The word was that he had met and married Agnes in Washington. New members of the court circle were always bright torches for a while; the couple, making their appearance in such a dismal social season, burned a bit more brightly because of it perhaps.

But Paola was right about one thing: Princess Agnes was the more incandescent of the two newcomers. She reveled in court life, and it did not seem to trouble her that her husband was seldom around. Perhaps she looked on his absence as a blessing, at the very least a convenience. Her undisguised, highly vocal infatuation with Maximilian the past few months—even if she had never yet been alone with him—bordered on the scandalous. Sarah wondered idly—and took herself to task for it—if the rumored gardener's daughter at Cuernavaca would be replaced if Max and Agnes ever really found themselves thrown together. The woman was certainly attractive enough to catch the Imperial eye.

"Make no mistake, though, *liebchen*," Paola said now. "I am happy for *you* that Charlotte wants you to walk with her. You deserve some *good* fortune for a change, since you still seem to think having *two* eligible men courting you is *not* good fortune."

* * *

At first Sarah thought Charlotte's suddenly rekindled interest in her was due to the hubbub at the dinner about her "engagement" to Henri. She wondered if she could now begin to work free of the trap she had entered so unwittingly, and let Charlotte break the news to Max that she had no intention of marrying Monsieur Le Comte de Bayeux. She was not afraid to tell the emperor herself—provided he would make time for her—but there was little point in risking injury to his Imperial feelings and to the career of Jason James.

It would be difficult enough telling the empress, she thought when she met Charlotte at sundown by the postern gate in Chapultepec's high west wall.

With relief she realized she could tell neither of the Imperial couple about her decision until she told Henri first.

"I would like to hear *everything* about the trip to Zacatecas and the meeting you and Colonel James had with Benito Juárez," Charlotte said.

I would like . . . ? No royal "we"? Sarah was not sure whether it was the suddenly expressed interest in the trip north or the restored intimacy subtly implied by Charlotte's use of "I" which pleased her most.

There came now a deep swell of satisfaction that Charlotte had expressed interest in Jason's and her journey and the upshot of it. At least someone in the Imperial bed seemed to care. She still did not know how Max had greeted Jason's account of Zacatecas, but from the fact that she had picked up no rumors around the castle, and that Felix Eloin was apparently avoiding her, she could guess.

The flowered path they walked led around to the north wall, and they soon stood under the battlements where she had gone to Jason the day Ignacio Comonfort took them to the roof.

She glanced up just once. The two old cannons seemed in the same place, still aimed at some vanished army. Some day, perhaps, Jason would tell her what had gone through his mind as she watched him.

Charlotte broke into those thoughts as sharply as if one of the cannons had spoken.

"What went wrong in Zacatecas?"

Sarah related the story of their meetings with Juárez, fully expecting when she finished that Charlotte would heap all the blame for the breakdown in the negotiations on him. It did not happen.

"My heart is sick, Sarah, that this *rapprochement* did not work. I was ready to accept President Juárez as a partner, and so was Max."

Genuine sorrow played a counterpoint to the words, but Sarah wondered if the last bit, about *Max's* willingness to have the embattled president of the Republic join him in his government, was really true. Charlotte probably thought it was, but perhaps, for all her keen interest in the workings of the Imperial government, she was not privy enough to the influence of Felix Eloin, even if Max's private secretary was a Belgian like herself and as much a faithful servant of King Leopold as of Max.

"I suppose it cannot be helped now, Sarah," Charlotte went on, "but I do so wish the attack on the president had not happened. Someone committed a blunder that comes dangerously close to treason."

"I must confess, Your Majesty, that what happened has brought me almost to the point of leaving my position here at court."

"Heaven forbid! Sarah! We need you."

"It must come someday . . . Charlotte." The old first name had slipped out, but a quick glance told her it apparently met with no objection.

"Please, please do not mention leaving again, *ma chère.*" She placed a hand on Sarah's shoulder. "We have not spent the time together I would have liked—but I cannot bear to think of Chapultepec without you. *Je t'aime. Vraiment.*" The Charlotte of St. Catherine's had returned. Sarah felt a glow of warmth toward the sad, dark woman such as she had not felt since her first days at the castle.

Charlotte continued. "I can assure you Max regrets what

happened to President Juárez, too. Unfortunately he does not think it quite the disaster I do. He is always too much the optimist. He believes all will turn out well in the end. I, on the other hand, fear for Mexico. This terrible war must stop. Sadly, because I am more of a realist than most people close to Max think I am, I know that since this attempt at treating with the president of this so-called Republic failed so miserably, we and the French will unfortunately have to crush Señor Juárez and his followers now. I do not think they will trust any offers of peace we make after what happened at Zacatecas. I cannot blame them, but it now means there is no other course but continuing the war."

She shuddered and drew her wrap more tightly around her slim shoulders, but not because of any sudden cold. "I only hope we can achieve victory quickly; the cost to both sides might not be so great in that event. I do not wish the death of one single Mexican." She paused. Something like a sob came, and she covered her mouth quickly for a moment before going on. "There is another reason to move rapidly in a military way. Please do not repeat this, Sarah, but I fear as much as anything else that Emperor Napoleon is losing his enthusiasm for this venture. It would be more difficult to defeat the Republicans without the French." She paused for a moment, then went, but now her tone became as sharp as a stiletto. The Imperial Carlota was back again. "I fear I *know* what is in Louis Napoleon's mind. And it is not *fair!* He seduced Max and me into accepting the crowns we wear. He cannot shirk his responsibilities, either to Mexico or to us. If he does, I will shame him before all of Europe—and the world. I swear I will!"

At the last a terrible, wild gleam lit her dark eyes. The gleam dwindled in seconds, but its afterglow lingered in Sarah's vision long after they turned and retraced their steps to the postern gate.

One thing the walk had provided Sarah: a new view of Her Imperial Majesty Empress Carlota as a knowledgeable and courageous practitioner of the art of statecraft. Except for that one heartfelt moment Charlotte von Coburg was no longer the impulsive, moody, but all-too-often frivolous schoolmate from St. Catherine's. She was now a shrewd, thoughtful, mature, and quite obviously intelligent woman. Her husband Max would be well advised to listen to her at least as attentively as he listened to Felix Eloin.

He needed one more advisor.

After watching Jason deal with President Juárez at Zacatecas, Sarah was fully persuaded that Maximilian could do far worse than listen to Sarah's colonel.

Only two things worried her aside from why Jason had not come to call or gotten a message to her much sooner since their return: the manic glint in Charlotte's eyes still danced in front of *hers* even after she closed them in bed that night; and the vulnerability the empress had revealed when she implored Sarah not to leave the Imperial service lingered, too.

A letter from Jason came at last, delivered to her by José Luis Blasio, the modest, reticent young Mexican whom Max a few months earlier had appointed as his personal private secretary. She liked José Luis, but she almost screamed at him when she discovered the letter had been in his hands two days.

"I am sorry, Doña Sarah. It was mixed in with the correspondence that came from French headquarters at the Palacio."

She did not even wait until she got to her room. Her hands shook as she tore it open.

My dearest Sarah—

Please accept my apologies for the tardiness of this letter. It was necessary to hold its delivery back for several days for compelling reasons of security.

By the time you read this, Marshal Bazaine and I will be with the armies in the north. With the failure at Zacatecas behind us, it has now been decided that all-out war against our Indian friend must be pressed in earnest. I feel deep regret that this has come to pass, but it does mean that certain personal advantages may come my way.

If all goes as the marshal plans, I will be given command of an army in the field. I know this sort of thing brings you no pleasure and I fully understand that.

Please believe me when I tell you that this might, in the long run, bring us even closer than we found ourselves to be at Zacatecas.

I also feel, and I trust this *will* bring you happiness, that this campaign will be my last. For the moment I cannot say more, but my career as a professional soldier could end with the next series of battles. Please believe me when I say that I have absolutely no misgivings about that possibility. Am I being too hopeful when I tell you how happy it makes me that there is a chance I may become more of the man you wish me to become?

I trust I am not living in ignorance or in some fool's paradise in thinking that you indeed do care.

As for myself, all that remains to be said—and I say this with all my heart every moment of every day—is that . . .

—I love you
Jason

It brought her mixed feelings of joy and sorrow. Joy to have heard from him, sorrow that it meant she still would not see him for a torment of time.

The sticky task of telling him about Henri, and Henri about him, could wait.

Charlotte could not possibly desire a quick end to the fighting more fervently than did Sarah Anderson.

From everything she saw, read, heard, or felt it seemed as certain as the never-failing sunrise that Maximilian I, Emperor of Mexico, and Benito Pablo Juárez, President of the Republic, had now set themselves upon a course straight for Armageddon—for at least one of them.

In this struggle she had run a narrow road between the thickets on the one side and the marshes on the other; she had tried with all her might not to wish failure—or success—for either one of them.

What she told Charlotte on their first vesper walk together, that the betrayal at Zacatecas—she could no longer persuade herself even for a second that it was an accident—had caused her to consider leaving, had slipped out. She had not known before the slip that her doubts ran quite so deep, but when she heard herself say it, she knew it for the truth.

Her consideration of the rights and wrongs of what was happening in Mexico was no longer—if it ever truly had been—a purely intellectual exercise; real people were shedding real blood, dying real deaths, and filling real graves.

There were real people still living, too.

After the affair at the *hacienda* her long-time respect for Benito Juárez had turned to genuine affection. She knew she would feel more than a little of the agony the president would feel if he lost. To Juárez, his dream for Mexico was not just a special something; it was *everything*.

For Maximilian, on the other hand, who could always return to Miramar, Mexico was a fascinating, complicated toy, one that he showed signs of losing interest in whenever it failed to work exactly the way he wanted it to work.

It should be an easy matter for Sarah Anderson to decide exactly where her loyalty should be given in this hateful conflict.

But there remained one other real, living person to unbalance the equation.

Charlotte.

Wait. There was Jason, too.

PART FOUR

▲▲▲▲▲▲▲▲▲▲

THE HOLLOW CROWN

". . . and humour'd thus,
Comes at the last, and with a little pin
Bores through his castle wall . . ."

— RICHARD II

39

▲▲▲▲▲

Bazaine erected his headquarters tent, the same bright, billowing pavilion he used at Puebla and San Lorenzo—flying his personal battle ensign and the faded old tri-color he had taken to every war he had fought for France through Sebastopol and Spain—in the rolling *lomas* eighteen kilometers northeast of Ciudad Chihuahua, nearly at the foot of La Sierra de la Virgen.

James thought the position a trifle exposed if Republican reinforcements for the defense of the city, or some new striking force, were to come down the El Paso del Norte–Chihuahua highroad in any strength. But it did afford an excellent view of the other main road, from Ojinaga, the border crossing-point facing Presidio, Texas across the Rio. And it gave the three new Chasseur cavalry regiments under General Aymard which had come north with them—one of them commanded, James was happy to discover, by Pierre Boulanger—a chance to monitor the munition and supply trains from Juárez's agents in the United States as they crossed the high Chihuahuan desert. When Bazaine had James pass on orders to Aymard and his Chasseurs that they were not to offer or provoke combat, but only to look on and make tallies—and put on a brave show—he wondered about the wisdom of the marshal's decision. But French Army intelligence must have discounted any effect the supply trains might have on the outcome of the battle for Chihuahua.

"Tell General Aymard and his Chasseur colonels that interdiction will come in due time, colonel. At the moment we have not built up the strength in this sector necessary to stop every one of them," Bazaine said. "So, *mon ami* . . . since we *can't* stop them all, we shall go ahead and let them supply the Chihuahua garrison, and try to make it look as if we had planned it this way. It might give them pause .if we do *not* attack their trains. Mejía and Brincourt will have to keep the city under heavy siege and force them to use up that valuable ammunition while we await more infantry and artillery from the capital. Patience, Colonel." He smiled. "Such advice applies to me as well."

Clearly, James was not to get his army quite yet. Only three squadrons of his own regiment, the Imperial Seventh, had reached the staging area assigned to it, and Bazaine had so far made no mention of any additional troops, horse or foot, Imperial or French, scheduled to report to him. He wanted to hurry the process along, and to that end he decided to try to talk the marshal into pulling Pierre Boulanger's Chasseur regiment away from General Aymard and the inconsequential duties of scouting, and placing them under his command. It would be a grudging assent if he got it. Bazaine did not really relish the idea of throwing together French and Imperial commanders at anything less than brigade level, particularly when the French officer did not have at *least* equal standing to his counterpart of any other nationality: Austrian, Belgian, Mexican, or in James's own unique case, American. Even in "the finest army in the world" everything still came down to politics.

James finally turned the trick by gaining an audience with Bazaine in his tent and reminding him of how well he and Pierre had worked together in the great victory at San Lorenzo and then by adding, "It would probably solve things from your point of view, sir, were you to promote Major Boulanger to the rank I hold."

Bazaine, shaving at the time, waved his razor as if it were a saber. "If I promote Boulanger, would there not be morale problems among the Chasseurs, as you feared in the case of Captain Gallimard?"

"None, sir. Unlike Gallimard, Major Boulanger has far more than enough time-in-grade for promotion, and he is also one of the most popular Chasseur officers in the army. I truly believe there would be general rejoicing at his good fortune."

Marcel Gallimard had not come up the line with Bazaine and James, as had Boulanger, so no one would hear a complaint from him very soon. To be charitable, the Comte de Bayeux's brother was not shirking combat; Emperor Maximilian himself had asked Bazaine to place him on temporary duty at Chapultepec, to serve as an equerry to his brother for the next month. And to be fair as well as charitable, he could guess the hot-headed, foolhardy Gallimard already steamed with frustration.

"*Très bien,*" Bazaine grunted, not too grudgingly. "Have Lemonde cut the order promoting Major Boulanger to colonel, and I will sign it." He laid his razor in the wash basin, toweled the last of the lather from his face, rolled his eyes up toward the ridgepole of the tent, and sighed. "I dread the day, James, when you at long last begin to labor as diligently on your own behalf as you do for your friend. A mere Marshal of France would be a poor match for your powers of persuasion. I am not surprised that you did so well with our enemy Juárez when you met with him. I think I would even trust you with this whole campaign sooner than I would any of my *present* generals."

"*Merci beaucoup, Monsieur le Marechal.*"

"Something I must also tell you, James," Bazaine went on. "In spite of what you described as a somewhat bald and brutal report you made to His Imperial Majesty about the happenings at Zacatecas, the Austrian bears you no ill will. Quite the contrary. When I saw him just before we came north he told me he was actually very pleased with the way you conducted matters with the Indian. He hinted at plans for you, saying that if or when you decide to leave the Imperial Army as a serving officer, there will be a high position waiting for you in his civil government. I would do some serious thinking about that, *mon cher ami.* The empire of Mexico bestows much greater financial rewards on its administrators than it does on its generals. I know as a matter of cold fact that the salary of Felix Eloin is three times that of General Miramón."

While James reeled a little at this disclosure, the marshal went on to offer another odd bit of intelligence, vaguely disturbing in the light of what he had just confided.

"By the by," he said, "I have also discovered something that might be of interest to you. I shared a camp dinner with some Mexican friends in Mejía's army last night. I was quite surprised to find that you will not be the only American officer taking part in the battle for this sprawling pigsty called Chihuahua. Nor, oddly enough, the one of the highest rank—at the moment."

"Sir?"

"Since your country's own civil conflict ended, a number of generals from the defeated Confederate forces have apparently drifted down into Coahuila and Nuevo Leon, looking for work. Some of them even have some insane idea that they can re-establish their Confederacy in Mexico's northern states. Most are military men of great professional reputation even before the war between your states, graduates of Point West or whatever you Americans call your St. Cyr. I understand some civilians have made the move down here, too, buying land for plantations in the hope of re-creating the South they come from. A few actually brought black slaves with them." A shudder signaled his disgust.

"But the emperor will not permit them to settle in Mexico if they still hold slaves," James said. How had Maximilian put it that night aboard the *Novara*? *"Slavery is an abomination under heaven, and it revolts us."*

"I would not be too sure of that, *mon ami*. Emperor Max has in recent months developed an extraordinary fascination with expedience."

Surely Bazaine was wrong about that. But then Zacatecas came to mind. "Do you have to accept these Confederate officers, sir? You are, after all, the emperor's commander-in-chief."

"I command all his *armies,* true—but I have little say in how they are put together. You yourself are one of the last officers for whom I was able to secure a good posting. There are limits to my power. These Southern generals have an envoy on his way to the capital to confer with Emperor Max at the moment. No one asked me about any of this. A year ago they would have. I really only mentioned all this because I thought perhaps it would amuse you to socialize with some of your countrymen, whether you share their views or not."

Jason remembered that Bazaine had never once pressed him for his beliefs about the causes of the violence that had raged across the entire eastern half of the United States this last four years.

And the marshal probably would never inquire as to whether he had "socialized" with these new arrivals or not.

He had absolutely no intention of doing so.

With nothing demanding too much of his time, he found the forward bivouac area occupied by the 14th Regiment of the Legion, and had a talk with Jean-Claude duBecq. He did not recognize a single face among the Legionnaires lounging nearest him and the sergeant. Casualties in his old unit must have been horrendous. His old comrade seemed glad to see him and returned James's embrace wholeheartedly, but turned guarded and faintly distant when the new commanding officer of Compagnie Rouge, one Captain Gaston LeRoi—a suave young man with the unmistakable whiff of St. Cyr about him—wandered up and demanded an introduction to "his excellency the Imperial Colonel," said as if James were the only such creature in existence.

James left quickly after that, to the obvious relief of Jean-Claude. DuBecq was probably going to have to answer a lot of questions about the "Imperial colonel," and what in the name of propriety he was doing embracing such an exalted personage as if he were a brother.

James shook his head in sadness after he mounted his horse and rode off. There were, it seemed, some places to which one could never return. But there was, too, still a lot of soldiering left to do.

With only one regiment, Boulanger's, and only a fraction of the Imperial Seventh in the field, his command—if it were truly *his*—hardly constituted an army. Jean-Claude's St. Cyrian captain would rethink "Imperial colonel," and then sniff contempt if he knew the present minuscule size of James's force.

The way things were going it might take a while before he became a general, although Cipi, as was to be expected, made his usual sanguine prediction.

"You are headed straight for the Imperial general staff, *mi colonel.* Cipi guarantees it."

"When?"

"That, of course, is impossible to tell, but it most certainly will happen."

Lord how he wanted to believe him! Of course, if he took the little brute's pronouncements about his professional future as gospel, would he not have to credit as well the dwarf's prophecy about his death which Sofía reported in that last, painful talk they had together? He could not ask Cipi.

For weeks after that difficult talk with Sofía strong doubts had eaten at him about his decision to let her stay in his service, but gradually, as they both seemed to ease their way back into the master and servant roles—he felt disgusted at that characterization—of the earliest days in Jalapa, he began to feel it *could* work out as she promised. He could not be sure she deliberately avoided all close contact with him, but he saw very little of her. There was some residual, acid guilt whenever he thought about how the severance must seem to her—as it still did to him—that he had used her cruelly, but on the few occasions when their eyes met he found not a shadow of accusation. At last he stopped looking for it. Since that night when she left his room with the door ajar, they had not uttered a single word to each other except those few necessary to her management of his household. He could not remember one time when Cipi spoke to him about her in any other way than as a servant, either.

But he knew that sooner or later he would have to tell Sarah about Sofía, would have to in order to live not only with Sarah, but with the man he saw in his mirror each morning; when that happened, the girl simply could not be part of the *menage* of Jason James, no matter how far in the past their affair might by that time have become.

Funny that Cipi had made so few predictions about *Sarah*. His restraint was not due to any sense of circumspection. If anything, he was an even bolder rascal since he masqueraded as Benito Juárez in the great escape from Zacatecas, at least now that his salt-and-pepper beard was reaching something of its former fullness. The dwarf and Sarah had been thrown together with increasing frequency in recent months, and James thought it might prompt something. Perhaps the answer to Cipi's silence in this regard lay in that same close proximity; perhaps his powers as a seer worked better at a distance. He was, for instance, turning his inner eye—and his perpetually wagging tongue—more and more on the doings in the capital and the south now that he and James seemed to be settling into preparations for what Bazaine swore would be the final battle for the north and one of the very last for total control of all of Mexico. He still did not bring Sarah's name up in his predictions, but there were enough of them dealing with politics and the war. Some of it, of course, sprang as much from the darts of gossip that came to him like flies to honey as it did from any exercise of his self-proclaimed "black powers."

"By the end of this year, *mi coronel,*" he announced one day in front of Pierre, "there will be an heir to the throne of Mexico."

"Nonsense," James said. "When I saw the empress a mere three weeks ago, she certainly did not appear as if she could possibly give birth to a child by New Year's Day."

"Of course not. Cipi did not say she would. She will never produce a child. It is impossible for her to become *embarazada;* she is as barren as a dry well in the *desierto.* You must have heard 'Mama Carlota,' the vulgar song about her failure to conceive which the Republicans and even some of the Conservatives have been singing this past year. She and the emperor will adopt a child."

Pierre laughed. "This opinionated miniature may just be on to something this time, Jason. The 'heir' he speaks of may be *le petit enfant* Agustín Iturbide."

"Who?"

"The two-year-old grandson of that martyred old fraud Agustín I."

"Where did you hear all this?"

"Paola. Just last month the emperor brought the infant and his aunt to live in the castle. The reason given out was that it was done for their protection, but hell, they were living in complete safety somewhere in the United States. Cipi is quite correct when he says the empress cannot bear children. Publicly she stands four-square behind our magnificent Max on this Iturbide business, but Paola says that in private she is hurting terribly. I personally think she is lucky her husband has not chosen to provide himself with an heir in the more usual way. He could have quite easily gotten one from that *señorita* in Cuernavaca with whom he makes the beast with two backs whenever Carlota is out of town."

"This, I suppose, comes from Paola, too?"

"*Certainement!* The Austrian virtually lived at La Borda something-or-other, the *estancia* in Cuernavaca where the young lady's father is head gardener, while the empress made her triumphal tour of the Yucatan last year."

"Also from Paola?"

"*Oui, mon ami.*"

"You're as much of an old woman for gossip as this little monster here, Pierre. And Countess von Kollonitz is not a bit better."

"Be that as it may, Jason," Pierre went on. "There may be an Agustín II in the offing if this Hapsburg house of cards holds up."

He wanted to ask Pierre if, in his opinion, the house of cards *would* hold up, but for some strange reason he did not want to ask him in front of Cipi. Was it because of that other prediction, the one about him and some man he had known a "long, long time" that the dwarf monster had hallucinated?

When he questioned Cipi about where *he* had picked up the Iturbide rumor the dwarf waved his hand loftily. "I *saw* it, *señor*."

Cipi's next prophecy, about something touching on the war, was straightforward, to the point, and—unlike the vague one of James being "headed straight for the Imperial general staff," when he refused to name a time—so specific as to constitute a risk to its tiny author, if only to his own view of himself. James and Boulanger could easily check this one when the time for it to happen came and went.

"*Señor El General* Porfirio Diaz will break out of the mountains of Oaxaca by exactly this time next year and will fall on the capital itself less than six months after that."

Pierre, on hand this time, too, with a bottle he had brought along to celebrate his promotion, gave a low whistle. "*Sacrebleu!* What response will *le maréchal* make, Cipi? How will he go about crushing General Díaz, because he *will* crush him, mark my words." That Pierre had not laughed outright persuaded James the Chasseur still put considerable stock in Cipi's predictions.

"*Señor* Marshal Bazaine will have taken ship for France by that time, Colonel Boulanger. The French Army will have left Mexico by then, too."

Well, the little weasel had very definitely put himself on the hook this time. To the surprise of neither James nor Pierre, he did not look remotely worried. He probably thought his swift tongue could explain everything when events proved him wrong.

Part of the prediction could well be a possibility, though. James remembered Bazaine's warning that Maximilian could not expect French help forever.

In the not too distant past he would have soon forgotten even something as stunning as this, but the episode triggered his thinking about some things to which he had never given deep, serious consideration.

For three years he had come close to only two men other than Jean-Claude duBecq—he surely could not call his relationship with Bazaine a close one—and now the good old Alsatian seemed lost to him. It left only Cipriano Méndez y García and Pierre Lucien Boulanger. He had fought alongside both of them, faced death with Pierre more than once, and he could never let himself forget how Cipi had saved his life on the field of San Lorenzo.

But—although he had watched their several reactions to individual occurrences, he truly had no genuine knowledge of how either of them felt about the things happening on the grand scale here in Mexico.

Cipi was not—as he had been quick to point out the day he and James met in that smoky cantina in Veracruz—a native Mexican, although from what James ultimately learned in bits and pieces about his history, some of it from Sofía when they were still talking, he might as well have been.

His parents, Reynoso and Favela Méndez y García, both normal sized, poor but somehow well-educated Madrilenos, had come to Mexico from Spain when the little man was only three, brought to this country as high level household servants by an enormously wealthy Spanish *hennequen* planter in Campeche who wanted to keep his children's, and his own, Iberian heritage intact and simon pure. The mother was employed as a companion and *dueña* to the planter's three daughters, the father as a tutor to the son and heir. The planter took a liking to Cipi—he swore he brought him good luck according to the dwarf—and raised him virtually as a second son. It answered the question about Cipi's devotion to René Descartes.

Whatever luck Cipi brought the old man, it did not sustain him long.

Irregulars serving under Padre Hidalgo murdered the entire family, along with Cipi's mother and father late in the War of Independence. Cipi's memory of how *he* escaped the massacre was unclear, had apparently fogged over as he grew to pitifully stunted manhood. One thing *was* clear, however. From that date forward the dwarf harbored sublime contempt for politics. One other thing was clear as well: Cipi was somewhat older than James had thought him the first two years they were together.

Pierre—almost from the first day they met on the mission to bring French wounded out of Orizaba, which resulted in the "incident" at Fortín—had been an incessant outspoken critic of his country's *military* conduct of the war. But he had been fairly noncommittal about its grander policies and politics. Perhaps he was exactly what he appeared to be and nothing more: a professional soldier.

James now found he had little but some sporadic training exercises to keep him occupied during the buildup Bazaine was masterminding before he lifted Brincourt's and Mejía's siege of the city and sent out his mighty, combined Army of the North on a genuine offensive against Chihuahua. It gave him entirely too much time for thinking.

He shook his head at just how much that thinking had changed since the meeting with Juárez in Zacatecas.

The things he had said to the president in those last doomed seconds before Antonio Pérez rode up Sierra Verde's road with the warning that vaporized their agreement had not been mere, convenient contrivances uttered only to *secure* that agreement. Although they were sentiments he had never actually voiced before, he found he meant every single one of them as sincerely as he had ever meant anything in his life.

But his oath to the emperor as a soldier still bound him to the Imperial cause.

He had lived by oaths since long before he reached full manhood. Along with all the Voltaire, Keats, Gibbon, and Macaulay, Aaron had pounded the sacredness of a soldier's oath into his young head, and he had remained grateful to his cousin at least for that; living by his oath had simplified his existence.

There had been the one cataclysmic moment of doubt when he finally faced up to the unwelcome knowledge about exactly who had ordered the dishonorable attempt on Juárez, something so threatening to his oath he had deliberately folded it away from his memory. In some ways he had walked through a mine field ever since.

But he could not let that deter him now. He could not harbor doubts about the days immediately ahead of him, even if he was preparing to do battle with a man his heart was begging him to follow, not oppose.

All he could do was to hope and pray that no one would trigger mines in the somewhat unsteady ground he had traversed since Zacatecas. He had to hold fast to his plan—and Bazaine's, perhaps the emperor's, too—for his future. He owed Sarah that.

As if all this were not enough, before he was in the field a week, part of his past came rushing at him like the bull out of the black mouth of the *toril*.

The buildup for Bazaine's attack progressed more rapidly now. French Zouaves and Tirailleurs, some drawn from the smaller front facing Díaz in Oaxaca, and scores of batteries of field guns just off freighters newly docked at Veracruz and Tampico moved up the road from the old Sierra Madre lumber town of Torreon. No major additions were made to the armies of Tomas Mejía or the other Mexican general, Méndez. None at all were made to the small forces already under the command of Jason James.

The intermittent sounds of the larger guns massed against the southern bulwarks of Chihuahua began to meld into an almost solid, sustained, deep roar. It would only be a matter of days before Bazaine sent the vanguard of his infantry crashing against Juárez's barricades.

James waited.

* * *

If the army of "General" Jason James, as Cipi insisted on calling him to his annoyance, had not yet materialized, and if those of Mejía and Méndez had not increased measurably in size, there *were* those new and different fighting men on their rosters, some of whom, he smiled to learn, still wore the gray uniforms in which they had faced their Union enemies through the course of the long and bitterly savage struggle north of the Rio Grande. It was, he presumed, their way of saying that the War Between the States had not ended for them, that in their eyes top-hatted Benito Juárez had become a surrogate foe for top-hatted Abraham Lincoln.

Had the emperor considered for even a solitary second how much more animosity toward him would build in that great, exhausted, but still restless giant of a country north of the border if he goaded them into making Benito Juárez's cause *theirs?*

Then Pierre Boulanger brought unsettling news.

The Parisian, true to everything James had come to learn about his habits, proved to be as peripatetic on this far northern front as he had been in all their campaigns together. He wandered from bivouac to bivouac almost every night, explaining to James that listening to the talk around campfires gave him insights on the men he would be fighting with. Pierre would not need such schooling had he patrolled the Sahara with infantry Legionnaires as James had.

While the new colonel eavesdropped principally on the talk of enlisted men and that of lower-ranking commissioned officers, now and again in his nightly peregrinations he was invited to mess with regimental and corps commanders, something that probably would not have happened without his Chasseur uniform displaying his recently awarded colonel's pips.

"Whenever I can, I assiduously avoid St. Cyrians, *mon ami,*" he said late one evening after he had made his rounds. "They still have an unlimited capacity to bore me beyond endurance. I do not wish to offend your American sensibilities, but I have found that those ex-Confederates who came out of *your* military academy before your war of rebellion—while none I met seemed to be the same spectacular clown Marcel Gallimard is—have every bit of the capacity for generating ennui my own compatriots possess."

James squirmed a little at the name Gallimard.

"I found one exception earlier tonight, however," Pierre continued. "A very impressive former general now breveted as a colonel under Mejía. Unless I am mistaken he will soon be a general again, in the Imperial Army this time, of course. Tomas could make good use of this officer; he seems utterly ruthless in a keen, cold way, just the sort of man Mejía likes. One of the other Americans, a former general named Sibley, told me his Confederate comrade commanded an army corps at a place called the Wilderness. Sibley said no general in the Confederate Army had more *personal* experience of combat."

"Fine, but do we have to go on with this? I'm tired."

"I would think you would find him *très interessant* for quite another reason. He fought here in Mexico with you in '47. Perhaps you knew him."

"Not likely, unless he was an enlisted man in my company. I don't believe officers in either the Union or Confederate armies mix with the ranks much today. They didn't even *know* us back then."

"He also comes from that same dreary place in *les États-unis* you told me you come from. What is its ridiculous name?"

"Kansas."

How many high-ranking Confederate officers from Kansas who had been in Mexico in '47 had ultimately served in the armies of Jefferson Davis? He could probably count every one of them by simply holding up his index finger.

There was no need to ask Boulanger this former general's name.

"I'll turn in now, Pierre."

Should he find Aaron and face him?

The question shot through the long minutes of wakefulness that made a silent limbo of almost the entire night. It seemed written before his eyes in a script of flame as he stared into the dark vault of his tent, and it even invaded the few short, wild dreams he had.

Did Aaron Sheffield remember the last thing he said the day they left Mexico eighteen years ago, as they stood together on the dock at Veracruz just before they boarded the two different ships which would take them home—that someday they would fight each other? And that one of them would die? *"It is carved in stone, Jason."*

Aaron had been wrong. Fate had once again brought them together, but on the same side as before: they would fight Mexicans again—not each other.

If what he told Sarah in his letter held, the end of his career as a soldier might be close at hand. He thought about what Bazaine had told him of Maximilian's "plan" for him. By God, he *could* make it all come true. Aaron Sheffield could not stop him. For all James knew Aaron could have changed. *He* had. Aaron might even be pleased to find that the young rifleman he had advised not to make soldiering a career had done fairly well in the profession.

He would ride to Mejía's headquarters after breakfast with Pierre and find him.

His mind made up, he slept without dreaming.

He had hardly scraped the uneaten food from his mess kit in the morning when a runner from Bazaine arrived at his tent, summoning to a meeting of the general staff.

The general staff?

In his sudden high excitement he forgot all about Aaron Sheffield.

40

▲▲▲▲▲

He dismounted in front of Bazaine's great tent and handed the reins to an orderly. Inside, the marshal was pacing back and forth behind a long camp table covered with maps and papers, hands clasped behind his back, taking strong, lunging steps.

"Colonel James reporting, sir," James called through the opening of the tent.

"Come in, come in, James!" Bazaine shouted back. "Come, come, come! *Vite!*"

The marshal stopped pacing as James entered and now turned to face him squarely. He wore the same clothes he had worn at Puebla and San Lorenzo: the sweat-stained slouch hat, the dingy tan vest, and the trousers that bagged around his thick legs and drooped over lizard skin boot tops.

The cascading "Come, come, come! *Vite!*" was nothing new. This was the third time James had been with this energetic old soldier when he neared the time to take an army into action, and on both earlier occasions the same exuberance had erupted, the booming voice a trumpet call to battle. It would have amused James as it had the first time he experienced it, at Puebla, had not his mind been on what Pierre told him last night.

"There is a question on your face, James," Bazaine said. "I can read it. The answer is a resounding *oui!* We are ready now to strike!" He lowered his voice. "I wish a few moments alone with you before generals Mejía, Méndez, Aymard, and Brincourt arrive. I want you to know where you will fit in when we proceed to the last stages of this battle."

Once before, on that Sunday evening at his office in the Palacio Nacional a year ago, Bazaine had brought James into a meeting some moments before the higher ranks put in their appearance. When they filed in the old soldier left them gaping as he informed them that the young major standing at the side of his desk—whom he promoted to colonel in almost the same instant—would be his deputy with full authority over all of them while he marched off to conquer San Luis Potosí. That was three cities and God knew how many towns ago—four cities, since they had taken Saltillo twice. Bazaine had led the recapturing of it after winning it once and then pulling back, letting Juárez's General Doblado and his badly mauled Republicans get away. That business had bothered both James and Pierre Boulanger at the time, raising some doubts about Bazaine's abilities as a strategist that were not quite resolved for months.

During a rare noon meal James later shared with him, the marshal finally brought the subject up himself, in what began as comments on the news from Appomattox which had just arrived in the capital and what that event might mean to the armies arrayed against Benito Juárez. That talk had ended in a very uncharacteristic attempt on the part of Bazaine to justify his decisions about Saltillo.

"You had questions about the conduct of the campaign, did you not, James? I am not surprised. You should have," he said as they shared lunch in his office one day late in May. "Letting Doblado escape was not *my* idea. I would have sent my army out in full pursuit to finish the enemy once and for all, just as your friend Boulanger recommended, but Emperor Napoleon thought it unwise to provoke a possible response from the United States at the time. I was unable to persuade him that your country was still too heavily involved in its own war to turn its attention on us. Also, wise as he is, Louis Napoleon does not really know the geography of this continent."

Bazaine had been gnawing at a shank of mutton as he spoke and now dropped it in his plate. He carefully sucked every one of his fingers before going on.

"Even if the Union had been able to spare a few troops to come our way when we were besieging Saltillo that first time, I could have fought off any such small army very easily. However, it is true that now that the war north of the

Rio Grande has ended, the United States could create a bigger problem for us. Consequently, we will have to end this struggle quickly. I do not believe your country would invade after a *fait accompli*. When we beat him here, Juárez's battle wagon will be empty and its axles broken."

But that had been rhetoric. James wondered what Bazaine wanted him to hear this morning that could not wait until the four generals reached this meeting. Did James dare embrace the wild hope that he would get his promotion when the others came to this meeting? Did he really want the promotion now?

Certainly not in the next few minutes and certainly not here. Bazaine must have recognized that he had made no friends for his protege that Sunday in his Palacio office, and he surely knew he would make none for him this time, either. It would be a disaster if he chose this moment to tell these proud, hard, older men that the same young man who had, if only temporarily, vaulted over them would now be a general. It would in all likelihood disturb the Indian Mejía.

"*Assieds-toi, mon ami,*" Bazaine said. "Over there." He gestured toward the hard, narrow cot tucked into the farthest corner of the huge tent. As James walked to it, the powerful Chihuahuan sun penetrated the tight weave of the multi-colored canvas panels, staining the earthen floor with stripes of yellow, red, and green. The much-traveled, tattered battle flags were stacked in another corner. He would have been mildly disappointed if they had not been somewhere in the tent.

"All right, James," the marshal said. "You must be wondering why I called you here so early."

"Yes, sir."

"I may wish to employ your diplomatic skills in dealing with General Mejía. Somehow he has learned of my plans for his army in the battle for Chihuahua, and has voiced his displeasure to his staff—and to the other commanders, too. Have *you* divined my strategy and my plans for Mejía, James?"

"No, sir."

"The defeat of the Republican Army turns on him and his cavalry wing. And collaterally on you. I want to hold his army, and the force we are building for you, out of the heavy fighting of the first week of the final move on Chihuahua. Mejía does not like it, but I am reassigning his infantry to General Méndez, so both his command and yours will be composed almost entirely of cavalry. There will be little use for horse squadrons in the initial stages of our advance. I want to position the two of you northwest of Chihuahua, ready to fall on the retreating enemy when they try to evade us after we take the city, the way they did at Saltillo. As you have probably determined for yourself, even though I am a marshal of France I do not think it politic to simply *order* Mejía to agree. We must win his mind and will."

James saw the wisdom in all this, but it was a disappointing that Bazaine had said "force" instead of "army" when he spoke of his command.

The marshal continued. "Tomas will strain at the leash to get into the battle early, and he would ride right over other Imperial units to do so. With the regiment of Chasseurs under your friend Boulanger on his flank and the rest of your command between him and the early action, we might be able to restrain him until we need him. And we *will* need him. Pay close attention to him. Where we can, we must give him what he wants."

"I would have only the single regiment of French cavalry which has already been assigned to me, sir?"

"Unless I can take the two Chasseur regiments away from General Aymard without offending him. Handle Aymard *avec politesse, aussi.*"

"Yes, sir."

"Your paramount task will be to work out the details of a tactical plan with Mejía that will fulfill his desire for glory without jeopardizing the rest of us. We will not have time for that today, so I wish you to call on him at his army headquarters in the morning." Bazaine glanced toward the

entrance of the tent. "Ah . . . I see my generals have
arrived. We will talk privately again tomorrow, James, after
your conference with General Mejía. In the meantime, *en
garde.*"

General Ramón Méndez entered first. Aymard and Brincourt followed him into the tent. The two Frenchmen
looked to be reserved professionals, St. Cyrians, most likely.
James had never met Méndez before.

Behind them, James could see horses being led away from
the tent, and several armed escorts and five or six aides who
would have to wait outside at least until Bazaine finished
with his generals.

Tomas Mejía was the next man through the opening.

The other generals saluted the marshal as he motioned
them to the folding camp chairs near the battle flags, but
Mejía merely nodded and turned his face toward James.
There was a glint of curiosity and steely, cold assessment.
Well, as the only officer in the tent not a general, he might
have expected such scrutiny.

Bazaine faced his generals.

"*Messieurs!*" he said. "We are met to plan what should
be the last great battle of this war."

He wasted no time. The tent was shot through with a
palpable electric charge as he spoke, and even the colors of
the canvas panels seemed to brighten. The briefing became
perhaps the most stunning performance of a long string of
them James had witnessed. "*You have hitched your carreta to
a very bright star,*" Cipi had said to him once. The grasp of
grand strategy was hardly more impressive than the marshal's knowledge of the most minute detail. Bazaine etched
a tactical picture at once simple and complex, and as he
neared the end, the heads of three of the generals were
nodding as on marionettes.

"We shall make an effective end to this war this coming
week! *Vive La France!*" He smiled, and added, "*¡Viva
Mexico!*"

Only Mejía seemed to withhold full approval. He had

shown no surprise, though, at any part of Bazaine's projected battle plan.

"You do not seem completely pleased, General Mejía," Bazaine said. "Is there something about our strategy, particularly in the way we wish to use your fine army, that troubles you?"

Mejía shrugged. "I have no objections to any part of it in theory, marshal, but . . ." He turned and looked at James again, then turned back to Bazaine. "I simply do not feel enough confidence in the young officer you have selected to command the army which will be arrayed next to mine. I would feel much better if a more senior soldier held that post."

The first faint sounds of the crumbling of the hopes and dreams of Jason James worked their way up from somewhere deep within him. He tried to block them out, but they persisted.

"You have someone in mind who would suit you better?" Bazaine said.

"I do."

"And he would be . . . ?"

"A colonel I have but recently added to my staff. I have brought him here with me today. I think you should meet him, marshal. May I bring him in?"

Bazaine paused. His big face tightened. He stroked his nose as James had seen him do when contemplating some decision he had no wish to make but which he felt he must. "Yes, general. But before you do, may I ask if you or this officer will accept Colonel James in an only slightly lesser post?"

As Bazaine spoke, Mejía had kept his eyes on James. "My colonel and I will gladly accept Colonel James as his second in command."

Bazaine turned to James. "Would you object to stepping down in order to assure the success of our endeavors, colonel?"

"No, sir." Refusing a blindfold when facing a firing party

must feel something like this. Jason James may as well have disappeared. Bazaine had sacrificed him with only a brief moment's hesitation. No matter how high the great marshal's estimation of him had soared, the winning of this battle, perhaps Bazaine's last in Mexico, was everything. As a professional James knew that he would probably have done the same himself.

Mejía had indeed learned of—or made a damned shrewd guess about—the marshal's plans for both of them. James fought against the notion that it had all been prearranged. Bazaine was ruthless, and possibly as much a creature of expedience as he had accused Emperor Maximilian of becoming, but he had never once been devious in all their time together.

Mejía spoke again. "*¡Bueno!* This will give me all the confidence I require. You did not need to persuade me to accept Colonel James as *second* in command, marshal. My colonel has specifically *asked* that Colonel James serve under him if he is approved as commander of the other force."

Asked for him? There was only one man in Mejía's army now who would *ask* for him.

"Bring this officer in then, general," Bazaine said.

Mejía stepped to the opening of the tent, beckoned to someone in the group outside, and returned to his seat.

The tall, gray-uniformed, elegant figure of Aaron Sheffield filled the opening.

At sundown Jason James sat in his own tent, his head in his hands. He certainly would not cloak himself in any prideful Achillean sulk at the way Bazaine had jettisoned him; he had known too many other setbacks in his life to begin indulging himself that way.

Aaron Sheffield had looked first at the marshal and saluted with the same remembered smartness. Only when Mejía introduced him to Bazaine, and he had shaken hands with the other three generals, did he turn his eyes on James. They still held the same dark fire that flickered in them when they left each other on the dock at Veracruz eighteen years ago. He had the same thin smile of that moment, too.

James looked hard for the wounds, the half hidden hurts, the indelible marks of suffering that a four year traverse of the hell of war would have left on an ordinary man. He found none. He had not truly expected that he would.

"This colonel," Bazaine said to Sheffield, "is Jason James, an American like yourself."

Without a word to James, Cousin Aaron turned back to the marshal. "The colonel and I are acquainted, sir."

The rest of the meeting took no time at all.

Mejía gave a brief, matter-of-fact resume of the American's career as a Confederate general under Lee, and by the time they left Bazaine's tent, Aaron Sheffield had become a general again, and three more regiments of Imperial cavalry, as well as the Chasseurs under Aymard, had been placed under his command.

Outside the tent, under the blazing sun scorching the scrub-covered ancient talus slope at the foot of La Sierra de la Virgen, James's new commander finally spoke to him.

"Report to me at General Mejía's headquarters tomorrow morning at nine, Colonel James. Before we go into battle together one more time, I must discover what sort of soldier you have become. It now seems you and I are to fight together again. But never forget for one moment what I once promised you. That promise *will* be kept when this war is over."

He mounted and rode off without waiting for a reply, and without looking at James again.

"Come to my tent for a bit, Jason," Pierre Boulanger said after the evening meal in the officers' camp mess was over. "I have acquired a bottle of multi-starred cognac, and as you know, I no longer drink alone."

"Let me beg off, Pierre. I have some thinking I must do."

"I have something I must show you, *mon ami*. It is quite important."

"What is it?"

"A letter from Paola. Much of it concerns Mademoiselle Sarah."

Strange. Pierre had not called Sarah "mademoiselle" for more than a year. "Is she all right?"

"You will have to be the judge of that, my friend."

In the tent, the Parisian lit the oil lamp hanging from the ridgepole, and fished an envelope from beneath the pillow on his cot.

"There are three pages to Paola's letter. Forgive me if I do not show you the first and third; they are, as you might expect, *très intime*." He leafed out the middle page and handed it to James. "I feel devastated, Jason. I would rather take a bullet or a meter of steel than show you this, but I felt you had to know . . ."

James lifted the page to the lamp, and the heat from the flame revived some of the scent Paola must have drenched it with.

> . . . at Charlotte's dinner just last night.
> The emperor has offered them a wedding
> gift of an *hacienda* right next to his
> own, La Borda Quintas at Cuernavaca.
> They have not as yet said anything at
> all about when the event might take place.
> Sarah is strangely silent for an about-
> to-be-married woman, but I expect that
> to change. It promises a splendid future
> for her. Henri is a prize. Jason, of
> course, must be told. I will leave that
> to you, *liebchen*. He will wish her well,
> I know . . .

He sat on his camp chair outside his tent and gazed at the Chihuahuan sky while Ursa Minor revolved almost all the way around Polaris.

His life had nearly come full circle, too.

He would soon fight side-by-side with Cousin Aaron here

in Mexico again—subordinate to him as he had been the first time.

Nothing much had changed.

> *What can ail thee, knight-at-arms*
> *Alone and palely loitering?*

41

▲▲▲▲▲

Sarah took advantage of Henri's sojourn with Max in Cuernavaca to visit the house on Avenida Moctezuma.

There had been times in the past when she had to plead with Melanie Zichy for even a few hours away from her duties at the castle, but the countess seemed eager to grant any of her wishes these days. It was no secret why Melanie—ordinarily a fairly stern taskmistress—had suddenly turned so accommodating. Sarah's "engagement" to Henri had subtly elevated her to a slightly higher level in the Chapultepec hierarchy, and she did not occupy that new tier solely in the first lady-in-waiting's eyes. Everyone at court she had anything to do with—excepting the irreverent Paola Kollonitz—had begun to treat her with a new, and mildly unsettling, deference. It would end in a hurry, of course, when the news worked its way around the Imperial inner circle that she had absolutely no intention of becoming La Comtesse de Bayeux. In the meantime she felt she had every right to turn the masquerade to her advantage in these little ways. She had been a faithful worker in the court vineyard, and she would probably pay for all this sudden respect swiftly enough when it ended, when she announced that she would not marry Henri Gallimard.

As vexed as she had been with Solange, it was good to relax in her company again—to a point. The Frenchwoman had heard, through her own grapevine, of Charlotte's dinner, and she now used her newfound knowledge for her own gushing celebration.

"Monsieur and Madame Pelletier will be so pleased and proud when they hear, *chérie!*" she said. "A noble marriage and a *hacienda* of your very own. *Merveilleuse!*" This, or something like it, came in maddening repetition.

Sarah kept her counsel. The tendrils of Solange's grapevine doubtless ran two ways, and were Sarah's long-time companion to be indiscreet, it could easily carry the news back to Chapultepec that there was no engagement, would be no marriage.

Sarah had to tell Henri first, before the news reached him by accident or design.

She was only slightly irritated that Paola shrugged off her insistence that she simply could not go on with what had become a charade.

"I still don't believe you," Paola said, "but I still think it wise to keep Jason on hand as a *divertissement.* You will soon find you have needs, if you haven't already."

So, it was doubly good to return to Avenida Moctezuma for the week.

There was correspondence to catch up on: a sweet letter from Uncle Tobias in Cambridge inquiring about her health and pressing her to return to Boston and home; a note from Alberto Moreno assuring her things were going well at the mine, but demonstrating the mine manager's fine sense of discretion by making no reference to the meeting with the president; and five pages from Monsieur Auguste, with far fewer diatribes aimed at Napoleon III this time. Her foster father expressed his pleasure that the French press and important members of the Corps Legislatif were urging the French emperor to pull the Army out of Mexico, something the monarch in Paris had not for once rejected out of hand. "*Perhaps this counterfeit Bonaparte is beginning to learn,*" he wrote. "*I do not think he is at last listening from any sense of moral imperative; it is far more likely that he fears American intervention now that the flow of blood from your Civil War has at last been staunched.*"

She had a slight twinge of longing for the Champs Elysées as she reread Monsieur Auguste's letter and leafed through Solange's Paris newspapers. The City of Light was enjoying a dazzling social and cultural season. She wrote Monsieur Auguste, playing perhaps too broadly on the season here in Mexico, but not mentioning that Sarah Anderson was expected to be part of it. It surely *would* be a fine season once she had her talk with Henri and was back with Jason once again.

But the time spent away from the castle brought its own special worries. Perhaps it was because her associations with Jason were more strongly remembered here in her quiet house than they were at often tumultuous Chapultepec. She was distinctly her own woman here.

There had been no more letters from Jason after the one telling her of his departure for the north with Marshal Bazaine, but from what she heard from Matt O'Leary of the sudden expansion and intensification of the war, and the heavy fighting at the gates of Chihuahua, she had not expected any. Her correspondence with Alberto Moreno at Zacatecas had moved back and forth sluggishly, and Chihuahua was even farther north, well beyond range of the regular postal coaches.

She coped well enough in the daytime, but long moments of almost every night became agonies of black wakefulness when fear for him nearly paralyzed her. How had women down the centuries borne this burrowing pain? If only he had made the decision to end his career as a soldier *before* this campaign instead of after it.

Matt's look these days disturbed her as well. His boyish face had the same cast of sadness she had come to know all too well since Veracruz in '62; he still grieved about not fighting in the War Between the States—even more now that it was over and all chance was gone.

Despite this she was overjoyed to be spending time in the company of the Marine captain. Her journey with Jason to Zacatecas to meet with President Juárez, her time at the castle dealing with its rumors, the never-ending communiques about the successes of French and Imperial arms, and now what had turned out to be two walks with Charlotte and the conversations that went with them—all of it had taken place inside a cocoon of sorts. Nothing from the outside got in. She needed a fairly impartial, fairly objective view of things, something hard and sharp enough to jolt her into awareness. Matt provided that even if it was not always an unalloyed joy.

"I believe I've said this before, Miss Anderson, but the military picture in Mexico is highly deceiving. It looks like Bazaine is beating the Republicans hands down, and I will agree that he has the *chance* to do just that right now at Chihuahua. But Ambassador Corwin is persuaded that Napoleon III will pull the rug out from under him at almost any second—even before this battle is history."

"And you don't believe Max's own army could perform the task by itself?"

"No, ma'am, I don't. What the French and the Conservatives have done so far is to roll Juárez back on his own supply lines. On the surface it looks as if they're driving him out of the country, but he somehow has managed to keep his enemy in the field since long before Maximilian arrived in Mexico. In actuality, Bazaine and Mejía are only compressing him against the southern border of the United States. They've never once tried to position an army *between* him and his supporters north of the border. Now that the war is over up there . . ." He paused and swallowed hard before going on. "Juárez will have a much easier time of it getting arms and supplies. The French know that, of course. That's why they sent those gunboats into the mouth of the river at Matamoros. Unfortunately for them it was too little, too damned late. The Conservatives don't even *have* gunboats. And except for Márquez, who's somewhere in Turkey now, they don't really have a commander with a genuine will to fight. Well, Mejía, maybe. In my opinion Miramón, for all his reputation, is a joke. He has yet to take the field with the army he is holding here in the capital. The least he could do is move south into Oaxaca and support the Conservatives who are trying to hold Díaz there. I understand Bazaine is disgusted with him.

"Oh, and there's something else. I'm not telling tales out of school, but there are strong indications that General Grant, who is, as President Lincoln was, a staunch admirer of Benito Juárez, as well as a champion of the Monroe Doctrine as you might expect, is about to send Phil Sheridan to the Texas-Mexico border with upwards of fifty thousand troops."

"You don't think the United States would actually invade Mexico, do you?"

"No. But I'm not sure it *wouldn't*. Napoleon won't be sure, either. Just the *threat* of a Yankee army in Mexico will tip things heavily toward the Republicans."

"What you're saying is that if Bazaine and the French leave, there's no chance for Max and his government."

"Exactly. I would give them two years at the outside from the day Napoleon *begins* a French withdrawal. Morale in the Imperial Army will drop like a stone the day the first homeward bound Zouave or Tirailleur takes ship at Vera-cruz."

"You would never know any of what you've told me by listening to the talk at Chapultepec."

"That's the way of a world like that, isn't it?"

As good as it was to see and talk with Matt, and particularly to listen to him, the conversation sobered and depressed her.

Part of her, a large part, perhaps the largest, hoped for the eventual Republican victory that Matt was more or less forecasting. Her remembered and constantly re-emerging affection for the little Mexican president and the "people" he cherished would not allow her to wish otherwise.

But her affection for Charlotte was every bit as strong, and had gripped her for a much longer time.

Charlotte had been responsible for her embarking on an adventure she could never have dreamed about.

She could not bring herself to reject or regret altogether her time at Chapultepec.

There remained in her nature something frivolous which reached out and embraced a little of the frivolity of Charlotte and her court. Wait. That was not *quite* right. The court, yes; Charlotte, no. Some of the women around the empress might have been frivolous enough—Paola certainly verged on it—but there was no longer anything of the perverse, playful female about Charlotte von Coburg-Hapsburg. Certainly no frivolous creature had made an appearance in the walks Sarah had taken with her in the twilight gardens of the castle.

Max was the one who indulged in frivolity.

For a long time, this side to his character had gone undetected, due to his sober mien, his soft, musical voice, winsome, winning smiles, and his exquisite manners. It had been disguised, too, by the way he backed every one of Charlotte's more earnest and ambitious social schemes: the announced hospitals, the food distribution for the poor, and the grandiose plans to educate every Indian child in the realm at government expense. That all of these things had still to be funded or implemented, however, seemed to have gone unnoticed.

Matt had talked of these things, too. "I hear it when I go to church, Miss Anderson. All these great programs, and mind you I think they're fine, even if the native Catholic Conservatives are outraged by them, have begun with fanfares and important sounding *pronunciamientos* on the part of the emperor—not one of them has come to anything. People like the archbishop, General Salas, and Juan Almonte have turned away from him for even suggesting such 'recklessly progressive' things, and on the other hand, the Liberals left behind here in the capital have begun to hate him because he hasn't followed through on a single one of them. It isn't that the emperor does so little for the people of Mexico; it's just that he promises so *much.*"

"I suppose he hasn't left the French too enamored of him, either," Sarah said. "Jason has never given away any secrets, but he has let slip that Bazaine, for one, looks upon

Max as a dilettante. Emperor Napoleon is beginning to have doubts, too, from what I read in the French newspapers Solange subscribes to, and from what my friends in Paris have to say."

"Yes. The Second Empire is footing a gigantic bill for this war while Emperor Max is throwing his own treasury to the four winds. In my view the Empire of Mexico has embarked on a race between defeat and bankruptcy. His Austrian and Belgian favorites are getting richer by the second, and if he now is running out of hard cash, he apparently hasn't run out of castles and *haciendas* to give away."

Had even Matt heard about her "wedding gift"?

"Probably the biggest mistake of his reign, though," he went on, "was the fiasco at Zacatecas. Tell me, Miss Anderson, was it the emperor himself who ordered that attack on the president?"

"I don't know. I honestly don't know. I am afraid Jason thinks it was. For a bit there I thought he might call it quits."

"I wouldn't blame him. He's a good, faithful soldier, though. Maximilian should not play fast and loose with men like Jason James, from what I know of him. Well, no matter, I guess. The emperor *is* getting the blame at the embassy for the attempt on Juárez. One more apparent breach of faith like that could do him in. And I've got the funniest feeling he is about to commit another one."

"You know something?"

"Not really. As I said, it's just a feeling. Word *has* reached the embassy that he has called a meeting of all his closest advisors to announce some new policy. When Ambassador Corwin saw him last, the emperor raged at the Republicans for fifteen minutes in a way he never had before. Before he excused the ambassador, though, he reverted to his regular charming self. The meeting I spoke of will take place when he gets back from wherever he's off to this week."

"Cuernavaca."

"Yes. I just hope he doesn't announce any Draconian

measures. For *his* sake. I didn't want him to come to Mexico, and I don't approve of his regime, but I don't wish him any harm."

"Surely you don't think he could actually *come* to harm, do you?"

"You never know in Mexico. These are violent times in a violent country."

He left, promising to return to take her to the opera the same night. Angela Peralta was singing in Mozart's *The Marriage of Figaro*, which Sarah had found much less connubial than its name suggested when she saw it in Paris. She was mildly curious to see whether or not there would be a some sort of reprise of the diva's challenge to Max and Charlotte last winter. It could not be precisely the same; the monarchs' box, with Max and Henri still in the south, and Charlotte not attending without her husband, would be as empty as a cave.

Solange declined Sarah's invitation to go along. "It is not a *French* opera, *ma chère.*"

She spent the afternoon visiting Sor Francesca at the orphanage, but even with that to take up her time, and as she checked some household accounts with Solange and dressed for the opera, she spent long moments in contemplation of everything Matt had said, and in wondering what Jason would have said on the same subjects. She pretty well knew how he felt about the situation in Mexico; she had seen it clearly when they talked with President Juárez, and in other little things he had come out with on the trip back to the capital from Zacatecas. Deep in his heart he was—at least emotionally—as much in the Indian's camp as she, and these trying days must be twenty times as difficult for him as they were for her.

Her only consolation came in remembering his words in the letter:". . . *this campaign will be my last.*"

Ángela Peralta seemed a more sprightly soprano, much more effervescent, in the *Marriage* than she had been in *La*

Juive, and at first Sarah put it down to the fact that as a superb operatic actress she was merely treating her audience to a new coloration due to the difference in the two roles. But there was something else. All through the first act she displayed some of the same defiance as when she stepped before the curtain for her withering rendition of "La Libertad" on the prior occasion.

On an impulse, Sarah sent her card around to La Peralta's dressing room at intermission, and just before she and Matt took their seats again, a girl in a maid's uniform handed her a note that said in brief that yes, the singer would be glad to receive her after the final curtain call.

Ángela Peralta did not *look* glad. There seemed to be flame in her eyes.

To begin with, she asked Matt to wait outside the dressing room, dismissing him with an almost brutal abruptness. "Señorita Anderson and La Peralta have private matters to discuss, *señor. Vamos, por favor!*"

She turned her great, dark, smoldering eyes on Sarah, but all Sarah really saw was the shadowy outline of the magnificent animal body under the flimsy dressing gown, the same body she had seen naked in the daguerreotype in Samuel's room at the Zacatecas *hacienda*. In a way it looked even more sensual than when it was fully exposed, exuding not only sex but passion.

"You knew my brother, Señorita Peralta. I wished so much to make your—"

"*¡Sí!*" It was an explosion, her voice raw and harsh, unbelievably so for the delicate true instrument that had rendered the Mozart so lyrically from the stage. "I mourn him! From the look of you I do not think you know the meaning of that. You look bloodless. You do not have enough *amor* in you!" She may have spoken of mourning, but only *seething* could describe the way the words came out.

"I had hoped we could be friends."

"*¿Amigas?* You and me? *Pero, no!* Did you really expect that La Peralta could be a friend to a *puta* in the filthy court of the usurper? Now that I have seen you at last, I find we do not have anything to say to each other, private or otherwise, after all. I cannot believe you are Samuel's sister. You may leave now."

"But . . ."

"*¡Ahora!* Leave!"

"Perhaps another time . . ."

"Impossible. My performance tonight ends my career in Mexico. I leave tomorrow to take a position with the company of Opera Cuba-Lirica in Havana. I will not stay another moment in a land governed by the pathetic weakling who subsists by sucking the blood from my people. And I wish nothing to do with one of the whores he surrounds himself with. Your brother would disown you if he were still alive. He would take a bullwhip and drive you from Chapultepec!"

Outside Sarah reeled and feared for a moment she would have to ask Matt to support her lest she fall.

She turned down his invitation to a late supper at the Mirador and did not speak until their carriage turned into Avenida Moctezuma.

"Matt," she said, "you know pretty much how I feel about Mexico. Am I a fraud, a hypocrite, staying on at Charlotte's court?"

"Good heavens, no! You and I are Americans. Nothing we do or don't do can alter matters very much. We have to get along with everyone here in Mexico."

It was not nearly enough.

Back at Chapultepec the next day she learned from Paola that Max and Henri had returned from Cuernavaca the night before. To her surprise and slight chagrin it seemed that Henri had not even inquired about her. Coming right after her terrible experience with Ángela Peralta, it disturbed her. She wanted things in some reasonable stasis before she had her talk with him.

"He is still the shy Henri we knew in Paris, *liebchen*,"
Paola said. "I would not put too much stock in this. He
loves you. I am sure of that." Despite the assurance, it was
clear that Paola was as puzzled as she. Paola went on.
"Besides, Max is keeping him very busy. The emperor
began his big important conference this morning, and he
has asked Henri to take part in it."

It must be the series of meetings Matt had mentioned,
the ones which had troubled him.

She had little time for conjecture. Charlotte was giving
another dinner tonight, and had also asked that Sarah join
her for another walk.

The afternoon post brought a letter from Jason. She so
desperately needed to hear from him she ripped the envelope open.

My Dear Miss Anderson—

The salutation staggered her. *Miss Anderson?*

I have heard the wonderful news of your impending
marriage to the Comte de Bayeux. Allow me to offer
my warm and sincere congratulations and heartfelt
best wishes. It will set your mind at ease, I am sure, to
know that you will not hear from me again.

Please do not trouble yourself about me in this
happy time of your life. I have my own life to live, and
I will get about the living of it forthwith. A change of
assignment makes it certain that I will be making no
more visits to Chapultepec, so my promise not to see
you will be an easy one to keep.

Nothing, however, will change my feelings for you;
that will remain a constant of my existence until the
day I die.

Pierre joins his congratulations and best wishes to
mine.

Your Obedient Servant,
Jason James

The shock of it left her numb, empty.

But the emptiness lasted no longer than a dozen muffled heartbeats.

She had to see Henri tonight.

Her very life—the life she wanted—depended on it.

42

▲▲▲▲▲

Cipi, probably because he knew his predictions about his master's military fortunes had come to nothing, was giving James a wide berth, and there had been no sign of Boulanger, although the Chasseur and his cavalry regiment had moved northeast of the city to bivouac less than a kilometer away.

He had not seen Bazaine since he reported to Aaron Sheffield almost a week ago.

Aaron had effectively reduced him from a true second-in-command of a legitimate army to exactly what he had come north as—a colonel with one patchwork regiment stationed far to the rear of the French and Mexican forward cavalry brigades. The vanguard of General Sheffield's army, with Boulanger a part of it, would see action whenever the outnumbered Republicans under Doblado, whom Bazaine's artillery batteries were still hammering so mercilessly, moved out of Chihuahua trying to escape the massed infantry of Aymard, Mejía, and Brincourt. Before they could find haven at El Paso del Norte, Sheffield and Mejía would fall on the enemy and hack them to pieces.

But James and *his* Mexican cavalry might never lower a lance or fire a shot.

"You will hold your regiment in reserve, Colonel James," Aaron said. From the look of him as he said it, James knew he was tossing it into discard. He had not even added "and await orders." James suspected that even had he done so, none would come. "With any kind of luck, Colonel, you will not have to join in our attack; if your past is any indication, you would not relish the work we shall have to do when we go into action. It is not General Mejía's intention—nor mine—to take prisoners."

Aaron had effectively buried him.

He had dug the grave when James reported to him at Mejía's headquarters the morning after the meeting with Bazaine, and his cousin's first conversation with him—if he could call the few words they had exchanged in front of Tomas Mejía a conversation—had been brief and coldly formal.

"I have read the military record of this officer, which Marshal Bazaine was kind enough to send us, General Mejía," Sheffield said in James's presence. "It speaks well of Colonel James's fighting abilities, but I have a personal recollection about him. He has in the past demonstrated troubling behavior *after* combat. Colonel James, I fear, is too full of the 'milk of human kindness' where the defeated enemy is concerned. But despite this weakness, perhaps we can make some use of him. Only time will tell."

Aaron's remarks and Mejía's contemptuous snort should have humiliated him, but he was already so beaten down by his demotion—and the shattering news in the letter from Paola Kollonitz that Pierre had shown him—that he did not react.

It was trivial at a time like this, but all he could do was wonder how long Aaron was going to wear the gray uniform of the Confederacy. If he rode at the front of his first attacking regiment—and James knew he would—he would shine through the waves of red and green Imperial cavalry like a lighthouse beacon, a target for scores of Republican riflemen.

There was never any real doubt about whether the combined French and Imperial armies would win the city itself, of course, at least in the way such things are measured. Each day brought fewer volleys from its defenders in answer to the attackers' guns, but it was taking far longer than expected to reduce the Republican batteries. Ten days of ceaseless pounding failed to open the breaches in Chihuahua's southern breastworks the infantry would need, and it began to feel to James as if they were fighting the second and much longer battle for Puebla over again.

The ten days lengthened to two weeks and then on to three without the breakdown in the defenses of Chihuahua that Bazaine insisted on before he ordered the final assault.

Then James discovered that everything in Mexico was about to change.

Bazaine had ridden to the headquarters of Mejía and Aaron Sheffield late one day midway in the fourth week of the siege, on a rare, dreary, overcast afternoon when James had called there, too, seeking his regiment's payroll. They met quite by accident at the entrance to Mejia's tent.

"Stay, Colonel," Bazaine said when James tried to excuse himself. "I am meeting with General Mejía, although he does not know it yet. What I am here to tell him concerns you, too. My news would have come to you as a matter of course in any event, but I would just as soon you heard it directly from your old commander."

A nervous and stammering Mexican major informed the marshal that General Mejía and his ex-Confederate partner were off on an inspection tour of the latter's still idle army, but were expected back soon.

Bazaine steered James aside for a few words in private while they waited.

"I am sorry, of course, for the way things turned out for you, James." Bazaine seldom admitted error, and *never* apologized, but he did look at least vaguely regretful. He also looked uncharacteristically dejected. Genuine as the apology sounded, the François-Achille Bazaine whom James knew best would never let anyone hear or see anything beyond that. Something else was gnawing at the marshal now.

The full reason for the seeming depression unfolded in a moment, after Bazaine settled into a camp stool an awe-struck orderly provided. "If I remain long enough in Mexico, I will try to make it up to you, *mon ami,*" he said.

"Is there some question about how long that will be, sir?"

"I received new orders from Emperor Napoleon today. Most of the French Army will leave this country in the next six or seven months," Bazaine said. "It is time for the Imperial Army to take over this war *in toto.* When that happens I may be able to make things right with you, *mon ami.* I will not, I trust, lose all influence with the Austrian, and I *will* remain on duty in the capital until the last of our forces have embarked for the mother country."

"Will these new orders affect our battle here at Chihuahua, sir?"

"*Oui,* I regret to say. I am under strict orders from Paris not to pursue the Republicans one kilometer closer to the United States than we are at this moment. It will be necessary to change the strategic thinking of the two officers we are awaiting. I am a little surprised that Paris even knows the name of this city. Perhaps someone has given my emperor a lesson in geography. You know what this means in the long term, James?"

"Yes, sir."

"It could eventually spell *finis* for the Empire of Mexico. I fear it could end with a victory by the Juáristas within a year after our departure. My next instructions from France will probably be to persuade that gilded puppet in the capital to abdicate. I do not relish that particular task."

On rare occasions James had thought it *could* come to this, a tacit surrender on the part of France's Second Empire, and with it what would amount to desertion of its surrogate government in Mexico and this planned request for the emperor to step aside.

But so soon? This battle was still raging, and staunch and heroic as the city's Republican defenders had shown themselves to be, they could not survive this grinding war of attrition more than a few days longer.

And Imperial forces still had a firm grip on the states

making up central Mexico. Surely there should be no cause for panic.

But—the concern about possible intervention by the United States, whispered in the officers' messes of all five armies on the northern front ever since the news from Appomattox avalanched down the continent, must have become even deeper than James had thought. In fairness to the French officer corps, there was no fear evident in the whispering. The St. Cyrians in particular looked on the possibility of fighting Americans as a challenge.

"The Imperial Army could still have its way if Miramón would get off his *derriere* and move on Díaz in Oaxaca," the marshal said. "If he crushed him quickly, he could join Méndez and Mejía here in the north and win the day even after my French and Legion soldiers leave. Díaz will soon begin to receive the new American arms now arriving in the west coast ports. Unless he is forced to fight before he is ready, he can control the entire south by next summer at the latest. The Austrian would then have to face the enemy on two fronts. He does not have enough men, guns, or treasure for that—*and not nearly enough will.*"

Bazaine looked smaller and less commanding perched on the camp stool, his hard belly suddenly gone soft and bulging almost comically. He was taking this curtailment of his authority very hard, seeming but a faint shadow of the powerful Marshal of France James had known.

A group of riders, dots quickly becoming larger, were now approaching on the long slope leading to Mejía's headquarters tent and compound. Tomas Mejía and Aaron Sheffield rode well in front of three mounted flag bearers. Off to the west French guns were still battering Chihuahua, but at this distance the sound was just a series of muffled thumps, punctuated from time to time by the faint, eerie notes of a trumpet.

Bazaine lifted a pair of field glasses to his eyes. "Tomas's new general is a fine looking officer, *n'est-ce pas?*"

"Yes, sir."

"He said the other day you two were acquainted."

"We did know each other, Marshal, many years ago. We both fought here with General Winfield Scott."

"On the same side, I presume."

"Yes, sir."

"I have never pried about this, and I would not now except that your civil war is over, but . . . if you had stayed in the United States, would you and General Sheffield have fought on the same side *there?*"

"No, sir."

"I thought not from what I think I have learned about you, James. I would never ask *you* this, but do you suppose this General Sheffield believes in slavery?"

"I don't know, sir." Aaron had never been that specific about any of his beliefs save those which had to do with honor, but in the long years apart James had often wondered exactly what *had* caused him to join the Army of the Confederacy. While James was still in Africa his mother had written to tell him that Cousin Aaron had donned the gray uniform. Her fears that her nephew and her son might some day have to fight each other pulsed between every line, causing James to abandon his first plan to plead his way out of the Legion, return home, and join the Union Army. Before he could ever consider it again he had embarked for Mexico.

Through his mother he had also learned that Aaron had served as an instructor at West Point under Commandant Robert E. Lee in '52 or '53.

He was sure Aaron had honored no deep-dyed philosophical or political beliefs that turned him toward the South. Something which had taken root in Aaron Sheffield's soul back in Kansas had flowered tragically long before the war. When fourteen-year-old Jason James saw the banked fires in the gray eyes staring out over the winter stubble of the farm, he had somehow known—even if he could never have articulated it then—that Aaron Sheffield would always search for causes that were already lost.

Aaron Sheffield had never been a simple soldier—he was even then a cavalier.

And he looked one now, as he and Mejía reined up in front of Bazaine and dismounted.

"*¿Como esta, mi mariscal?*" Mejía said.

"I am not feeling as well as I would like, Tomas," Bazaine sighed, "but it is not my health. May I have a moment of your time? I have received orders from Paris which I fear will disappoint you."

"*Por favor, señor.* Let us go inside my tent."

Mejía led the way. Bazaine caught James's eye for an instant just before he entered. He raised a finger and touched it to his lips.

James was alone with Aaron Sheffield.

The marshal's strong voice was coming from inside the tent, but through the heavy canvas James could not make out the individual words.

"You know what is going on in there, don't you, Colonel James?" Aaron said.

"Yes, I do . . . general."

"Would you care to tell me?"

"No, sir. I would not."

The perpetual dark fire in Aaron's eyes turned even darker.

"Not even if I order you to tell me?"

"No, sir."

Aaron smiled. "You realize, do you not, Colonel James, that this is one more insubordination to add to your list in our history together?"

This was the first admission since Veracruz that they *had* a mutual history. "I know that, sir."

"Have you never really considered the consequences of such an act? Have you not yet divined my capacity to discipline you, are you so obtuse that—"

He broke off as Bazaine and Mejía emerged from the tent, with the Mexican finishing a remark in a voice that verged on hysteria, ". . . disgraceful and dishonorable, *señor el mariscal!* No matter what *your* orders are, General Sheffield and I will attack tomorrow—and we will drive the few we leave alive in that pitiful army of traitors north of the river and into the very lap of the *norteamericanos* who terrify your Emperor Napoleon." His stocky Indian body quivered with fury.

Incredibly, Bazaine's face had turned white, and he looked almost defeated.

But only for the moment. He stiffened. The marshal of France had returned. "*Très bien, Monsieur le General!* I wish you well." There was a stinging bite in Bazaine's voice. "There is one thing I must ask of you and General Sheffield, though. I would like Colonel James here seconded to my command again. He has done magnificent work for me these past two years and I want him at my side during the withdrawal."

"Take him, *señor!* We will be well rid of him. From what General Sheffield tells me, he is probably better suited for withdrawal than for attack."

"*Gracias,* General Mejía," Bazaine turned to James. "Move to my command post tomorrow, colonel. I will have Lemonde find a billet for you." The voice was now as firm and vigorous as it had been at any time in James's memory. He turned back to Mejía. "One more thing, general. The three regiments of Chasseurs in General Sheffield's army will not be available for your attack. They are French and consequently under Emperor Napoleon's orders as am I. I want them placed under the command of Colonel James immediately. *Merci beaucoup et au revoir, messieurs.* My horse and that of Colonel James, *s'il vous plait.*"

Mejía turned and made his way back inside the tent.

James turned toward Aaron Sheffield.

The smile was still there, but even more wintry than before, an icy contrast with the hot, burning eyes.

"I am sorry General Mejía let you get away from me . . . Jason," Aaron said. "But remember, your marshal of France protector will not be there for you forever."

As he rode off, James felt the eyes of Aaron Sheffield on his back, piercing as a lance.

But Aaron had called him "Jason."

The circle of the years had nearly closed.

43
▲▲▲▲▲

"You have not seen Henri *yet?*" Paola said. "What is the matter with him? Perhaps he is not as French as I thought he was." She cocked a quizzical eye at Sarah. "Did you say something to put him off before he went to Cuernavaca with Max?" Her eyes narrowed. "Did you tell him about your affair with Jason in spite of all my warnings?"

"No. I wanted to, but I never got the chance. We hardly talked at all before he left. I saw him for just a few minutes after he returned that night, and he was so exhausted from the trip up the valley he went off to his suite and bed before we had five words. Outside my door he nearly fell again. Since that night he has been closeted with Max and his cabinet ministers at the Palacio. I haven't seen him since."

"I suppose all you can do is be patient then. I worried that you might have expressed the same doubt about the marriage you did to me."

There was no point in telling Paola yet again that it constituted far more than doubt.

For all their differences, they *had* become sisters as Paola predicted that day on the train. There had been no jealousy at Sarah's reborn closeness with Charlotte. Paola could not suppress her curiosity at what Sarah and the empress found to talk about on those twilight strolls, but Sarah resisted the urge to tell her. The countess, her instincts unerring on things like this, did not demand answers. It was different with the marriage.

Sarah did not tell Paola about her brief, disastrous

exchange with Ángela Peralta. The memory of the visit to the dressing room and the diva's insulting accusations and assumptions continued to haunt her.

She had plied herself from time to time with questions about what she was actually doing here at Chapultepec, but none of them had been the only legitimate one she *should* have asked.

When would she resign her position at court and leave here?

The answer still had a lot to do with seeing Henri.

It had even more to do with seeing Jason James again, and recovering what his last letter revealed they had lost since Zacatecas.

She had not quite begun to prepare herself for bed when someone knocked at her door.

"If it is not too late, *ma chère*," Henri Gallimard said when she let him in. "We can have the talk I promised you."

He made no attempt to embrace or kiss her. As he sank into the one big chair in her small parlor, she searched his face. She had never seen it look so troubled.

"It is not too late for something that important, Henri," she said. She braced herself.

"*Merci, mon amour.* Unfortunately, there is no easy way to do this," he said now. "I cannot tell you how sad it makes me."

Did he already know what she was going to say?

He sighed, and the sound was as empty as any she had ever heard. "I have avoided you—and the truth. I can do so no longer . . ."

"First . . ." He seemed to struggle with every word. "I must tell you once more something you already know, but which will always bear repeating. I love you. You are the greatest, indeed the only, love of my life. That will never change, believe me . . . but . . .

". . . I cannot marry you."

He lowered his face into his hands, lifted it again. "Please hear me out, Sarah. This is as difficult for me to say as it will be for you to hear."

Oh, she would hear him out, at least *try* to hear him out, even though it would be hard to follow whatever it was he was going to say with the way her head was spinning.

"You see . . ." He began again, stopped, fought with himself, it seemed, before going on. "Long before we met in Paris, and I swear to you it *was* long before, I contracted a disease. I fully thought I was cured during our time together, but it was only the calm period which follows the first stage of this affliction. After you left Paris my condition worsened again, with new and different symptoms. My doctors in Switzerland assure me I present no danger of infection to anyone any longer. Even so, I would have forsworn the few embraces I have given you since I arrived in Mexico, but I could not help myself."

Had she heard him right? Her mind was not working well.

"You might, Sarah—" he continued, his voice flat, dead, "knowing your courage and your forgiving nature—think that since I am no longer a threat to *your* health, that we could proceed with our marriage. *Helas*, it cannot be. I am moving now into the final stage of this hateful illness. My doctors tell me now it will be marked by the failure of my motor skills—something which has already begun to plague me a little as I am sure you have noticed—and . . ." he stopped again, then went on with even more apparent effort than before.". . . end with the complete loss of my mental faculties in just a few more years . . .

"I could never burden you with the care of the crumbling ruin I most certainly and inevitably will become."

His declaration that he would have "forsworn the few embraces" finally came through.

She knew the name of this disease. It was one of two whose names she had never heard uttered, and had certainly never had said out loud herself. She had only seen its name once in print, in the medical history of some forgotten

Italian duke in the time of the first Napoleon which she read in the Sorbonne, and even in her ignorance at the time, some sixth sense—prompted by the forbidding way the strange word "syphilis" appeared in context—had admonished her never to ask about it.

She recoiled. *Please, Dear God, do not let him try to touch me now. It would break his heart to see me shrink from him, and as much as he takes full blame for this, he deserves much better.*

Then the wave receded, exposing a wide, dismal strand of sorrow and sympathy.

"But surely, Henri, there is something your doctors can do about it."

"Nothing, *ma chère*. There is no hope. None at all." He slumped deeper into the chair as he spoke. "I beg you not to grieve. I am fully resigned to it. The loss of myself is as nothing compared to my loss of you." He straightened up. "I will leave for France within the week."

He stood, started for the door, but turned back to her. "One other thing, Sarah. In order that there will be as little embarrassment for you in this as possible, I have told no one here at court of my predicament. Please tell everyone that breaking our engagement was your idea. Only you, I, and my doctors know of this. I will have to tell my brother Marcel when I see him tomorrow night. I would not tell him, except that he will succeed to the title when I am gone. He can be trusted with our . . . secret—for the sake of the family name."

He bowed to her then and left without another word.

Part of her heart followed him through the door. If it had not been for Jason she might have loved Henri Gallimard the way he wished.

But she knew what she had to do. She had to get north to Jason.

"Impossible, Señorita Anderson," Colonel Miguel López, the officer Jason had named as commander of the Household Guard said. "There has been sporadic but fierce guerrilla action the entire length of the road between here and Chihuahua. Even *large* bodies of troops have come under attack from time to time. I could not get you through even if I could spare a squadron of the Guard. Talk to Blasio. *Lo siento.* I truly *am* sorry."

"No, Doña Sarah," José Luis Blasio looked horrified. "I just *can't* ask the emperor. He would think I had gone completely insane to ever consider helping a woman get to a fighting front. Perhaps Señor Eloin . . ."

"I'll find another way. *Gracias,* José Luis."

Marcel Gallimard, due to be excused from his duties as his brother's equerry in order to rejoin Pierre Boulanger's Chasseur regiment in a day or two, could not help her, either—or would not. Suspicion darkened his face when she told him what she wanted. Henri apparently had not told him of the broken engagement yet.

She ordered a carriage from Chapultepec's vehicle park and had the driver take her to Imperial Army headquarters in the Zócalo, but no one there would even listen to her.

She was about to return to the castle in frustration when she remembered she would pass Jason's house on the Paseo.

Cipi, of course, would probably be in the north with his master, but perhaps some other servant there could help—as a colonel of the Guard, Jason must employ people to look after things when he and the dwarf were gone. It was probably a futile hope, but her only remaining one.

It was midafternoon when she reached the house.

There was someone in residence, all right.

The dark, ornately carved door opened on a vision in white.

The Mexican girl she had seen in the carriage outside the Banco Central two years ago stared at her.

She had to force a greeting. *"Buenos dias, señorita,"* she

said. "I am Sarah Anderson, a . . . friend of Colonel James."

"I know who you are, Señorita Anderson."

"And you . . . ?"

"Sofía, *mi doña.*"

"May I come in . . . Sofía?"

"*Sí.*" The girl turned and led the way down a narrow hall that opened on a sparsely furnished parlor with bone white walls, where the sun streaking through tall, undraped windows and a skylight more typically left bank Parisian than Mexican caught motes of dust and turned them into microscopic diamonds. She turned back to Sarah and motioned her to a settee. The gesture was a graceful swing of her slim arm, worthy of an actress.

"May I serve you something, Señorita Anderson?" she said. "Tea, *quizá?*"

"*No, pero muchas gracias.* I shall not stay but a moment."

The girl stood with her back to the tall windows, her eyes fixed frankly on Sarah. The light streaming through the windows made a sepia silhouette of Sofía's body under her white cotton dress, and for one weirdly distracting moment it was as if Sarah were looking again at the daguerreotype of Ángela Peralta in Samuel's room at the Zacatecas *hacienda.* No young creature Jason had seen most days for two long years had any right to look this beautiful.

"I want to get north to see Colonel James, Sofía. Could you help me, *por favor?*" she said.

"*Pero* . . . I cannot help you, *mi doña.* I would go myself if I knew how."

Disappointment and satisfaction waged a small battle. "When did you last hear from Colonel James?"

"Not since before he went to Zacatecas."

"Did he not return here to the Paseo before he left for the war?"

"No, *mi doña.* The colonel lived at the palace his last few days in the city. He sent his *hombre* Cipi to pack his things."

Satisfaction had the better of the struggle by a tiny margin.

"Thank you, Sofía. I will leave now."

It had been a useless exercise. There was nothing to do for the moment but write a letter.

Darkness had fallen by the time she reached the castle, but two or three score flares and bonfires lit the outer grounds, turning the old cypresses into strange, phantasmagoric creatures, a bigger display of light than was usual for this hour.

The hall just inside the western sallyport was crowded. There had been no word of any special function for this evening, but a number of men in uniform and even more in civilian clothes thronged the huge hall. Some she recognized as dignitaries from the other foreign legations, one of them, to her surprise, Ambassador Thomas Corwin, frozen-faced and watchful. Solitary figures paced back and forth in agitation, others in small groups bent their heads together and spoke in whispers. None except Corwin, who barely nodded, seemed to notice her as she threaded her way toward the central staircase, and from their sober looks she decided they were definitely not here to attend a party of any kind.

As she walked the upper terrace toward the wing that held the chambers of the ladies-in-waiting her mind teemed with ideas on what might have happened or was happening, but then she saw Maximilian's personal ensign flying from the flagstaff on the outer balustrade. The pennant only flew when His Imperial Majesty was actually in residence and receiving at Chapultepec. The conferences at the Palacio must have concluded.

In her suite she discovered a note from Paola.

Liebchen—
      See me before you talk with anyone.
          —P. von K.

She hurried down the hall and found Paola in her sitting room, reading from a long document of some kind, a box of chocolates open on the crescent table by her chair, and a liqueur glass in her hand. The table held a cognac decanter which had been almost full last night. It was empty now, yet, except for the occasional one-glass-too-many of Champagne at a party, Paola was not much of a drinker.

"Where have you been, *liebchen?*" Troubled excitement filled the Austrian countess's huge brown eyes. The document slipped from her lap.

"What in heaven's name is going on?" Sarah asked.

"Today's two things have great importance, *liebchen*. The one about the French might be bad news for all of us foreigners here in Mexico; the other, of course, is something I think the emperor should have done a long time ago. I do not know how you feel about it, but I trust that—"

"For the Lord's sake, Paola, begin at the beginning."

"Then you have not heard?"

"I've been in the capital all day."

Paola's face turned grim. "That upstart, Emperor Napoleon—may the nasty little commoner fry in hell—has informed *our* emperor that he is pulling the French Army out of Mexico."

"What?" The news stunned her.

"It is true. Every Zouave, every last Tirailleur, every Chasseur—including my Pierre—and every single Foreign Legion *bleu* will be gone within a year. In less time—if Marshal Bazaine can manage it. Our Max will have to face the Juaristas on his own."

"So that's what the crowd down in the great hall is gathered for."

"*Nein, nein!* They are here about the *other* news. They may have heard rumors about the French withdrawal, of course, but it has not yet been made public by Max or his council. Max is furious that Napoleon apparently informed Marshal Bazaine even before telling *him*."

"How did you learn about it?"

"Charlotte. It distressed her that you were not there

when she told Melanie and me. She wants the three of us to breakfast with her tomorrow morning. The empress puts great store in our opinion, *liebchen*, especially in yours these days."

"Of course I'll be there. Now—what is the '*other* news'?"

"The emperor has issued a decree. It was the reason for the long conference your Henri has attended instead of attending to his Sarah. The decree *is* official. Copies were distributed in the castle and throughout the capital this afternoon, and more are on their way to Marshal Bazaine and the armies in the north. It brought every foreign diplomat in the capital here to Chapultepec on the run. I have no idea why."

"What does this decree say?"

Paola bent from her chair and retrieved the paper that had fluttered to the floor. "Read it for yourself."

She handed the long scroll to Sarah. It was gray with tiny print, but eyes that had pored over reams of legal and historical papers in the library at the Sorbonne had little trouble fastening on its important elements.

It began innocently enough. Following the expected stilted opening that *pronunciamientos* of any kind usually had, it actually praised Max's nemesis, the Republican president, going on to say, "the cause which has been maintained with such courage and constancy by Don Benito Juárez has failed, defeated by the national will and the will of Almighty God." Sarah drew a breath of hope. Was the emperor pleading once more for a *rapprochement*? Another try for the "accommodation" she and Jason had almost won for him at Zacatecas?

No. The decree became more ominous line by line. It went on to say that it was the "regretted" decision of the government and crown of the Empire of Mexico that anyone found carrying arms against the Imperial or French armies, or demonstrating a desire to resist them—as irregulars or even in uniformed opposition—would be put to death within twenty-four hours. No petitions for clemency would be accepted, no requests for pardon by the emperor or for redress or reprieve would be so much as entertained. Commanders in the field were ordered to execute prisoners captured in a military operation and without civil trials or courts martial.

It was signed "Maximilian I, Emperor of Mexico" and carried the signatures of every one of Max's cabinet ministers.

"My God, Paola! Max simply can't do this."

"But he *has* done it, *nein?*"

"What is the talk around the court?"

"Most, like me, are pleased. It is time the army stops the depredations of Benito Juárez and his barbarians. Some are displeased with the words of praise he showered on that wicked savage. I will admit that a few seem afraid of some imagined consequences. Oddly enough, Felix is one of them."

"I can understand that," Sarah said. "Felix Eloin, for all his faults and seeming deviousness, is more in touch with the world than some of the other people close to the emperor. This decree will outrage the foreign press, particularly in the United States, and it will disgust every civilized leader in the world. It will win Max no friends outside of Mexico, and will lose him many here, even among those who have supported him against Juárez."

Paola shrugged. "It simply cannot be all that serious, *liebchen.*"

She would think no more about any of this tonight. She would think no more about it until morning, when she told Charlotte of the decision which had just clicked into place like the sharp closing of a lock—or the opening of one.

She would give the empress her resignation when they met for breakfast.

Melanie Zichy had often dined with Charlotte on the sunlit balcony outside her sleeping chamber in the past, but it was the first time here for Sarah, and for Paola, too.

The empress looked as if she had slept no better than Sarah had herself. The shock of the French announcement of their planned withdrawal surely went deeper for her than for any of the three of them, although Melanie had clearly been shaken and tearful, when they met at Charlotte's door.

But there was infinitely more than tears or sleeplessness in Charlotte's face.

Beyond a whispered greeting she met her three ladies in silence, and stayed that way until the Indian servant cleared the last of the dishes away, leaving them only the sterling coffee service with the etched Imperial crest and the fragile Limoges cups which had somehow survived the *Novara*'s bumpy voyage to Veracruz.

A squawking red-and-yellow parrot-like bird flashed over the four of them a mere five feet above the table, and its cry and the whir of its wings startled Charlotte. A few drops of coffee spilled from the cup halfway to her lips, and with the cup still held in front of her, she wiped the table covering with her serviette, scrubbing it as if she were rubbing a hole in the tablecloth itself.

"Thank you all so much for coming," she said when she looked up at last. "You are no doubt wondering why we have called you here this morning." She paused. "The emperor has conferred all night with the members of his council about the disturbing news from France. His Imperial Majesty and your empress will concern ourselves with little else in the next weeks and months. We will bend our all effort toward persuading the French to change their minds, and in consequence we fear social life at the court will suffer." She fastened her dark eyes on Sarah. "We must ask you not to set the date for your marriage without consulting us, Sarah."

"But Your Majesty—"

"Hush, *ma chère, s'il vous plaît*. We know how that must grieve you, but there is a reason for delaying it. We will shortly leave for Paris, and we do not want to miss your wedding."

Sarah wondered if Charlotte meant both she and Max were returning to Paris, or if it was only that annoying royal plural again.

The empress settled that with her next words. "Maxl will, of course, stay here in Mexico. These are dangerous times, and there is much that only the monarch can accomplish. In Paris your empress will secure an audience with Emperor Napoleon and remind him of his promises to us and to the House of Hapsburg. She will not return to Mexico until she has new French guarantees that they will keep their forces in Mexico until pacification is complete."

Charlotte looked at Sarah again. "That should not take long," she said. "We are sure you will be the Comtesse de Bayeux by Christmastime, and we should return *long* before then." Now she turned her gaze on the other two. "Countess Zichy will accompany us to Paris and Countess von Kollonitz will assume Melanie's duties in running the Imperial household for Maxl during our absence. If Paola thinks it would be helpful, we shall appoint Princess Salm-Salm as a lady-in-waiting to serve at least until our return." She turned then to Sarah. "You told us recently, Sarah, that you were considering leaving our court. Your resignation would devastate us . . ." Charlotte actually looked stricken. She trembled. "Now—we do not think anything untoward will happen, but there is the remote possibility that the emperor could confront danger to his person. You are the only one of us with any links to our enemy, Benito Juárez. We implore you to stay in our service, and ask that you give us your promise that you will remain in our court at least until I return from France. If necessary, my dearest friend, your empress will go to her knees if she must . . ."

Paola and Melanie stared at Sarah. If Charlotte's calling her her dearest friend had brought any rancor to either of them, they failed to show it. A protest died on Sarah's lips.

She *could* delay her leaving for a bit. In the long run no more emotional harm could befall her in this brief extension than had already befallen her one way or another since she came to Mexico. She could wait for Charlotte's return, but not a second longer.

"You have my promise, Your Imperial Majesty."

"You swear it, Sarah?"

"Yes, I do . . . Charlotte."

No one had mentioned the decree.

And no one did all that day, until she met Colonel Miguel López while she strolled on the terrace trying to sort out her thoughts.

"You have read the Imperial decree, have you not, Doña Anderson? I fear it is as injudicious as anything the emperor has ever done. It is a *black* decree—*de veras un bando negro.*"

44

▲▲▲▲▲

He reported to Bazaine's tent as ordered, to find the Hero of Sebastopol in a magnificent rage.

"The fool!" the marshal bellowed. "The idiotic, adolescent, utter fool! I swear I despair of all aristocrats."

"Sir?"

Bazaine held out a long sheet of paper, a document of some kind. "Read this, *mon ami,* and even though you are a soldier and not a woman, shed a few sad tears for the Emperor of Mexico and his cause. If it was not a lost cause before, this exercise in lunacy will almost certainly insure that it will become one. And sooner than I thought."

The paper was a decree of some sort. As James read, Bazaine raved on. "I am certainly not squeamish, and I do not totally disagree with the intent of this thing, James, but why did he issue it *now?* A year ago I might have welcomed it. *Le bon Dieu* knows that Márquez, and even our own Dupin, killed enough Republican prisoners without any legal sanction. But making it an announced, *official* policy that we will execute *military* prisoners might bring the Americans into this war forthwith. And it most assuredly *will* send the anger and subsequently the morale of his enemies soaring, and at precisely the time when my French armies are preparing to withdraw. The Conservatives who might have welcomed this will be outraged by the praise for Juárez in the opening. If the Austrian should lose this struggle now, it almost guarantees he will forfeit his life as well as his tilted crown. I for one—should the Imperialist generals some day fall into his hands—would not blame Juárez if he sent every one of them to the wall, and if I *were* the Indian I would not exempt his Imperial Majesty."

James heard all the marshal's words, but they scarcely registered. The smell of battle had reached him, the odor of the fires burning inside the city strong enough, fortunately, to mask that of the rotting dead no one on either side had risked pulling away from the enfiladed ground before Chihuahua's barricades. None of those odors, though, was quite as repugnant as the one rising from what he had just finished reading.

He handed the document back to the marshal.

"I suppose," Bazaine said, "that this was met with much enthusiasm at the camp of our friend General Mejía. This 'Bando Negro,' as Lemonde tells me this filthy scrap of parchment is being called, must have reached Tomas, too. I wonder how his new colleague, General Sheffield, feels about it. If my reading of recent history is correct, Confederate officers were a devoutly chivalrous lot. Perhaps he is as disgusted with this as you quite obviously are, James."

"I cannot speak for General Sheffield, sir."

He knew what he had to do, and it would bring the end of something.

Bazaine proceeded. "I am returning to the capital to meet with Maximilian, James. This battle at Chihuahua, since Emperor Napoleon sent me his new instructions, has become a game not worth the candle. It can continue to its conclusion quite well without me. Brincourt can finish our

French part of it before we pull back to the South. I will miss you, *mon ami.*"

"May I return to the capital with you, Monsieur le Maréchal?"

Bazaine's mouth fell open. "You want to go back with me?"

"Yes, marshal."

"You surprise me, James. Do you not realize that taking you back from General Sheffield was the prelude to giving you an army of your own? With our withdrawal imminent, the Imperial Army has no course but to expand, and your career would take flight like a rocket."

"It no longer matters, sir."

The fierce, questioning eyes of the old soldier fixed him with an even more pinning gaze than had any of the myriad, sharp gazes of the past. "I am not trying to read your mind, Colonel James, but are your intentions what I think they are?"

"Yes, sir. I will resign my commission in His Imperial Majesty's army."

"And you wish to tell him of your decision to his face?"

"Yes, sir."

Bazaine walked to the array of battle flags, put out his hand and brushed it across their folds in a movement that could not have been more loving if he had touched a woman.

He turned back to James.

"Of course you may accompany me to the capital, colonel. I will make no attempt to dissuade you from the course you are setting for yourself—our time together has convinced me of your determination in everything you do—and I will arrange an audience for you with the emperor immediately after we arrive." He paused. "One thing more, sir: you are the finest and most honorable officer it has ever been my privilege to serve with. I wonder if the Austrian has the faintest notion of the value of the man he is losing through his consummate folly."

He brought his tough, square hand to his forehead in a salute.

James rode to the camp of Pierre Boulanger.

"*Sacrebleu!* I can see you *mean* this, *mon ami.*"

"I do, Pierre."

"Will you rejoin the Legion?"

"No. My days as a soldier are at an end."

"You can't mean *that!*"

"I have never meant anything more seriously in my life."

"But what will you do? You are still a young man, Jason."

What *would* he do? All that concerned him was how he could best avoid any embarrassment to Sarah. Bazaine had assured him there would be no need to go to Chapultepec; he could meet with the emperor at the Imperial Palace in the Zócalo. He would leave the capital immediately afterward, of course.

"I don't know yet what I will do, Pierre."

"Will you return to America?"

"There is, if anything, less there for me than here." He could not return to his own country yet. In a way he had forfeited the right to even *call* himself an American. "I probably will stay in Mexico, for a while, at least. I think you know I have developed a strong affection for this country." When he left Sidi-bel-Abbés the last place on this earth or in the next that he wanted to go was Mexico. Now . . .

"Tell me what prompted this Draconian decision of yours, *mon ami,*" Pierre said. "Does it have something to do with what happened in Zacatecas?"

He started, until he realized Pierre was only referring to the meeting with the president and the Imperial attack there; he had never once let slip what else had happened. "It began there," he said.

"I know you became quite enamored of the Indian, and I have long suspected that you were at least partly in sympathy with his cause, not that you ever betrayed your oaths to the French or to the emperor. Have you considered going over to Juárez and his government?"

"Not for a moment. I will no longer fight for Maximilian, Pierre, but I will not fight against him. My fight is finished."

"Then it is this Bando Negro that tipped the scale?"

"Yes."

"*Zapristi!* I admire you, Jason. This new decree outrages me, as well. I would like to think I would do as you are doing, had I given *my* oath to Maximilian, and not to France, but I am glad I am not being tested. I fear I do not have your strength of character."

The subject must be changed. "When do you take the field again, Pierre?"

"Tomorrow. Since the word came down from Bazaine that we will begin our withdrawal when this battle ends, I confess I do not have the heart for it I might once have had."

He hated to see his friend go into battle lacking the "heart" for it. "*Bonne chance,* Pierre."

"*Merci.* I have this feeling that from here on out I *will* need luck, as well as skill. I wonder if this might be the last time we shall see each other."

"Of course not. You will still be in Mexico for quite a while."

Boulanger laughed. "Just so long as I am not here forever, *mon ami.*"

Back at his own quarters he told Cipi of their impending return to Mexico City.

"Your predictions have come to nothing."

"Cipi is not perfect, but if the colonel studies *all* the news from the capital, he cannot fail to note that there *is,* as Cipi did forecast, a new heir to the crown already residing at Chapultepec. The emperor has adopted *el niño* Agustín Iturbide. Of course the infant prince will never ascend to the throne of Mexico."

PART FIVE

THE HILL OF
THE BELLS

"... let us sit upon the ground
And tell sad stories of the death of kings"

— RICHARD II

45

With Charlotte gone to France accompanied by Melanie Zichy and an entourage of advisors that included, to Sarah's surprise, Felix Eloin, the castle of Chapultepec became a giant stone cavern.

At Veracruz, Henri Gallimard, whom Sarah—to her mixed sorrow and relief—never saw again after his shocking revelation, boarded the *Imperatrice Eugenie*, the same ship the Imperial party was taking to Le Havre. The vessel's name stirred up some ironic thoughts. In the last days before her departure, the empress had taken to blaming the wife of Napoleon III for the French decision to withdraw from Mexico every bit as much as she blamed the husband. Sometimes she voiced her anger in shrill outbursts that went on at such length and with such ferocity Sarah wondered if by the time she reached Paris Charlotte could settle into the kind of regal calm that the protocol of audiences at the Tuileries required.

"Of all people, Eugénie Bonaparte should feel tremendous guilt!" Charlotte had screamed to a dozen of the people closest to her, Sarah Anderson among them. "The empress of France is even more responsible for our predicament than is Louis Napoleon. She *begged* us to come to Mexico. She is leading a conspiracy against us."

Those in the inner circle who had been with Max and Charlotte since Miramar supported her criticism of Empress

Eugénie, but it did not assuage Sarah's worries about *her* empress. In the last weeks she had become again the old, caring friend from St. Catherine's, but sometimes as fragile and moody, too, and sometimes even more eruptive than in their days at school. Her thin, wild voice seemed to echo in the corridors of Chapultepec long after she left the castle.

The emperor, who accompanied Charlotte and her party only twenty-five kilometers east of the capital to say good-bye and bestow his final blessing on her mission, now spent almost all his time at the Imperial Palace in the city. The news issuing from his offices there reported that Marshal Bazaine had returned from the siege of Chihuahua to confer with the monarch, and there were more reports that there had been a violent, crackling confrontation about what everyone now called the Bando Negro when Max and the marshal met. However bright the pyrotechnics of that meeting, the decree remained in force.

Sarah saw less of Paola. The Austrian countess, when she did catch a glimpse of her, seemed overwhelmed by her new duties as the acting head of the Imperial household, and uncharacteristically out of sorts when dealing with the castle's scores of servants. Social functions of the more elaborate kind had come to a standstill, but there were still high teas and dinners to be planned with the three kitchens and their staffs. The wine cellar had to be checked daily and accounts pored over. Paola Kollonitz turned into a frequently wild-eyed tyrant by day, and Sarah began to avoid her until she finally settled her nerves by evening. She offered her help, but Paola declined with thanks. "After all, *liebchen*," she said once. "At least I am losing weight. I may have to borrow a gown or two from you until I can meet with my couturier."

With Henri, Charlotte, and Melanie gone, and distanced from Paola much of the time, Sarah felt as if she had been cast loose from all her moorings.

She thought of quitting the castle more or less permanently and moving back with Solange on the Avenida Moctezuma. Her promise to Charlotte did not forbid that, and she certainly had little enough to keep her occupied here. Living at Avenida Moctezuma had much to recommend it. The distance between Chapultepec and Sor Francisca's orphanage demanded an overnight stay every time she visited, and she felt herself falling behind in the attention she really wanted to pay the mother superior and her charges. It was a more convenient one-day trip to the mission school from her own home than from the castle, and it would be particularly more convenient to have old Pedro drive her there at a time of her choosing, day or night, than to have to wait sometimes hours for a vehicle from the castle carriage park furnished on the whim of some officious ostler. From Avenida Moctezuma it was also but a short ride to Jason's home on the Paseo should she decide to ask the girl Sofía for news of Jason.

There remained only one compelling reason not to move back to the city.

Jason.

She was positioned better here at the castle to get word to him than she would ever be on Avenida Moctezuma.

A blizzard of letters to him had so far brought not one reply. She tried to be patient. Mail from the north came here more quickly than it did to backwater Avenida Moctezuma, although it certainly did not arrive with the speed it would have in France or back in Boston; the fastest post from the northern states took nearly three weeks to make the journey. Paola had heard from Pierre a month ago, but although she had written back to him the same day—a new diligence on the part of the carefree, slipshod countess—she still had no idea of whether or not her letter to the Chasseur had gotten through. Sarah felt helpless.

A trip to the Imperial War Office elicited next to nothing.

Jason, they told her, had gone north with Marshal Bazaine as a member of his staff, but she already knew that much. According to the uneasy clerk in the payroll and records department she spoke to, the marshal had assigned him to an Imperial regiment, but no word had come from Bazaine's headquarters as to where that regiment could be found. She suspected, from the way the clerk diverted his eyes when he told her what little he knew, that the Imperial Army was at last keeping secrets. Security must have tightened on the fighting front and along the roads there and back. She could, of course, send a letter in the personal care of the marshal, but she suspected it might be examined by the prying eyes of army censors somewhere along the way, and she wanted what she had to say to him to be seen by Jason only. She finally decided it was perhaps just as well. She still did not know how she could deal with that heartbreaking line in his last letter: ". . . *you will not hear from me again.*"

But she *would* see him again. She would have to wait . . . as she had waited once before. And for the moment at least, she would have to wait for him here at Chapultepec.

If the Imperial Army and the government of Emperor Max had at last learned the art of keeping secrets, it had been a selective learning process, confined to little things such as hiding by intent or accident the whereabouts of one of its serving officers.

But if the authorities in the capital had mastered secrecy about minor matters, they draped only a skimpy, threadbare cloak over the larger one.

It was no secret whatever that the Empire of Mexico, bastard child of the overweening ambitions of the emperor of France, who was now denying his paternity and abandoning his unwanted offspring, was drifting into mortal danger as a result of that abandonment.

To be sure, dispatches from the north claimed the Battle for Chihuahua had been another resounding victory for France and its Conservative allies, but it still cast shadows hinting at ultimate defeat. The main Republican Army had escaped destruction yet again. Matt O'Leary had predicted that if the enemy eluded Bazaine's last grand trap, and if the French withdrew—something that was also common knowledge and already underway—Chihuahua would prove to be but a small step backward for the Republicans before they began a series of crushing forward paces that might not end until their boot marks covered all of Mexico.

In the weeks after Charlotte left for France, Sarah had the first of a number of conversations about the military situation with Colonel Miguel López. The handsome colonel was more in evidence these days as alarming news trickled down from the north. The castle guard doubled in size, and for the first time since Sarah had been at Chapultepec, uniformed men outnumbered civilians at the dinners Paola oversaw. López himself frequently dined with Sarah and the Austrian countess.

Remembering how Paola had teased Pierre that day in the Plaza de Toros with her remarks on López's presumed amorous talents, Sarah wondered if her friend might now— with Pierre off to the wars again—set her cap for the colonel.

That Paola showed nothing more than polite interest in López made Sarah realize how deeply her affection ran for Jason's best friend.

López seemed every bit as knowledgeable as Matt O'Leary—if not as gloomy. And like the Matt she had known for more than five years now, he lusted after combat.

"I will not see action unless the emperor orders General Miramón and his army north. That is unlikely for a while at least. Some forces must be kept in the capital to stop Porfirio Díaz if he breaks out of the mountains and attacks Oaxaca City."

Strangely, the tall, young officer did not seem particularly disturbed by the dismal outlook for the Imperial armies once the French withdrawal was a reality. More intellect than emotion seemed to invest everything he said. He was full of some elaborate ideas about the path the emperor's grand strategy should take, and while his oddly dispassionate explanations of them interested her, they did not interest her as much as did his discussion of the armies and the smaller units and the commanders who would have to tread that path. He named names. At last she heard the one she had been listening for all along, but that she had not actually expected to hear.

"It is unfortunate that Marshal Bazaine has lost the one

officer on whom, in my humble opinion, he and the emperor could have relied even more than they could on some of the more famous generals serving under them."

"And who would that officer be, colonel?"

"A friend of yours, I think. My former superior and mentor, Colonel Jason James."

Lost? What had happened to him?

"Por favor, colonel . . . what *about* Colonel James? He has not . . ." She could not bring herself to complete the question.

Miguel López obviously read her mind or saw the black distress that must have darkened her face. "No, no, no, Doña Sarah! I presume Colonel James . . . former Colonel James . . . is alive and well. At least he was when he returned to the capital with the marshal to see the emperor and resign from the Imperial service."

Relief and gratitude swept over her. Then she took in the last of López's remarks. "Colonel James resigned?"

"Sí."

"But when? The marshal came back to Mexico City more than a month ago. I heard nothing at the time about Colonel James."

"They met with the emperor at the palace. I only learned about it a day ago myself. Actually, it was two months ago to be exact, *mi doña.*"

Jason had been in the capital two months? His vow not to see her must be as strong as when he wrote that letter. "Where is Colonel James now?"

"I have no idea. Perhaps he has settled into that house he keeps on the Paseo."

This time she could not wait for a vehicle and driver from the carriage park. She ran most of the way to the castle's stables in a frenzy and had a groom saddle her a horse.

The ride to the Paseo, although shorter and certainly less physically demanding than those to Zacatecas and back, was every bit as emotionally wearing. Thoughts raced through her mind infinitely faster than the horse traveled the capital's cobbled streets, hammering her with far more insistence than did the drumming of its hooves.

What had prompted Jason's resignation? She could guess, but it was better far to let him tell her, if he would. How would he greet her announcement that there would be no marriage to Henri Gallimard? Would he display joy or disbelief? With what he must have thought about her these last two months, would he even see her?

As she reached the sedate city block on the Paseo that held his house, the pounding of the hooves faded beneath the pounding of her heart.

Then that pounding gave way in turn to silent anticipation when she reached Jason's tree-shaded drive. She held her breath until she reined up at the portico.

What she saw stunned her.

The old baroque stone mansion was boarded up, with heavy planks nailed over the tall windows through which sunlight had silhouetted the lissome body of the girl Sofía.

Someone had posted a sign on the front door. The relentless Mexican sun had already faded it, and its edges were tattered and curling away from the mahogany.

¡RENTA!
Sr. Refugio Velarde
Bienes Raices, Fincas
19 Calle Brillo Sur

She rode to Avenida Moctezuma to spend the night with Solange and get a change of clothes. She would not give up.

An inquiry of the rental agent Señor Velarde, when she found him in his dingy office the next morning yielded nothing. He professed to have no idea where Jason had gone after paying the last of his rent and vacating the house on the Paseo.

Her immediate visit to the war office provided no help,

either. "No, Señorita Anderson," the same furtive clerk of her previous visit said. "Colonel . . . now *Señor* James . . . left no forwarding address. He collected his back pay and left. It was a lot of pay. He is now *un rico.*"

Marshal Bazaine. He should know of Jason's whereabouts.

It took three days to get a meeting with the premier French soldier in Mexico.

"I am very sorry, Mademoiselle Anderson. When Colonel James resigned and ended his military career, he left me with a handshake, but without a word as to his intentions. Perhaps he has returned to the United States. If you find him, tell him his old commander would like to hear from him."

Could he have left Mexico? She went straight from the war office to the American embassy and recruited Matt.

"I don't remember the name of his town in Kansas," she said, "but can there really be so many Jameses in such a thinly populated state? He fought here in Mexico with General Scott. I know that's a long time ago, but doesn't the American army keep records of its soldiers' hometowns and families? They would *have* to know where to send a . . ." She shuddered, but then remembered she was not searching for a dead man. Jason had not disappeared from the face of the entire earth, just that part of it she occupied. While nothing she had discovered meant he had actually left the capital, he would not have given up that house if he were staying.

"If he has gone back to the States, Miss Anderson," the Marine said, "I'll find him for you if it's the last thing I do."

She had never told Matt of her feelings for Jason, but the earnestness of his promise left no doubt he knew.

"And if he hasn't gone back?" she asked.

"I'll put out feelers here in Mexico, too. May not even have to. Most U.S. citizens who reside here for any length of time eventually register with the embassy. I presume he still considers himself a citizen." The Marine looked doubtful. "One other thought. Since he served so long in the

Foreign Legion, he might have re-enlisted. The Legion will be here for a while."

"Would not the marshal have known if he returned to the Legion?"

"Not necessarily. If he did go back he might have re-enlisted under an assumed name."

This chilled her. She and Matt would have a much harder time of it finding him if he returned to Africa no longer calling himself Jason James.

"Checking Mexico and Kansas," Matt said, "will take time, of course, particularly . . . and you have to consider this, Miss Anderson . . . if he doesn't want to be found."

She bit her lip, knowing she had to take a grip on herself and let Matt do his searching for Jason without her looking over his shoulder.

The Marine's phrase echoed in her brain.

"*. . . particularly . . . if he doesn't want to be found.*"

46

▲▲▲▲▲

"This is the most ridiculous idea you have ever had, *mi coronel!*" The furious little man driving the wagonload of household goods had been transformed from Cipi. He had puffed up into the Cipriano Sebastian Jesus Camarga Méndez y García who had forced himself on James in Veracruz more than four years ago.

From her seat in the overstuffed chair balanced on the settee in the bed of the wagon Sofía laughed. "See," the dwarf went on. "Even this simple minded *niña* knows what a farce this move will be; and *she* usually thinks every one of your most feeble farts is the utterance of some sacred oracle."

"I think Sofía is laughing at something else," James said. "If my plans upset you so, you don't have to stay with me."

"Don't have to *stay* with you? If Cipi does *not* stay with you, who will look after you? You would only make more idiotic decisions like this one. Besides, where would Cipi go? You have stripped him of his options. It would be different if we could have stayed in the army."

There indeed was the rub. When they left the army together seven weeks ago, the daily tantrums had begun. Since they closed the house on the Paseo they had worsened. The dwarf had turned petulant the moment James told him he would have to give up his uniform.

"Why is my idea so idiotic?" By rights James should not put up with this, but Cipi's eruption *was* providing some comic relief at a time when James sorely needed it. At worst, he might be right. This could very well turn out to be another idiotic notion.

"Why, indeed! Cipi will gladly tell you why. You, *mi coronel* . . . but Cipi forgets . . . he should no longer *call* you '*coronel.*'" He turned his ugly little head and spat into the roadway in disgust. "But that *is* only the beginning of this nonsense. In your stupidity you gave up a high position in the Imperial Army, where with Cipi's help you had become a man of prominence."

"Let's not get into that again."

"Cipi does not think he would have minded half so much if you had bought a silver mine like Señorita Anderson's— or a cattle ranch. You could even have invested in some dignified business in the city or used the money to buy some high office. Do you never think of faithful Cipi and *his* desires?"

"Any of those things would have cost a great deal more money than I had. It was all I could do to swing this thing. Imperial Army colonels are not made of money."

"But to take almost all the *dinero* you had and buy a *bean farm?* Why in *el Nombre de Dios* would a man who nearly became a general want to become a *farmer?*"

"I don't think you would understand if I told you."

"Probably not." He unleashed the whip over the mules'

backs. "Is Cipi permitted to ask when we leave for this pitiful bean farm, *por favor?*"

"Tomorrow at first light."

"And this farm is exactly where?"

"At San Pedro, half a league west of Querétaro."

Cipi whipped his head around and glared at Sofía. "This was *your* idea, you stupid, meddling woman!" His sizzling tone could not have been more accusing were he a vindictive judge ruling on a conspiracy of murder.

"No es verdad, Cipi," the girl said. "I only told the colonel I *come* from San Pedro. I swear I had nothing to do with his decision. The colonel does not share confidences with me."

True enough. At least it had been true since their talk together the night after the bullfight. Her mention of San Pedro had only come out reluctantly when he asked her once about her origins. In almost every other thing she had remained a mystery. But when he perused the list of farm properties for sale three weeks ago, San Pedro had leaped from the page.

The girl continued. "But I will not deny I will be happy to be close to my *familia* once again. And San Pedro is a fine village. The farms around it are small but they all do well."

James knew the dwarf would not let either of them forget this. He would burn with rage for hours, thinking Sofía had learned something before he had. He was already growling at the girl every chance he got.

"And your crotch itches now to take once more the cock of that *sucio puerco* who ruined you and made you run to Querétaro. Have you no shame, *puta?*"

"Cipi!" James broke in. "Watch your filthy tongue."

"She has not told you about him, has she?" He looked back at the girl again. "You have *not* told him, have you?"

Sofía bristled. "That *hombre* no longer lives in Querétaro."

"He could return."

"He no longer lives at all. *Mis hermanos* saw to that."

"And what will your brothers think about the *coronel?*"

"There is nothing for them to think."

The dwarf was not through. "They may not agree. If the colonel gets a knife in his back it will be your fault. They were none too happy with you five years ago, if you will bother to remember. They would have administered a *bastinado* to you if Cipi had not taken you away from that *mujer* in that house in Querétaro who wanted to make a whore of you . . ."

"*Basta,* Cipi!" James shouted. "*More* than enough!"

The dwarf became even busier with his whip. The girl looked at James sheepishly.

This business might bear looking into. He had always thought the dwarf had found Sofía in Jalapa. Now it turned out he must have hidden her in Veracruz when they first met. Of one thing he was sure: Cipi and Sofía had never been erotically involved. Sofía was not one of the fleshed-out women he liked, and when he was not bullying her, his attitude was almost fatherly. Somehow this new revelation sounded as if he had rescued the girl. He had lost none of his capacity for surprise.

Cipi's question about why he wanted to become a farmer was a good one. He thought he knew the answer.

He had been wrong when he decided his life had come full circle when Aaron Sheffield appeared in it again. But this *would* close the loop. Going back to his beginnings and starting over with what he had been as a boy was the only thing he had considered for more than a brief second after he saluted the emperor and left his service, receiving for his pains no argument from that vague man but a limp handshake and a casual sigh carrying only a tinge of regret.

It was turning back the clock, in a way.

This time there would be no Aaron Sheffield to teach him, fill him with dreams, make him wonder at—and worship—honor, toy with his mind, break his heart, make him doubt his world and himself. His cousin would still be in Mexico, but he would occupy an entirely different universe from James. There could not be even the slimmest chance of that "*carved in stone*" promise ever coming true.

Cipi was still savagely attacking the two poor animals drawing the wagon, and doing a lot of low muttering that James, while not exactly silencing, had at least muffled. Every last syllable, though, was clearly meant to be heard. James, smiling broadly, only heard part of it.

". . . humiliating . . . we have done great things for nothing . . . a *farmer* and a miserable hired hand . . . *caramba!* . . . what would Colonel Boulanger say? . . . it is criminal to hide a city man like Méndez y García in a field of beans . . . it amounts to indecency . . . has this stupid colonel no pride at all? . . . no compassion or respect? . . . and does this *norteamericano* fool think he can please his elegant *norteamericana* with this foolishness?"

The last phrase stopped the smile. Sarah. Yes, *she* would still be in Mexico for a while, but the move to Querétaro would take him from her orbit long enough for her to get back to France with Henri Gallimard. Would they marry there or in Mexico before they left? Were they already man and wife, *Comte et Comtesse?*

And for Lord's sake when would he stop torturing himself?

Cipi turned the wagon north. He knew the road to Querétaro, all right. James suspected that the devious little beggar had already known the location of the farm James had bought with the cheque that came close to stripping every last *peso* from his bank account.

The angry little man driving the wagon turned to him. "You will grow a beard and get fat and wear a big, dirty, straw sombrero and stink of beans, onions, and pig shit!"

"Nothing wrong with that. There will be rewards. We should bring in our first crop next spring. In late May or early June, I should imagine," James said. "You have never brought in a crop before, I take it. You will take more pleasure in it than you think."

"*¡Si!* Cipi will sing and dance," the dwarf said, the acid

sarcasm in his voice something to marvel at. "It will, without a doubt, be the greatest day in the entire history of Querétaro, past, present, or in time to come."

47
▲▲▲▲▲

To shield herself from the cold wind of her fear that Matt's search would end in failure and she would never see Jason again, Sarah turned her mind toward the worsening news from the north—and toward the mystifying lack of *any* news from Paris about the empress.

Miguel López told her and Paola one night at dinner that Marshal Bazaine had ordered the withdrawal of all his French and Imperial forces from Ciudad Chihuahua. "Juárez's army reoccupied the city without a shot being fired, and the president has seated his government there again." Maximilian, he went on to say, was outraged, and he had demanded Bazaine retake Chihuahua one more time, but the marshal refused. "He was not even courteous about it."

Since then the flow of arms and ammunition and other supplies to the Juaristas—scores of cannon, thousands upon thousands of new, modern rifles from the United States, mules, foodstuffs, freight wagons, medicines, and other supplies—had broadened and deepened to a powerful stream that threatened to become a swollen river by summer's end, and a tide by early autumn.

Christmas had come and gone, as had Easter—indeed both were now months behind them—without a word about when Charlotte might return from France. Whatever Max heard from her he did not share with the rest of the suddenly bewildered residents of the castle on the few occasions when they saw him.

Sarah had never expected the empress would make it

back in time for the holidays as she had promised, but her extended absence spoke of deep trouble for her fateful, emotionally charged mission to change the mind of Napoleon III. Its purpose clearly had not been accomplished yet; the French retrenchment and withdrawal continued unabated. Bazaine's Tirailleurs, Zouaves, Legionnaires, and Chasseurs no longer even looked for the enemy. As they moved southward league by desolate league, they only fought when the Republicans attacked, and the only government troops still on the offensive at all were those of Maximilian's Imperial Army. *Their* actions, even though bloodier after the return of the savage Leonardo Márquez from Turkey to fight alongside Tomas Mejía, became defeats more and more often.

The roll call of the places—large and small—that López said had fallen to the Republicans in the long, hot summer of 1866—now almost at an end—became a litany of Imperial defeat. Village and city names she had never heard before ran through the reports she got from López. It shamed and saddened her to discover how little she knew of the country she had come to love. Her mental map of Mexico north of Zacatecas was very nearly an unrelieved blank. She knew Tampico, Matamoros, and Monterrey, of course, but when López rattled off Saltillo, Guaymas, Tuxpan, Alvarado, and Tlacotalpan as also having fallen to the Republicans, he might as well have spoken of places on another planet.

"These losses, Colonel López," she asked, "I realize they are serious, but are they irreversible?"

"*Quién sabe*, Doña Sarah?"

Friendly and engaging as the Household Guards commander was, he sometimes made her uneasy with his air of eerie calm as he told her about military catastrophes she would have expected to alarm one of Max's most trusted officers. To her discomfort he even made a dark joke about one of the defeats, at Alvarado, where a thousand captured Mexican troops went over to the enemy.

"In the long run it is probably a boon. If they fight as badly for Don Benito as they did for the emperor, we have a chance."

To be fair, López was not the only one who seemed untouched by the reverses. His almost casual attitude about what was happening not too far to the north was typical of the attitudes of too many other residents of Chapultepec, including the emperor. But Maximilian's concern had sharpened recently. Now, at least, he was spending much more of his time in the Imperial Palace, conferring with Miramón and the other generals who would defend the southern sector if the Republicans were to get that far. No one in the castle, soldier or civilian, thought they would.

Summer gave way to a dry autumn in the quietly subtle way of the change of seasons in the Valley of Mexico. The leaves on the *ahuehuete* trees in the forest now called Parque de Chapultepec, where they had dined with Ignacio Comonfort, gathered enough dust to turn them as gray as ash. It began to seem—to Sarah if to no one else—as if something might be coming to an end.

For her the stream of time had forked, and was now running in two currents of vastly differing speeds. One, carrying the splinters of her hopes that Matt would find Jason, was a wide, sluggish channel that scarcely moved; the fierce waters of the other fork, the war, raced as if through a giant sluiceway.

It seemed only yesterday that Charlotte left for France with Chihuahua under siege and the French and Imperial Armies still in the ascendancy. Now, as suddenly as a sunset over the Sierra Occidental, places in the northeast, the north, and as frighteningly near as Mazatlan in Sinaloa on the northwest coast, were in Juarista hands.

Even more ominous, at breakfast one October morning, a long, vicious lead article in a box on the front page of the Conservative newspaper *La Sociedad* reported that General Porfirio Díaz had captured Oaxaca City. The boxed column blamed "Imperial indifference" for the defeat—in impassioned language. It surprised her that a journal that claimed to back the emperor would give the fall of Oaxaca so much space, and turn so much criticism, some of it cruel and all of it disrespectful, on what it perceived as the weaknesses of the monarch. Then she remembered that the journal was the personal trumpet of Max's nemesis, Archbishop Labastida.

"The tone is excessive, *sí*," Miguel López said. "But Oaxaca *is* a devastating loss. It is no more than a week's forced march from Chapultepec and the city of Mexico."

Maximilian acted decisively enough this time. General Miramón and the army that had guarded the capital and the castle roared out of barracks as if scourged, pounding down the road south to meet the challenge of Juárez's most talented commander.

Some agonizing thoughts about her deepest desires for this country plagued her. She wished passionately that Jason was with her. What were his thoughts on the precarious state of Mexico now? She needed his strength and understanding—and above all his example. His resignation from the Imperial Army had been, if her guess about his motives was correct, a stronger and certainly more honorable declaration of principle than any she had made.

But she could only wish; so far Matt's efforts had met with no success.

She wished fervently for the return of Charlotte. Until that event released her from her promise, she could make no rational decision about her future, with or without Jason.

She wanted to turn to Paola for solace, but when the Austrian woman was not in a frenzy of activity about her duties at the castle, Sarah found her sulking and ended up consoling her friend rather than being consoled.

Paola's sullen mood darkened their relationship for weeks before Sarah pinned her down about the cause of her malaise.

"Agnes Salm-Salm," Paola said.

"What about her?"

"The reason I did not let you help me with my duties was

because Melanie assigned Agnes to assist me. Max is at the castle so seldom nowadays that I need his full attention whenever he does spend a few moments with us, but Agnes throws herself at him like a harlot."

News—not from Charlotte, but about her—came at last from Paris by way of two letters, one to Paola from Melanie Zichy and another from M. Auguste Pelletier to Sarah.

Separately they told a disturbing story. Read alongside each other and reflected against Sarah's last moments with the empress, it became a frightening one.

The first audience with Napoleon III had gone badly. The French monarch had apparently tried to be as gentle as possible with Charlotte, but he had been adamant that France was going to wash its somewhat sullied hands of Mexico.

According to Melanie—who had not been present, but who had gotten the story from Felix Eloin, who had—Charlotte had gone berserk, accusing the French emperor of yielding to the demands of "that whore, your wife!" Empress Eugénie had tried to calm her down, to no avail.

M. Auguste reported that Louis Napoleon was so shaken by the confrontation he had taken to his bed, and had avoided Charlotte ever since, doggedly postponing any further meetings with her. Empress Eugénie hid from Charlotte too.

During a nightmarish stay at the Grand Hotel in the French capital Charlotte had become completely divorced from reality and shrieked to anyone who would listen—including a journalist friend of M. Auguste's from *Le Temps*. The writer did not try to publish the shocking story, but he did tell his friend Professeur Pelletier that Charlotte claimed Eugénie was bribing the chef at the Grand to poison her food. Panicked, Eloin and Melanie had spirited Charlotte off to Miramar and had called in a specialist from Vienna's largest hospital for the insane. Melanie's letter to Paola said the plan was to bring her back to Mexico once she recovered, but it contained no guess as to when the recovery might be complete. Instead it hinted that the Viennese doctor held out little hope.

Paola and Sarah did not breathe a word of what they had learned, but someone else at court must have heard from Paris. The news ran like wildfire through every nook and cranny of Chapultepec.

From the look of him, Sarah decided Max knew. But of course he *would*. Adroit Felix Eloin, even though probably all too aware of the fate of so many of history's bearers of bad news to the mighty, could not keep anything of this magnitude a secret.

At least no one poor soul here at the castle or at the Palace had the sole responsibility for being the messenger for Imperial Mexico's more immediate mounting misery.

The casualty lists from the fighting fronts lengthened. The early battles in 1862—the two at Puebla and the one at San Lorenzo—had been huge, deadly affairs, to be sure, but Matt had said at one point during the pacification that the French were conquering Mexico with their feet. Márquez and Colonel Dupin had been ruthless marauders, showing their defeated foes no quarter, but their engagements had been relatively small in number and in casualties. This had now all changed.

The Republicans were not retaking the country merely by walking over it as the French had. Men were dying in great numbers on both sides.

She could and did console herself with the thought that Jason, wherever he was, was no longer involved in the fighting.

Then something happened that began as another castle whisper, a mere rustle of a rumor, something that struck her as outlandish, but that in the end made more sense than anything since Charlotte's departure for France.

Maximilian I, the Emperor of Mexico, the hushed gossip had it, was considering abdication.

She remembered the Max von Hapsburg of almost three years ago on the train from Veracruz to La Soledad surveying the bright, singing colors of the land he had come to rule, colors heightened and intensified even more by his own bright hopes and dreams. She remembered, too, Max and Charlotte turning their faces down to the silent white ocean of *calzone* clad Indians which had lapped against the steps of the cathedral in Puebla in a tide of love. The memories of the pair were vivid, and . . . yes . . . admit it, Sarah, affectionate. She could take no joy—ever—in their leaving even this *papier-maché* throne.

She shrugged off the rumors, did not even discuss them with Paola. Max would never even think of abdicating. The whispers would surely soon fade to nothing.

But they did not.

Three envoys from the court of Napoleon III, with faces grimmer than those usually seen on diplomats, arrived at Chapultepec, loosing still another chorus of innuendoes that for the first time had a basis in fact. No one in the castle's secretariat could keep a secret any better than could the war office. Max closeted himself with his generals at the palace and kept the envoys waiting for three days before he granted them an audience, but José Luis Blasio told Agnes Salm-Salm, who told Miguel López, who told Sarah, the purpose of the visit.

The French emperor was begging, almost demanding, that Max abandon the throne and return to Miramar. According to Blasio the envoys played heavily on the state of Charlotte's health, hinting strongly that her only hope of full recovery was for Max to come back to Europe and work in concert with her Viennese doctors. One of the three, a Baron Phillipe d'Antoine, of whom Sarah had heard but whom she never met during her time in Paris, had gone to Miramar to assess Charlotte's condition for Louis Napoleon. But if he confided in Blasio, at least this time Max's junior secretary kept discreetly mum, although José Luis did disclose that the baron had brought a letter from the empress, a thick packet, actually, page after page filled with

Charlotte's patently pathological rantings about Napoleon and Eugénie.

If the blandishments of the three envoys had any effect on the emperor when he finally met with them—for a total of nineteen minutes according to the Blasio-Agnes-López telegraph—Sarah failed to see it in his face.

In any event she had little opportunity to study him. He left Chapultepec the very next day for a holiday stay in his summer residence at Jalapilla, near Orizaba.

Unlike his visits to La Borda, made with only one or two other people, a dozen members of the court went east with him to Jalapilla, among them—and presumably in charge of the party—Agnes Salm-Salm.

"That minx has wormed her way into Max's confidence. Managing an Imperial journey was always Melanie Zichy's responsibility," she said, in a fine aristocratic fustian. "Any examination of protocol should have told Max to take *me* with him to run things, instead of that brazen *parvenu. Gott im Himmel!* All he had to do was read his own silly book." Paola made life miserable for the kitchen and household staffs for a week, despite Sarah's best efforts to soothe her injured feelings.

Sarah could not know that within ten days she would wish desperately for a display of even this kind of petty outrage from her friend, demeaning as it seemed now.

Miguel López expressed doubt about the wisdom of the junket of the emperor and his traveling companions.

"The emperor apparently does not know or care about the bad effect this excursion might have on his soldiers. The commander-in-chief should not be perceived as taking time off to idle when things are going so badly on every battlefield."

The idea of Emperor Maximilian abdicating left the realm of speculation when López received a message from José Luis Blasio at Jalapilla.

According to Miguel, Blasio said Maximilian was not only *considering* vacating his throne, but had more or less made up his mind to do so. Apparently the three-man delegation from Paris had been more persuasive than Sarah had thought possible.

No mention of such a decision, if it actually had been made, appeared in the official dispatches from the temporary Imperial residence, but they contained other news almost as electrifying.

The emperor had repealed the Black Decree, the infamous Bando Negro.

"It is a useless gesture," Lopez said. "He cannot undo the damage. The only result of the Bando Negro was to stiffen the resistance of his enemies, here *and* abroad. Most of his *supporters* were dismayed by the edict when it was first announced. The repeal, I fear, will be not looked upon as evidence of repentance, but of weakness. With the emperor pressed on every front, it was at the very minimum the wrong time for this."

A new view of the abdication rumor appeared in the front page of *La Sociedad* in the form of a "letter" addressed to "His Imperial Majesty, Maximilian I, Emperor of Holy Catholic Mexico." The letter praised Max's and Charlotte's reign, and implored him, indeed *commanded* him, not to consider abdicating for a second, ". . . lest the forces of the Anti-Christ prevail in this struggle between Light and Darkness." It never could have appeared without the full approval of Labastida, and indeed, for all its promise of support for Max and the regime, it carried the claw marks of that *eminence grise* in every line. The archbishop must have written it himself. "It is the Catholic duty of the monarch to stay on watch for God," the letter continued, "should he not, Holy Church may have to perform its painful duty and leave the Emperor's soul to His dreadful and eternal wrath by excommunicating him."

Almost as an afterthought, another column on the front page of the paper announced that the army of Juárez's General Ortega had now captured Durango, San Luis Potosí, and Zacatecas, and that Marshal Bazaine had hinted that these would be the last actions of the French Army in Mexico. It quoted Bazaine as saying that the battle for

Zacatecas had resulted in extraordinarily high French casualties and that, ". . . it is time for the forces of His Imperial Majesty to assume full responsibility for the war."

Sarah was too stunned to look at the casualty lists, beyond noting that they seemed even longer.

She wrote to Alberto Moreno at Sierra Verde, begging for his story about what had happened in Zacatecas, and mentioning her prayers that nothing had happened to him or his people.

When the emperor returned from Jalapilla a day later he asked Paola to plan a huge dinner, a banquet, in order that he might address the entire court.

Princess Salm-Salm occupied the place usually reserved for Charlotte. At Sarah's elbow Paola sat as silent as a wisp of smoke, but Sarah could feel the heat from her friend's body, radiating as if from a poorly banked fire that could burst into flame at any moment.

When the meal was finished Max rose.

A hush of anticipation blanketed diners who were usually a fairly noisy lot, and for the first time in Sarah's memory there was no need for Max to tap his wine glass for silence and attention. Even the servants seemed to know that something important was about to happen; they stood in mute ranks against the walls.

The emperor looked even paler than usual, and his tall figure was bent into an even more pronounced stoop than in the past.

"*Mes cher amis . . .*" At least his voice was strong and firm as he began. "It is time for us to put all conjecture about the future of the Imperial Monarchy to a rest.

"Because of the temporary military reversals suffered in this past year, much pressure has been brought to bear on your emperor to forsake his Crown and abandon you. Some of those who have felt this to be a correct and honorable course are dear, loyal friends and faithful subjects, but they are sadly misinformed as to our character if they think we could ever be persuaded to this course.

"*We shall not abdicate, now or ever!* By Divine appointment and intercession we shall hold our crown, our throne, and our empire—as Almighty God himself intends.

"We shall not only not abdicate nor surrender, we shall take personal command of our armies in the field. Next week we leave for Querétaro, the closest of our cities to the enemy, to establish ourselves in that forward position and hold it until our valiant Imperial soldiers achieve the final victory.

"There is no need for us to tell you that each of you individually and all of you severally have our unbounded love and trust."

As he neared the end he became more erect with every word, every breath. His light blue eyes glowed as Sarah had never seen them glow before. At this moment he would appear an emperor to even the most skeptical.

Two mornings later a jubilant Paola told Sarah that Max had sent around a note. "He wants me to go with him and run his residence at Querétaro, *liebchen*. Perhaps Princess Agnes has worn out her welcome!"

But that evening Paola missed dinner in the small salon she usually shared with Sarah, Miguel López, and the two Belgians and three Austrians who had been, month in and month out, the most congenial of Chapultepec's European contingent. With her enormous appetite Paola never passed up a meal. Perhaps she was too excited about Max's taking her to Querétaro.

Although none of the regular diners were impolite enough to comment on it, the dinner, without Paola to remonstrate with the servants, was a minor disaster, as if it had been as totally unplanned as it was unsupervised. When she heard about it, Paola would be beside herself. It would go hard with old Rafael, the Mexican *mayordomo* who had the chief responsibility for the dining room. When the affair ended Sarah sought him out and asked him what had gone wrong.

"*La Condesa* left no instructions for this evening, *Doña*

Sarah." The old servant was trembling; he knew how badly things had gone. "I have not seen her since early afternoon."

"I will speak with her, Rafael."

She hurried to Paola's suite. There was no answer to her knock, but a crack of light showed under the door; Paola *must* be in. She knocked again. Fifteen or twenty seconds went by before she heard a weak, muffled voice, speaking in German. She only made out the last word. *"Kommen."*

The last rays of the dying sun revealed that the door to the bedroom was ajar, and when she entered it she found Paola face down on her four poster bed. On the floor beside her lay the ripped pages of a newspaper. Paola clutched a torn half-page of the paper in her hand.

Sarah stepped closer to the bed and as she did Paola lifted the hand that held the scrap of newsprint. Even in the faint light Sarah could make out that it was from the section of *La Sociedad* with the list of casualties from the north. She eased the half-page from Paola's grip. There was not enough light under the canopy of the bed for her to read by.

"Light my lamp, *liebchen*." Paola still had her face deep in the pillow. "There is a story, too."

Sarah lit the lamp and held it over the printed sheet. Each of the recent battles had its own list of the dead and wounded.

Pierre Boulanger's name headed the list of those killed in action at Zacatecas.

> *Boulanger, Pierre—Colonel,*
> *3rd Chasseurs d'Afrique*

The story ran in the column alongside the list.

CHASSEUR AWARDED CROIX DE GUERRE
Colonel Pierre Boulanger of the 3rd Chasseurs Regiment has been awarded the Croix de Guerre by Marshal François-Achille Bazaine for courage above and beyond the call of duty in the recent action at

Zacatecas. In utter disregard of his own personal safety, Colonel Boulanger rode alone to the rescue of a fellow Chasseur officer who had become separated from his command, only to meet lethal Republican fire. The rescued officer, Captain Marcel Gallimard, also of the 3rd Regiment, has requested a Requiem-Mass for Colonel Boulanger when the regiment returns to the capital next week.

By the time she finished reading it, Paola had turned over and sat up. Her eyes were dry, but makeup had streaked her cheeks. Tears had stained the lace pillow case behind her.

"How long have you been alone here, Paola?" Sarah asked.

"All afternoon . . . years. What difference does it make?"

"You should eat something."

"No."

Sarah stayed with her until full dark and for hours longer. They did not talk. There was nothing much to say.

The Requiem Mass had more celebrants at the great, golden altar than mourners in the pews. Except for Sarah, Solange, Matt O'Leary, and Paola, the other five or so were all in the uniform of the Chasseurs d'Afrique. She saw Henri's younger brother. He looked different, genuinely crushed and sad.

She sought one special face. If Jason was still in Mexico and knew about Pierre's death he would be here. She did not see him.

Marcel Gallimard, a major now, and in a dress uniform, approached them when the Mass was done.

He spoke first to Paola. "I am so sorry, Countess von Kollonitz. I am afraid it was my fault." Sarah had never expected to hear such contrition from Marcel, and neither she nor Gallimard were prepared for the fierce heat of the response Paola made.

"It was not *your* fault, *monsieur!* It is the fault of *France!"*

It withered young Marcel, who moved quickly on, and Sarah might have felt embarrassment had this not been the first sign of life from Paola since the emperor's note that she was to join him at Querétaro.

Paola had been virtually catatonic since Sarah found her face down in her bedroom. That things had been going on in that once lively mind became apparent, though, in her next words.

"I have written to Charlotte at Miramar and to the emperor at Querétaro, Sarah. I am resigning from the court. I will take Pierre back to his family in Paris. I have gotten Max's agreement to have you take my place with him at Querétaro."

Something twisted inside Sarah, but she gave Paola no argument. By not speaking she knew she was making another promise to add to the one she had made to Charlotte.

The emperor left for Querétaro as promised, and three weeks later word came for Sarah to come there with an escort composed of those members of the Household Guard Max had left behind, including its commander, Miguel López.

Paola came down to the sallyport to see the party off, an "auf wiedersehen," she said, not a good-bye.

But something told Sarah Anderson it *was* good-bye.

48
▲▲▲▲

Life at the tiny farm as the time for the first harvest neared would have been a near perfect existence for Jason James had there been someone with whom to share it.

Someone? Thinking about that would bring not a single *peso* of emotional profit. Even if things between Sarah and him had worked out differently, he could never have brought her here. The idea of taking her from her life at Chapultepec or wherever she more likely lived it now, and bringing her to a marginal farm in a Mexico far different from the one she had known, was preposterous.

It had constituted enough of a plunge into the ridiculous at the beginning for Cipriano Méndez y Garciá, but it seemed at times during the past months that the dwarf was at last making a satisfactory if grudging adjustment to pastoral life.

But Cipi's past had been vastly different from that of Sarah Anderson. James could never have asked *her* to adjust.

And yet it was strange that Sarah might at this moment be a farmer's *wife*. Had she not told him—or had it been Marcel Gallimard—that Henri, le Comte de Bayeux, owned a farm on the Loire in France? Well, a chatelaine was not precisely a farm wife. An unbridgeable chasm gaped between a chateau on the Loire—hemmed in by faithfully trimmed, dense hedges, geometric emerald fields, pastures thick with sheep perhaps, and stables housing blooded horses—and James's leaky stone *casa* thatched with *maguey* looking out over a scrubby, weedy oblong of not even fifty hectares. The two outbuildings were flimsy *jacales*, sheds without doors or walls. His horse and Cipi's, perfectly adequate animals to ride to market in Querétaro while Sofía drove the wagon, had no pedigrees. Three *burros* rounded out his "blooded" stock.

He could not offer her Paris, either, just Querétaro, only half a league away in actual distance, but a thousand kilometers off in the way he had come to measure things deep inside him.

Querétaro, however, in his present circumstances, was more than enough for *him*, when he could take time from planting and digging irrigation ditches to go there. Or it had been, until just this month.

* * *

When Cipi, Sofía, and he reached the old colonial city on the way to San Pedro it was still full daylight, with more than enough time to make it to the farm before darkness fell. But after one deeply admiring look at the plaza, the cathedral, and the ancient buildings with their smooth, sepia walls broken by wrought-iron balconies filled with flowers, he decided they would stay the night.

"Aah . . ." Cipi said, "it is a reprieve, but not much of one." He had been an unhappy traveler since the first day out, carping about the clumsy wagon, the food, and every place they had slept. "Still, it will probably be Cipi's last decent meal for all eternity."

The dwarf found them a fine *posada* on the plaza and hired a rheumy-eyed old man to watch the wagon through the night.

Supper and rooms for the three of them cost rather more than James wanted to pay, and it reminded him that he would have to be a good deal more careful with his resources than he had been in the past. He would have had Cipi find less expensive quarters, but he decided that perhaps the girl and the discontented runt deserved one last night of comparative luxury before they settled into a life in which even an *approximation* of luxury would play no part.

Cipi knew Querétaro only a little, it turned out, but it was home territory to the girl.

"I came to market here every Saturday when I was a *niña, mi coronel*," she said in response to James's question about her knowledge of the city.

After supper she led them through the Alameda and a warren of narrow *calles* that finally opened on the cathedral plaza. She asked then if she could go to vespers, pray, and make confession.

With a dyspeptic grunt Cipi endorsed the idea. "We will *need* her prayers for this senseless enterprise. If he were a religious man, Cipi would go in with her."

"Too late for *you* to pray, *mierda pequeña*," James said. "After the life you've led."

Across the plaza stood the usual places selling religious medals and other objects of worship. The line of shops, some shuttered tight at this hour, made the plaza look like Mexico City's nighttime Zócalo in miniature, but without nearly as many blind and crippled *peones* sitting with their bent backs against the walls as in the capital.

Sofía had been even more silent than usual on the last stages of the journey from the capital, but here in this familiar city she had displayed a certain wary liveliness. Perhaps it was a matter of apprehension about the welcome she might find when she some day reached her family.

In their nearly five years together her age had always been indeterminate—and by him undetermined. Certainly he had seen no sign of aging, but at the moment some new surge of youth had made her look little more than a child.

She skipped up the broad steps of the cathedral, hardly touching them. It was like the flight of the *golondrinas* swooping and darting around the towering twin belfries that soared into the sky above them. He wondered what requests of her God, or more probably of the Virgin, she would make.

April. His first crop would be ready in five or six more weeks.

He knew now something of his father's deep satisfaction every late summer back in Kansas as harvest season neared. With any luck, and with enough hard work such as Cipi, Sofía and he had done these past few months, he could bring in two crops a year.

He had expected the hard work, had wanted it, in fact. He did not look upon it as a penance of any kind; he now had nothing to repent. Regrets, however, were a different matter.

If he had not stayed with Maximilian so long . . . if he had resisted Bazaine's request that he join the Imperial Army and had stayed with the Legion . . . if . . .

He spent long days in the sun, plowing with the team of

oxen rented from a neighbor Cipi had as usual bullied into accepting what James thought an insulting pittance. He tilled, planted, diverted the stream that ran through the northwest corner of his fields two hundred meters above where it cut a deep gorge with excrescent fangs of stone exposed, and built the gates for his irrigation system—with a surprisingly willing and knowledgeable, if foul-tempered Cipi laboring beside him. The work made it easier to keep his thoughts of Sarah successfully at bay.

But he still awoke in the middle of some long nights with her face looming in the darkness. Intellect did not function well in those black moments.

If Cipi still groused, and if James still had dark night thoughts, one of the three of them seemed completely happy for the first time since they met.

The third morning at the farm, as they finished breakfast, Sofía had asked James if she could make the visit to her family she must have looked forward to in mixed joy and fear every foot of the journey from the capital.

"Could I take one of the *caballos, por favor?*"

Before he could answer, Cipi intruded. "Why do you need a horse? It is less than two kilometers. Take a *burro!*"

James had not known until then that her old home was that close by. One look at the girl's face—doubt and nervousness showing in it—told him this matter of riding there must be of some importance to her. "Of course you may take a horse, Sofía. Cipi will be happy to saddle one for you. Won't you, Cipi?"

The little man grunted something unintelligible, but left the table and stumped out the open door and toward the shed they had pressed into service as a stable.

"*Grácias, mi coronel,*" Sofía said. Ordinarily as poised as a pontiff, the girl suddenly looked agitated. "If I am on horseback it will look as though I have become someone. My family never owned a horse when I lived with them, and probably does not own one now."

He noticed then that although she still wore the familiar

white cotton dress, she had slipped on the pair of sandals she had bought just before they left Mexico City, and had draped her graceful neck with the silver necklace which Cipi—in an unexpected show of generosity for all his reputation as a pennypincher—had surprised her with last Christmas, shaming James into buying her a lace *mantilla*. When she protested that the necklace cost too much, Cipi had growled, "*Es nada.* I found it." James knew he was lying.

She looked fresh and lovely. But she also looked apprehensive, perhaps frightened.

"Would you like Cipi to ride there with you, Sofía? Or better still, should I?"

"No, no, no, *mi coronel!* This is something I must do by myself."

He shouted to Cipi to saddle the black, far the handsomer of the two horses, and as she rode off minutes later, a tiny, erect figure in white, she looked as much a queen as Empress Carlota had on *her* black horse in a parade he had seen once on the Paseo.

When Sofía returned in the late afternoon she did not come alone. Cipi and James had been working the field closest to the house, but they dropped their hoes as if on a signal and hurried to the corral to meet her. As much longer as James's strides were than Cipi's, he was hard put to keep up with the dwarf.

Two young men on *burros* and trailing a third with deep wicker baskets strapped to its flanks rode beside Sofía. A smile brightened the girl's face and James's sudden, irrepressible sigh of relief made him aware of how he had unconsciously worried all day long about her and the reception she might get as a probable prodigal daughter. The dwarf must have been nervous about this trip, too, the way he scampered out of the field to greet her.

The two men must be *los hermanos*, the brothers Cipi had invoked in his warning to the girl back in the capital.

"*¡Gemelos!*" Cipi said just before the threesome arrived at the gate to the corral.

"Twins? They could be two of triplets."

"You may be right, *mi coronel.*"

"You don't know?"

"I must not have noticed the startling the resemblance when I saw them in Querétaro five years ago. I was, of course, in a hurry to leave that town of *rústicos* at the time. Those two were very angry *niños locos.*"

It was a relief to see that the young men were smiling now; they were shy, but he could see the sinewy strength in their lithe bodies. Pushed to anger, they very likely would have been formidable foes. They paid no attention to the dwarf, but they looked James over very carefully between warm glances at Sofía.

"These are my brothers, *mi coronel,*" Sofia said. "This one," she pointed to the one who had hopped from the back of his *burro* to hold the head of the black horse while she dismounted, "is called Vicente. The one back there is Armando. They bring gifts of welcome from *mi madre.* She would have come to show respect, *también,* but she does not walk too well these days, and she does not ride at all."

The one called Armando was leading the trailing *burro* forward. One of the wicker baskets overflowed with foodstuffs: huge round loaves of bread, melons whose rich aroma overpowered the sharp smells of the farmyard, other fruit, and vegetables. The companion basket held big chunks of some dressed animal, deep red meat veined with streaks of pure white fat.

Vicente and Armando did not stay long, and while they were within earshot of James and Cipi, neither of them said a word, merely nodding when James thanked them, but when Sofía walked them down the drive just before they left, a good deal of unheard conversation took place amongst the three. *Los hermanos* sent a dozen or more inquisitive looks James's way. This time a few were directed at Cipi. James was glad to see the ones directed toward *him* were of curiosity, not enmity. He could not be sure about those they gave Cipi, but they did not look threatening at least. Sofía must have made her peace complete enough to include the little man.

The talk ended with a round of *abrazos*, and when the brothers were at last on their *burros* again and moving down the road in front of the farm, Sofía returned to James and Cipi.

"Armando and Vicente do not think you look much like a farmer, *mi coronel*," she said. Unless James was mistaken there was a touch of satisfaction, perhaps pride in her voice.

"Your homecoming went well, Sofía?"

"*Sí. Muy bien. La Virgen* has answered the prayers I made to her in the cathedral the other night. My brothers wish me to come home and live with them and *mi madre* once again."

"Is that what *you* want?"

"*No, mi coronel.* My place is here with you and Cipi for some time yet. I have told *mis hermanos* that, and they accept it." She smiled. "It did not go so easy telling *mi madre* that, but I think she understood."

He would not ask how long "some time yet" might be.

"Enough talk!" Cipi shouted. He pointed to the two wicker baskets. "Let us haul these fine *comestibles* to the kitchen. Cipi is hungry enough to eat a vulture—feathers, head, beak, and all."

After supper James moved out to the bench on the western side of the house and stoked up the pipe he had begun smoking on the trip from the capital to Querétaro. The sun was just beginning its final dip below the tops of the distant hills. Its rays were silhouetting a nearby stand of *maguey* he and Cipi would eventually have to eradicate. The black shadows from the spiky fronds inched across the yard like the bayonets of a line of advancing skirmishers. He smiled. He should put the metaphors of his old profession behind him now, but the habits and thinking of nearly twenty years died hard. Never again would he face sharp steel, not the shadow nor the substance of it—unless it was an ax or a scythe.

"*Mi coronel*," Sofía had emerged from the house to stand beside him.

"Yes?"

She had removed the silver necklace and her feet were bare again.

"Does the colonel remember the promise he made me once . . ." she said, "that someday he would do something for her that, as he said, would make things right at least in part? Those were the colonel's words, not mine."

"Yes, I remember."

"You have done it now, *mi coronel*."

"In what way?"

"You have brought me home."

His pipe had gone out. "But that was mere coincidence. I can take no credit."

"Ah, but you can, *mi coronel*. The colonel held in his *corazon* what I wanted more than anything. *Muchas gracias*."

He had held it in his *heart*?

By the first of May the bean plants had stiffened into near maturity. Almost the last weeding had been done, and there was no more heavy work ahead of them until the actual harvest sometime around the middle of June. James chuckled at Cipi's behavior. He knew that when the dwarf thought his master was not looking, he walked between the long row of green vegetation, almost tall enough to hide his short body now, and beamed at the plants as an indulgent father might smile on precocious children. In front of James or Sofía, though, his comments still echoed with the same consistent cursing.

"Méndez y García a *campesino*? A pimp for *frijoles*? *Mierda!*"

Sofía spent almost every Sunday with her family now. She no longer rode the black horse; apparently her one appearance on it had served her purpose. She returned to the farm every Monday morning renewed and glowing. When she worked alone she sang sometimes, her voice drifting flute-like out of the stone house to where he and Cipi bent their backs over the bean plants and swung their hoes. Perhaps he *had* done something wonderful for her, if only inadvertently, as he had protested in all sincerity. And her obvious happiness did lessen—a little—the sense of guilt he had felt in varying degrees ever since he broke things off with her the night after the bullfight.

Actually, his memories of that awkward, wounding time were growing blessedly dimmer by the month—in every detail but one. He still had perfect recall of her telling him of the sole prediction Cipi had made which he had never discussed with his diminutive companion of five years, the one about James facing death at the hands of man he knew . . . *"He saw you dying,"* Sofía had said. Well it was too late to challenge Cipi on it now, and besides, had not Sofía sworn him to secrecy about it?

Time to banish *all* thought about the past.

His future was growing in those verdant fields stretching away from the house. Not much surely, but at the same time everything. Life, in these bright days of spring at least, was no longer the dreary parade of quiet desperation it had been after he resigned from Emperor Maximilian's army.

Of course those troubling, haunted *nights* still came, but perhaps they would come with less frequency in the years ahead.

Then, on a morning in the first week of May when a strong wind blew from the east, he heard something through its gusts that had once sent his blood racing, but which now froze it in his veins.

It was the low, grinding, faint concatenation of noises he would have recognized at any distance, in any country, and in any clime—the rumble of caissons and muffled marching feet, the low, throbbing thunder of hundreds of horses' hooves, the clang of metal on metal, and now and then the rattle of drums and the shrill, piercing notes of insistent bugles.

An army was moving into Querétaro.

49

▲▲▲▲▲

"In the name of God, mademoiselle, *why* have you brought me here?"

If the duenna had asked the question once she had asked it a dozen times since they arrived in Querétaro a week ago. *Mademoiselle* again. As usual, there would be no hope of *"ma chère"* or *"chérie"* until her fit of fury passed. The Frenchwoman's spiteful little ploy failed to amuse Sarah as much as it had once, probably because she was still questioning her own wisdom in coming here.

"Our rooms," Solange went on, "are no bigger than jail cells in the Bastille. It is insulting for a lady-in-waiting to the empress. José Luis Blasio should be taken out and shot for doing this to us!"

"Don't blame José Luis, Solange. I made the room assignments. He only approved them."

Their accommodations did leave much to be desired. While the old tiled-roof Spanish buildings and the grounds of the Convent of Santa Cruz where the court had established residence were quietly lovely, the sparsely furnished, closet-sized *dormitorio* rooms with their unforgiving, narrow cots had not been designed for members of an Imperial court. They were intended only to house nuns like those the army moved across the city to the Convento de Santa Rosa Viterbo before the emperor settled in here at Santa Cruz. Each of the pious sisters probably owned nothing more than a missal, a rosary, and a change of habit.

But Solange would have sniffed in contempt at their new

circumstances had Sarah housed her in the finest hotel in the realm. For all her often expressed affection for their adopted country, she had turned a vitriolic tongue on everything Mexican the moment she learned Marshal Bazaine had ordered the French Army to march to Veracruz to leave for France and Africa, and had announced loudly that she and Sarah should leave as well.

Sarah pointed out that even the quarters she had selected for the emperor were Spartan.

"There has been no complaint from His Imperial Majesty, Solange. I think *we* can suffer this minor privation in silence, too. After all, we each have a room of our own. I was forced to make some of the *generals* double up."

A plethora of generals: Márquez, back from abroad; Mejía; the other Indian general, Méndez; Vidaurri; and a score more; had joined the emperor in Querétaro. While none of them slept here at Santa Cruz, a never-ending parade of them filed down the covered walks that led to Max's quarters and office whenever he was in residence.

Actually, he had lived first in a rough camp on the rocky top of the Cerro de las Campanas, the high "Hill of the Bells" just west of the city. General Mejía, according to López, had pleaded with him to relocate to Santa Cruz, much less exposed to enemy fire if the Republicans managed to beat their way down from their new positions at San Luis Potosí to lay siege to Querétaro.

"That, of course," López said, "is not expected to happen. Generals Márquez and Mejía are clamoring to take the offensive, and there will be much more pressure on the emperor to do so when General Miramón arrives from the south. He has suddenly become an even more aggressive commander than Márquez. Mejía is very cautious for an old cavalryman."

"I thought General Miramón was fighting Porfirio Díaz in Oaxaca."

"He was, Doña Sarah, but Díaz broke off their engagement unexpectedly and moved his army to the east. A very skillful move. Apparently now that he has gotten out of the mountains he has no intention of pushing toward the capital until he picks up new recruits in the central states. My speculation is that he will strike out for Puebla when he does. The Republicans have something to prove there."

Before they left Chapultepec she had already begun to wonder why Miguel López seemed so willing, so eager in fact, to feed her information that could even be called secret, speaking freely in a way men virtually never did with women.

Solange had an answer.

"Colonel López has designs on you, particularly since Countess von Kollonitz is no longer here. He talks of important things to make *himself* seem important."

Sarah supposed it could be true. López had been energetically charming. It was the last sort of attention she wanted in these hectic days, but she was glad she had the opportunity to learn what was going on. These were, after all, momentous times. As much as she wished she could be somewhere else, and with *someone* else, it was a small price to pay to be this close to the center of history.

Solange was not through. "It would be disgraceful for you to lose Monsieur le Comte—and even that Colonel James who seems to have left you *aussi*—only to take up with a man who cannot even pay his honest debts."

"What are you talking about, Solange?"

"Hah! You have lived in the same castle with this colonel for a year and you have not found out what *pauvre* Solange found out in five minutes from his and the other servants."

"Tell me."

"He owes every tailor in the capital, two of every five wineshops, and more than half the cantinas and restaurants. His army pay is pledged to his creditors for the next two years. He does not have a *sou* he can call his own! It is plain you don't know very much about the people you have associated with since we came to this despicable country."

Solange could well be right. Paola, for instance, had

surprised her with her quite possibly unwarranted jealousy of Agnes Salm-Salm. She had judged her friend to be totally free of envy or fear. And she never had thought her capable of the love and grief she displayed at the Requiem Mass for Pierre. Charlotte, for her part, had run up storm signals even when they were at St. Catherine's, early warnings of the mental slide which had now apparently taken place in Paris. She *might* have recognized the onset of the empress's spiral into what the latest reports bluntly called lunacy, but something in her had refused to face that particular knowledge as squarely as she should have.

Friendly as they all appeared, and seemingly forthcoming, aristocrats, she knew now, always held something of themselves hidden from the likes of her.

She most assuredly had not known Max von Hapsburg.

But considering that she saw no more of him than she had in her three years at Chapultepec—he had not since her arrival attended a single dinner she supervised—she *began* to know him a little. She felt strangely closer to him. Perhaps it was the physical proximity brought on by the modest size of the *convento* compared with that of the great, rambling, multi-storied castle. Perhaps it resulted from her talks with the ubiquitous Miguel López.

Solange had more to say about the Guards colonel. "He is a very bitter man."

"Why?"

"The emperor promised to make him a general a year ago. It has not happened."

López did not reveal any intimate secrets about the monarch, if he was privy to them, but a word dropped here and there alerted her to things and people she had not paid much attention to before, and that turned a new kind of sight on Max himself.

There were two men in the emperor's entourage López mentioned frequently whom she had known before, but not well. Their names kept popping into his conversation. One was Herr Doctor Basch, the hefty, hyper-dignified old physician with a fleshy, but not unpleasant, face whom Max had summoned from Prague a year ago during a debilitating bout of fatigue—and melancholy, it was reported in whispers at the time—which had laid him low on one of his longer stays at Cuernavaca. The second member of the emperor's small entourage was named Tudos. Court records listed this short, funny, gentle Hungarian as his valet, but he served principally as Max's personal chef.

Here in Querétaro, since Max invariably dined alone, Tudos had far more opportunity to exercise his culinary skills, whatever they amounted to, than he had at Chapultepec with the complex dining protocol Melanie Zichy had originated and then bequeathed to Paola Kollonitz.

The portly doctor in his funereal morning coat and the almost scruffy little Tudos both seemed to worship Maximilian. Lopez said the emperor, in spite of all the hours spent with his army chiefs, somehow managed to make time for long conversations in Hungarian with the valet-cook. Maximilian obviously considered Basch as much friend as physician. The doctor, his omnipresent black-and-gold stethoscope draped around his neck, never strayed more than a few steps away from Max even when the emperor closeted himself with López and his gold-braided generals in the departed mother superior's office that had become the absolute center of the empire.

Whenever the generals and López left, the soberly gray-suited emperor, the two other Europeans, and shy, bespectacled José Luis Blasio seemed to snap together as part of the same jigsaw puzzle, becoming a withdrawn, tight little group not too unlike some of the families that formed around professor emeritus bachelors of the Harvard faculty. At these times Max looked pensive, fragile, but comfortably *en famille*.

That impression faded quickly, though, when the generals came to call again, or when the four of them were joined by two or three, sometimes as many as six, of the convent *padres*.

Max seemed to find some new, delicately balanced strength within himself whenever he was surrounded by his military or spiritual advisors—or when he left the *convento* to visit the troops at the new barricades north and west of the city. In the convent's halls or in his morning and evening walks about the grounds, even more markedly in the greetings he gave his generals, and particularly when he rode out on his horse, Anteburro, to make his rounds of the defenses of the city with them—wearing the white sombrero he had affected since coming to Querétaro—Max floated on a dreamy cloud of confidence. She detected a serene determination and sense of purpose in him she had never seen before.

The last battle for his empire had not been fought. There had been no Mexican Armageddon. He was a man in seemingly superb command of himself. And yet . . .

There came, with increasing frequency as the days went by, the dread sense that this new force had come too late for Max von Hapsburg to do more than stand nobly against the tide rising in the north.

She could not avoid some troubling thoughts that she and Solange might be in considerable danger themselves when Benito Juárez's army reached the city, if it did, and although she felt guilty at exposing the duenna to the perils of war, she wondered why she was not more concerned about herself. She did not consider herself a particularly courageous woman, but it was doubtful that even were the worst to happen, actual fighting would reach the convent's gates.

When a letter arrived from Matt telling her he still had discovered nothing about Jason's whereabouts, she decided she knew why she felt no great fear.

Staying here in a place that might become a maelstrom of conflict kept her mind off Jason most of her waking days.

In the days and weeks after she heard from Matt, any need she had to rely on Miguel López's marathon lectures on the gloomy military picture diminished rapidly.

A clear picture was emerging that the Imperial forces of Maximilian I of Mexico were facing imminent collapse. She could see the future writ plain on the drawn countenances of the generals and other high ranking officers entering and leaving the mother superior's office. It was no secret to anyone in the convent that Márquez and Mejía had failed to check Juárez's army on the northern approaches from San Luis Potosí.

She began to hear the name of a new Republican general—Mariano Escobedo was driving down toward Querétaro as relentlessly and freely as François-Achille Bazaine and the then-invincible French had marched north two and three years ago. The word spread that Escobedo would have the city under siege in days, and another Republican army under the better remembered Doblado was streaming southeastward out of Guanajuato to join forces with him.

And then the first rift between Max and one of his generals appeared.

López told her that Márquez wanted to take his army out of Querétaro and meet the smaller of the two advancing armies, Doblado's, on the open road, before the junction could be made. "General Miramón agrees with him, but General Mejía has vetoed the plan, saying he wishes to face the enemy with all the empire's strength intact. He has received the backing of the emperor."

"But isn't Miramón senior to Mejía?" Sarah asked.

"Nominally, yes. But the emperor has turned a stone ear to Miramón's and the Leopard's pleas. Miramón took it well, but General Márquez has not attended a staff meeting since the decision was announced."

If the faces at the convent looked glum at the approach of the enemy, that of Maximilian did not, nor did that of Sarah's persistently faithful informant, Miguel López.

The Household Guards colonel's demeanor did not display the confidence that Max's did; in his case it showed what, for lack of a more fitting word, she could call diffidence. It could easily be mistaken for serenity. She could understand this. He certainly inched closer to the emperor every day. Perhaps he still hoped for the promotion denied him a year ago.

But López had not lost all his effectiveness as a harbinger of doom.

"The combined armies of Doblado and Escobedo number more than 40,000 troops. All the emperor can muster here in Querétaro totals slightly over 9,000. Even though the advantage, at least initially, lies with the defense, I fear it will not be nearly enough. The emperor's soldiers know how desperate the situation is, even if the emperor himself does not. What the French, who have words for everything, call *morale*, is ebbing in the army. Some of his advisors have tried to persuade the emperor to flee. His Imperial Majesty does not listen. What they call prudence he sees as cowardice."

The numbers López tallied for her could be a quantified formula for disaster, but it did not surprise her that the Max she had watched so closely in recent days refused to run to safety. He lived now in a world realists could never visit.

Against López's report of a Republican Army of more than 40,000, the Imperial 9,000 seemed pitifully small, but it was an enormous number in one worrying respect. With the regular civilian population of Querétaro, it formed a gigantic, cavernous stomach. There was a noticeable pinch on foodstuffs for both the garrison and the populace.

She began accompanying her harried chef, Silvano Tafoya, on his daily trips to the market. At first, merely by means of smiling moral suasion, she got everything she wanted from the vendors, but day by day they grew more resistant to her good natured nagging to fill the convent wagons even at prices they hiked shamelessly, sometimes doubling them while she looked at the produce in the stalls. She finally sought out José Luis Blasio and found him in a *tête-à-tête* with Miguel López.

"My household funds are nearly exhausted, José Luis. I must have more money if we are to eat. I need a great *deal* more money."

"And I would like to authorize it, Doña Sarah," Blasio said, "but the treasury is seriously depleted. We are having difficulty paying the *soldados*. *También*, we need more horses, water wagons, clothing and firewood for the front line troops, and so many other things it makes my poor head spin. I do not relish the idea of asking the emperor to advance *dinero* out of his own privy purse, but within a few days I fear I will have no choice."

López broke in. "May I offer the services of a half dozen soldiers of the Guard to help you buy food, *mi doña?* Bayonets can take the place of *pesos.*"

She stalked away from Blasio and López in a righteous rage—but two days later, after she and Tafoya returned from the market center with their two wagons empty, and with the knowledge that no more than half a week's supplies remained in the convent's larder, she knew she would have to avail herself of Miguel's help.

It horrified her even more when she learned that bayonets and *pesos* were being linked in another equally vicious financial manner. Imperial troops were banging on doors in every quarter of the city, from the most poverty stricken *barrios* to the neighborhoods of the rich, collecting "special taxes" disguised as loans.

"The empire will need a lot of treasure for the future, no matter what transpires here in Querétaro," Lopez said.

She wondered if Max finally regretted his open-handed, carefree profligacy of the past three years.

Then, on successive days she reeled from shocks as severe as any she had ever felt. The first filled her with a sadness she had not known since Samuel died; the second, in some ways the heavier of the two, brought a flicker of hope.

Max had finally agreed to come to dinner with everyone living at Santa Cruz and some of his generals, as well, and Sarah was conferring with her *mayordomo* and Dr. Basch in the convent's foyer about what the emperor could and could not eat that night, when Miguel López and a uniformed man carrying a dispatch case brushed by them. Sarah recognized the man as a courier she had seen frequently at Chapultepec. He must, from the exhausted look of him, have ridden straight through the night. They stopped at the door of the emperor's office, and the bedraggled rider said something to the colonel she could not catch.

After López ushered the courier in to Max, he came out again and summoned Dr. Basch, showed the physician inside and followed on his heels, closing the door behind him.

Sarah dismissed the *mayordomo* and walked toward the kitchen wing to see her chef. She stopped. Something alarming must have happened. The courier had not looked like any happy bearer of glad tidings. Her curiosity pulled her back to the foyer. Had the courier brought news of still another military disappointment, something in the south? Could Diaz possibly have attacked at Puebla so soon?

She stationed herself in an alcove that gave a view of the door to Max's office down the hallway. The alcove held an alabaster statue of St. Sebastian with the saint's polished white body pierced by copper arrows. Painted blood ran down from the arrows's entry points.

As she watched the office door, the morning's allotment of generals and their aides, Miramón and Mejía among them, began filling the benches outside the office of the mother superior and clogging the hallway. Some of them fixed Sarah with stern, questioning looks as they passed the alcove. She must, she realized, have looked a little silly, as if she were hiding yet not hiding well.

After what must have been ten or twelve minutes the door to the emperor's office opened and López stepped into the hall and closed it behind him. The generals converged on him like a pack of hounds closing on a fox. López spoke to them in tones so low she could not hear the words, but even as he spoke he caught sight of her. If he ran true to form he would extricate himself as soon as it was acceptably possible and hurry to her to tell her the news. The passing of information to her had by now become a compulsion with the handsome colonel.

Not one sound came from any of the generals. One by one they turned away from the Guards colonel, their faces—some of them, at least—blank and frozen. The door to the office opened again. The stout figure of Dr. Basch filled it. He crooked a finger at Mejía and Miramón, calling them inside. The door closed again.

The Imperial blue-and-gold clot of high ranking officers dissolved, and they began to leave the hallway. As they walked past her she knew they no longer saw her. They were almost all gone before López could free himself and make his way to her.

He looked up at St. Sebastian for a moment, then motioned her deeper into the alcove.

"Terrible news, Doña Sarah," he said when they faced each other. His voice was flat, dispassionate. He drew a breath. "A message has come from Señor Felix Eloin at Miramar.

"Empress Carlota is dead."

She did not see Max the rest of that day. Even before she and López left the alcove, with her body numbed nearly to immobility and thinking that the lifeless plaster saint felt more from its copper barbs than she did, little Tudos raced by them on the way to the office and disappeared inside it. He must have heard the tragic news from one of the departing officers or one of the aides.

There was no one to tell her the details of Charlotte's death. She returned to her job. She had an Imperial dinner to cancel. And there would be no need to go to the market today with her squad of soldiers and their *peso*-bayonets. Some of tonight's food would go to waste.

Charlotte von Coburg was dead. Hours dragged by before she could even *begin* to cope with it. Then she realized with a start that she was now released from her promise. No one could point a legitimate finger of blame at her were she to leave the court this minute. It surely would make sense to leave Querétaro before the Republican ring of steel closed around the city and travel between here and the capital came to a halt. If Miguel López's last assessment of the situation was anything like accurate, that might happen within a fortnight. With the battles, large and small, now being fought in most of the central states, trying to get to the capital might be too dangerous by far, but if she and Solange left now it surely would be possible to get to Zacatecas by way of Irapuato and reach what sanctuary Alberto Moreno could provide. She and Solange could find safety at Sierra Verde. The Republicans had Zacatecas now, of course, but the mine manager had maintained strong links with Juárez through all this turmoil.

Convoys were making sporadic trips to the capital and other places still in Imperial hands. One was due to leave for Irapuato soon. Solange could easily have them ready to travel with it.

"Pack all the larger things," she told the Frenchwoman. "Keep out only the things we have to have, the bare minimum."

She would market one more time with Silvano Tafoya. Until she left she would keep dead Charlotte's house for her.

The bayonets of Miguel López's guardsmen would make no substantial purchases today.

The canopied stalls in the market were nearly empty. The meats smelled rancid, and the fruits and vegetables were past their peak, the lettuce streaked with rust, the squash shrunken and often rotted. At only half of the locations did the vendors so much as glance her way. A few apologized. One vendor told her food would not be truly plentiful until the spring bean crop in the Bajio was harvested and brought to market. That could be any day now, he said, but . . . "*Quién sabe, mi doña?* The farmers may not be able to get it through the enemy lines to *nuestro mercado* then."

Chef Silvano Tafoya looked as if he might begin to weep. "I cannot make a dinner of just onions and *calabazas*, Doña Sarah."

They did not find enough pork, beef, and greens to cover the wooden bottom of the smaller of the two tiny wagons.

"We shall just have to make do with what we have, *Señor* Tafoya—and fill our guests with soup. We might as well return to the convent. Most of the vendors are closing shop. We'll try again tomorrow."

"*Sí,* Doña Sarah."

The chef helped her up to the seat of the wagon, climbed in on the other side, and took the reins. He had to wait for a long column of Imperial infantry to clear the road before he could whip up the mules. As they straggled by, the soldiers of the column looked as dispirited and defeated as she felt.

Then, as her gazed lifted over the moving mass of capped heads, two people on the far side of the column caught her eye through the rising dust.

Jason's man Cipi and the girl Sofía!

They were on horses, not on *burros* as were most of the other riders in the market place. The dwarf was turning his animal and moving it off, but the girl held hers in place.

She was staring straight at Sarah.

Then, her face impassive, she turned her mount and started to ride away.

The sound of the marching men made it senseless for Sarah to shout to her, but she had to get her attention, or Cipi's.

She started to step down from the wagon and found her eyes level with the head of another rider a dozen feet away, a military man of some indeterminate rank, an officer, and a high one from the way he carried himself. He was outfitted in an unfamiliar uniform, and looking out over the heads in the column, as she had.

She jumped from the seat, and ran to the column of marchers to push her way through, but when she reached them she knew her slight body was unequal to the task.

In a near panic she raced back to the wagon and scrambled up on the seat again for another look.

Cipi and Sofía had disappeared.

"May I be of assistance, *señorita?*" It was the officer on the horse. He had moved his mount closer to the wagon.

"Did you see those two riding together, sir . . . the girl in the white dress and the dwarf?"

"Yes, I did." •

In her excitement she had not noticed his speech at first. Now she did and it dawned on her he was as American as she was.

"I must speak with them."

"I am afraid you can't. They rode off at great speed. They must be well out of the market now. You could not possibly catch them in your wagon. I am terribly sorry, miss." His use of "miss" told her he had spotted her for an American, too. And now she knew the uniform. It was the dove gray of the Confederacy. She remembered Matt telling her of Confederate officers now serving in Maximilian's army, but she had more or less expected to see an Imperial uniform if she ever met one of them.

She readied herself to plead with the officer to ride after Cipi and Sofía, but before she could, he touched his gauntlet to the brim of his campaign hat, laid the reins across his horse's neck, and turned it away. He was lost to sight in a blink of an eye, just as Cipi and Sofía had been lost a few moments earlier.

The column had cleared their path and the way was open for her and Silvano to return to the convent. The chef waved to the driver of the other wagon to follow along behind them.

When they were under way she forgot the man in the gray uniform.

If Cipi and Sofía were in Querétaro, could Jason be far away? She would have to return to the market tomorrow, and for as many days as it took if there was a chance of seeing the dwarf and the girl again. Perhaps one or more of the vendors knew them. It was too late in the day to make inquiries; most of the stalls had closed while the infantry column passed.

But she would be here bright and early in the morning.

She had been unaware of the strong impression the man in gray had made on her in their few seconds together, but as Silvano guided the team and the wagon into the grounds of the convent his image kept returning.

He was a strangely handsome man, but with a face she felt sure was not given much to smiling. His voice had been like ice, and the memory of it chilled her. His manner with her had been impeccably courteous, gentlemanly, but she could not shake the notion that somehow he did not like her. No, that was not quite it. He had not *seen* her. There had been something frightening about him that was only beginning to register now.

She turned her thoughts back to the other semi-encounter.

Cipi probably had not seen her, but Sofía had.

It seemed manifestly unfair to think it on the slight evidence of the one brief look, but she had caught something in Sofía's stare that made her certain the girl would not tell Jason of the near meeting.

No matter. If Jason was in Querétaro or near it, she would find him. She would not join that convoy to Irapuato.

Her heart had pounded so on the trip back from the market she had failed to hear the other pounding. She heard it now.

It was a sound she had never heard before, but she needed no one to tell her what it was.

The distant *crumpf . . . crumpf . . . crumpf* of field artillery and even heavier guns echoed from the convent walls.

The attack on Querétaro had begun.

"Solange respectfully requests the *mademoiselle* to make up her mind." The duenna, in black to mourn the empress, and who had at first almost collapsed at the prospect of the impending battle and the sound of the opening guns, was now back on the *qui vive*, and thoroughly enjoying a steaming Gallic mood. "She sometimes pushes a woman's privilege far too far!"

50

▲▲▲▲▲

For the third time in a week James rode to the top of the small hill half a kilometer north of the farm, digging his spurs into the flanks of the black horse harder than was necessary, feeling a twinge of shame at the smoldering anger that caused him to abuse the baffled, willing beast.

He reined the black to a halt and pulled his telescope from the saddlebag.

The telescope, and his pistol and saber back in the house, were among the few possessions he brought from Sidi-bel-Abbés in '62. He had saved little else from his time with the Legion there or here in Mexico, or from his service in the army of the emperor. He had kept his greatcoat, but he had disposed of all his uniforms and accoutrements, Legion and Imperial alike, before he, Cipi, and Sofía left the capital. The telescope and pistol could still be useful, and a heavy wool coat to turn the chill north winds away next winter would probably be hard to find in Querétaro.

The saber? Well, he could use it for chopping *maguey*, or as a scythe to cut down the plants Cipi and the two *peones* the dwarf intended hiring would strip of beans two days from now. He would never again put it to the work it had been designed and meant to do.

The anger that caused him to use the horse so hard on this short ride had first sparked and flamed three weeks ago, when the sound of armies reached the farm, and it had burned inside him ever since.

He railed silently at his own stupidity in coming here.

From his recollection, clear as crystal, of the military map of Mexico that hung in Bazaine's office, he should have known that the last great battle of this conflict would be fought at Querétaro. Its central location offered an escape route to the east and Veracruz if Maximilian's forces lost. The way was well north of the usual path to the great gulf port, through Puebla and Orizaba, where some Republican commander and his army—Porfirio Díaz if he had fought his way out of Oaxaca—might block the way. Querétaro opened, too, on a wide, smooth road for a triumphal march back to the capital if by chance the Imperial Army won.

He had no special recent knowledge pointing to either possible outcome of the struggle, of course, but the very fact that the emperor's army was making its stand here, rather than at Guanajuato, San Luis Potosí, or even farther north, seemed to him to presage defeat. There must have been Imperial losses he had not heard about since he left the capital for the farm, and there had already been a few before then.

Was it mere coincidence that he now found himself in such proximity to what could be the empire's last battle, win or lose? Perhaps there was something else at work here, something deeper.

There is a destiny which shapes our ends . . .

Nonsense.

Cipi had brought him the biggest news about events going on inside Querétaro when the little man discovered that the emperor himself had come to the city and was taking command of the armies there. He was a dilettante, but James had seen brilliant strategy from even more unlikely men than Maximilian of Mexico.

At the first, faint sounds of the coming battle he had been tempted, even as his resentment mounted, to ride into the city for a closer look at things before the lines hardened and made such an excursion an impossibility. He would have ignored any risk had the French still been involved. He might have been able to find old comrades like Pierre and duBecq, or even Marcel Gallimard. But they must have left Mexico by now. He had written Boulanger, but to this date there had been no answer.

In any event, it was too late now. Cipi and Sofía had made their last trip to market two weeks ago without him. When they told him they had been followed by an officer and half a dozen armed cavalrymen almost to San Pedro, he had forbidden any more such ventures. The sometimes insanely cocky dwarf—after making a great show of patting the old pistol James had forgotten he possessed, and boasting he was a match for any number of soldiers, Republican or Imperial—had finally if reluctantly admitted there would be no chance of worming their way through the packed front ranks of the two opposing forces.

Sofía had been almost in a trance since that day. The officer and his men must have frightened her more than he would have thought possible. She had known far too many soldiers in their time together.

They would have to stay on the farm as tight as ticks until the bitter end. A passable road leading to the fighting front ran past the farm, and although there had been some minor military traffic on it, all of it Republican, no foragers had come their way . . . yet.

He raised the telescope to his eye and swept it slowly from north to east. The small hill gave a good view of the dispositions of both the attackers and defenders. It was like looking at the terrain box in Bazaine's headquarters tent at Puebla before Pierre and he had taken the decoy force to San Lorenzo. How he missed his sardonic friend. The Parisian was probably on the high seas at this very minute, bound for France.

In the foreground he saw clearly the gun emplacements and the staging areas overflowing with the massed Republican infantry that would soon make its last advance, but beyond the most forward of the Imperial breastworks the Cerro de las Campanas blocked any good look at the northern precincts of Querétaro itself. The southern and eastern limits of the city still looked relatively untouched.

The guns were mute this morning, had been for two days now. The first salvos had gone screaming into Querétaro the afternoon Cipi and Sofía returned from their last market trip, and had shaken the earth and sky for nine straight days and four of the intervening nights before the barrages stopped. Even with that two-day respite, smoke still rose in twenty or thirty places behind the Hill of the Bells. The city had taken a fearful pounding. When the guns shattered the silence again—tomorrow or the day after, he guessed—the final action would be truly joined.

He turned the telescope due south and his little farm appeared in the chromatic world it revealed. Images were blurred, and colors ran in crazed bands around the *casa*, the wagon, the sheds, and the tiny figure of Cipi carrying two wooden buckets to the corral. Sofía came into view in the doorway of the house, standing motionless in that almost transfixed state she had lived in since returning from that last day of marketing.

Whatever disturbed her, he had not heard her sing once since then. Her smile had disappeared, too. He had thought at first that some new trouble had arisen with her family, but when the brothers came to call on their last two regular Monday visits he detected no sign of any rift.

He caught her glancing at him from time to time, but she always turned and moved quickly away before he could ask what troubled her.

Perhaps when they began the harvest the day after tomorrow her mood would change again.

Day after tomorrow.

If his experience had taught him anything, the Republican attack should start just then.

While the attack proceeded, Jason James, a professional soldier, hardened by two decades of wars on two continents, a man still young and strong enough to lead fighting men and wield his saber, would be using that saber in a placid patch of beans less than three miles off.

Perhaps after harvesting his crop—and when the other field fell silent, too—his *"transient madness,"* as ancient

Horace called it, would pass away forever. The last time he
even *thought* of Horace, he had Aaron Sheffield leaning
over him, pointing at that very line. A harvest neared at
that time, too.

He rode a good deal more gently as he eased the horse down
the hill and back to the farm.

When he reached the outer gate Sofía still stood in the
doorway, but as he lifted the latch bar she disappeared.

The bean plants nearest the stone *casa* bent almost
double under the weight of the swollen pods.

51

"General Márquez has left Querétaro, Doña Sarah," Miguel
López said. "He swears he will go to the capital and return
with reinforcements, but I truly believe the emperor has
seen the last of him. He would have to resort to a *leva* to
form another army, and I seriously doubt that such forced
recruiting would produce enough new troops to make a
difference, anyway."

She had heard the rumor of Márquez's leaving just this
morning, but this was the first confirmation of it. "Has he
taken his own army with him?"

"A good part of it. The emperor permitted him to take a
thousand men as an 'escort.' A generous but foolish move.
General Miramón has added what strength Márquez left
behind to his own, but since the Leopard rode out desertions have risen at an alarming rate. His troops always have
had more loyalty to him than they did to the cause of the
emperor. The desertions have not only occurred in Márquez's former command; men are slipping away from all the
other armies, and with the losses since the siege began, the

emperor now has less than six thousand men to defend him and this city."

Again Sarah was struck—troubled, this time—by what she had previously characterized as Miguel's air of diffidence. She now fought hard to keep from thinking of it as satisfaction, but in a brief moment that turned her cold, she knew that had she been talking to a *Republican* officer, Miguel's attitude and demeanor would have been much the same.

It had to be her imagination. The trust and confidence in Miguel which the emperor had displayed this past year now seemed heightened. Strange, though, that he had failed in his promise to promote the colonel.

Maximilian saw even more of his Household Guards colonel these dark days than he did of Miramón or Mejía. No doubt López did not speak of defeat when with the emperor.

Miguel's next words did at least a little something to reassure her.

"I plead every day with the emperor to leave for the coast. My guard is ready to ride with him. If we depart within the next few days, before the Republicans crack the defenses under the Cerro de las Campanas, we could be halfway to Jalapa before the Republican general, Escobedo, even knows he is gone."

"He will not even *consider* going?"

"No. He says he cannot leave Querétaro and still keep faith with Mexico. Since there seems no likelihood of him changing his mind, I have strengthened the Guard by placing two squadrons of Márquez's cavalry around the perimeter. I will turn the *convento* into a fort. When the enemy discovers what it will cost to storm our position here, they might decide to permit him to go his way. Even as determined as he is to stay, the emperor surely will see the wisdom of leaving once the city falls. With my best efforts I will not be able to hold the convent for more than a day or two when the Republicans have taken the city."

There was no need now to ask if the city *would* fall. It was no longer a question of *if*, only *when*. She had shuddered when Miguel said, *"storm our position here."*

But neither she nor Solange could leave. By the emperor's order the gates were as closed to those trying to quit the convent as they were to anyone trying to get in, as she discovered the morning after her glimpse of Cipi and Sofía at the market. When she tried to make a trip there to look for the dwarf and the girl, a sentry stopped her and turned her back. Maddening as it was to be locked inside the convent walls when Jason could be out there somewhere, she fully understood the emperor's edict.

The Republican bombardment moved closer to the convent by two and three hundred meters a day. By the sixth day the market itself fell under enemy fire, and she resigned herself to the idea that she could not look for Jason until all this ended. The entire assault to this point had been made by artillery alone, but she knew that men with rifles and bayonets would soon be killing each other in the city streets.

The only exceptions to the order forbidding entrance to the convent were the wounded arriving every day. Fortunately they were the less serious cases, the *walking* wounded, the overflow from the hospitals closer to the city center.

An infirmary had been set up by Dr. Basch in the convent chapter house, and straw pallets had to be laid down to supplement the five beds already there. The doctor begged Sarah to lend him Solange. "We badly need nurses, or women to act as nurses," he said.

A strange metamorphosis took place in Solange when she began her duties in the infirmary. She had trembled and clutched her rosary when the detonations from the first shells and projectiles inched closer to the section of Querétaro that held the convent, but with the arrival of the wounded, and Dr. Basch's need for her services, however unskilled they were, the Frenchwoman's fear seemed to ebb, and the *"chérie"* and *"ma chère"* returned. Her essential peasant toughness had resurfaced. It worked a world of wonders for Sarah, and she herself fought any other fears by paying even closer attention to her tasks as the emperor's housekeeper.

Surprisingly, food became marginally more plentiful, even though the size of the garrison had increased with the addition of Márquez's always famished cavalrymen. She guessed at last why Silvano's pantry filled a little, and it bothered her some. Without her along to temper their excesses, Miguel's peso-bayonet squad brought far more provender into the convent kitchen in a day than she and the chef had managed to garner in a week. She knew without being told that the extra food did not come from the market; López's roving squads were pillaging the homes of the emperor's supporters across the city, and hunger was probably growing in the old residences nearest the convent.

Then for two days the Republican guns were silent.

"When they begin again," López said, "they will send out skirmishers under the covering fire of the guns. It will be only a question of time then, and not much of that."

The prohibition on excursions outside the convent now applied to the emperor himself. He no longer rode out on Anteburro to visit his soldiers in the line and distribute words of Imperial cheer. She had pictured him wrapped in his cloak, coming out of the dark of night to surprise the men at the breastworks and the gun positions as Henry V had surprised his archers at their watchfires the night before Agincourt.

No matter what happened in Querétaro the image had been apt, but with some differences looming now. King Harry had won his battle. There was no longer any hope for Maximilian. The Welsh and English knights and pikemen under Henry were sure they faced defeat, and the English monarch himself had not known he was going to win. Obviously, Max von Hapsburg, from his looks, especially after the news about Charlotte came, still did not know he was going to lose; his soldiers—from General Tomas Mejía down to the newest recruit—did.

Even though she hardly saw the emperor in person in

what she now felt in her heart to be the last days of his reign, she began to get a picture of him from a source other than Miguel López.

Since the locking of the convent's gates she had moved—not by choice—a little closer to Dr. Basch, who had been civil and friendly since their first meeting at Chapultepec, but decidedly formal and a bit distant, a man not given to idle chatter. She had never dined with the portly physician at the castle, but since the court moved to Querétaro he had revealed a ravenous appetite which the enforced small portions Silvano Tafoya now served could not satisfy. One morning in the first week of May he had come to Sarah and begged her to intercede with Silvano to open his pantry for between-meals tidbits or savories to see him through until lunch or dinnertime.

"Tudos, fine, faithful chap that he is," Basch said, "is a parsimonious little wretch at times, *fräulein*. He will give me absolutely not one nibble from the emperor's private larder. There is more than enough food there, I assure you." It was a weak little whimper, all at odds with the doctor's size.

She had no wish to show preferential treatment, but the doctor, after all, was running the infirmary and in need of all his strength. When she told Silvano to grant him a modicum of freedom in the convent kitchen, the physician turned as grateful as if she had settled a king's ransom on him. He became suddenly talkative, too. Basch was close to Max in a way Miguel López could not hope to be.

She asked the one question she wanted answered. "How has the emperor reacted to the tragic news about the empress, Doctor Basch?"

Basch looked stricken.

"He is a changed man, *fräulein*, although he hides it quite successfully most of the time, and always when he is in the public rooms of the convent or with his military people."

"Changed?"

"*Ja.* In all my years of medical practice and dealing with

the bereaved I have never seen a man grieve so deeply. He does not speak of her often, but he spends a long time each night looking at the miniature portrait of her that he carries always. He weeps then."

"Understandable, sir."

"Indeed, *fräulein*, but the report of Her Majesty's death may have a disastrous effect on the future. Before it came, the emperor talked to me and Tudos, regularly and seriously, of surrender and abdication. I do not believe his military chiefs and other advisors knew that."

"They must not have, Doctor Basch. At least none of them have said he entertained such ideas." By "none" she meant Miguel. She had spoken to no one else about the emperor.

"Well," Basch continued, "such talk on His Majesty's part has stopped entirely since he learned that Empress Carlota is no longer with us, and I do not think he will ever again consider anything but continuing the struggle to its conclusion, even if that conclusion is defeat and exile. Just last night he said that if he lost his throne and crown after losing the empress, there would be no point in living. Remaining emperor of Mexico, His Majesty said, is the only fitting memorial to the empress he can make. He feels he *must* prevail."

The next morning something happened that sent a wave of disbelief and horror all through the convent. The wave crested and broke at the door of the mother superior's office, where Maximilian and his generals were having a meeting that López had predicted at breakfast would be one of desperation.

"He betrayed no emotion at all when he received the news," the Guards colonel said now.

Someone had brought half a dozen copies of the Republican journal *La Independencia Mexicana* through the convent gate. The editorial staff of the newspaper, first published in San Luis Potosí after the Republican government fled the capital, had followed Benito Juárez in all his peregrinations since the French occupied Mexico City in '63, finally returning with the Indian president to the paper's birthplace. Sarah, thanks to Matt O'Leary, had been a regular reader until she joined Charlotte's court at Chapultepec. Although *La Independencia* laid no claim to being an official Liberal publication, she knew its columns echoed the views of the president unfailingly.

One of Miguel's aides rushed a copy to Max's meeting. All but one of the others were snapped up in seconds by officers waiting in the hallway to see the generals after their meeting with the emperor. Dr. Basch, showing amazing speed of hand, snatched the last copy from the hands of a burly colonel.

As he scanned the front page the doctor's face blanched. Sarah hurried to him.

"I cannot believe this, Fräulein Anderson," Basch said when he lifted his eyes from the newspaper. His puffy features registered a mixture of rage and terror. "Civilized states and their leaders simply do not behave this way." His hand shook as he handed the paper to Sarah.

The lead article, with a dark band of indigo ink around it like the border of a black-edged letter, proclaimed that after "the man falsely calling himself the Emperor of Mexico," was captured, the government of Benito Juárez would try Maximilian von Hapsburg, Archduke of Austria, for treason to the Republic and for other criminal acts against the state and the People, among them the issuance of the Black Decree, known as the Bando Negro. "If the court finds the usurper guilty, it will, by the authority of the Decree of 25 January 1862, sentence him to death with no appeal."

She had to swallow down the bile that suddenly filled her throat.

She had never thought Benito Juárez, the man she met at Samuel's dinners and again with Jason at Zacatecas, would implement the death penalty called for in the January *pronunciamiento* of five years ago. *La Independencia*, and even the old, suspended *El Siglo* of her first days in the capital, bombastic and retributive as their editorial policies had been, had never hinted that the decree should be invoked. Calling it up must be only a *pro forma* threat solely in answer to the repealed Bando Negro, and something Juárez would disregard now that he had won his war against the Conservatives and the French, and when all his political goals were within easy reach.

But she recalled his rocklike determination in the talks at Zacatecas, and the look on his swarthy Indian face when she and Jason said good-bye to him that night and watched the Sierra Verde carriage take him off to safety through the high desert *maguey* . . .

"This is a monstrous declaration," Dr. Basch said. "It demonstrates an implacable lust for vengeance. He must hate the emperor to the point of insanity."

"No, doctor." She had to say it. "There is much more here than that. This is policy as Señor . . . as the Republicans see it, not vengeance."

If it were only a desire for revenge, there would be some hope that the intention stated in *La Independencia* could be averted. The Juárez she had come to know in those long visits to the *hacienda* when she was just a girl, and in their two meetings since she came to Mexico this time, would never set himself on any such tragically cosmic course out of *personal* desire for retribution. But if this decision had been made for *Mexico*, it was a different matter. And she could understand how it could have been. The president had obviously decided that a living emperor, even dethroned and in exile, would always be a threat to a Republic that held so many factions unalterably opposed to its aims and dreams.

Her heart broke at how close she and Jason had come to bringing these two men together.

At dinner that night, which would have been far more silent than any wake were it not for the sound of the heavy guns—some already within the city now—she spoke with López.

"Surely you can persuade His Imperial Majesty to leave Querétaro now, Miguel."

"*Puede*, Doña Sarah . . . possibly." He did not look at her. "I will not be able to speak with him tonight, though. I must absent myself from the convent for a day or so on a matter of overriding personal importance."

"This personal matter cannot wait?"

"No, *mi doña*, it cannot."

She wanted to ask more, but López abruptly left the table.

Solange, seated next to Sarah, stared at his back as he left the room. Sudden contempt twisted her mouth. "He is running for cover, just like General Márquez did," she said. "The emperor should have done more to keep his Frenchmen with him."

"Solange! The colonel just said he will return."

"If he does, it will not make matters any better for the emperor."

52

▲▲▲▲

That Querétaro had fallen to the Republican Armies became apparent to Jason James half a day before news of the emperor's defeat reached Sarah Anderson in the embattled Convento de la Santa Cruz.

The sound of the guns had stopped again and Sofía, Cipi, and he had just begun their first harvest sweep through the fields when he heard horses' hooves clattering on the hard-packed road that ran past the farm. When he straightened up to look, he saw through the rising dust a body of uniformed, mounted men approaching from the east, thirty of them, maybe forty. For a second he wondered why cavalry would be heading out of the city instead of into it while a battle raged. On his trip to the top of his small hill earlier in the morning he had seen that the firing line had moved well past the Cerro de las Campanas, and that the Republican forward skirmishers were now moving through the streets in the neighborhood of the cathedral plaza. There was still a lot of fighting to be done, of the most vicious kind, and he could not understand why whoever was commanding Benito Juárez's army was not now deploying every fighting man he had, horse soldiers as well as infantry. These riders should be in the thick of things.

As the horsemen neared he recognized their uniforms.

These were not Republican troopers, they were Imperial!

Yes, some wore the distinctive scarlet sashes of the cavalry of Leonardo Márquez belted around soiled green tunics. Several of them wore filthy, blood-soaked bandages. The formation was a shambles. There were no guidon bearers, no officer out in front or bringing up the rear, no lances, and hardly any other weapons, save for a few sidearms.

James had never seen a Márquez unit of any size in such disarray. The Leopard's cavalry had always been the smartest soldiery of the Imperial armies, nothing like the often ragged hordes in some of Tomas Mejía's infantry regiments.

When they passed the farm's rickety gate he saw their faces. None looked his way; they kept their eyes fixed on the road ahead.

The faces put to rest his wondering of a moment earlier.

He had seen faces like these many times before, on his own Legionnaires at Marrakech when they scurried from the field under the Koutoubya Mosque, for instance, and on the defeated and panicked men of Ignacio Comonfort at San Lorenzo, when Bazaine's Chasseurs gave chase.

These riders were not soldiers any more; they were men bent only on escape . . . deserters.

The city of Querétaro, and possibly all of Mexico, now belonged to Benito Juárez and his Republic.

Maximilian must have left the city before it fell. He could rally and fight again, but more likely he was heading for Veracruz and the vessel that would take him home. James hoped so.

How would Sarah—wherever she was—take the news of what had happened in this wrecked city? It might be that she would now think of it as of no more importance than that Jason James had become a farmer.

When the last of the riders disappeared in the west and the dust had settled, James, Sofía, and Cipi went back to picking beans.

Two more days at most and the harvest would be in.

In another ten the Querétaro market should be in full swing again.

Cipi would have to find another wagon to go with the one they had. It would be a bumper crop.

The victors would need food as much as the vanquished had, and within a month the three of them would grub out the field and get ready to plow and harrow for the second planting of the year.

He watched Sofía and Cipi as they dragged their sacks through the rows of beans.

He should be satisfied. By and large he was.

Why then did he know he would not sleep tonight?

53

▲▲▲▲

"I knew it, absolutely *knew* it!" Solange Tournier said. "That deceiving colonel was a traitor all along, and Solange knew it from the start!"

She had *not* known it, but in these black moments it would serve no good purpose for Sarah to correct her.

The end, or rather the beginning of the end, had come to the convent with harrowing swiftness.

Miguel López had returned, all right, as he had promised, but he had not returned to plead again with the emperor to ride with him to safety.

Actually, he returned to the convent twice, the first time

to order his Household Guard and the cavalrymen who had once fought under Leonardo Márquez straight into the flaming vortex the center of Querétaro had become. To Sarah's surprise, he did not report to Maximilian. He spoke to no one but the officers under his command, and rode out after them as they marched their men through the gate, leaving it wide open and unguarded.

Sarah's heart turned heavy. Miguel was taking these men into their first combat in this battle, and probably their last. He might very well die himself. He been invaluable to her since they came to Querétaro. No matter what doubts had plagued her in the past few weeks, he looked every fine inch the faithful defender of his emperor as he rode away.

But she did see him again, and sooner than she would have thought. And this time he looked different.

He rode back within the hour, leading a squadron of cavalry through the convent's gate into the courtyard.

Dr. Basch, Tudos, José Luis Blasio, Sarah, and three of the court regulars had rushed from the building when they heard the horses, and now stood in the shadows of the portico and watched the squadron come to a halt. Sarah had never seen this unit before. Most of the uniformed riders dismounted, but López stayed in the saddle. Sarah sought his eyes, but he kept them away from hers. A lower ranking, younger officer rode by López's side, saber drawn.

"They have come for the emperor!" Dr. Basch almost shouted it. "Our splendid colonel had come to rescue His Majesty."

A low, strangled cry came from someone in the group under the portico. "*Sí, mi doctor,* they have indeed . . . come . . . for the emperor," the shy secretary Blasio said, his voice half sob, half gasp. "But not for what you think. There will be no *recobro,* no rescue, here at Santa Cruz today."

José Luis had seen what *she* had seen.

The soldiers filling the courtyard all wore the blue-gray uniforms of the Army of the Republic of Mexico.

* * *

She entered the dark, empty office which had been the last headquarters of the emperor of Mexico, and put her lamp on the immaculate mahogany desk. Only a week had passed since Maximilian sat behind that desk, but it seemed a century.

He had sent word from his prison that he wanted books brought to him at the Convento de las Capuchinas, where General Escobedo had him taken two days after his surrender. Sarah had not seen him since Republican soldiers bundled him rudely into a closed box carriage—a black twin of the one Juárez used—and drove him through the gate of Santa Cruz, leaving behind the deadliest silence she had ever known.

In the darkness of the office the lamplight flooded a full length portrait of Charlotte which Max had ordered brought from Chapultepec two weeks after Tomas Mejía begged him to move down from the Cerro de las Campanas and installed him in the Convento de la Santa Cruz. Sarah had heard of this portrait, from Paola or Melanie, she could not remember which, but she had never seen it; apparently it had hung in Max's bedchamber at the castle. It had been done in Brussels when Charlotte was about seventeen, close to the time when Sarah first knew her at St. Catherine's.

She picked up her lamp again, held it to the picture, and tried to read the artist's signature. L. de Prieux, or something like that; she had never heard of him. Small wonder. Most likely this was the first and certainly the last commission the painter had ever received from the court of Leopold of Belgium.

Royal patrons did not often care for this kind of brutal honesty.

The first glints of the insanity that engulfed poor Charlotte in Paris and washed her away to her death at Mirama were already frighteningly revealed in the black eyes.

Why had Max had it brought here?

Perhaps in these last days he had not seen what Sarah saw there on the shadowy wall. Perhaps he never had.

He may never have seen the incipient madness, but the

other things the painting radiated into the corners of the room, the unyielding will and the ruthless, hot ambition evident even then in the face of a mere headstrong girl. Had Max reflected in those last, gradually despairing weeks that it was *this* Charlotte who had kept him on the self-destroying course which had led him to the tragedy of Querétaro? Perhaps he had never had any true, inner ambition of his own—only hers.

What had Dr. Basch told Sarah? *"Remaining Emperor of Mexico, His Majesty said, is the only fitting memorial to the Empress he can make."*

Was *dying* as emperor then, in Max's mind, an even *more* fitting memorial? If so, it answered a lot of questions.

She found the books. She would take them to him tomorrow, resigned in advance to the certainty that his jailers would not permit her to see him any more than they had permitted such a visit yesterday, when she delivered his fresh linen. The doctor was still sleeping and eating at Santa Cruz, but he was granted a few moments with the emperor twice a day. Only little Tudos had gotten to live at Las Capuchinas with his master.

Basch sketched out a heartbreaking picture of Max and his new surroundings.

"His Majesty's circumstances are barbarous! Two steps with his long legs carry him across his cell, and five take him the length of it," the Czech doctor said. He had begun in outrage, but subsided into lament. "He writes to the empress every day, just as if she were alive."

It came as no surprise that Maximilian's room was so confining. Las Capuchinas was more monastery than nunnery, and Sarah had already guessed from what little she had seen of the place that the monk's quarters there must be even more cramped and bare than the rooms she and Solange occupied here at Santa Cruz. The cell was on the upper floor, Basch said, opening on a gallery overlooking a garden with orange and lemon trees in bloom. "That would be of some comfort if the emperor could see or even smell them," he went on, "but his guards keep the door to the gallery locked, to prevent escape! Ludicrous! Where on earth do they think His Majesty could find refuge now?"

Max did have some other company besides Tudos and Basch twice a day. Escobedo, while forbidding entrance to any of the clerics from Santa Cruz, had furnished him with a confessor, a *padre* named Manuel Soría. And there were two other prisoners on that upper floor, too. Tomas Mejía and Miguel Miramón were housed in adjoining cells, and were permitted visits with Max every evening. A Republican rifle ball had creased Miramón's temple in the last day's fighting, and the general wore a bandage around his head that Basch changed when he was allowed to, something that did not happen often enough to satisfy the earnest old physician's sense of how he should best honor his Hippocratic oath.

"The generals' wives are permitted to see them every day," Basch told Sarah. His face lost its fullness, was instantly drained of color. "If only the empress were still alive."

Thinking of the trial that was to begin in another week, and of what she knew in her heart of hearts would be its fatal outcome, the wish was not one Sarah necessarily shared.

Sarah herself had a visitor at Santa Cruz.

Matt O'Leary—in civilian clothes!

"Ambassador Corwin wanted an observer at the trial, Miss Anderson. I suppose I'm about the only man in the Embassy insignificant enough so as not to attract too much attention." After the chill despair of the past ten days the Marine's familiar broad grin was like a warming fire. "I have no idea whether the Court will let me in, of course."

"Tell me how things are in the capital, Matt. We've been cut off from all news here since the emperor surrendered, and we never did get much during the battle." Except from Miguel López, but she was trying hard these days not to think about *him* at all. It had been made easier by the fact that in their horror at what Miguel had done, no one at the convent—except Solange—had breathed his name.

"Then you don't know that Díaz has laid siege to the city?" Matt said.

"No! We thought here he was heading for Puebla." Miguel López's idea again.

"He did. He took Puebla in two days, turned and beat Márquez badly at San Lorenzo—where Comonfort lost to Bazaine in '63—and then marched on the capital. Márquez has disappeared, along with the money he extorted from Liberals and Conservatives alike after he came down from Querétaro. Things have been pretty bad in Mexico City—food and water shortages, people starving, a nasty outbreak of cholera. What's left of the Imperial Army can't hold the place. Díaz had already moved his headquarters into Chapultepec and brought the rest of the city under his guns by the time I left."

"My God! What happened to the people at the castle?"

"Gone. Most of the Europeans have packed up and left for Veracruz to catch ships for home, the Mexican conservatives who hung around the court have just disappeared into the city. They sure can't stay there long. Díaz will probably occupy the rest of the capital within a week. Archbishop Labastida has discreetly moved to Manzanilla, but I think some of his more prominent supporters should give some thought to skedaddling. It's about all over with in the South as well as here, Miss Anderson. Juárez has won his war."

"You and Ambassador Corwin must be pleased about that."

"I will admit I am pretty happy, Miss Anderson. Are you?"

"I think I might be, if it were not for what the emperor is facing."

"I forgot. You and the emperor and empress go back a long way, don't you? Or in her case *went* back a long way. No one at the embassy wished that kind of end for her—or the kind of end her husband faces. But speaking of the emperor's predicament, that's the reason the ambassador sent me here. There's been a lot of outraged fuss in London, Paris, Vienna, and even in Washington, both by the governments and the press, at what will happen at Maximilian's trial next week—and afterward. There will be a lot more angry noise when the Republicans sentence him to death."

"When, Matt? Not *if?"* Was she trying to pretend the grisly thing now looming would simply go away? For her own fragile peace of mind it was best to change the subject. "Did you have a lot of trouble getting here, Matt?"

"Actually, no. I came north with the one European I know of who didn't run to Veracruz. Díaz gave her a safe conduct and an escort to get her through Republican lines. Decent of him. I just tagged along with her, safe as if I was in God's pocket."

"Who was she?"

"A Princess Salm-Salm."

"Agnes is here in Querétaro?"

"No. She has gone on to San Luis Potosí. Says she will try to intercede on the emperor's behalf with Juárez. I wish her luck, but from what we know of the president I wouldn't hold out a lot of hope. Juárez *can't* back off now. Some of his own supporters would try to tear him down in a second, and this business would be followed by a civil war that would make the one with the French look like a picnic. At any rate, this princess has raised a lot of money to either ransom Maximilian, or buy his escape. If she fails in San Luis Potosí, she intends coming here. A very dramatic woman. Says she will see her emperor if she dies in the attempt."

Agnes coming to Querétaro? Would Escobedo *let* her see Max? Bribes probably would not secure Max's freedom, but they could gain Agnes entrance to him. She smiled. It was just as well Paola was no longer in Mexico.

"One other thing, Miss Anderson. I'd give my right arm not to have failed you like this, but I must tell you I have had no success trying to find Colonel James. I will keep on trying."

"That may not be necessary Matt. I believe he might be somewhere in or near Querétaro right now." Seeing Cipi and the girl that day was no guarantee they were still with Jason. There could be a hundred reasons for them to have been in the market that had nothing to do with him. But she knew he was near for all that.

Silvano had told her at today's lunch that the market had again reopened. She would resume her watch tomorrow.

"Miss Anderson," Matt asked, "may I see Miss Solange, please? I can't tell you how much I have missed the old girl. Now that this city seems to have settled down a little, I want to take her to church. Something else I want to show her. Did you know that Querétaro was the home of La Corregidora, the lady who was one of the great figures of Padre Hidalgo's war for independence back in 1810? Kind of a far off echo of what's happened here now."

54

▲▲▲▲▲

The brief career in agriculture of Jason Jeremiah James came to a sickening end on a bright and beautiful morning in the middle of June, when his first patiently awaited crop became his last.

Another band of deserters—on foot this time and silhouetted against the sun rising over the low crest between the farm and Querétaro—appeared on the road. Even when they loomed half a kilometer from where he stood in the middle of the yard, something told him that Cipi, Sofía and he would not be as fortunate as when Márquez's cavalry deserters passed them by and headed west. Something about the way *these* men moved almost screamed "hunger"—with mordant echoes of menace.

From their uniforms—filthy and sweat-stained as they were—and their almost universal Indian look, they came from Mejía's infantry. None appeared armed; they must have thrown away their rifles on the battlefield. He did not see a pistol or a knife, but that did not mean there *were* none—knives at least—tucked into belts or hidden under tunics.

As they neared the gate, he called Cipi from the shed where he was hitching the mules to the wagons. The dwarf and he had already loaded the sacked beans they would take to the market if Vicente and Armando reported the way was open when they joined them with *their* crop a mile down the road that led to the silent city.

He kept his voice low; he had no wish for the men on the road to hear the faintest sound of alarm. "I think we're about to have visitors, Cipi," he said when the dwarf reached him. "Don't run, but get into the house as fast as you can, load our pistols, and for God's sake don't let Sofía so much as show her face at the door."

The first man on the road reached the gate and pulled it open as Cipi walked to the *casa*, stumbling once as he looked back over his shoulder toward the wagons.

Sofía had stubbornly insisted on bathing before they left for the city. After their early breakfast she had laid out a fresh white dress, the silver necklace, and her lace *mantilla*. James had teasingly asked if she was meeting someone at the market, and got a strange look, but no reply.

She had drawn her bathwater from the well only half a minute before the first of the deserters came in sight. Without this delay, James and Cipi might have been pulling the two wagons out into the road at this very moment, weaponless, and with the girl—even more vulnerable then than they would be—riding the black horse beside them.

Two or three score men were nearing the gate. A lifetime of sizing up dangerous situations in seconds told him that when he and Cipi stood in the doorway of the house they would have little chance to turn them from their purpose, even with guns in their hands.

He walked to the corral, trying not to appear as if he were rushing, and was able to get a hackamore on the head of the black before the ragged soldier at the gate was joined by perhaps a dozen others. There would be no time to chase down the sorrel and still make it to the *casa* before the intruders reached the outbuildings or the yard. He half ran the black across the yard to the little house and tied it off on a post of the *portal*.

Cipi burst out of the door, handed James his French service revolver and pulled his own cumbersome old pistol from his belt.

"I will run to the sheds and unhitch the mules, *mi coronel*. We should not make it *easy* for them."

"No time. We can't stop them. I need you here beside me. If they don't have firearms, we maybe can keep them out of the house."

Men were now pouring down the cart path, some chasing the two pigs, and grabbing chickens whose squawks sounded like the cries of damned souls. Others now ran toward the wagons.

James heard a rustle from inside the *casa*. He looked over his shoulder. Sofía's white clad figure appeared in the shadows of the doorway. He looked back toward the sheds.

"Hide, *pronto!*" He prayed his fierce stage whisper had not reached the vandals filling the yard. "Under the bed in my room. Don't make a sound until Cipi or I come to get you."

The horde at the wagons were probing the hemp sacks fat with beans. Four of them broke away from the others and started toward the house.

"Cipi will begin with the two on the left, *mi coronel*," the dwarf said. He cocked the pistol and at the sound the quartet coming toward them halted for a moment, then took another pace or two, stopped again. "Do we start firing now?"

"No, not yet. If we made every shot count with this first lot, we couldn't hold off the ones at the wagons. Even if they're not armed they could kill us with their bare hands. This bunch doesn't look very determined, anyway. Let's not bring on the others before we have to."

"If we are not to fight, then Cipi suggests we *smile, mi coronel.* No man likes to face a death that smiles at him."

They grinned like cretins.

By God, it seemed to work! The four disheveled soldiers in the middle of the yard huddled together. The largest of them whispered something to the other three, and then, after one more look at James and Cipi, they turned and walked to where their comrades were busy with the wagons.

In less than a minute, Jason James's first crop was on the road, the sorrel and the burros trailing behind the wagons, chicken feathers filling the air like snowflakes, saddles, tack, mattocks, hoes, poultry, pigs, and everything heading westward just as Márquez's cavalry deserters had.

In a minute more the yard was empty.

Their noon meal was the most silent of any since they had come to the farm.

Sofía kept her eyes on her plate, but did not eat. Cipi gazed out through the door into the yard.

If anything the dwarf had been even more wounded by the rape of their hopes than James had—a strange turnabout for the little man.

It was time for Jason James to take stock of his situation.

He had hardly enough money left in his account at the Banco Central for another planting. Those miserable, mute marauders had carried off almost every bit of what future remained to him here.

If he could find a buyer for the farm it would probably bring enough to settle a little something on Cipi and Sofía and get him back to Kansas.

No, it would not be Kansas.

It made more practical sense to return to doing what he had done since that day in Marseille sixteen years ago. It would not be the Legion again, but mercenaries with his credentials could easily find other soldiering to do. There were probably a dozen wars raging around the world he had not even heard about.

He had buried himself in this remote part of Mexico for

an assortment of complicated reasons which even now showed little promise of becoming clear. Leaving the service of the emperor had not at first meant he was ending his life as a soldier. To begin with, it was only due to his revulsion at the issuance of the Bando Negro coming on top of the dishonorable attempt on Juárez at Zacatecas. Soldiering could not be blamed for either betrayal. Men had been responsible . . . flawed men who for their own purposes had used him: Maximilian casually, Eloin with cold intent, even Bazaine, although the marshal had never tried to hide it.

That he had been used was not the answer; a soldier had no realistic expectation *but* to be used.

Perhaps this dilemma had come about because he had tried to be more than a soldier. When he faced things honestly and truthfully—and it was high time for that—he knew he would have fought for the emperor in Querétaro to the end, had he not spent that time with Benito Juárez in Zacatecas.

That left Sarah. Losing her should have kept him in uniform, if not happily at least with no lament. Her essential unhappiness with his profession would no longer matter.

But oddly enough, if he had *not* lost her, the same rationale applied. In the last of their time together she seemed not to despise with the same intensity what he did—as once she had. To be with her, to earn what he told himself was his *right* to be with her, he had doggedly pursued the generalcy Bazaine had grandly held out to him.

There remained something he had not yet faced.

55

▲▲▲▲▲

"Let us return to *el convento, por favor, Doña Sarah.*" Silvano Tafoya's deeply lined, flat brown face had turned gray with worry. "Darkness comes fast in Querétaro. It is safe enough here in the market by day, but at night there are still many bands of armed *ladrones* and cutthroats roaming the *avenidas* and *calles* of the city. And if I may remind *la doña*, I have many mouths to feed tonight."

The old chef must have wondered why she had stayed in the market until closing time every one of the last three days, but of course he had not asked.

There had not been so much as a glimpse of the girl or Cipi. How long could she maintain this hope? They could have gone almost anywhere in Mexico since she had seen them, and she had a nagging, drowning fear that Jason might not be with them, in any event. The trips to the market had become fool's errands.

"Take me back to the convent, *por favor*," she told Silvano.

She did not spend every moment thinking of Jason's whereabouts.

Matt persisted in his gloomy forecast of the outcome of Maximilian's trial. "Every indication we've received from San Luis Potosí indicates Juárez's government will not be content until the emperor goes to the wall," the marine said.

She argued with him, almost fought him. "No! It will not happen. I don't care what the Republican spokesmen are saying, until the president himself makes such an announcement I will not believe it. And I most certainly won't give up hope even then."

"Well," Matt said, "maybe that princess I traveled north with can talk the Indian into granting clemency when the trial is over."

"That's just it, Matt. I think Agnes is putting the cart before the horse. The trial hasn't even *begun*, the emperor hasn't been found guilty, and he hasn't been sentenced to death. If I thought there was a real possibility of that happening, I would ask to see the president myself."

* * *

She had enough to keep her occupied. The number of people eating and sleeping at Santa Cruz had declined sharply after Miguel López and his Republican troops took the emperor into custody, but her guest list had swelled again with a host of new arrivals. She found quarters in the convent for Matt O'Leary, and there were a couple of dozen other newcomers she had to feed and billet. Officers from the Austrian and Belgian brigades were flocking to Santa Cruz, allowed there by General Escobedo, all of them under self-policing house arrest. Escobedo sent a letter to the convent informing everyone there that even the civilians such as Dr. Basch and José Luis Blasio were under a similar order of confinement. Women in the convent were free to leave for the capital or the coast, but were forbidden travel to any other part of Mexico. She and Solange were the only women left at Santa Cruz.

The incoming officers all bore chits from the Republican general, which she accepted gratefully. She and Blasio were running out of money and she seriously considered issuing a draft on her own bank account in Mexico City to cover the cost of food and to pay the servants.

She knew many of the newly arrived officers from her days, months, and now years in the capital. Most of them she had seen either at the Imperial Palace or Chapultepec, at balls, *fêtes*, and Charlotte's little dinners. She remembered dancing with at least ten of them. They were a different lot now, subdued and haunted. Paola's distinguished Belgian, Alfred van der Smissen, was one of them, his arm still in a sling from a shoulder separation incurred in a bad fall from his horse in the recent fighting. Bandages swathed half a dozen others, two of whom had sustained wounds at which Dr. Basch sadly shook his head in helplessness. Those two ate in the infirmary where they were bedded. She offered to have them carried to the dining room if they could not make it on their own, but one was in too much pain from a terrible chest wound to even try. The other just waved his hand weakly. "Things are . . . gloomy enough . . . without my comrades having to . . . look at me, *fräulein,*'' the young Austrian Major Horst von Kleinem told her. He could scarcely get the words out past a jaw a rifle ball had shattered as it tore away half his face. Von Kleinem had sustained a hideous leg wound, too.

Had he not resigned from the emperor's service, Jason could have been lying there.

One of the newer resident officers caused a good deal of talk. Agnes Salm-Salm's husband Felix had somehow managed to get to Querétaro with a troop of lancers after the defeat at San Lorenzo, and in the last week of the failed battle to save the Empire had performed prodigious feats of arms. The German prince was the only semblance of a universally acclaimed hero in attendance at the evening meals—except that they all were heroes, if in a doubtful cause.

Prince Salm-Salm confided in her that he expected Agnes to journey south from San Luis Potosí and join them at the convent in a few more days, her self-appointed mission to wring a pardon from Benito Juárez a failure. She had written, "The beastly little savage told me that the fate of the emperor will serve as a warning to other similar 'adventurers,' as he called them, and as a signal to other nations to let Mexicans run Mexico. As if these backward people could. Imagine this barbarian trying to teach civilized behavior to genuine, sovereign states!"

Although Sarah did not hear any of it herself, a good deal of bitter talk circulated around the convent about one other person. Matt reported it was now common knowledge the length and breadth of Querétaro that Miguel López had been paid 100,000 *pesos* to betray the emperor. "There have been guesses and accusations, Miss Anderson, but so far no one has determined exactly *who* paid him his thirty pieces of silver."

One name, that of Maximilian I, did *not* make it into the dinner conversations, nor, as far as she could tell, into the talks in the room to which she herded her officers every night for cognac and cigars. Perhaps it was due to the horror engendered by what Matt was still convinced would be Max's fate.

She wanted to scream at all of them that it would not happen.

One thing: she need not wonder how her own soldier felt about it.

Jason James had quit the service of the man now imprisoned in the Convento de las Capuchinas disillusioned and probably poisonously embittered by all that had happened to Mexico, and to *him,* but she knew his soul to be too great to take any joy from any outcome of the trial scheduled to begin on the thirteenth of June, less than a week away. Jason must know of it. Even if he had now gone abroad, the news of what was about to happen in Querétaro would have found him.

A deeply troubled Dr. Basch sat with her at dinner one night. She put his discomfiture down to his omnipresent concern for the prisoner at Las Capuchinas, but after he stared at an untouched plate of food that she could not believe failed to appeal to a man with such an enormous appetite, he suddenly turned to her.

"I lost a patient today, *fräulein.* Horst von Kleinem."

"The young man with the ruined face? For all that he suffered I thought he was on the mend, Doctor. What went wrong?"

"Infection. In a way it was my fault. *Ja.*"

"How so?"

"When his comrades first brought young von Kleinem in he was already near death from a massive loss of blood from his leg wound. To save him I tried a procedure that the medical fraternity has not yet approved. Indeed, few physicians have even heard about it. Before last week I had never done it myself. I had seen it performed twice—in a hospital for paupers in the east end of London—by a fearless English doctor named James Blundell. Both times it succeeded. Near miracles."

"What procedure, Doctor?"

"Dr. Blundell calls it a 'transit infusion.' He has had some success drawing blood from a healthy person and infusing it directly into the systems of otherwise utterly doomed patients—as in von Kleinem's case."

"And you tried it with Horst?"

"*Ja.* One of the wounded Belgians offered his blood. Ever since I saw Dr. Blundell I have carried in my bag the equipment he provided me, and I took good notes in London, but I have never had the opportunity to attempt this thing. I must confess I have long wanted to try. Refined, the procedure may some day save many lives. It seemed to work with von Kleinem, but then the infection set in and he died today."

"Surely you do not blame yourself. You said he would have died *without* your attempting this . . . 'transit fusion.'"

"I may have jumped to a conclusion about that because of my own desires. I do know I will not even *suggest* doing the procedure again unless I am more sure the patient will die without it."

Unburdening himself must have revived the doctor's hunger. He attacked his meal with gusto.

Princess Agnes Salm-Salm gusted into the convent three mornings before the trial began, trailing whiffs of cologne behind her.

She had not been there twenty minutes before Sarah came to a full and sympathetic understanding of the indignation of Paola Kollonitz in those last days at Chapultepec.

With hardly more than a nod to Sarah, Agnes ferreted out the convent's old *mayordomo* and ordered him to find larger quarters that would accommodate her and her husband in higher style than that afforded by the already comfortable room—for Santa Cruz—Sarah had assigned him to. That done, the princess marched into the kitchen and bearded Silvano Tafoya, handing him a handwritten menu for the dinner she wished served that night in the prince's quarters.

The beleaguered Mexican chef stuttered in misery as he tried to explain to Agnes that the foods she insisted on were not available within a hundred kilometers of Querétaro. "And I regret *también*, Your Highness, we no longer have the staff to prepare and serve private dinners."

"Were I not in such a desperate hurry, I would have your head, you simple peasant!" she raged at poor Silvano. "All right, but make sure the wine is right." She turned to Sarah, who had followed her into the kitchen, and who was about to indulge in a little satisfying outspoken rage of her own. "I do not have time for idle chatter, Mademoiselle Anderson. I made a slight detour on my way here from San Luis Potosí and had a talk with General Escobedo. He is granting me a visit with His Imperial Majesty this afternoon. At long last I will have a private audience with His Majesty."

Apparently, for all Paola's jealous fears, Agnes had *not* had her chance to get Maximilian alone at Jalapilla.

She scurried off in her cloud of cologne before Sarah even had a chance to vent her own mounting anger—as much for Paola as for Silvano or herself.

By the next afternoon a story began to circulate in the convent so bizarre Matt blushed when he repeated it to Sarah. The Marine's assessment of her innocence touched her.

Agnes had indeed had her audience with Max, had in fact spent more than an hour with him, but what Matt had heard did not concern the visit. After Agnes left the emperor's cell, she almost pushed the officer in charge of his guard detail—a Colonel Villanueva whom Matt had met in the capital once and whom he said was a "paragon of truth"—into an empty room across the hall, somehow found the key, locked the door behind her, and offered him a hundred thousand U.S. dollars to arrange the emperor's escape. The startled colonel—no Miguel López, obviously—refused, and Agnes began to remove her clothes.

"If the money is not enough, colonel," Agnes was supposed to have said, "take *me* as a bonus. I doubt if you will ever get another chance to bed a princess!"

Whether or not the tale was true, Sarah agreed with Matt's assessment of it.

"It sure as hell—pardon me, Miss Anderson—won't do the emperor a bit of good. Nor will the way she is rumored to have badgered President Juárez when she went to San Luis Potosí."

It seemed ridiculously painful but true that at the last Max von Hapsburg might need nearly as much protection from his friends as he did from his enemies.

But what about her? Benito Juárez might not accede to her pleas any more than he had to those of the Salm-Salm woman, but perhaps he would listen. She castigated herself cruelly for not thinking of this before Escobedo had sent his letter prohibiting travel. There was no chance now to get north without the permission of the victor of Querétaro.

She scribbled a note, and Matt took it to the general. Would she ever be able to repay him for all he had done for her—and Solange—these past five years?

Matt was back within two hours with Escobedo's polite but flat refusal. All she could do now was to wait in silence with everybody else.

"I don't think anything you said would have changed the president's mind, Miss Anderson," Matt consoled her.

The trial of Ferdinand Maximilian von Hapsburg, Archduke of Austria, and of Tomas Mejía and Miguel Miramón, began as billed at eight o'clock in the morning, June 13, 1867. The proceedings took place at El Teatro Iturbide, the theater named for the man Comonfort had called "that comic old fraud," when he pointed to his portrait in Chapultepec the day Sarah, Jason, Solange, and Matt had toured the castle with him, and whose grandson, for a pitiful, fleeting moment, had been heir to the throne of the Empire of Mexico.

The public had been invited to attend the trial, but seats

for foreigners were in short supply. According to Matt, who returned to the convent for two hours when the court recessed at noon, the only women who came to the theater were the disconsolate wives of Mejía and Miramón.

"It's not a trial," Matt said. "It's a star chamber as bad as any I've heard about. A theater is exactly the right place for it. The court itself is composed of seven officers, four captains and two majors, presided over by a supercilious young colonel who proves the French and the Conservatives have no corner on foolish officers. I would have expected Juárez to throw in at least a couple of his veteran generals. The prosecutor is another colonel, Manuel Aspiroz, and he appears to be good, very good."

"And Max's lawyers?"

"From Mexico City. Riva Palacio and Martínez de la Torre—and, strangely enough, a countryman of ours named Frederic Hall who's been practicing law in the capital for a while. They're actually pretty able men, I think, but I also think they're spitting against a hurricane."

"I know the charges against Max, but what about Mejía and Miramón?"

"They're going after them under the provisions of that January decree of '62, for taking up arms against the Republic in the service of a foreign oppressor, but they're also bringing up the old stuff on Miramón about the Massacre of Tacubaya. His only defense is that he swears Márquez did it on his own."

"How is the emperor taking it all?"

"He wasn't there. Your Dr. Basch furnished him with a medical certificate for something or other I didn't catch, and I guess the court had no choice but to excuse him. They seemed pretty sore about it. They wanted him on display."

She did not see Matt again until the following night, and by the time he reached the convent the news of the verdict had preceded him. He only provided the details.

"Guilty on all charges, Miss Anderson. All three of the defendants. The judgment was unanimous."

"And the sentence . . . how did they vote on that?" She already knew.

"Three of the judges cast their ballots for banishment for life, I think to make it look a little more legitimate. The three others didn't blink. That ass of a colonel had the deciding vote. Death by musket fire."

"When?"

"Day after tomorrow. The sixteenth. On the Cerro de las Campanas. That's the Hill of the Bells, isn't it?"

This time Solange made no objection to packing their belongings. She apparently had no more wish to be in Querétaro when the emperor walked to his death on the Cerro than Sarah did. But neither of them spoke of what would happen the day after tomorrow.

Public transportation between Querétaro and the capital had virtually ceased to exist, but Silvano had found her a coach and a driver for hire. It would cost a small fortune, and she had misgivings when she met the driver, a fat, sleepy-looking, but frightened old man, a Mexican St. Nicholas in appearance—full white beard and all—who mumbled vaguely when she asked when he would be able to bring his vehicle to the convent. At first he tried to put her off for two more days, but finally stroked a bulbous, red-veined nose and agreed to come at ten the following night. *"Pero*, we cannot leave before four in the morning, *mi doña*,*"* he said. "when the robbers all have left the streets."

It would be a close thing.

She wanted desperately to be far along the road to Mexico City before the sun came up and lit the tragic scene on the Hill of the Bells. That road led right by the rocky hill, and according to Matt the execution would be held at dawn. She knew it would drop her straight into some bottomless emotional purgatory were she to hear the actual firing.

She could not remember falling victim to such an attack of despondency in all her life, but by noon the next day, things eased—a little.

"The emperor's lawyers have wrung a three-day reprieve out of San Luis Potosí," Matt said. "So they can get up there and beg the president for a pardon. Fred Hall talked the others into letting me go with them. With the . . . thing on the Cerro . . . postponed, you and Miss Solange won't have to rush now. You can still be gone by the time it happens. There is supposed to be a storm rolling in from the west, anyway."

"We'll go as planned, storm or no. I don't completely trust my driver, Matt. If I change my mind now he might back out. Solange and I will try to get some sleep this evening before we leave. Good-bye, Matthew. And thank you for everything, dear friend."

56

▲▲▲▲▲

Vicente and Armando brought the news from Querétaro to the farm.

"When?" James asked. He felt curiously detached, almost as if he were reading this in a history book, as if it had already happened to some unknown king in another age and in another country.

"It was to have been done *mañana,* but that has changed. They will kill *el empereador* three days from now instead, *mi coronel,*" Vicente said. As with Cipi and Sofía, James had discouraged the brothers calling him "colonel," and also as with them, his protestations had fallen on deaf ears.

The veil of defeat and hopelessness that the loss of the crop had dropped over the *casa* had not lifted. It had turned everything as dark and dismal as the gray clouds now racing across the skies of the Bajio from the great Sierras. Heavy weather all the way around, more for the unfortunate Max von Hapsburg than for Jason James.

After Vicente and Armando left, James sat in the wicker

chair on the *portal*. Sofía had earlier prepared his morning coffee, but he had not touched it.

Cipi had wandered into the high stubble in the fields. he had growled that beans were not much of a loss, but he spent a lot of time walking through the fields, sadly shaking his great head.

The mottled pewter sky promised rain, a downpour. The storm would not break much before nightfall, though; in this desiccated air the temperature would have to drop five or six degrees to wring moisture out of those fast moving, rolling clouds. But when it came, it would come in torrents.

He picked the cup up from the table at his elbow.

Someone on the road, a man on horseback trailing a second horse, had crested the rise between San Pedro and Querétaro while James had looked at the sky.

Even at this distance, even in this morning's ghostly deep shadows, and even though the rider's gray uniform blended almost invisibly into the matching gray clouds behind him, Jason James knew this rider.

"You know why I've come, don't you, Jason?" Aaron Sheffield said. He sat across the table from James and sipped at the coffee Sofía brought him.

The wooden box with the great brass hinges that Aaron had pulled from a pack on the trailing horse before he even greeted James rested between them on the table.

"Yes," James said, "I know why you have come. How did you find me?"

"Not that it matters, but I saw your dwarf in the market in Querétaro. I remembered him from Chihuahua. I would have been here sooner, but I had one last battle to fight. There will be no more battles for me in this dreary country, but *one* thing remains for me to do here. I made you a promise once, remember?"

"Yes."

Aaron leaned forward, turned the wooden box around until its latched clasp faced James and with his eyes still fixed on him, reached across the top, undid the latch, and opened the box's lid. He pushed the box toward James as if it were a gift.

Nested in a brilliant, velvet interior as red as blood, were two onyx-gripped, silver-mounted dueling pistols.

57
▲▲▲▲▲

"Wake up, wake up, Doña Sarah!" A hand shook her shoulder roughly. "Wake up, *por favor!*"

"Solange! It can't be three o'clock already." Solange? She would never call her Doña Sarah, or say *por favor*. She came instantly awake and reached for the lamp on the bedside table.

Even before the lamp blazed up, a flash of lightning lit the room and limned the face and figure of the girl Sofía.

Her clothes were soaking wet and water dripped from her long black hair. A heavy rain drummed against the window panes. The bedroom trembled from almost continuous rolls of thunder.

"*¿Que pasa, Sofía?*"

"Colonel James, *mi doña*. The colonel is badly wounded. I fear he will not live to see the morning. He calls for you. Come, please. I will take you to him. *De prisa, por favor!*"

Dr. Basch stopped at the carriage and looked aghast as Sarah pushed the fat old carriage driver out of his seat and into the mud of the convent courtyard. Thank God the drunken brute had the horses already hitched. She had not been able to rouse him from his stupor with the hard slap she had given him, and it terrified her that Basch looked ready to change his mind about accompanying her. It had proven difficult enough to get his agreement in the first place. When she went to his room and pounded on his door, half a minute went by before she heard a sound. At last, growling something unintelligible, he opened his door a crack. She could not see him, but she could almost feel the violent shake of his head when she told him why she had awakened him.

"No, *fräulein*, no! In this storm? Impossible."

"I implore you . . ."

"No! Forgive me, Fräulein Anderson, but no!"

She did not want to remind him of the favors she had done him, but she had no choice.

"*Ja*," he said. "*Das ist richt.* And I am grateful, *fräulein*. But there is my duty to the emperor. I must be with him when . . ."

"I promise I will get you back long before . . ." She could not bring herself to say it, either. "Besides, you can't help *him*, doctor!" It was all she could do to keep from screaming. "Did you not take a sacred oath once to do everything you could to heal the sick and injured, to help them live? I've known the emperor even longer than you, sir. I *know* what *he* would want you to do. His Majesty sets great store by oaths . . . *Doctor!*"

A clock ticked from somewhere in the doctor's dark room.

"Stay there in the hall while I dress, *bitte*," he said at last. She exulted in relief as he went on. "As I do so, tell me what you can of the patient's condition at the moment."

"I don't really know much, except that it is a deep wound in the lower left leg—from a bullet, I presume. Sofía—the girl who came—says he has lost a great deal of blood, that he is delirious, and getting weaker by the minute. We have not really had much time to talk."

"When did this gentleman sustain his wound?"

"Early this morning. Yesterday morning, actually."

"As long ago as twenty hours? *Ach! Das ist nicht gut.* Where is our transportation, *fräulein?*"

"In the courtyard, near the covered walkway."

"I will meet you there in five minutes, *fräulein*. I must ge to the infirmary for my bag, dressings, and . . . some other things."

As she returned to her room to dress herself she wondered why in the name of God Jason had fought a *duel*.

Basch shoved his black leather bag and a voluminous canvas carry-all in his other hand into the space behind the driver's seat and climbed up beside her.

Sofía sat on the glistening bare back of the black horse she must have ridden to the convent. Cold rain pelted her. She had to be freezing now. Sarah wondered how she had managed to control the horse and stay on it, riding bareback, and against the storm.

Sarah had a problem of her own. Although she had handled the reins from the seats of countless buggies and sleighs even as a little girl in Cambridge, she had never driven a two-horse hitch before.

But there was no time to worry herself about that now. Sofía beat her heels against her horse's flanks.

"*¡Vamonos!*" the girl cried through the black rain. "Follow me, *por favor!*"

58

▲▲▲▲▲

The leg began to throb again, burning away the fog of delirium that had enveloped him since darkness fell, bringing him to semi-wakefulness. Perhaps he would sink into that final oblivion, the other darkness he was now ready for, in just a few more moments, when the pain stopped again.

The dwarf sat on the bench at the doorway to the bedroom, his back toward it. It almost looked as if the little monster stood guard, trying to *keep* him here.

He could not see the girl. Of course not. In his last time

of consciousness—had it come minutes, hours, or days ago?—the little man had told him she had taken the black horse and ridden off. He did not know where she had gone; probably to her family.

Who could blame her? The stink from the shattered, swollen leg would turn any stomach. It had obviously revolted *his* at some point or other. His half-dried vomit was sticky on the sheet that covered him.

His last memory of the girl, a shadowy, shapeless image, was of she and the dwarf dragging him from the yard through a blinding rain. He could not remember them getting him to his bed.

There were bits and pieces of recollection of some of the real, agony-filled minutes since, but none of them clear.

His last clear memory of anything was of the thirty unreal minutes before the storm had broken.

"You can't be serious, Aaron," James said when he lifted his eyes from the dueling pistols.

"Oh, but I am. I have never been more serious."

"But why?"

"I tried hard to make another Aaron Sheffield of you when you were young. I failed. I must atone for my failure."

"By killing me?"

"Yes. But by also giving you the chance to kill *me*—with honor."

"And when did you decide all this?"

"Before we left Mexico the first time. At Chapultepec."

"Why did you not do it then? It would have been so easy."

"Yes, Jason. But the rub's right there. It would have been *too* easy. You have the skills to face me now. You didn't then. Whether or not you have the courage—and the will—remains to be seen."

"Don't try to goad me into this insanity with any talk of courage. I might have responded to that once, but I know better now. *I won't 'face' you!* Not now or ever."

There remained something else to say, something prompted by the sudden, full, horrifying realization of just what a tortured, crack-brained man Aaron Sheffield had become, as Danno Sullivan had said . . . and something else. The man across the table from him, slouched comfortably in the other wicker chair, had lived with death too long, fairly reeked of it, had become now what Jason James might well have become himself. God bless Sarah. She would never know it, but she had saved him from being what he now looked at. He had become a soldier because Aaron Sheffield said he could not. *"You have no talent for it."*

"Aaron," James said, "this is madness. I truly believe you have actually lost your mind."

Aaron Sheffield's body snapped to rigidity. His eyes flared red and hot, a startling contrast with the glacial face. His right hand shot to his belt and came up with a service pistol, a twin of the one in James's room, unloaded and packed away after the misadventure with Mejía's deserters a week ago.

Aaron laughed. "Very good, Jason! Very good indeed. You almost made me forget myself." His eyes narrowed. *"Never even SUGGEST that I am insane again!"* He leveled the pistol at James's forehead. "Now, *Cousin*, let us proceed to the work at hand."

"Be on your way, Aaron. I will not in any way be a party to this."

"There is a way. I am sure that if we sit here quietly for a while, that way will manifest itself. We may not be able to read it yet, but as I told you once, *it is carved in stone.*"

Out of the corner of his eye James could see Cipi, still drifting morosely through the rows of bean plants, stopping now and then to strip away a pod missed during the harvesting. He hurled each one of them to the earth with a gesture of disgust. Why had he not come up the lower path to the *casa*? What had happened to his usually insatiable curiosity?

Sofía came through the door with the coffeepot.

"*Gracias, señorita,*" Aaron said. He swung his pistol until it pointed toward the girl. "Stand right there and do not move, *por favor,*" he said. "I have no wish to shoot you, but I will." His eyes flicked to James and then back to Sofía. "I do believe our impasse is at an end, Jason. You have only until I count to ten to give me your word of honor that you will answer my challenge—or I will put a ball through this lovely young creature's head."

They faced each other across the yard as the clouds lowered even more.

Aaron had held his service sidearm on Cipi until the dwarf loaded the dueling pistols, laid them on the table, and backed away. Then he ejected the cartridges from the service pistol, stuffed them in his pocket, and tossed the pistol at Cipi's feet. He motioned James to the table. "Your choice, Jason."

James followed Aaron into the center of the yard, turned his back on him, and stood silently until he felt Aaron's shoulder blades snug against his own.

"You know how this works, don't you?" Aaron said. "We walk when your grotesque little man begins to count. At the count of thirty we turn and fire. There will be no other command or signal."

"Begin your count, Cipi," James said.

There was no sound but a distant, soft peal of thunder.

"Cipi!" he shouted. "Let's get this over with!"

"*One . . . two . . . three . . .*"

The count and the walk would take forever—and no time at all.

"*. . . thirteen . . . fourteen . . . fifteen . . .*"

Twenty years of soldiering without a single wound. DuBecq had once said God smiled on him. Pierre, probably more accurately, said it was the Devil.

"*. . . twenty-three . . . twenty four . . .*"

God bless you, Sarah.

"*. . . twenty-eight . . . twenty-nine . . .*"

He did not hear Cipi's *"thirty."* He spun around just as it would have come, and faced a white brilliance that blinded him. Lightning had stabbed the crest of the little hill north of the farm. Even before the ripping clap of thunder he heard the report of Aaron's pistol.

Only when his left leg was torn from under him and he felt his lower leg bone splinter and the pain turn every shattered piece to a flaming fragment did he realize he had not fired yet himself. Down on his knees, he tried to stand, could not. The sky was turning dark.

As if inside a long tunnel, he heard Aaron's voice.

"You may kill me now, Jason."

Then the pain reached his brain. His head swam.

"Jason," Aaron called again. "Fire! Or don't you have the stomach for it? You never did, did you?"

The yard tilted. He raised his pistol, leveled it on Aaron Sheffield's chest.

"Kill me, Jason. Kill me. That's an order!"

James lowered the pistol, and discharged it into the ground a meter ahead of him.

"I can't kill a man who is already dead, cousin."

Had Aaron Sheffield heard him?

It did not matter.

The skies opened as Sofía and Cipi dragged him to the house.

The dwarf pulled at him with just one hand, handicapped as he was by the saber and rifle he had stripped from Aaron's horse seconds before Aaron got there himself. He had kept the rifle on Aaron as he rode from a yard that had become a wide, deep river in seconds.

Aaron had reined up once, turned and shouted.

"This is not over, Jason!"

The amorphous fog settled over him again. Surely this process would not consume much more time.

The pain at least had stopped; a mixed blessing. When the pain stopped long enough, death would step in to take its place. He had seen it happen too often to other wounded men.

The storm had abated some, but the raw arroyo in the northwest corner of the farm still ran full.

59
▲▲▲▲▲

"Jason!"

She pulled the wet cloth from his forehead and covered his face with kisses. His skin burned her lips and he gave not the slightest sign he felt the touch of them, but he was still alive and she leaned back to take her first real look at him.

"*Achtung, fräulein,*" Dr. Basch said, "please step away from him so I can begin my examination."

She had never fainted in her life, but she very nearly did when Basch pulled the sheet away and bent over Jason's inert body. Cipi or Sofía had removed his left boot and cut away his trouser leg and applied a crude tourniquet above his knee. They had wrapped an even cruder bandage around his lower leg, hiding the wound itself. The tourniquet must not have worked too well; the makeshift dressing was crimson, and the bed a swamp of blood. Above and below the bandage bluish-purple and sickly yellow streaks discolored the ugly, puffed flesh of his calf and shin. His bare foot had swollen and had already turned black.

Basch straightened up, turned and faced her.

"This, I believe, is where part of the oath you reminded me of takes effect, *fräulein.* I must tell the truth. There is only one chance in a thousand I can save this man. Of course I must remove the leg."

Sarah's gasp was smothered by a cry from Cipi.

"No!"

"If I do not remove it," Basch said to the dwarf, "the gentleman will surely die."

"Pero—the colonel would not let *Cipi* do it."

"The patient is hardly in a position to decide for himself now, my little friend, is he?"

Basch was no longer the terrified, quaking passenger of the nightmare carriage ride from Querétaro.

"Shall I begin, *fräulein?*"

She did not hesitate long enough to take a breath. "Yes."

"Danke, fräulein. I can save the knee. It is actually a simple piece of surgery, but . . ." He looked down at Jason. His voice had trailed into uncertainty.

"What is it? Tell me, sir!" Near panic seized and shook her.

"Before I start on the leg there is something else to consider."

"Yes?"

"Herr James has already lost an enormous quantity of blood and is in deep shock. The renewed heavy bleeding resulting from the amputation will probably still cost him his life. There will be very little hope."

"Dear God in Heaven! Is there *nothing* you can do?"

Basch reached out and touched her shoulder gently. "I think you know, *fräulein.*"

She looked down at Jason. "Do it!"

"First we must have what the Englishman calls a 'fully consenting donor,' the person who gives the blood. It is not only that Blundell has experienced frequent failure with the recipient, but the donor should know there are grave risks facing him or her as well: infection and, as in the all too frequent result with the patient . . . death."

There was not a moment's doubt in her mind as to who that donor would be, but before she could say a word, Cipi and Sofía both stepped forward.

"No. *Muchas gracias, mis amigos,*" Sarah said.

Basch touched her shoulder again. "You are *certain* you wish to do this, *Fräulein* Anderson? You know you will put your own life in danger . . . when it is by no means certain you will be saving his?"

"I *must* do it, doctor."

Cipi and the girl looked crushed at her insistence, particularly the girl. Basch turned to them. "Do not grieve, dear people," he said. "There will be much for you to do to help your friend as we proceed." He turned to Sarah. "I *would* use one of them and spare you pain, *fräulein*, but my friend Blundell says—for some reason he does not understand—that blood should only be taken from racial types similar to the patient. I pray these two fine, caring friends of Herr James will not take offense." Cipi and Sofía both shook their heads. "*Sehr gut.* I will first set up my apparatus for the 'transit fusion.' Once I am satisfied the flow of blood is under way and going well, I will take the patient's lower limb. If the little man will bring my carry-all from the other room we shall begin. I fear old Basch has now proposed more than any of us bargained for."

It was the second time she had shared a bed with Jason, but now his body radiated an altogether different sort of heat.

Her right arm pained fearfully where Basch had plunged the thick needle into it, but other than that she felt nothing . . . physically. She had no feeling that anything was being taken from her, only that she was *giving*. The doctor was now conducting his grisly business with Jason's leg. She did not dare raise her head to look. She could hear the long, drawn out, cruelly uncompromising rasp of the saw, and she wished she could cover her ears, but Basch had cautioned her against even the slightest movement of the arm connected to Jason's, and all she could do was clap her free hand over her mouth to keep herself from screaming.

She thanked God that Jason was now so deep in some nether world of mindless, numbing delirium he probably felt nothing, either. But he almost jerked free of *his* needle when the saw must have cut through the thickest section of the bone, and although she tried to will his pain into her own trembling body, she knew he felt *something*. It told her he was still alive.

Then he spoke, twice. She could not be sure of exactly

what he muttered the first time, but a long string of clouded whispers ended with the names "Aaron" and "Chapultepec." Then his mumbled "Sarah" made her think he knew she was beside him, and a bell in her heart rang with joy.

"Jason?" she said. He did not answer.

The rest was frightening silence, broken only by the rustling sounds of Basch and Sofía as they tended him.

She prayed.

The storm cleared before dawn.

"I cannot tell yet whether or not our efforts with Herr James have met with success, Fräulein Anderson," Basch told her when he let her rise, "but although he has not regained consciousness, he seems to be sleeping somewhat normally. The fever I feared would take him two hours ago has broken, and that brings hope. If there are no indications of a general infection in two days' time we will have succeeded. The same holds true for you, *fräulein*."

She had left the bed faint and dizzied, but heartened.

Sofía served breakfast on the *portal*, now bathed in the morning sun, while Jason slept. Mist rose from the bean fields and their naked plants. Strange to think of Jason, the immaculate military man, grubbing in the earth, a gringo *campesino*.

Sarah had never had soup for breakfast before, but the blistering potion the girl concocted could perhaps start to rebuild the blood she had lost, and restore the strength she would need so badly.

Basch repacked his medical kit, and Cipi waited at the carriage to drive the doctor to Querétaro and his emperor. He intended going straight to Las Capuchinas instead of Santa Cruz.

She had forgotten Max.

Two more days. There would be no "transit infusion" to save the life of Max von Hapsburg.

She had a minor standoff with Cipi before he went to the

shed to hitch the horses to the carriage. She offered him money to pay the fat driver when he returned the mud-spattered rig, but Cipi refused it. "Such a *borracho sucio* deserves not a *centavo solo* for the way he treated you, Dona Sarah! If you press money on him he will only waste it on *cerveza* or *tequila.*"

"In a week or so, sooner if all goes well," Basch said as she walked him to the carriage, "I want you to bring Herr James to the infirmary at the convent. Sooner if infection sets in. If I am not living there at the time, I will somehow get back to examine him. I have instructed that beautiful young woman in how and when to change his dressing. Have no fears on that score. I left him an excellent stump." She shuddered at the ugly phrase. "He will come back to the land of the living sometime this morning, but I want him to sleep as much as possible for the next few days. Do not stint with the sleeping draughts I left with you. Give him one the moment he awakens. They will help ease his pain, as well."

She stood in the yard until Cipi whipped the horses and the carriage through the gate.

Something had worried her when she had risen from the bed, so weak she could scarcely stand. Basch, still occupied with Jason, had instructed Cipi in how to clean and bandage her arm, and while the dwarf worked, his stumpy, horny hands surprisingly gentle, she questioned him.

"Do you know the man who did this terrible thing to Jason, Cipi?"

"*Sí.* By sight, *mi doña.* His name escapes me, but I know him from Chihuahua. He is an American like the colonel and *la doña*—a general in the army of Tomas Mejía in the battle there."

"Do you think he might come after the colonel again?"

"*Sí, mi doña.* This *hombre es muy loco.* He is a very dedicated madman. But *la doña* must put her mind at ease. Cipriano Méndez y Garciá will not *allow* this *lunático* to fight his master ever again. *¡Lo prometo!*"

Before Sofía had served breakfast, and while Basch was

washing up, Cipi told her about the duel, in more horrific detail than she really wanted. But he professed himself as much in the dark about what had passed between Jason and his antagonist in their histories as she was. From Cipi's description of the American she suddenly realized he had to be the same officer who had ridden away from her before she could ask his help in the market in Querétaro. She knew, too, that this man in gray and Jason had traveled a long, dark road—together or apart—and she had the strange but sure feeling—brought on no doubt by his muttered invocation of the castle as she lay beside him—that it had something to do with that still disturbing episode on the rooftop of Chapultepec so long ago.

There remained a great deal about Jason James for her to learn.

She took comfort from the dwarf's fierce promise that he would not allow the man in gray to fight Jason again, but she could not dismiss the possibility of him returning to the farm. She made up her mind to get Jason to the convent the very moment he could travel.

The carriage, Dr. Basch, and Cipi had now vanished behind the rise in the road to Querétaro and she returned to the *portal*.

Sofía was clearing away the breakfast dishes.

"You have looked in on him, Sofía?"

"*Sí, mi doña. Mi coronel* sleeps. His head is cooler."

My colonel?

She had never deliberately tried to delude herself about this; she had only refused to *think* about it.

"Sit down Sofía, *por favor*. I must ask you something." She took one of the wicker chairs and watched the girl lower herself into the other, her back straight, almost defiantly straight. She knew what Sarah was about to ask. Her black eyes met Sarah's, frankly, fearlessly.

"You are . . . in love with Colonel James . . . aren't you?"

It was like watching the swelling of a hot summer thundercloud.

"*¡Sí!*" It came as an explosion. "I love the colonel with all *mi corazon.*"

"And Colonel James?"

"No. The colonel does not love me. It is all on my side."

The answer to her next question might stab her more deeply than Basch's needle had, but she had to ask it. "Was it always this way, Sofía?"

She could almost read her mind. The girl understood clearly. Sarah suddenly remembered her own outrage when Paola asked her once if she had slept with Jason. This was different. Whether she had any right to know or not, her need was paramount.

"*Sí* . . . no. Sofía was the colonel's lover . . . for a while."

Her heart almost emptied. "Are you his lover now?"

Did she really want this answered?

"No, *mi doña.*"

"When did it stop?"

"The day the colonel took *la doña* to the bullfight. He never so much as touched me after that."

It *had* to be true, but her joy ran headlong into something close to heartbreak for this sad, excruciatingly lovely woman. "Loving him as you do . . . why did you bring me here to him?"

"He loves *la doña* too much for me to have let him die without seeing her one last time. He has been too kind to me, means too much . . . for me to deny him that."

"You know I love him, too, don't you?"

"*Sí.* But such things are in the hands of God. Sofía is content to let them stay there. *Dios* has already kept her colonel alive."

The shift from "*my*" colonel to "*her*" colonel covered an aching, interstellar distance, to somewhere well beyond the point of no return.

Three days later she decided to move Jason to Querétaro and the infirmary.

The left leg seemed to be giving him no great problem—

his recuperative powers were remarkable—but she did see him wince from time to time, and it hurt her, too, to see the effort he made to disregard the pain. She thanked God that the feared infection made no appearance in either of them.

They had not talked much; the deadening effect of Dr. Basch's sleeping draughts kept him asleep or in a hazy limbo. He knew her, but his face, even tinged by the last of the fever, remained frozen. He must be terribly confused. She did not want to guess whether or not he knew that part of his leg was gone.

"One thing I must warn you about, *fräulein*," Basch had said some time during the night when she had lain beside Jason and his agony. "The missing leg may give him pain long after he recovers. It is what we call 'phantom' pain."

That information had brought her the first bright ray of hope. Basch had said "after he recovers"—after, not *if*.

She had not yet told Jason that her tie to Henri Gallimard had been irrevocably severed. His mind had to be crystal clear for that. He could not be left with any doubts.

As she had more or less expected, he made a mild objection to leaving the farm for the infirmary, but Cipi, bless him, helped her browbeat him into accepting her decision.

She thought there would be a problem securing transportation for him, but Sofía solved it before it arose.

"*La doña* would not know it, of course, but my family has a farm less than a kilometer away."

The girl rode off on the black horse and returned with a wagon drawn by two mules. Two young men, apparently her brothers, accompanied her.

They made a bed for Jason in the bottom of the wagon. Cipi and the two young men carried him out of the *casa* and eased him into it. His jaw set grimly at this assistance.

With Cipi at the reins they set out.

With a determined shake of her head Sofía refused Sarah's request that she go with them.

* * *

As they pulled into the outskirts of Querétaro Sarah realized she had pushed something to the farthest corner of her mind and had not let it out.

Max . . .

The black crepe hanging on almost every door on the *avenida* leading to the convent told her there had been no more reprieves.

She turned and looked down at the drowsy man in the bottom of the wagon.

"The emperor is dead, Jason."

60

She thought she had already made her final farewell to Matt O'Leary, but after she got Jason into a bed in the infirmary, found Solange, assigned her to nursing duty, and took her first bath since leaving the convent in the storm, she discovered the Marine in the smoking room.

"Matt! I thought you were in San Luis Potosí."

"I came back with the emperor's lawyers the night of the eighteenth, Miss Anderson. As you may know, they failed to get things changed. It was an unhappy trip, believe me."

"Then you were here when Max . . ."

"Yes."

She did not want to think about that now. Matt must have realized it.

"President Juárez asked about you, Miss Anderson. He was surprised to learn you were in Querétaro. He inquired after Colonel James as well. He seemed gratified the colonel had resigned his commission in Maximilian's army, and very pleased that he had done it before it was at all certain the Republicans would win. Colonel James made a big impression on the president when you three met at Zacatecas. He said that even though the colonel is a Yankee, he hoped he would stay in Mexico, said he is the kind of man the country needs in the years ahead. I disappointed him when I couldn't tell him if the colonel has remained in the country."

"As a matter of fact, Matt, Jason *is* in Mexico, and not two hundred meters from where we are sitting at the moment."

She went on to tell Matt the entire story of how she had found Jason and what had happened to him, growing impatient as she neared the end. She had been away from Jason for more than an hour now, and it seemed a month. Long months *had* gone by without their seeing each other; this brief absence from him seemed somehow much more agonizing.

"When may I see him?" Matt said.

It would be probably be good for Jason to see another familiar and friendly face, even if part of her begrudged the few moments loyal Matt might spend with him.

"I'm on my way to the infirmary now, Matt. Come along if you like."

As they walked across the convent courtyard Matt said, "One thing I forgot to mention. President Juárez is stopping here in Querétaro on his way to the capital. He should be here in day or two. When I saw him with the emperor's lawyers, he struck me as just as saddened by what happened on the Hill of the Bells as anyone here."

She had managed to find Jason a room all his own in the infirmary, and Solange met them at the door.

"Matt!" she cried. She threw her arms around the Marine. When she released him she turned to Sarah. "*Les hommes!* Men are such fools! This stubborn colonel of yours, *ma chère*, has refused to take any of the medicine you old me to give him. And he insisted on bathing himself! As if Solange had never seen a man."

"Perhaps he knows what is best for him. Matt would like

to see him." Solange's complaint about Jason lifted her
spirits marvelously. She wondered if the "old girl," as Matt
called her, had in fact ever "seen" a man, no matter what
she might like to claim. "Give us a moment with him, *s'i*
vous plait, Solange, and I'll send Matt out to you. It should
not take but a minute."

It took considerably more time than that.

Jason sat half upright in the bed. His eyes had cleared,
and even though he gave her a strangely uncertain smile,
she knew he had at last emerged completely from the semi-
drugged state of the past week. He looked wonderful.
Solange must have helped him shave, probably arguing with
him about that simple, practiced male task at every stage o
it.

She sank on the bed beside him and kissed him, wishing
fervently that poor Matt would simply disappear.

His lips and face no longer held the heat of fever she fel
when she arrived in fear and trembling in his room at the
farm that night. They were almost cool. And he *saw* he
now.

But even though he saw her, he did not seem to see the
things she wanted him to see.

"Hello, Captain O'Leary," he said.

"Colonel James."

Jason looked at Sarah. "I don't know how long I've beer
out of things, Miss Anderson. But it seems I hear
someone, somewhere say the emperor is dead."

She almost said something about the "Miss Anderson,"
but, ruefully, she realized her concerns about the two c
them would have to wait. He still could not know the wa
had been totally cleared for them to be together, and o
course he would want to know about the man he had serve
for as long as his conscience let him.

"Yes, Colonel," Matt said, "he died on the Cerro de la
Campanas on the nineteenth of June."

"Were you there on the hill when it took place?"

"Yes, sir. I had not wanted to be, but Ambassado
Corwin telegraphed me that he felt the United State

should be represented. He could not get here from the capital in time, so it had to be me."

"I don't have to ask if he died well, do I?"

"No, sir. He . . ." Matt glanced at Sarah.

"Go on, Matt," she said, "I should hear this, too."

Matt told the tragic tale quickly. Short as he made it— out of concern for her sensibilities, she knew—it would stay with her all her days.

"The emperor went first. He offered Miramón the center as a mark of honor. Apparently General Mejía had some deep prejudice about taking the left, so the emperor himself stood there. There were not nearly as many people present as I expected. Aside from his confessor, Padre Soría, the only company Maximilian had—other than the two generals—were the old doctor you introduced me to here at the convent, Miss Anderson—Basch?—and that funny looking little foreign fellow."

"Tudos."

"Before the proceedings began the emperor asked the officer commanding the firing party if he would instruct his men to aim for his heart. 'My mother might look upon me some day, sir,' he said, 'and I do not wish her to shrink at the sight of my face were the volley to strike me there.' To ensure that result he gave each of the six riflemen a small sack of gold, begged them to aim true, and forgave them for what they were about to do. He faced the firing party squarely, gave what Mexicans call the *grito,* ¡'Viva Mexico!,' his voice quite firm, betraying not a particle of fear I could detect—and died.

"Instantly I hope," Jason said.

"Absolutely. He did not suffer. What I will carry with me forever is the image of his utter calmness. I never thought much of him, as I am sure you both know, but I will admit he impressed me in a way he never had. No matter what he might have been all his life, in the end he *was* an emperor." Matt fell silent. "Oh, I talked with the firing party's officer afterward. He told me the *grito* was not actually the very last thing he said."

"What was it, Matt?" Sarah knew.

"Charlotte."

After the young Marine left them it was a long minute before she spoke.

Certainly she owed Max von Hapsburg one brief, momentary tribute of reflection.

Now she had to turn her thoughts to the man in the bed It would be difficult to begin.

"Has Doctor Basch seen you?"

"He was in this morning."

"And . . . ?"

"He says I am doing well."

She could wait no longer.

She told Jason then of the end of her involvement with Henri Gallimard.

". . . and now there is *nothing* keeping us apart, not tha there ever would have been any insurmountable bar to u being together if I had only found a way to tell you of thi before. We have wasted too much time, Jason. Let us no waste another second."

Her heart had leaped with joy at his look as she said th last, but it almost stopped beating when his face suddenl clouded.

"Sarah," he said, "you make it sound easy, but . . ." H nodded toward the end of the bed. The sheet had flattene where the lower leg had been. "You are forgetting *that*. I ar no longer a whole—"

"Don't say it, Jason! *I will not listen!*" She should hav expected this, should have been prepared.

He went on. "And you must know that what happene to me at the farm could happen again."

"These are *excuses!* What is the real reason you ar resisting me?" She could not help herself. For the first tim she had given way to the forces which had hammered he thin. "Be honest with me, Jason. I know you love me; yo even showed it when you almost died last week. You don have to say it if you feel it will entrap you, but you do have to tell me why you are apparently willing to give up on us."

"Sarah . . ." he said. He laid his head back against the pillow and closed his eyes. Oh, how she wanted him. He breathed heavily. "You are quite right. I do love you. Before I met you I had *never* loved. And I owe you so much now. Doctor Basch told me how you saved my life, and I am grateful to you. It means everything that I will be able to go on loving you somewhat longer, even if we cannot be together—"

"Jason!"

"Please let me finish, Sarah . . . I must be honest with you." He fell silent for a moment. "You have a *place* in the Mexico that will come out of this. I have none. You own a prosperous mine, your people count on you, and through your brother you have roots here. I suppose you have places in France and Boston you could return to if you choose to do so. I am virtually penniless, and after I sell the farm I will no longer even have a home. I have no profession. I am not a soldier any more, nor will I be again. The most I can claim to be is a failed farmer. You deserve much better than me. I have nothing to offer you."

She thought then of something her mother had told her once and that she had all but forgotten. "I don't claim to know a great deal about men," Abigail Anderson had said, "but I do know this. No matter how they love or need us, and they can love and need very much indeed, there is one other thing they have to have. *Their work defines them.*"

A bolt of lightning could not have lighted her way with any more brilliance.

She knew what she had to do.

When Benito Juárez, President of the Republic of Mexico, arrived at the headquarters of General Mariano Escobedo in Querétaro in the last week of June 1867, a host of military men sought conferences with him, but the first person on the list of the petitioners for his time and attention he agreed to see was a civilian—Sarah Kent Anderson of Boston, Paris, Mexico City, and Zacatecas.

61
▲▲▲▲▲

He got about on crutches now, handling them with skill but not without looks of self-reproach whenever she or Solange had to hand them to him. He made it vexingly plain that he bitterly resented help of any kind.

Dr. Basch, who moved to a private home near the convent when Escobedo lifted his order of house arrest even for civilians, came to see him again and pronounced him fully on the mend. "His life as a soldier kept him fit *fräulein*," the Czech told Sarah, "as did his hard physical work on that farm we visited. He will do well if his attitude is good. I am every bit as pleased to see that *you* suffered no ill effects from our happy experiment."

The convent had begun to empty now. Mexican officers had been collected by Republican soldiers, but so far the government of Benito Juárez was acting with admirable restraint. The expected bloodbath rash of executions had not come and seemed unlikely to. A few went to the wall, among them Ramon Méndez, the Imperial general who had dined sometimes at the convent.

Escobedo had released the Austrians and Belgians from their personal paroles and almost all of them had gone, Alfred van der Smissen taking forlorn little Tudos under his wing, to see him safely back to Europe. Jason, Solange, and Sarah would have to depart soon, as well. The sisters of the order were pleading to get their convent back.

Of the erstwhile confident and brilliant crowd which had

accompanied Max von Hapsburg to Querétaro, only self-effacing José Luis Blasio remained. Correspondence addressed to Max still came from abroad, the first messages swearing strong support for the emperor, then turning plaintive and bittersweet since the grim tableau on the hilltop. These soon gave way to those of condolence mixed with outrage, and from some quarters even pathetic vows of vengeance.

One morning the secretary brought her an astounding piece of news just arrived from Felix Eloin at Miramar, one that first brought her an ecstasy of joy, but which on reflection broke her heart.

"Empress Carlota is *alive*, Doña Sarah!" José Luis told her. "No one knows the origin of that false report of her death, but she is alive and . . ." He could not finish even his happy declaration by saying "well."

Charlotte would live at Miramar, but deranged irrevocably, according to the letter from Felix Eloin Blasio handed her.

One question would haunt Sarah forever. Would Max have fled Querétaro when there was still a chance, had he known Charlotte was alive?

She and Jason took long walks every morning in the convent gardens. His facility with the crutches amazed her. He seldom seemed to tire.

They talked, but although every fiber in her being clamored for such an exchange, they never spoke of love. She had to bite her tongue twenty times a day to keep from blurting out her own burning feelings.

He asked about Paola, and wondered if she had heard from Pierre Boulanger.

When she told him what she knew he turned his face away.

"Boulanger. Poor wonderful devil . . ." He said. Tears ran down a suddenly ravaged face. "Pierre said once Marcel would lead good men to their deaths. I don't believe Pierre thought *he* would be one of them. There will be an empty place inside me with him gone."

On one of their morning walks he pointed with scorn and disgust at the shortened leg.

She knew what he wanted to say and reacted before he could utter a word.

"For God's sake, Jason! These are not the Dark Ages. You can be fitted with an artificial limb and lead a decent productive life. You're not a soldier any longer. There will be no more charges at the enemy, no more parades." She paused, added, "Did you ever wonder what it must have been like for Cipi, going through life with others considering *him* half a man?"

That seemed to stop him. But it brought something else from him.

"The little wretch hasn't been to see me. I wonder if everything's all right at the farm."

She felt some curiosity herself about the dwarf's absence. Sofía would not come, she was sure of that, but she had expected Cipi to attend his master.

Jason's mention of the farm worried her. If he decided to return there, it could signal the beginning of the end for them. As much as she loved him, she could not chase after him. She felt as if she were waiting for some impossible *deus ex machina* to save the day, and for the moment it seemed that just such a miraculous eventuality, or the appearance of some genie, was all she could hope for.

Days went by with no word from and no sign of Cipi.

Then Matt, who had left the convent for a room in *posada*, came to say good-bye before he returned to the capital. Just before he left he solved the mystery of the dwarf's whereabouts.

"A weird thing happened somewhere on the road to Irapuato," he said. "It seems we have had another casualty in this war I thought was finished. One of Mejía's officers, former general with the Confederacy, an American, was found murdered a few days ago, still wearing his old gray Rebel uniform. He had been stabbed at least a dozen times. It might not have caused such a fuss, but the assassin pinned a note to the dead man's tunic that said, 'Cogito ergo sum.' No one has yet discovered the identity of the man General Escobedo has taken to calling 'the Cartesian Killer.'"

The Marine's bland face as he related the story told James he had not made the connection, but Matt would not have known of Cipi's worship of the French philosopher. He tried to keep his face a blank as he glanced at Sarah. Something in her face said she knew. James had never told her of the duel, but Cipi or Sofía must have, describing Aaron Sheffield in the process.

When Matt left she demanded the full story.

"Who was that man, Jason?"

He gave her only a hurried, sketchy revelation, but when he ended, she knew what he must have lived through in memory that day on the rooftop of Chapultepec. Aaron Sheffield had wounded Jason much, much earlier than when the pistol ball left him on those humiliating crutches. She regretted then the way she had thrown Cipi at Jason as a model. As a young soldier this man she loved so deeply had been damaged every bit as much as the accident of birth had damaged that formidable little man.

On the Fourth of July, no Independence Day for *him*, James thought, the grinning gargoyle face of Cipriano Méndez y García appeared in the doorway.

"You have been a busy little *hombre*," James said.

"With no work to be done at that ridiculous farm, Cipi had to find *something* to occupy his time."

"It did not occur to you that I could handle this problem myself, or that I might want to?"

"*Sí, mi coronel.* But I made a promise to *Doña* Sarah."

"Since when do you make promises to her? Am *I* not your master?"

"Of course, my colonel. But *la doña* will be Cipi's mistress when she and the colonel marry."

"Another prediction?"

"*Sí.*"

His heart turned cold. For a moment, in spite of the cold implication of Aaron Sheffield's death, the banter had warmed it.

"I fear this prediction will never come to pass, *amigo.*"

When Sarah joined him for his lunch he asked her if she could arrange to get him back to the farm the next afternoon.

Then, on the morning of the fifth, a letter arrived from Benito Juárez, sent in care of Doña Sarah Anderson, but addressed to "Colonel Jason James."

62

"You know what this letter from the president contains, Sarah," Jason said when he looked up at her after reading it. It was not a question, but she thanked God it was not an accusation, either.

"I do not, Jason." It was not *quite* true. She had not told him she had seen the president since his arrival in Querétaro, and she would not tell him for a long, long time.

He must have read the letter three times over; it had taken nearly five minutes for him to look up and meet her eyes from the time he started on it. Now he turned and gazed through the courtyard, where the first of the convent's nuns were alighting from a wagon. She waited until she was sure one more second would drive her mad.

"What does it say, Jason?"

"The usual. He sends greetings and felicitations, he inquires as to the state of my health after my calamity, he recalls—with fondness he says—our meeting at your *hacienda* in . . ."

My God! He was *teasing* her! His voice carried the first note of levity she had heard in it since they left the farm, and one of the few she had ever heard from this sober man. She listened, not patiently, but she listened.

". . . and he sends his regards to you, of course. He says he is leaving for the capital in the morning—that would be this morning, naturally—the letter is dated yesterday, and—"

"*Jason!*" She could stand it no longer. "What does it *really* say?"

He looked at the letter again.

"The president wishes me to assume the governorship of Zacatecas State until elections can be held, in about a year. He says he would want me to stand for the office in those elections, but were I to be defeated, he assures me there will be an important position waiting for me in his central government."

"What will you tell him?" Her voice was a whisper.

"Benito Juárez is as persuasive in writing as he is in person."

"*What will you tell him, Jason?*"

He shrugged. The gesture maddened her, but his face now wore the faint beginning of a smile.

"We shall see, Sarah."

Now they had reached what he had called the moment of truth at the Plaza de Toros the afternoon she first kissed him on the cheek.

"What about *us*, Jason?"

Again it came. "We shall see."

It was not *everything* she wanted, but life had never promised her everything.

Then his smile broadened, deepened.

She flew to him, threw herself in his lap, placed her hands on his shoulders, bent her head to his, and kissed him.

His arms slid around her waist and he kissed her back,

more fully and freely than he had even at Zacatecas, and it suddenly *became* everything she wanted. She would not get enough of him through a thousand lifetimes—and somehow they would live them all.

She leaned back and cocked her head.

"Oh, yes, Jason James," Sarah Kent Anderson said. "We shall see. Indeed . . . we . . . *shall* . . . see!"

AUTHOR'S NOTE

In *Chapultepec* the author has made an honest attempt to be true to the history which serves as background for his imagined story, but he will not try to delude the reader into believing he has told the *whole* truth. The cast of real historical characters in Mexico, Europe, and the United States during the French Intervention of 1862–1867 and the Maximilian-Carlota-Juárez drama was an enormous one, and it was only possible to permit a few to perform on the stage of this novel.

It was difficult to prevent the rich, romantic lode that was the Mexico of the middle third of the last century from overwhelming the characters and their stories. While this novel had to be securely fastened to the recorded events of those turbulent times, the author had constantly to remind himself that he was a storyteller first, and only in the business of giving history lessons—no matter how compelling—in the most collateral and coincidental way.

Thus, while the *facts* of the Maximilian-Carlota tragedy as set forth in *Chapultepec* are true, the author used only those historical personages and events he thought would bear most directly on the stories of Sarah Anderson and Jason James.

Charlotte von Coburg, Empress Carlota of Mexico, deranged beyond recovery and all but forgotten, lived until 1927, dying in Belgium at the age of eighty-six.

In the Franco-Prussian War, François-Achille Bazaine surrendered the fort of Metz to the enemy, was court-martialed for abandoning his post, escaped from a French prison, and lived out his days in exile in Spain.

To the author's great surprise, Countess Paola von Kollonitz eventually married Felix Eloin. Perhaps—as "survivors" of the tragic three years which ended on the Hill of the Bells—they moved toward each other despite their differences.

Benito Juárez remained president of the Republic of Mexico until 1872. Mexicans still revere him as the principal architect of their modern nation.

The dashing cavalry general Porfirio Díaz, at the time of the Intervention a dedicated follower of Benito Juárez, discarded his democratic ideals and rebeled against the "little Indian" and his constitutional government. With one short period out of office he served as president himself from 1875 until 1910, when his dictatorial rule ended with the Mexican Revolution.

In 1895, Leonardo Márquez, the "Tiger of Tacubaya," ill and impoverished, returned to Mexico City after years of exile in Havana. The government of Porfirio Díaz took no action against him, and he faded from history a second time.

One of the riflemen in the firing party that executed Maximilian, Mejía, and Miramón was still alive in Mexico in the 1950s.

The traitorous Miguel López died of rabies.

The Austrian frigate *Novara*, which brought Maximilian and Carlota to Veracruz in 1864, bore the emperor's body home after his execution.

Solange Lucille Tournier returned to Paris and served the Pelletiers until their deaths in 1877 and 1892, dying herself at her family's home in the Pas-de-Calais in 1896.

Brigadier General Matthew Joseph Aloysius O'Leary won the Medal of Honor posthumously in his country's war in Cuba.

Sofía Elena Chacon ran the farm at San Pedro until her death in 1909. She never married.

Jean-Claude duBecq served with the Legion in Indo-China, winning the Medaille Militaire. He retired there, married a village girl, and fathered three children. A grandson fought the French at Dien Bien Phu.

Cipriano Méndez y García died in the shade of a mimosa tree in the *alameda* of Zacatecas in 1894, reading Descartes.

Sarah Kent Anderson and Jason Jeremiah James? They lived happily, if not quite forever after.

N.Z.